THE ANGOLAN CLAN

CHRISTOPHER LOWERY

urbanepublications.com

First published in Great Britain in 2014
by Urbane Publications Ltd
20 St Nicholas Gardens, Rochester
Kent ME2 3NT

A CIP catalogue record for this book is available
from the British Library.

Paperback ISBN 978-1-909273-15-3
mobi ISBN 978-1-909273-16-0
epub ISBN 978-1-909273-17-7

Cover design and typeset at Chandler Book Design,
King's Lynn, Norfolk

Front cover images sourced through royalty free photo libraries:
© Dunca Daniel | © Billyfoto | © Zim235 | Dreamstime.com

Printed in Great Britain by
CPI Group (UK) Ltd,
Croydon, CR0 4YY

urbanepublications.com

The publisher supports the Forest Stewardship Council® (FSC®), the leading international forest-certification organisation. This book is made from acid-free paper from an FSC®-certified provider. FSC is the only forest-certification scheme supported by the leading environmental organisations, including Greenpeace.

Dedicated to the two ladies in my life,
Marjorie and Kerry-Jane

My thanks for their advice
and assistance go to:

*UK: Nick Street, Mike Jeffries, Sig Ramseyer,
Francoise Higson*

*Switzerland: Kerry-Jane Lowery, Jeremy Lowry,
Martin Panchaud, Carlos Lopes da Silva*

Spain: Mo Nay

US: Dan MacDuffie

"For the love of money is the root of all evil"

Timothy 6:I King James Bible

PROLOGUE

January, 1960
Peniche, near Estoril, Portugal

Almost at the limit of their eastern reach, the massive waves of the North Atlantic Ocean pounded against the rocks of Peniche peninsular. Intermittent flashes of light illuminated the darkness of the walled fortress as they had done during every storm since it was built in the sixteenth century by Manuel I, fourteenth king of Portugal and Algarve. Now, almost five hundred years later, the fortress was called Peniche Prison. Under the regime of the Prime Minister-Dictator, António de Oliveira Salazar, it was used to house political opponents of the New State and on this freezing January night, despite the raging storm which battered the peninsular, the bursts of illumination that broke the darkness were not from flashes of lightning, but gunfire.

Followed by the staccato chatter of submachine guns, a group of fifteen prisoners were racing towards the protection of a buttress at the south east corner of the star shaped battlements, where the rocks rose to meet the fortress wall ten metres above a small cove. The men were almost all unshaven, many with full beards and unkempt hair. Their ragged prison uniforms were soaked through by the freezing rain lashing down in torrents from the storm clouds which darkened the sky. Some struggled to keep up the pace and were helped along by the stronger members of the group.

For the moment, the advantage was with the four guards who were less than fifty metres behind them in the prison yard. The prisoners were crossing the pool of light created by one remaining searchlight and were easy prey, even for the poor marksmanship of the warders and the limited range of the Portuguese produced FBP m/948 submachine guns, designed before World War II. One of the prisoners turned and took steady aim, shooting out the searchlight, but was then catapulted backwards by a burst of shots to the chest. The remaining men spread out, to reduce the chances of being hit by a random shot as they ran through the dark.

The leader of the group, a tall, heavily built man, clean shaven and in the uniform of a prison guard, reached the buttress and threw himself behind the remnants of a low, crumbling wall. He pushed the pistol into his belt and checked his watch. They were five minutes behind schedule. He estimated that the remaining guards would break out of the cell he'd locked them into at any moment. He shouted orders over the noise of the shooting. The other men sought shelter behind tumbled rocks and masonry. Now, for at least a few minutes, the advantage was with the prisoners, as five of them aimed a wave of pistol and submachine gun fire at the guards who found themselves silhouetted in the middle of the desolate prison yard.

Three of the warders ran back to reach the shelter of the prison buildings in the centre of the compound. One of them made a charge, emptying his weapon madly as he ran forward. He was cut down within a few steps, falling in front of the other dead and wounded. Extending the trail of bodies of both guards and prisoners that led from the main fortress building on the western wall. The 'death house', as it was known, that contained the interrogation rooms, the solitary confinement cells and the torture cellars.

The remaining prisoners spread out to surround two men, creating a human shield. The smaller of the two was a wiry figure with a shock of white hair and thick, black eyebrows. The other, a stocky man with long hair tied in a ponytail, pulled him to the ground and covered him with his own body, as if he was a helpless child. "*Álvaro, fique em baixo!* Álvaro, stay down! Wait for Alberto's signal." he told him.

Alberto, the leader, shouted out again. "Give me covering fire." Adding their firepower to the gun squad, the bodyguards discharged their Russian supplied APS Stechkin machine pistols and AK-47 Kalashnikov assault rifles indiscriminately at the guards' positions. Bullets ricocheted off the ground and the walls, screaming past them as the warders aimed from the protection of the buildings at the flashes of fire from the muzzles of their guns. A rifle shot came from the nearest watch tower and one of the group cried out and fell to the ground. The others squeezed closer to protect the two men in the middle.

Under the cover of the group's barrage, Alberto scrambled through the rocky debris to the buttress wall and pulled himself up to the top of the weathered stone parapet. He reached down between the metal spikes towards the sea, his hands feeling about, searching for something. After a few moments he grunted, "*Bom, está aqui.* It's here." He pulled up a thin cord until a rope ladder came snaking up to the parapet. When it was clear he fastened it across the metal spikes and threw it down again over the wall to the rocks. He turned and shouted to the two men on the ground, "*Álvaro, Mano. Vamos!* Álvaro, Mano. Let's go!"

They scrambled to their feet, and ran towards the wall. Mano climbed over the spikes on the top and turned, kneeling on the parapet to pull Álvaro up and help him over the top. He caught his foot in one of the rungs and scrambled down the ladder to the bottom of the rocky face. Mano and the others followed in turn, until there was only Alberto and the gun squad left behind.

He shouted at them, "*Agora! Fora.* Let's get out. Now!"

They moved back, firing as they went. Two prisoners fell immediately as the guards started to advance again, attempting to cut off their escape. A light came on at the fortress building and they could see six more guards running out towards the battle. Two of them set up a Madsen light machine gun in the middle of the yard and a salvo of US manufactured 7.62x51mm NATO type cartridges exploded against the walls and rocky debris around the prisoners. Alberto pushed the remaining three men over the top then he climbed up. He undid the ladder, threw it down and prepared to jump to the rocky shelf at the foot of the wall. A stray round from the Madsen caught him in the leg and he fell onto the rocks. The others manhandled him down the cliff to a waiting fishing boat, moored in the partially protected inlet beneath the fortress walls.

The men cast off the ropes and the skipper throttled the diesel engine to the full. Those with ammunition remaining used it to give covering fire, aiming up at the fortress wall where the guards were now shooting down into the darkness. When the boat cleared the rocky cliff, the skipper fired up the specially fitted twin outboard motors and the craft leapt forward, smashing through the battering waves out to the open sea. Leaving the huge outline of the fortress and the sound of gunfire behind in the pitch black night.

The eleven survivors of the group held desperately onto anything they could find to keep themselves from being thrown overboard, as the boat breached the enormous waves and the adrenalin surge drained away from them in the freezing cold spray from the sea.

Alberto ripped a long strip from his shirt and tied it around his calf to staunch the bleeding from the gunshot wound. It felt as though the bone was damaged and the bullet was still lodged in the flesh. After binding his leg, he limped into the cabin and emerged with a flashlight. He stood on the deck rail and, holding onto the cabin roof, pointed the lamp out to sea, in front of the boat. He signalled with it, switching it on and off. The beam cut through the black void ahead.

Álvaro was in the cockpit of the cabin, looking at a chart with the skipper. He came to the door. "Wait, Alberto," he said. "Try again in a minute."

He sat on the deck with his back to the door, holding the binding tight around his leg to try to halt the bleeding.

They were now a kilometre away from the shore and the boat was bouncing about on the sea like a toy, climbing on top of the enormous waves, halting for a sickening moment then dropping almost vertically into the trough below, only to repeat the movement every few seconds. The men were terrified, even more than during the gunfight. Hardly any of them could swim. Even if they could, they wouldn't have lasted more than a few minutes in the savage, freezing ocean. Several of them were puking over the side, retching their guts out while they tried frantically to hang on for their lives.

"Mano, come over here." Álvaro yelled from the shelter of the cabin door.

The ponytailed man staggered across and they stood inside with him. He and Alberto bent low, straining to hear Alvaro's voice against the screaming wind and crashing waves.

"When we get there I'm confirming you, Manolo, as my deputy and you, Alberto, as my bodyguard. You'll be well rewarded for tonight's work and for everything you've done to get us out. Thank you, comrades."

The two men shook hands with him and he kissed them both on each cheek.

After a few minutes Alberto went out and tried signalling again.

"*Lá está!* There it is!" The men in the boat cheered with relief. A yellow, blinking light could be discerned, shining faintly in the darkness ahead. The skipper switched on his searchlight and slowed the engines down, moving towards the source of the yellow signal. When the slowing boat started to wallow in the sideways swell the effect was more sickening than crashing through the waves. More of the men started vomiting and the boat stank with the mess floating in the ankle deep water on the deck.

As they drew closer, they could make out a darker shape on the surface of the sea. A grey cylindrical object appeared ahead of them, about eighty metres long. It was the submarine they had been promised. A coastal patrol, Whisky Class vessel, known as Project 613 in the Soviet Union. The men were still cheering. After years of privation and abuse, their dreams of freedom were finally within their grasp.

"*Está perfeito. Muito bem Victor. Obrigado,* Well done. Thanks, Victor." Álvaro clapped the skipper on the shoulder.

In the beam of the searchlight, they saw that the conning tower was open and a couple of sailors were hanging on, roped to the ladders on the tower. A voice boomed over the Tannoy system and said in English, "Come alongside, Captain. We'll throw ropes down to you. Take great care."

The skipper carefully brought the boat to the leeward side of the submarine, seeking protection from the wind and the raging sea. He manoeuvred the craft close enough for ropes to be thrown to the bows and the stern. The men caught and tied them to the deck rail and the sailors pulled the boat to a distance of about fifteen metres. The skipper played with the throttles and rudder to keep in position as best he could without crashing into the sub.

The Russian sailors ran another rope around a stanchion and threw both ends across to Alberto. A two man inflatable dinghy was fastened to the deck rail and the men took it down and held it in place on the decking. He threaded and knotted the rope through the two eyeholes at the front and rear of the dinghy, attaching both rope ends to the deck rail. They lowered the light craft over the side nearest the sub. The men kept it in place with the tie rope as it bounced about on the waves.

"You first, Álvaro," he shouted. "We'll go one at a time to keep the load light. It'll be safer and quicker."

Tying another rope around Álvaro's waist, he made it into a harness over his shoulders then threw the weighted end across to the sailors. He and Mano helped the smaller man over the deck rail and into the dinghy, where he lay face down and spread-eagled, hands and feet through the straps attached to the sides. Alberto hauled on the tie rope and it ran around the stanchion like a pulley, dragging the dinghy across the surface until it slid onto the side of the sub. The sailors pulled on Álvaro's rope, dragging him up the slippery metal. He helped them, drawing himself up hand over hand, until he was standing on the deck of the submarine. He threw off his rope and looked back at the others, "Come on," he yelled, above the noise of the storm. "If I can make it, so can you." Then he disappeared down the inside of the conning tower.

Alberto quickly hauled the dinghy and the rope back to the boat, and one by one, he and Mano helped the others to tie the rope around themselves, then hauled them across onto the submarine. Several of them slipped down into the freezing water, but the sailors pulled them up the sheer steel skin onto the deck until only the two of them remained.

"Here, Mano." Alberto tied the rope around the other's waist and threw the end across to the sub. Mano grabbed hold of the cabin roof and stepped up onto the rail. As he prepared to clamber into the dinghy, the fishing boat wallowed sideways away from the sub and his feet slipped from the slick, wet rail. With a cry he fell straight down between the boat and the sub, disappearing beneath the waves. The skipper immediately heaved the wheel around to try to increase the gap between the two vessels.

"Pull him up!" Alberto screamed at the sailors on the tower. They were already pulling on the ropes and Mano's head reappeared, his eyes bulging with fear. He coughed violently, sea water spewing out of his mouth as he gasped desperately to get some air into his lungs. He tried to grab the side of the dinghy, but it was bobbing about like a cork. Realising the impossibility of the task, he started swimming strongly towards the sub. The sailors helped, pulling him across, until he reached the metal hull. There was nothing Alberto could do to help, just watch, as Mano was pulled slowly up the side of the submarine. The deck suddenly slid away from him and he fell on his face, damaging his injured leg again. He reached out to cling onto the metal rail as a giant wave lifted the forward hull of the fishing boat up like a feather and pushed it towards the other vessel. The skipper desperately tried to turn the boat away, but the hull crashed down on the side of the sub and then slid back into the swell. The rope holding Mano was torn from the sailors' grasp and he was pulled down into the sea.

The impact of the crash pushed the fishing boat away and the gap of boiling sea between the vessels was again visible. Alberto leaned over the side, peering desperately into the waves that crashed around the boat, screaming out Mano's name. But there was no sign of the stocky man. He had disappeared from the surface of the ocean as if he had never been there.

He climbed back to his feet and scrambled across to the skipper's cockpit. The seaman said, "There's nothing you can do, Alberto. He's gone, God rest his soul. And I've got to get out of here. My boat is going to break up if I don't."

The big man stood for a moment, wondering how he could tell Álvaro that Mano, his deputy, closest friend and ally for twenty-five years, a fellow prisoner in Peniche Prison for eleven of them, was gone. Captured by the waves of the Atlantic Ocean, just as his comrades had finally found freedom. He shook his head. There was no time to think about it now.

He took out a wad of banknotes in an oilskin pouch, handed it to the skipper and embraced him warmly. "*Muito obrigado, camarada. Até logo, nós estaremos de volta.* Thanks comrade. We'll be back."

The dinghy was still attached to the deck rail, but floating upside down, a ragged tear in its skin. He climbed onto the metal rail and, ignoring his wounded leg, leaped onto the dinghy, grabbing hold of the tie rope. Half swimming and half pulling on the rope, he hauled himself across to the sub and was pulled up to the conning tower. He shook hands with the two sailors and climbed down inside. The sailors cast off the ropes and the dinghy blew away on the wind. They turned and saluted the skipper, then scrambled back into the submarine.

The conning tower closed up and huge air bubbles broke the surface as the grey, tubular vessel sank below the waves. In the control room, the navigation officer set a course for Murmansk and the Captain ordered, "Engines full ahead."

After eleven years in Peniche Prison, Álvaro Cunhal, the leader of the Portuguese Communist Party, was escaping to Russia. But it would be many years before the rest of the world would discover the reason for his escape.

BOOK ONE

PART ONE: 1973 - 1974

ONE

November, 1973
Johannesburg, South Africa

Rachel Harrington was sitting on the living room floor of her apartment in Clanwilliam Drive, Johannesburg, sobbing her heart out. The tears were running down her face and soaking into her yellow blouse. Her normally pretty Irish complexion was flushed and blotchy and her nose was red and swollen from constant blowing. She had been sitting like that for half an hour since Nick walked out the door. He had only a small case with him, but she knew he wasn't coming back.

This last row made the others pale into insignificance. She'd called him names that could never be recalled. Said words she didn't even know she knew. Nick was gone and she was alone. Ever since his promotion three months ago she'd known this might happen. He'd started to move in elevated circles, mixing with people that she didn't know and didn't want to know. Company executives that he went out boozing with or invited home. Bigoted people with attitudes that made her want to slap their faces. People who thought that she was worth talking to just because she was white. It didn't matter whether she had anything to say or not, they would talk for both of them. It was just as well, she would soon have been classified as 'nigger lover'. That's what anyone who didn't believe in apartheid was labelled by those people.

Rachel had moved in with Nick three months after they met at the Imperial Diamond Exploration Company's Christmas dance. He had just obtained his BSc. in Mining Engineering at Wits, the University of the Witwatersrand. Already a certified diamond expert, he'd studied for his degree on a part-time evening course while working for Imperial Diamond as a mining engineer. After three years of studying almost every night he'd gone to the dance with two agendas. Get pissed, find a girl.

Thanks to his mates, who plied him with beers all night, he achieved the first objective before ten o'clock. Then he encountered a redheaded girl standing at the side of the dance floor. Taking her by the waist, he asked, "How would you like to dance with the best looking man in the room? "

Rachel gave him a withering look. "Just point him out and I'd be delighted." She was not in a particularly good mood, having arrived with another chap who'd disappeared after half an hour.

"It's Rod Stewart. Come on, everybody can dance to Maggie May." He pushed her onto the floor and she managed to hold him up while he tried to dance to the jive beat. It was fortunate that Rachel was a nurse and had experience of holding up sick people. Although he wasn't actually sick until they went outside into the steaming hot night. She found out where he lived, got him back to his flat and put him to bed. She thought he was rather good looking, but she didn't approve of drunkenness.

She went back to her own place and decided to forget all about men for the foreseeable future. At the time she was on a two year leave of absence from her nursing job at the General Hospital in Durban, working on a cancer research project with the Faculty of Medicine at Craighall Clinic. When Nick walked into her office the next day, stone cold sober and with a box of chocolates, she happily went out for dinner with him and then one thing led to another.

When Nick asked her to marry him she was deliriously happy. She was twenty-seven, three years younger than him. They planned to wait eighteen months to save up some money. In June they'd gone down to meet her parents in Durban, then to see his divorced mother in Port Elizabeth. They rented the apartment on Clanwilliam Drive when they returned to Joburg and moved out of his flat where they'd lived for the last three months.

Craighall offered her another two year assignment at their Research Faculty, studying cancer causes, prevention and treatment. At that time the disease was still little understood, but since the mapping of DNA in 1953, research had begun, to understand the causes of cancer at a molecular level and to devise new treatments based on this knowledge.

Rachel was given access to information from other hospitals and research centres. Analysis of this data showed the background to genetic changes in cells destined to become cancerous. Studying the nature of the genetic damage and the affected genes revealed the consequences of those changes on the biology of the cell. This led to understanding the defining properties of a cancer cell and the additional genetic events which led to further progression of the cancer. All of this work provided vital data for remedial research.

Her research work was social as well as medical. She carried out studies into life style or dietary patterns which modified cancer-causing factors, collating the data and other input to assist in the creation of preventative programmes. As she became more involved in this research, she began to be known among her peers, both in South Africa and abroad.

She threw herself into her new role with passion and conviction. A challenging new man in her life and a challenging new job, marriage in view. Rachel was a happy, fulfilled woman.

It seemed to her such a short time ago. *What a record to be proud of. Meet a man, fall in love, live together, get engaged. Fall out of love, separate. All in less than twelve months! Oh God. What am I going to tell my parents?*

Rachel pulled herself together, dried her eyes, stripped off and had a cold shower. But she was still thinking about the last few months. *If only he hadn't joined the bloody golf club at Hyde Park. It was full of those people.*

Nick didn't have a prejudiced bone in his body. At Wits, he'd been involved in their very active anti-apartheid movement. He didn't notice whether someone was black or white. They were just people who were fun and interesting to be with, or not. Then three months ago he had been promoted to Director of Diamond Mining Operations. The money was good, the work was challenging, but the price in terms of compromise was exorbitant. He didn't actually change his views, he pretended to change them, which to Rachel was even worse. It was pure hypocrisy. It was no longer Nick. It was someone she didn't know.

He started making plans without consulting her, getting friendly with people for the wrong reasons, suppressing his better instincts so he could fit in with the big brass.

"Darling," he'd say. "Just because the guy's an apartheid supporter it doesn't mean he's a bad person. He has a point of view. We all have the right to our point of view."

The business at the golf club was the last straw. In order to become a member he needed three sponsors. It so happened that the three members with whom he'd played several times were all from Imperial Diamond, all part of the drinks parties' circuit and to Rachel they were all racial bigots. She pleaded with him not to ask them for their support.

"It's only a golf club membership. My God, you'd think I was plotting the assassination of Mandela." Nick was adamant. He wanted this membership and that was the price he was prepared to pay. So he had his way. From that day, Nick seemed to become a captive of these people. He spent more time with them, drinking and politicking, than he did with Rachel. She couldn't speak out to them so she had to take it out on Nick and it was destroying their life together.

The previous month, he had sprung a surprise. "I've booked a long weekend at the Mount Nelson, in Cape Town, Thursday to Monday. Garden suite, champagne, the works!"

"Oh Nick, that's a marvellous idea. Oh my God! To get away for a few days. That's what we need, just the two of us, like before. You're a genius."

The weekend was a great success. The weather was warm and dry. They spent long lazy hours lying by the pool, sipping cool drinks and talking about nothing in particular. They took a taxi down to the harbour and had dinner at a bistro on the waterfront.

On the last day, Nick hired a dinghy with an outboard and they sailed down the coast to Clifton Beach. He made a barbecue on the beach from fish they caught on the way. He'd put two bottles of rosé wine in the dinghy, covered in ice under a tarpaulin, cold and delicious with the fish. They were both still tipsy when they got back to the hotel.

He carried her into their suite and laid her on the bed. "I love you so much Rachel. I'm sorry for being such an asshole. I'm sorry for everything."

"Shut up and come here, you idiot."

He gently removed her blue halter top and shorts. She had on only a flimsy pair of panties. He kissed her breasts, her stomach, between her legs. They made love as they had when they first met, tender and passionate.

Then Rachel climbed on top of him, her legs astride. She pushed herself onto him, thrusting herself against his body with a violent fury. As if to wipe out the memory of the last couple of months, the arguments, the scenes, the awful people, the breakdown of their relationship. She cried out and bit his neck as they both climaxed. Then she slid down to lie alongside him. Nick's arms came around her and she fell into a deep sleep.

When she woke he was snoring gently. She sobbed quietly until he stirred and they went down for breakfast.

Nick didn't return and she heard nothing further from him. He was gone from her life and she didn't know where he was. He had always wanted to visit Europe and she wondered if he had decided to take this opportunity. He had withdrawn exactly half the money from their joint account. *He won't last long on that.* She stayed in the apartment and continued with her work at the Faculty.

Nobody came to see her except Nick's boss from Imperial Diamond. He looked at Rachel as if to say, *I know whose fault this is!*

After a few days, she called her mother. "We're having a bit of a break, Nick's got a job overseas and we're going to see how things go. I'll join him when he gets settled down."

Her mother didn't believe a word. "Why don't you come up to stay with us at home? Daddy and I would love to have you with us, just until Nick decides what he's going to do."

But she stayed in Joburg. Partly to continue with her research work, which was becoming an all consuming passion, but also in the faint hope that Nick would walk back through the door. Not the man that she'd been living with for the last three months, but the old Nick, the man she'd first met and who'd taken her to Cape Town. But he never came.

The following week, her period was late. She was a nurse, she didn't panic. Stress and trauma often manifested themselves in such ways. Two weeks later she woke up feeling nauseous, so she went to see her doctor. She couldn't remember whether she'd taken her pill that day in Cape Town. She'd been too emotionally upset.

The baby was due in August. Rachel was a fine specimen of a pregnant twenty-seven year old with no vitamin or hormonal deficiencies. She fleetingly thought of suicide, then abortion. Finally she called her mother and just before Christmas she arrived back in Durban. The Faculty had been sad to see her go. Her parents were delighted to welcome her home.

They threw a big Irish Christmas Party for the family and some friends. Rachel had four brothers and a sister, and there were three sisters- in-law and three nephews and nieces and a dozen more guests. No one said anything about Nick. Her parents had obviously spread the word about their break-up, but not about the baby. It was to remain a closely guarded secret. No one except her parents and her sister would know of her condition.

After dinner she left the other guests at the big table and went up to sit on the terrace. Her sister, Josie, was sitting alone on the swing bed, smoking.

"Better give it up Josie." She admonished. "It's been medically proven that.."

"Doctor Rachel! For your information, I am absolutely convinced that you're right, and that smoking causes cancer and if I continue I will suffer a long and lingering illness, followed by fatal death. However, I am definitively quitting for ever on New Year's Eve. So, if it's going to kill me, then it had better be quick. So there!"

Rachel laughed. "Well, you make it sound so harmless I'm tempted to have a smoke myself. Except that I'm equally convinced that smoking is a definite no-no for expectant mothers. Besides, I don't think I want anything further to do with cancer research. That was chapter twenty-seven of my previous life and I'm starting chapter one of my new life."

"What's it like being pregnant, Rachel? Is it magic and fulfilling and all the wonderful things people say? Or are they all lying?"

Rachel sat down beside her sister. "It's bloody terrifying, to tell you the truth. Especially when you haven't a husband, and I haven't even got a boy-friend any more. My life is not working out the way I expected. Not at all."

Josie put her arm around her. "Everything will be just fine. You'll see."

Hanny Peterson was a friend of Rachel's father. He had lost his wife two years before, giving birth to their third child, a girl, and was still only in his early thirties. Hanny owned three jewellery stores in the Durban area and lived in a villa overlooking the harbour, just a couple of miles from the Chukka Country Club. He had been invited to the Christmas Party with his children and had spent as much time as he decently could, talking to Rachel, watching Rachel and enquiring after her to her parents.

On January 11th, Hanny phoned and asked to speak to her. "I wondered if you'd like to join me for dinner at the Country Club, tomorrow night?"

Although she didn't really know him, Rachel was too polite to refuse. They drove out to the club in a smart limousine. Hanny was good company, relaxed, considerate and interested in her. He asked about her work in cancer research. Her father, who was on the senior staff at the Royal Albert Hospital, had obviously been boasting of his daughter's capabilities. He was impressed. "You must be proud to have done such ground-breaking work. There can't be many young women who have become renowned cancer researchers."

Hanny was descended from Norwegian stock. Baptised

Johannes, he'd been Hanny since he was a child. He told her his grandfather had come to Durban on a steamer at the turn of the century. He'd fallen for a girl on the trip over and they decided to get married and settle there.

"He had an amazing life. Just went off and did his own thing. Can you imagine? A Norwegian, who couldn't speak a word of any other language, gets off a ship in Durban and seventy years later, here we are, dining in a fancy country club, all because of what he did."

Rachel encouraged him to recount the story. "He was lucky enough to be befriended by a very wealthy man, another Norwegian. He started as a truck driver then became his chauffeur and finally he looked after him when the old man was widowed and sick.

"He left my grandad a nice legacy, so he started up his first jewellery store with a partner, a Dutch gem expert. They did well when Durban was expanding and there was a lot of money around. Then he bought out the business when his partner went back to Europe."

"And so it got handed down to you in due course?"

"I took it over when my dad passed away, four years ago." Hanny looked a little sheepish. "That's the Peterson saga, three generations of boring jewellers!"

Rachel enjoyed his company. It felt good to be with someone who obviously liked her for herself, and when he suggested meeting again, she happily accepted and they went out often over the next few weeks. Hanny never went further than a couple of goodnight kisses, somehow sensing that Rachel wasn't yet ready for a physical relationship.

He invited her to his home to meet his children. The twins, Catrine and Gregor, were three years old and Birgitta was a year younger. They had Scandinavian colouring, with fine features and blonde hair. They latched on to Rachel like a surrogate mother. She read the signs well enough, but her emotions were still concentrated on Nick and her unborn child.

After several outings, she realised that Hanny's feelings were more than just a casual affection, and decided to confide her story to him. They sat in the garden of his house above the harbour and she told him everything. About Nick, their relationship, the problems in Joburg, their falling out and her pregnancy. She was happy to have her child, even without a father. Finally, she told him that she didn't think she would ever get over Nick. He was her first true love and the father of her child. Rachel liked everything to be clear, no misunderstandings.

Hanny said nothing for a while, then he took her hands. "Rachel. That was a different life. It's over, but you will always have the memory of it because of your child. You need to concentrate on your new life now and not dwell on the past. I'm flattered that you confided in me and I wouldn't wish you to be any different than you are. I don't expect you to forget Nick. I'd be disappointed if you did. You can't change your true feelings. It's not in your nature. "

They continued to go out together and Rachel saw that Hanny didn't seem to be troubled by her story. It was true, he wasn't bothered by it. He was falling in love with her, but he knew that he had to handle the situation very carefully.

In February he invited her to a St. Valentine's dinner at the club. As usual, he picked her up at her parents' house, wearing his black tie and dinner jacket. He was a fine looking man. A true Norwegian, just under six feet, slim and upright, very fair hair and blue eyes.

After dinner they danced a couple of waltzes then went outside to walk around the beautifully manicured gardens, admiring the varied colours of the many tropical plants and flowers, and breathing in their heady fragrance. Hanny plucked up his courage. Pulling her closer to him, he said, "Rachel, you must know what I feel for you."

Even though she'd been half expecting this, she was flustered. "I don't want anyone to feel sorry for me."

"That's impossible. You are the cleverest, most charming and lovely woman I've ever met. My feeling for you isn't pity. I'm in love with you and I want you to be my wife and I want your child to be our child. We both know that it's the best solution."

Rachel said nothing. She liked Hanny and could probably get to love him. He was a good man and a loving father to his children. But she knew she couldn't feel the passion for him that she'd felt for Nick.

He went on. "I already have three lovely children and I know how much kids need a mother *and* a father. It doesn't seem right that my family should lack a mother, whilst yours will lack a father." He paused, waiting to see if he'd said too much.

"Do you think that Catrine and Greg would take easily to having their mother's position usurped? And Birgitta, she's still very young and vulnerable."

"They would all scream with delight if I told them that they had a new mother. You!"

Two weeks later she surrendered. Hanny had played his cards well, but there was only one thing that counted. He loved her, and his children loved her. Her parents were relieved. Fatherless babies were still frowned upon in Durban. Hanny had saved the family's reputation.

They were married in a quiet family ceremony on March 10th. The Harringtons were an Irish catholic family, but the ceremony was held in the Peterson's family church, the Bayhead Presbyterian. Her wedding gown was a primrose colour, loose and flowing to hide the slight baby bulge. Hanny thought she looked adorable. He was the happiest man on the planet.

What an incredibly lucky woman I am, Rachel thought. Then, she fleetingly wondered where Nick was. *What is he doing? Who is he with?*

TWO

April, 1974
Brighton, England

"And our sixteenth contestant is Portugal. Please welcome Paulo de Carvalho, singing *E depois do adeus, And after the Goodbye*."

It was Saturday, April 6th, 1974 and in the Brighton Dome concert hall, British TV personality, Katie Boyle, was nearing the end of her presentation of the entrants in the nineteenth Eurovision Song Contest. After Portugal, only Italy's performance remained to be viewed before the voting began.

Portugal's three points would earn them an equal fourteenth place. Well behind the twenty four points gained by *Waterloo*, which won the contest for Sweden and launched ABBA, an unknown rock band, on their glittering career. However, in Portugal, some of the viewers and listeners to the programme were disinterested in the result of the voting. They had more important matters to attend to.

Lisbon, Portugal

Late in the evening of April 24th, *E depois do adeus* was played on one of Portugal's most popular radio stations. Then at quarter past midnight on the morning of April 25th, the presenter introduced a well loved song that had been banned by the dictator, Salazar, many years before. *Grândola Vila Morena,* written by the Portuguese folk singer, Zeca Afonso, had been branded subversive and suspected of promoting communist ideals. This was the first national performance of the song since its banishment.

The two songs were heard by hundreds of thousands of listeners all over Portugal, but the combination was understood by only a few hundred. It set in motion a sequence of events that would cause the deaths of millions of people and upset the world balance for more than a quarter of a century.

Prague, Czechoslovakia

The white-haired man was reading in his apartment on Wenceslas Square when the telephone rang. It was after four in the morning, but he was waiting for the call.

"Good morning, comrade. Vasco here." The voice said, in Portuguese. "It's done. You can come home."

"*Vivo a revolução!*" he replied and replaced the receiver.

He poured himself a glass of white porto, drank a swallow then he dialled a local number.

The phone was picked up immediately. "*Sim?*"

"You can book the tickets, Alberto. We're going back to Lisbon."

"At last," said the bodyguard. "At last. Well done comrade Cunhal. Congratulations! Now it's our turn to change things. Let's get back and change history."

Lisbon, Portugal

At five forty-five, Nick Martinez walked out of the foyer of the Tivoli Hotel onto the Avenida de Liberdade in Lisbon. After a couple of stretching exercises on the front step, he turned right as he'd done almost every morning for the last three months and set off at a steady jog down the footpath between the main road and the lawns sprinkled with sweet smelling mimosa.

It was still quite dark and the street lights were on, but the temperature was pleasant, no breeze and a slightly heavy atmosphere. The summer was on its way. Martinez breathed in the fragrant, warm air and adjusted his stride for a comfortable half hour run. He had a pretty full programme, but this early jog was an essential part of the rehab programme he'd been following since leaving South Africa. Being addictive, he'd had to replace unhealthy addictions with healthy ones. So, out with the booze and cigarettes and in with the running and the yoghourt.

After the excesses of colonial style life in Johannesburg he was appreciating the lack of temptations in this simpler environment. He'd been helped out in this by having only two hundred dollars left in the world when he arrived in Lisbon and got the assignment with *APA*. His body was appreciating it too. Just over six feet and broad framed, his weight was now down to ninety kilos. He hadn't needed to throw out many clothes, since he'd left most of his stuff behind when Rachel finally kicked him out last November.

He was now turning towards the Alfama district, past Rossio station and back up the other side of the Avenida. His inherited Patek Phillipe watch, the only thing of value that he owned, told him it was six o'clock in Lisbon and eight in Johannesburg. So that was useful, even though he was about to leave the former and wasn't going to the latter. His flight to Luanda was at nine thirty, but he had a few jobs to get done before going out to the airport. He listed them in his mind. *Get the samples back from the assessor with his last data analysis. An hour with the hotel photocopy machine, cutting and pasting. Type up a one page report on the Remington. Then pack a quick bag and off to the airport. No sweat.* He wasn't going into the *APA* office this morning, his schedule was too tight.

Loping across the soft grassy surface of the Parque Eduardo VII, the South African looked up at the Ritz Hotel, which he'd recently discovered had a magnificent wine cellar. *Too bad I quit,* he thought to himself. Picking up a sprint to cover the park he dropped back into jogging mode again. His black tee shirt was soaked through and he was on a high, oblivious to everything except his body. A final turn onto the Praça do Marquês do Pombal and at six ten he was heading back down to the Tivoli.

The perspiration was dripping down his face and neck when he ran up the two flights of stairs in the hotel. His key was in his shorts pocket and he was back in his room at six fifteen, having neither seen nor spoken to anyone since he'd left it. The yoghurt, orange juice and fruit that he'd ordered were on the table with the Herald Tribune. He stripped off and did a few stretches and push ups before taking hot and cold showers, spending a couple of minutes luxuriating under the heavy flow of water beating down on his body.

Nick towelled off and shaved then glanced at the headlines while he ate his breakfast and dressed. Navy double-breasted suit with flared trousers, wide collared white shirt and maroon tie. Putting his wallet into his jacket pocket, he paused and took out a photograph. The pretty, red-haired woman in the snapshot was wearing a blue halter top and shorts and standing in the surf on the edge of a beach. It was just a few months ago, but it seemed like a lifetime.

What an asshole I turned out to be, he thought. *Getting dumped by the girl I wanted to marry.* Coming from Durban to Joburg was tough enough for her without having to put up with him behaving like a total prick. He'd been too wrapped up with his new job, his new so-called friends. He'd frightened Rachel off and he was paying for it now. *Still, she's young, and better off without a loser like me. She's probably already found somebody else.* He felt a momentary surge of jealousy and put the photograph back in his wallet.

He looked in the mirror to straighten his tie and dusted off a few imaginary flecks from the shoulders of his jacket. The dark-haired, tanned, Latino reflection in the glass smiled back at him. *Looking good, Nick. This is going to be a big day, a very big day.*

He had no idea how big it was going to be.

At six thirty-five, Martinez picked up his briefcase and walked down the stairs and out the hotel exit. He had taken to keeping his key with him since a recent scene in reception when he had been accused of trying to get a different room key. This was due to his incomprehensible Portuguese which he insisted on trying out on the desk clerk. Ironically, Nick came from Portuguese origins, several generations ago and it was spoken in his family, but he hadn't been brought up to speak it. It was considered by non-Portuguese speakers to be an 'inferior language'. His full name was Nicolao Jorge Martinez, after his grandfather. And though he also spoke Afrikaans, his English had a softer than usual South African accent. This background was the reason that he'd gravitated from Joburg to Lisbon, of all European cities.

Turning left out of the hotel, he headed up towards the Avenida Fontes Perreira de Melo, where the assessor had his small ground floor office. It was still dark, but he noticed that the city was unusually quiet. There was no traffic to be seen and he walked straight across the main Avenida without waiting for the light to change. He tried to remember if it was yet another religious holiday, but gave up on it.

The assessor's office was two blocks up the street in a smart new office building that, like everything else in Lisbon, wasn't quite finished. Nick wondered vaguely how the guy could afford the rent, but given the last ten years' enormous increase in oil and mineral exploration and production in the Portuguese African colonies, he supposed that he had more than enough work to make a living.

Martinez arrived at the door of the office and pushed. The door was locked, the lights were out, there was nobody there. He checked his watch. It was six forty-three precisely. The man had promised to be there by then, to do business before his flight departure to Angola. There was no doorbell, so he rattled the handle noisily. When there was no response, he rapped on the glass panel with his knuckles. *Hell, the guy knows I need the stuff this morning. What's his name again? Afonso, that's it.*

He banged on the door again and shouted, "Afonso, it's Nick Martinez. Open up."

He knocked and shouted until a light appeared in the back of the office. He waited for the Portuguese to open the door. Instead, Afonso approached the glass panel and gestured for him to go away. He was mouthing something, seemingly in Portuguese. Nick couldn't make it out. He was getting mad. He wasn't going to let some obscure Portuguese religious holiday destroy his plans for the day. He knocked and gesticulated until finally Afonso motioned to him to stop and began to fumble with the locks and bolts on the door.

Martinez's naturally good humour returned and he stepped back with relief. The door opened an inch. "*Bom dia,* Afonso. I suppose it's a holiday, but if you'll just give me my stuff, you can lock up again and take the day off." He didn't want to upset the Portuguese when he had the most important samples in his office with the analysis.

The man didn't reply. He poked his head out of the door, looked up and down the street, then at Martinez. "*Senhor nao sabe?* Don't you know?" He asked in a whisper.

"Afonso, you know I don't talk your lingo and I have to get ready to fly off to Luanda in a couple of hours. Will you please just give me my stuff and I'll leave you in peace?"

Afonso came up so close to him that he could smell the breakfast coffee on his breath. "Senhor not understand. Portugal has revolution today."

Martinez's brown eyes widened. He stared at the Portuguese, who was already locking and bolting the door again. As if in a dream, he turned and looked around him. The sun was just coming up and he noticed for the first time a group of soldiers with rifles outside the doors of the Banco Atlantico. Another group was marching down the Avenida. He heard shouting from the park behind him and the blunt shapes of three steel-grey tanks came into view, turrets open and soldiers standing with machine guns at the ready. Crowds of cheering people were climbing up onto the tanks. The women were kissing the soldiers and offering them red carnations from the bunches in their hands.

He turned back to the office door and saw Afonso looking out at him through the glass panel. "Oh, Fuck!" he said.

It was the morning of Thursday, April twenty fifth, 1974.

THREE

September, 1974
Near Ambrizete, North-western Angola

"Congratulations, Sergio, you have a fine, healthy son. Three kilos eighty exactly." The midwife picked up the newborn baby boy from the kitchen scale and placed him carefully into his father's hands.

Sergio Melo d'Almeida beamed with delight, kissed the woman and gave a loud hoot of happiness. He gazed through the pebble-thick lenses of his spectacles at the naked infant. The child was screaming at the top of his lungs and squirming so much that he held him tightly for fear of dropping him onto the sisal covered floor.

"How is Elvira? Can I see her? Is she OK?" His wife was in the bedroom upstairs to the kitchen where they were standing. The cottage was really nothing more than a two up, two down terrace apartment, one of the six that his father had built for the senior workers when the mine became operational, ten years before.

"She's upstairs with Manuela, sleeping. She's in good health, just very tired after so many hours in labour. It's best to let her rest for a while. No working for two weeks at least." Elvira was the accountant in the business, so Sergio was going to have to replace her for a while by doubling his own work load. *Sociedade Mineira de Angola,* The Angolan Mining Company, was a family affair and there weren't many office-trained people to share the load.

The midwife wrapped a cotton wrap around the baby then went back upstairs to Elvira. Sergio walked along to the offices to show off his latest offspring to his brother, Henriques.

It would have been impossible to guess that the two men were brothers. Small and skinny, Sergio had a light brown skin, inherited from their Portuguese father, and wore thick lenses in his plastic framed spectacles. He seemed to be constantly peering through a fog, his eyes screwed up in his sharp, bird-like face, in a head that looked too big for his body. Henriques was the exact opposite, a massive, heavy-boned man, whose colouring was a throwback of the true African black skinned people, like their Angolan mother.

Henriques was sitting at his desk with three year old Alicia, Sergio's first child, on his knee. His wife, Manuela, had been assisting at the birth and was still upstairs with Elvira. They had no children and spoiled Alicia as if she was their own. "What news, brother?" he asked.

"Wonderful news! We now have a girl and a boy. My work in the child production department is progressing well." Sergio laughed out loud with joy and placed the tiny baby in his brother's enormous hands. The baby was no longer screaming and seemed to gaze curiously up at Henriques.

"Thank God he and Alicia look like Elvira and not like you," he said. "Good Portuguese stock, not scrawny Angolan rejects."

Sergio just smiled at his brother's chiding. They were as close as two siblings could be, despite their contrasting personalities and physical appearances.

Henriques gently lifted the child and held him on his niece's lap. "See what we've found, Alicia, a little brother for you."

The three year old girl stared at her new brother in wonder. The little boy was the image of his Portuguese mother. Dark, curly hair and enormous brown eyes looking out from a round, olive-skinned face.

She reached carefully out and stroked his head and face, still damp from the midwife's washing. "He's beautiful," she said. "Can we keep him?"

The child was christened on the second of September at the Catholic Mission in Ambrizete, on the coast about thirty kilometres from the mining property. Sheltering from the blazing hot sun in the shabby clapboard building, the small group of family and friends listened to the Pastor, Father Cristóvão, as he blessed the newborn child and named him Raymundo Jesus Melo d'Almeida, after his uncle Henriques's middle name. The christening was the last joyous event that the family would share together before the aftermath of the Revolution of the Carnations would sweep their homeland into a maelstrom of terror, privation and death.

Durban, South Africa

Rachel's son was born on September 4th, two weeks late. His step-brothers and sisters were too young to understand the significance of this six month pregnancy, and his fair colouring and looks favoured the mother. He could have passed as Irish or Scandinavian. Hanny treated the new baby as if he were his own son. The rest of the family would never divulge the secret. It would never be known. He was christened Adam Johannes Peterson, and for thirty- three years he didn't know who his real father was. And his father didn't even know that he existed.

BOOK TWO

PART ONE: 2008

FOUR

Wednesday, April 2nd, 2008
Verbier, Switzerland

It was a cold, raw morning in the Swiss Alps and a heavy mist cut the visibility down to less than twenty metres. A *jour blanc,* as it's known in the mountains. The tall, slim man in the dark-blue ski outfit wasn't worried. He was a highly skilled skier who knew the area like the back of his hand. There had been a heavy snowfall over the last day and night and there was about fifteen centimetres of fresh powder which he wanted to enjoy while it was still untracked. This would be his last run of the season. He'd been ready to go back home until he saw the weather forecast and decided to stay for one more outing.

After getting into the Medran lift in Verbier when daylight still hadn't permeated the mist, at eight forty he was skiing down below the Lac des Vaux towards the Vallon d'Arby. Now into his retirement years, he was still skiing as well as he'd ever been. He also played low handicap golf and enjoyed a couple of weekly tennis games when he wasn't up on the slopes. All this was courtesy of a healthy life style, a hip replacement and no financial problems.

He stopped at the entrance to the gulley and peered around in the limited visibility. There was no one in sight. Easter had been early that year, the holidays were over and the mountain resorts had entered the quiet, end of season period. There had been some good snow earlier in the season, but until this last fall it had been getting thin. The relatively poor snow conditions meant that there were few visitors around and the lack of visibility had apparently put them off.

He had gone for a nightcap at the Crock bar the previous evening, chatting with a young American-sounding guy who said that he might join him, but it looked like he had opted out. The man didn't mind, he loved the feeling of space and freedom that an empty, snow-covered mountain can give. His wife had passed away two years previously and they had no children, so he preferred to spend his time skiing alone, in the quiet solitude of the Alps, away from the more socially active life style of his home country.

Verbier had become a large village in the thirty or so years since he had built the chalet, but he enjoyed the atmosphere, the proximity to Geneva airport and the better than average snow conditions, compared to other lower resorts, which had hardly received a covering of snow this winter. With most runs at over two thousand metres, Verbier's large skiable domain offered many itineraries. This morning he was in his element, skiing a long challenging run, away from lifts and other artificial infrastructure.

The Vallon d'Arby was officially closed off. The orange cord and the 'Danger' signs were designed to discourage less competent skiers. This meant that the tractor had not yet been sent out. The machine was taken out after each snowfall to pack down the snow on the famous, or infamous *path,* a long narrow track which led from the exit of the opening gulley, five hundred metres further down the slope. The path led to several kilometres of fairly precipitous descent, with the poor visibility and fresh powder snow coverage adding extra spice to his morning outing. The quiet solitude and beauty of this itinerary made it even more special. After the initial entrance gulley and the path, the skier was faced with several options, steep powder slopes and narrow gullies, or gentler, wider slopes and many routes through a large mountainous forest.

Today, he would ski right along to the end of the path and across to the forest, which provided better visibility for the run down. It culminated in a picturesque, protected valley, with a stream running parallel to the track towards the village of La Tzoumaz. There he would enjoy a coffee and croissant before a few more runs and then back to his chalet for lunch.

He ducked under the cord and adjusting his snow goggles, he set off through the mist in a tight line, turning expertly around the large moguls, slaloming his way through the light powder to the bottom of the gulley. There was a sharp, rocky turn to the left to negotiate then he would follow the path to the forest at the end, before starting his descent through the trees.

It was a narrow track, only wide enough for one skier. No more than a gash cut across the mountain, it was well covered in fresh snow with no other tracks to be seen. The start was between two steep slopes and visibility was better than further along, where it disappeared into the foggy gloom, snaking between the snow-covered mountainside tight on the left and a precipitous drop down the right side to a large field of jagged, icy rocks below. His heels tight together, he skimmed along the narrow, uneven surface and then started side-slipping to slow down before a hairpin bend to the left, which led down to a series of bumps with no room for speed or error.

Exiting from the hairpin bend, he heard the sound of someone behind him. He came to a stop and standing precariously at the first bump, the gaping void disappearing into the mist below his skis, he looked back. Behind the tinted goggles his eyes opened wide with astonishment. Another skier, in a black outfit, appeared from the hairpin bend, just a few metres behind him, coming down the slight decline without slowing, now virtually on top of him. *Merde! What the hell?*

He frantically turned back and stepped sideways, left, to the high side of the path to leave room below him, but the oncoming skier had already gone higher. As he sped past, he struck the tall man hard on his left shoulder. Completely off balance, he was thrust sideways to the right and projected straight out into the misty void towards the rocks ten metres below.

Instinctively he turned desperately in the air, trying to pull his skis below him to land feet first. The skis collided against the cliff side, propelling him headfirst into the rock field. He put his arms up to cover his head, his ski poles still hanging from his wrists by their straps, and landed in the middle of the rocky ground, breaking the clavicle of his right shoulder,.

His left knee smashed against a massive boulder and his skis flew off and clattered down the mountainside as he skidded further into the rocks, trying vainly to protect his head with his sleeved arms. One of the ski poles caught amongst the rocks, and his arm was pulled down behind him. A wrenching pain tore through his left shoulder as his body twisted unnaturally. A root of bracken trapped his boot and his knee cracked as it was torn sideways by his falling weight. The snow goggles were broken and ripped from his head along with his ski hat, as his body was thrust between two large jagged boulders. A ragged outcrop tore into his right eye. Then his head smashed into a corner of the rock and he lost consciousness at the impact. He slid limply to a halt, trapped between the two rocks, unconscious and bleeding.

The stranger halted sharply on the path and removed his skis. Looking around, he ensured that there was nobody in sight, then using his batons, he carefully scrambled down over the icy rocks to the unconscious figure. The victim's body lay twisted in a grotesque position. A massive gash was oozing blood from his forehead and one of his eyes seemed to have been penetrated by a sharp rock. He felt the side of his neck, there was still an unsteady pulse.

After peering around again carefully, he removed his ski gloves, under which he was wearing rubber kitchen gloves. He pushed up his goggles then took out a leather box from the inside pocket of his anorak. It contained a small phial and syringe. He filled the syringe from the phial and injected it directly into the gash on the injured man's forehead, withdrew it and replaced the box in his pocket. He searched through the pockets of the man's torn ski jacket and found what he was looking for, zipped into the inside pocket. Slipping it into his own jacket, he replaced his fur gloves and climbed carefully back up over the rocks to the path. After checking his boots for snow, he stepped into his skis and pulled down his goggles.

He looked around again at the deserted scene and skied off along the path towards La Tzoumaz.

In the village, the stranger took the skis, batons and boots back to the ski shop, where he reclaimed his cash deposit. Up in his room in the Hotel de la Poste he changed out of his ski gear then carried his overnight bag down to reception. He paid his bill in cash and walked along to get the bus to Martigny station. The Geneva train arrived at Cointrin Airport two hours before his flight. He had time for a sandwich and a beer before leaving.

The body wasn't found until nine thirty, when the mist cleared a little and the first tentative rays of sunshine started to warm up the mountain. A group of three young snowboarders stopped on the path above the rocks to negotiate the bumps and saw what looked like a bundle of clothing below. They scrambled down to where the crumpled, semi-frozen body lay. Then one of them pulled out his mobile phone.

Twenty minutes later, the paramedics arrived and tried vainly to find a pulse. The body was carried up to the path, wrapped in blankets and laid on a sled. They skied along to a large open area called the Col des Mines, where a helicopter from Air Glaciers had landed. It transported the man to the nearest hospital, the Cantonal, in Martigny, where he was pronounced dead on arrival.

The pathologist found several broken bones, a ruptured spleen and very severe trauma to the head and eye. She didn't find any trace of nitroglycerin because she wasn't looking for it. The death became a statistic, added to the seventeen other skiers and climbers who had already lost their lives in the Swiss Alps that season. A season ski pass was found in the man's blue ski suit, together with two hundred and fifty Swiss Francs and the keys to his chalet in Verbier. The file was passed to the Martigny police.

They called the Verbier Gendarmerie, who sent two gendarmes to the chalet. There were documents with the man's permanent address and several thousand francs in a drawer in the bedroom. A copy of the file was sent down to the authorities in his country of residence. The local police entered the magnificent penthouse apartment and were able to open the safe with a key found in the

Regency style desk in the office. There was little of interest except for a large amount of Euros in cash and two envelopes addressed to Sra. Angela Soto-Mendez, in Montevideo, Uruguay. The first envelope was marked, "Will and Testament". Apart from some charitable donations, she was the only beneficiary. The other envelope was marked, "Only to be opened by Angela". It seemed to contain a key. The executor, a local attorney, was advised, and the police in Montevideo were asked to contact her.

A week later they heard back from Uruguay. Señora Soto-Mendez was travelling in the Antarctic and couldn't be reached for at least a month. The police were undermanned and overworked and in any case saw no reason to mount an investigation into the accidental death of a foreign resident, so the file was put aside until her return. It subsequently transpired that the dead man left no direct descendents.

FIVE

Friday, April 11th, 2008
New York, USA

New York was having a freezing cold, late winter spell. It was pouring in Manhattan and the wind was blowing the rain sideways. The wet, slippery pavements had become even more dangerous than usual. The temperature in the night club however, was suffocatingly warm, either as a result of the central heating, or perhaps the floor show that was just terminating.

Cinderella's was a very private and discreet club located a few hundred metres to the north-west of Broadway and Times Square, in the basement of a small office building with a greasy spoon café and a greengrocer on the ground floor. Unlike the fairy tale, at midnight Cinderella's didn't turn into a pumpkin and mice. Instead it became even more private and a lot less discreet. The decor was in various shades of pink, which must have looked odd in daylight, but at night the lights were dimmed, so that it wasn't a garish, but more a relaxing, almost cosy environment. Despite the smoking ban in most New York clubs, there was a smoky haze across the room, and the smell of cigars pervaded the atmosphere.

At midnight on this particular Friday, in fact on almost any given Friday when he was in New York, Rodrigo was lounging in a wide leather chesterfield, watching the floor show, a glass of Chivas Regal in one hand and a Romeo y Julieta Cuban cigar in the other. He was in his early forties, but looked younger. A taller than usual Portuguese, well built, with the dark complexion and curly black hair of his race. He was based in New York since leaving London in 2000, although his sexual preferences required him to make frequent visits to Kuala Lumpur, Bangkok and other destinations which fuelled his alternative lifestyle choices.

He had been back in New York for the last week, after spending a month in Cape Town, where his particular fantasies were well catered for. A few days in a private safari park in the Kruger had rounded off his winter break and he was feeling good. Fortunately, his extravagances were financed by a substantial inheritance from his father, who would certainly not have approved of them, God rest his soul.

He took a sip of his whisky and settled back to watch the floor show.

In front of him, a sinuous, large busted blonde wearing nothing but a leopardskin g-string was sexually harassing a similarly dressed, huge, muscular black man. For some reason, a silver and yellow Harley Davidson motor bike was involved, as they pranced around the catwalk that served as a stage in the middle of the floor.

There were fifty or sixty people in the club, mostly men, some of whom were with younger male partners. A number of women, professional and others, several of them topless, were drinking with customers. The remaining single clients were looking for a partner for the weekend. They were all mesmerised by the dancers, watching and waiting for the denouement. A tense atmosphere of sexual excitement pervaded the scene. They knew what to expect and they waited with bated, and in some cases panting breath.

The music climaxed and so did the dancers. After one last thrust of the hips, the black man lifted the girl up over his head and supporting her with just one hand, ripped off her g-string, baring her carefully shaved pubes. Then he stripped his own garment off, proudly showing a massive penis, aroused and rigid. Still carrying the girl above his head, he backed off along the catwalk and out of the room to the blaring finale of 'Sex Bomb'.

After a palpable sense of anticlimax, the audience applauded and went back to their primary occupation, partner hunting. Rodrigo surveyed the room, looking both for the waitress and also for some interesting company.

"Hi, Roddy." The girl who appeared from behind him was a striking redhead. She was topless, showing expensively enhanced breasts with large pink nipples. She had on a tiny mini skirt, with apparently nothing underneath.

"Hello! How do you know my name?" Rodrigo was particularly attracted to redheads of both sexes, preferably younger, but he was intrigued by the novel approach.

"Trade secret. I hear you're an old customer. I'm Cindy, I'm new around here. Mind if I join you?"

She dumped herself in the chesterfield beside the Portuguese, almost on his lap. Her skirt rose up and he saw she was wearing a flimsy pair of panties. Turning towards him, she brushed her breast against his hand. It was surprisingly soft, despite its firm shape. She had a beautifully clear complexion, with a small freckle on her upper lip. He estimated that she couldn't have been more than twenty or twenty-one and he suddenly felt rather old and jaded.

"How about a drink, Roddy?" Her breath smelled of peppermint toothpaste. Her short hair was fragrant with shampoo and he could also detect a subtle perfume. Rodrigo was an aficionado of odours of every kind. The girl was very clean, he decided. He signalled the waitress. What's your fancy?"

"Champagne of course, I wouldn't insult you by drinking anything else." She laughed. A nice sound, rather naive and childish.

The waitress was wearing nothing but a miniscule red tartan kilt. She stepped nearer and Rodrigo ordered another Chivas, his third that evening, adding, "Bring a bottle of champagne for the young lady." He knew that Cindy would get a twenty per cent commission on the bottle, but he figured it would be a good investment.

"The barman said you're a gentleman." She kissed his ear and stroked his inner thigh.

"So you're Cindy, of Cinderellas. Which part of the States are you from? Do I detect a southern twang there?"

"I'm a country girl from Florence, South Carolina, just arrived from the farm." She laughed again. "And you, Roddy, where're you from? I'm figuring you for a European."

"A bit complicated, you know, but basically Portuguese." Rodrigo licked his lips in a greedy, almost predatory manner then pulled on his cigar, inhaling deeply, his eyes half closed.

"Does this bother you?" He blew the cigar smoke away from the girl, who smiled and shook her head.

"There are worse things in life than Cuban cigars. Is that your only vice?"

Before he could answer, the waitress brought his whisky, added a little water and, with a flourish, opened the champagne and poured a glass.

"Here's to us."

"Cheers, my dear. A pleasure to make your acquaintance." Since arriving in New York, the Portuguese had taken to affecting the expressions of the English upper classes. It seemed to get him special service wherever he went.

They clinked their glasses and took a drink just as the music started to blare out again. This time it was a tall black girl and a small white man, both dressed in bowler hats and Y-fronts. They began an intimate samba, involving more and more lewd, crude movements which brought louder and louder bouts of laughter from the now very rowdy, inebriated crowd. The unmistakeable odour of marijuana overcame even the smell of Rodrigo's cigar smoke and the atmosphere began to change, to move to another level.

"Have you ever been to South Carolina?" Her hand caressed his thigh, moving higher.

"Too puritanical for me I think."

"Maybe I can prove different." She moved closer to Rodrigo and pulled his head down to her breast. He nuzzled the nipple, it tasted of vanilla. He was enjoying this. Her hand moved insistently up his thigh until she was stroking his crotch.

He was not alone. Looking round he saw several couples sliding lower in their settees and chairs, trying to preserve some semblance of anonymity in the noisy, smoky room. He covered Cindy's hand with his own and leaned over to whisper in her ear, "Quite a few well known people here, you know." He licked his lips again and drew on the cigar, this time blowing the smoke towards the girl, who blew it back at him.

"Is that so? Well, I'm not surprised, we have just the same phenomenon in the south. Sexual tastes respect no boundaries."

Her probing fingers had found his aroused penis through the cloth of his trousers. She started gently rubbing it along its length, until he felt he might lose control.

He stopped the movement of her hand and asked, "Do you have a place?"

"I have a small apartment, just around the corner." She took his hand and placed it between her warm thighs.

"OK, let's go," he whispered, quaffing the remainder of his drink. "We'll get our coats."

He signalled to the waitress for the bill, added a generous tip and signed it, reclaimed his overcoat from a tough looking bouncer at the door and slipped him a twenty dollar note. Cindy put on a woollen jacket over her naked breasts and then a furry coat and suede boots. She pushed her purse and high heel shoes into a canvas bag and took out a folding umbrella. They exited into the cold, rainy night and she put up the umbrella, which gave virtually no protection. Walking a matter of two or three hundred yards, they reached a shabby, five story building with an Irish pub on the ground floor. The pub lights were on and the place was still fairly full. Music could be heard and a couple of people were smoking outside, huddled up in overcoats under the entrance porch.

Cindy entered a code and pushed open a door at the side of the pub. In the small, stale-smelling lift, she pushed herself against the Portuguese, kissing him artfully and pushing her hand down inside his coat to caress his crotch. He clasped his hands around her backside. At her touch and the sensation of her thrusting tongue in his mouth he felt a return of his arousal.

He said, "How much for the whole night, Cindy?"

"Let's don't talk about sordid things like money. Anyway, I'm worth it. You'll see."

They stepped out of the lift on the third floor, and she took some keys from her purse and opened a door on the left into a darkened hallway. They left their outdoor things in the hallway and she led him through a second door into a studio flat of about thirty square metres.

The cheap fitted carpet was partly covered by a colourful rug and there was a patterned quilt on the oversized bed. A large flat screen TV and a few pieces of battered furniture completed the furnishing and several coloured prints decorated the off-white painted walls. There were no personal possessions to be seen. Doors leading to what looked like a small bathroom and kitchenette stood ajar at the back of the room. The flat was warm and smelled quite clean to his nostrils.

"Nice place." He gestured in a deprecating gesture, "You're lucky to find it."

The girl shrugged out of the woollen jacket, revealing her amazing breasts again. "Girl friend of mine was leaving town, I'm sub-renting it. I got a good deal. It's just for friends."

The Portuguese looked at her and nodded. He licked his lips again, "That qualifies me as a friend I guess." He gave a short, rather mirthless laugh. "What do we have to drink?" He looked around and spotted a bottle of Chivas and some glasses on a cabinet against the wall. "Good taste, Cindy. Make one for me, will you? I have to hit the john." Rodrigo squeezed her breasts playfully as he went to the bathroom at the back of the flat.

"Same again? I'll have one as well. That champagne tastes like cat's piss." Cindy went to the cabinet and fixed two glasses of whisky, adding a dash of water from a jug.

When Rodrigo came back into the room, he was wearing his shirt loose over his trousers. He pulled down the quilt, sat on the bed sheets and removed his shoes and socks.

Cindy came over to him with a tumbler in each hand. "Here you go. To new friends."

She proffered one of the drinks and knocked back her own in one long gulp. He saw this and did the same. She took the empty glasses and placed them carefully on the cabinet. "Now, lie back and get comfortable. I'll show you what we learn in school in puritanical South Carolina."

The Portuguese lay back on the bed, his head on the pillow. The girl kissed him wetly, her tongue thrusting into his mouth. He pushed his hands inside the back of her skirt and massaged her buttocks. She unbuttoned his shirt, kissing down his chest and stomach until she reached his waist, teasing the curly body hair with her teeth. He pulled his shirt off and threw it onto one of the chairs. She noticed that he looked to be in pretty good condition, not fat at all. She undid his belt then slid the zipper down on his fly. Rodrigo breathed deeply. This girl was good, probably expensive, but worth it.

Cindy stroked his crotch through his shorts then slid her hand inside the leg, rubbing his penis until it pulsed into its full length. Pulling the organ free she licked all round the inflamed head. She looked up at him, "I like big men, Roddy."

"Wait!" He kicked off his trousers and shorts and she threw them on a chair. She smiled at him, then took his member deep in her mouth, sliding it faster and faster between her slick lips until he could no longer control himself.

SIX

Friday, April 11th, 2008
New York, USA

"That was just a starter. Let me get something to clean up with. Then we can enjoy the main course." Cindy got off the bed and went to the bathroom.

Rodrigo lay back against the pillow, staring at a stain on the ceiling. His eyes were clouding over. There was the sound of the toilet flushing. When Cindy returned, he was wiping his forehead. There was a sheen of sweat on his brow.

"Are you feeling OK? You look kinda pale."

The dark complexion accentuated the pallor which had suddenly appeared on his face.

"God, I feel terrible. I must have caught a bug, I'm sweating like a . . . ." He sat up again, looked at the girl standing over him. "*Não compreendo.* What the hell's happening?"

The last thing he saw was the face of the girl looking down on him before he slipped into unconsciousness and fell back onto the pillow.

Cindy went to her bag in the hall and pulled out a cell phone.

"You can come now."

By the time she had cleaned off the bed sheets, the door opened and a man came in. He was wearing a fedora and a navy blue raincoat, with a scarf around his neck and a pair of leather gloves against the cold. He didn't appear to be very wet, he must have been waiting in the downstairs hall and come straight up.

The man removed his hat and placed it on a chair. He looked with distaste at the unconscious Portuguese lying naked on the bed. "Did you have to go all the way like that?"

"No, but it's good practise. Besides, I never did a Portuguese before."

He laughed and took out a handful of notes from his wallet. "Another two thousand dollars, as agreed." He counted out the hundred dollar bills onto the cabinet.

Once again she noted his slight accent and wondered where it originated from. She asked, "What you want me to do now?"

"I told you. Just a few photos. It's a divorce scam, I've got a camera."

"OK. Wait 'til I put this away." She turned to take the cash to her bag in the hall.

Before she could do so, he said. "What time's your bus?"

"Not 'til six am. I've got plenty of time to do this then pick up my things and get to the bus depot. Why, you lookin' for a freebie?" She laughed at him, shaking her breasts.

"I've got a little bonus for you."

She followed him to the bathroom, where he took a packet from his raincoat pocket and spilled some white powder onto the marble surface of the wash basin. He rolled another hundred dollar bill into a tube. Cutting the powder into a couple of lines, he said to Cindy. "Best stuff in town. Treat yourself."

"Well, I guess it's my lucky day." Cindy placed her two thousand dollars onto the wash basin, took the tube and bent over to snort the powder into each nostril. The man put his hand into the side pocket of his coat and pulled out a long rubber band, the kind you use for physio exercises. As she came up, she sneezed and rubbed each nostril then shook her head, her eyes closed. He threw the band over her head and around her neck, crossed his hands over and pulled it tight from behind.

Cindy's eyes opened wide with shock and she saw the reflection of the scene in the small mirror over the wash basin. She tried to scream, but no sound emerged from her mouth. She struggled to pull away, but the band just got tighter. She tried to force her fingers beneath the rubber, but it was biting into the flesh of her neck. In the mirror, she could see the man pulling the band tighter, a savage, arrogant sneer on his face. She flailed about with her arms and legs, trying to escape from the suffocating stranglehold. Her breasts swung from side to side as she struggled, like a macabre sexual ritual, and her kicking legs revealed her flimsy underwear. Cindy's eyes bulged and her face became suffused and crimson. Her tongue protruded from her gasping mouth then her movements ceased and she hung limply from the rubber band in the stranger's hands.

The man carried Cindy's body over and laid it on the bed alongside the naked Portuguese. After replacing his leather gloves with a pair of thin rubber gloves he took the empty sachet the girl had used for Rodrigo's drink from the cabinet. He sniffed both glasses then flushed the dregs from the drugged glass down the toilet with the sachet, washed the glass and dried it off with some kitchen roll. He poured some whisky and water into the glass then threw the liquid into the toilet and flushed it away. Going back to the bed, he put the glass into the unconscious man's hand, clamped the limp fingers around it, pressed it against Rodrigo's lips then replaced it on the cabinet.

From the inside pocket of his coat he took out a rubber band and a small leather box, containing a disposable syringe in a plastic sleeve and a small phial. He filled the syringe from the phial and tied the band around Rodrigo's left bicep. Pressing carefully, he found the vein, and using the other man's right hand, he injected the contents of the syringe into his arm. He withdrew the syringe and the band and dropped them on the floor by the bed.

After closing the fingers of Rodrigo's left hand around it, he put the phial onto the wash-basin. Next, he poured a small amount of the powder from the packet into the banknote tube. Kneeling at the side of the unconscious man, he carefully blew a little of the powder from the tube into each nostril, ensuring that it didn't touch his lips and that it touched the inside of the nostrils. He pressed the limp fingers several times onto the tube and the paper packet then replaced them on the wash basin.

Finally, the man went over to the bed again and removed Cindy's skirt and knickers. He threw them onto the floor, then taking the ends of the rubber band, still around her neck, he pressed Rodrigo's hands onto the band and dropped it back onto the bed. He looked down at the girl. She was lying on her stomach, her head turned towards the Portuguese, as if she was sleeping. Her legs were slightly akimbo and the cheeks of her backside were invitingly open. Reluctantly, he tore his eyes away, went to the door and looked carefully around the studio for any slip-ups. Suppressing a laugh, he went back to take the two thousand dollars from the wash basin. He had another thought and took the wallet from the trousers on the chair. In it there were eighteen hundred dollar bills. He took out ten and replaced the wallet in the trousers.

The man went out to the hall and closed the apartment door, took Cindy's purse and cell phone from the bag on the floor, dropped the keys into the bag and picked up the umbrella. Closing the outside door, he went down the stairs and exited to the street without seeing anyone. As he walked back to the Grailton Hotel he removed the twelve hundred dollars and the few papers that were in Cindy's purse. He extracted the SIM card from the phone and threw them with the rubber gloves and the purse into a skip at the side of the road. The papers from the purse he dropped into a trash can outside a restaurant.

He was back in his room by two in the morning and got five hours sleep. After showering and shaving, he paid his bill with cash then took a cab to Kennedy. He was in time to have breakfast before his flight and he got a few more hours sleep after take-off.

The bodies were not discovered until Sunday, when the neighbours in the apartment opposite called the rental agent about a noxious smell. When she opened the living room door, the smell was so appalling that she screamed even before seeing the bodies on the bed. Panicked, she went down to the pub, where the manager took charge of the matter until the police arrived.

The rental agency confirmed that the apartment had been rented by Cindy, two weeks previously, under the name of Mary-Lou Graham. She had paid one month's rent in advance plus a month's deposit, in cash.

Rodrigo's membership card for Cinderella's led to an investigation which revealed that he had left with a girl at some time before one in the morning. The girl, whom they had never seen before, had arrived just after midnight and asked for him by name. Her canvas bag, which was still in the hall, contained a pair of high heel shoes and a pack of multi-coloured condoms, but no identification.

There were no fingerprints other than Rodrigo's and the girl's to be found on the glasses, syringe and other items. Semen from the Portuguese was traced on the bed sheets, on the girl and on a hand towel.

The pathologist identified a large quantity of heroin in his body and traces of cocaine in both his and the girl's nostrils. The Rohypnol had already been metabolized and eliminated by his system and was untraceable. The condition of the internal organs showed that neither Rodrigo nor Cindy was a habitual drug user. Subsequent analysis of the remaining contents of the syringe showed it to be heroin of a high purity and strength.

The girl was a natural brunette, her hair was dyed red.

The police developed the theory that Rodrigo had strangled the girl, perhaps during a sex act. Then, being unused to drugs, he had succumbed to a fatal mixture of cocaine and heroin. Whether or not this had been accidental or deliberate was impossible to determine.

When the police entered Rodrigo's apartment on Central Park West, using the keys they had found in his overcoat, they discovered large quantities of pornographic material of a very depraved nature, involving children. Inspection of his laptop and mobile phone revealed thousands of images and many email addresses. The machine was sent to the Child Exploitation and Obscenity section of the Justice Department in Washington.

In his office safe they found even more revolting pornographic material, twenty thousand dollars in cash, and several keys. The keys were unlabelled and there was no way of identifying them. Amongst the few pieces of documentation was a file containing bank statements, an address book and a computer printed first class return ticket to Geneva, via London, for the last week of April.

The police finally picked up Cindy's trail. Her name was actually Dolores Jean Lane. Her mother, who lived in a trailer park in Dallas, Texas, was distraught when she sobered up enough to be told of her death, three months after the event.

As far as the demise of the Portuguese was concerned, the coroner recorded an open verdict, and the police began a very slow and inefficient investigation. The Justice authorities concentrated their attention on his laptop and the address book. They were more interested in Rodrigo's life than his death. It transpired that he had no traceable descendants.

SEVEN

Sunday, April 13th, 2008
Marbella, Spain

At 7:00 am, before his golf game, Charlie Bishop walked up the stone staircase to the lake on the land above his house to throw some fish food onto the water. After he and Ellen had finished building the house about five years ago, they'd held a garden party for almost two hundred people. Cecilia, a friend from the golf club, brought as a gift, three tiny goldfish in a plastic bag full of water. When they put them into the lake, he never imagined that in a few years he'd be feeding fifty or sixty enormous carp. Blue, gold, red, silver, white, these beautiful fish just kept on growing and reproducing year after year.

Nature is an amazing thing, he reflected. *Eat, shit and have sex. Nothing else to do, I suppose, if you're stuck in a garden pond.*

The lake was fed with fresh water by a stream which meandered down the slope of the upper garden area towards the house from a natural spring near the perimeter wall, a hundred metres higher. A series of waterfalls and ponds broke the stream's course, each one raucous with the sound of dozens of frogs, calling to each other, day and night.

I've become a breeder of carp and frogs. Could be a new business opportunity. A retirement project.

Charlie went up to the very top of the garden where the spring had been tapped to feed the stream. There were even some smaller fish in the top pond. He wondered how on earth they got up there. He looked down over the gardens, full of flowering plants, eucalyptus trees, bushes and many varieties of palm trees. A large part of the western side had been planted with fruit trees and left in an unkempt state, like the old fashioned orchard they'd had at the previous house. It was a bright, clear morning and from his vantage point he could see over the gardens to the swimming pool, and beyond the pool, across the golf course to the Mediterranean.

He remembered vividly the first time he and Ellen had come here. The hillside had been marked out in *parcelas,* lots, of about two thousand square metres each. They had scrambled up from the bottom of the hill all the way to the top, through bushes, scrub, undergrowth and trees. They weren't dressed for mountain climbing and arrived at the top of the small wilderness breathless, hot and dusty, scratches on their bare legs. Charlie looked over the uncultivated hillside at the view below. The golf course was already open and a hotel was under construction with a few villas being built around it. The main perimeter wall was being erected and there was a temporary guard house, with a security man already installed.

"Let's buy it, Ellen."

"Which plot do you have in mind?"

"The whole hillside!"

That was seven years ago. Once the main house was under way, about half way down the hill, Charlie turned his attention to the land above. He flattened out a plateau above the level of the house that would accommodate several short golf holes and a small lake. He hired a tractor and brought it onto the top of the land, sat in it and released the handbrake, letting the tractor find its own way down the line of gravity. When he reached the plateau he looked back up the hill. The tractor had marked out the line for a stream to run down the hill.

It took almost two years to finish the house, the gardens, the lake, the waterfalls. Then…Ellen disappeared from his life the following year.

I was still a young man when we built this house. Hardly sixty. What happened? Charlie suddenly felt very old. He strolled back down the long staircase to the pool, mounted the top step and threw off his bath robe. Under the robe he was naked, because neither Juan, the gardener, nor Leticia, the housekeeper, worked on a Sunday. So at least once a week he got to enjoy the feeling of warm fresh water against his skin, without the sight of his sixty-eight year- old body being the cause of any domestic upheaval.

Like everything else about Charlie's property, the pool was very large and the water was pleasantly heated. But he never swam for longer than ten minutes, just enough to freshen him up for his golf game, tee-off at eight thirty. Since the triple bypass he didn't dive anymore, but he pushed himself down and swam a circuit of the pool, returning to the shallow water by the steps. He did this a couple of times, doing a flat breast stroke with his face in the water, stretching his shoulders and chest, as the physiotherapist had advised. Got the blood running through his system, lifting his head out of the water to breathe deeply between strokes.

He surfaced at the edge of the pool, rubbed the slight prickle of oxidised water from his eyes and ran his hands through his still thick, curly hair. He heard a soft voice behind him. "Good morning, Charlie."

He stiffened and let out a deep breath. "What? Who's that?" he rasped, "What the hell is..?" He looked up to see a hand, gripping a short cudgel aimed at his head. He had no time to react, the weapon caught him exactly on the temple above the right eye and he fell back onto the steps. The intruder grabbed hold of Charlie's head and carefully banged it against the tiled edge of the pool exactly on the mark of the wound, then let the limp body slip back to drown in ninety centimetres of crystal clear water. There was virtually no blood, but after a few minutes the dark rinse from Charlie's hair began to colour the water brown.

The intruder looked carefully around, then walked up the staircase to the terrace level and slipped into the house by the kitchen door. After about thirty minutes, he re-emerged and climbed the staircase alongside the stream and the waterfalls to the top of the garden. Stepping onto a tree branch, he slipped over the wall where it became the perimeter wall, surrounded by the forest and out of sight of the security cameras. He walked carefully through the trees to his waiting car and drove out by the unguarded dirt track at the rear of the urbanisation. Turning back onto the main road several kilometres further along, he headed down to access the highway, on his way to Malaga.

Without a sound, a creature emerged from the flowering bushes that surrounded the end of the pool and leaped down from the decorative wall onto the tiled surface. The long haired cat crept forward and crouched by the steps. Its thick, lustrous fur was jet black, only the tip of the tail marked with a white flash. Stretching its head towards the water the animal lapped up some of the fresh liquid, its pink tongue flicking in and out. Its huge green eyes seemed to be fixed on the body hanging in the water in front of it. After refreshing itself, the cat strolled back to leap up onto the wall and disappear into the spacious garden.

The sun was already warm in the Costa del Sol. Another beautiful day had begun.

At nine fifteen, Charlie's body was found floating by Juan, who had come in on his day off to water the upper gardens. He managed to pull the eighty-five kilos dead weight out of the water and tried unsuccessfully to resuscitate his employer. Then he called the security service and Leticia, the housekeeper, on his mobile phone.

The local security guard arrived within a few minutes and also vainly attempted to revive the body. The housekeeper arrived ten minutes later, followed by a green car with two Guardia Civil officers. Then two officers of the Policia Nacional drove up, accompanied by an ambulance. The police took statements from the two servants and the security guard and looked at the body. There was a tiny fragment of blue mosaic tile on the wound. They found a corresponding smudge on the edge of the pool. The investigation seemed conclusive.

The body was taken to the morgue in Marbella, laid out on a slab and pushed in the freezer. A report was sent to the Comisaría of the *Policía Nacional* in *Malaga.*

EIGHT

Monday, April 14th 2008
Ipswich, England

At three thirty in the afternoon, UK time, Jenny Bishop was in the kitchen preparing a pot of tea when she received a phone call from a Sergeant Harris, the duty officer with the local police in Ipswich. He asked to speak to her husband, Ronald Bishop.

Jenny went into a blind panic. "What the hell are you talking about?" she shouted into the phone. "Is this a practical joke? My husband passed away last December. You're supposed to be looking for his murderer, not making stupid phone calls."

The policeman was apologetic. He wasn't aware of Ron's death, he'd only been with the Ipswich force for a few weeks. He explained that they'd been contacted by the Malaga police department. Ronald Bishop was registered with the Spanish authorities as the nearest of kin to a Mr. Charlie Bishop. He was sorry to report that he had apparently died from an accident in his pool in Marbella the previous morning.

Jenny's mind went numb at this news. *Charlie's dead, so soon after Ron,* she registered. Suddenly, she couldn't think any more, she couldn't continue with the conversation. "I just told you that my husband is no longer here, so I don't see how this concerns me."

The officer apologised again and said he'd call back when he'd made further enquiries.

Jenny put the phone down. She was in a cold sweat. It was three months since she'd had to discuss Ron's death on the phone with anyone. It was hard to continually face up to the fact that she'd been widowed at the age of thirty-six by a hit and run driver. It was even harder to get up every morning, knowing that there was a murderer out there who had knocked down her husband and left him dying in the street like an animal and then disappeared into the night.

She sat in the living room with a cup of tea and tried to practise the deep breathing and calming thoughts that were getting her through therapy since Ron's death. Four months later and she still couldn't sleep without a sedative. The empty bed at her side was a constant reminder of his absence and she missed the feel and the smell of him next to her. Every night as she lay there, waiting for the unconscious state induced by the sleeping pill, she would relive the day of Ron's death, searching for answers. Then after finally falling asleep, her mind would be invaded by vivid, frightening dreams, until she awoke, exhausted, in a sweat. Her mother was reputed to have a kind of sixth sense, dreaming of events before they occurred and from a few similar experiences it seemed that Jenny had inherited this gift, or curse. But now her dreams were not of future happenings, but of past events. Unhappy, black dreams, ending in frightening scenarios, which, fortunately, her memory failed to retain when she awoke.

Two years ago Ron had gone through his 'silly season', having an affair with a young secretary at the garage. When Jenny was told about it, typically by her best friend Audrey at the tennis club, she went into a rare rage and rushed home to confront him.

She screamed insults at him when she saw from his face that it was true. "What the hell do you think you're doing, making us both look like idiots in front of our friends? Am I so bloody repulsive that you can't keep your hands off the office girls?"

After he confessed and swore that it would never be repeated, she went out with Cooper, her six year old Westie. It was a warm, clear night and as they walked along by the river, Jenny realised it wasn't the end of the world. Ron provided for her well and apart from his occasional childish moods he was a good husband. He didn't deserve to be kicked out because of a twenty year-old tease who wanted to brag to her friends about sleeping with the boss.

Jenny had spent four years tutoring difficult youngsters at the Teesside Secondary School in Sunderland and she had soon learned that it paid to tackle problems head on and not avoid them so that they returned later on in a more virulent form. She went home and gave Ron a severe talking-to as if he was an unruly adolescent, and it worked. She never heard any more of the matter. Life got back to normal and it was fine.

But now it was no longer fine. It was horrible and miserable and lonely and there seemed to be no end to it. *Will it be like this until they find his killer?* She had to force herself not to keep thinking about his death on a dark street, on a wet and cold night, his body left broken and bleeding, to be found by a young woman cyclist who almost ran right over it. *Poor thing. What a sight to discover on a dark night.*

It was ten days before Christmas, the saddest and most unhappy Christmas she had ever spent. The funeral had been on the day they were due to fly off to Dubai, to get away from the freezing weather in Ipswich. Afterwards, Cyril, Ron's salesman, had arranged with the travel company to refund the cost of the holiday. As if that was any consolation. She had gone through the New Year in a daze, impervious to the activity around her, hardly stirring out of doors except to walk Cooper. He seemed to miss Ron too.

Now, he jumped up onto her lap and she stroked him absentmindedly, thinking about the phone call. An unknown voice telling her that Charlie had died, in his swimming pool, thousands of miles away in Spain. She had only met him four times in her life and although he was Ron's father, she didn't like him. And now he was dead, so soon after her husband. By another fatal accident. She shivered. *Father and son, both killed in accidents,* she thought. *A strange coincidence. Maybe.* Jenny didn't believe in coincidences. Everything happened for a purpose.

Ron had adored Ellen, his mother, but he said he'd never been at ease living with his father, leaving for England as soon as he left school. He hadn't talked much about him, or his background. There seemed to be something there that he didn't want to discuss and she had never pressed the point. Then after the wedding, although his mother had visited frequently, Charlie had never been to see them. And she and Ron had been together to his house only for the housewarming party and then sadly, just a year later, for Ellen's funeral.

The only other time that Jenny had seen Charlie was in December, when he came over for Ron's funeral. He seemed to her to be greatly diminished from their previous meetings. He was a large, imposing man and she had always thought him rather arrogant, fit and in control of things, seeming younger than his age. But suddenly she saw an old man, worn out by a heart condition and the loss of his wife and son in just a few short years.

"I don't know what to say, Jenny. You don't deserve this, nobody deserves it. I'm so terribly sorry." For the first time she saw Charlie cry. He hadn't cried at Ellen's funeral, but now his wife and his only son were gone. Jenny hadn't produced any grandchildren, so for him it was the end of his whole family. He wasn't crying for her. She didn't figure in it, she wasn't a Bishop. Even though she had lost her husband it was Charlie who had suffered the greatest loss. His relationship with his son had never been easy but he must have loved him a great deal.

Although Christmas was just a week away, he left on the day after the funeral, telling her that he would be there if she needed him. But she knew that he was just saying the words. He was returning to his home in Spain, truly alone in the world, and that was the way he would continue. It seemed that Charlie had never easily made friends and it was now too late to start.

"Goodbye, Jenny. Look after yourself."

"Goodbye, Charlie, you take care too."

After half an hour, the officer called back. Jenny was calmer and he was gentle and understanding. "I'm only ten minutes away by car. Why don't I pop around and we can sort this matter out? It seems to be a bit complicated."

She went upstairs to change into a skirt and blouse and was at the door when the bell rang a few minutes later.

Sergeant Harris was a big, bluff, old fashioned looking police officer with kindly brown eyes and a little sandy moustache. Jenny decided he was probably what is described as a 'gentle giant', a big, soft teddy bear. He was accompanied by a female PC, about half his size, wearing a smart cap over her short, tinted blonde hair. She hardly looked old enough to be a police officer, chewing gum and carrying a red file embossed with the police department motif, labelled *Charles W. Bishop, Marbella.* They sat in the lounge and both accepted a cup of tea.

One more cup won't kill me, Jenny thought as she carried the tray into the room. Cooper jumped up on the settee beside the policeman, who stroked him affectionately.

"Officer Dawson is here to, er, provide company and comfort." The policeman coughed apologetically. "It's standard police procedure in the case of advising a death in the family."

"Tracy will do fine," the policewoman said. "We don't want to be too formal, do we?"

Diplomatically, the sergeant didn't quiz her about Ron's death. He mentioned that he'd only been in Ipswich for a few months, but she surmised that he must have been brought up to date by the other members of the force. The traumatic events crowded back into Jenny's mind.

A futile inquest resulting in an open verdict.

An unsolved death, hidden in a dossier ten inches thick, with no answers.

A murderer, still at large, with the death of her husband on his conscience.

She jumped slightly when he suddenly broke the silence.

"Well, Mrs. Bishop," he began rather formally, putting aside his tea-cup.

"Call me Jenny, it's what everyone calls me," she interrupted, from force of habit.

"OK, right then, Jenny. Anyway, the thing is, it seems from everything we can find out that you are now the only surviving relative of Mr. Charles Bishop. Were you aware of this?"

Jenny realised this could well be true. Ron was an only child, and his mother had died four years before. Perhaps because he'd been born in Spain, she'd somehow never thought about any relatives in the UK and he had never mentioned any, apart from his grandparents who had passed away before she met him. And now it seemed that there were none to disclose.

"Can you think of any other family?" PC Dawson helped her by listing the possible relationships in order. First, on Charlie's side. No uncles that she'd heard of, but an aunt, yes. She recalled that he had an older unmarried sister who had died in a nursing home that he had paid for. *A surprisingly out of character, generous gesture,* she thought. Or maybe she had just never bothered to find the real person behind the tough, rather distant façade. Who could tell?

Her thoughts were interrupted by Sergeant Harris. "What about your husband's mother?"

Jenny found herself suppressing a pang of guilt at the question. "She came from Middlesbrough, you know," she replied defensively. Ellen, an attractive, vibrant, wonderfully lovable woman, whom she still missed, had a strong and determined character, even in her later life. She couldn't have been more unlike her own mother, who had become weak and vacillating, her strength of character beaten out of her by twenty years of unhappy marriage ending in a divorce cloaked in shame and scandal.

Ellen was continually planning things for herself, her family and other people. She often visited her sister in the north, and since their marriage she would come down to stay with them in Ipswich. She seemed much more relaxed without Charlie and enjoyed her visits, showering them with kindness when she was there. Jenny suspected that it was partly because of her lost pregnancy. Ellen had been devastated at the accident. It was she who had suggested adoption and had given her the details of the orphanage

On her last visit, she was still busy decorating the new house they had built just above Marbella. In the morning she had come down to breakfast and announced, "We're going up to town for a few days to spend some serious money. We'll empty Bond Street and Knightsbridge and then take in some culture. Evgeny Kissin is playing at the Albert Hall, I've already booked a box, so we'll be treated like royalty. Champagne and caviar, that's what we deserve!"

They had a memorable trip. Jenny coming back feeling guilty, laden with gifts that neither Ron nor she could ever have afforded to buy. Excess spending always made Jenny feel guilty.

Some memories in life were difficult to get over, and for her that was one of them.

As Ellen was leaving, she said, "We'll do it again next time I'm over. I'll be back before you know it."

Just a few months later she contracted septicaemia on a cruise ship in the Black Sea and died in a filthy hospital bed in Yalta, waiting for a helicopter to fly her to Istanbul.

Ron had been distraught at losing his mother this way and Charlie had been suicidal. At the funeral in Marbella, there had only been Charlie, his lawyer, the housekeeper and gardener and a few local friends, some from the golf club. Ellen's sister was too ill to travel and Jenny assumed that not many people would want to fly to Marbella for a funeral. *A game of golf perhaps. But a funeral? No thanks.*

Such a waste. All that money and it makes no difference, Jenny thought. Her own mother, having gone from extreme wealth to almost abject poverty after the divorce, had been taken by cancer two years after their wedding, which had broken Jenny's heart the first time around.

She was still lost in thought again when Sergeant Harris coughed politely. "Sorry, Sergeant, I was thinking about Ron's mother. She had a sister, but she died two years ago. You probably know that Ron and I were unable to have children, so there isn't a grandchild either."

Remembering the adoption papers they had prepared after the accident and the children she met at the orphanage in Bulgaria, tears pricked at her eyes and she blew her nose violently.

She racked her brains, but couldn't for the life of her remember any other surviving family members. "There's my sister, Emma, but I don't suppose that counts. It's only Charlie's family that you're asking about isn't it?"

She looked up at their concerned faces. "Do I have to do anything? I don't think I'm up to facing death and funerals again so soon," she burst out, "I don't think I can handle it."

"Look, Jenny," Sergeant Harris said gently. "What we need to do now is to go to the station and look at all the paperwork. Then I'll call my opposite number in Malaga and we'll see what has to be done. There's been a death and we've got to follow the procedures.

Can't have the Spanish police criticising our ways. I'll help as much as I can, alright?"

Chief Inspector Espinoza, from the Policía Nacional in Malaga, spoke very good English, which made the conference call easier than she had feared. The death seemed to be an accident, but there were various formalities and administrative matters to be completed and she was the only person who could assist them.

He said, "I've now been in touch with Sr. Bishop's lawyer, Sr. José-Luis Garcia Ramirez, and he has also informed me that you need to come down here, Señora."

"Why can't the lawyer handle things without my involvement?"

"In the case of a suspicious death we need to have a member of the family to help us resolve the situation, you understand."

"Resolve what situation? You said it was an accident. No, I don't understand."

"Señora Bishop, it seems to be an accident, nothing suggests otherwise, but I am waiting for the results of this morning's post mortem to be sure. I will then prepare a report for the Examining Magistrate to determine whether to hold an inquest. In addition, it seems that Mr. Bishop's instructions are that he be interred here in Spain, but I would like to get a signed confirmation from you before we take any action. I would also like to meet you and talk to you for a few minutes before I write my report."

Jenny was shaken. *Meet me and talk to me?* She asked herself what the policeman could possibly want to talk to her about. Charlie's death was an accident, wasn't it? Her mind filled with foreboding. She thought again about Ron's death. *Everything happens for a purpose.*

She started to formulate another objection, but Espinoza went on, "I am sorry to insist, Señora, but you must come here as soon as possible. I can't force you to come, but you must."

So that was that, there was no point in trying to avoid the inevitable. She had another talk with Sergeant Harris and PC Dawson, who then drove her home and gave her a file with the relevant names and addresses.

The policewoman dropped her off at the door and said, "If you want, we could arrange to have someone travel down with you to make it easier."

Jenny didn't want a chaperone so she refused and thanked her, then went back into the dark, quiet house alone. Cooper was pleased to see her, it was supper time.

She prepared the Westie's meal, adding some raw carrots to clean his teeth. Then she went onto the Internet. She found there was a coach running between Ipswich and Stansted Airport every two hours. She opened up the easyJet website and booked a single ticket from Stansted to Malaga, for the next evening, Tuesday, for sixty-nine pounds. The coach fare was only fifteen pounds, so that wasn't too ruinous. She didn't book a return ticket, not knowing how long she would be there for and not wanting to risk losing the cost of a non-refundable ticket. Jenny liked to think of herself as a low-maintenance person, not a big spender.

She called Linda at the kennels, whom she knew would still be answering the phone in the evening. She could take Cooper the next morning. Another tick in the box.

Next, she called Cyril, who had now taken over the garage business on a buy-out arrangement. He was at home, she could hear music from the TV in the background.

"Everything is going fine at the garage. Lots of work, no problems at this end."

She explained that she'd be away in Spain for a short while. "Just some family business."

"Good idea, Jenny." His deep, cockney voice resonated in her ear. "'Bout time you took a holiday. Relax and get some sun. See you soon. Bye." *If only he knew.*

Her last call that evening was to her sister, Emma, in Newcastle, briefly telling her about Charlie's accident and her visit to Spain. She kept the call as short as possible, not wanting to get onto the subject of the investigation into Ron's death.

Emma was understandingly sympathetic, but said she couldn't come down to see her before she left. She was going up to Edinburgh to do a book signing the next day. She put the phone down and went back to picking up her teenage son's clothes from his bedroom floor. She wished she could have done something to help. Jenny was going through a difficult period.

Several more calls would be needed the next morning to cancel her hairdresser and therapists' appointments, some gym sessions and a tennis game. Jenny wasn't at all happy about this. She didn't know what she'd find in Spain and she didn't like not knowing things.

Cooper was ready for his walk, so she spent half an hour leading him around the park, a plastic poop bag in her hand, trying to sort out her confused mind. After the trauma of Ron's death and the months of anguish and unanswered questions, she had finally started to get her life under control again. A simplified version, with no complicated relationships. Just the pieces she could manage herself, until she could cope with new situations again. And now she was being thrown into events and circumstances beyond her control. Complications that she didn't want and wasn't ready for.

She shivered and looked around the park in the gloom. There was no one else in sight and the trees were depressingly bare. The evening was freezing cold, just like Charlie's body by now.

NINE

Tuesday April 15th 2008
Washington DC, USA

Sonia Nicolaides occupied a small cubicle on the third floor of the offices of the Child Exploitation and Obscenity section of the US Dept. of Justice, at 1400 New York Avenue. Since transferring from the New York Police Department to join the section two years previously, Sonia had been promoted to Senior Case Manager in CAPP, the Child Abuse Prevention Programme.

She was currently working on six projects in CAPP. By monitoring and manipulating the exchange of messages and material that the department found, by accident or by diligent detective work, the CAPP team could send out 'fishing' material to expose and trap members of paedophile and child slavery rings. It was delicate and painstaking work that could take months and even years to accomplish. But the satisfaction she enjoyed when these sick, murderous perverts were convicted and imprisoned was worth all the work and sleepless nights. Nevertheless, she wasn't sure how long she could cope with the dreadful, depraved, harrowing images and texts that she had to handle to obtain the proof necessary for conviction.

She concentrated on her latest and most promising assignment. *Project Fairy Tale* had been instigated by the fortuitous discovery of a global paedophile ring, probably centred in Eastern Europe. A member of the ring, a Portuguese national named Rodrigo Pires da Silva, had been found dead in suspicious circumstances in Manhattan the previous weekend. His laptop was opened up by the police department to find out what they could about him. Family members or friends who could help to find out more about him and the sordid life he obviously lived. The department hackers had no trouble in breaking through the multiple passwords and protective devices that he'd used to hide the contents. But instead of finding information about the man's family or friends, they found more evidence of his 'hobby', a treasure trove of the most revolting filth they had ever had the misfortune, or, in this case, the good fortune, to find.

They passed the machine to a senior officer in the Justice Dept. who immediately called the director of CAPP. By Monday morning it was in the hands of an IT expert in their Washington offices. Opening up the laptop was like finding an ABC guide to the most evil scum imaginable on this earth. Once he had found the paths through da Silva's cleverly conceived filing system, the technician uncovered dozens of files with names, email and physical addresses, web sites, bank account details and more. An Aladdin's cave of information which would keep them busy for a very long time. And which could lead to a major coup in combating at least one strand of the spider's web that was the global trade in the exploitation of innocent children.

The case had been labelled *Project Fairy Tale* because of the place where da Silva had been on the night he died. A strip club called Cinderella's, in New York. Some wag in case management had decided that it was an appropriate pseudonym.

On the Tuesday morning the machine had been given to Sonia to manage. She had spent the first few hours becoming accustomed to the laptop's log-ins and filing system. Da Silva had four log-in names, his real name and three pseudonyms. She had mentally labelled the three files 'dirty' and the fourth, 'clean'. The dirty accounts had large address books and many files to do with his sickening hobby and which contained the valuable information that she could use. Her first action was to create an automated reply to any incoming messages on these accounts. *"I will be travelling and unable to access my emails etc."* This would give her a few days to familiarise herself with the details of da Silva's abominable activity and to read correspondence from the other members of the ring. *Getting to know the game and the players.*

The address book for the clean *r.da.silva* account contained very few names, which didn't appear in the dirty accounts. There were no other files in this account and it seemed that all sent and received messages had been deleted just before da Silva's death, whether by him or by someone else, she couldn't discern.

There were a couple of messages received since his death in the infile, a British Airways confirmation of flights to London and Geneva and confirmation of a reservation at the Hotel Kempinski for April 24th to 26th. The BA flight would be a no-show, so it could be left without reply, but she wrote a quick message of cancellation to the hotel, in case the visit was somehow linked to his activities and might send a red flag to the other ring members.

The clean account was now neutralised and she started going through the dirty files, her notepad on the desk beside her. Sonia still had some old fashioned habits. Keeping hand-written notes and drawing pencilled diagrams to jog her memory was one of them, even though she found it difficult to write down certain words or phrases to do with the filth she had to read and look at. She steeled her nerve and opened up the first file, labelled 'Stuff I - 2005'.

TEN

Tuesday, April 15th, 2008
Malaga, Spain

Jenny was pleasantly surprised to have found herself a window seat. Unfortunately, she was sitting next to Melvyn, a rather flashy and pompous real estate agent, obviously doing well with the Marbella crowd. He was not in Ron's league, she thought, but trying to sound high class, with a fake swanky accent. Jenny was from Sunderland and proud of it and she had never felt really comfortable with people from south of Doncaster. She was a slight woman and looked younger than her thirty-six years, with fair hair tied back in a pony tail. Still attractive to Marbella real estate agents, apparently.

"So, I told the lady that I had five other offers for the house and she signed a cheque there and then for the deposit." She turned away in irritation as Melvyn took a gulp of his gin and tonic and fortified himself to recount yet another of his triumphs in the property market, when the Captain announced, "Ten minutes to landing."

The cabin staff started rushing around with rubbish bags, checking on seat backs and safety belts. Melvyn knocked back the remains of his drink too quickly and belched rather noticeably.

Those in window seats leaned forward, looking through the cloudy night sky as the plane banked over the ocean and started to descend towards the lights of Malaga.

Déja vu, thought Jenny, as she glimpsed the welcoming lights. It was just over ten years ago that she had first met Ron at his father's house in Spain. She was staying in Mijas Pueblo, the White Village, as the locals called it. The house was situated nearby, above the Los Lagos golf course. A big old hacienda with acres of land around. She was invited along with a couple she met at the Mijas Hotel during the summer break from her teaching job in Sunderland.

"Very pleased to meet a visitor from *oop North*. Come onto the terrace and have a drink, Jenny. Make yourself at home."

"It's a beautiful old house. Have you lived here long?" She hadn't lost her north-eastern accent and Ron was quite taken with the sing-song lilt which reminded him of his mother.

"It's actually my parent's house, but I came over from the UK to house-sit while they're away. You can't leave a big house for long without having problems when you come back."

His father was in Geneva on business. "Mother's in Middlesbrough, with her sister," he laughed. "Catching up on the Teeside news grapevine. How are things up there, anyway?"

"Cold and wet. I'd rather not think about it. Mijas suits me fine for a couple of weeks."

Ron was three years older than her, but she was taken by his flattering attention and relaxed by the easy, laid back life style of the expats who were present. They had quite a lot in common, since before setting up his garage business in Ipswich he had spent some years in Middlesbrough, fifteen miles away from where she lived and worked.

She came to the house several times to play tennis with him on an old clay court that had once had a proper net and lines. He was fit in those days and they sweated happily in the warm sunshine and had lazy lunches and suppers on the terrace. A magnificent old Steinway baby grand stood in the living room. Although she hadn't played for some time, she couldn't resist trying it and he was generous in his praise.

Charlie kept several docile horses in the adjacent paddock and Ron, a poor rider himself, took on the task of teaching Jenny until they were both saddle sore and in hysterics at their lack of skill.

There was a big unkempt orchard full of orange and lemon trees behind the paddock where they first made love after too much Rioja. They had got into a friendly wrestling match, in which she almost broke his arm, before succumbing to his love-making.

She told him afterwards that her mother had insisted that she take judo lessons when she started working with difficult students at the Teesside Secondary School. He was suitably impressed. "I suppose I'm lucky you didn't give me a real beating."

They continued to see each other back in the UK, and the following Easter, Ron proposed. Jenny wasn't one to chop and change. She decided she would be just as well off with him as with anyone, so she accepted.

Her mother had called her a stupid bitch, Ron wasn't good enough for her. But he made good money from his garage business and after witnessing her mother's miserable life as a divorced parent, struggling to pay the monthly bills, Jenny needed to find love, stability and financial security. And, at twenty-five, she was ready to get married and have children. They bought a small house in Woodbridge, near Ipswich, with good views, near to the river and the golf club. Ron enrolled them both for membership. He was planning to take up golf now that his business was established and he signed her up for lessons as well.

She stopped taking the pill and immediately fell pregnant. Jenny was more than content. A nice house and business, getting married next month, a child on the way, golf club membership. What more could she aspire to?

The wedding was at St. John's Church, in Woodbridge, on a warm, sunny July day. That was the first time she met Charlie and Ellen, who arrived the day before, stayed for the ceremony and the reception and left for Geneva the following day.

Ellen looked lovely in a blue outfit, her hair curled down to her shoulders. Jenny couldn't help comparing her to her own mother, who, even at the wedding, looked tired and listless.

"I'm so happy for you and Ronny. Now I'll finally have a daughter-in-law and a grandchild on the way! I can't wait to come back for the christening. I'm just sorry that we can't stay longer.

But there it is, Charlie's very busy." She was charming to her new daughter-in-law, but somehow rather stressed. Charlie seemed like a man in a hurry to get away, and Jenny wondered why.

Sadly, her aspirations of happily married life with lots of kids were short-lived. She lost the baby, a girl, at six months, after falling off her bicycle in the high street. What was worse, she couldn't have another child. They talked about adoption for a while and even visited an orphanage, but it was a complicated and somehow very invasive procedure. She also realised that Ron wasn't really cut out for fatherhood, he could be moody and sometimes behaved like a child himself, rather than like a father. So she bought a dog.

And that was Jenny's life at twenty-six years of age; a husband called Ron, a garage business, a West Highland terrier named Cooper, a semi-detached house in Ipswich and golf lessons twice a week, weather permitting.

It was after 11:00 pm when she pushed her baggage trolley out to find Juan carrying a card with the name *Bishop* scrawled on it. A nondescript, balding man in a black tee shirt, she had met him only once, at Ellen's funeral, so without the sign she would have missed him amongst the dozens of families, friends, rental car touts and tourists crowding around the arrival hall. She used up most of her Spanish vocabulary saying *Buenas Noches* and shook hands with him.

It was pouring with rain outside. Jenny couldn't believe it, she had never seen it rain in the Costa del Sol. Juan held an umbrella over her as they hurried across the wet pavement.

Juan was a shy, quiet man, happier working out of sight in the garden than trying to have a conversation. But tonight he was agitated, extremely jumpy. As they reached the ticket machine in the car park he started telling her something in rapid, voluble, Andalucian Spanish. He kept repeating "*Robo, robo,*" but she couldn't get the gist of it at all. Finally, he shrugged and put some coins into the machine. He said something about Leticia and then fell silent.

He stowed her bags in the boot of a metallic grey Bentley Continental and they drove to Marbella in silence, apart from the swish of the windscreen wipers. They went on the old coast road, which even at that hour was busier than she remembered. Jenny suspected that Juan didn't like using the toll road where you had to pay a few Euros. The oncoming headlights flashed on the wet windscreen. *It's just like being in Ipswich,* she thought. Juan put the radio on and she watched the coast slip by in darkness on her left.

Several years ago, Charlie had sold the hacienda and built an enormous new house situated on a hill overlooking Las Manzanás Golf Course, near Marbella. He and Ellen had moved in the year before her death, and she hadn't finished her final decorating touches when she died. The house, or mansion, more like, was up at the top of the exclusive Las Manzanás estate. Jenny didn't like ostentation and York House was the epitome of it.

The whole urbanisation was surrounded by a massive wall made of white Mijas stone, kilometres long, with a guard in a cabin down at the entrance. He was still on duty and waved as they started up the main street to Calle Venetia. Juan drove around the three metre high wall that surrounded Charlie's property and stopped at a pair of huge iron gates with CCTV cameras stuck on top of the gateposts. He fumbled with the remote control and the gates slid back.

York House looked as if it was lit up for Christmas. Every light in the house and gardens seemed to be on. There was enough light to illuminate a small town. As they pulled up in front of the four door garage, she saw Leticia come running down the staircase to meet her. The rain had stopped.

ELEVEN

Wednesday, April 16th, 2008
Marbella, Spain

It was a warm bright morning and the sunshine slanting in between the blinds caused Jenny to leap out of bed like a child. There was some humidity after the rain and just getting dressed after her shower caused her to perspire. She put on shorts and a tee shirt and decided to start the day with a swim from now on. Then she remembered Charlie's last swim.

She came down to the terrace just after eight and, breathing in the fragrance from the masses of flowers and shrubs that Juan tended with obsessive devotion, she marvelled at the vista before her. Across the swimming pool was the golf course, surprisingly lush and green despite the well advertised water shortage in southern Spain. Groups of olive trees and umbrella pines lined the fairways and she could make out the light blue reflection of the early morning sky glittering in a long, narrow lake which almost surrounded the nearest green. The lake seemed to be attracting regular visits from the golfers who could already be seen, either pulling golf trolleys or riding in electric buggies.

A couple of kilometres further down the valley was the azure line of the Mediterranean. The divide between the sea and the sky was still clear in the morning light, but she knew that as it got warmer that line would gradually disappear. Despite peering closely to the South she couldn't make out the far coastline of Morocco, but turning towards the west she was rewarded by a vague outline, bulging out into the sea. Gibraltar was almost sixty kilometres away, but it was unmistakably visible at that time in the morning.

She went in through the French windows to the kitchen. "Good morning, Leticia. Isn't it a beautiful day, as usual?"

The housekeeper was already fussing about with fruit and orange juice and toast. "Jenny, how are you?" She hugged her and kissed her on both cheeks. "I'm so pleased that you came here. Have you slept well? It was very late when you arrived."

She had welcomed her last night and offered to make her supper, in her melodic, Spanish-accented English. Too tired to eat, Jenny had sent her off to her family, dumped the bags in the hall and climbed into the bed that was made up in one of the five bedrooms on the second floor of the house. For the first time since Ron's death she hadn't taken a sedative and incredibly, she had slept like a baby and woke up feeling alive and well.

She sat on the kitchen bench and admiringly watched the young woman as she prepared breakfast. If she had been born into a family in Europe, Leticia da Costa could have been a supermodel. She had that extraordinary combination of fine bone structure and wide, slanted, brown eyes that always looked stunning, surrounded by curly, rich brown hair cascading down to her shoulders. At thirty-four, just two years younger than Jenny, she was one of the most beautiful women she had ever seen.

Jenny had only met her three times and had never met her parents, so she knew nothing of her family's background. Ron had told her only that they were originally from Angola and had come from Lisbon to the Costa del Sol twelve years ago. They lived in a flat in the old working area of Marbella, about fifteen minutes drive away, and Leticia had worked for Charlie since he and Ellen had moved into the new house.

Now, Leticia was fidgeting in the kitchen, moving things

unnecessarily from place to place and wiping imaginary stains away. Jenny thought of her own experiences over the last several months, realising that the housekeeper must still be affected by the accident.

She said, "Come and sit on the terrace for a moment, it's a change for me to be able go out without a coat and umbrella." They went out and sat on a large rattan settee. It was going to be a hot day, the sun's rays were already warming Jenny's body through her blouse.

Leticia sat looking down at the pool on the level below the terrace, without speaking.

"It must have been difficult for you since the accident. These things are never very easy. Do you want to tell me about it?"

The young woman remained silent for a moment, running her hand nervously through her hair. Then she turned. "Can I tell you, Jenny? I think it's better for me if I can tell you."

The words poured out of her as she described every event since the day Juan had discovered Charlie in the pool and the disruption it had caused to the tranquil life in York House. For the last couple of days the property had been invaded by security guards, policemen, forensic experts, lawyers and friends, or at least acquaintances, who had come to pay their respects or just to satisfy their morbid curiosity. "Everybody has come to the house since the accident," she said. "Just like going to the market place."

She took Jenny down to the swimming pool. It was still cordoned off with red and white plastic tape until the enquiry was ended. Pointing to the spot where she had seen her employer's body lying by the pool, she said, "Juan told me that Charlie was a very heavy body to take from the *piscina.* His head was not cut. *Una fractura,* the doctor said." She indicated her own temple, "*Ahí dentro, en la cabeza,* in Charlie's head. Then he drowned in the water." She pulled out a handkerchief, wiped her eyes and sighed, "The police say it might be robbers, but I don't believe it. I can see nothing missing in the house."

Jenny realised what Juan had been trying to tell her, *robo,* robbery, of course. But a robbery by burglars who stole nothing from an unoccupied house?

They walked around the pool talking until Leticia had calmed herself down then went back up to the kitchen. Like the rest of the house, Jenny thought the kitchen was way over the top. The marble floor must have measured ten metres by five, lined with every conceivable machine. A huge island of ceramic hot plates and other equipment stood in the middle and a series of cupboards lined the walls. The cupboards along the windowed walls were half height, with a counter along the top, and there was a long granite table with a row of chairs on each side and a bench seat built against the wall around the end. At the back of the room there was a large, cool pantry, where the household supplies and kitchen utensils were stocked on wide, deep shelves.

They took the breakfast things out to the terrace and sat together in silence for a while. Jenny pictured Leticia returning to the house to find her employer lying dead by the pool. She shivered, unwelcome memories of Ron's death flooding back into her mind. The housekeeper sat with a sad expression in her eyes and said nothing.

As she drank her coffee and spread her toast with fresh bitter marmalade, home-made from the Seville oranges in the orchard, Jenny felt a gentle stroking on her bare ankles. She looked down into a pair of huge green eyes. A magnificent black cat was looking up at her, purring and rubbing itself against her legs. She stroked the lovely creature on the top of its head and under the chin. The cat turned and lay on its back, purring happily, inviting her to rub its stomach. Its long, thick fur was so black that the reflection from its coat made it appear to be midnight blue. A small splash of white on the tip of its tail was the only identifying mark.

"Look what I've found, a new Spanish boy friend. Black cats are lucky, you know."

Leticia stooped to stroke the cat. "His name is *Fuente.* You know what it means?"

Jenny's Spanish vocabulary was minimal. She shook her head.

"It means fountain, Charlie told me the right word."

"He's really handsome, such a gorgeous thick coat." The cat returned to stroking itself against Jenny's legs. "I think he likes me. I must smell like fish or something"

"You're very lucky if Fuente likes you, he is a very fussy cat. I can tell you he doesn't like men. He was not friends with Charlie, he scratched him and he doesn't like Juan."

She went into the kitchen to put some cat food into a plastic dish, added some sort of fish supplement and placed it on the tiled surface beside them. The cat crouched down and ate hungrily, looking up at them after every few mouthfuls and licking its lips.

"So why on earth did he get him?"

"He never got him really. The cat came to the garden two years ago, just a baby, very wild. I think his mother is dead. He was trying to catch fishes in the lake and he fell in the water, beside the fountain." She giggled, a delightful sound. "So, Charlie called him Fuente."

"You mean he adopted you. He sneaked his way into your life, like animals always do."

"It's like that, yes. He was so wet and hungry, I gave him some food and now he comes a few times in the week, when he wants. It's a very independent cat."

Fuente finished his breakfast. He lay there for a moment, wiping his mouth on the back of his paws then he stretched luxuriously, and wandered off into the garden.

"See what I mean? He comes and goes when he likes."

They watched the animal depart and then the housekeeper lapsed into silence once more. Jenny tried again to shake her out of her melancholy mood. "That's enough mooching around," she said, "I want you to cheer up and tell me all about your family."

At this, Leticia started to talk in an animated manner about her father, José, who was about to retire from his job at the supermarket and Encarni, her mother, who still made almost all her own clothes. Jenny was impressed by her greatly improved English. She rarely switched into Spanish or Portuguese, as she had done when they had last met.

She turned to pour another cup of coffee and suddenly caught a Spanish word which she knew. "*Mi hijo,*" Leticia had said, "My son."

Jenny spun around and looked into her dark brown, liquid eyes. "You have a son?"

"Si, si, Jenny. I have a son, his name is Emilio Salvador."

"But, but, then you have. I mean, you are…"

Leticia interrupted her in turn. "*Casada,* married?"

Jenny nodded, looking at the young woman, with a puzzled expression.

She said shyly. "No, I am not a married woman. I am just a single mother without any husband or lover." While Jenny pondered this reply, she went to her bag on the counter in the kitchen and pulled out a small photo wallet.

"See how handsome he is already." A happy, smiling face looked out at her from the photograph. Emilio's curly black hair was just like his mother's, but his skin was a lighter, olive colour, enhanced by sparkling hazel brown eyes.

Looking at the photos of the little boy, Jenny felt a pang of envy. It seemed that neither of them any longer had a man in their life, but Leticia was left with a lovely child and she was left with nothing. *It doesn't seem fair,* she thought. Suppressing the feeling, she said, "He's gorgeous, Leticia. Congratulations! How old is he?"

"Just two years old now."

"A lovely son," she said. "You are very blessed, Leticia."

"Thank you, Jenny. I am blessed, you are right, only..." She didn't finish the phrase, but wiped her eyes again with her handkerchief and replaced the photos in her handbag. Jenny was puzzled, but said nothing further. She knew when it was best to leave things alone.

It was after nine when they carried the dishes into the kitchen and Jenny went to get the file given to her by the policewoman all that time ago in the cold, miserable UK. She went through the names and details to brush up her memory for the phone call. *Now for the difficult bit.* She dialled the lawyer's number.

Juan opened up the garage and drove out a silver Mercedes 500SL which was parked alongside the Bentley and a blue Mini Cooper. There was also a quad bike and a golf buggy in the cavernous space.

Leticia was to drive her to the lawyer's office, since he had suggested that they come together. She appreciated the lawyer's thoughtfulness, not knowing the way and glad of the company. Uneasy and apprehensive of what awaited her in the next couple of hours.

"What about Emilio?" She asked.

"There is no problem, I called my mother, she likes to have

her grandson with her. They will go for a walk at the beach today. Emilio, he loves to run on the sand."

So that was settled. Jenny liked the way that everything in Spain was settled so easily.

Leticia drove her Suzuki Vitara into the courtyard then got into the Mercedes. The two seater sparkled as if it had just come from the showroom and when she pressed a button, the roof folded away into the boot, making the car look even more sleek and flashy.

"Fresh air and sunshine, better than England?" Leticia said, a picture of health and beauty posing in the open top car. Jenny looked at her and laughed out loud, intoxicated by the sunlight and warmth.

God, that feels so good, she thought. She couldn't remember the last time she had laughed like that. Taking the file and her handbag, she climbed into the passenger seat and they drove out the gates and down to the motorway.

TWELVE

Wednesday, April 16th, 2008
Malaga, Spain

José Luis Garcia Ramirez must have been about sixty-five years old. A large, portly man in a smart, striped navy suit and maroon tie, Jenny had met him only once, fleetingly, at Ellen's funeral. It seemed like a lifetime ago. He had a full head of hair, which had now turned a pure white. He wore it slightly longer than before, which gave him a rather raffish air. He came to the reception area at precisely ten thirty and welcomed them in an old fashioned manner, calling Jenny "Dear Madame Bishop". Kissing her hand and sympathising with her over her recent losses. Apart from a slight limp, José Luis looked as well as he had done previously. He kissed Leticia on both cheeks and asked after her parents and her son in rapid Andalusian Spanish that sounded so melodic to Jenny's ears.

They were ushered into a comfortable conference room with impressive views over the Parque de la Constitución to the sea and José Luis took a seat opposite them across the conference table. Jenny hadn't had much to do with lawyers, but when he put on his spectacles and placed a fat dossier on the table, marked "C. W.

Bishop," he certainly looked like one to her. The only thing that spoiled the appearance was that he constantly wore a large smile on his face, even when delivering complicated or even disagreeable information.

This time it was he who said, "Please call me José Luis. It's so much simpler than Spanish double barrelled names without end." So they continued the meeting all on first name terms.

She felt a stab of apprehension when he pulled the big file towards him and opened it up. It seemed that she had spent the last four months doing nothing but looking at dossiers that got bigger and bigger without any end in sight. The lawyer extracted a few documents, then pushed the file to one side and smiled across the table at her. She immediately felt better.

"Now then," he said, "do you know much about your father-in-law's life or affairs?"

Jenny dredged her memory and told the lawyer the little she had learned from Ron about Charlie Bishop's life, in dribs and drabs, over the years. She knew he had lived in Portugal at the time of the revolution and had been involved in finance and banking, especially between Portugal and Africa.

Ron had told her he had been born in Portugal. "I remember leaving Cascais in 1975, when I was six. The communist party had taken control of the government and dad decided it was time to get out. We filled the car up with all the family stuff and drove off to Spain in the middle of the night. They made a bed for me on the back seat. I slept most of the time, but it was stifling hot in the car and I was as sick as a parrot." He said they had then flown to London, afterwards coming back to settle in Spain, never returning to Portugal again.

She also knew, because it was very obvious, that Charlie had made a lot of money along the way. He had set up Ron's garage business for him with two hundred thousand pounds, which was a substantial amount in 1995. The house in Marbella was further proof of wealth, in addition to the cruises and expensive cars. Ron had intimated that his father was extremely wealthy, but he never expanded on it and Jenny suspected that the source of this wealth was one of the reasons that he had fallen out with him all those years ago. So she knew that he had been in Portugal and that he had money, but she knew little more about him or his affairs.

"Yes, what Ron told you is correct." The lawyer removed his spectacles and looked at her pensively. "Charlie came here from Portugal in July 1975 and that's when I first met him. I have been his lawyer here in Spain ever since. I don't know everything about his affairs, but I'll tell you what I know, if you are patient.

"To start at the beginning, Charlie left England in 1969, when he was thirty. He had just got married to Ellen and they moved some months later to Cascais, just outside of Lisbon."

"So Ron was born not long after they moved?" Jenny was jotting things down in a note pad, in case she needed to remember anything when she went to meet the Chief Inspector.

"That's right. Just a few months after their arrival. He was born in the local hospital."

"But why did they move to Portugal when Ellen was pregnant?"

"Because of his job. Charlie was offered a senior position with *Aliança Portuguesa y Africana*, owned by one of the most influential banking and trading families in Portugal. The head office of *APA* was in Lisbon, so they had to move there.

"He was a clever man and became their specialist in banking and trade relations between Portugal and the African colonies, a valuable and highly paid officer in their group. One of the few non-Portuguese senior executives in Lisbon in those days, as a matter of fact.

"Charlie managed to stay with *APA* until July 1975, when the communist government was granting independence to Portugal's remaining colonial possessions, principally Angola and Mozambique. Nobody knows the full details because the Portuguese borders were virtually closed and the news was censored, but he told me that during 1975, life became really dangerous. Bankers, businessmen and landowners fled the country, or were thrown into prison, just because they were rich. It was a very difficult period but he somehow survived it."

"So Charlie's job disappeared just when the colonies were about to become independent? I would have thought that there would have been more opportunity than before." Jenny looked at Leticia, who was shaking her head vehemently.

"Not right," she said, a look of sadness on her face. "The Russians and Cubans invaded Angola. My parents' country was in war more than twenty-five years. A lot of their friends were killed and many ran away, like them. They came to Portugal with nothing."

Jenny realised that she hadn't understood the implications of the independence of Leticia's homeland. Like most people, she supposed, she knew nothing about the Portuguese revolution, nor the liberation of its colonies. The scant knowledge she had of Africa was through her sister Emma, who had been a delegate with the British Red Cross. She had worked in Rwanda after the genocide in 1994 but she never talked about it. Jenny could understand why. It didn't bear thinking about, never mind talking. She looked back at the lawyer.

"I'm afraid Leticia's right," he said. "Portugal just walked away from its African colonies and relations between them shut down overnight. Millions of Africans and Portuguese had to flee those countries. Wealthy Portuguese families lost everything they had owned and invested in Africa. Charlie's job disappeared along with everything else."

Jenny said, "I'm sorry, Leticia. I had no idea that your parents had such troubles. So," she calculated for a moment, "you were only a baby when you came to Portugal?"

"Yes. Myself, I remember nothing from Angola. Only what my parents have told me about that time. It was very bad for everyone. They all lost everything. The rich people and the poor people. It made no difference to the rebels and the Russian and Cuban soldiers, they destroyed everything. Murderers and robbers, killing and stealing and raping the women."

They sat for a moment in silence. Jenny was trying to take in what had happened in Portugal and Africa all those years ago. It had happened to Charlie and his family and it had happened to Leticia's family. Wrongly, she assumed the difference was that, unlike Leticia's family, Charlie's had apparently not been faced with a choice between flight or death.

She tried to picture Leticia's parents, perhaps in hiding, starving and terrified, surrounded by so-called soldiers committing atrocities and killing indiscriminately. Yet somehow finding a way to survive, to get out of that horror, and to make their way to a country where they could restart their lives.

She sighed and squeezed Leticia's shoulder tightly. She began to realise that her own losses, real and tragic as they were to her, didn't begin to compare with those of a whole nation, thrust from one occupation to another, with all of the human devastation that ensues and continues without end.

She turned back to José Luis. "So Charlie came here from Portugal in July 1975?"

"Yes, that was when we first met." The lawyer continued in a thoughtful voice, "It was rather a peculiar first meeting. He came to me when I was quite young and not well known. It's possible that he had been to see other lawyers, I don't know."

Jenny gave him a puzzled look. "Why? Was there something improper about it?"

"Improper no, but rather unusual. He introduced himself and explained that he had just brought his family out of Portugal. He had a leather briefcase with him and he asked me to look after it while he took his family to England. They were flying from Malaga the following day and he did not want to take it with him. He intended to return within a few days and then he would explain to me what it was he wanted me to do for him as a client."

"So, since he became your client, I assume that you agreed?"

The lawyer laughed. "Well, apart from the ETA terrorists, people didn't blow places up then as they do today, so I saw no reason not to do it. I put the case in the safe and kept it for a week until he came back."

"And then?" Jenny asked impatiently.

"He told me about his life in England and Portugal and everything I have recounted this morning. Then he explained to me why he had come to me in the first place."

The lawyer paused and picked up another paper, studying it for a moment before continuing. "That brings us to the second part of our discussion. I am going to tell you about his affairs. Your father-in-law came to see me about buying a property and opening bank accounts. Looking back, I suppose it's possible that he left the briefcase with me as a kind of test, to ensure that I was trustworthy.

Charlie was clever that way. In any event, if that was the case, I must have passed the test. You see, he then told me he had quite a lot of money. In cash. US dollars actually, quite a lot." He paused again in his rather theatrical style.

Jenny looked across at Leticia and then back to José Luis.

"Oh, sorry, Jenny. You want me to leave now?" She rose from her chair, ready to go.

"Well, it seems that we're going to discuss private matters, so maybe it would be better."

The Spanish lawyer interrupted quietly but firmly. "If you don't object, I would prefer Leticia to stay. In any case, don't forget that all of this happened over thirty years ago."

Jenny was mildly irritated. She didn't see why the housekeeper should be privy to this information. On the other hand she was only related to Charlie through marriage, so she didn't feel any ownership of his affairs. And something that had happened so long ago was almost in the public domain. *Maybe he wants a witness,* she thought, *because of the cash.*

She answered, "If you think it's appropriate, then of course she can stay." Leticia took her seat again and Jenny continued, "I suppose that the money was in the briefcase?"

"I imagine it was inside the briefcase, but it was locked with a combination lock and I had no wish to look inside it. I could listen to what Charlie said but I couldn't witness that he had a large amount of foreign currency illegally in Spain. I also asked him not to tell me anything about the origins of the cash. Even Malaga lawyers have scruples and it was better for him that I didn't know any details, especially when he told me how much he had."

Once again he paused, looking expectantly at them both.

Jenny decided to play his little game. "Very well, José Luis. How much cash did Charlie have?"

"Five hundred thousand US dollars." The lawyer replied dramatically. Then he sat quietly, watching their shocked reactions. After a moment, he called his secretary on the intercom and asked her to bring more refreshments.

THIRTEEN

Wednesday, April 16th, 2008
Malaga, Spain

Ten minutes later, Jenny was still trying to come to terms with the amount of cash involved. She tried to calculate how much it would represent today, doubling it every five years for inflation or devaluation, or whatever it was called. *That would make something like ten million dollars in today's money. In cash! Where on earth did he get it from? It's impossible to come by so much cash honestly.*

She asked many questions of the lawyer, but he insisted on continuing his story in his own way. "In 1975, there were strict controls on currency in Spain, so he couldn't announce that he had all that foreign currency. Nor could he buy a property or other asset without showing how the money was brought into the country. So, Charlie had all that cash but he couldn't use it. He had to get it out and bring it back officially."

"But I don't understand." Jenny interrupted. "My father-in-law was a senior executive with *APA*. Why couldn't he get the money out of the country with their help?"

"Because earlier in 1975, the communist government had

nationalised all banks and insurance companies. The owners of *APA* managed to run the business until the summer, but then things became so bad that they had to admit defeat. I believe that one of the family was lost in an accident. Then they moved the business to Geneva, so there was no one left in Portugal that he could turn to."

"So what did you do? Were you able to help him?"

"I'm afraid I can't say. That would be incriminating. All I can tell you is that I helped to arrange a safety deposit box for him at the Banco de Malaga. Then shortly after, he advised me that he had opened an account with a bank in Switzerland and I never heard anything more about the cash. A few weeks later, he opened an account at the Banco de Malaga. He transferred funds down and bought an old hacienda near Mijas village."

"That's where I met Ron, in 1997, the first time I came to Spain." Fond memories drifted through her mind as she made more notes and waited for the next revelations.

"Now there is someone I want you to meet." The lawyer called on the intercom and a young man entered the room. Early-thirties, medium height, he had a pleasant, sun-tanned face framed by curly, dark brown hair. Behind steel rimmed spectacles, his eyes were brown and kindly looking. He was dressed in a blazer and jeans, a white shirt open at the neck.

"Let me introduce my colleague, Francisco García Luna."

The man hugged Leticia and kissed her on both cheeks, simultaneously enquiring after her family. Then he took both of Jenny's hands, "A pleasure to meet you, Madame Bishop." He had a low, soft voice and spoke with an accent that sounded both Spanish and American. A soft drawl, very easy on the ear. Just as his appearance, she registered with some confused emotions, was very easy on the eye.

Feeling slightly flustered, she asked him to call her by her first name. He nodded and took a place at the conference table opposite the two women.

"Francisco is… How do I put this? He is my young legs. He looks after our international clients, which requires a wide knowledge of foreign taxation and a lot of travelling around the world which I can no longer cope with. So he does it for both of us."

The young man said to Jenny, "I got to know your father-in-law quite well over the last year. He was an impressive man, such a loss..." He broke off, looking lost for words.

"Yes," added José Luis, "when Charlie had his heart attack last August, it coincided with the start of this leg problem that is troubling me. So it was Francisco who had to follow his progress and look after his affairs."

"Francisco helped very much when Charlie was in hospital. Even coming to the house to make sure everything was alright." Leticia added.

"Francisco is as fully aware of Charlie's affairs as I am," José Luis continued. "In case I am not available, you can discuss matters with him, just as you would with me."

They talked for a few minutes about the police investigation and Jenny gratefully accepted his offer to accompany her to the Comisaría for her meeting with Chief Inspector Espinoza that afternoon.

"There is just one more thing to be settled," Francisco said. "Would you like us to take care of the funeral? Provided the Chief Inspector has no objection, we could arrange it for Friday, or at the latest, Monday. It would be unwise to delay any longer."

"Charlie's wish was to be buried alongside Ellen of course," interjected José Luis.

"Yes, we must arrange it, I wasn't really thinking. It would be a great help, if you don't mind the bother." Jenny's mind was forced back to the practical problems of the present. However, as she had already noted, things seemed to get settled easily in Spain.

"I'll get on with it as soon as we get the go-ahead from the police. I'll see you at a quarter past two then, after lunch. *Bueno apetito.*" Francisco made his excuses and left the room.

José Luis took several more documents and two envelopes from the file. He opened the first envelope. "Now we come to the last part of the morning's business. Charlie did me the honour of asking me to be his executor and I have here his will. This will was redrawn after..." He paused. "After the death of your husband, Jenny. It was written in February."

He went on, "The will is what is called an 'open will'. It is written in Spanish and English and was signed in front of a Notary Public. As executor, I have a copy and there is another in the central registry in Madrid. Charlie became a Spanish resident a number of years ago and because he had nothing left in the UK, we have only to consider the inheritance laws and taxes here in Spain, which are straightforward.

"We don't need to go through a probate procedure. I can arrange all the necessary transfers of title with the notary's consent. There will be some documents for you to sign, that's all. It isn't necessary for me to read the whole will, since it is extremely simple, so I will just tell you of the main provisions.

"Charlie has left the sum of twenty-five thousand Euros to Juan, with the wish that if the house is retained, he will continue to be employed. There are also some donations to local charities." José Luis paused once more, and looked straight into Jenny's eyes. "The balance of his estate is to be divided equally between Jennifer Margaret Bishop and Leticia Lurdes da Costa, in trust until the twenty-first birthday of Charlie's son, Emilio Salvador da Costa."

FOURTEEN

Wednesday, April 16th, 2008
Malaga, Spain

The two women walked in silence to the restaurant that José Luis's secretary had booked for them. Leticia was waiting for Jenny's reaction to the news about her and Charlie and she feared it wouldn't be good. She didn't know how she would handle a bad reaction after the stress and emotional strain she'd been through over the last few days. What she needed more than anything was an understanding friend. She waited for Jenny to speak.

She was right to be worried. Jenny had been astonished by the lawyer's revelation. Then she immediately berated herself for having missed so many signs that she should have spotted. *Charlie was lonely after Ellen's death. He had a beautiful, happy, single young woman to comfort him in his loss. Leticia must have spent lots of time at the house. She was reluctant to talk about the baby's father. Charlie didn't want Jenny to get involved in his life, he just wanted to return home to his new family. José Luis wanted Leticia to be informed of everything. So many clues,* she thought to herself.

She didn't harbour any jealousy over Emilio. He was Charlie's only surviving son and she was happy that he had left an heir after losing Ron. It was also none of her business how or why Leticia had replaced Ellen in Charlie's affections. But now, whether she liked it or not, she was stuck with Leticia and her son, because they were co-owners of the house and property and everything else. She had been trying to simplify her life after Ron's death and now it was becoming even more complicated than before. Jenny needed to blame someone, to get mad about something, to scream at someone.

She stopped and rounded on Leticia. "Why didn't you tell me about you and Charlie? You told me about Emilio but you missed out the main point, his father is my father-in-law. I feel an absolute idiot, always the last to know everything. Even the lawyer knows all about it and it's written into the will. It's bloody humiliating. How could you do such a thing?"

Leticia stepped back in shock, tears flooding to her eyes. "Jenny, I am sorry to not tell you about Charlie and me, but I didn't know when to tell you. We talked about his accident and then about Emilio and I got so upset that I couldn't explain. It's very difficult with my English. When I'm upset I don't talk well. I didn't want to explain it wrong and make you angry. It's the same reason I didn't say anything about Ron. I'm sorry about him, about Charlie. I'm sorry about everything, but it's just too complicated for me to talk about these things. Please don't be angry with me, I want to be your friend, not your enemy."

Jenny looked at her anxious face, the tears running down her cheeks. *She's still trying to get over finding her lover, her little boy's father, lying dead by his swimming pool,* she thought to herself. *And I'm just making it worse.* She flushed with embarrassment and took Leticia in her arms. The younger woman sobbed onto her shoulder, her body trembling with emotion.

"I'm sorry, truly sorry. Please forgive me. I've behaved like an absolute bitch." She took a deep breath, hugged Leticia closely and tried to find the right words. "Let's start again. I'm really sorry that you lost Charlie and I'm so happy that you have Emilio. And I'm happy for myself as well. You're not just a friend, you're part of my new family. I thought I had lost all my family and now I see that I've found a new one. It's marvellous news." She put aside her forebodings and mustered as much conviction into her tone as she was able.

"Yes, it's marvellous news. Thank you, Jenny."

Laughing and crying simultaneously, the women walked into the restaurant.

"Let's have a glass of wine." Jenny tried to maintain the positive mood, for Leticia's sake. She had inherited a fortune and a ready-made family. Maybe it wasn't such a bad thing. It would take some getting used to, that was all.

Leticia wiped away her tears as the waiter poured their wine.

"*Salud*."

They raised their glasses.

"To my new Spanish family."

"Yes. I think this makes you my daughter, Jenny."

After his momentous and theatrical reading of the will, José Luis had taken up a couple of financial statements. He explained that Charlie's fortune in Spain was tied up in the house and all the surrounding land and the cash and deposits in his bank accounts.

"The properties are owned by a Luxembourg Corporation, so they are virtually free of inheritance tax. They are also easier to transfer, we just transfer the shares. The bank accounts are at the Banco de Iberia, in Marbella. We know them very well, so there is no problem in dealing with the transfer of ownership.

"So," he finished, "all of this makes it very simple to settle the estate. Charlie has prepared his affairs in his usual competent and efficient manner."

The lawyer studied the papers again. "In the Banco de Iberia accounts, there is a total of about eight million Euros. Charlie liquidated all of his investments over the last few months. He was convinced that there would be a major crash. Everything is now in cash and deposits, as you can see from these statements.

"You'll need to take your time to decide what you want to do about the house and lands and we can discuss it again later. I would estimate the overall value of the property at fifteen to twenty million. In any case it will take me a little while to process the necessary documents with the notary. Meanwhile, if you need funds or anything else, I can arrange this by my position as executor."

Once again they both sat in silence, Leticia stunned by the amount of their inheritance and Jenny still stunned by the news of Charlie and Leticia.

Now," José Luis continued, "I believe that there may be other assets. For example, I think that there may be bank accounts in Switzerland. But I would prefer not to be informed about them. It would just complicate my declarations for tax purposes. That is something for you to resolve.

"I can provide you with any documents you may need to assist you in the event that you do discover such accounts, or any other assets outside of Spain, of which I am unaware." He looked at the two women, waiting for their nodded assent.

He handed the second envelope to Jenny. "This is from your father-in-law. I hope it's something good, something to bring you happiness and peace in your life."

Finally, he took both women's hands in his. "I have one last thing to say. Don't forget that I am always here, as I have been for the last thirty years. I will see you at the funeral, but don't hesitate to call me if you need anything at all. And now it's time for you to go and enjoy your lunch together. Time to celebrate your good fortune."

With that he accompanied them to the door and they stepped out into the hot, busy street, feeling as if they were waking from a dream.

Jenny realised her life had changed irreversibly since that morning. In addition to the problem of Leticia and Emilio, there was the money. A great deal of money. Even if the properties were worth only fifteen million, the estate was worth more than twenty million Euros. She had just inherited over ten million Euros and there could be more in Switzerland! Who could possibly need so much? Certainly not her. And where did all that money come from?

When her father had been imprisoned for embezzlement, when they lost the big house and expensive cars, when her mother divorced him and they had to move into a tiny flat on a housing estate in Sunderland, she had heard a saying for the first time, '*behind every fortune there's a crime*'. She shivered, thinking about Charlie's and Ron's deaths. *I wonder what crime is waiting to be discovered?*

There was nothing she could do about it, so she would just have to get used to it. *Better to start start right away,* she thought. She opened up the envelope while they sipped their wine. There was a single sheet of paper, dated February 26th 2008, printed out in dark blue text on a computer printer. She read it out aloud.

> *Dear Jenny,*
> *This is the second note I have written. First to Ron and now, since José Luis has delivered it to you, it must be that my days are over and you and Leticia and then Emilio, will succeed me. If I have seemed unloving or aloof with you in the past, I am sorry for that. I'm afraid that apart from Ellen, and then Leticia, I haven't been lucky in my life with close relationships. I would like you to know that I wish we could have been closer, but it would have been too complicated for me.*
>
> *Jenny, I am sorry that you lost Ron, as I lost Ellen and I hope that you will find someone else, as I found Leticia. She is a wonderfully loving and positive force of nature and I hope you will let some of her happiness rub off on you. You haven't had much of that and you deserve some.*
>
> *Please look after her and my son, Emilio, for me, Jenny. She is clever, but still young and unsure, inexperienced in her ways. She will need your guiding hand for a while. Just keep following the trail together. I promise you that the end is worth the journey.*
>
> *I wish you and Leticia and Emilio a long and happy life.*
> *Your loving father-in-law, Charlie.*

Underneath the signature there appeared several more lines:

> *Laptop password:* *Emilio_ 1975.*
> *My Computer:* *VAIO (C).*
> *File:* *Documents and Settings.*
> *Password:* *Middlesbrough*
> *Sub file:* *CB Private.*
> *Password:* *Ellen_1969*
> *Word document:* *Angolan Clan.*
> *Password:* *cascais.*

The two women looked quizzically at each other as the waiter brought their meal.

"What does all that mean?" Leticia asked.

"I don't know, but let's leave that for this afternoon, now it's lunch." Jenny called the waiter back. "Two more glasses of wine please."

FIFTEEN

Wednesday, April 16th, 2008
Malaga, Spain

Like most places in central Malaga, the Direccion General De La Policia, in the Calle José Iturbi, was quite close, so Francisco walked them through the bustling streets in the warm afternoon sunshine. Chief Inspector Espinoza's office was on the third floor and they were shown into a large room with a linoleum floor and at least a dozen metal filing cabinets. The office smelled faintly of carbolic soap.

The policeman was a surprisingly small man of about fifty. Full of nervous energy, he paced up and down his office, repeatedly removing and replacing his spectacles as he talked. He had red hair, which Jenny had never seen in a Spaniard, and which looked at odds with the smart blue uniform he had donned for the meeting. A holster at his waist contained a pistol and she wondered fleetingly if it was loaded. English policemen didn't carry weapons and she couldn't help comparing him with Sergeant Harris, the gentle giant.

He introduced himself as the head of the Homicide squad, responsible for the Malaga and Marbella region. Like José Luis, he had a large dossier lying open on his desk, this one a buff colour, labelled, *Charles W. Bishop. 13/04/08.*

"There is no need to identify the body, Señora Bishop." (He had ignored Jenny's usual plea to drop the formalities.) "We have already received all necessary information about Sr. Bishop. As far as the death is concerned, this seems to be a tragic accident, since the post mortem showed no evidence of foul play. We can find no trace of any intervention in the house or gardens. In addition, the house has a security camera at the gates and a CCTV system around the walls and there is no record of any intrusion."

Jenny nodded gratefully at the police officer, relieved that she didn't have to go through the same procedure as she had after Ron's death. It was too traumatic to contemplate.

"I have only a couple of questions to ask you, to... I would say... settle my mind about the death of Sr. Bishop, if you don't mind."

"I don't think I can help you, Chief Inspector, but I'll do my best."

The policeman sat at his desk, removed his glasses, placed them carefully in front of him and paused for a moment. Then he asked "Sra. Bishop, can you think of anyone who would benefit from the death of your husband or his father, or both? Can you think of anyone who had a grudge, or any kind of an enemy of either of them?"

Jenny was thunderstruck. She thought that she had finished coping with Ron's death, but now she was faced with a suggestion that it might not have been an accident. That it might be linked to Charlie's death That there might have been a motive. Fears that she had pushed away returned to her mind, like waking after one of her dreams. *Everything happens for a purpose.* She sat very still, her face blanched and Leticia put out her hand to hold her shoulder. Francisco looked at her with concern and then at Espinoza. They all waited quietly.

She breathed deeply, therapy style, pulling her thoughts together and trying to consider all of the aspects of the question before replying.

"Chief Inspector, I cannot imagine any connection between the two deaths. My husband was the victim of..." She took another deep breath, "a cowardly hit and run driver. This was last December, on a dark, rainy night in Ipswich. The driver has never been found, but I have always assumed that it was an accident caused by someone who was drunk or stupid and too cowardly to come forward. The police have come to that same conclusion. Ron had no debts, no enemies, or even unhappy customers. And apart from me, there was no one who could possibly benefit from his death."

The policeman nodded, replaced his glasses and made some notes in the file.

She paused again and considered the little she knew about Charlie, his life and his death. "As far as my father-in-law is concerned. First, I don't believe that he had many friends, but I don't think he had any enemies either. He was not a bad person, he was only a little unsociable. As a matter of fact, he and my husband didn't get on at all. They had been more or less estranged for many years.

"Next, Leticia and I have just been with Sr. Ramirez and it seems that we and his son, Emilio, are the only people who will benefit from his death. He was a wealthy man and there is no evidence of any debts, or other problems of any kind. Then, you have also told us that you believe it to be an accident since there were no other indications. So I can't see why you would imagine that it was not an accident, nor how an accident in his pool in Marbella on Sunday could be connected with a drunken driver in Ipswich last December."

Jenny sat back in the hard office chair. Her head was aching, whether because of the wine, or the emotional exhaustion of delving into her most intimate fears, or perhaps both.

"Yes, well, it's exactly what is supported by our own investigation." Espinoza looked disappointed. He closed the dossier and removed his spectacles. "I don't think the police can do any more in this matter, Sra. Bishop, and I will not be requesting an inquest. Thank you for coming here so promptly and I apologise if it has been a trying experience for you."

There was a sudden lightening in the highly charged atmosphere. Jenny breathed out deeply, as if she had just run a marathon. "Chief Inspector, thank you for your concern and for the time and effort you have invested into this matter. I'm glad that we agree on the outcome."

He nodded politely. "Sra. Bishop."

Francisco said, "We need to arrange for Sr. Bishop's funeral. Can we plan it for Friday?"

The police officer shook his head. "That's impossible Francisco. The magistrate will only rule on my recommendation tomorrow and the paperwork has to be done. As soon as I get the go-ahead, I will issue instructions to release Mr. Bishop's body. I suggest you arrange the funeral for Monday. Give me the details and I'll see that everything is done in time."

He opened the door. "Señoras, thank you for coming to see me and please try to put these matters behind you now. You have been through enough trying times." He handed a card to each of them. "If you remember anything further in connection with this matter, or you ever need to get in touch with me, you have my contact numbers here."

As they walked back to the car park to retrieve the Mercedes, Francisco sympathised with Jenny. "It must have been difficult for you to discuss those sad events."

Jenny wanted to talk about anything but the last half hour. "Where did you learn to speak so well in both Spanish and English? Have you lived in the States?"

"Well, I was born in California, but my father's Columbian and my mom's American. She wanted to speak his language, so I started out in Spanish. Then I studied modern languages at Berkeley and added a bit of French. I got my law degree in Washington DC and practised for a while in New York. I had some international clients, so I was able to keep up my languages.

"When I arrived in Madrid three years ago," he continued, "I met a girl who came from Malaga, so by the time I came to work for José Luis last year I spoke like a true Andalucian."

"So you're married now?" Jenny immediately regretted the question. It sounded to her own ears almost like a proposition.

Fransico shrugged. "Unfortunately not. Girlfriends and studying tax law are not really compatible. And now I'm travelling such a lot for the firm. But there's plenty of time for that."

They arrived at the parking and the lawyer left them, promising to call the next day with details of the funeral.

Their drive back to Marbella was more subdued than their departure that morning. Both women were silent, trying to come to terms with these changes in their lives. Regretfully putting the past in its place and cautiously looking forward to the future.

Jenny looked out at the vast amount of development that was taking place on either side of the motorway. Villas and apartments were springing up like mushrooms in the midst of bare, brown areas of earth, presumably destined to be golf courses and country clubs. There seemed to be thousands of unfinished dwellings in various stages of construction. Some looked fully completed, others were half-built. Many more were barely started, just concrete frameworks, like skeletons sticking out of desolate tracts of land. They were surrounded by pieces of every conceivable kind of construction equipment, standing idle, or lying where they had been thrown. Like sleeping creatures waiting to be woken up, ready to attack the defenceless earth.

They're destroying this lovely coastline, just for profit, she thought to herself. *But who on earth is going to buy all that property?* She closed her eyes and rested as Leticia drove them back to York House.

Chief Inspector Espinoza called his secretary into his office. He was going to dictate a recommendation to the examining magistrate not to arrange an inquest and he wasn't happy.

He reflected on the interview with Sra Bishop, especially remembering the points he hadn't mentioned to her. The tyre tracks in the dried mud at the edge of the forest path behind the Bishop's house and the footprints through the trees to the perimeter wall. The same mud was found on the wall itself and there was a footprint on the branch of a tree just inside the property. But the police had no idea when those tracks had been left, nor by whom. The weather had been dry and sunny for the last week, so they could have been several days old. In addition, Juan had hosed down the stone staircase before the police had the chance to cordon it off, so there were no prints or mud to be found on the steps.

Further investigation of the tyre marks and footprints had produced nothing. The tyres were well worn. A popular, inexpensive make and available from just about every garage. There must have been hundreds of thousands of them in the Costas. The shoes were from one of the big chains of stores and just as unidentifiable.

The questioning of Juan and Leticia had also proved fruitless and apparently no one had been in the area on that Sunday morning. Nobody had seen anything at all. No suspicious or unusual cars, people, noises or events. The investigation had come to a full stop, a dead end. But despite the lack of any real evidence, he had been a policeman too long to ignore his instincts and they told him there was something he was missing. But he had nothing to go on. Nothing at all.

His secretary arrived and he started to dictate from his notes. He wanted to get it done and out of the way before he changed his mind.

SIXTEEN

Wednesday, April 16th, 2008
Marbella, Spain

Charlie's computer was a slim, shiny laptop, plugged into a kind of cradle on his office desk, which was connected to a printer, a keyboard and a flat screen. At the side was a fax machine and a complicated looking telephone base station. It was now four thirty and they had brought a couple of mugs of tea along to sip while Jenny worked on the computer.

The laptop warmed up and the usual *Control, Alt, Delete* message appeared, then the password request. Jenny entered *Emilio_1975* and the desk top page came up. She scrolled across the screen and opened up *My Computer* and saw, under *Hard Disc Drives*: *VAIO (C)*. Opening this up revealed several folder names, including *Documents and Settings*. She typed *Middlesbrough* and the screen displayed another list of folders. Scrolling down through the dozen or so names, she came to *CB Private*. She entered *Ellen_1969* and the folder opened up. *Angolan Clan* was the first file in the listing. The machine asked for another password and she typed in *cascais*. She had to do it twice because she put a capital letter in the first time. The second time it worked and she saw a Word file with the heading ***Angolan Clan.*** It was dated July 2007 and typed in Times New Roman, size 10 font, with single spacing. Charlie was obviously not a man to waste space for the sake of presentation. At the bottom of the screen it told her that this was page 1 of 72 pages.

Leticia looked over her shoulder. "It's difficult for me to read, on the computer like that."

"Right then. I'll print it out and we'll read it together so we can find out why Charlie took so much trouble to hide it. I've never seen such a well hidden document in my life, although I haven't looked into anyone else's computer before. Maybe they're all like that."

She went to *Select All,* changed the font size to 12 so they could read it more easily, switched on the printer and hit print. Sheets of paper piled up onto the desk and slid down to the floor. The pages were numbered and while they were sorting them out, Jenny tried to estimate how long it would take them to read it all with Leticia's less than perfect English.

"Listen," she said. "Why don't you get your family to come up here for the night. It's going to take us hours to read this document and I don't want you to leave Emilio all that time. We can make something for supper here for everyone. It'll cheer us both up. Besides, it's about time I met my new family, especially my two year old brother-in-law!"

Leticia's mother, Encarni, was happy to comply when she called, and agreed to drive up as soon as her husband returned home from work.

They took the by now 94 sheets of paper into the kitchen and sat with the pages on the table between them. Leticia looked at the close-packed paragraphs and shook her head. "You better read it for me," she said, "I think it will take less time. If there is some things I don't understand, I'll tell you."

Jenny started to read aloud. *"Thursday, April 25th, 1974, Cascais."*

BOOK ONE

PART TWO: 1974

SEVENTEEN

April, 1974
Cascais, Portugal

When Nick Martinez got back to the Tivoli Hotel, he found an envelope on the desk. It was a telephone message from Charlie Bishop. "Call me before leaving the hotel. Cheers, CB."

Charlie was International Director of *APA, Aliança Portuguesa e Africana,* the large Portuguese finance, investment and banking company, and although only two years older, he was Nick's immediate boss. He had met the South African three months previously at a friend's drinks party, just after he'd arrived from Johannesburg. Nick was a diamond expert and a mining engineer. Charlie couldn't believe his luck. He immediately hired him as a consultant for his new Angolan project which needed both kinds of expertise.

Charlie answered the phone immediately. "You've probably heard about what's happening, so you'd better be careful in Lisbon."

Nick didn't let on that he'd already made a fool of himself that morning.

"We've told everyone to stay at home today, so can you hop

on the train and come over here? I don't think there'll be many taxis around, but there should be some trains running."

By nine o'clock, the two men were sitting on Charlie's terrace, drinking coffee.

"So, what have you heard?"

Nick shrugged. "Afonso, the assessor, told me there was a revolution. Go figure!"

"Was there much happening in Lisbon?"

"It was quiet earlier. Now it looks like the whole city's out celebrating. The Avenida's full of tanks and soldiers and there's crowds marching around, shouting and cheering, traffic all over the place, hooting horns and stuff. It looks more like a carnival then a revolution."

Charlie's wife, Ellen, was at the house with their son Ronnie. Not surprisingly, their maid, Maria, hadn't turned up, so Ellen was making a list of provisions and foodstuffs, ready to stock up as soon as the stores opened again. She was not as sanguine as Nick. "I got a call from Agnes and she said that Jorge has told everyone not to go into the office 'til next week." Jorge Gomez was the general manager of *APA*.

"Don't pay attention to him, Ellen. He's a spineless little twerp. I don't know why Olivier keeps him around."

Olivier Bettencourt was the Chief Executive, and his family the majority shareholder of *APA*. However, the Angolan project was Charlie's brainwave. Several months before, he had signed a joint-venture with one of their clients, *Sociedade Mineira de Angola,* the Angolan Mining Company, a diamond producer in the north-west province of the country. The new venture would mine, process and trade Angolan diamonds on a global scale, bypassing the major exporters and gem houses who dominated the industry. Their plan was to launch an IPO, a share float of the joint-venture company, on the London Stock Exchange.

Charlie had hired Nick to set up the structure for the business. They were looking to sell off a quarter of the new company for ten million pounds, giving it a total value of forty million. It was a great opportunity, Charlie's baby, and now Nick's too.

Because of its sensitive nature the project was treated with complete confidentiality. Only Olivier, Charlie and Nick were fully informed and in direct contact with the Angolan diamond company. Nick had a suite at the Tivoli which he used as his office and he came into *APA* rarely, where he was introduced only as a business development consultant.

"So what's this all about, Charlie?" Nick asked.

"OK, I'll explain the background to what's happening." He lit up a cigarette and took a deep drag. "Portugal is almost the only remaining European country with African colonies. They all had them once, Germany, Belgium, France, Italy and of course England. They've been pumping resources out of Africa for over five hundred years. First, slaves, then minerals, precious stones, agricultural produce and now oil. Then they either left or got kicked out, all except the Portuguese. They've got Angola, Mozambique and Guinea and a couple of small possessions. The big one is Angola. Over the last ten years it's become an absolute goldmine for Portugal.

"The problem is that, behind the scenes, there's only a few hundred wealthy Portuguese families benefitting from these colonies. This is all courtesy of Salazar, the previous Prime Minister, who died back in 1969. He was a real dictator and under him the rich stayed rich and the poor stayed poor. And if a few thousand Portuguese soldiers got shot by rebels in the process, well that was a price he decided they could afford."

"You mean the independence guerrillas in Africa?"

"That's right. As far as I can recall, there are three separate movements in Angola and another two in Mozambique and Guinea and they are all trying to grab independence, for their own benefit and for their sponsors. They are funded by just about everybody and his brother. The Cubans and the Russians are on one side, the Americans, Chinese and Brits on another, and so forth. South Africa is also becoming very agitated about developments down there."

"I didn't know we were involved in Angola." The South African looked slighted that his government was acting without his knowledge.

"Think back, Nick. Verwoerd, Vorster and Botha were all paranoid about communism. They outlawed the Communist Party in 1960, but even Mandela was suspected of being linked to the

Russians. Portugal is just as paranoid, and it's easy to understand why. In Angola you've got Agostinho Neto, who runs the *MPLA*. He practically lives in Cuba, he's on first name terms with Fidel Castro and used to lunch with Che Guevara. In Mozambique there's Machel's *FRELIMO*, same story there. And last year I heard the Portuguese assassinated Amílcar Cabral, the boss of the freedom fighters in Guinea. No prizes for guessing who funds those guys.

"The communists have been waiting for years for a breakthrough in Africa and maybe now they've finally got one. It seems from what I've heard that the soldiers are fed up getting shot to pieces to keep fat Portuguese families driving Mercedes limousines."

"Have you ever gone past the military hospital behind your hotel, Nick? Young boys with legs and arms missing, just come back from Africa. It's horrible. If that's the reason for this revolution, then I agree with the army." Ellen shuddered at the memory.

"Well, it seems that the army agrees with you too, Ellen, and has taken over and kicked out the government."

"So you're saying that this revolution is all about the wars in the African colonies?"

"That's my take on it, Nick. But we'll just have to wait to find out the full story. Right now, I'm going to call Mario, ask him how things are down there." Mario Ferro was the local director of the *APA* office in Luanda. A third generation Angolan, he had been trained at *APA* in Lisbon by Olivier and Charlie and had turned out to be a born trader. Using his inbred talent and local relations, allied to the commercial knowledge he'd acquired from his two mentors, he had helped *APA* become one of Angola's main trading partners.

The international call came through. "Mario, it's Charlie Bishop."

"Welcome to the revolution, Charlie. Have you been liberated yet?"

"No, I'm still married to Ellen and to *APA*. But I'm working on it."

"I have exactly the same problems. Maybe we should organise our own revolution." Mario had a highly developed English sense of humour and the two men got on well.

Charlie continued. "How are things with the staff?" *APA* Angola employed over a hundred hard working local people, who were well looked after and loved both their boss and the Bettencourt family. Olivier's father had set up the company thirty years before and he was a local hero. The Bettencourt Comprehensive School, in the courtyard behind the office, had educated hundreds of children from all over the province and many of them, including Mario, had ended up working for the company, either in Luanda, or in Lisbon.

After ten minutes chat, Charlie rang off and said to Nick. "It seems the streets are full of gossiping crowds and there's a thousand different rumours, including that the Americans have invaded. Anyway, things are fairly quiet, but he doesn't recommend any flights down there for the moment. He'll look after the shop and we can maintain contact by telephone and telex."

"But where the hell does that leave us? Is this going to blow my business out of the water? God, I don't believe it!" Nick was suddenly scared to death, and for good reason. A few months ago he'd been at a drinks party, acting like a millionaire, with only two hundred dollars left to his name, not knowing how long he could survive without finding a job. He was missing South Africa, missing Rachel. He was so depressed he was almost suicidal.

Then, by an incredible stroke of luck, he was offered a well paid job and the opportunity to make a fortune, doing what he liked best. And now it looked like it was all going to slip from his grasp. He would be back on the street in a country that was going down the drain, with the same few hundred dollars to his name. He felt sick at the thought.

"Bloody hell, Nick. This is not just your business, it's our business, so calm yourself down. I already spoke to Olivier, he's in Paris this week. He thinks things will settle down. We'll proceed with the plan and review the situation as and when we get a clearer picture."

"But should I go down to see Henriques or not?" Nick wasn't good at surprises, he just wanted a clear plan of action.

"Mario's advice is to wait and see. Besides, we don't even know if the airport will be open. We'll call Henriques, but he's sure to know what's going on. Bad news travels fast."

Henriques Jesus Melo d'Almeida was the owner of *Sociedade Mineira de Angola*. A big, smiling black man, he was one of the cleverest people that Charlie had met on the African continent. He also smoked two packs of cigarettes and drank a half bottle of whisky a day and was surprisingly foul mouthed, employing a large vocabulary of English swear words.

In business however, nothing escaped him. He ruled his mining operation fairly and humanely, but with a rod of iron. In the last ten years, Henriques had carved out a healthy market share of Angolan diamonds, amongst the finest in the world. His mine in north-west Angola produced about thirty thousand carats of rough alluvial diamonds per year, worth twelve million dollars in uncut form and several times more after cutting and polishing. *APA* had been the company's banking partner since the inception of the business by Henriques's father.

The proposed joint-venture would be producing fifteen thousand carats of top quality finished stones per annum, with a market value of over fifty million dollars. Henriques estimated that the alluvial deposits on his property contained enough stones for more than twenty-five years supply. Those were the stakes they were playing for.

Nick pulled himself together. "OK. I'll call Henriques and make sure he knows what's going on. If I can get the samples and the report back from the assessor I can at least get some work done on the prospectus. I just hope it'll be worth the effort."

Henriques told him that things were still quiet in his neighbourhood. But he added, "It's probably the calm before the storm. It'll be pissing communists before you know it." The Angolan had a talent for inventing colourful phrases spiced up with swearwords, but today he sounded worried. Nick agreed to call again the following week.

Rather than have a confrontation with Jorge Gomez, Charlie decided to leave the offices closed until Monday. It was safer to let a few days pass for tempers to calm down.

Ellen persuaded Nick to stay with them in Cascais over the weekend. "Just until things get more settled. I'm not keen on you being stuck in a hotel in Lisbon in the middle of a revolution. If anything happened, I wouldn't like it on my conscience."

Over the next few days the atmosphere in Lisbon was tense with suspense and apprehension. Rumours abounded about the recent events but it seemed that a group of army officers had organised the coup d'état. The story was that the housewives of Lisbon, when they saw the armed soldiers marching along their streets, had cut carnations and stuck them into their rifle barrels. In any event, hardly a shot was fired and the coup became forever known as the *Revolução dos Cravos,* the Revolution of the Carnations. Both the current President, Américo Tomaz and the Prime Minister, Marcelo Caetano, were immediately exiled to Brazil.

Charlie told Nick and Ellen what he'd gleaned from TV, newspapers and friends on the local grapevine. "It's almost impossible to know what the hell's going on. It's changing every minute. But we know that the *MFA*, that's the Armed Forces Movement, is the top layer of power. They're the officers who organised the revolution. They've set up a military Junta to replace the government. So, although we're now living in a bloody military dictatorship, we can stop worrying, we'll be saved by the Junta of National Salvation. We've also got a new President, General António Spinola. The problem is, he's a right-wing moderate and the rest of the Junta members are left-wing activists or even more dubious characters."

He opened up that morning's newspaper and indicated a photograph of a prematurely balding, lugubrious looking man in his early thirties. "That's Vasco dos Santos Gonçalves. He's one of the officers who pushed this revolution through. He's an out and out communist."

The 'strong man' of the *MFA* was indeed a left-wing activist. He seemed to exert more power than António Spinola, the titular President. Under his influence, the new military regime began to undo the very fabric of the government structure put in place and maintained by Salazar and then Caetano for over forty years.

The Gestapo-inspired Secret Political Police, set up by Salazar, was immediately disbanded. Thousands of them tried to flee the country and many were caught and thrown into prison, to suffer the same fate as their victims – beatings and torture, and sometimes death.

Wealthy businessmen and landowners saw their assets confiscated and bank accounts frozen by the Junta. They also started to run to the borders.

Left-wing, self appointed vigilantes set up road blocks and manned the border posts, to trap and imprison the capitalists and other right-wing loyalists. Riots broke out all over the country. The newly liberated left-wing was determined to depose the fascist heirarchy.

The Junta immediately took control of the Bank of Portugal and its hundreds of millions of dollars of gold reserves.

Workers' committees and groups of employees kicked out the legitimate owners and seized their businesses. They took over huge tracts of agricultural and development land in the Alentejo and the Algarve from absentee owners, together with their homes and belongings.

The *PCP*, the previously banned Portuguese Communist Party, was legitimised and thousands of new members rushed to join the small number who had been waiting for over twenty years for this moment.

From one day to the next, Portugal was transformed from a right-wing capitalist society to a left-wing military dictatorship.

After the *APA* staff started coming into the office on Monday, Charlie somehow managed to maintain order in the business. He spent most of his day hearing reclamations from executives and employees, but he held things together pending Olivier's return. Nick was working back at the hotel, occupied with the material he'd recuperated from Afonso, the assessor.

That evening, Charlie got a call from Olivier. "I've been in contact with the *MFA* and fixed an appointment with one of their top people on Friday. I'm flying in from Paris on Wednesday and we can prepare for the meeting."

Charlie agreed to meet him at the airport and invited Nick to come along. When he told Ellen, she marked it in her diary. "You do know that it's May 1st, Labour Day, don't you?"

EIGHTEEN

May 1st, 1974
Lisbon, Portugal

The car park at the airport was barred and Charlie had to leave the Peugeot in a nearby side street. His Triumph TR4 was only a two seater, so he'd borrowed Ellen's car. He and Nick stopped in amazement in front of the airport building. There were a dozen tanks ranged around the roundabout in front of the arrivals exit. Several vans with loudspeakers fixed to their roofs were parked between the tanks. There was a cacophony of sound from the klaxons of those cars which had been allowed into the parking area. Dozens of soldiers stood in a circle in front of the crowds of people marching around, singing and carrying red flags, banners and placards. They were chanting at the top of their voices, *"PCP, MFA, JUNTOS!"*

Nick had to shout to be heard over the row. "What are they saying?"

"It's the Communist Party. They're demonstrating in favour of the Junta."

The shouting and cheering increased in volume as the arrival doors opened and a group of men emerged. They were welcomed by the soldiers and two of them were embraced by several officers in turn. They helped the smaller of the two up on top of one of the tanks and gave him a microphone. He was a lean looking man, shorter than medium height, with a mane of white hair, dark eyebrows over a lined face. Handsome in an aquiline way.

The man struggled to be heard over the cheering of the crowd. They were heaving with excitement, shouting communist slogans, waving their banners and screaming, "Álvaro, Álvaro, Álvaro."

He held his hands up until the crowd calmed down, then said, "*Bom dia, Lisboa.* I have come back home after fourteen years, to lead you to socialism, to equality, and to prosperity." The uproar from the crowd escalated to a roar. Pausing to be heard after every few words, he spoke for five minutes, finally shouting the same slogan as the crowd, "*PCP, MFA, JUNTOS!*" The soldiers helped him back down as the crowd again erupted with roars of approval.

Finally the row diminished until Nick could be heard. "Who the hell is that?"

Charlie was looking around, counting and calculating in his logical fashion. He turned back to Nick, a worried look on his face. "*That* is Álvaro Cunhal, the leader of the *PCP*, the Portuguese Communist Party."

"So how come he's just flown into Lisbon? What's the big deal?"

"The big deal is that he escaped from a Portuguese prison in 1960 and he's been in exile in Moscow since then. Another big deal, Nick, is that there must be a couple of thousand supporters here and an army contingent to help him get his opening message across. Look at those banners and placards. How long do you reckon it took to prepare them, to organise this demonstration and to get the army to orchestrate it all? This must have been in preparation for months. And it's certainly no coincidence that today is May 1st, Workers' Day. This is not looking good. In fact, it's looking bloody awful!"

"There's Olivier." The two men fought their way through the still raucous crowd to the doors where the rest of the passengers were finally emerging. They shook hands and Charlie picked up his suitcase and led the way out of the airport grounds to the car.

Olivier took his arm, "Guess who was sitting across the aisle from me. Álvaro Cunhal!"

"You just missed seeing his triumphant return ceremony. What was he doing in Paris?"

"Apparently he's been in Prague for a couple of years and just came through Paris to get here. Flying first class. Tough life being a communist exile!"

Like many well educated Portuguese, Olivier spoke perfect, unaccented English. He had spent twelve years in boarding school and university in the UK before returning to Lisbon. After a few years in Aliança Portuguesa y Africana, which had been started by his father, who was still President of the group, he had taken over as Chief Executive and the business had never looked back. *APA* was now one of the leading commercial banks in Portugal and handled a large percentage of the trade between the African colonies and the rest of the world. The international trading was Charlie's responsibility and he had built it up massively since joining the bank five years before.

Olivier continued his story as Nick drove them to the office. "But that's not the strangest thing that happened to me on the flight."

"You got laid by a communist supporter?"

"Well, almost as good. Was there a big, swarthy looking guy with Cunhal at the arrivals? Walked with a limp?"

Charlie could still picture the scene. "He and Cunhal got hugs and kisses from the army."

"Well the big guy's name is Alberto Pires da Silva. He told me the most incredible story I've ever heard."

"How come, did you already know him?"

"Never seen him before, but he was sitting next to me, and Cunhal was on the other side of the aisle. He had three or four glasses of champagne and decided he loved me like a brother. "Turns out da Silva is Cunhal's bodyguard, has been since 1960."

"1960? Isn't that when...?"

"Exactly. When Cunhal escaped from prison. That's the incredible story and I got it right from the horse's mouth." Olivier settled back in the car seat. "This chap, da Silva, was one of Cunhal's guards in Peniche Prison. The only thing is, the Portuguese didn't know that he is actually Angolan and had been working for the Russians for years."

"He told you this? He's crazy."

"Charlie, these people think they've won the jackpot. They've returned from a very comfortable exile. They're probably getting paid gazillions by the Russians and now Portugal is their oyster. Did you see those crowds, the army? They've got it made."

"So, da Silva was strutting his stuff to the first person he met after he'd had a skin full?"

"And by lucky chance I was the guy in the next seat."

Nick pulled the car up in Charlie's reserved space and they walked into the offices together. Olivier put his key into the elevator lock and pressed six for the executive level. Isabel, his secretary, greeted her boss, installed them in his sumptuous office and took his suitcase.

"Can you fix a meeting of senior staff in the conference room in an hour, Isabel?"

"Four o'clock? As good as done." She brought in three coffees then retreated to her guard post and they heard her start calling on the interphone.

"Right. Let's have part two of the Cunhal mystery story." Charlie took his coffee, lit up a cigarette and sat in one of the armchairs opposite the others.

"OK. It seems that da Silva is a dyed in the wool communist and was a member of the outlawed Angolan Communist Party. The *PCP* had also been outlawed and in the 1950s, hundreds of people in Portugal and in the colonies were imprisoned by Salazar for communist activities. Some of them were sent to the political prison colony in TarRaffal, in Cabo Verde. Talk about Devil's Island. It was a hell hole with no escape. Cunhal was lucky. Even though he was the de facto leader of the *PCP*, he'd been in Peniche prison, beside Estoril, since 1949.

"Da Silva told me that in 1958, Agostinho Neto, the leader of the *MPLA*, the Marxist rebel group, sent him from Angola to Lisbon with the best references that could be forged. He got a job with the military prison service and ended up guarding Cunhal in Peniche." Olivier shook his head in disbelief. "And all this time he was spying for the Russians and was a go between with them, the *PCP*, the *MPLA* and the communist leaders who were in prison."

"So they were being guarded by an Angolan Communist who was a Russian spy." Charlie looked at Nick, a wry smile on his face, as if to say, *I told you so.*

"In 1960, and this is the scary part, he helped to organise an escape plan to get Cunhal and the other *PCP* leaders out. Not just out of Peniche prison, but right out of Portugal. There were about fifteen of them and if what da Silva told me is true, I have to say it was a brilliant plan. Dangerous, but brilliant. A bit like those 007 spy movies they're making.

"The Russians, can you believe, sent a *submarine* to pick them up. Da Silva and his communist comrades killed the guards in a gun fight and he got Cunhal and the other survivors to the sea. Da Silva almost got his leg shot off in the process. Then a fishing boat took them out to a Russian submarine. A bloody Russian submarine, in the Atlantic, just up the coast from Estoril, and it shipped them off to Moscow, all of them!"

Olivier calmed himself down. "Apparently Manolo de Siqueira, Cunhal's deputy, was killed and I don't know what happened to the others, but Cunhal and da Silva's families joined them and they spent 10 years in Moscow and then went to live it up in Prague."

"But why was Cunhal so valuable to the Russians?" Charlie was asking himself why an insignificant Portuguese communist politician was worth the risk of sending a submarine to cruise off the coast of Estoril in the middle of the Cold War. "There must be more to this than da Silva told you. Cunhal had been in prison for eleven years, supposedly out of all contact with his party. It doesn't make any sense to run such a risk to take him back to Russia to cool his heels, doing bugger all there for another ten years. Not to mention Prague!"

Olivier shook his head in puzzlement. "After twenty years out of circulation you'd wonder what remaining value he'd have. One thing I do remember, is that in 1961, Cunhal went from de facto boss to actual boss of the *PCP*, when the previous leader, Gonçalves, died in TarRaffal."

"And do you remember when the rebels started rattling their sabers in the colonies?"

"I do. One of my uncles worked for the radio station in

Luanda, and he was killed in the first wave of violence. It was in 1961. I think Mozambique and Guinea were not very long after. In any case we were fighting in all of our colonies by the middle sixties."

"So, Cunhal escapes to Moscow in 1960. In 1961 he becomes King of the *PCP* and suddenly all hell breaks out in the Portuguese colonies. And we know that it's the Russians who are financing most of the fighting there. Quite a coincidence, eh?"

"And today, fourteen years later, he gets the "Welcome Home" reception from the new army Junta and the outlawed and supposedly non-existent Portuguese Communist Party!" Nick looked over at Charlie. "You weren't wrong my friend. You had it right on the nose."

"I wish I had been wrong. This business must have been in preparation for years. The army captains and everyone else are being duped. There was no revolution. This is a Russian-orchestrated communist move to take over a European country."

"And there's something else I haven't told you," Olivier added. "Da Silva said the signal to start the revolution was given by two songs played on the radio, just before and just after midnight. These guys in Prague knew all about it. They've had their trip prepared for months."

He looked worriedly at the others, trying desperately to find a positive spin to the situation. "The only thing is, we must never forget that there are opportunities with every regime, with every situation, with every change in circumstances. We have to recognise the authority of the new order and we have to work with it and not against it. This could be a blessing in disguise. We've already fixed up a meeting with the Junta, so let's get our act together and see how we can help them. It's the only way to help ourselves."

At the executive briefing meeting later, despite Olivier's calm demeanor and motivating words of encouragement, Charlie noticed that some of the company managers were distinctly jumpy about the recent events. Jorge Gomez, the general manager, could hardly sit still, looking as if he wanted to get out of the meeting as quickly as possible. Other executives were more sanguine, some of them contributing fairly positive remarks.

I wonder which of them we should worry about the most? Charlie asked himself.

NINETEEN

May, 1974
Belem, near Lisbon, Portugal

The Palace of Belem, a magnificent complex of buildings on the bank of the Tagus between Lisbon and Estoril, dates back to the 16th and 17th century. Amazingly, the buildings were spared during the Great Earthquake of 1755, which destroyed a large part of Lisbon. The palace is the official residence of the President of Portugal and is where the highest ranking ministers and government officials of the country have their offices.

Olivier and Charlie were stopped at a recently erected guard post to produce their papers and have their appointment confirmed. There were so many soldiers and military vehicles around, it looked more like an army barracks than a historical building. They were taken up from the majestic entrance hall to the second floor where a young officer led them along the corridor. Another officer welcomed them into a palatial room, full of antique furnishings and paintings which must have needed a team of housekeepers to look after. Huge windows with heavy drapes gave superb views straight across the Tagus. It was so clear that they could see the unspoiled beaches of

Caparica on the other side of the river.

Major Manuel Nunes Furtado was a self-confident man in his early thirties, with a luxuriant, British Air Force style moustache. His uniform was so crisply starched and pressed it must have hurt him to sit down. He seemed pleased to be able to show off his English when Charlie apologised for his limited Portuguese.

Olivier gave him a short description of *APA* and its activities. "I think you'll agree, Major Furtado, that it has to be in the interests of the Junta to maintain Portugal's economic activity, and especially exports. The new Government must show the world that the revolution has been a positive move, not just for the population, but for the country's finances."

Furtado wasn't impressed by this not so subtle hint of the danger of a run on the currency. He had fulfilled his duty by removing the corrupt government and giving the country back to the people and he didn't seem to be very concerned about the consequences.

"That may be true, but you are speaking from the point of view of a capitalist. It will be up to the new Government to decide whether capitalism is still a viable policy for our country. I'm not convinced it is."

Charlie tried talking about Portuguese-African relations, but here Furtado was even less impressed. "Our intention is to stop the senseless slaughter of our comrades in Africa. Portuguese soldiers have no business in Angola, Mozambique or any place outside of Portugal and we do not intend to continue with the murderous colonialisation policy that has killed so many of our compatriots. We will bring them safely back home just as soon as we are able."

The meeting ended after just twenty-five minutes and the officer led them back down to the entrance hall. He assured them that he was at their service at any time and left them.

"Well that was a 'Major Success' if you'll excuse the pun," Olivier said as they headed towards the exit. Charlie was just as disappointed, but he said nothing. Just then the main doors opened and three men entered the palace.

Olivier stepped forward and addressed the tallest of the three in Portuguese. "*Bom dia,* Alberto. A pleasure to see you again." He put out his hand.

Da Silva was wearing the uniform of a major of the Portuguese army. He hesitated, then smiled agreeably and shook his hand. "Olivier, welcome to Belem. This is Sr. Álvaro Cunhal."

The smaller man smiled reservedly and shook hands.

"And this is Major Otelo Saraiva de Carvalho, the hero of the Portuguese Revolution." The major bowed low, basking in the praise. His tunic was garnished with a dozen medals.

Olivier introduced Charlie then they continued speaking in Portuguese. Cunhal was warming up a little, since Olivier was complimenting him on his return to Portugal. Alberto seemed genuinely pleased to see him again and after a short conversation they shook hands and exchanged cards.

Before turning to leave, the Angolan leaned down to listen to Cunhal, then said, "Olivier, we are having a small celebration dinner tomorrow night, at the Ritz Hotel. Perhaps you'd care to join us at 8:00 pm?"

"I'd be delighted, Alberto. *Muito obrigado. Até amanhã.* See you tomorrow."

"Thanks for not getting me invited." Charlie opened the car door and climbed in. "The last thing I need is a cram course in Portuguese. I've got enough on my plate."

"Did you see that guy Carvalho bow down? He had so many medals I thought he was going to collapse on the floor."

Charlie laughed, "Well done, boss. You jumped in there like an insurance salesman with his foot in the door."

"Well, this could be the break I've been talking about. Work with them and not against them. Let's see what happens. You never know, we could come out smelling of roses."

TWENTY

May – July, 1974
Lisbon, Portugal

"The situation is even more complicated than I thought." Olivier was with Charlie in the office, reviewing his Saturday night party. "Spinola has been forced to share power with the Junta, the Armed Forces Movement and the Communist Party. That's one hell of a committee. They're going to build a camel at this rate. But I've met them all now, so if we play our cards right we can ally ourselves with whoever comes out on top."

"Was there anything specific that you could get progressed?"

"They're all concerned about the problems in Angola and Mozambique, but for quite different reasons. On one side there's Spinola and the other army factions who want to save soldiers' lives and get them out of Africa. On the other there's Cunhal, who's backing the rebels who are killing them. He asked me a lot about our businesses over there, especially our contacts in Angola."

"Did he know much about it?"

"He knows of my father's reputation down there, which is a good thing. I suppose that's why he invited me, getting some local input. He'll know that Mario's people are ultra loyal to the family and to *APA*. No leverage for him there."

"Did you tell him about Henriques?"

"Only that we do some banking business with him. Nothing about the joint venture."

"Some bloody joint venture. It's on the back burner until God knows when. We don't know if it'll ever come off it." Charlie was furious that the opportunity might be lost.

"Cunhal did tell me one thing which I wasn't expecting."

"And that was?"

"They're reopening diplomatic relations with Moscow. It's already in the works."

"What did I tell you? Now we'll be living in a Russian suburb. I suppose you offered to be the new ambassador?"

"They can't afford me. Besides, I don't speak communist."

Olivier would try to maintain close contact with this new source of information. If nothing else, *APA* might be better informed than their competitors.

This state of uncertainty continued for the next several months. The political scenario changed incessantly and daily life became a dangerous and sometimes terrifying experience. Tanks and soldiers were ever present throughout Lisbon and other large cities, and street searches were common. Anti-fascist demonstrations occurred almost daily, some of them very violent. Cars were burned and homes, shops and offices vandalised if the left-wing crowd believed they were owned by capitalists. More properties and businesses were taken over by the workers and the mood of the people shifted more and more to the left. The communist faction was taking control.

On July 15th, at nine in the evening, Alvaro Cunhal and his bodyguard, Alberto Pires da Silva, arrived at the Palace of Belem and were taken up to the first floor. Leaving Alberto seated outside, Cunhal was shown into a palatial reception room. Seated around a table were four left-wing members of the Junta of National Salvation: de Azevedo, Neto, Rosa Coutinho and da Costa Gomes. Also present was General Vasco dos Santos Gonçalves.The remaining three moderate members of the Junta, including the President, General

Spinola, were noticeably absent. After about an hour, Cunhal left the room and Alberto drove him back to his apartment.

On July 18th, General Vasco dos Santos Gonçalves, the Marxist 'strong man' of the *MFA*, replaced the moderate Adélino da Palma Carlos as Prime Minister of Portugal.

"I've just heard that the *MFA*, that's the Communist Committee who are in charge of the army now, have set up something called *COPCON*."

It was a warm summers' evening, with not a breath of wind. Charlie and Ellen were strolling around the garden in Cascais. Ronnie was in bed and they had just finished dinner on the terrace. The smell of eucalyptus and jasmine pervaded the air. Apart from the sound of crickets chirping in the bushes, there was no noise at all. A tiny sliver of a moon was slowly making its journey across the backdrop of stars.

Charlie's words dragged Ellen reluctantly back from this idyllic moment into the reality of the politics of post-revolution Portugal. "What on earth does it stand for?"

"I don't know the exact name in Portuguese, but it's a new secret police force, run by the army. It's just like the Secret Political Police that Salazar set up to destroy communism. But this time it's to convert everybody to the Russian flag. There's five thousand of them and they're going to beat the crap out of the right-wing and moderate citizens until they turn the entire population of Portugal into red flag carriers. It's insanity! They disbanded the Fascist secret police and now they've replaced them with the Marxist secret police. I suppose they're going to bash people on the other side of the head, to show the change in their political stance."

Ellen shivered. "You don't think any of this is going to affect us here in Cascais, do you? I mean, Ronnie and school, the club, our family life and everything. And what about you, your job, the *APA* business, our livelihood?"

"I honestly don't know, Ellen. The communists are winning every point for the moment but I can't believe the international community will let the country become an outright communist state. It's in nobody's interests for that to happen, especially the Portuguese people.

"And if it does happen, you don't get changes like that overnight. We'll have time to pull up sticks and get back to the UK, or wherever we decide to go. I'm quite capable of starting again, it won't be the first time. But for the moment, I don't think we should panic. Cascais is just a tiny fishing village. We're not in the eye of the storm, we're not Portuguese and we don't own big properties or businesses. I'm making good money here and we're saving a lot. I think we should wait until we see a change in the things that really affect us."

"That's more or less what the British embassy said when I called them yesterday. They haven't given out any panic instructions, so I suppose you're right." Ellen was a pragmatic Yorkshire woman who liked to form her own impressions, with the maximum amount of input. "And I'm not so sure it's the best time to be thinking about starting again. My father says things in the UK are really bad. With a Labour government and an oil crisis, unemployment is bound to be on the rise again. We'd best wait and see what happens.

"I've been thinking about Nick," she continued. "He shouldn't be taking risks in Lisbon if we're not. He should move in with us until we see what happens. You might find you need to go into town less often. He must be fed up living in that hotel, it's no fun on your own."

Won't it be a lot of work for you?"

"Charlie, you know very well that Maria does just about everything in the house," Ellen scoffed. "It won't make any difference to me at all."

Charlie liked the suggestion. This change might help to remotivate Nick. He had little to do since his project had been shelved, so Charlie had brought him into his international business team. He was a clever worker, quick on the uptake and with a mind for detail. More importantly, he was one of the few men he could trust. His time could be spent more productively than moping around, waiting for a solution to the Angolan project.

He told Nick the next morning at the *APA* offices. "It's Ellen's idea, she thinks you need mothering. The property is big enough for ten. You don't have to worry about treading on our toes. It'll be just like staying in the hotel except you'll have company."

Nick cheered up at this invitation, he had been feeling lonely and depressed He still missed Rachel and being in the almost empty hotel was not helping. He had also dropped his morning jog, the city had become far too dangerous. He could take it up again in Cascais.

They drove down to the hotel that afternoon to pick up his bags. As they walked from the car, Charlie was looking around, sniffing the air, like a bloodhound on the trail.

"What's up?"

"Have you noticed the difference?"

"You mean the soldiers and tanks and stuff?"

"No. Those are the obvious things. I mean the other changes, the ones you can't see."

"Like what?" Nick wasn't following Charlie's drift.

"It's hard to put your finger on it. It's just that nothing seems the same. There's a different smell in the air, you know? Not that soft, warm, fragrant smell like before. That's gone. It's more like a hard, impersonal smell now. There's a different mood, a different tempo. You can actually feel it, smell it, hear it. Something precious is gone and I doubt it'll ever return."

Charlie was right. Things would never be the same again, there were too many changes which were now irreversible. However, for most people, it would take time for those changes to become apparent. Time for them to mature. Time before they would wreak their eventual havoc on the lives of everyone concerned. Inside and outside the state of Portugal.

Nick moved in that evening, happy to be with friendly company and away from the capital in the frighteningly chaotic ambience that had enveloped the country. They spent the weekends swapping rumours with the other members at the tennis and golf clubs. Everyone seemed to know someone who had already left the country.

"At this rate we'll be the only ones left," Nick cracked as they drove back to the house one Sunday evening. The remark was truer than he could foretell.

Apart from the fact that life was still comparatively tranquil and there were fewer disturbances in Cascais, Ellen had other reasons for wanting to stay. She didn't want to disrupt Ronnie's school life. He had just started at St. Julien's English School in Carcavelhos and had made friends and was doing well at his lessons. She enjoyed her tennis and her golf and Charlie had a well paid job which he loved. As long as they were safe, she would give things a chance to get better.

At the tennis club singles championship, she was beaten by a new member, a young Australian woman called Maggie Attwell. It turned out that her son, Alan, was a schoolmate of Ronnie's at St. Julien's. The two women became friends and started playing together regularly.

Ellen rationalised her losing streak. "She's much too good for me, but I don't mind her beating me all the time. My game is actually improving with every match I lose."

Divorced, Maggie worked with the Australian Consulate in Lisbon as a Commercial Attaché and lived in a flat along the road in Estoril. They invited her to bring Alan round to swim with Ronnie at the weekends. Then they would enjoy an al fresco lunch together.

Ellen would often play the piano for them and the kids adored it. "Play the ABBA song, Mammy. *Waterloo*." It wasn't what she was trained for, but it helped to keep them happy, especially over the occasional rainy weekend. Nick printed out the words so they could all sing along. ABBA had no need to worry about the competition.

Ellen was also happy to have a new source of information to update her on events in Portugal. Every week, Maggie briefed her on the latest diplomatic moves and likely happenings. Like the British, the Australians hadn't issued any leaving instructions to their staff or expat residents. This constant flow of information comforted her in their decision to remain, but she was prepared to get out at a moment's notice if the news changed.

Charlie and Nick stopped going into Lisbon on the train, it had become too dangerous. Bands of demonstrators and hooligans roamed the carriages, terrorising anyone who looked like a capitalist, especially foreigners. They drove in on the Marginal, the coast road, although they were constantly held up by army convoys, political rallies and occasional road blocks.

Then Charlie's beloved Triumph TR4 was written off by an apparently deranged driver on a perfectly clear morning, near Ronnie's school. Only the sports car's "A" frame chassis prevented them both from being killed. The driver denied that he'd been driving at over a hundred an hour on the wrong side of the road. The police came to the scene, but went off without making a report when they saw it was a Portuguese driver against a foreigner.

Charlie was able to get a statement from a teacher at the school who witnessed the 'accident' and he invested the insurance money into a fairly new Morgan, offered at a bargain price by a friend at the golf club who was returning to the UK.

Nick was convinced that the man had deliberately driven into them, but Charlie couldn't credit it. "There are easier ways of killing us than by a suicidal crash on the Marginal."

"Not if you want to make it look like an accident. Nothing would surprise me these days."

The political situation made business increasingly difficult, both inside and outside of Portugal. Charlie had to continuously replace left-wing employees who walked out of the company, as well as disillusioned outgoing trading partners with incoming ones. But he somehow managed to juggle all of the conflicting balls in the air and maintain traction in his international division.

Thanks to his skilful management the division was doing well, exceeding their annual targets. Nick flew down to Luanda on a couple of occasions to see Mario, the local *APA* director, about shipments and new business opportunities, which were surprisingly numerous.

Henriques, the mine owner, came to Luanda to meet him and they tried to salvage a business opportunity from the joint-venture. It was a compromise approach, using Nick's contacts to process the rough diamonds in small batches and go directly to the market with finished stones, to increase sales prices and profits. The strategy was feasible, but the timing depended on developments in Portugal and Angola, which were not looking promising.

Olivier and Alberto met together frequently, the banker's initial reason being to maintain a contact in the political arena. Surprisingly, the two of them became friends, despite their widely differing points of view. The Angolan turned out to be a very cultured person, well read and speaking French, Russian and English besides his own language. Born in 1920, Alberto was a third generation Angolan from Spanish and Portuguese blood. His great-grandparents had left Portugal to establish a smallholding near Luanda, farming and raising livestock.

In 1950 he had married Inês, a niece of a senior official in the Portuguese Colonial Administration in Luanda. He was soon offered a job in the administration service and five years later he was promoted to senior liaison officer. Disgusted at the sight of so much undistributed wealth shared by just a few hundred Portuguese families, he joined the *PCA*, the Angolan Communist Party. At that time, there was little communist activity and it was hidden deeply underground. Salazar's secret police quickly snuffed out any political movement that he didn't control. The information that Alberto could obtain through his key position in the administration was highly valuable and he became an influential member of the *PCA*.

In 1956, the *PCA* was merged into Agostinho Neto's *MPLA, Movimento Popular de Libertação de Angola* and he became a prominent member, happy to help a group of apparently impotent intellectuals to fight the occupation of the fascist Portuguese regime. He was proud to be chosen to go to Portugal in 1958 to organise Cunhal's escape, although he told Olivier, "I'm sure it was only because I was big enough for the job, not smart enough."

When Neto and his *MPLA* supporters were exiled from Angola in 1959 his ambitions of being involved in a swift rebellion, leading to independence were thwarted, but now that he'd returned to Lisbon, he was witnessing the resurgance of a movement that he'd believed in and fought for for over twenty years.

He tried to convince Olivier that the only solution for his country was Marxism. "Angola is not ready for democracy. If we can get rid of what is in reality a Portuguese dictatorship, my country will need time to adjust, time to educate and train people who have been treated like slaves for many, many generations. This can not be done in a capitalist environment. It will be just another form of slavery. Our way is the only way."

Olivier couldn't convince Alberto otherwise. *It looks like we have to go through another failed communist experiment to get back to where we started,* he realised.

Apart from the occasional public demonstration and the inevitable interruptions to services and utilities, things remained fairly quiet in Cascais. After Maggie Attwell had been over to the house several times, Nick invited her to dinner and they started to see each other regularly. He bought an old Opel Kapitan. A huge, six cylindered battleship of a car, with an enormous interior and a boot big enough for the contents of a small house. Nick called it the 'Tank.' He would stay over at Maggie's flat in Estoril and take her and Alan out on the weekends.

Maggie was great company, always in a good mood and he started to put the disappointment of his failed project behind him and enjoy himself again. He found that Australian women were very liberated. She taught him a lot of interesting things in bed. He never forgot Rachel, but he was not in a hurry to leave Portugal.

It seemed that from one day to the next, the tourists stopped coming. In July and August the beaches at Cascais and Estoril were deserted of holiday-makers. Charlie's parents and Ellen's mother had usually come down for a couple of weeks' holiday in previous years, but they decided that tanks, soldiers and machine guns were not the most inviting welcome to Lisbon.

During these months, hundreds of thousands of Portuguese ex-patriots and first or second generation African settlers returned home from the colonies. The numbers of homeless and jobless rose on a daily basis. There was no plan to look after them, no money to help them.

On the other side of the street from the Bishop's house in Cascais there were no houses, just a small copse of trees, where some immigrants had set up tents, like a small shanty town. The newcomers hadn't disturbed the Bishop's daily life except to make Ellen feel guilty.

She said to the others, "Can you imagine this happening in England? These poor displaced people have been dumped here and they've got nothing. The only thing they can do is to go begging in the Cascais market place. The whole town is full of beggars. Where do they all come from? Nobody cares about these people. They're not criminals. It's disgusting, I wish we could do something about it."

But there was nothing they could do. It seemed that there was nothing anybody could, or would do. Even though Ellen was possibly right and the immigrants were not criminals, they were obliged to turn to petty theft and pick-pocketing to survive. But there was no evidence of increased police presence. The bars in Lisbon were full of prostitutes, both female and male and seemingly younger and younger. Crime began to be a real problem, people were afraid.

TWENTY-ONE

August – September, 1974
Lisbon, Portugal

In August, Charlie's secretary, Bella, came to him with an invitation to her wedding to Carlos Souza Machado. The date was set for Saturday 21st September. The ceremony was to be held in the sixteenth century Jeronimos Monastery church in Belem and the reception at the Cocina del Palacio Nacional de Sintra, a famous restaurant to the north of Cascais.

Charlie hugged her. "Congratulations, Bella. You've finally decided to tie the knot?"

"Well, you know that Carlos is a member of the Mozambique Independence Party."

Carlos was a Mozambique national, a trading account manager at *APA*, specialised in business with that country. His parents still remained in their homeland, despite the fighting between the *FRELIMO* guerrilla forces and the Portuguese army.

"He has good information that the Portuguese are preparing to pull out of his country. Apparently they're about to sign an agreement that independence will be declared in nine months time and it's *FRELIMO* who'll form the government. They have a moderate ideology and Carlos is keen to go back and be involved in helping to form the new government."

Charlie was sceptical that anyone could determine what might happen in such a volatile situation but he just said, "This is a real case of mixed emotions for me. I'm happy that you and Carlos are getting married, but then I'll have to replace two of my most trusted assistants. How will I cope?"

"Don't worry," she said. "We won't leave you in the lurch, you'll have plenty of notice."

Carlos asked for the day off on 13th September. It was a Friday, so Charlie didn't know whether he was attending a pro-independence rally, or maybe holding his bachelor party. He was happy to grant the absence in any case. Carlos had brought good profits to the division over the last two years.

At the golf club on Saturday morning, Ted Carpenter, one of his partners, came up to him. "Did you see the telly this morning?" Charlie hadn't seen it.

"The police broke up a rally in Porto last night. With bloody guns! Dozens of people were injured and someone was killed. I saw some of the live footage. It was horrible. Things are going from bad to worse in this country."

"What kind of a rally was it?" Charlie had a bad premonition.

"Pro-independence for Mozambique. Some woman was preaching peace and brotherhood, and then a riot broke out and the police started shooting people. I don't understand why the hell they were involved. The police are supposed to be on the side of the army and the army is supposed to want to get out of that country and give it back. I thought everybody had agreed on independence and now they're killing each other. It's bloody madness!"

Carlos had gone up to Porto on the train with four Mozambican activist friends on Thursday night. Joana Simeão was coming to the city. Known as the 'Mother of Mozambique', Joana was head of the moderate movement, United Group for Mozambique, *GUMO*, and was negotiating with Samora Machel, the leader of *FRELIMO*, to introduce democratic elections after independence. Carlos had been contacted by one of her team in Mozambique to help with Joana's visit to Porto.

They spent the night sleeping on the floor of Bella's sister's flat in the textile manufacturing quarter. The next day they were the first to arrive in the Jardim da Boavista in the city centre and by four in the afternoon there were thousands of people in the park. Carlos and his friends had set up a platform from packing cases, with planks of wood and a carpet on top. They installed a primitive amplification system with a microphone and some loudspeakers around the platform. A van from the national television company was parked nearby, and a reporter with a handheld movie camera was walking around interviewing people in the crowd.

When Joana Simeão walked onto the platform the scene erupted with cheering and whistling. Men and women alike were crying "*Joana, Joana. Nossa Mulher Mocambicana.* Our Mozambique Mother. Independence for Mozambique now!" The cameraman, in front of the stage, was filming the whole spectacle.

The leader of *GUMO* was a bespectacled, middle aged lady, suited to her nickname. She took the microphone, "*Bom dia Porto!*" She spoke fluidly, exhorting her supporters to greater efforts for independence. The crowd cheered incessantly, straining to hear her words blasting indistinctly from the loudspeakers.

In front of the stage, a gang of rough looking Mozambique men in worker's overalls were drinking beer. One of them turned to Paolo, a friend of Carlos, who had handed the mike to Joana. "Get that bloody bitch off. We don't want another right-wing, fascist government stealing our country."

"So, you'd rather have the communists murdering and pillaging, would you? What's wrong with a moderate consensus?"

The man's response was to crash his fist into Paolo's face. He fell to the ground, blood pouring from his broken nose. The rest of the gang started kicking him, shouting and screaming in a frenzy. Carlos and his friends tried to protect him, fighting the men away. Some of the assailants produced short cudgels that they could wield in the restricted space. They swung them around, smashing heads and faces indiscriminately.

Within minutes there were injured people lying all over the

ground. The TV camera man ran to the back of the crowd, away from the fight. Marxist extremists spread the fighting further afield, until there was a general riot in the park. Moderates and Marxists alike were lashing out at each other. Carlos and his friends were prime targets, right in front of the platform.

Those on the outskirts of the crowd started hurling rocks, stones, bottles, anything they could find, into the melee. Duarte, who was engaged to Bella's sister, was hit by a flying beer bottle. The bottle shattered on impact, shards of glass ripping the flesh from his face and splintering into his eyes. He went down into the heap of bodies, falling on top of Paolo. More troublemakers rushed in to kick and punch the defenseless bodies senseless. After filming the riot from the edge of the crowd for a few minutes, the reporter raced off to the safety of his van.

Joana Simeão tried to calm the crowd. She called for order and quiet. When that didn't work she called for the police. "*Buscar a Polícia,*" she cried vainly. The fight in front of the stage threatened to bring down the primitive pile of packing cases. Carlos managed to climb up beside her and pull her to the back of the stage, away from the fighting. Just then, a detachment of police came running up. They had dogs on leads and they were carrying rifles and pistols.

The leading officer was shouting through a megaphone. "Clear the area! Anyone still here will be arrested and put in jail. Clear the area now!" Trying to disperse the maddened crowd, but only succeeding in creating more panic.

The women in the crowd tried desperately to escape from the pandemonium, but many of them fell and were trampled by the surging fighters. The police pushed forward, they were now wielding their weapons like clubs, laying about them with relish. Then the militants stopped fighting each other and started attacking the police. They were met with rifle butts and batons. The dogs barked and strained on their leashes as they were used to push back the crowd. More of the crowd started to take out their hatred and venom on the police.

First one, then more of the officers started shooting into the air, shouting at the struggling, bloodied demonstrators. The dogs were frightened by the pandemonium, barking and jumping, fighting to get free from their leads. Two policemen were pulled down to the ground, boots and cudgels smashing into them. A woman was screaming, a dog had grabbed her ankle in its jaws. The blood was pouring from her leg, running onto the mud-baked ground. The gang of Marxist militants moved about the crowd, manipulating the situation, pumping up the crowd's animal ferocity until it was a frenzy. The panic got worse. The noise was infernal.

Carlos led Joana down the stairs and away from the stage towards the top of the park where it was quieter. A policeman looked over and saw Carlos pulling Joana away. She was still crying out to try to calm the crowd. He took aim and fired his rifle at Carlos.

Afterwards, the officer testified that Carlos had been threatening to kill Joana, but by that time she was already on her way back to Mozambique and couldn't speak in the dead man's defence.

Everyone was devastated by Carlos Souza Machado's death. His funeral was a reality check to the large number of family and friends who congregated in the churchyard by the grave. The weather had changed. A cold wind was blowing in from the Atlantic, bringing heavy, bitter rain with it. The sky was leaden with black clouds and the ground was saturated underfoot.

The sods of earth clung to the shovel then clunked down onto the coffin like giant slabs of chocolate. The wreaths and garlands of flowers were soaked and limp looking, their colours muted by the gloomy half light. It was a sad, desolate scene. The congregation vainly tried to keep dry under a panoply of umbrellas, huddling together as if to ward off the malignant aura of death. Suddenly, the impersonal threat of change that had surrounded them since April had materialised into the murder of someone they knew. And a wedding had become a funeral.

The priest spoke out with a firm voice, straining to be heard against the beating rain. "Carlos was a fine young man with an admirable purpose in his life. To bring independence, freedom and prosperity to his homeland and to resettle there with his new wife, Bella."

Instead, he had been shot down like a criminal, his body thrown into the back of a police truck, together with other wounded friends whose only crime had been to love their country.

Bella quit her job and went to live with her parents in Setúbal. Charlie had been right. He had lost two of his best colleagues, although he could never have foreseen the tragic circumstances that would cause the losses.

And she and Carlos were not the only employees that *APA* had to replace over the next few months. Now, more and more communist activists were showing their true colours in *APA* and the growing, insidious influence of the Marxist group caused many departures. Jorge Gomez, the general manager, had gone from being frightened and scared of the revolution, to embracing it with open arms. He was a small man, both in stature and in strength of character. It seemed that he had been totally converted to the Marxist propaganda. He had also subverted a number of the bank's middle management and some younger employees to join him. The group always left the offices early on the day of a left-wing rally or demonstration. Gomez tried to organise political meetings in the bank, as was happening in many businesses, but the majority of the staff was still loyal to the Bettencourt family and so far he had been unsuccessful .

The problem was that under new government directives, employees could not be sacked or made redundant without a full enquiry. These enquiries became political demonstrations and were totally destructive. So they stayed, fomenting discontent, like worms in a barrel of apples. In the case of Gomez and his henchmen, plotting to overthrow the corrupt capitalist owners of the business, along with their star executive, Charlie Bishop.

After attempting and failing a coup d'état, President António Spinola resigned from the Junta on September 28th. His troops, all afilliated to moderate political parties, were outnumbered and soundly beaten by the forces of *COPCON*, the Operational Command of the Armed Forces and the puppets of the extreme left. Several of his closest aides were thrown into prison, where they would stay for God knew how long. His resignation left the field open to the Marxists. He was replaced as President by General Francisco da Costa Gomes, a left-wing member of the Junta. Another nail in the coffin of democracy. Day by day Charlie's prophecy was becoming a reality.

TWENTY-TWO

October, 1974
Cascais, Portugal

The attack on Charlie's house came on October 25th. He and Nick returned home early for the weekend. They took the stairs to the kitchen and dumped their briefcases, grabbed a couple of beers from the fridge and went to sit on the garden terrace.

The garden door into the kitchen was ajar. The door had been forced, the wood around the lock was splintered. Racing back through the house they saw two men running from the hall out the front door and down the driveway. They sprinted after the men towards the road, where a white Fiat had just come racing up. One of the men turned. He was wearing a balaclava which hid his face. He held a pistol in his hand and he raised it up, aiming.

"Christ almighty!" Charlie pulled Nick down behind the bushes at the side of the driveway. They heard the crack of two shots and spurts of gravel came up from the path. Looking up they were in time to see the men jump over the wall and climb into the car. It shot off up the road towards Cintra. They ran to the gate but were too late to see through the back window and there was no number plate on the back.

They went through the house, checking every room. It seemed that nothing had been touched, until they got to the office. The room had been ransacked. The desk drawers and filing cabinet had been forced open. There were papers and books thrown everywhere and the files had been emptied all over the carpet. An attempt had been made to open the safe. There were scratch marks around the lock, but it was bolted to the floor and wall and still intact.

"Did you have anything worth stealing in here?" Nick was picking up papers and trying to get them into some semblance of order.

"Absolutely bugger all! Ellen's couple of rings and bracelets are in the freezer drawer. Our personal papers are in our safety deposit box at the bank. All I've got in the safe is *APA* stuff and this is the only place they've looted, so I'm just wondering why anyone would be interested in burgling my office. This is not a typical burglary, it has to be a political thing. Someone looking for something incriminating, something to do with me, Charlie Bishop, director of *APA*." He opened up the safe and ensured that its contents were untouched. "The other thing is that it's Maria's day off. Somebody's been doing their homework on the Bishop's household routine."

"Did you notice the tall guy in the black jerkin? Not the one with the gun, the other one?"

Charlie shook his head vaguely, still coming to terms with two intruders in his house and being shot at in his driveway.

"Who did he remind you of?"

"I didn't get much of a look. Who do you mean?"

"I'm almost certain that it was that tall skinny guard who started at the bank last year. He's been very thick with Jorge Gomez recently if you've noticed."

"Shit, that's just great. So we're being burgled and shot at by our own employees now. What in hell is going on in this country? Who do they think I am, Salazar's long lost son?"

Charlie called a local handyman to come over to fix the door and put additional locks on all the outside entrances. Next, he called the Cascais police station who said that they would send someone right away.

By the time Ellen got back with Ronnie the two men had managed to clean up the office so that it looked reasonably tidy again. She was horror struck when they told her about the aborted break in. They didn't mention the gunman. "Can you imagine if they'd come when we were in the house, or even worse, at night? What if Ronnie had been at home?"

Shortly after, two police officers arrived. They were totally disinterested. One of them who spoke English said to Charlie, "It's time rich people like you stopped exploiting the poor. Either that, or you should go back where you came from, we don't want capitalists or foreigners in our country." They walked out without acknowledging anyone any further.

"Well, that's encouraging." Nick smiled sarcastically. "As long as we know we have the police on our side, we won't worry, will we?"

Ellen calmed herself down. "Let's not blow this out of all proportion. It's a minor incident and compared with what's going on elsewhere, we're very lucky. Petty crime happens all the time, it doesn't matter where you are. There's no harm done."

That night in bed, Charlie said, "Listen, Ellen. When you decide you want to leave, you just have to say it's time. I'll understand."

She kissed him and switched off the light. "I'm not going to let a couple of petty thieves chase me out of my home. We'll leave when we're ready and not before."

Charlie said no more. He didn't want Ellen to know that they seemed to have become targets of the new regime. There was no point in worrying her. He could worry for them both.

In the Toston Bar in Cintra, five men were sitting drinking beer in one of the back rooms. Cigarette smoke swirled up through the light from the ceiling lamps. The air was thick with the acrid smell of cheap tobacco.

Jorge Gomez, the smallest of the group, asked, "So, you found nothing?"

The man in the black jerkin shook his head. "There was nothing in his files. He might have had something in the safe, but we couldn't crack it."

The other intruder interrupted, "If I'd nailed them in the drive, we might have been able to go back and break it out."

"Don't be a fucking imbecile. I've told you. No guns, no trouble until we're ready. We want to get rid of all of those fat bastards in the bank together, in one fell swoop. The whole rotten lot of them, pay-off time." Gomez took a drag on his cigarette. "I'm certain there's something going on. That new guy, Nick Martinez, is involved with Angola, money smuggling or something like that. But we need real proof. Bank account numbers and names, copies of transfers, that kind of thing."

"Well, that's it for me tonight." The tall man emptied his glass and got to his feet. "I've got a hot date, that new receptionist from Angola. Bloody animals, these Angolan women. See you in the morning, I hope." He led the way out and the men dispersed in separate cars.

Despite Ellen's apparent calm, Charlie knew she was on the verge. The uncertainty and fear was taking its toll on all of them. If they weren't safe in their own home in a sleepy little backwater like Cascais, then where were they safe? He hired a security company to check on the property day and night. They advised him about buying a shotgun and, despite her protestations, he showed Ellen how to use it. The security companies were doing great business. Some people were happy with the situation.

TWENTY-THREE

November, 1974
Lisbon, Portugal

On Friday, November 29th, at eight in the morning, Jorge Gomez, General Manager of *APA,* arrived at the *COPCON* headquarters in central Lisbon and was met by two army majors. He was carrying a cardboard box-file under his arm. They spent almost an hour inside the building, then emerged with two other soldiers and climbed into a canvas-covered lorry. They sat on the wooden seats along the interior of the vehicle for the ten minute ride to the *APA* head office on Avenida Duque de Loulé.

Just after nine, a smug smile on his face, Gomez bustled ahead of the soldiers up to the reception counter and asked the Angolan girl to call down Sr. Bettencourt. Olivier came out of the elevator and after a brief discussion he left with two soldiers on either side of him. He wasn't permitted to make any phone calls but was taken off to the *COPCON* barracks for questioning, then to Lisbon prison and no one could contact him.

His wife, Cristina, called Ellen. She was crying and distraught. "Olivier's brothers have been arrested as well," she sobbed.

The two younger brothers, Ruiz and Andrès, ran a property development business, also started by their father. They owned hundreds of hectares of beach front land and properties in the Algarve.

"It's all been confiscated by the government. We're losing everything. I took my father-in-law to the airport yesterday and put him on a plane to Geneva. He's seventy years old, he can't take this kind of thing. What's happening Ellen? Why won't they let me see them?"

Ellen was shaken. "I'll call Charlie. I'm sure he can fix things. Try not to worry. I'll get back to you as soon as I know anything."

Charlie was visiting a bank in Milan. She called him at his hotel. "I'm not sure that you should come back here. You were right about Jorge Gomez."

"What on earth are you talking about?"

"Cristina called me. It seems that Gomez has talked *COPCON* into putting Olivier and his brothers in prison and the government has confiscated their properties.

Charlie was dumbfounded. Olivier's father was the Duque de Santiago de Compostela, and Olivier would inherit the title, although it had long since lost any significance. He couldn't believe that the Junta was starting to imprison the aristocracy of Portugal. "Ellen, just stay calm. Call Cristina back and tell her not to worry." he said. "Let me make a couple of calls and I'll ring you as soon as I've sorted something out."

He called Nick, at the office. "I've been trying to get hold of you," the South African was speaking quietly and quickly. "Apparently that bastard Gomez walked in this morning with *COPCON* officers and they took Olivier away. We can't contact him. I even sent Isabel to the barracks and to the prison and they just sent her away. *No comment.*"

"What about the rest of the staff?" Charlie tried to organise his mind. He was being worn out by the continual confrontations in their lives but he was now the most senior executive in the business and he had to take charge.

"Couple of account managers and admin guys stayed away, but so far the fall out is minimal. Even some of Jorge's gang are still here. I don't think they're very happy with this turn of events. Some people want to keep their jobs. They need the pay."

"OK. It's Saturday tomorrow. Get Bill to send everyone home early for the weekend and tell them I'll talk to them on Monday morning. Go back to Cascais and expect me home tonight about eight thirty. Look after Ellen and Ronnie until I get there, Nick. We'll sort this out."

Charlie thought for a while then took his address book from his briefcase. He looked up a name and number, picked up the hotel phone and dialled the operator.

"Yes, Mr. Bishop, what can I do for you?"

He hesitated for a moment. *What the hell,* he thought. He asked her to call the number.

Sitting in the army truck Olivier was trembling with reaction. Nothing could have prepared him for being betrayed by one of his most senior executives, then arrested by soldiers of his own country. He was guilty of nothing, but he was being treated like a criminal, as if he was a danger to his nation. Now he was being taken to the army barracks and God alone knew what awaited him there.

"What's going on, Jorge?" Gomez was sitting opposite him in the truck, the smug smile now a wide grin. Neither he nor the officers spoke and they drove in silence to the barracks.

He was bundled out of the truck and pushed into a small office furnished with a metal filing cabinet, a desk and three chairs. A young lieutenant told him to sit down and pulled up a side table with a battered Underwood typewriter on it. Taking from the drawer three identical forms, he placed carbon sheets between them and inserted them into the machine. He asked Olivier for his personal details, laboriously typing out his answers onto the triplicate forms.

The soldier left with the forms and after ten minutes, he returned to escort Olivier into a larger office with a conference table and six chairs. Five minutes later, Gomez came into the room with another officer that he hadn't seen before. He introduced himself as Major Eduardo Tavares, Director of the Bank Fraud Investigation Committee. Gomez opened up the cardboard file. It was full of notes and lists, a few typed pages. He pulled out a page and showed it to Tavares. Then the questions started.

"On November 6th, at four o'clock, you called the *Banque Privée de Genève* and spoke to M. Guigneaux, the assistant manager. Is that right?"

"I don't remember the date, but it's probably right. Why?"

"We're asking the fucking questions here." Gomez snarled, banging his fist on the desk. "Why did you call the bank?"

"We've been doing business with them for twenty years. We call them all the time about transfers or transactions we're doing. I can't remember every call I make, that's ridiculous."

"You were recorded as saying," Gomez read out from the page, "*my father will be there on the 21st November. Please arrange to have him picked up and put the funds at his disposal.*"

Olivier suddenly felt sick. "Why the hell have you been monitoring my phone calls?".

"I told you we're asking the questions. But for your information, we've been listening to your calls for the last month. Very interesting. Very incriminating. That right Major?"

"What was the call about, Sr. Bettencourt?" The officer was more circumspect than Gomez, he wasn't sure of the facts. Most of it was hearsay, there were very few recordings that could be considered incriminating. Gomez had wanted Olivier's home phone tapped, but they'd drawn the line at that, so they didn't have much to go on.

"My father has gone to live in Geneva. He's too old to put up with the situation here. I was arranging for his trip, that's all."

"So, what funds were to be *put at his disposal,* eh?"

"He's had an account there forever. It's nothing criminal, it's been on his tax returns every year. Have you looked at them?"

Major Tavares glanced uncomfortably at Gomez. "We haven't had a chance to check everything. Sr. Gomez has been investigating this matter. We've got his reports, that's all. He believes you've been transferring funds illegally."

"I run a bank, Major. It's my business to transfer funds, but not to break the law. And I'm not stupid enough to do it under the nose of the general manager. The whole story is a load of rubbish, nothing more or less."

For the next half hour, Olivier was shown transcripts of telephone calls, lists of numbers, details of meetings he'd never been in and names of bankers and clients, mostly in Switzerland. Gomez had prepared his attack cleverly. It was totally unfounded, but the circumstantial evidence was overwhelming. He controlled himself, replying to the questions quietly and respectfully, determined not to buckle under the pressure. If he did, he knew he was lost.

Suddenly, Gomez leaned across the desk and grabbed Olivier by the lapels. He shouted into his face, "Bettencourt, you're a crooked capitalist bastard! You've been stealing from the Portuguese people for years and you're going to pay for it."

"You lying little shit! I should have fired you years ago for your incompetence. The only thing you're good at is screwing things up and lying to cover it up." Olivier had boxed for Christ Church College and now his reflexes took over. He stood up, pushed Gomez away and hit him with a right cross to the cheekbone, knocking him back over the desk onto the floor, where he lay still, his head touching the major's boot, blood running from his nose.

Tavares jumped quickly to his feet, moving away to avoid ruining his gleaming boots. He pulled out his firearm. "That's enough, Sr. Bettencourt. Step back and sit down again."

Olivier slowly sat down, looking at the inert figure on the floor and cursing his reaction.

The major called the other three officers into the room and told them that Bettencourt was arrested for illegal money transfers and fraud. They left Gomez on the floor and Olivier was frogmarched out to the truck and driven across Lisbon, to be imprisoned in the city jail. When he resisted being pushed into the dank cell he was struck on the head with the stock of a gun. Then another soldier smashed his rifle barrel into his back and legs and he was pushed headlong onto the floor, the sound of the cell door clanging shut behind him. He lay there all day and night in the pitch black, desperate with fear and anxiety for his wife and children, wondering what was going to happen next. He had no food nor drink. He was left alone, lying frightened like a little child in the dark, and after many hours, he finally fell into a troubled sleep.

He was woken by the sound of the cell door swinging open

and the footsteps of two men at the entrance. He peered through the gloom, trying to make out who was there. He didn't know if it was night or day. Then he heard, "*Bom dia,* Olivier. How are you feeling?"

"Alberto? What are you doing here?"

"Get up. We're going to talk in the warder's office. Come on." He turned and waited outside with the other man.

Olivier struggled to his feet and followed the bodyguard to an office near the entrance. Once in the morning light he saw that the other man was one of the soldiers who had arrested him the previous day. The officer who had not spoken a single word.

Alberto was wearing his major's uniform with *COPCON* badges and had the cardboard file with him. "I just want to ask you a few questions," he said. Olivier looked nervously at the Angolan. He was frowning, avoiding the other man's gaze. He looked like a man on a mission. A mission he wasn't enjoying.

On Monday morning, Charlie and Nick were standing in front of the *APA* employees in the staff canteen, the only place big enough to house everyone. There was an uneasy atmosphere in the room. Most of the staff were standing silent, waiting apprehensively for news of their boss. Others whispered together, swapping the many rumours which were doing the rounds. Everyone knew of Olivier's arrest and imprisonment. Gomez had made sure of that.

Charlie was rehearsing a plausible story to calm them down and avoid too many leading questions. As he was about to step up on the small platform to speak, Olivier entered the room. He was wearing a silky grey suit with a red handkerchief in the breast pocket. He looked in much better shape than Charlie felt. They shook hands and he climbed onto the platform. The mood in the room immediately lightened. People began to talk together, there were one or two cheers and a round of applause. Olivier started speaking, sounding confident and convincing. "Good morning, everyone. Thanks for coming to this meeting, there are some things I need to tell you. I'll be very brief. "First, I was unfortunately obliged to fire Jorge Gomez last week, he was causing us problems and neglecting his responsibilities. I'll take over his tasks pending a replacement.

"Second, I had a long meeting with *COPCON* when I went over there on Friday and we are now back on their 'Be good to them' list. So I don't expect any further mishaps.

"Third, I'm pleased to announce that business has never been better. You will all be receiving a bonus at the end of next week. That'll give you time to spend it before Christmas." He paused, waiting until the cheering and laughter died down. "That's all for now. Let's get back to more productive matters and thanks again to everyone."

He stepped down from the platform and several employees and executives came forward to thank him and confirm their commitment to *APA*.

"Bloody hell, that was a close call!" Nick shook Olivier's hand. "Well done."

The Portuguese winced and withdrew his hand, bruised and cut from the cell floor. They could now also see that he had a nasty cut along the hairline. He'd hidden it by combing his hair forward. "Thanks, but you've got the wrong man. That genius standing behind you fixed things, otherwise I was a goner. How did you manage it, Charlie?"

"You were right. Alberto loves you like a brother. Five minutes on the phone and he agreed to pull rank on the prison service. He's got a lot of experience in that department."

"Well, at least I didn't have to escape in a Russian sub." The three men laughed, not so much at the feeble joke, but more from the sense of relief.

Sitting back at his desk, Olivier relived the weekend's events. Shivering at the memory of the stink and filth of the prison, the noises of the suffering of unseen people, the tiny barred cell with no toilet facilities where he had been locked up for two days. The feeling of helplessness, in the hands of a communist-led army that preferred to believe a corrupt little Marxist spy like Jorge Gomez rather than an innocent man. Alberto had told him his brothers had been arrested and were in the same prison, but he hadn't been allowed to see them. If it hadn't been for the Angolan's intervention they would still all be lying in the filthy confines of a Portuguese prison.

After examination of Gomez's file, Alberto and the army major had agreed there was no case to answer. Olivier and his brothers could be released as soon as they got the paperwork organised. But it was Sunday morning before he got home to his wife and family. And it was Monday morning before he pulled himself together enough to face the outside world again.

What was happening to his country? His father had been forced to flee his own homeland. The country in which he had strived for over forty years to make a better place for his fellow citizens, by creating businesses and jobs to support the economy. And now this! What would be next? In his confused mind he couldn't work out whether his release was an act of friendship and justice, or the next step in a plan to trap him, his friends and family in an even greater fabrication. He felt physically sick at the thought.

Back in Cascais, Ellen and the two men once again discussed the worsening situation. It was becoming more dangerous every day and no one knew how it would end. Pragmatically, Ellen pointed out that it was getting near to Christmas, and after the awful year they'd had she wasn't going to let anything spoil the plans they'd made to make the holiday a special one with Ronnie and Alan. There was nothing they could do but wait to see what the New Year held for them.

Who knows?" She told them. "There could be good surprises in store. Maybe the communists will run out of steam. There are lots of decent, sensible people in Portugal. They just need to organise themselves as well as the communists. Then we'll see what happens."

It was impossible to argue with Ellen's common sense, so they decided to prepare for the holiday and ensure that the kids had a Christmas to remember.

On December 4th, Jorge Gomez was appointed Deputy Director of the Bank Fraud Investigation Committee and given a small office in the building next to the *COPCON* headquarters. His first action was to apply for permission to tap over fifty private telephone lines, including Olivier's and Charlie's. Afterwards, he went home, had dinner with his wife, kissed her goodnight and left the apartment, "for an important meeting." Then he went out on the town, with the *APA* Angolan receptionist.

TWENTY-FOUR

December, 1974
Lisbon, Portugal

The week after his release from prison, Olivier visited Alberto to thank him again for his help. His mind was working clearly now and he knew the Angolan had acted out of fairness and friendship. But nothing in Portugal was as simple as that any more.

He greeted Inês, Alberto's wife, then the two men went into the study.

"What the hell's going on, Alberto? It wasn't an accident, me being arrested, it was a frame up. And if you hadn't come along I'd still be rotting in jail along with my brothers."

Alberto took a drag on his cigarette, considering how much to tell the banker. Finally, he said, "There's been a lot of activity around the colonies. You already know about Mozambique and it looks like there will be some more announcements soon. This is causing a lot of tension in Portugal and the left-wing extremists are taking advantage of it. You were a victim of this because Gomez is a troublemaker and for some reason he's out to get you."

"So, what's your advice?"

"Olivier, I'll let you into a secret. I've never mentioned this before, but I know a lot about your family. They've been in Portugal forever. Your ancestors were of the aristocracy, which I despise, but your father was one of the greatest businessmen we've ever seen. I used to hear his name when I was a kid. He was a hero to us, even in Angola. One of the few capitalists who worked for the good of the Portuguese and Angolan people, not just for himself. I didn't go to the school he built in Luanda but I knew kids who did. They were lucky. It was the best school around and they were able to go because of your father. He's a fine man.

"He's old and tired now, but you're not and you've got to follow in his footsteps. Believe me, Portugal is not going to erupt into civil war. The political changes will sort themselves out and we'll find a new equilibrium. It will take some more time but it will get done in the end. There are difficult times ahead but they won't last forever. Nothing in life ever does.

"So, if you stick it out, toe the line for a while and get through this period, then Portugal will need you like never before. I know you're a clever and honest man like your father was and I'll support you as best I can. I have a little influence and if I can help, I'll try. And if I see things change for the worse, I'll let you know. That's all I can promise."

Olivier thanked him and left the apartment. Alberto watched from the window as he went to his car then he picked up the phone. "*Bom dia,* Alvaro. Bettencourt was just here." He listenened for a moment then replied, "I don't anticipate any more problems with him."

He rang off and looked back out the window. A drunken man was vomiting into the gutter, surrounded by vandalised buildings and burned-out vehicles. This was not what he had planned for in helping to bring communism to Portugal. He lit another cigarette, reflecting on the situation. For the moment, Cunhal had the power. But Bettencourt still had a fortune. He would continue to back both men until it was time to choose.

At *APA,* Olivier relayed the bodyguard's message to Charlie and Nick and they told Ellen when they got back to the house.

"I told you there would be good surprises in store," she said triumphantly. "I'll bet there are more on the way." Just to be sure, she called Maggie to ask if the Australian embassy agreed with Alberto's opinion. It was still the case.

Nevertheless, to be on the safe side Charlie and Nick went less often to Lisbon and worked from home. But they were forced to travel more to maintain the overseas business. There were now very few finance houses prepared to issue credits for Portuguese transactions.

Charlie returned from Frankfurt having sewn up a contract for Angolan oil. "We're still ahead of the game, guys. With our financing relations we're picking up business where other companies can't compete." Olivier and Nick knew this was true and that it was largely due to Charlie's expertise and international relations.

The two main, practical problems were getting into Lisbon and getting in and out of the airport. Despite the VIP travel cards that Alberto had obtained for them, it was a continual nightmare getting past the check points on the main roads to the city. And airport security was so tight they had stopped taking a travel bag, just a briefcase with their personal items inside.

In December, Nick went down to meet with Mario in Luanda. Before leaving for his return flight, he called Henriques at the mine, to keep up the contact in case things changed.

"It's an insane situation, actually," Henriques told him." "The *FNLA* have taken over the place because we're close to the Zaire border. Roberto Holden's the boss and he's up there in Kinkuzu, jerking himself off at his success in occupying the north-west. Everybody knows he's been on the CIA payroll for years and apparently he's now done a deal with Mobuto and with the Chinese for soldiers and arms. Clever sod!

"Now the Portuguese have disappeared from everywhere except the main cities, and the *MPLA* haven't come up here yet, so we're sitting in an *FNLA* occupied zone, pretending nothing has changed.

"But the funny thing is, they're leaving us alone. I don't think they want to piss off the local people because they'll want our support if those *MPLA* bastards do come up here. I hear that around Luanda and in Malange the *MPLA* have got a working alliance with the Portuguese, so they'll be busy getting organised down there. But once they're sorted, they'll be heading up to the north-west. Then you'll see things change around here faster than a farting cheetah.

"The only thing that's certain is that the Portuguese are doing what they've done in Mozambique. Getting ready for independence. Independence and democracy! That's a joke. Everybody talks about it and no bugger can do anything to make it happen." From his fouler than usual language, Nick guessed the Angolan was getting weary and fed up with the uncertainty and escalating violence in his country.

Despite the high profile international plan to prepare for democracy in the Portuguese colonies, behind the scenes nothing was changed. Henriques was right, it would be a guerrilla war. The best funded group would win, whatever the politicians wrote into the history books.

Nick wished him well and took the next flight back to Lisbon. As Henriques had said, central Luanda and the airport were still under Portuguese control and fairly quiet. He prayed that it would stay that way, for everyone's sake, especially Mario, Henriques and their families.

On December 6th, Jorge Gomez, Deputy Director of the Bank Investigation Committee, and his boss, Major Tavares, entered the offices of the Portuguese PTT, the national telecoms operator, and met the director. They provided him with a file full of executive orders signed by a member of the staff of Major Otelo Saraiva de Carvalho, the head of *COPCON*. Twenty minutes later, the two men left and the director called his manager of network maintenance.

The next morning, two telecoms engineers came to work on the Cascais substation near Charlie's house. When they left, after only a half hour's work, a small monitoring device had been connected to the line going from the substation to the house. The machine started automatically every time there was an incoming or outgoing call and registered the third party number. It also activated a miniature tape recorder.

After leaving Cascais, they went to the Alfama district, a very old part of central Lisbon. It took them longer to connect the monitor and recorder to Olivier's line, because the copper wire installation was much older and more difficult to identify amongst the masses of lines going into the densely populated area.

The recording tapes could hold only two hours of conversation and had to be changed regularly to maintain semi-permanent monitoring. Unfortunately, the engineers had many other things to do and changes were not as efficient or as regular as they should have been.

On December 7th, they were all at Olivier's house in Lisbon with the children, it was Cristina's birthday. The house was an 18th century palace overlooking the old part of the city, which had been rebuilt after the Great Earthquake. The rooms were vast, with high, ornate ceilings, enhanced by graceful mouldings designed to show off the many paintings which still hung on the walls. Every surface was covered with family portraits and fine masterpieces dating from centuries ago. It was more of a portrait gallery or a museum than a family house. Thanks to Alberto, the house hadn't yet been seized by the workers or the government, but they knew that time was running out. His brothers had already left for Geneva. It was too dangerous for them to go back to the Algarve, so they had been forced to turn their backs on ten years of development work and hundreds of millions of escudos of land value.

Those members of the family who hadn't yet fled the country were at the house with their children. Olivier's extended family was very numerous. The kiddies were playing five a side football in a beautiful ballroom which was now also used as a gymnasium and sports room. The women were gathered together in the enormous kitchen, still equipped with old-fashioned service bells and speaking tubes connected to the many bedrooms in the building. The men congregated in one of the ornate reception rooms, swapping rumours and opinions, like everyone in Portugal. There was to be a party that evening and the rooms were decorated accordingly. Olivier and Cristina were convinced that it would be the last time they would entertain in the house.

Olivier took Nick and Charlie aside and they stood looking over the rooftops of the city. He said, under his breath, "I just heard from Alberto. That little shit Jorge Gomez is working for *COPCON* in the bank fraud committee, so I'm sure that he's already tapped our private phone lines, as well as the bank's. Be careful who you call and what you talk about."

Both men nodded their agreement. They were not surprised at this news.

Olivier continued, "You know the Angolan rebel groups have agreed to sign the Alvor Accord?"

The treaty was a compromise, negotiated between the US and Russia, to leave Angola with a democratic solution after independence, by creating a transitional government between Portugal and the three rebel groups. Despite the chaos in the country, the gossip grapevine ensured that every piece of news was immediately disseminated around Lisbon.

"Even if they execute the treaty I'm certain they won't stick to it." Charlie's analytical mind had been dissecting the matter. "The Russians have fooled the Americans again. They are behind the *MPLA* so there's no way they'll stick to a power sharing deal with the other two parties. The communists don't share power, they take it, whatever the cost. Look what happened in Mozambique. The minute *FRELIMO* was nominated as the next government, Machel started turning the country into a Marxist state and he's murdering everyone who doesn't agree with him. The treaty won't be worth the paper it's written on."

"You're right, but my point is that I reckon we are now looking at the end game. The very existence of this agreement means that Portugal is pulling out of Africa completely and quickly. Mozambique, Guinea, Angola. It's just a matter of time, a very short time, in my view."

"Agreed."

"I have some news for you," Olivier lowered his voice again, "We're moving the business to Switzerland."

"What about Alberto's assurances?"

"I think he's underestimating the effect the withdrawals will have on Portugal. If our colonies go, we'll have nothing left. A civil war could easily be on the cards and we'll lose everything. So we have to plan for it now and save what we can. If he's right and I'm wrong, it won't matter, but if I'm right, we can still survive. In the meantime, with Alberto's help we can continue for a while, until we're in a position to move.

"We've set up a new Geneva company called Bettencourt SA. My brothers are working with my father to rebuild the business. They're arranging a banking license and we're hoping to be up and running by the summer. After what happened last month I've decided to join them. I can't expose my children to any more risk of losing their father."

"Can you salvage anything from Portugal?" Charlie was thinking of the huge loss that the family would face. The *APA* companies employed almost six hundred people, most of them still loyal to the family. Olivier's father had started the business forty years ago, it was his lifetime's work, but it was coming to an end. *He must be heartbroken,* thought Charlie.

Olivier replied, "So far we've managed to get about half of our capital out and we're working on the balance. There's not much we can do about the physical assets. We can move our international business and whatever profits we can shift, and that's about all."

"I suppose that's where Nick and I come in. The international business."

"Exactly. You know that we would like you to join us. Our success in Portugal has been a combination of banking and trading and we want to do the same in Geneva. Will you come?"

"Let's work this out," said Charlie. "Today's December 7th. What's your timetable?"

"We should have the banking license by April and I expect it'll take that long to salvage as much as we can of the capital. We won't get it all out, but we'll do the best we can. Also, we need more capital in Geneva than in Portugal, so that's something else I'm working on."

Olivier lowered his voice again. "Outside of the bank assets we own about fifty buildings, offices and factories, around the country. We own them through a UK Plc and there's no link to us. They're UK registered, clean as a whistle. The government won't dare to grab them, they've got enough problems with the British Embassy as it is. I'm negotiating to sell the UK company to a Swiss property group. We swap our shares for cash in a Swiss bank.

"The problem is that the price is going down every day that the communists increase their power. They're worth at least thirty million dollars, but I'll be happy to get between ten and fifteen. I reckon it'll take a couple of months, then we can plan our move.

I want the maximum cash and assets in Geneva before the Swiss Banking Commission rules on our application."

"Listen, Olivier," Charlie interjected. "We have several very profitable contracts to ship in the next few months and there's a few more in the offing. I'm confident that we'll get most of them because there's nobody else can do them. We can easily divert part of the profits from these deals to Geneva. We use *APA* to negotiate the deals and we set up a Geneva trading company, an indirect subsidiary of Bettencourt SA, to pass the business through."

Olivier was already ahead of the game. "If we can show a well-capitalised bank with a profitable trading subsidiary the banking license is a piece of cake. My brothers can acquire one through our Panamanian company, so there's no trace to the family or *APA*. Give us a week."

"Right." Charlie turned to Nick, "We haven't done the Frankfurt contract yet, have we?"

He shook his head. "We could easily pay a fifteen percent commission to a Swiss agent."

Charlie continued on his line of thought. "There's something we'd like to propose to you, Olivier. We'd both like to join you in Geneva, but as minority partners, not as employees. If we can bring extra profits and commissions like this, would your family allocate shares to us?"

"I guarantee it. We just need a formula to calculate the shareholdings."

"Then it's agreed. Right, Nick?"

When he confirmed his agreement, Charlie continued. "I figure we can squeeze four or five more months of good business here, so how about a first of June start in Geneva?"

Nick was sceptical of this time-frame. "What if we don't have that long?"

"Oh, don't worry. With Alberto's help, we'll have it. We just need to manage it well."

InterCommerce SA, a Swiss trading company established in Berne for over five years, was bought on December 13th by a lawyer acting on behalf of MultiTrans Ltd., a Panamanian company with bearer shares. On December 17th, InterCommerce signed a contract to buy the Angolan oil contract from *APA*, simultaneously signing a contract with the Frankfurt buyers, and Charlie and Nick started to earn their shareholdings in Bettencourt SA.

In his little office next to the *COPCON* building, Jorge Gomez and his assistant/secretary, Lía, read through over two thousand transcripts of taped phone calls during the month of December.

Lía was a tall, big breasted Angolan refugee, who wore a thick layer of makeup on her cheeks to hide the scars remaining from the chicken pox she'd had as a child. She had been the *APA* receptionist until Gomez made her a better offer. The downside of the job was that he expected her to spread her legs for him or give him a blow job several times a week, but the work wasn't hard and the pay was better than at the bank. In addition, she was right next door to hundreds of the most powerful men in the country and she hoped to take full advantage of it.

The changing of the tapes was sloppy and there were usually long intervals between the transcripted calls. This was for two reasons. There were now hundreds of wire taps in place in and around Lisbon and there were not enough technicians to attend to them regularly. Dozens of untrained army conscripts were being seconded to the task of managing the recorders and typing out the transcripts but the whole project was a shambolic mess.

However, the automated register of caller's numbers from the machines was complete. When they found Swiss, Luxembourg or similar *offshore* numbers, they would look for the transcripts to try to find incriminating conversations. Usually they heard anodine, innocent talk, since many of the callers knew that their phone had been tapped and were using code words. But their hit rate justified the cost of the operation in the eyes of their paranoid left-wing bosses at *COPCON*. Several bank or business managers had received early morning visits from them and were now lying terrified in filthy cells, just as Olivier had done.

In the transcripts for the end of the month they started to find calls between *APA* and InterCommerce SA, a Swiss company that Gomez had never heard of. He found out from the Swiss commercial register that it was a well-established company, but he was convinced it was a front, set up to funnel money out of the country and he was determined to expose it. Day by day he was preparing his attack on the remaining pieces of the capitalist system and especially on *APA* and Olivier, Charlie and Nick.

In Cascais, Charlie hadn't told Ellen about the phone tapping. It would have looked suspicious if she suddenly stopped using the phone to call her friends and family. In any event, she was unlikely to say anything of a compromising nature, since she didn't know anything. But he was ill at ease knowing that Gomez was looking over his shoulder. The man was determined to bring him down and would go to any lengths to succeed. He found himself needlessly double-checking the doors and windows when they went out or up to bed and he ensured that either he or Nick was always there and they never left Ellen and Ronny alone.

On Christmas Eve the three men went out for a celebration drink. They had won a reprieve. God knew for how long, but at least they could enjoy Christmas and New Year with their families and worry about 1975 later on.

BOOK TWO

PART TWO: 2008

TWENTY-FIVE

Wednesday, April 16th, 2008
Marbella, Spain

It was eight o'clock by the time the two women had read to this point in the narrative. Leticia's parents had arrived earlier with Emilio. At first, he sat on Jenny's knee quite happily while they continued reading. When he started yawning, they realised that they were as tired as he was.

"Time for supper. We'll finish reading in the morning." Jenny switched the laptop off and they went into the kitchen with Encarni, to scavenge what they could and prepare some supper.

Leticia's parents spoke no English but they were the most friendly and natural people Jenny had ever met. José was a small skinny man with skin so clear that it appeared to be transparent in the lamplight. He looked more like a doctor or an artist than a check-out clerk in a supermarket. His wife was quite the opposite. Large, ample bosomed and dark skinned, with her hair tied back in a typical Spanish bun, she could have been an ex-flamenco dancer.

Together the three women made up dishes of tapas from what they could find in the kitchen, while José opened a fine bottle of

Rioja from the wine cellar. Despite the recent traumatic events, the ambience was relaxed, mainly because of little Emilio, who was a born clown. He laughed and chattered at the table and had them all in stitches with his antics. Clearly he had inherited his mother's cheerful, outgoing personality. His grandparent's lack of English didn't present a problem. Smiles and gestures were sufficient to complete the conversation. It was a long time since Jenny had felt so at ease and she began to revise her feelings about her new 'family'.

Leticia also felt uplifted by the happy atmosphere and managed to put aside her private grievings. They had agreed not to discuss or even think about Charlie's extraordinary story until they finished it the next day. Tonight was a family affair and it was a great success.

They made up beds for everyone and by ten thirty they were all asleep. In Jenny's case, benefitting from the second full night's dreamless sleep that she had enjoyed for many months.

The man in the small black car had been sitting outside the da Costa's apartment building since six o'clock. Although it was a warm evening, he had parked the car in the sun where he could see the entrance clearly, but he couldn't be seen. He had waited there for each of the last four evenings, but there had not yet been a night when the whole family had gone out and left the apartment empty. He hoped that tonight would be an exception. Leticia had been out all day and still hadn't returned. Would the rest of the family follow her?

After about thirty minutes wait, he saw Leticia's father park his battered red Volkswagen on the other side of the street, walk into the building and get into the elevator. Then just after seven, both her parents came out with their grandson and drove off. His patience had finally been rewarded.

The man moved his car into the shade at the side of the building until darkness fell. It was eight thirty when he went into the hall and pressed the button for the fifth floor. In less than a minute he had picked the Yale lock and entered the da Costa's dwelling.

He spent a full hour searching the five-roomed apartment meticulously, methodically and expertly, leaving no visible trace of his visit. He was especially painstaking in his search of the bedrooms which were obviously Leticia's and Emilio's. But despite his expert examination of the apartment, he didn't find what he was searching for. Supressing his disappointment, he ensured that he'd disturbed nothing, then left as quietly and efficiently as he'd arrived.

Shortly after nine o'clock, Chief Inspector Pedro Espinoza finished editing his report for the Examining Magistrate. He handed it to the duty officer to be delivered the next morning and went out into the fresh air for the first time that day. There was a tapas bar just down the street from the Comisaría and he sat at an outside table, lit up a cigarette and ordered a cold beer.

He had spent a couple more hours rereading the Bishop dossier once more. Trying to find some common thread between two deaths, months apart, in different countries, seemingly accidental, seemingly unrelated. He knew there had to be something, but once again he had found nothing.

Espinoza had a *sine qua non* approach to his investigations. *Find a motive for the crime and you'll most likely find the culprit.* In his experience, he'd found there was often motive without crime, but seldom crime without motive. So his only possible access into the criminal's mind, if there was a crime, was to find that motive. Not just for Jenny's father-in-law's death, but her husband's too. His instinct told him the deaths had to be connected. The Ipswich police had sent him a copy of the verdict of Ron's inquest. It was totally non-committal, but he didn't believe that fatal accidents to both father and son could be a coincidence. He knew there had to be a common motive and he had bluntly asked Jenny exactly that.

It wasn't a subtle approach, but it might have produced something. Unfortunately it hadn't. Sra. Bishop was understandably nervous and had seemed overwhelmed by his question, but she obviously knew of no possible connection. So he had been obliged to rule out foul play in his report. He had never handed in a report with such a feeling of uncertainty and he didn't like it at all.

The Chief Inspector ordered some tapas with a large glass of Rioja and ate his supper at the pavement table. He did that more and more these days. Since his separation from Soledad there was no reason to go home for his meals. It was easier and cheaper to eat tapas for one than to buy groceries, then cook and wash the dishes. And it was more sociable to be surrounded by several other diners than to sit with a television screen in front of his eyes.

He paid the bill and walked back to his office. There were still a few matters he wanted to finish before he went home for the night. He would have another look at the Bishop file the next day, if he had the time. Maybe the night would help him to find a fresh approach.

In Washington, Sonia Nicolaides was diligently trawling through the files in Pires da Silva's laptop, vainly trying to detach her conscious self from what she was reading and viewing. She had already been physically sick several times, but she overcame her nausea to continue drilling down into the mass of dreadful depravity to reveal the full extent of the ring's activities.

She had now uncovered a number of "shadow sites", containing the most repulsive filmed material she had ever come across. The shadow sites were hidden behind respectable web sites, possibly even without the domain owner's knowledge. By entering certain coded instructions these apparently innocuous sites opened up to display their filth to the members of the ring. She had identified sites in France, Belgium, Russia, Ireland and South Africa and had started compiling a list of the email addresses which accessed them. Sifting for information which could lead to identifying the originators of the material. Those who made fortunes in this inhuman activity. When she felt confident that she could fool these evil perverts, the next step was to start impersonating da Silva and continuing his communications with the other members of the ring.

Sonia brought herself up to speed on the day's new messages. She saw there were no new emails on the clean address, but there were a number of fresh messages received on the three dirty addresses that morning. It was now evening in Europe, so the time difference worked in her favour. She could study the messages, compile her notes and files and prepare her replies in her own time, when she was ready to start playing the game. When she was ready to start dismantling at least this one strand of the global spider's web of depravity.

The following morning, everyone in York House was up by seven. After a quick breakfast, Encarni took Emilio out for a walk on the beach and José went off to his job at the supermarket.

The two women started reading the rest of the history.

BOOK ONE

PART THREE: 1975 - 2007

TWENTY-SIX

January - March, 1975
Lisbon, Portugal; Geneva, Switzerland

In January, hundreds of activists, both right-wing and left-wing, were killed or injured during a right-wing congress in Porto. For the first time, *COPCON,* the armed forces communist political secret police force, fought with the *Guarda National Republicana,* the National Republican Guard. Other Portuguese cities were affected the same way. Violence and political stand-offs were more and more frequent.

Public demonstrations became common and more violent as agricultural workers fought over the farms and landholdings they had stolen from absentee owners. All agricultural production had stopped and even the families of the usurpers were facing lean times. Moderate political meetings were invaded by communist supporters, often resulting in fatalities and wounded. Lisbon became a very dangerous place, with thousands of homeless immigrants and criminals eagerly taking advantage of the uncertain situation. Vandalism was ripe and burned- out cars and broken shop and office windows lined every street. Despite the increased resistance of active moderate and right-wing supporters, the militant left was pushing the country on an irreversible slide towards full Marxism. Civil war seemed more and more likely.

In the midst of this anarchy, the *APA* international team was still doing great business. Thanks to Mario Ferro in Luanda, who was digging up deal after deal, they signed up several more profitable contracts, all through InterCommerce. Charlie had been right, business was booming and there was more in the pipeline to fulfill their commitment to Olivier and to Bettencourt SA. After the disappointment of Portugal and the failure of the Angolan project, he and Nick were determined to get to Geneva in style and make their fortunes as shareholders in their new business venture. But it was not to be as simple as that. Events got in the way.

On February 12th, Jorge Gomez took the midday flight to Geneva. He visited several banks and company offices which were on his list of active investigations and stayed that night in the Hotel d'Auteuil. The next morning he had more meetings then lunched in the Café du Commerce. After lunch he took the train to the Swiss capital, Berne.

He was disappointed to find the InterCommerce office where it was supposed to be, at 413, Veldenstrasse, and to meet the young Swiss German director, Herr Marcus Schügler, who seemed to be running a genuine Swiss business. Herr Schügler showed him around their small, but well appointed offices. Full of industrious, efficient Swiss employees, processing contracts and making telephone calls in various languages. He was well acquainted with *APA*, a large client of theirs, but had never heard of the Bettencourt family. Gomez swallowed his disappointment and promised to be in touch, then took a train to Zurich to continue his investigations, before flying back to Lisbon with several pieces of incriminating evidence for his files, but still nothing concerning *APA*.

Marcus Schügler called Ruiz Bettencourt in Geneva to advise him of Gomez's visit. The message was transmitted to Olivier and Charlie. Their security barrier was working well.

Towards the end of February, Nick called Henriques in Angola to get an update. The mine-owner sounded more worried than before. "There's a lot of bad things happening around here now that the so-called 'Transitional Government' is in charge, he said. There's hardly any Portuguese troops anywhere and the rebels seem to have a free hand everywhere. We've had the *MPLA* up here, marching around the compound, showing off with their guns and terrifying everyone. The only thing that's saving us is the *FNLA* contingent that's north of us guarding the coast road to the border and Cabinda. Mobuto's sent a unit down from Zaire to strengthen their hold up here. The *MPLA* aren't strong in this area so they don't want to get into a fight, yet. They're coming in small groups, probably spying out the land, getting ready to make a move when they're ready. It's just like a bloody rehearsal! There's talk of the Americans funding the *FNLA*, so we're praying that's true, but if it's bullshit, we'll be finished here."

Nick tried to talk him into getting out, but soon realised he was wasting his breath and gave up on it. Apart from offering his sympathy for the Angolans' plight, there was nothing he could do and little to discuss, the diamond project was panned. Their grand plan to float an Angolan diamond business on the stock exchange was bust and there was no way that they could manage to operate the InterCommerce arrangement for diamonds from Angola.

He and Charlie resigned themselves to missing a great opportunity. They just hoped their friends would emerge unscathed from the chaos that was engulfing the Portuguese colonies.

"You know, Olivier, I simply can't get my head around this at all."

"Around what, Charlie?"

They were in Olivier's office at *APA*, reviewing the status of the remaining international contracts.

"The whole, insane political bullshit in this country."

"Well, I'm with you all the way, but what particular insanity do you mean?"

"Let me ask you a question. OK?" Charlie had never looked more serious. "If you made a Balance Sheet of Portugal's assets and liabilities, what value would you put on anything, or everything? I mean, what is the value of the State of Portugal, as a going concern?"

"Well, the whole country is virtually bankrupt. And those few pieces that aren't, like *APA*, will be very soon. So, I suppose the answer is that the only value is in the colonies, with their oil and mineral resources, agricultural and fishing production and low cost labour force."

"Exactly right! So why is the whole agenda with the army, with Cunhal and his Russian cronies, with the government, in other words with everybody, to move the country further and further towards a communist regime? Apparently with the objective of handing Portugal over to the Russians, when there is nothing left of any value? It simply doesn't make any sense.

"Remember what I said before? Why did they bring back Cunhal, twenty-five years after he dropped out of sight, just to bankrupt the country? They've saved this guy, taken him to Russia, paid a fortune to support him and his entourage, brought him here and backed him again. They've bet the house on him for twenty-five bloody years, for what?"

"There's only one possible answer. They want the colonies."

"Well, mark my words, Olivier, they're going to get them, and it won't be pretty."

"Things are getting out of hand, António. You have to intervene. You still have massive support in the country. You must show the people that the right-wing still has a voice in Portugal. Show them you're not finished, that you're determined to find a fair solution." Alvaro Cunhal was speaking at a clandestine meeting of twelve men at Tancos military airport, about sixty miles north of Lisbon.

Ex-President António Spinola looked bewildered. "I can't believe I'm hearing this from you, Alvaro. For the last year you've been fighting me and undermining my position and now you want me to intervene. What's going on?"

"Civil unrest in Portugal. That's what's going on." Cunhal tapped the table with his knuckles. "If we don't calm things down we'll have a civil war on our hands. If that happens, what do you think the chances of a political compromise are?"

"Is that what you want, a compromise? I thought it was communism or nothing."

"António, I believe in communism. I'm a Marxist, I always will be. But first and foremost I'm a Portuguese and I love my country. I don't want communism in Portugal at the cost of civil war, so we have to do something before it's too late."

So what do you want me to do?"

"Take over the Presidency again and force the Junta and the *MFA* to see sense. Most of them are ambivalent. Communism is the soft option because there isn't anything else to attract them. They want a strong personality, someone who can offer a real alternative to left-wing fanaticism. You're the only man who can do it. Get Soares and Gonçalves to sit down together and hammer out an agreement. The others will follow like sheep. I'll support you, if you do it."

"You can count on our support too, General." Air-Vice Marshall Coelho Dominguez was commanding officer of Tancos air force base. "I can have ten thousand paratroopers around the Lisbon barracks so fast the *MFA* won't know what hit them."

"Of course you also have our unconditional financial support." The speaker was a member of the Espirito Santo family, one of the richest banking dynasties in the country.

"Now you're talking." The tall thin American civilian smoking a cigar in the corner of the room spoke for the first time. "Sounds like we have a plan. Let's get down to the detail."

The next day, Cunhal visited the Prime Minister in Belem. Vasco dos Santos Gonçalves was not the brightest star in the firmament, but he was a fanatical Marxist. After listening to the *PCP* leader's summary of the meeting, he asked, "So how do we take advantage of this?"

Cunhal gave him his advice and after a few more minutes discussion, he left the palace and Alberto drove him back to Lisbon. He said nothing about his plan to the bodyguard. The man seemed to be becoming a bit too friendly with the remaining capitalists.

On the morning of March 11th Nick was driving Charlie to the airport when they were turned back at a roadblock. All the roads into Lisbon were barred with wooden barricades. They were manned by workers, men and women, from adjacent offices and factories.

General Spinola, the ex-President, had attempted another unsuccessful coup d'état, sending two Fiat T-6 fighters and two helicopters from Tancos airforce base to bomb the barracks south of Lisbon. Immediately after the departure of the aircraft, the air base commander and his two senior officers were arrested and imprisoned by *COPCON* officers. The paratroopers sent to take the Lisbon barrackes were left leaderless and began to fraternise with the left-wing members of the *MFA*. By eleven o'clock, the attempted coup had failed and Spinola and his closest aides had already fled to Spain by helicopter. The rest of his supporters were rounded up and thrown in prison alongside those who had been festering there since the last failed coup in the previous September.

Within hours, banks, factories, schools, offices and shops were occupied, closed down and encircled by pickets. Left-wing fanatics rampaged through cities and towns, vandalising cars and buildings and running riot, attacking anyone who looked wealthy. It was a witch hunt. It was not safe to go outside.

Cunhal's cynical duplicity had paid off. The last remaining threat from the military right-wing was removed and the popular mood was murderously anti-fascist. He was particularly pleased that the simpletons from the CIA had suspected nothing. Now he was free to execute the remaining steps of his long-prepared plan to capture the ultimate prize for his Russian masters.

Charlie and Nick drove back to Cascais and called Olivier. "Looks like it's really getting out of control. What do you think?"

"I'll call Alberto. See what he has to say."

The bodyguard was unaware of Cunhal's involvement in the aborted coup. His advice was still the same. "It's just a knee-jerk reaction to that asshole, Spinola. It'll settle down. Sit tight and I'll keep you posted "

Ellen called Maggie. "Still no panic stations," she told her. "The Ambassador has spoken to Gonçalves, the PM, and he's stationing extra troops around the main cities to maintain order without bloodshed. It seems to be just a storm in a teacup."

Ellen was comforted by this report and by Alberto's assurances. Somehow, things didn't seem too bad in Cascais. They decided to wait and see what happened.

The *MFA* moved rapidly to consolidate all power into the hands of the Marxist military government. They abolished existing levels of control and set up a Council of the Revolution consisting of two hundred and forty of the most radical left-wing members of the officer corps. The council could control the presidency and exercise a veto over the legislative process.

For a couple of days it seemed that the optimists' opinions were justified. The army presence was more evident and it was effective. Street violence and vandalism were less frequent, the streets were full of people trying to buy the few supplies that were still available in the stores. Lisbon was almost a beautiful city again.

On Friday, March 14th, Charlie and Nick were in Olivier's office when Alberto called. Olivier listened for a few minutes then put the phone down.

He turned to the others, his face ashen. "It turns out that amongst Spinola's supporters, there were seven members of the Espírito Santo banking family. They've all been thrown in prison for treason and bank fraud. There's even a rumour that the CIA was involved in the attempt. But that's not the worst part." He stopped, gathering his wits about him. "As a result, that communist bastard, Gonçalves, has just nationalised all commercial banks. That means us!"

Nick and Charlie looked at him, then at each other. "Oh shit," they said simultaneously.

TWENTY-SEVEN

April – June, 1975
Lisbon, Portugal

In practise, the nationalisation programme was a combination of incompetance and treachery. A Nationalisation Committee was created for each large enterprise, reporting to the Council of the Revolution, the new Marxist military government. The *APA* committee was named in the third week of March and held its first meeting with Olivier and his senior staff on Thursday the 20th. The members of the committee had no business experience at all. Two of them were from the Ministry of Tourism, which was now virtually inoperative, and the third was an army captain, seconded to the Ministry of Finance. They had a list of documents which they required and it was clear that they wouldn't be able to understand anything they were given. Rather than antagonise them, Olivier and Charlie befriended them. Explaining various points until the men were completely befuddled. Their next meeting was arranged for the following week.

"How did it go?" Nick hadn't been in the meeting.

"Piece of cake, we're their new best mates. With their help I think that we can get more money to Geneva, not less." Charlie was confident, but there were unseen forces at work.

Manuel de la Peña, the army captain, sat in the Toston Bar in Cintra with Jorge Gomez and three of his informers from APA. The soldier didn't understand the APA business, but Gomez did. He had begged his boss, Major Tavares, to be seconded to the nationalisation committee, but the major had ruled it out. Gomez had spent thousands of francs in Switzerland and come up with virtually nothing. And he didn't want a repetition of the embarrassment of last December's arrest of Bettencourt. His ears were still ringing from Alberto's scolding.

"Intercommerce is the key to the money smuggling. It has to be." Gomez took a drag on his cigarette. "There's more than half their business going through that company now. They're obviously skimming a margin off in Switzerland and handing it over to the Bettencourt family. You must be able to find something, something to do with Bern." His obsesssion was becoming apparent to the soldier. "I went up there a few months ago and I don't trust the people. I know they're crooked. You've got to look at those contracts. It must be there somewhere."

De la Peña nodded and promised to dig deeper into the business. But there was nothing to find. The contracts were perfectly in order, and showed a reasonable margin. Goods were shipped and money was received and paid and that was all he understood. Charlie and Nick were running rings around the nationalisation programme. During April and May, they and Mario worked diligently to sign up and execute more deals with the few remaining Portuguese manufacturers and Angolan producers, and InterCommerce in Berne continued to be their biggest trading partner.

The committee listened carefully as Charlie explained that since the revolution it had become almost impossible to find a credible business partner. "We've been lucky to find a prestigious company like InterCommerce, since almost nobody wants to do business with Portugal anymore. Of course they take a margin on the contracts but we don't have any choice. This seems like an expensive solution but it maintains *APA*'s activities and produces enough profits to pay our expenses and salaries until times change."

They nodded their understanding of this requirement. They were on salaries too.

By this time most business owners had fled the country, leaving their companies in the hands of the nationalisation committees, guaranteeing that the business would quickly fall into bankruptcy. Thanks in great part to Alberto, *APA* was the exception, with its two top executives still running the company. The government was already selling off the countries' gold reserves to bail out the companies that had been nationalised. The members of the committee were delighted to find themselves running one of the only remaining profitable businesses in Portugal, and they were not slow in bragging about this to their communist bosses.

In late May, Manuel de la Peña announced that *APA* had been chosen as the best run and most profitable nationalised business in the country. "The *only* one, they mean," quipped Nick. The Prime Minister, Vasco dos Santos Gonçalves, would come to the offices the next day, to congratulate the nationalisation committee and their management team.

Shaking hands with the Prime Minister, a dyed in the wool Marxist, and posing with the nationalisation committee for the television cameras, Olivier and Charlie almost peed themselves with laughter. They had become the most famous capitalist-communists in the country by diverting profits to Switzerland and leaving just enough to pay the salaries for the Marxists in Portugal. It was a surreal moment in the midst of the chaos going on around them.

Alberto called when he saw them on TV. He just said, "You owe me. Big time!"

When Jorge Gomez saw the news report he was incandescent with rage. He stormed into his boss's office and demanded to be appointed to the *APA* nationalisation committee. He was certain there had to be something going on.

It was the third time that Major Tavares had turned him down. "You've still produced nothing but innuendo about *APA* and I don't intend to be embarrassed again. You've found nothing here nor in

Switzerland, and until you do, you'll keep your head down. Stick to your investigative duties and find some proof. Then we can discuss this again, not before."

The major was becoming tired of Gomez's obsession with *APA*. According to the members of the committee, the business was sound and healthy and Bettencourt's team were hard working and honest. Alberto had told him the same thing when he had casually posed the question at a recent meeting of *COPCON*. He was not about to be made to look a fool again in front of the top brass. Not after last Christmas's fiasco and certainly not after the prime time TV item with the PM. He filed the request and resolved to forget about it.

On May 29th, Nick called Mario to check on a contract for delivery of coffee to Italy. "The InterCommerce people are bugging me. We're two weeks late on completing." They had decided it was too dangerous to disclose to him the true relationship with the Swiss company.

"It'll leave on Friday, barring acts of God or the *MPLA*." Mario sounded tired. He had worked miracles to create and execute business for them over the last few months, but Nick didn't need to tell him it was about to come to an end, he'd already worked it out for himself.

"Sounds like things aren't going so well down there. How bad is it?" He asked.

"On a scale of ten, I'd say it's about seven and a half. They say the airport's still under Portuguese control and functioning, although it's becoming flooded with families trying to get out of the country. I hear there's thousands of them camping around the airport grounds and car park already. The roads around Luanda are fairly safe until you get further out of the city. The MPLA is getting stronger by the week, we're hearing that they've got massive shipments of arms from Russia. Now they're more occupied with trying to grab other chunks of the country than consolidating their hold on Luanda, so it's not as bad as it might be here in the city. In any case there's no real opposition to them here. They'll just come back and take it when they're ready. When the last Portuguese troops leave in a few months, it'll fall into their hands like a fat plum. All juicy and ripe for the Cubans to rape and plunder."

"What the hell have the Cubans got to do with this?" Nick was confused.

"Haven't you been listening to the Lisbon grapevine? Everybody knows the Russians have enlisted thousands of Cuban troops and instructors to come down and teach the *MPLA* how to behave properly when it comes to a democratic takeover."

Nick called Henriques. He was now seriously worried about the safety of the Angolan and his family. He repeated what Mario had told him.

For the first time, Nick detected a nervous tremour in Henrique's voice. "I know the situation in Luanda isn't too bad. But up here it's getting worse. The Zairian soldiers that Mobuto sent down have pissed off and the *MPLA* has moved in just south of us. So we're trapped between units of the *NFLA* and the *MPLA*, and now they've cut off our bloody supply route to ship the merchandise out."

Henriques's only export arrangement was an official contract with *ANDEC*, the Angolan National Diamond Export Company, who bought the diamonds in their rough state at a fraction of their ultimate price. If he couldn't deliver his diamond production, he was finished.

"So how are you surviving? You've got about a hundred people working for you. What's happened to them?"

"Easy. We're still surviving by the oldest way in the world, bribery." Nick heard the scratch of a match and a deep drag on a cigarette at the other end of the line. "I've made deals with the local unit commanders of both the *FNLA* and *MPLA*. They open up the road and let us through once a week, so I can ship the merchandise to *ANDEC* in Luanda. I get paid in cash, although it's a real crap price, and then I split the cash with the rebels. They leave me enough to pay the wages and expenses and for Manuela and me to eat. So we're surrounded by corrupt bastards who are stealing from us. But don't knock it. It works!

"For the rest of the time we've got to find out every day which way they're going to move, so we can sneak around between them without getting caught in the middle. There's only about fifty or so soldiers on each side so it sounds easy, but it's a fucking nightmare. Still, so far we're managing to survive."

"But, why the hell don't they just kick you out and take over the mine and sell the production to *ANDEC* themselves. Are you sure they need to keep you alive?"

Henriques laughed. "Are you seriously suggesting that the rebels could actually agree on anything, even on screwing me out of my business? No bloody chance. And if either of them tried to take it over, my people would be gone like a shot. Nobody to operate the equipment, to dredge, to pressure hose, to manage and maintain the screening machinery, the grease table controls. And that's just the extraction. There'd also be no bugger who knows about sorting, grading and valuing. They wouldn't know a diamond from a piece of shit! The mine would be as dead as a doornail. For the moment, they need us alive and working to keep making money, so we'll stay until they don't."

"But if it's that close to drop dead, why hang on?" Nick insisted. "It's one thing to lose your business and your money. But it's better than losing your lives. Just get out. Take what you can get away with, jump in the van and drive away from it all."

Despite Nick's arguments, Henriques was adamant. He had now learned that the *FNLA* had received arms shipments from China and he was convinced that they would get funding from the US and South Africa and be able to fight off the growing strength of the *MPLA*. He and his family would stay until he was convinced there was nothing left to stay for.

By the end of the month, Portugal suffered regular riots and violent demonstrations, fire-bombings, sacking of political premises and bloody head to head confrontations between moderate socialists, extreme right-wing elements and the ever more powerful left-wing extremists, under the control of *COPCON*, the communist controlled secret police. Every day saw an escalation in the numbers of injuries and deaths occurring throughout the country.

Hundreds of thousands of Portuguese and African colonialists had now fled back to Portugal, swelling the numbers of unemployed, and the economy continued to slide towards total bankruptcy. Immigrants and workers fought for ownership of abandoned properties, shops, cafés, farms, anything that they thought might help them to earn a few escudos to feed their starving families. Portugal continued to drift inexorably towards civil war.

Despite the increasing influence of the moderate socialist members of the *MFA*, grouped around Ernesto Melo Antunes and Mario Soares, the Marxist Prime Minister, Vasco dos Santos Gonçalves, continued the nationalisation of virtually all the remaining large companies in the country. All key industries, utilities, support services, insurance companies newspapers, radio and television stations, were taken over by the Council of the Revolution, who censored all media reports. By the end of the year, the government's share of the country's gross national product would reach seventy percent.

Astonishingly, Cascais was still relatively untouched by this nationwide hysteria and mayhem. It was still just a quiet fishing village. An island surrounded by a raging sea of political madness and hatred. They were now used to the shortages in the shops and regular cuts in electricity and water and managed to cope with them, thanks to Ellen's planning. The continual processions of right and left-wing demonstrators and workers in the streets had become more boring than frightening. Ellen still played tennis and golf with Maggie and their friends, and the two families spent their weekends together. Ronnie and Alan and the other children were happy and industrious at St. Julien's, apparently oblivious to the chaos that surrounded them.

Maggie reported back regularly from the Australian Embassy. So far, neither they, nor the British Embassy had given any evacuation instructions. Charlie relayed the same information from Alberto. There was still no need to panic, things would settle down. But Ellen knew that their time in Cascais couldn't last much longer. It was coming up to the end of the school term and she wanted as little disruption in Ronnie's life as possible. It was a logical time to take a decision about their immediate future. She asked Charlie what his plan was. Shouldn't they start preparing to make a move?

He told her about his agreement with Olivier. "Nick and I will get four percent of the capital of Bettencourt SA. Our contribution is one million dollars of profit, plus we're signing five year contracts. The whole capital will be fifty million dollars, so our shares will be worth two million and that's just for starters. The value of the company is likely to go through the roof once we get into business properly. So, I think we've solved the problem of starting again."

"Well, why on earth are we still hanging around in this pathetic excuse for a country? Let's just get out while we can."

"We need to bring another quarter million dollars of profit, Ellen, that's why."

"How long is it going to take?"

"Another month. The contracts are already signed, we just have to ship them. If we jump ship now, we'll lose them. Nick and I need until June 30th and we're out of here."

At the prospect of restoring their fortunes and moving to a new life in Switzerland, Ellen was convinced, despite her misgivings. She agreed to see it through until the end of June. *It means Ronnie can finish his school year,* she reflected, *less disruption for all of us.*

Charlie was relieved. He and Nick could concentrate on shipping the remaining contracts and building their stake in the Geneva business.

In the second week of June, Olivier, Nick and Charlie were lunching in a restaurant in Estoril. They didn't have meetings in the bank any longer. In addition to the nationalisation committee, they knew that Gomez had many more informants inside of *APA*.

"I have good news. I signed the deal for the sale of the property company this weekend." Olivier raised his glass in a mock toast.

"Well done." Charlie was impressed. It wasn't easy to sell Portuguese real estate these days, even at a knock down price.

"It always takes longer than you expect. But twelve and a half million dollars was worth the wait. Ruiz says we should have the banking license next month so I think it's time to make a move. Things are completely out of hand here. I'm becoming seriously concerned about getting out of the country alive. We're going to leave it too late if we wait any longer."

Olivier was right. The violence that was engulfing the country had now come to *APA*. Amost every day there were fights and stand-offs in the offices or corridors between the various political affinities. Just the previous week, a full fledged battle had taken place in the car park between militant left and right extremists. Two Marxist militants had been almost kicked to death and six more employees were taken away with knife wounds. Olivier had hired an armed bodyguard to escort the senior staff in and out of the building and the executive level sixth floor was now sealed off from the other floors, accessible only by the restricted elevator.

The hospitals were overflowing and tents had been erected in the car parks and surrounding gardens. The Hotel Tivoli, where Nick had stayed, was closed to visitors and the rooms had been taken over to accommodate some of the growing numbers of starving, sick and wounded that the hospitals couldn't hold.

Even their unusually friendly relationship with the members of the nationalisation committee and the behind the scenes support that they received from Alberto were wearing thin. They were, after all, capitalists, and they were still running a nationalised company in a Marxist environment. The country was reaching breaking point. It was ready to explode and they were right in the line of fire.

Charlie understood the concerns expressed by his boss, he had to cope with them every day. He also remembered the promise he'd made to Ellen, *get out by the end of June*. But he figured that they were still in control of the game and he was confident in his ability to get the job finished and move to Geneva knowing that he'd fulfilled his promise. And because of his north-east of England upbringing, he couldn't tolerate being told what to do by people for whom he had no respect. As long as Ellen could hold on, he would leave Portugal when he decided and not before. And certainly not because some incompetent and corrupt communist government or committee thought he should go.

He reached absent-mindedly for a cigarette, then remembered his decision to quit. Instead, he drank a sip of the fine white Douro wine. Olivier really knew his vintages. *I hope the Swiss wines are up to this standard,* he thought to himself.

He told Olivier the same thing he'd told Ellen. "I don't think it's time for us to jump ship. We've got three more contracts to deliver, which will bring another quarter million dollars to Geneva. You've kept your end of the bargain and we have to do the same. This will take us from the three percent that we've earned to date, to the four percent we agreed on."

"Charlie, I've already told you that I'm going to allocate four percent, whatever. You've done enough. It's simply too risky. We've been lucky until now but it won't last for ever."

"We're not looking for any favours. It's only fair that we should deliver what we promised." Nick was as adamant as his friend.

Charlie said. "You know, I'm quite enjoying running rings around these idiots in the so- called nationalisation committee, and the Marxist creeps in the bank. They haven't got a clue what's going on. If we can't fool them 'till the end of the month and contribute a few more dollars to Geneva, then my name is not... What's my name again?"

Olivier smiled, but was still concerned. "What about Ellen? Is she OK with this?"

"I've talked to her and she's up for it. Cascais isn't Lisbon, she doesn't see much of the stuff we see. She gets regular updates from Alberto and Maggie and our embassy, so she knows the score. We're all determined to see this through for another couple of weeks."

Olivier pushed his plate away. "Right. We'll do it your way. I'm sending Cristina and the kids to Geneva this week to stay with Ruiz but I'll organise my timing to fit in with yours. I'll stay here until the end of the month. You obviously can't continue if I'm not around. In any case, as you say, whatever we can squeeze out in the next couple of weeks will make progress in Geneva that much easier. Let's make our starting date July first."

The three men raised their glasses and toasted the vision of a new start, in Switzerland.

But once again it was not to work out quite like that. The pace of change was accelerating, and not for the better.

TWENTY-EIGHT

June, 1975
Lisbon, Portugal; Luanda, Angola

On Friday June 13th, Nick received a call from Angola. It was Henriques.

"Have you seen what's happened in Mozambique? They haven't even signed the bloody decree yet and it's civil war already. And it's starting in Angola. I've been assuming things might get sorted, but I was wrong. The shit's already hitting the fan. Can you and Charlie come down? I need to talk to you. It can't wait, it's bloody urgent!"

The declaration of independence of Mozambique for June 25th had been announced several months before and already over a quarter of a million white ethnic Portuguese, *retornados,* had fled from the Marxist *FRELIMO* government-in-waiting and returned home, leaving virtually no qualified workers to manage the delapidated infrastructure left behind by them.

APA had closed their office there earlier in the year, exactly six months after the death of Carlos Souza Machado. Now it seemed the country was in civil war. Rumours abounded of a bloody massacre in the capital, Lourenco Marques, with thousands of civilian deaths at the hands of Samora Machel, the leader of the *FRELIMO* movement.

Nick hesitated. "What's happening with the *MPLA* and *FNLA*? Is it the same as before?"

When Henriques confirmed it was, Nick agreed to do his best. "I'll talk to Charlie. If he's OK with it we'll be there as soon as we can get a flight. *If* we can get a flight."

Charlie called Henriques back immediately. "What's this about? I'm not sure that flying down to Luanda is a great idea at the minute."

"Not to put too fine a point on it, Charlie, it's a matter of life and fucking death. And I'm talking about the life and death of me and Manuela and all my family. If the *MPLA* get hold of us we're dead. Those maniacs are meaner than a pride of three-legged lions. I think you can help us and I'm begging you as a friend to come here one last time. Please don't let me down."

"Let me check with Mario what things are like in Luanda. If it seems safe we'll come as soon as we can. If not, well, let's wait and see."

Charlie made the call to Mario. He knew that Henriques didn't panic easily. If they were going to do something, it had to be quick. "What's the situation at the airport, is it still safe?"

"It's still being run by the Portuguese and they're operating evacuation flights every day. There's thousands of families camping all over the place and the UN and some other agencies have set up a camp and food kitchens in the grounds. But the army's patrolling the area, so the terminal itself is fairly safe. Around Luanda it's very complicated. The Portuguese are assuring safe passage on the perimeter roads around the city and the *MPLA* are basically in control of the centre. But they're all waiting for the starting pistol to fire, so it's just a matter of time."

"How about driving up the coast road towards Cabinda, is it safe?"

"It depends how far. It's controlled by the Portuguese when you leave the city, then there's an *MPLA* unit further north, and then the *FNLA* are in charge up near the border."

Mario's information confirmed what Henriques had recounted. He rang off and looked at Nick. "Are you up for this?"

When Charlie told Olivier of their decision the banker was dead set against the idea. "Why the hell would you want to go back down to Angola? Don't you think we've got enough problems here in Lisbon? Look, Charlie, it's only two weeks to Geneva. Why take any risks?"

Charlie thought for a moment before replying. "Wouldn't you do it for me?"

TAP, the national airline, was still flying to Luanda, but since hardly anyone except army personnel and politicians was going down there now, the departure times varied from day to day. They easily got first class seats to go down the following Wednesday morning, but it required a lot of bribery and persuasion to book the return seats for Thursday evening.

Most passengers in Lisbon airport were going to the UK, or other European countries, but even at seven in the morning the soldiers at immigration spared nobody. They searched every bag and many passengers so thoroughly that they had the women in tears. Their passports and travel papers were inspected by four officers before they got through passport control.

The departures hall was milling with people. "It looks like everybody who hasn't already left is leaving today." Nick held his nose against the smell of unwashed bodies.

As they fought their way towards their Luanda flight, they passed the departure gate for the Swissair flight to Zurich. There was shouting and a scuffle broke out in the packed crowd.

"What the hell's going on over there?"

Before Charlie could answer, two men in business suits carrying briefcases broke free from the crowd and ran towards them. The queue at the gate split apart and two soldiers appeared by the passport control desk, fighting their way into the clear. One of them had a pistol in his hand. He shouted out, "*Parem ou dispararei!* Stop or I'll shoot!"

The second officer kneeled down and raised a rifle to his shoulder. People started screaming as the other passengers threw themselves to the floor. Parents pulled their children down to the safety of their arms. Two women were standing next to Charlie, totally confused, panic stricken, incapable of moving.

"On the floor, stay down!" he yelled at Nick. He pulled the women down to the floor and lay flat on his face. The fake marble surface was thick with greasy dirt. It stank in his nostrils.

Nick was mesmerised by the sight of the two men running right at him. He didn't move. Suddenly there was a gap all the way from the desk to the running men. The soldier aimed his rifle and loosed off two shots. Blood spouted from the head of the second man, and he was propelled to the floor, right at Nick's feet. The other man grabbed hold of his jacket and ran behind him, trying to shield himself from the gunmen.

Nick snapped out of his trance. He fought the man off and scrambled behind a metal bench. The man looked towards the soldiers. He was shouting, appealing to them. Two more shots rang out and he fell to the floor, clutching his chest, almost on top of Nick. A bloody pool appeared under his lifeless body.

There was silence for a few moments. Then the sound of hysterical crying, shouting and screaming broke out. People were grabbing their bags and dragging their families away from the bodies lying bleeding on the floor. Shielding their children from the sight of the massacre. Others lay still, not yet daring to move. The soldiers pushed aside the crowds and marched up to the victims. One of them checked them for a pulse, then shook his head at his partner, "*Nada.*" They stood over the two dead men, still holding their weapons at the ready. Looking round at the crowds, hoping to find more prey.

Charlie was sitting on the floor beside the two women. They grabbed his hands, talking away to him. Thanking him, thanking God for their escape. He helped them up then dusted himself off, picked up his case and went over to Nick.

"You bloody stupid South African!" He shouted at him. "What part of "On the floor, stay down", do you not understand? Lesson one in survival, hear bad noises, dive for cover!"

"Jesus Christ almighty!" Nick got back to his feet. He was trembling uncontrollably. He looked for his bag. It was under the body of the man who'd tried to use him as a shield.

The passengers were calming down again, most of them keeping well away from the soldiers and the corpses. A few came up to look at the bodies, pointing and gossiping as if it was an insignificant incident. The crowd had reformed at the gate, eager to get their flights.

Charlie couldn't believe the lack of reaction from many of the crowd. *What will it take to make them understand what's going on in their country?*

By this time another half dozen soldiers had arrived on the scene. They chattered away for a few minutes, inspected the two dead men then shook hands with the gunmen. Everyone looked pleased with the carnage. The soldiers fetched a baggage trolley, loaded up the two bodies and carted them out of the hall. A cleaning woman came over with a mop and bucket. She wiped Nick's bag and gave it to him, then started slopping water over the blood-covered floor.

A middle-aged man standing nearby had heard the talk between the soldiers. He whispered to them in English, "They were two of the officers who planned the coup with General Spinola in March, they've been looking for them for months. The rest are all in prison. Now they've got them, they're happy." He picked up his suitcase. "Thank God I'm getting out of this bloody country. I just hope the flights will operate. Nothing else does any more."

They made their way shakily to their departure gate and ordered a couple of brandies at the bar. Nick decided to give up his no booze vow until he recovered his nerves. He knocked back the liquor in one swig. "In the middle of a bloody airport. What the hell are we doing here, Charlie?"

They ordered another drink then sat quietly for a while, waiting for the boarding announcement and trying to settle themselves before their departure.

The flight itself was very quiet. Mostly military staff and a couple of men in business suits. A few Angolan families with children were in the back. Álvaro Cunhal was also on the plane. Charlie acknowledged him and introduced Nick. He wasn't sure whether the *PCP* leader remembered him but he figured it was better to be safe than sorry. The plane departed at nine am, only an hour late. After a light snack they managed to get some sleep.

At about seven in the evening, an hour before the approach to Craveiro Lopes Airport, they were woken by the erratic movement of the plane. A violent thunder storm was raging around the aircraft. It was pitch black outside and they could hear rain lashing against the portholes. A jagged lightning flash lit up the sky for a moment. They were flying through a thick bank of cloud, black and grey, impenetrably dense. The plane was buffeted from side to side by the storm, heaving and bucking like a child's kite blowing about in the air.

Nick gripped the seat rests until his knuckles were white. Suddenly they dropped several hundred feet through an air pocket and his face turned the same colour. A woman in the back of the plane started screaming and set off the other women and children. It was bedlam.

Coming in to land, the wind was gusting violently across the runway. The pilot came in at high speed, one wing lower than the other, until they were sure he would turn the plane over. At the last minute he accelerated and righted the trajectory, bouncing the aircraft onto the tarmac with a bang. The noise of the reverse thrusts screamed in their ears as they slowed and came to a rest in front of the terminal. The passengers in the back clapped and cheered with relief.

Charlie grimaced at Nick. "Welcome to Angola!"

The sweat was running down the South African's face, he'd never been a keen flier. He didn't know which was worse, the shooting in the departures hall, or the last hour on the plane.

The immigration desk was manned by civilian staff working under the close scrutiny of four heavily-armed Portuguese soldiers. After showing their documents and opening their bags, they walked through to the arrivals hall. It was chaos. Hundreds of people were crammed into the area like sardines in a can. Africans and Europeans alike were loaded down with trunks, bags, children, boxes, parcels. Women in brightly coloured wraps, bandanas and scarves carried bundles on their heads. Some were carrying crates of chickens in each hand. There were children leading goats, pigs or dogs on pieces of rope. Families were camped out on the floor, many of them eating their evening meal, bags and possessions strewn all over the place.

Would-be passengers were screaming at the one or two airport employees or UN representatives who were unlucky enough to pass by. Waving bundles of escudos, they were pleading for tickets on outgoing flights. Any flights, it didn't matter to where, just as long as it was somewhere else. They both fought feelings of mounting claustrophobia as they struggled through the sweating, frightened crowd amid the cacophony of noise that surrounded them.

Henriques was waiting inside the main doors, a cigarette hanging from his lips. "Nice flight?" They ignored the sarcasm and said nothing about the shootings in Lisbon airport, he seemed to have enough to worry about.

He gestured around at the melee. "These are not people arriving in Angola. There's hardly anyone coming here now. These are people who are trying to leave. The departures hall is full, so they overflow everywhere in the terminal. And just wait 'till you see the car park."

Another unit of armed soldiers was stationed at the main doors, studying the faces of the crowds flowing in and out of the building. They were not stopped and made their way out to the covered walkway. The blast of humid air hit them like a hot, drenching shower and made the sweat pour out of their skins. The rain was beating down so hard that it was bouncing up off the ground. The air had a fetid, animal smell, as if they were in the middle of the jungle.

Henriques had fetched oilskins for them to put on before leaving the relative protection of the walkway. As they ran to his Transit van in the car park, they saw that half of it had been cordoned off for the campers that Mario had described. Thousands of exhausted, filthy-looking Portuguese and African men, women and children of all ages, holding umbrellas, tarpaulin sheets, coats, blankets, even plastic shopping bags over themselves. Some had erected scruffy canvas tents, anything to provide some protection from the downpour.

A marquee with a UN flag flying over it stood in the middle of the campsite, queues of clamouring people lined up at its entrance. Trying to get onto the increasing number of emergency flights that were leaving every day. Another marquee was set up as a soup kitchen. Lines of people jostled and pushed in the pouring rain, hoping to get something to eat before night. Others were sitting patiently, desperately waiting for someone to get them out of that

God-forsaken country and back to the relative civilisation of their home country. Henriques drove slowly and carefully past the crowds of people and out onto the perimeter road.

From the shelter of an army hut at the side of the car park, Jorge Gomez watched the three men drive away in the van. He had arrived on a military flight late the previous night and had got a few hours sleep at an army barracks before returning to the airport to mingle with the crowds of refugees. The phone tapping system had finally thrown up something worthwhile. He was now absolutely certain that *APA* was planning something with the Angolan company. The only way to find out was to come to Luanda himself and see where they went and who they met.

He ran through the driving rain to the closed jeep waiting for him in the car park. The army corporal at the wheel opened the door for him and he climbed in, his shirt already soaked through. "See the white van that just went out. Follow it!"

TWENTY-NINE

June, 1975
Ambrizete, Angola

Henriques's Transit was a converted coach, with the back closed off behind two front bench seats. It was reinforced to transport goods and materials at the mine. The three men shared the driver's bench seat as he drove across the city and picked up the coast road leading north to the border with Zaire. His mine was located near Ambrizete, about two hundred kilometres away.

Even considering the storm that was following them, the road was much worse than they remembered. It was rutted with pot holes, a stream of water running down the middle of the cracked surface. In the ditch at the side of the road a filthy flood roared alongside them, threatening to inundate the remaining tarmac at any moment.

On the outskirts of the city, Portuguese soldiers in rain gear were gathered at every crossroads, rifles and automatic weapons in their hands. They had to show their identity papers several times but were left to continue. The last check point was near Sassalemba, about thirty- five kilometres north of Luanda. They passed intermittent groups of pedestrians, wearily plodding along the side of the road, soaked and miserable under the pouring rain.

"Displaced families and refugees," answered Henriques, to Charlie's question. "There's more and more coming up from Luanda, looking for safety in the north-west, away from the centre, where most of the shit will hit the fan."

As they continued north the state of the coast road became worse and their progress slower. At one point, they saw lights coming towards them, several kilometres off in the pitch black distance. Henriques rightly guessed it was a rebel contingent and drove off the road onto a shallow decline. They waited behind a screen of bushes until the convoy passed them. As the van climbed back onto the road, he lost control of the vehicle and the back wheel slid almost into the ditch. They manhandled the van up onto the tarmac and climbed back in, filthy and soaked with the muddy ditch water.

About ten kilometres before Ambrizete, Henriques left the road and took a dirt track that led east, towards Bembe. He lit up what must have been his twentieth cigarette. "There's an *MPLA* unit on the coast road south of the town and an *FNLA* unit on the north side, They're both my business partners. If we all leave each other alone, we should be OK."

The track turned north towards Tomboco, then west again to rejoin the coast road north of Ambrizete. After another couple of kilometres, they reached the Mbridge river, driving over an old stone and metal bridge, that even in the dark looked as if it was about to collapse at any moment. Turning east again, another dirt track took them alongside the north bank of the river for about ten kilometres. The river was running high with the torrential rain and the track, flooded by the overflowing river water, became more and more difficult to follow.

The last ten kilometres took them almost an hour, making the drive almost six nerve-wracking hours instead of the five hours it took under normal conditions. By this time they were exhausted and as completely soaked as if they hadn't been wearing the oilskins.

Located between the towns of Ambrizete and Quimencunco, the mine was sited on a junction of the Mbridge River, which flowed down from its source on the Angola-Zaire border and then met a tributary of the Sembo, coming down from the mountainous area to the south-east. It was this confluence which caused a high concentration of alluvial gravels to be deposited in the riverbank at that point. The property was completely surrounded by the river on the south side and a high barbed wire fence on the north, stretching off into the distance.

They drove alongside the fence for about five hundred meters and pulled up in front of wide metal gates with a blockhouse built next to them. An army jeep was parked alongside. The door of the building opened and a well built, tough looking black man came out into the rain, a submachine gun in his grasp. Henriques spoke to him for a minute then he saluted and opened up the gates so they could drive into the compound.

"That's Joaquim. He's a war orphan. Been with the family for years. He patrols the perimeter every half hour, all night long. Not the best job in town on a night like this."

Inside the compound, several concrete constructions surrounded a small office building in the centre. The rain splashed down on the fast-flowing river which ran alongside them in both directions, with a deep, wide bank of gravelly sand running alongside the water. Lamps positioned along the bank illuminated machines, like large vacuum cleaners, with pipes running from them to the waterside and they could discern the steady thumping noise of a generator.

The diamonds which lay in the gravel beds of Henriques's mining property had been formed billions of years before, up to a hundred and fifty kilometres underground, by the heat and pressure caused by the constant shifting of the earth's upper mantle, forcing carbon atoms deep into the planet's molten core. Over the following millions of years, volcanic magma exploded upwards to form cone-shaped pipes of molten rock and minerals, called kimberlites. These were pushed to the earth's surface, often finishing in the sea, or in lakes in the craters of volcanoes or other mountainous terrain. The magma in many of these kimberlites contained diamonds and other gemstones mixed with the rock and other mineral material.

The subsequent erosion of the kimberlites over the course of thousands of years released the rocks and diamonds, in the form of gravels, into rivers and lakes, to be washed along in river currents and deposited in the banks alongside bends and intersections of the river. This was how the alluvial, or 'placer' diamonds, had been transported, wrapped in a blanket of rocks and gravel, all the way from southern Zaire to Henriques's kilometre-long stretch of the Mbridge River in north-western Angola.

The Angolan gestured in both directions along the property. "Seven years ago, my dad spent the little bit of family money we had on a fifty year concession on this property. He borrowed every penny he could, to build the compound and the security fence and blast away the banks to expose the terrace gravels. Two years later he went and dropped down dead, God rest his soul. Since then I've managed to pay off the loans and started to make a small profit.

"All this equipment was designed and built by my brother, Sergio. It's way ahead of anything being done elsewhere. He's a genius. A bloody boring nerd, but a genius. The gravel is blasted by high-pressure hoses and the larger debris is channelled into those machines you can see." He pointed to the pipes running from the machines. "There's a kind of X-ray screening process inside and then the debris that might contain placer diamonds is filtered out onto belts that run inside to the grease table and sorting enclosure."

"Once inside, the material runs across the grease table and the key workers pick out the rough diamonds by hand. The stones go to the graders and so on and so forth, until we've got batches of priceable merchandise. Then Sergio and I do the pricing and production inventories and prepare the shipments and documentation for *ANDEC*. We don't have big losses through thieving because Sergio's processing system quickly moves the diamond carrying gravel inside, where it's easy to control. Our security is tighter than a tree frog's ass! I don't mind if the workers grab the occasional small gems from the river. It keeps them keen and working hard.

"So," he finished, "We've got a good work force, a great process producing good diamonds and we've got a thousand meters of gravels to work on, which I reckon is twenty to thirty years of production, and that's our entire lives work. And now we've got to run away like fugitives and leave it all behind. It's fucking heartbreaking." He spat into the river with frustration. The others said nothing.

They went into the building, glad to get out of the rain. Manuela, Henriques's Portuguese wife, welcomed them, kissing them on both cheeks and taking their oilskins and jackets. She appeared tired, as if she hadn't been sleeping well. Her young, pretty face looked lined and weary. She gave them dry towels, made them some hot coffee and put out sandwiches. It was almost three o'clock in the morning when they sat with the snack in Henriques's office, drying off.

"So, what's up, Henriques? Why are we here?" It was Nick who broke the silence.

"Right." The Angolan lit up another cigarette. "Well, first off, thanks for coming down here. It's not the best time to fly out of Lisbon or to fly into Luanda and we really appreciate it. We needed to have this talk with you before it's too late. The fact is that we were praying that things would get better, but they're not. There's no hope left for this country, or for us."

The other men exchanged glances. Henriques was never like this, he was the original happy, smiling African giant. He must have a good reason for asking them to risk coming down to see him, they just had to wait for him to get to it.

"We're listening." Charlie sat back. They had all night to hear what he had to say.

"This granting of independence to the colonies is going very fast." Henriques ticked off on his fingers, "Timor went last December. Mozambique and Guiné-Bissau have already started their own civil wars with Russian arms. Cabo Verde and São Tomé e Principe went this week. The only place left is the jewel in the crown. My country, Angola. But not for long.

"The transitional government is supposed to hand over power in November to a tri-partite government, formed by *UNITA, FNLA* and *MPLA*. But now it's clear what the Portuguese game is. Those Marxist bastards in Lisbon are pulling their troops out and leaving the *MPLA* in charge everywhere, so the transitional government won't last another month. They'll piss off and leave us to sort out independence for ourselves. The problem is that here in the Portuguese colonies we don't know how to be independent. We've been virtual slaves for so long we're just like a bunch of naïve virgins waiting to be raped."

Unknowingly, he paraphrased the very words that Alberto had used when speaking to Olivier, a year before.

"Look what happened in Timor. Just nine days after getting rid of the Portuguese, the bloody Indonesians marched in. Some change there! Same shit, different flies. Mozambique is going to be even worse, that communist bastard Machel is already slaughtering his own people. And here in Angola we have three independence movements who will never, ever agree. Either with each other, or with anyone else. The Russians are pouring money and arms in and it's easy to see what's going to happen, there will be a civil war. It's unavoidable. Right, Manuela?"

His wife nodded her agreement.

"You know that Cunhal has been here every month since he came back to Lisbon?"

"He was on our flight today" confirmed Charlie.

"Do you know who he meets when he comes down?" He took another deep drag of his cigarette. "Agostinho Neto, the boss of the *MPLA*, the rebel group that's funded by the Russians. Those guys are thicker than an elephant stew. On the other side you've got the moderates, Savimbi's *UNITA* and Roberto Holden's *FNLA*, but they can't agree on anything except killing each other. We're in a classic fight between democracy and communism, and the communists have got the most money and they've been around the longest.

"And what do you think the Americans are going to do about it?" He asked with a laugh.

"Not a lot, after the Vietnam fiasco," replied Charlie.

"Dead right. They're so traumatised after Vietnam they'll do bugger all. Roberto Holden's in bed with the CIA and we heard that Kissinger convinced Ford to send funds to the *FNLA*, but all they sent was three hundred grand. It's like pissing in the wind. Without funding and arms from the US, the *FNLA* is dead. I thought they'd link up with *UNITA* and with the Americans behind them, they might have been able to create a democratic system. But I was wrong. Three hundred grand. Big deal! The Russians are pouring money and troops into the country and they want the *MPLA* to take over. So that's what will happen. And Cunhal licking Neto's balls is proof positive of what Portugal wants, so it's a fait accompli.

"Ask yourself why the communists have taken over Portugal? It's so bloody obvious. Because it's the key to the door to Africa, especially Angola, that's why. The *MPLA* is going to open the door, then the Russians and Cubans are going to march in and rape and pillage like Attila the Hun and his merry men. It's already happening, for Christ's sake."

The other two men said nothing, but they both knew that Henriques had finally reached the same conclusion as them. The Angolan was definitely in the wrong place at the wrong time.

"And how do you think they're going to fund their bloody war?" he continued. They're going to steal my mine and everybody else's and they're going to hack out diamonds with their fucking machetes and sell them at rock bottom prices to pay their soldiers, to buy their weapons and to send dividends back to their masters in Cuba and Russia. As soon as the *FNLA* gets pushed back from this territory and the *MPLA* has a free hand, we're all dead."

He flopped back in his chair. Manuela took his hand. They were facing ruin. Not just financial ruin, but the ruin of their lives in their birthplace, the only country they had ever known.

After a moment, Charlie asked, "So, what can we do to help you?"

"Well." For the first time, Henriques's mood seemed to lift, becoming more positive. "Apart from convincing Kissinger to get off the pot and shit on the Russians, I think there is something you could do, and I may have a plan. For the last few years I've been holding back our best stones from *ANDEC*. At first I put them aside as an insurance policy, just in case the problem with the insurgents got out of hand. Then when we signed the joint-venture I was going to use them to launch our new business in a blaze of glory. Since that project is totally fucked, I've got another proposition for you and that's why I asked you to come down."

Henriques lit up another cigarette. "Right now I've got about twenty thousand carats of rough stones of outstanding quality and size hidden away. I know these diamonds, even before they're processed. They'll be graded either flawless or VVS, and finest white or fine white in colour. They're washed, but uncut, un-booked and unseen and they're in a safe place known to no one else but Manuela and me." His wife again nodded her agreement.

"We don't have kids or parents to worry about, just us and my brother and his family. We can get out and start again. And if we can get these diamonds out we can set up a new business in a safe place with the best merchandise in the world. The problem is how do we get them out? And the other problem is what do we do next, even if we do get them out?"

"So you want us to get them out for you?" Nick leaned forward excitedly. His project could be back on track. There was fabulous business to be done. For the Angolans and for themselves.

"Look. The truth is, we've.. I've waited too long. It's too late for us to make a run for it with these stones. We stand absolutely no chance of getting them out of Angola, let alone into Portugal or anywhere else. The minute we leave this property we'll be hunted prey and we can't risk being caught with anything at all or we'll be dead.

"And it'll be even worse on the outside. We're Angolans, we don't know how to survive in your business world, London, Johannesburg, New York. We wouldn't last a minute if we tried to set up a business. But you know all this shit, you do it every day. If we do something together we can combine our forces and all make a fortune. It stands to reason, nobody has diamonds like these and there'll be no more for a long time. Anyway, Manuela and I think you are the best, probably the only option available. What do you say?"

"Well, Henriques." Charlie hesitated for a moment before replying. "On the one hand, we would love to do it if we're able. It's unthinkable that you and Manuela will lose everything that you've worked for all your lives. And on top of that it also seems like a very profitable opportunity for everybody concerned.

"But on the other hand, it's a bloody risky business. Every time we come down here it gets worse and it's going to get worse still. This place is now a definite war zone, and in wars, people get killed. Getting killed is not high on my agenda of things I want to risk.

"The other thing is that if we get caught with that kind of merchandise, we'll get shoved in some stinking jail and we'll never see daylight again. This needs some thinking about."

Henriques looked at Manuela. She nodded her assent. "OK, I never expected you to agree today, but I'll make you a specific proposition so you can come to a definite decision. In addition to the diamonds..." He took another drag on his cigarette. "We have half a million US dollars in cash. We'll split it with you if you'll do it."

THIRTY

June, 1975
Ambrizete, Angola

Jorge Gomez sat in the jeep with the army corporal, looking at the lights of the mine, just one hundred metres along the track. The rain had lessened and they could make out the shape of the blockhouse and the jeep standing outside. He reasoned that there were probably guards in the blockhouse, armed guards, and neither he nor the driver was equipped for a battle. After thinking for a few minutes, he told the corporal to drive back to the coast road, where they would wait until the morning. Depending on what transpired, he would decide on their next action when daylight came.

Charlie and Nick sat in a state of shock for several moments.

"Run that by us again, Henriques?"

"Right, listen. I told you that my dad put everything he had into the mine. It wasn't strictly true. A few months before he passed away he told me about a debt that he had from a guy in Nueva Lisboa, a Portuguese. The guy had been the Governor of Zaire province, that's this area, where we are now. It was him who arranged for my father to buy the fifty year concession on the mine property at a really good rent and helped him to raise some financing. When he decided to go off to make his fortune in Nueva Lisboa my dad loaned him a batch of diamonds as security to help him to finance a real estate development, when the town was starting to grow fast. Cut a long story short, he made millions.

"We went to see him and believe it or not he was an honest man. Except he didn't have the diamonds any more. We worked out that they would be worth about five hundred thousand dollars, so he took us to his safety deposit box and counted out a bundle of thousand dollar notes and gave them to us. I almost shit myself. Half a million dollars in cash! If I'd been smart I should have pissed off from Angola there and then with the money, but my dad was sick, the mine was producing and Manuela and I had just met. Anyway, that's why we've got that cash.

"Now we're screwed, because I can't show the money. We'd lose every penny and be shoved in jail into the bargain. I've been really stupid not to get it sorted before, but it's too late to cry about it now. If you can help us to save the situation, that's all that matters.

"As far as the diamonds are concerned, they're worth an absolute minimum of four hundred dollars per carat in their rough state. That's eight million dollars. You have to figure a fifty per cent loss on processing, but the value is then several times more when they're finished. So, I reckon they're worth between ten and fifteen million dollars.

"Here's our proposal. I'll give you the five hundred grand and the diamonds up front. You get the merchandise out and we make a joint-venture deal to process and market the diamonds together once Manuela and I get out. When we reach Europe, we'll start the business. Nick and I will handle the processing and you do the marketing and manage the finances.

"We'll put the diamonds in at a value of five million and you pay us back half of the cash – quarter of a million dollars. We fund the business together from the cash. Then we split the increase in the value of the diamonds two ways, you and us, when we sell them. We get our cost back first, then we split the profit, fifty-fifty."

He took his wife's hand again. "Manuela and I have built this business up for the last five years. With the cash, the diamonds are all we've got. We don't have properties and bank accounts all over the world. This is our only chance to get out of here with something to show for our life's work. And it's also a great business opportunity that can make us all very wealthy people."

He lit up another cigarette and added, "Manuela agrees with this one hundred per cent. In fact, she came up with the idea. She's the smart one in the family."

"It's the only way, Charlie. You and Nick have to help us. What do you think?" Manuela looked pleadingly at the two men. She was at her wit's end. A broken spirit.

Charlie's brain was going at a furious pace, his emotions too. Suddenly, he was faced with the choice of either leaving two friends to an almost certain death, or at least the loss of everything they possessed, or taking a gamble which could result in a successful and profitable outcome, or a catastrophic conclusion, for everyone involved. He came up with and discarded several ideas until he could see a possible solution. Then he started to talk it through logically.

"OK. Let's talk about what we actually have to do. First, how many stones are there?"

"I put aside good sized stones that we can cut large, medium or small. They're not big enough to cause an investigation and not small enough to be rubbish. They go from two to four carats. In total, about seven thousand stones."

"Next. How much do they weigh and how large will the package be?"

Nick interjected quickly. "You remember the finished stones I showed you in Cascais? They were smaller, sample stones to grade the colour and clarity. These are bigger stones, they're worth much more than the small stones. The value that Henriques's talking about is a low estimate." He was getting keener by the minute. "I reckon the weight would be four to five kilograms, about ten pounds. A pretty small package. Right, Henriques?"

"Absolutely right. We're not talking about a massive shipment here. It's high value, low volume." He took what looked like a dull, crystal pebble from his pocket. It was smaller than the size of his thumbnail. "This is four point two carats in the rough. You can get more than two clear carats after cutting. The finished stone would take your breath away."

"So the package would fit into an ordinary briefcase?"

"Right."

"And you're valuing the rough stones at eight million dollars for twenty thousand carats?"

"That's right, but I'll put them into the partnership at five million."

"And they'll produce about ten thousand carats of high-grade finished stones?"

"At least. Probably a little more."

"And you'll split the half a million dollars with us to get them to Europe and then go into a fifty-fifty joint venture with you?"

"Right."

"And the currency is in one thousand dollar notes, so that'll also go in a briefcase?"

"Right. And before you say anything, I know those notes haven't been in circulation since 1969. We've had them well hidden ever since my dad died. They've always been our last- chance ticket out of here. It's much easier to carry five hundred notes than five thousand."

"Are you certain they're still legal currency?"

"I'm absolutely certain. But I'm sure you'll check it out, so don't take my word for it."

"How about you? How will you get out?"

"Leave that to us. Penniless ex-capitalists are a dime a dozen in Angola. We'll get out."

Charlie brought up several more detailed points, until he was satisfied that he understood every angle of the proposal. He told the Angolan that he would provide him with a secure phone number in Portugal, so they could talk without fear of interception. It was now up to them. Henriques and Manuela were ready to go, desperate to go.

Manuela took Charlie and Nick by the hands, "Promise you won't let us down."

"Give us a week. We'll either say no before that or we'll plan in that time frame."

They were now dead beat and Manuela showed them to quarters behind the offices where they could get some sleep. Charlie

dreamed of Ellen and Ronnie. Nick dreamed of diamonds.
They had been able to book first class seats for the flight back the next day, but it made almost no difference. After struggling to the departure gate, Nick had to give the ground staff manager a thousand escudos to let them on the plane. He told them it was overbooked three times.

For the second time that week, Nick gave up his no-booze vow for the duration of the flight back. He and Charlie shared a bottle of champagne, courtesy of TAP's first class service.

Charlie was quiet, pensive. He was thinking about Henriques and Manuela, and Álvaro Cunhal. While the Angolan couple were desperately making plans to survive, to try to mitigate the loss of everything they had worked for all their lives, Cunhal was coldly preparing the rape of Angola. He was planning to open up the floodgates of independence to let in armies of Russian and Cuban soldiers to steal away everything from the Angolan people. To take away their country from them again. Just when they believed they were finally getting it back.

The only sin that Henriques and Manuela had committed was to succeed. To work day and night for years, to take risks, to build a business that they believed in, and to succeed. To give employment and commerce to hundreds of local people and to contribute to the national economy. And now they would see it taken over by a mob of murderous Marxist thugs, dressed in army uniforms and preaching about the joys of equality under communism.

He poured himself a glass of champagne. "Cheers, Nick. What do you reckon?" He clinked his glass against the other man's.

"Cheers." The South African wasn't as introspective as Charlie. Spending his life under apartheid had forced him to acquire a fairly thick skin, and leaving Rachel and his homeland had been a hard-learned lesson. He was more excited by the business opportunity than concerned about the potential consequences for Angola and its people. After all the frustration of the last eighteen months, this was his chance of finally getting his project off the ground.

The only appropriate response he could come out with at that moment was, "Unfuckingbelievable!"

Henriques was talking to Joachim, the security guard. A man called Gomez from the Portuguese Junta had arrived in an army jeep after they had left that morning. He had asked questions about the mine, the owners and the visitors and had then left and hadn't returned.

"What did you tell him?"

"I told him to fuck off, like you always tell me to." The guard was nervous. Gomez had looked like a man with an agenda and those days in Angola most agendas were not pleasant.

Henriques felt a shiver of apprehension at the news, but he knew he had to hold things together until they could get out. He calmed the big guard down. "You did great, Joachim. There's lots of crazy people around these days. It's probably nothing to worry about, but keep your eyes open. Watch out and let me know if he comes back or if anything transpires."

He went into the office to talk with his younger brother, Sergio. Putting his arm around the smaller man's shoulders, he said, "Looks like we might get out of here in good shape."

Not mentioning the cash or the diamonds, he went on, "You should be ready to leave within a month, with Elvira and the kids. Don't worry about the problems on the outside. Manuela and I've got it sorted with the people from *APA*. We'll take care of you and the family when we get out."

Sergio was not a planner and had little knowledge or interest in anything outside of his job, his wife and their two children. He managed the technical and production operations of the mining business with the detailed, precise attention of an accountant, which was a prime reason for the commercial success of the business. Despite the danger surrounding them, he was content to get on with his job and leave the strategic thinking to his brother. If Henriques said they would be OK, that was good enough for him. He went back into his office and started on the day's production numbers.

When Jorge Gomez got back to Lisbon, he went up to see Major Tavares. "I want a check made on all flights to Angola and Geneva until further notice. When any of the *APA* people book a ticket, I want to be there before them. This time I've got them with their hands in the till."

He went on, excitedly, "And I want phone taps on *APA* in Luanda and a company called *Sociedade Mineira de Angola* and its owner, Henriques Jesus Melo d'Almeida. They're north of Luanda, near Ambrizete."

Tavares sat for a moment, thinking about the requests. "Right. I'll authorise the check ups on the flights and have them call you direct at your office. As far as Angola is concerned, there's no way we can do anything."

"What the fuck are you talking about? Do you think I trailed those bastards half way across Africa and then waited all night in the pissing down rain just to come back and hear that. Do you want to nab these capitalist sons of bitches or not?"

"What I'm *fucking* talking about, Gomez, is that first, we have no authority to intervene in Angola without written orders from the Prime Minister, and I'm not about to ask him on your say so. And second, there isn't a single trained technician left in Angola, there isn't any tapping equipment and we have no idea where the lines are, or how to tap them, without sending down a team of people we don't have. So forget it, OK?"

He then questioned his disgruntled assistant about his information. Why was he so sure there was something going down?

Despite his bosses' questions, Gomez refused to explain any further. "I'm going to give the Bettencourt family and their sidekicks to you on a plate," was all he would say.

Instructions were given to the TAP and Angolan airline offices in Lisbon and at the airport to watch for and report any bookings in the names of Bettencourt, Martinez and Bishop.

Then Gomez went back down to his office, locked the door and pulled his secretary down onto the filthy sizal carpet.

THIRTY-ONE

June, 1975
Cascais, Portugal

On Friday, June 20th, Olivier was sitting on the terrace at Charlie's house. They had called him over that morning to give him a blow by blow account of their trip.

When he heard about the half million dollars in cash, he choked on his coffee, spilling it onto his immaculate outfit. "Bloody hell! Where did he get that kind of money?"

He quickly assessed the benefits of the plan. They could save Henriques and Manuela from total disaster and help to restore their fortunes, as well as everyone else's. In addition, from a purely selfish point of view, this single deal could provide enough profits to boost the successful launch of the new Bettencourt bank and businesses in Geneva.

Once again he could prove himself to be the right man. The man who could restore his father's businesses and reputation. To prove that he hadn't wasted forty years of his life and to show that the Bettencourt family was still a force to be reckoned with. He owed it to his family and to himself to give it his best shot. He knew he had to do it.

After asking the same questions as Charlie about the weight and size of the package, he sat back, analysing the possibilities in his head. "There's probably only one person in the world who can help us to get this merchandise safely out of Angola," he finally said.

"I know." Charlie nodded in agreement.

Nick looked puzzled, but they didn't expand on the exchange. Instead, Olivier changed the subject. "You have to understand we can't bring this deal anywhere near the bank, it's too risky. It's risky for the bank and for us, and even more so for Henriques and Manuela. If the Nationalisation Committee caught wind of this we'd all be shoved in prison for the rest of our days and they'd never be heard of again.

"It has to be quick, slick and totally confidential, or we'll be in deep shit. We have to make this a private project and run it from your house, Charlie. We'll agree on a split between us, both the cash and the future profits from the diamonds. I'll make the arrangements with my family in Geneva afterwards, if it works."

"Your deal is mine," said Nick. "Anything you and Charlie agree on is good with me. I'll do my part and you can be sure I'll multiply the value of those stones to a very big number. You just need to give me the chance." Nick could smell, feel, taste the diamonds. He would be back in the business he'd been trained and hired for.

The next evening, Saturday, June 21st, Olivier sat in the dining room of the Hotel Ritz with Alberto Pires da Silva, Cunhal's bodyguard. The hotel had been nationalised, however apparently nobody had told the chef and he still served the best food in Lisbon. They sipped the last of a 1962 Dão Caves Velhas Tinto as they finished their rack of lamb. The Angolan had been pleased to receive Olivier's call and even more so to join him for dinner at the Ritz. The banker calculated that it would rouse less suspicion to meet him there, where members of the government often dined, than to go to a smaller, more discreet restaurant. He had thanked Alberto once again for his help over the last year and the other man had shrugged it off, but he was looking shrewdly at him, guessing that this was not just a casual supper together.

They sat back, relaxing with a glass of Adega Velha brandy and Alberto lit up a huge Montecristo Cuban cigar with evident pleasure. "I got the taste for these in Moscow. An expensive habit, but as you'd imagine, we have a special deal with the manufacturers."

"*Boa saúde, Alberto.* Good health."

"*Para ti também, Olivier.* And to you." He sipped the amber liquid appreciatively.

"Tell me. How old are you?"

"I was fifty-five last month," the Angolan replied.

"You have just one child, don't you?"

"Yes, a son, Raffael. We call him Raffa, he'll be ten this year."

"I suppose he was born in Moscow?"

"Yes. Inês and I always wanted a family, but at the time we were married we felt that Angola wasn't a safe place to bring up a child. Then, during the mission in Peniche we didn't know what was going to happen. So when we got settled in Russia we decided to go ahead with a family. We were late, but lucky. Raffa's a great kid. Although I suppose I was a bit old to become a father at forty-five."

Olivier decided to get to the point. "Are you a wealthy man?"

Alberto stiffened imperceptibly, carefully weighing his words. "Well, I wouldn't say I'm wealthy. We don't own our own home but we have some savings. I am well paid for what I do and frankly, these days I don't do very much. So, all in all, I'm not too badly off."

Olivier leaned closer to him, lowering his voice. "How would you like to become wealthy enough to do nothing for the rest of your life? Make sure that Inês and your boy never have to worry, despite what might happen here. I think that both of us know the present situation won't last forever, Alberto. A good insurance policy is worth its weight in gold."

He sat back, waiting, trying not to show the tension in his body. *This could be worth ten million dollars or the rest of my life in prison.* His relaxed appearance belied his thoughts.

A gamet of emotions ran across Alberto's face. At last he replied, "You know I won't betray my convictions?" He was ready to make his choice between power and fortune.

"I would never ask you to do that. We may have different points of view, but I know a man of conviction when I meet one and I respect you for it. This is purely commercial" Olivier let out a sigh of relief and the two men sipped their brandy contentedly.

"Well done, Olivier. That was a risky move. I'm glad you didn't tell me what the secret weapon was. I'd have been pissing in my pants in case it backfired."

It was Sunday morning and Olivier and Nick were back at Charlie's house. Olivier's wife and their two children were already in Geneva and Ellen was at the beach with Maggie and the kids.

Nick's compliment was well earned. Alberto had taken the bait, hook line and sinker. He had even advised Olivier that he was scheduled to go down to Luanda on the following Thursday morning, "just to deliver some papers." His only condition was that he wanted Olivier to go with him to Henriques's mine and assist in the handover of the merchandise.

"That was inevitable." Charlie said. "I already told you he loves you like a brother and he obviously trusts you, which is the clincher. He doesn't know Henriques so there's no way that he would go down there without having his insurance policy at his side. Our insurance policy too," he added, unaware that those words would come back to haunt him, very soon.

"I'll call TAP in the morning," said Olivier. "Alberto's going on a military flight, so I need to get there ahead of him on Wednesday. Henriques can pick us both up somewhere without us being seen together. Same thing coming back. We can't take any chances by being sloppy."

"I'll confirm it with Henriques for Thursday. He told us that he's ready to leave with Manuela immediately after the shipment." Nick was making notes.

"How's he getting out?"

"He didn't tell us and we didn't ask him. I think it's better like that."

Charlie said, "I'm not keen on these arrangements being made on the phone. It would blow the whole business out of the water if that shit, Gomez, gets wind of this." He turned to Nick. 'What do you think Maggie would say if we asked to use her phone as a contact number? Not even *COPCON* would dare to piss off the Australian Embassy."

"*No sweat,* as she's always saying." Nick laughed. "Maggie's always hankered after a job as an Australian spy, now's her chance. I'll talk to her when we get home. Good idea."

"OK, that's great. If she agrees, we'll make our calls from her apartment until this is sorted. Charlie was thinking ahead. "What about the next part, Olivier? Lisbon to Geneva sounds easy, but how do we actually do it?"

"I'd rather say nothing until we have the merchandise safely here. I have the beginnings of a plan I think we can organise with my brothers. But let's take it a step at a time."

Maggie was happy to help, her apartment was at their disposal. She didn't bug Nick for any details, but she knew their time together was coming to an end, so he told her that he would soon be leaving Portugal. It was only fair, she was a marvellous woman and he would miss her.

She was relieved to hear that he planned to leave. "My contract's up in August," she told him. "It's time to take Alan home to Melbourne. I was worried about breaking it to you."

After that, they spent every night together, making the most of their remaining time. They had always known that the separation was inevitable, but it would be a difficult break. Maggie was a real brick, a pragmatic Australian girl, who knew the rules of engagement.

On the Monday, Olivier made calls from her phone, booking a TAP flight to Luanda on Wednesday morning, returning on Friday morning. Nick set up the arrangements with Henriques to pick them up at the far end of the car park, next to where the campers were installed. He transmitted the details to Alberto, who confirmed he was set to go. He was arriving late at night, so there was little chance that they would be spotted in the dark.

Nick also called Mario at *APA*. He was closing the office at the end of the month, after paying off the remaining workers. The last few months of business had been very profitable and their longstanding employees would receive generous bonuses. After ten years in the job, Mario could hardly bear to watch it all go to waste but he knew there was no alternative. He'd already sent his family to Lisbon the previous week. Just another few more days of this hellish existance to endure and he could join them. He agreed to Nick's request and promised to be at the airport at the agreed time. He didn't ask any questions. If this was the last service he could perform for the Bettencourt family he would be happy to comply.

That afternoon, Olivier told Charlie that he had to make a quick trip to London. "I'm going tonight and I'll be back tomorrow afternoon. Something I need to sort out before I go down to Angola. Look after the shop for me, OK?"

Jorge Gomez received a call from his contact at TAP on Monday evening. Olivier de Bettencourt had booked a return flight to Luanda, leaving on Wednesday morning, returning on Friday morning. *This is it,* he thought to himself. *I'm going to catch the bastards redhanded this time.*

He informed Tavares that he was going back down to Luanda and got his approval to catch a military flight on Tuesday evening. Cryptically, he told his boss, "I said I'd bring the Bettencourt family and their sidekicks to you on a plate. Well, get the champagne ready."

Charlie bought a leather briefcase with a flap over, fastened by three locks. Two side fastenings were operated with a key, and the central one with a four digit combination code. It was strong and capacious, like a lawyer's briefcase. He entered a combination in the central lock and placed it in the office at home.

On Tuesday evening, Olivier returned from London and came over to the house to eat. Nick, Maggie and Alan were already there. While the women were preparing supper, Charlie gave the briefcase to Olivier with a set of keys and a slip of paper with the combination.

They went to sit on the terrace with a beer. "I've put the house up for sale, not that it makes any difference these days." Olivier shook his head. "I just wanted to show that we've finally thrown in the towel and we're leaving the country. It might take the heat off for a few days at the bank, give us time to get things done."

Charlie nodded in agreement. "I've let it be known that we've given up the lease on this place for July 31st. Let's hope that those communist bastards in the bank spread the news around. 'Two more capitalists forced to leave the country!' The Nationalisation Committee is going to be pissed off, running just another bankrupt company. No more kudos in it for them."

"Seriously, Charlie, this is a pretty risky endeavour for everyone. If it works, we'll be in great shape when we kick off the business in Geneva and you and Nick will have earned a bigger chunk of share capital. On the other hand, if something goes wrong, and I can think of a dozen things that might, Alberto might be OK, but Henriques and I'll definitely be in the shit and maybe you two as well. I haven't told Cristina or my family. It'll be time enough if it works out. I just told them I'll be out of contact for a day or two, handling some business in Angola."

He took a sip of beer. "If anything goes wrong, I mean, if I get into trouble, I want you to tell Cristina and the family yourself, if you're able. I don't want you to tell them about this deal, it's better if they don't know. Just say I was in Angola, closing off business arrangements before leaving. OK with you?"

Charlie murmured his understanding. The future Duque de Santiago de Compostela had to avoid bringing shame on his family. It was more or less the same story he'd told to Ellen.

Olivier reached inside his inside pocket and handed him an envelope, letter size. "I'll collect this from you when I get back. Alternatively, open it and inform my family. Please don't show it to anyone else, anyone at all."

THIRTY-TWO

Wednesday - Friday, June 25th - 27th, 1975
Luanda; Ambrizete, Angola

Luanda airport was in indescribable chaos. The building was filled to overflowing with thousands of people trying to find a way out of the country. Men, women and children were standing, sitting, kneeling or lying in the middle of the chaos, by now many of them crying and wailing, their hands held out, begging for anything they could get, money, food, anything. UN officials were bustling about the terminal, organising a group of passengers on another emergency flight for Lisbon, the fifth that day.

Olivier once again asked himself how his country could have come to such a pass. To stand by and permit this humanitarian nightmare to occur. To walk away from their once most productive and stable African possession, rich with every conceivable kind of resource, and see it reduced to a shambolic, war-torn hell-hole. And then, as the coup de grâce, to hand it over to the Russians and Cubans, knowing full well that they would destroy all hope of a normal life for its citizens for the foreseeable future. He couldn't comprehend it at all.

The soldiers at immigration were inspecting every bag and parcel, body searching many passengers and generally demonstrating their importance. The mass of people pressing around was an advantage, the immigration officials checked his VIP papers and waved him through to the arrivals hall, where Mario was waiting to meet him. They drove to his apartment and Olivier spent the night and the next day there, not going outside at all, for fear of inviting trouble. The plan was too important to screw up now.

Alberto's military flight arrived just after eleven on Thursday night. The Angolan bodyguard had informed his master that the Bettencourt family had finally given in to the inevitable and were pulling out of Angola. He told Cunhal that Olivier had arranged for him to meet the boss of *Sociedade Mineira de Angola*. After delivering the documents to Agostinho Neto's adjutant, he was going to see the mine owner and try to get him to agree to continue running the production if they got the *MPLA* to guarantee protection.

Cunhal had agreed to his request without hesitation. He had condoned Alberto's friendship with the *APA* people in the hope of just such an eventuality. The diamond mining business could be an immediate funding source, but almost all qualified workers were fleeing the country. If Alberto could help them to take over a profitable, operating mine, they could fund a lot of activities, including some special bonuses for the right people.

During his time as a soldier, Alberto had been trained to grab any sleep he could, when he could. He had thrown some blankets across the hard metal seats of the converted Boeng B727 and managed to catnap for part of the almost twelve hour flight. Now, it felt as if every bone in his body was aching. He pulled himself together and washed his face in the lavatory wash basin before climbing painfully down the aircraft steps. He was wearing his major's uniform and carrying the documents for Neto in Charlie's briefcase. A jeep, waiting by the side of the runway took him to the airport building where an army captain saluted and showed him into the small office adjacent to the arrivals door. As usual, Neto's adjutant was waiting for him and they quickly exchanged files of papers, shook hands and separated.

Alberto went back outside then came in through the arrivals door to walk along the empty corridor towards the immigration desk. He suddenly felt a shiver of apprehension. He hadn't been through immigration into his own country for several months, always meeting at the outside office before returning quickly to Lisbon.

He turned the corner into the entrance to the arrivals hall and stopped in shock. Beyond the immigration desk the whole space was a solid mass of stinking humanity of all races and genders. Europeans, Africans, men, women, old people, children and babies. Every one of them seemed to be shouting, screaming or crying. Hanging onto everyone who went by in any kind of a uniform; soldiers, aircraft crew, aid helpers, even mechanics and baggage handlers.

He walked towards the desk, trying to block out the sight and sound of the seething mass of misery that lay ahead of him.

One of the soldiers at immigration recognised the figure of Cunhal's tall bodyguard limping toward him and whispered excitedly to the others. The soldiers and immigration officials stood to attention and saluted, shouting, "Welcome to a hero of the revolution." The officials casually looked at his papers and cheered him through without searching his case. A couple of soldiers manhandled people out of the way to clear a path for him and he emerged from the building into the torrid heat of the night.

At the exit, one of the soldiers asked him, "Is your driver waiting, or can we take you somewhere?"

Before he could formulate an answer, an attractive young woman walked up to him and kissed him on the lips. "Alberto, how are you my dear?"

He shrugged to the soldiers as Manuela led him across to the car park.

"I don't think he needs any help from us tonight," the soldier said to his comrade.

"But I think he might in the morning!" the other replied with a lewd smile.

Alberto whispered to Manuela, "Sra. d'Almeida, I presume. *Obrigada*."

"*Prazer*, Alberto. The others are over here."

He hung on to her arm as she steered him through vehicles, tents and families to the end of the car park, trying not to look at the thousands of people milling about in the chaos around them. His mind was too stunned to cope with the stark reality of what his regime had created.

Olivier fell into step beside them. "*Bom noite, amigo,* how are you feeling?"

"I'm absolutely knackered, to tell you the truth. Twelve hours in a military plane and you can't wait to become a civilian."

Henriques was waiting with the Transit van in the darkest corner of the car park and after introductions, they climbed in, Manuela and Alberto on the back seat to give the bodyguard more room for his long legs. "Get some sleep on the way. It's a five hour drive, minimum."

Olivier hadn't been down for some time and was astonished at the increase in the number of soldiers and roadblocks. They were flagged down by a military unit, with armoured cars and a tank, deploying at a large intersection about ten kilometres north of the capital. Several jeeps and trucks were overturned at the side of the road. They could see bodies lying beside the wreckage and, as they waited, a truck arrived and the soldiers started loading the bodies, throwing them up over the tailgate.

"God almighty! What the hell's going on here, Henriques?"

"It's what I told Charlie and Nick." The soldier with the red flag waved them on and the mine owner picked his way carefully through the remaining vehicle parts and debris on the road. "The *MPLA* are finally ready to kick the *FNLA* out of the north-western territory. There's been new fighting around here for the past couple of days. The Portuguese are pulling out and the *MPLA* are moving up towards the border and clearing everything out of their way, so they'll be in Ambrizete in a day or two. Then they'll join up with the unit that's already there and push up to the border and we'll be fucked like an impala by a water buffalo. We're down to the wire, we've got to get things done now or we'll be too late. It's time to get out."

Alberto said nothing, he was too confused by conflicting emotions to speak. He lay back on the seat and tried to sleep. Memories flooded through his mind.

He was ten years old, running around his parent's small farm outside of Luanda. He fell in a stream and his mother pulled him out, slapped him across the head then kissed it better.

He was fourteen, at school, listening to the children of wealthy Portuguese landowners talking about their holidays in exotic sounding foreign places and ordering their negro servants to carry their bags and serve their lunches.

He was thirty, standing for the photographer under a baking sun with his new bride, Inês, wondering what the future held for them in Angola, under Portuguese occupation.

He was thirty-five, secretly providing information to the Angolan Communist Party and planning to save his country from the Portuguese fascist occupation.

He was thirty-eight, proudly sitting in clandestine discussions with the cream of Angola's intellectual radicals, convinced that the MPLA really was the road to independence.

He was forty, helping Álvaro Cunhal, the infamous leader of the Portuguese Communist Party to escape in a submarine to Russia, to start a war by proxy in his homeland.

He was fifty, sitting in a shitty little apartment in Moscow, reading Karl Marx, attending brain dead communist conferences and dinner parties and wondering if he would live long enough to see his country emerge from the shackles of colonialism.

He was fifty-five, in Lisbon, twelve months after the revolution of the carnations, watching crowds of starving workers looting, rioting and burning cars and buildings in the streets outside his comfortable apartment.

Alberto could still see, hear and smell the panic and fear of the seething masses of his fellow Angolan citizens at Craveiro Lopes Airport. Desperate to get out of their country, his country, before they were consumed by the onslaught of civil war.

What happened? He asked himself. *Where did we go wrong? This is not independence. This is not democracy. This is just madness. I want no more part of this murderous conspiracy.* Then he realised, *I have to get these diamonds out. So Inês and Raffa and I can start again, before it's too late.*

After a short while he fell into a dreamless sleep. He was a soldier. He'd taken his decision, now he had to execute it.

This time it took them less than five hours to get to the mine. The weather was good, the road was fairly clear, apart from a continuous line of refugees trudging along the roadside, and they met no rebel units, neither *FNLA* nor *MPLA*.

Joaquim was waiting at the blockhouse to let them into the compound. He saluted and they drove inside and parked the van. It was four in the morning but they didn't have time to waste, not even to sleep. The military flight was leaving at eleven and Olivier's plane was at midday, so they would have to catnap on the return drive and on the flight. Henriques would drive Alberto back and then Manuela and Olivier would follow later, to avoid any chance of them being seen together.

Charlie had prepared a simple form of agreement, spelling out the deal. Henriques read it through and signed it without question. "So, we're partners now. Let's get out of this shithole and make a fortune in a new country." He poured a glass of whisky for each of them and they toasted their new partnership. "To Angolan diamonds, without Angola."

Alberto didn't react to this provocation. *Amazing what the promise of a fortune can do to your principles,* reflected Olivier. He had no idea what was going through the Angolan's troubled mind.

Henriques went through the sorting plant to a windowless, single story concrete construction with a massive, iron bound door. It was fastened by three bolts with large padlocks attached. He unlocked the padlocks and entered the building alone with the briefcase. When he returned, it was impossible to tell that the diamonds and cash were inside it.

Olivier locked the case with both the key and the code and passed it to Alberto with the key and a scrap of paper with the digits.

"*Boa sorte,* Alberto. Good luck, I'll see you in Lisbon."

Before Alberto could reply, the door burst open.

They all turned in shock at the sound. In the doorway stood Jorge Gomez, flanked by two Portuguese soldiers, each carrying submachine guns.

"What the fuck?" Henriques stared with astonishment at the three men. Manuela stood in a daze, frozen to the spot by this nightmarish interruption.

Olivier looked at Alberto in disbelief. This little bastard had followed them here, all the way from Lisbon. *He must really hate our guts,* he thought to himself.

Gomez shut the door behind them and the two soldiers took up positions at either end of the room, their weapons trained on the bewildered group.

Gomez strutted up to Olivier. "Patience is a virtue, wouldn't you agree? It's taken me nine months to catch you redhanded, but what a bonus I've earned by waiting."

He turned to the Angolan bodyguard. "The exalted Sr. Alberto Pires da Silva, a hero of the revolution, caught with his hand in Angola's till. I love it." He gestured to the case in Alberto's hand. "Let's see what's in that briefcase."

Alberto tried to tough it out, the Portuguese knew nothing, yet. "You impudent bastard. Don't threaten me with guns and treat me and my friends like bloody criminals. I'm a major in the Portuguese army. Stand back and put those arms down!"

"Shut the fuck up and put the case on the table. These men are under my orders and they've got instructions to shoot if you piss me off. I personally don't give a shit what happens, just another dead crook, that's all."

Alberto placed the case on the table between him and the Portuguese. "It's full of papers concerning the mining operations. I'm down here on official business. Just wait until Cunhal hears about this. He's going to have your balls for breakfast." Despite the bluster he knew they were cornered. He had to prevent Gomez from opening the case.

"I don't believe a word of it. You people have been as thick as thieves and there's more to it than mining papers. Money or diamonds is more likely, so let's see, shall we?

"And just try to do something stupid," Gomez continued, "these soldiers can't wait to exercise their trigger fingers. Ask your dead guard outside if you don't believe me." He picked up the case and tried to release the two catches. "Give me the fucking key, you stupid Angolan prick. I've told you what'll happen if you try to play any tricks."

Alberto's mind was working furiously. Although he hadn't been active for several years, apart from his injured leg he was still strong and had always been a tough fighter. Gomez was no problem, but the two armed soldiers might stretch the odds. He clumsily threw the key on the table. It fell to the floor and he stooped to retrieve it, stepping nearer to the Portuguese. The soldiers' attention was diverted by the clatter of the falling key and they failed to notice Henriques slowly inching towards the filing cabinet standing against the wall.

"Give it here, you Angolan imbecile!"

Gomez snatched the key from Alberto's hand and opened up the two side locks. "What's the combination?" he snarled.

"I can't remember. I've written it down here somewhere." Alberto fumbled through his pockets, desperately trying to think of a plan of action.

Gomez snatched the pistol from the holster of one of the soldiers and pulled Manuela over to his side. He held the gun to the terrified woman's head. "I'll count to three, then you lose your girl friend. One, two.."

"I thought I told you to fuck off!"

Suddenly the door had burst open again and Joachim was standing in the opening, his big silhouette outlined against the darkness. His left arm was hanging down uselessly at his side, blood covering his shoulder and chest and dripping from his sleeve, but his right hand was aiming his submachine gun into the room. The soldier on the far side had no chance to react and was cut almost in half by the hail of bullets, but the other turned swiftly and a burst of fire brought Joachim to his knees. Just as swiftly, Henriques grabbed his pistol from the top of the cabinet and fired three times into the soldier's chest. As the man was blasted backwards against the wall, Alberto threw his arm around Gomez's neck and twisted viciously. There was a sickening crack and the Portuguese traitor dropped lifeless to the floor. A moment later, Manuela fell down beside him in a dead faint.

THIRTY-THREE

Friday, June 27th, 1975
Ambrizete, Angola; Leopoldville, Zaire

The telephone in Maggie's apartment rang at six in the morning.

"It's Olivier. Sorry to call so early, but I need to speak to Nick."

He gave the South African an abbreviated version of the night's events, emphasizing that they were all safe, except for the unfortunate Joachim. The merchandise was in the briefcase, on its way to the airport with Alberto. He was obliged to return with the military flight to avoid suspicion but they had agreed that it was too dangerous for the others to go back into Luanda. Gomez probably hadn't suspected Cunhal's bodyguard's involvement until he'd arrived at the mine, but he may have told the local authorities about his suspicions of Olivier and the others when he enlisted the soldiers. There might already be an alert out for them. They couldn't risk it. Alberto had therefore driven off alone in the jeep to get to the airport in time for his plane.

Despite Nick's requests for more details, he told him only that they had got rid of the bodies and it was unlikely that they would ever be discovered. Henriques' plan was to drive up the inland road, going through the border at Noqui, to Matadi, in Zaire. Matadi was the principal port on the Zaire River and there was a good highway to the airport in Leopoldville, the capital. Henriques had made the trip before, taking about eight hours, including the border crossing. There they could find flights to Paris and on to Lisbon. Henriques and Manuela couldn't fly anywhere else without first getting visas for their Angolan passports.

The Angolan's reasoning was sound. He had established good relations with the *FNLA*, the only forces they were likely to encounter on their way through the north-western province. In addition, under Mobuto's rule, Zaire was treating Angolan refugees kindly, having already accepted many thousands of them since the announcement of independence. With a vehicle and enough money to bribe the rebels and the authorities, they should have no trouble getting through the border and even less trouble flying out of Leopoldville. It was a good plan, Olivier was confident they would be back in Portugal within two days, ready for the next step.

Nick could do nothing but take note that Alberto should be arriving at Lisbon airport at ten that night and was expecting to meet them there. He wished Olivier and the others the best of luck. "See you in Lisbon, then Geneva. Travel safely."

He put the phone down and said to Maggie. "I have a very bad feeling about this."

At twenty minutes to eleven, Alberto walked into the departures hall at Craveiro Lopes Airport, carrying the briefcase. He strode confidently through the hall, carrying the case lightly, as if there was nothing in it but the file of documents from Neto. Inside he was shaking with nerves. *What if they've had news of the attack? What if that bastard Gomez knew about me before and has advised the authorities? What if he was in league with Cunhal and it's a trap? What if they want to open the briefcase?*

He pushed his way through the milling crowds and approached the immigration desk. A group of passengers was being led past the border guards at the desk by a UN official. People in the crowd were trying to push into the group. Scuffles and fist fights were going on all around the desk. Four soldiers were pushing back the angry, frightened mob. Beside the desk was a young woman carrying a small baby. She was screaming at the officials, desperately trying to convince them to let her go through. The baby was making as much noise as the woman.

One of the men shouted at her, "When you come back with a ticket, you can get through, not before. Now get back to where you came from and stop hassling us, we've got important work to do." One of the soldiers turned her bodily around and pushed her into Alberto's path.

The woman saw Alberto in his major's uniform and grabbed him by the arm. She thrust the screaming baby at him. "Take my baby to Lisbon. We've been here for days, we can't get out. We're going to die here, we're all going to die. Please take my baby with you, I beg you."

Trying to prevent the baby from falling, he dropped the briefcase on the floor. He ignored it and gently placed the baby back into the mother's arms. "I can't take the baby and I can't take you, Senhora, I'm on a military flight. But there are a lot of refugee planes scheduled to leave. You'll get on one. They're helping people with children."

He turned to the soldier who had picked up the briefcase. "I am Major Pires da Silva. Here are my documents. Bring a UN official over here immediately and get this woman and her child on the next flight. Now give me my case and let me through, my plane leaves in ten minutes and I don't want to arrive in Lisbon late for Sr. Álvaro Cunhal."

Alberto could hardly force his legs to climb the steps up to the 727. He was a nervous wreck, his mind numbed by the multitude of emotions he'd experienced over the last few hours. He was sweating freely and his limbs were shaking as if he had a palsy. He'd managed to extricate himself from the pathetically grateful embrace of the woman and get through the barrier. The guards had not tried to stop him. There was no alert for him. He walked past the control desk to the accompaniment of their salutes and cheers. Now, all he wanted was to have a whisky, grab some sleep and get rid of the briefcase as soon as he arrived in Lisbon. He didn't want to hold it for one minute longer than necessary. He was getting too old for this kind of thing.

Olivier and the others drove away from the mine at seven o'clock on Friday morning. They needed to get on their way quickly in case a warning notice about them had been issued.

After Alberto left for Luanda in Joachim's jeep, the men's first action was to take the bodies away from the compound before the workers started to arrive. They left Manuela to clean up the office and then sleep for a few hours while they manhandled the four corpses into the Transit van. Without waking anyone in the cottages, they drove downstream for several kilometres to a high area of the riverbank, surrounded by a copse of trees. It took them over an hour to bury the bodies and they came back bone weary and covered in mud and gravel.

His brother Sergio was already in the office when they returned and Henriques recounted the night's events. He introduced Olivier as someone from *APA*, with no further explanation. His brother didn't seem particulary concerned about the deaths, except for Joachim. They had been childhood friends. All he said was, "Are you still going to get us out and look after us?"

"Absolutely," replied his brother. "Wait until we're sorted out and I'll tell you the plan."

They cleaned up the Transit van and filled it with gasoline, food and water and additional jerrycans of fuel in the back. Then they showered off the night's filth and Henriques found some overalls for Olivier which almost fitted. Manuela was now rested and ready for the journey.

Sergio and Elvira brought out their two children to see them off. Henriques took his brother aside. "Take this pouch and keep it safe until you leave." He sprinkled ten cut, polished diamonds into Sergio's hand. "They're worth forty or fifty thousand dollars, but don't use them until you get out of the country, it's too dangerous. Hide the pouch in Raymundo's clothes when you leave and show it to no one." He handed him a wad of fifty and twenty dollar bills. "Use this cash until you get out of the country."

He explained their itinerary and promised to call when they reached Leopoldville. "Then I'll tell you what you should do. Say nothing to anyone. Don't take the risk that there's rebel spies about. Get the truck ready to leave and wait for my call. Don't worry, look after Elvira and the kids and we'll soon be seeing each other again somewhere safe."

Henriques took the first shift, driving back along the dirt track to take the road up towards Lussenga, leading to the border post at Noqui, about a hundred and sixty kilometres north-east of Ambrizete. He knew the road, which was little more than a track. It was dry and in fairly good condition, so his time estimate should have been accurate. But he hadn't taken into account the thousands of inhabitants who were fleeing their homeland for the safety of Zaire. The trickle of refugees had now become a flood heading for Noqui. The narrow road was packed with families struggling to escape the imminent *MPLA* onslaught that would come from the south and the east to smash the *FNLA* forces and take the north-west province.

It took them six hours to get to the outskirts of the border town. The van had no air conditioning and as they moved slowly along under the blazing sun it was like being baked in an oven, the sweat running down their bodies until they were soaked and dehydrated.

They picked up Avelina, a young woman with a small baby in her arms and dragging along a little boy and girl trudging wearily beside her. Besides helping the exhausted family, it would provide more camouflage if they were stopped by a patrol and also at the border. Avelina's husband had been killed by the *MPLA* the previous week in a shoot-out with the *FNLA*. She was desperately trying to escape from the country before she and her children suffered the same fate. The incident had taken place at Quimavongo, a town just forty kilometres south of Ambrizete. Henriques was right, the *MPLA* were starting to move north.

At the entrance to Noqui, their passage was blocked by an *FNLA* unit. Olivier was driving and the women were in the back seat with the sleeping children. They were now in the midst of a mass of refugees, not just from the north-west, but from towns towards M'banza Congo to the east and from the south as far as Uíge, even Luanda. They took up the whole width of the road. Young men and women. Adolescents and children. Old people, healthy or crippled. Walking, cycling, pushing prams, carrying infants, riding horses or in horse-drawn carts, a few in ramshackle old cars. It was a heart-breaking sight.

"Have you ever seen anything so fucking tragic in your life?" Henriques struggled to contain his anger and sadness at the devastation of his country and the plight of his fellow Angolans. The only advantage of the milling crowds of refugees around them was that with their cheap, worn clothes, they were not worried about attracting attention.

There were about twenty rebel soldiers standing with their weapons in the midst of the procession of refugees who were trying desperately to get past them to freedom. A wooden barrier was erected across the road and they were extracting a toll from the exhausted travellers. Those who couldn't, or wouldn't pay, were pushed back, to join the growing numbers of people sitting by the roadside, wailing and crying in their fear and misery.

Around the area where the barrier was erected, Olivier could see the burnt-out wrecks of a dozen vehicles; cars, vans and a couple of army trucks. On the other side of the road another thirty or so rebels were sitting around a makeshift campsite of filthy tents, alongside a brackish stream and a pond that looked and smelled like a cess pit. He didn't want to imagine what was below that greasy, turgid surface. Under the remorseless heat of the scorching sun, the whole place smelled of corruption and death. There was an overriding aura of rank terror.

"Stay here and don't move or make any noise," said Henriques. He went to talk to the guards whilst the others sat silently, sweating in the van.

Five of the rebels came over with him to the vehicle, machine guns and pistols in their hands. Teenage kids, skinny and wide eyed. Arrogantly waving their guns at everyone and everything. The testosterone emanating from their pores was almost tangible and the rancid stink of their sweat was overpowering. They pointed their weapons at the group inside the van, laughing at the fear they induced. Then they lined them all up with Henriques in the hard-baked mud at the side of the road, a pock marked youth left to cover them with his machine gun, high on chewing iboga bark, jittery and jumpy, as if he had the St. Vitus dance. After the murder of her husband, Avelina was shaking with terror and could hardly hold her baby. Manuela took the child from her and they held the other children against them, sweating and trembling in the torrid heat, praying to be delivered safely from these teenage killers.

The youths ransacked the vehicle, taking the few items of any value. Then one of them, apparently senior to the others, started bargaining for a payment to open up the road. Finally, Henriques negotiated a fee of ten thousand escudos for them all to get through. The kid took the money, seeming to agree, then he turned to Avelina. She was a buxom, pretty woman, about twenty-two, still with the extra weight in her breasts and bottom after her recent childbirth.

"The others can go, the kids as well, but you stay." He pulled the young woman aside.

"No! No! Pity!" Avelina started screaming and struggling and the other youths came up to help him drag her away. Olivier jumped forward to pull her back and one of the youths smashed his rifle butt into his kidneys, knocking him flat, then pushed his face into the filthy ground. The others grabbed Avelina again and her shift was torn off her shoulders, revealing her large, milk-filled breasts. At this, two of the adolescent rebels pulled her to the ground and started pulling the garment off her, the others laughing and cheering them on.

Henriques looked wildly about him, the woman would be raped in front of them and he would be shot out of hand if he interfered. Avelina was shrieking hysterically, begging for mercy. Manuela and the older children added their screams of terror, pleading for her. Another soldier came over to see what was going on. He looked about twenty-two years old, wearing a shirt with the epaulettes of a Portuguese major, badges and ribbons on the front. Henriques stepped out and grabbed him by the hand, smiling and talking, pulling out a wad of escudos. It was an officer from the unit near Ambrizete he had been bribing for the last six weeks.

The man looked around at the scene. Now, Avelina was naked under the remains of her shift, vainly trying to pull it across her body to hide herself. One of the youths was undoing his flies while the other two held her down. Other rebels had come across to join in the rape. Olivier was kicked back down each time he tried to climb to his feet. He was bruised, bleeding and frightened for his life. Another of them tried to grab Manuela, but Henriques pulled her back and stood in front of her, turning the children away from the terrifying scene.

The 'major' pulled out his sidearm and shot it into the air. "Stop! That's enough! Let them go and get back to your duties. Get this van out of here. We've got enough problems with these people, don't make it worse." He pocketed the wad of notes and pulled Avelina to her feet. Olivier staggered up and the two men helped the women and children into the van and locked the doors. The soldier waved them on through the barrier.

The rebels fired their guns over the heads of the other refugees, warning them to stay back. Their frightened, defeated faces looked on resignedly as the Transit drove through the roadblock. Avelina was weeping with relief and fear, hardly believing she'd escaped the ordeal. She took her children in her arms and held them fiercely to her, safe for the moment. Manuela found some underwear and a wrap for her and wet a rag to wipe the blood and filth from Olivier's face. They were too exhausted to show their happiness and relief as they drove on to Noqui, to tackle the last hurdle in their escape from Angola.

Here, the situation was less perilous. Under the pressure of the thousands of refugees who were now fleeing their country, the border guards had given up asking for proper documents. They seemed happy to see the backs of the Portuguese and Angolan families who were leaving, as long as they could extract their last few escudos for an exit visa. This time it cost them twenty thousand escudos and they were out of Angolan territory.

Henriques looked back at the border, his last sight of his homeland. He had never dreamed that the day would come when he would be glad to leave his country, his family's home since generations. But now he was just glad that he was alive, that they were all alive and headed for a new life in a civilised place. They drove slowly along in the midst of the crowd. Just eleven kilometres more and they would reach Matadi, in Zaire.

Maggie's phone rang again at about five fifteen on Friday evening.

Nick jumped up and grabbed it. "Olivier! Thank God. It's great to hear from you. Is everyone OK? Where are you?"

"I'm at a public phone at a filling station on the highway to Leopoldville. We're an hour from the airport, all completely knackered, but doing well."

"When are you getting back? Have you checked the flights?"

"I just called the airport and booked us on an Air France flight for Charles de Gaulle Airport in Paris, at nine this evening, with a TAP connection to Lisbon tomorrow morning at nine fifteen. So we should arrive at about eleven o' clock."

"Terrific. We'll be at the airport to meet you tomorrow. Well done, Olivier."

He called Charlie straight away. "They're safe and sound in Zaire. Next stop, Lisbon."

At ten o'clock that evening, Charlie and Nick parked the Opel in the airport car park. They showed their papers at the terminal entrance then went to have a drink inside the arrivals hall. Two refugee flights had just landed and the terminal was pandemonium. Half an hour later, they saw Alberto struggling through the crowds of passengers. He was carrying the briefcase.

On the way to his apartment he recounted all that had happened in Angola. The other two men were astounded to hear the details of Gomez's relentless pursuit. Charlie had the same thought as Olivier. *He must have really hated our guts.*

Alberto was relieved to hear that the others had managed to get out to Zaire. That meant that so far there had been no alert. They should have time to make their escape when the others arrived in Lisbon. He said nothing about his own decision to leave Portugal. He needed time to work it out, time to organise his family's lives before taking any action. At his apartment he removed Neto's documents and passed the briefcase and the key to Charlie.

"It's up to you two now," he said. "I've played my part and you have to make it happen and look after me correctly. I have a feeling I'm going to need my share. My advice to you is to get out as soon as the others get here. You can't risk one day more than you need to."

An hour later, the briefcase was in the safe in Charlie's house. He didn't open it, he thought that Olivier should have that pleasure. They told Ellen nothing of the events in Angola, only that she should get ready to be on her way out of Portugal.

"Thank God!" she said. "Let's get out of this hell-hole and move to a proper country."

Manuela was driving the last leg of their journey to Leopoldville airport while Henriques dozed in the seat beside her and Olivier slept in the back seat. They had left Avelina and her children at Matadi and were all dead beat, looking forward to sleeping on the flight. The two way road was built along an escarpment, with a narrow hard shoulder on the right, the hillside falling steeply away to a rocky valley. Like most African roads, it was full of every conceivable type of vehicle, many of which looked as if they would fall apart at any moment. The drivers were typically aggressive and dangerous, overtaking whenever a few meters of empty space were available. Risking everyone else's life, almost forcing the oncoming traffic off the road.

Manuela drove cautiously in the right-hand lane, following the signs for the airport, now only fifteen kilometres away. It was six fifteen and she had covered almost fifty kilometres since their stop at the petrol station. Dusk was falling, but the light was still fairly good.

Then from one moment to the next, the twilight ceased and the night set in. There were no road lights and she suddenly found herself in pitch black darkness, the lights of oncoming traffic flashing onto the windscreen and momentarily blinding her. Never having driven the Transit van in darkness she ran her hand over the dashboard to find the light switch.

"Damn!" She glanced down to find the switch. It was a button that pulled out from the dashboard. The lights flashed on full beam and she looked up just in time to see a sign pointing off to the airport on the left. Panicked, she signalled left and pulled over to the turning lane. An old, battered Renault was already moving into the lane from the blind spot on her offside. She pulled the wheel back and turned into the right hand lane again, simultaneously braking, hoping to catch the turn after the Renault.

Manuela didn't see the rusty, blue flatbed truck that was coming up behind her, because it had no lights on. When he saw the van come back into his path the driver stamped down on the brake, but the truck was piled high with scrap iron and the ineffective brakes strained to slow the momentum of the heavy load. As the Transit van slowed, the wheels still turned to the right, the truck piled into the back of it, pushing it forward and to the right. Manuela braked again and desperately pulled the wheel around to the left to avoid driving off the road.

The crash of the impact and the swaying of the vehicle woke the two men from their doze. Startled, they both shouted conflicting instructions.

"Pull over to the right and stop on the verge!"

"Straighten up and accelerate away!"

In her panic, Manuela did the worst possible thing. She accelerated while still going towards the left. The van overshot the turning lane into the path of the oncoming traffic.

"Jesus Christ!" Henriques grabbed the wheel, desperately trying to pull the vehicle back to the right. They looked in horror at the headlights coming straight towards them. The driver of the oncoming lorry had no time to avoid them. The offside wing of his vehicle smashed into the van at a combined speed of one hundred and seventy kilometres per hour, pushing the engine through the front seat and killing all three of them instantly. The van was thrown back into the path of the truck behind, which smashed into it again, shoving the vehicle across the hard shoulder and over the edge of the escarpment.

The rocks and rubble at the top of the slope turned the Transit over and it started a mad descent down the hillside, rolling over and over, the three lifeless bodies being thrown around inside like dolls.

The fractured remains of the van reached the bottom of the escarpment and it lay motionless on its side, its headlights still cutting through the blackness of the night, illuminating the barren, rocky surface around. The only sound to be heard was the hissing of the punctured radiator, breaking the blanket of silence that surrounded the bent and broken metal casing that was now the tomb of the three occupants.

THIRTY-FOUR

Saturday, June 28th, 1975
Lisbon, Portugal; Ambrizete, Angola

Nick and Charlie arrived at the airport five minutes before the TAP flight from Paris was due in, and waited in the arrivals hall. Their friends had no luggage and they expected them to emerge amongst the first passengers. Half an hour later, when the last passenger had departed, they went to the TAP desk and spoke to the attendant.

She consulted the passenger manifest. "I'm sorry, none of those names are on the list."

Charlie made her check again all the way back through the list and then asked her to look through the bookings. When she hesitated, he added, "These are friends of ours who are refugees from Angola, flying from Leopoldville. They could have only come to Portugal. They don't have papers for any other country."

The woman studied her computer screen. "I can find their reservations, but they didn't fly, so they must have missed the plane. It happens a lot with African connections. There's another flight tonight, but there are no reservations for them on that, and it's the same tomorrow. I can find no bookings at all."

"Can you check with Air France and any other airline coming here from Paris?"

The young woman called Air France and Air Zaire and after a few minutes of discussion in French with each, she turned to the two men. "I'm sorry, but there's no trace of your friends with any of the airlines for today or tomorrow."

Charlie had a sick feeling in his stomach. He said,"We need to get back to Cascais."

Sergio d'Almeida knew that he had to be ready to leave with Elvira and the children when his brother called. He forced himself to try to think like Henriques, to plan for any eventuality. It was twelve thirty on Saturday afternoon and the plant was closed for the weekend. Only a couple of guards and maintenance people were working. He went to the workshop area and started up their last sizeable, roadworthy vehicle. It was a Chevrolet truck, with the back closed, two bench seats and a storage space full of tools and equipment behind them. He drove it over to the house and helped Elvira and the children onto the back seat and they went out through the compound gates. Telling Joachim's replacement that they were off for a picnic, he headed east for about two kilometres until they reached an area where there was a small lake, fed by the Mbridge river. They had often gone there with Henriques and Manuela for picnics.

While Elvira played with the children in the warm, shallow water, he ripped out the racks and fittings that were used for the tools and equipment that the truck usually carried, and created enough space to put in a mattress where his family could sleep. He cleaned up the mess, threw the tools and broken fittings into the river then went to join his family for a swim in the lake.

At the mine, the phone rang out, but the office was locked and there was no one to hear it.

When Charlie and Nick got back to the house, there was a note from Ellen, "Gone shopping, back soon." He went to the safe to retrieve the briefcase. The two men looked at each other anxiously.

What was happening here? Was this some kind of a trap, a trick to fool them into giving themselves away? What could have happened to delay Olivier and the others, except for something that they didn't even want to imagine?

Charlie opened the three locks. "Check it out, you're the expert."

Nick undid the flap and emptied the case onto the desk. The contents were exactly as Henriques had promised. There was a package of five stacks of one thousand dollar bills, each containing one hundred notes, fastened with wrappers marked *Banco de Portugal y Angola*. In addition, there were ten chamois leather pouches, tied with a string, like an old fashioned lady's purse. Inside each pouch there was a handful of stones that looked like cheap beads, most of a dirty crystal colour, others a light brown. He examined the contents of each bag and nodded his head. "It's the real deal alright, Henriques hasn't let us down."

"And neither has Alberto. So what in God's name has happened to Olivier? We need to make some phone calls."

"If this is some kind of a trap or a double cross, we are in really deep shit, Charlie. You know the phone's definitely tapped." Nick was pacing up and down the office.

"It can't be helped. We have to find out where the hell Olivier is."

He dialled Henriques's private number. There was no answer. He called the office number, still no answer. He didn't know if they worked on a Saturday afternoon, but, if they did, no one was answering the phone, not even Sergio. He didn't like the fact that Henriques's brother wasn't there, but he said nothing to Nick.

Charlie thought for a moment, then picking up the phone once more, he looked at Nick for confirmation. The South African said nothing. He dialled Alberto's number.

Alberto didn't call back until the next afternoon. "We need to meet," he said, with no further comment. They arranged to see him immediately in a bar in the Alfama, the old town.

The Angolan's face was strained, he looked all of his fifty-five years and more. He avoided looking at the others. "I got a call from the Angolan Consul in Leopoldville this morning. The news is very bad."

Charlie and Nick said nothing. They waited, fearing the worst.

"The van was involved in a crash outside of Leopoldville last night, only fifteen kilometres from the airport."

"God almighty! Olivier and the others?"

Alberto continued as if he hadn't heard. "Apparently, they were all killed, instantly. The van was virtually destroyed. It took the police some time to identify the victims and advise the consulate." He breathed in deeply, then expelled the air through pursed lips. "I'm sorry, I'm really sorry. Olivier was a good man. He was a friend. This situation in Angola, it's..." His voice trailed off.

The others were incapable of speech, and after a moment Alberto continued, "You remember what I told you on Friday about getting out. It's now vital to do it immediately. You can't explain Olivier's absence to the Nationalisation Committee, and Tavares is bound to be looking for Gomez when he doesn't turn up tomorrow. You've got no time to waste."

He asked for the Bettencourt's address in Geneva. He would arrange with the Portuguese embassy in Leopoldville to contact the family to inform them of Olivier's death and ask what arrangements they wished to make for the body. He also promised to organise a decent burial for the d'Almeidas. It was the least he could do.

Somehow Charlie managed to drive back to Cascais. He couldn't help repeating, "Fifteen kilometres from the airport. My God, just fifteen bloody kilometres." Apart from that, he and Nick hardly said a word.

They hadn't mentioned their anxiety to Ellen when she came home the previous night, but her instinct had alerted her that something was wrong. After Ronnie had gone to bed, they went to sit in the warm evening breeze in the garden. The two men told her everything. Every detail of the plan, from start to finish. The last part, the contrary twist of fate that had caused the loss of their friends, three innocent civilians, caught up in a bloody, senseless, political death trap, brought tears to their eyes.

Ellen was sobbing uncontrollably. She wanted to blame Charlie, or Nick, or anybody, for this awful situation, but she knew it was useless. She knew they were all trapped in this nightmare, and the only way to get out of it was to leave, now. It would never get better. It would only get worse. They had to get out while they still could, before it was too late. For them, for Ronnie, for their future lives.

When Ellen had finally fallen asleep, exhausted with emotion, and Nick had gone off to his bedroom, Charlie went to the safe in his office and took out the envelope that Olivier had given him. He turned it over in his hands, wishing himself back in the past, before the accident, before the communist takeover, before the revolution. He also knew that they could no longer stay, that they had to leave immediately.

But there are still things to be done. Things that only I can do. He had to fulfill Olivier's wishes. He had to contact his family. Somehow he had to find a solution for the money and the diamonds. Olivier's and the others' deaths mustn't be in vain.

He was tired and depressed and his head ached. He opened the envelope. It contained two sheets of paper.

The first was a receipt for a premium on a life insurance policy from Frazer, Robinson, Lloyd's Insurance brokers in London, for seventeen thousand six hundred Pounds Sterling. It was dated June 24th 1975.

The second document was a cover note confirming a policy on the life of Olivier Cabral e Mendonça Borges de Bettencourt de Santiago de Compostela. The policy itself was in preparation and would be delivered within two weeks. The capital sum payable on death was two million five hundred thousand Pounds Sterling. Charlie quickly calculated that this was equivalent to about five and a half million US Dollars at the current exchange rate.

He continued to read the cover note. There was a double indemnity clause for accidental death. That meant the policy was worth eleven million dollars, since according to Alberto's account, Olivier's death could certainly be shown to be accidental. *What about exclusions? Foreign territories, war or insurrection?* He scanned the document, looking for any excluded conditions. There appeared to be none.

Finally, he looked at the beneficiaries of the policy. They were Cristina Alves Cabral e Mendonça Borges de Bettencourt de Santiago de Compostela, Olivier's wife, and Bettencourt SA, the family's Swiss company.

Charlie sat in silence, absorbing yet another twist in this tragic series of events. *What an incredible man.* His admiration for his Portuguese friend knew no bounds. By this simple act, executed in London the day before his fatal trip to Luanda, Olivier had ensured financial security for his wife and children. He had also achieved his objective of bringing his father and brothers the capital they needed to develop their new Swiss endeavour. In death, as in his life, he had found a way to fulfill his duty.

Sitting alone in his office, in the quiet of the night, the tears streamed down Charlie's face. He wept for Henriques and he wept for Manuela. But most of all he wept for Olivier, a brave, clever, far-sighted man. A true and loyal friend, whom he would never, ever forget.

THIRTY-FIVE

Monday, June 30th, 1975
Cascais, Portugal

Charlie hardly slept that night, his mind going over and over the recent tragic events and their present dilemma. This wasn't a game of outwitting the Nationalisation Committee any longer. It was now a matter of life and death. Three of his friends had already lost their lives and no one knew what danger they and their remaining friends faced. When he got up, still feeling tired and depressed, he asked Nick to take Maggie and the kids to the beach so he and Ellen could be alone. He called Olivier's latest secretary with a story to cover his absence. Then he explained to Ellen what the insurance policy meant to Cristina and the Bettencourt family's Geneva plans.

After that, he unburdoned his deepest feelings to her about the money and the diamonds. About their plans for Geneva and their future. Despite the tragic outcome, the plan to retrieve the valuables had worked, but Charlie had had his fill of Portugal and the whole horrible experience. He'd seen enough cruelty, corruption and fear for a lifetime. He wasn't prepared to take any more risks with their lives or their friends' lives. He wanted to pack up and get out.

Start again somewhere new. To hell with the diamonds and cash, it just wasn't worth it.

He finished by repeating Alberto's warning. "We've got to get out now. Tomorrow, or Wednesday at the latest."

Ellen listened until he had exhausted his emotional outburst then she walked with him into the garden and they sat quietly together.

After a few minutes silence, she said, "We've been here now for six years. That's a long time, almost as long as our marriage. Ronnie was born here, so if we leave with nothing else, we'll at least have achieved something in this country."

"I'm not following you, Ellen." His wife was a Yorkshire girl, shrewd and pragmatic, and Charlie was normally used to her thinking process, but now he had no idea what she meant.

"I mean that apart from our child, who could have been born anywhere, we've made no progress at all in our lives here. We'll have to start again in some other place with nothing, because we both know that without Olivier, there'll be no place for you in Switzerland. It's clear, the Geneva dream is over and it's all because of a government full of Marxist dupes who have terrorised us and caused the deaths of our friends for no apparent reason at all."

"So, what's your point?"

"My point is that in the safe there's millions of dollars worth of reward for your six years of hard work in this country. Don't you think that at least we should get out in good shape? We've suffered enough over the last year, more than anyone deserves. We can't throw in the towel now, when we've got the chance to make it all worthwhile. This is an opportunity to achieve financial independence, maybe the last chance we'll get. It's also a chance for Nick and Alberto to get through this nightmare with more than just bad memories."

"So, you're saying we have to get out with the valuables. You're willing to take the risk?"

"I'm saying that no bunch of communist thugs should stop us from keeping what's now ours. You've almost given your life to try to save your friends. That fortune that was given to us would have been stolen by some murderous crook if you hadn't got it out. We're entitled to it. And if the government, or the army, or anyone else doesn't like it, well, I say *Screw them*!"

When Nick returned, Charlie told him that he and Ellen had decided to try to get out of Portugal with the valuables. Nick tried to hide his immense feeling of relief. He'd been desperately afraid that Charlie would drop the project, and him with it. After all the disappointments they'd been through, he didn't think he could have coped with yet another. But he knew they still had to find a way to get the goods out of the country.

Nick was not good at strategic thinking. He was a technician, an engineer and a diamond expert. "But how do we get the stuff out without Olivier? Can we use Alberto again?"

"No. Alberto has taken this thing as far as he can. He's fifty-five years old, with a wife and a kid and I'm not about to see him get locked up in a Portuguese prison after everything he's done for us. Angola to Portugal is one thing but going through immigration and customs into the big outside world is quite another. I can't let him risk it. We're on our own.

"But I have a kind of plan, or at least the outline of one. I've been worrying about this since we left Luanda and I've come up with only one possible way. It's not clever, it's down and dirty and it's probably fraught with danger, but it's the only way I can think of."

The South African waited without speaking. This was Charlie's forte.

"Almost every day there's more and more people leaving Portugal. There are thousands of people getting out every month. A lot of them travel by car across one of the border posts with Spain and it's impossible for the border guards to effectively search every car. It's a logistical nightmare, it can't be done. So they randomly select every fifth or tenth car, or whatever, to search. And even then it's almost impossible to search a car thoroughly unless you pull it to bits, and they don't have time for that. At night, or early in the morning, it's even more difficult for them because they're tired and irritable and just want to get rid of you."

"So we drive through the border at night with the goods hidden in the car. Right?"

"No, Nick. I don't want you to drive anywhere. A single man, or two men in a car, will draw much more attention than a family. I want to drive Ellen and Ronnie through, like a fed- up, law abiding, English family, going back to the UK via Spain, in a car piled high with belongings. Clothes, pictures, books, family possessions of every kind, so that it would require an X-Ray machine or a mind reader to find a well hidden package."

"So what do you want me to do?"

"Right now, nothing. But tonight I want you to come here with Maggie and we'll plan the move. We've got to be out of here by tomorrow, so we'd better get started."

When Jorge Gomez hadn't returned by Monday evening, Major Tavares called Colonel de Mouro, the commanding officer at Craveiro Lopes Airport. The colonel confirmed that Gomez had asked for two soldiers to accompany him on a sortie on Thursday evening. They hadn't yet returned and the sortie request said only Bettencourt, Ambrizete. He knew nothing more and he didn't have time to spend in trying to find out. He sounded tired and overwhelmed by the worsening situation at the airport. Tavares was irritated that Gomez hadn't told anyone what he was up to, but he agreed to call the Colonel the next day to check again. Meanwhile, he would look through Gomez's files to try to locate their destination.

That evening, Charlie explained his plan to the others. As he had said himself, it wasn't particularly clever and might be dangerous but he didn't know what else to suggest. In the absence of anything better, they agreed to execute it the following day.

The next morning, they went to the *APA* offices as usual and talked as if they were staying until the end of July. They concocted a story to explain Olivier's absence and, by good fortune, there was no meeting of the Nationalisation Committee until the following day.

Charlie called a friend from the golf club and sold Ellen's Peugeot to him at a bargain price. They had rented the house furnished and Nick's only possession was the Opel tank, so they would leave nothing of any value in the country when they escaped, except the Morgan and the tank, and they needed them both for his plan.

Jorge Gomez still hadn't returned by Tuesday afternoon, so Major Tavares went next door to his office and got Lía, the secretary, to check through his files. They found the request that he had made a couple of weeks previously to tap the phones at a mining company in Angola. He called Colonel de Mouro at Luanda airport again and gave him the details. The officer reluctantly agreed to send a couple of soldiers up to Ambrizete the next day to check out the situation.

Major Tavares invited Lía for dinner that night. She readily agreed and put on her best outfit for the date. She was starting to move up the ladder of powerful men. Mostly on her back or on her knees, but it was better than living in a filthy hovel in Angola.

THIRTY-SIX

Tuesday, July 1st, 1975
Cascais, Portugal; Malaga, Spain

That evening, Nick drove over with Maggie and Alan in the Opel and parked it by the Morgan in front of the garages at the side of the house, so they could come and go to the cars in the dark without being seen from the road.

Charlie opened up the boot of the old car. "Give me a hand, Nick. All that stuff piled in the garage is going in here. I reckon it'll just about fill this monster."

They packed the boot until it was overflowing with every conceivable thing, including Ronnie's games and their golf and tennis gear. The clothes and items that they needed for their trip were packed into two suitcases.

"OK. Now for the clever bit, I hope. Can you get the back seat out of there, and open up the tool compartment?"

They wrapped the cash, the diamonds and their few family valuables in a plastic tablecloth, hid them inside the tool box and placed the box back in the tool compartment, under the back seat. Then they put the seat back in place.

"Now for the camouflage."

They loaded layers of clothing, beach towels and blankets onto the back seat, until it was as high as the door handles. Then Charlie laid a sleeping bag bed for Ronnie on top of all the layers. He placed some family papers into the briefcase, and stood it on the floor in the back.

Stepping back, he inspected the old car. There wasn't an inch of wasted space. "Right. It'll have to do. Let's have a drink with the ladies."

Ellen and Maggie put the boys to bed, then made some sandwiches and they opened a bottle of wine. At the table they discussed the details of their plan.

"We'll set off at about eleven. I'm going to drive down to the Algarve and then through Spain to Malaga." Charlie held Ellen's hand. "It'll be fine, it's just a day and a half's drive. We'll be there tomorrow lunch time. Nothing is going to go wrong, I'm sure of it."

Nick, Maggie and Alan would spend the night at the house then drive back to Estoril next morning in the Morgan. Anyone watching would assume it was Charlie and Ellen. They would go out to the airport in the afternoon and dump the Morgan nearby. Nick would leave on the Madrid flight and check into the Hotel Plantamar. Maggie's diplomatic immunity would help if there was a problem at the airport. Then Maggie and Alan would take a cab back to Estoril.

Charlie would call Nick at the Plantamar in the afternoon. If he couldn't make the call, well that was pretty self-explanatory.

"There's one more thing." Nick got up and raised his glass. "Here's to all of us. Good luck and good health."

They clinked their glasses and drank a toast, then he fished in his pocket and took out two ring boxes. "For two wonderful ladies. Thanks for everything."

The women opened up the boxes.

"Oh my God! Nick, how fabulous!" Maggie slipped the solitaire diamond ring onto her engagement finger. Ellen did the same. They were equally stunning. Nick had mounted them on white gold, to show off the exquisite lustre of the diamonds, each of which was just over one carat. He was embarrassed at the grateful thanks they showered on him.

"They look better on your fingers than in the *APA* vault."

"You'd better not wear them at the border, or it might scupper our plans. Nick, you're a real gentleman." Charlie shook his hand. Both women were in tears. It was going to be a difficult parting for them all.

They said goodbye just after eleven o' clock and Charlie drove the Opel out of Cascais to Lisbon and then down the main southbound highway, towards the Algarve. He didn't drive fast. First, because he didn't want to attract attention, and second, because he was worried that the tank couldn't take it. He knew the radiator tended to overheat, so he stopped twice to fill it up. They passed several check points, but they were not challenged. He was wearing a black tee shirt and had not shaved. Ellen had pinned her long dark hair into a bun and could easily be mistaken for a Portuguese Senhora. In the old car, Charlie hoped they would be of too little interest for the soldiers to bother them. He was partially right.

It took them just over five hours to reach the Algarve coast road. For the first couple of hours, the three of them sat on the front bench seat and played word games. It was a very hot night and the car had no air conditioning. By the time they reached Grândola, Ronnie was tired and looked pale from the heat and the lack of air, so they laid him down in the sleeping bag on the back seat.

They were stopped for the first time at the coast road. There was a small wooden guard post at the junction, and a soldier with an automatic rifle stepped into the road and asked for their papers. He perused them for a moment, looked into the car and at Ronnie's sleeping form then waved them on. They followed the road east, all the way past Loulé and Faro. At about half past five in the morning they stopped in Tavira, to fill up with petrol and pour water into the radiator. It was just after six thirty when they got to the Castro Marim border post. Ronnie was still fast asleep in his make shift bed. There were no other cars waiting. The place was deserted. Charlie had got it wrong.

The border post was a concrete building, with barbed wire running north and south from each side. There were four soldiers on duty, two were inside listening to the radio, and the other two were sitting smoking on a bench outside the door. One of them stood up and came to the driver's door. Charlie spoke to him through the open window. "*Bom dia Senhor.*"

The soldier ignored him. "*Passaportes e documentação.*"

Charlie gave him their two passports and the car documents. The soldier examined the passports, looking at the photographs and back at them. He looked at the sleeping child on the back seat. Ronnie's name was added to Ellen's passport. He closed them after a careful examination. Then he checked Charlie's driver's license. Finally, he looked at the car registration document and the license plate. He said in Portuguese, "So, this is not your car?"

In halting Portuguese, Charlie said, "*Não, Senhor.* It belongs to a friend"

The soldier looked inside the car, at Ellen, at Ronnie and all the stuff piled inside. He opened up the passports again and looked at the photographs. "Why are you driving it across the border?" he asked.

When Charlie started to speak in English the man silenced him. "*Fale em Português!* Speak Portuguese!"

Charlie couldn't answer the question, so he just shrugged and said nothing.

The soldier said, "*Para fora,*" signalling to him to get out of the car. They went round to the trunk. "*Abra!* Open!"

As he opened the boot, the other soldier walked across from the bench. Charlie noticed uneasily that he was wearing a captain's uniform. The two men conversed and then signalled to Charlie to empty the trunk. It took him a couple of minutes to take out the golf bags, the suitcases, the tennis kit, the books, toys, clothes and all of the rubbish that he had piled in the previous evening.

The two soldiers examined all of this, then started on the trunk. They lifted up the cover to the spare wheel and searched the compartment with a torch. They prised away the side and back panels and inspected every cavity. Going underneath the car they searched the chassis with their torch. Then they told Charlie to load it up again and open the bonnet.

He released the bonnet catch, propped it open and came back to the trunk. Didn't bother fixing the panels back, just hurled the stuff in as fast as he was able. During this time, he saw a couple of other cars arrive alongside them at the post. A third soldier casually examined their papers and waved them across the border. *Typical bloody Bishop's luck,* he said to himself.

The soldiers searched the engine compartment and the underside of the engine and chassis with the aid of their flashlight. As Charlie finished repacking the trunk, they pushed the bonnet closed again and opened up the back doors of the car from each side. The captain picked up the briefcase, looked through the papers inside and replaced it without comment.

The other soldier spoke and gestured to Charlie, clearly instructing him to empty the back seat. In the front, Ellen was terrified, pressing her legs together desperately, trying not to pee herself with fear. Charlie was sweating and hyperventilating, at his wits end. *They're going to find everything. What the hell can I do?* He didn't know how to stop them. He gestured at Ronnie, lying in his sleeping bag. "My son is asleep. *Meu filho. Dormir.*"

One of the guards shouted from the block house and the captain walked back over to the building. Charlie could see him speaking on the phone, he was looking out towards the Opel. Charlie started to feel very frightened. *Jesus Christ. They've found out about Gomez and Henriques and Olivier, everything. We're up shit creek!*

The remaining soldier again shouted his instructions to empty the back seat and banged the roof of the car with his fist. Then the most extraordinary thing occurred.

Ronnie sat up, yawned and rubbed his eyes. He looked around the car and saw his mother. He said, "Mummy, I don't feel..." Then he vomited all over the sleeping bag and the blankets on the back seat.

"*Mãe de Deus!* Mother of God!" The soldier stepped back, disgusted. The stench was appalling. He slammed the door and threw the passports and documents at Charlie. "*Para Fora!*" he shouted, adding in English, for good measure, "Get out of Portugal, filthy pigs!"

They drove across the bridge over the Guadiana River to the Spanish immigration buildings in Ayamonte. Charlie showed their papers and explained to the officer in English what had happened with Ronnie. He pointed to a washroom adjacent to the customs building. They pulled the car up in front of it and took the dirty blankets and sleeping bag into the toilet. Charlie had never smelled such a divine fragrance as Ronnie's vomit.

"How did you get him to do that?" he asked Ellen.

She shook her head, still not believing that they had escaped. "I have no idea. I think he's just a clever improviser, like his father."

They stopped for breakfast at a small hotel in Huelva, all of them practically asleep on their feet. Charlie extricated the package from the tool compartment and carried it with him in the briefcase. After three cups of Spanish coffee he was ready to drive all the way to London.

Taking the inland road up to Seville and back down to the coast road at Cádiz and on to Algeciras, they bypassed Gibraltar, then continued along the coast and arrived in Malaga at three thirty in the afternoon. They checked in for a couple of days at the Hotel Majestic, which had a suite available. Ellen and Ronnie lay on the double bed and immediately fell asleep.

Charlie went back down to reception and deposited the briefcase, fastened with all three locks, in the hotel safe. Going outside to the faithful tank, he tore up all the documents and threw them into the hotel rubbish bin. Then he drove to an open car park on the other side of town, where he left the car unlocked with the key under the mat and the family stuff inside. He was sure that when he returned, the Opel would be gone.

When he got back from disposing of the car, it was six o' clock in the evening. He called the Hotel Plantamar in Madrid and was put through to Nick. "Thank God you're safely out. I've got an incredible story to tell you, but not right now."

"Well, if it's better than my story of getting walked through immigration by a lady with a diplomatic passport, I'd love to hear it. I've decided I really like empowered women. Shame she's going back to Oz."

Charlie confirmed that they were ready to get started and that Nick should arrange to come down to Malaga. But first he was taking the family to the UK and would return on Monday. They arranged to meet at the Majestic in Malaga on the Monday evening.

He then called Iberia, and booked three seats to London for them on Friday's flight, and a single return for himself on Monday morning.

Ellen called her family in Middlesbrough. "I'm coming this weekend with Ronnie to stay for a while." Her mother and sister were relieved to hear that they were out of Portugal. They'd been reading some worrying articles in the UK newspapers.

Sergio d'Almeida hadn't heard from his brother since he'd left on the previous Friday morning. It was now Wednesday night, and he knew something must have gone wrong.

On Monday, he had placed guards at each end of the dirt track that ran alongside the property so that he'd have advance warning of any unwelcome visitors. On Tuesday night, he and Elvira had prepared bundles of clothes, food supplies and plastic bidons of water and fruit juice and loaded everything into the Chevrolet with several jerrycans of gasoline. He had managed to fit in a mattress and bedlinen for his family. The maintenance truck now resembled a mobile home. They were ready to make a move. If they heard nothing from Henriques the next day, he would assume the worst and try to take his family to safety .

He said nothing to his workers, not even the senior employees. He remembered what his brother had told him. He waited anxiously for news.

At Craveiro Lopes Airport, Colonel de Mouro was inundated with work. In addition to the commercial flights that were still operating, the number of refugee flights had doubled that week and were now coming in from five different agencies and three countries. On top of that he had almost twenty thousand people camping inside and outside of his airport and representatives from the agencies and embassies were knocking on his door all day long. Jorge Gomez was not high on his list of priorities.

Nevertheless, by Wednesday evening he managed to find the time to order two soldiers to drive up to Ambrizete, with instructions to locate *Sociedade Mineira de Angola,* question the owner, Henriques Jesus Melo d'Almeida, and find Jorge Gomez. There were few vehicles available, so the soldiers would set off first thing in the morning in an open jeep.

On Thursday morning, Charlie obtained the local phone book and looked up *Abogados,* Lawyers. He called the first number on the list and asked to speak to the senior partner. An English-speaking man came on the line and after a short conversation Charlie thanked the lawyer and rang off. He rang a second number and arranged an appointment at 4:00 pm that afternoon.

After lunch, Ellen went to discover Malaga beach front with Ronnie. As they walked along the sand together, Ellen tried to explain to her son, in simple terms, why they had been forced to leave their home and friends in Portugal. She needn't have worried, Ronnie was a smart boy. He'd already figured out that bad things were happening in that country. Now he was looking forward to seeing his cousins in the UK.

Charlie recovered the briefcase from the hotel safe. He walked out to get a taxi to the lawyer's office, thinking through the past events and the tasks ahead. Suddenly, he had a sick feeling in his stomach. *Sergio. Henriques's brother!* He'd completely forgotten about him.

He went back to the suite, opened up his address book and asked the switchboard operator to connect him with the number of the mine in Ambrizete. The call might cost a fortune from the hotel but he owed it to Henriques to try to contact his brother, to see what was happening and if he could do anything.

The number rang out, but, like the Saturday before, there was no reply. He put the receiver down, wondering what was happening, or what had happened in Ambrizete. What had happened to Sergio and his family. He didn't think it could have been anything good, but there was absolutely nothing he could do about it.

He picked up the briefcase again and went to find a taxi for the ten minute drive. At one minute past four in the afternoon of Thursday, July 3rd, 1975, Charlie met José Luis Garcia Ramirez for the first time.

THIRTY-SEVEN

Thursday, July 3rd, 1975
Ambrizete; Santo Olivier de Zaire, north-west Angola

At eleven thirty on Thursday morning, one of the guards rode his motor cycle back from his post at the coast road end of the dirt track and ran across to Sergio, who was outside the sorting plant.

"There's a jeep just come up the road from Luanda with two soldiers in it."

During the night, Sergio had been considering the little that he knew of the recent events and current situation. *Two weeks ago Joachim had told him of a man from the Portuguese Junta who'd been around the mine, asking questions. Last Friday, there had been killings at the mine, involving the Portuguese man and two soldiers. Henriques and Manuela had left that morning with an APA director from Lisbon, promising to call him that afternoon from Leopoldville.*

He'd heard nothing since then and now there were two soldiers driving up to the mine. He could wait no longer to hear from Henriques, it was time to get out.

"There's no problem," he told the guard. "Go back to meet the soldiers and bring them along here. I'll be waiting for them."

The man rode off again and Sergio went to get Elvira and

their two children. He helped them into the back of the truck and made them lie down on the mattress, out of sight. Saying nothing to anyone in the offices or plant, he drove out of the gate, stopping only to speak to Joachim's replacement, who was standing outside his blockhouse.

"There's some soldiers coming from Luanda. I'll drive along and see what they want. I don't want them disturbing the workers, it's bad enough without the army parading around."

Sergio's plan was simple. His brother had driven north-east to Noqui, to go over the Zaire border at Matadi. He had to assume that they hadn't made it for some reason and he didn't want to risk making the same mistake. He knew there was an *MPLA* unit on the coast road just south of Ambrizete and he'd heard there were more rebels coming to join them, so he couldn't head south towards Luanda. In a few minutes, there would be two soldiers coming east along the dirt path towards the mine. There was only one remaining alternative.

Sergio drove about five hundred meters east along the dirt track until he came to an even narrower and rockier track going north, towards Tomboco. A couple of kilometres up the winding gradient, he stopped and helped Elvira and the children out of the rear door of the truck. The sun was already high and the interior of the vehicle was unbearably hot.

"God," she complained. "It's like a furnace in the back. There's no air." She was coughing and wheezing with the heat and lack of fresh air. Elvira was asthmatic and the stress and worry of the last several months had made her condition much worse.

He helped her and the children up onto the bench seat behind his and made them comfortable. He opened all the windows and listened helplessly to his wife panting for breath, trying to suck the hot, humid air into her lungs. After a few minutes he started up the truck and set off again.

Driving up the narrow track his forearms began to ache with the effort of gripping the wheel to keep the shaking and bouncing truck on the uneven surface, its worn-out suspension creaking and groaning with every rock or crater in their path.

At two o'clock they stopped for a rest and a snack under a huge banyan tree, its high branches and foliage creating a pool of shade, which made the heat just about bearable. Sergio and Elvira were already sore and aching from the rocky, tortuous road. The children had slept a little, but were in a fractious mood now. Four year old Alicia was continually asking why they had to sit in the horrible van for hour after hour and Raymundo, less than a year old, was crying and wailing with the heat and the jerky motion of the jolting vehicle.

At three thirty Sergio found the track going west, back towards the coast road, and they started to make better going on the slightly improved surface. They were driving along a series of irregular escarpments in the foothills of the mountains and the landscape was stunning. Rugged, barren expanses of mountainous terrain stretched off towards the distant horizon in the north and east, interspersed with bands of forested savannah-like plains.

At four thirty, just short of the coast road, he pulled the truck off the track into a rocky area and walked carefully forward to check the road for potential problems. Apart from a crowd of refugees trudging wearily past him, he saw nothing to alarm him. He could now increase his speed and at five o'clock they reached Manga Grande, about half way to Santo Olivier de Zaire, their ultimate destination, now just about one hundred kilometres away.

Sergio's plan was working. They had encountered no soldiers or rebels of any kind. This north-west corner of Angola was completely isolated, because it led nowhere but to the southern bank of the mouth of the Congo River. From there, they had three choices. To go east across impossibly difficult terrain and cross the border at Nóqui, where his brother had been heading. To traverse the twenty kilometre mouth of the river, to Banana, in Zaire. Or to try to get on a passing ship that was heading to a hospitable destination, wherever that might be. He would decide when they reached Santo Olivier de Zaire.

THIRTY-EIGHT

Monday, Tuesday, July 7th-8th 1975
Malaga, Spain

"So, tell me about this lawyer. Why did you seek him out? How did you find him, for that matter?"

Charlie and Nick were sitting in the bar of the Majestic Hotel in Malaga. It was six o'clock on the evening of Monday, July 7th. Charlie had returned that morning from England and had his second meeting with the Spanish lawyer that afternoon.

He assembled his thoughts. "Have you ever heard of IOS, Investors Overseas Services?"

"Nope."

"OK. IOS was a major offshore investment company, run out of Geneva, but operating in just about every country in the world, including Spain."

"That's why I never heard of them. I never had any money to invest. Go on."

"Unfortunately they went bust a few years ago, and I lost five thousand pounds."

"Tough." Nick was having difficulty following the story.

"In every country where they operated they had political contacts, salesmen, banking relations and lawyers. Their specialty was to get money from, let's say 'inhospitable climates', to more hospitable places."

"You mean they smuggled cash to Geneva?"

"If you want to be crass, I suppose you're right. Anyway, they had a great international network of smart people. At one time, I heard that they were receiving over ten million dollars *per week* in Geneva. The money would come in every possible currency and it would end up in US dollar mutual funds. It was a really neat business, I was a big fan."

"So I suppose that José Luis was their lawyer in Spain. How did you know?"

"Exactly right and it was easy. I called a firm of lawyers and asked them who used to be the lawyer for IOS and they gave me his name and number."

"Good thinking. But if the company is down the drain, how can he help us?"

"Because today I told him I want to move half a million dollars out of Spain."

"You did *what*?" Nick was almost apoplectic.

"Just wait." Charlie took a slip of paper from his pocket. "Here's the name he gave me."

Nick took the paper. "Who's Laurent Bonneville?"

"He was Mr. IOS down here until a couple of years ago."

"So where is he now and how can he help us?" Nick sounded exasperated.

"Sorry, Nick, here's what I know. Laurent Bonneville is a Frenchman who was a Regional Manager for IOS. He was one of the big sales chiefs. His territory was Iberia, as in Spain and Portugal. Apparently he speaks a dozen languages like a native, Spanish, German, Portuguese…, well, you get the picture. He made a fortune with IOS and was one of the few who didn't sink all of his money into the company stock. So he's still well heeled and still apparently involved in 'international financial transactions'. He lives in Monaco and he's coming down to see us tomorrow."

"You've already spoken to him?"

"I figure that we need to move quickly to finish off what we've started. José Luis tells me that he is absolutely trustworthy and a very fast worker. Well, in that kind of business you have to be. One wrong move and you're out of business, or fairly dead, I suppose."

"What if José Luis is not what he seems?"

"All I can tell you is that he didn't ask me anything when I left the briefcase with him, and today he asked me even less. I told him the bare bones about coming from Lisbon, the family, etc. and that's all. I didn't mention you, Olivier, Angola, nothing. I simply told him that I have this cash and asked him if he could help me. He obviously hadn't opened the briefcase and he didn't want to know anything about it. I left it with him as a test, to see what he would do. He did absolutely nothing, except to look after it, which greatly impressed me.

"Today, he gave me this Frenchman's details and made me promise that I would never divulge that he had done it. Don't forget he was the IOS lawyer, and he's still in business. In my book he's the real deal. When we get things sorted out, I'm going to hire him for my own affairs."

"If you trust him, that's fine, no problem." Nick thought for a minute. "There's just one thing though. If this guy Bonneville was the big IOS man in Portugal, why didn't you find him before?"

"Because sometimes I'm really stupid. I just didn't think of it until I was busy cleaning sick off Ronnie's sleeping bag. I was asking myself if there wasn't an easier way to get cash moved, and bingo, the light came on. In any case it probably wouldn't have mattered. Apparently Bonneville is *persona non grata* in Portugal. Or maybe I should say the communists would love him to go back, so they can throw him in prison."

Laurent Bonneville was a tall, slim, fit-looking man with an angular jaw and a head of blonde hair swept back in a film star style, smartened down with hair cream. He appeared to be in his early to mid-thirties. It was easy to see why he'd been so successful in persuading wealthy people to trust him with their money. He had intensely piercing blue eyes and he used them to great effect. Sitting in the park near the Paseo Maritimo, he seemed to be looking through the two men to glean the truth of their story. They had agreed to tell him simply that the cash was from Portugal and they wanted it in Geneva. They wouldn't mention the diamonds. That could come later, if the first step went successfully.

"So." He had a softly modulated voice with a recognisable French accent. "It's really very simple. You want me to move half a million dollars in cash from Spain to Geneva, and you'll make your own banking arrangements when it's there."

The other two nodded their agreement.

"Where's the cash?"

"It's five minutes away from here in an easily accessible, safe place, under our control." Earlier that morning, the two men had visited the nearby Banco de Malaga. With the help of a telephone call from José Luis, they had been able to arrange a safety deposit box. They were relieved to be able to store the briefcase in the safety of the bank vault.

"When do you need the money in Geneva?"

"That depends on you of course, but as soon as possible."

"It'll be there next week if we start today."

Nick frowned. "How can you start today? You didn't know what we wanted until you arrived here."

"My resources are always prepared. Clients are usually in a hurry, if you see what I mean."

The others exchanged glances and Charlie said, "You have local associates." The Frenchman inclined his head.

"So, how does this actually work?"

"It's very simple. You go to the butchers at El Corte Inglés and you buy some chicken pieces. Ask them to wrap them in some waxed paper with newspaper around it and then put it in one of their shopping bags. You go back to your hotel with the chicken and the cash. Throw away the chicken, put the cash inside the waxed paper then wrap the newspaper around it again. You tie the parcel with cheap string, and put it back into the shopping bag.

"This afternoon at four o'clock, you sit on this same bench, with the shopping bag. A young Spanish woman called Angela will stop to say hello.

"You will tell her that you're a great admirer of "Manolote", the famous bullfighter.

"She will tell you that his real name was Manuel Rodríguez Sánchez.

"You will give her the bag, and she will walk away."

"Just like that? We give half a million dollars to some kid we never met? Jesus!" Nick wasn't used to financial transactions of this kind, nor to trusting people he didn't know.

To defuse the situation, Charlie asked "Which way will she go?"

"Again, it's very simple. There's no point going north, because the French have had exchange controls since 1945, so we'd be swapping a Spanish Prison for a French one."

"Well, you can't go west to Portugal, so I guess that leaves you with one or two options."

"Our best route is through some part of North Africa, but that's all I'm going to tell you. It's better for you not to know."

Charlie laughed. "It's amazing how many times we've been told that lately. OK, Laurent, last question. What's your commission?"

"Ten per cent."

The Frenchman lit a cigarette while the other two conversed quietly on the other bench. Finally, Nick said to him, "It's a deal. We'll do it this afternoon."

"Good. As you can imagine, I don't make contracts or agreements, so my word is my bond."

This sounded so old fashioned that Nick almost laughed out loud, but instead he asked, "So what guarantee do we have, once we turn the cash over to you?"

"None at all." The Frenchman turned his steely blue eyes on Nick and said nothing more.

The young woman looked as if she was only about nineteen years old. She was slim and tiny, coming only up to Charlie's shoulder. Good looking, in a handsome Spanish way. Her hair was jet black, very thick and long, hanging loose down to her shoulder blades. She pronounced the "G" in her name with an "H", sounding like *Anghela.* She took the carrier bag, gave them a shy smile and disappeared into the crowd.

THIRTY-NINE

July 14th-18th, 1975
Malaga, Spain; Geneva, Switzerland

On Monday, Charlie received two messages. The first was a telegram telling him the person he was expecting was at the Hotel *Les Ambassadors* in Geneva.

He called Ellen. "Good news, darling. You and Ronnie can plan to come back to Spain in a week or so."

She sounded happy and relieved at the news. It was pouring with rain in Middlesbrough.

He had hardly put down the phone when it rang again. It was Ruiz Bettencourt. Charlie had called him the previous week to convey his sadness at his brother's death. He'd told him that he had some important news that he couldn't discuss on the telephone. Now it seemed that Olivier's body had arrived in Geneva and the funeral would be held on Thursday morning. They would be pleased if Charlie, Nick and Alberto were able to attend.

He called Alberto to thank him for arranging the transport of the body and to give him the news. The Angolan apologised that he couldn't come to the funeral. He said, "It would be difficult for me to travel to Geneva at the moment. Things are becoming very complicated here. Please let the family know how sorry I am. Olivier was a good friend. I'll miss him."

He also told Charlie that Henriques' and Manuela's remains had been properly buried in the graveyard of a catholic church in Leopoldville. Charlie reflected that Alberto had turned out to be a true and loyal friend.

The two men flew up to Geneva on Wednesday afternoon and booked into the *Hotel d'Auteuil*. They couldn't know that Jorge Gomez had stayed there just six months before in his relentless attempt to find the information he needed to destroy them.

Charlie told the Bettencourt family nothing about the reason for Olivier's trip, only that he was tying up some loose ends with Angolan trading partners. He gave the insurance documents to Ruiz, who immediately contacted the Lloyds' brokers. They advised him that there were no exclusions on the policy. Ruiz would obtain a death certificate from the Portuguese embassy in Leopoldville. Olivier had thought of every eventuality.

The funeral the next morning was a tragic affair. Cristina was still in a complete state of shock. Surrounded by her family, she looked small and vulnerable, with her children weeping and miserable about her, not understanding why their daddy wasn't there. Olivier's father sat on a bench in the churchyard between his two remaining sons. He seemed lost and detached from the reality of his bereavement. The ceremony was short and Charlie left the family with fond words and hugs but he knew that Ellen had been right. There was no longer any place for him in their future plans.

That afternoon, Charlie visited several banks in Geneva. He didn't want to use any of the banks which he knew through *APA*. It was better to start a new relationship. He had obtained a list of the members of the Private Bankers Association and had selected five of them. He went into each bank in turn, asking if they would accept a substantial deposit in one thousand dollar notes to open a banking relationship for current, deposit and portfolio banking. They all offered him coffee and assured him that their services were the best in town.

He chose Klein, Fellay SA, whose offices were near the railway station, because they spoke perfect English, they were conveniently situated for trains and for the airport and because the young lady who interviewed him was clever, an absolutely stunning brunette and had a great sense of humour.

Afterwards, he and Nick went along to *Les Ambassadors.* Laurent was there with the parcel, unopened. The funds were safely in Geneva, another step accomplished. They had dinner together. Laurent was also a wine connoisseur.

At Klein, Fellay the next morning, they sat in the conference room adjoining the young woman's office. Her name was Miriam Constance and she was a *fondé de pouvoir,* a senior customer relations officer. Charlie and Nick opened a joint account, just until they decided how to set up the accounts and structure for the new business. The young woman asked for their personal details.

When she asked, "And what's your home address, Mr. Bishop?" he couldn't help laughing. Since he was presently homeless, he gave a temporary address at Ellen's sister's house in Middlesbrough. He would fix it later.

He handed Miriam the five packs of thousand dollar bills and she looked at them in astonishment. "I've never even seen one of these bills before, never mind five hundred. You should frame them, not change them. They'll be collector's items one day, worth a fortune."

Charlie took her advice and kept back one of the notes, "for sentimental reasons." He replaced it with hundred dollar bills. She sent the notes to be counted and checked by a counter-forgery specialist before giving him a receipt for the cash. He placed four hundred and fifty thousand dollars on a thirty days deposit and asked for a cheque, made out to bearer, for fifty thousand.

He said quietly to the Frenchman, "That's for your commission, Laurent, with sincere thanks from Nick and me."

Laurent called the young woman back. "Don't bother with the cheque, I'd like to open an account with you as well. You can transfer the funds directly when the accounts are in place. *Merci d'avance, Mademoiselle.*"

Charlie and Nick agreed to meet Laurent for lunch, then they walked back to their hotel to discuss the structure of the business and the reward for each of the 'partners' involved.

As usual, Charlie tried to bring a logical approach to working out how to slice up the cake. "First off, we know that however much we would like to, we can't include Olivier, or his family. He didn't want them to know about the real reason for his trip to Angola, so we can't reveal it. In any event, thanks to his incredible foresight, they're all in good shape and they don't need our help. And, of course, we did provide a lot of the profits that have gone into the new business. So in all honesty I don't feel that we have any obligation there."

Nick nodded his agreement.

"Now we come to Henriques and Manuela. They are both gone, God rest their souls. They have no surviving parents or children, and as far as we know, the only people in Angola who depended upon them were Sergio and his family. The problem is we don't have a clue where they are. I've now called the mine several times, no reply. I'm sure they must have got out when they didn't hear from Henriques. It must be anarchy down there since he disappeared.

"As far as finding them goes, you remember how many refugees there were at the airport last month? There's probably ten times more by now, and that's just one departure point. They could be anywhere in Angola, lost amongst hundreds of thousands of stranded people. Or they could already be out, in some safe place or, God forbid, they could be dead, just like our friends. This morning I read in the Herald Tribune that the whole country's now in a state of all-out civil war. Mario's already gone back to Lisbon and we don't know anyone else down there, so I wouldn't know how or where to start to look for them."

"It's a crap situation," agreed Nick. "If the Russians and the Cubans are in there, it's not going to be tea at the Ritz. There's not a snowball's chance in hell of going back there and finding them." Charlie had long ago noticed that his friend was not one to use a single cliché when he could squeeze in two or more.

"I suppose we could make some kind of a reserve in case we ever hear anything in the future, but apart from that, I don't see any solution. Let's put that one aside for the minute."

Charlie continued his analysis. "Now it's clear we have a big obligation to Alberto. He's turned out to be an honest, decent Marxist, which in my book is an oxymoron. That's a contradiction in terms," he added, before Nick could ask.

"I know that! You shouldn't assume that all South Africans finish school at age ten."

Charlie continued. "I have another suggestion. It turns out that Laurent is also the real deal. We're going to have more shipments to make if we do this. We have to get the diamonds to Geneva and then you'll regularly have to send stuff around for processing or for selling and then the proceeds have to be repatriated. His contacts are great for this.

"We're both going to have our hands full with setting up and managing the business and we'll need some help. In addition, I have to say that Laurent is the best sales guy I've ever met. When he hits you with those steely blue eyes, all you want to do is sign. So I think we should ask him to work with us, if he's willing. How do you feel about bringing him in as a partner?"

"If he'll join us, I think it's a great idea."

"Good, then that's settled. Is there anyone I've forgotten about?"

"I can only think of two more. You and me."

"Right, let's take you first. Assuming we can get the stones here without problems, can you have them cut and polished and market them at anything like finished prices?"

Nick sat forward in his chair and cleared his throat. "I've given a lot of thought to this. We're going to have to be really careful how we operate, or else we'll find ourselves in deep shit. When we were going to do it through a public company, it was easy. Nobody asks too many questions if you're worth forty million quid on the stock market. But now we're not. We'll be just a pipsqueak, tiny little company, selling fabulous diamonds from Angola and making an awful lot of money. See what I mean?"

"You mean that if anyone sees all these diamonds, they're going to assume we stole them, or smuggled them out of Angola, and we'll get done?"

"Stands to reason. Angola's already going down the pan. Nobody's going to believe that we were handed these stones as a going away gift by the owner of the mine, just before he disappeared. They know exactly what's happening down there and they'll be on our tails like a shot. If we start to flash thousands of Angolan diamonds around, the big guys are going to get wind of it and they'll find a way of screwing us. They didn't become monopolistic monsters by being nice guys, believe me. In South Africa, we saw some very nasty incidents when the smuggling rings were discovered. Literally hundreds imprisoned or killed, and they were the lucky ones."

"So, what's your plan?"

"Well, I've never tried to sell high quality loose stones on the market. But the way I think we have to do this is to start with maybe fifty rough stones and gradually increase to a few hundred every year. That's my gut feeling. Start very small, feel our way and see how it goes. I already have two cutters and polishers that I know, up in New York and Montreal. I don't want to go anywhere near the big boys in Belgium, London or Joburg."

"So the answer is yes, you can do it, but it'll take forty years?"

"Charlie, the honest answer is that I haven't a bloody clue. I've never done it. But that doesn't mean it can't be done, and we probably stand as much chance as anyone else. Once we actually get started we'll learn fast. Maybe I'm being conservative and we can run the numbers up when we get the processes sorted and efficient, time will tell. Anyway, unless something happens to change the status quo, I'm all systems go."

"What kind of prices are we talking about?"

"Good question. Look at it this way, these diamonds need a lot of work to get them into finished form. African diamonds are very hard and it's not an easy process. And we want them to be perfect, high quality. These are not industrial diamonds, they're "*Oh my God. I have to have that*" diamonds." He said this latter in a posh English lady's accent.

Charlie laughed, Nick knew his stuff. "Get on with it, you idiot."

"Selling rough stones through Henriques's wholesale channel, they're worth maybe four hundred dollars per carat. That was his low estimate, eight million for twenty thousand carats. But we don't want to go that route. We want to cut and polish these diamonds and sell them higher up the food chain. We'll lose on average about fifty percent on processing, but that's why it's great to have two to four carat sizes. That means an average of one to two carats net after processing, so we can cut one large, high value piece, or split them into two or three lower value pieces. Not too big, not too small. It's easier to market them, because we can adapt our product to current demand and to the quality of the stones. And we'll get better prices, because bigger stones are valued higher than smaller ones, even if the quality is the same.

"As far as costs are concerned, doing anything on a small scale is always more costly than in big quantities, plus we want to keep a low profile. So our processing is going to be more expensive and slower than the big houses. If we estimate total costs and expenses really high, say a thousand dollars per rough stone, we can produce diamonds that are worth five thousand dollars per carat. But that's a top-end price, with visibility. If we market them like that, we'll get caught, just like if we flashed thousands. So we need marketing without visibility."

"You mean small dealers and jewellery manufacturers, that kind of thing?"

"And don't forget about the auction houses. Christies, Sotheby's, Phillips, etc. They're great places for anonymous sales and good cash prices. Laurent would be perfect for this type of business. A suave, elegant Frenchman who speaks a dozen languages, what could be better?

"But we still have to sell under the market, because we can't give any kind of certification and we want to stay invisible. So, let's take a really serious discount of fifty per cent. I think that we should be able to achieve two thousand five hundred dollars per carat."

"So, let's see." Charlie did the maths in his head. He jumped up from his chair. "Bloody hell. We could make a lot of money from this deal!" He stopped and thought for a second. "And that's exactly why we can't make a song and dance about it, we've got too much to lose."

"You're dead right. So I'll need, say a hundred thousand dollars to get things going, then I'm prepared to take responsibility to turn those little rocks into gems worth a fortune. You have my solemn promise, partners for life."

Nick's assessment of the risks and potential was probably the longest speech that he'd ever made. He sat back again, glad to have got it off his chest. "How do you see it?"

Charlie had digested Nick's concerns about avoiding high profile activities, and his technical and marketing analysis. Now, he was thinking about the timing, psychological and valuation aspects of the project.

"I agree with you, we have to look at this as a long term business. We have to start slowly, and if necessary, stay slow, so that we don't blow the opportunity. That means that we have to build a business that makes enough each year for us all to be motivated to stay involved, until we can see an end game or an exit strategy."

"The thing is this. Suppose we were to set up a kind of pension fund. We couldn't have a better investment base than in a precious commodity, and diamonds are a perfect example. I'm sure that diamond prices will match or even beat inflation and will increase in value year over year. So we'd be pretty stupid to sell too quickly if we can sell later at a better price. Cash devalues, but good assets don't. For all of these reasons, low profile processing and marketing, value protection and a regular revenue stream, my vote is a slow, steady business, until we're ready to exit at some future date."

Nick nodded his agreement with this analysis.

"I'll give some thought to the structure, but I think it has to be a partnership of some kind, or an offshore, private company. You and I have to be fifty-fifty majority partners so that whatever happens we are running the show. I'll manage the corporate, banking and investment side of things. You manage the product development and processing and Laurent will look after marketing, delivery and repatriation. What do you say?"

"Agreed. And what about Alberto?"

"Alberto won't be involved in the business, it's not his thing and we don't know when he'll get out of Portugal. But he has to be in for a good share. He took terrific risks on our behalf and without him we'd have nothing. And remember how he looked after our friends."

Relieved that they had agreed on the nucleus of a partnership plan, the two men shook hands and went off to join Laurent for lunch.

Bonneville ordered a Pinot Noir from the Valais. Nick thought he was showing off, but the wine was delicious. After they toasted the success of the transfer of the dollars, he said, "Interesting wrappers on the bills, Portuguese Angolan Bank. I used to know them well, once upon a time."

"I had no idea that you'd done business in Africa?" Charlie was intrigued.

"That's not something I like to think about too much. Because of my activities in Portugal, we helped thousands of Africans and expats to transfer some of their savings to a safe place. I personally did this in good faith. It's true I made a good living from it but I really felt that I was providing a valuable service. Then, because of the big banks who didn't like to see an offshore outfit doing better than them, the whole business was blown out of the water."

"Then Robert Vesco stepped in and hijacked the rest?" Charlie remembered the American fraudster who had suckered the IOS Board into giving him control. At the last sighting he was in Costa Rica, with almost three hundred million dollars of stolen funds, having executed the *coup de grâce* on the once enormously successful investment company.

"That's what makes no sense. There was a fortune of money there, no reason for it to fail. Then some American *voyou* comes along and rips off hundreds of millions of dollars. Insanity!

"And those trusting people that I thought I was helping lost just about everything. That was not a good result. Not what I intended. And since then I can't tell you how many of those friends I made down there have been hounded, imprisoned or murdered. Just because they had a few thousand dollars and they'd tried to protect their family's future, or because they happened to be in the wrong place at the wrong time.

"These people trusted me. They became my friends. I went to their homes, their parties, their weddings, their christenings, their funerals. I just about became a member of their family. And then

I let them down. And it was because I trusted others, just like they trusted me!"

Laurent took a large swallow of his wine. He was trembling with rage at these memories. Charlie and Nick said nothing, waiting for the Frenchman to calm down.

"Anyway, that's all in the past. Do you want to tell me how you came into half a million dollars from Angola?"

"Well, there's a similar story behind that. Do you want to tell it Charlie, or should I?"

FORTY

Monday, July 21st, 1975
Santo Olivier de Zaire, North-west Angola

Sergio, Elvira and their two children had been living in the truck in a wooded area near the beach at Santo Olivier de Zaire for the past two weeks. He knew they had to make a move soon. This state of anxiety and fear was taking its toll on his wife. The occasional slight cough and shortage of breath that she had suffered was now becoming a constant wheezing gasp as she desperately sucked air into her lungs. It was breaking his heart.

When they had arrived at the beach, there were about a thousand people there, waiting patiently for some kind of deliverence. Since then, some had moved out but a lot more had arrived. There were now several thousand refugees sitting around the beach and it was becoming crowded and unruly.

An *FNLA* unit was stationed a couple of kilometres from them. There had been no serious incidents, but when the teenage rebels got high on drugs or drink, they could hear them rampaging about, shooting off their guns and looking for trouble. Sergio was afraid for his family. He had already decided that it was futile to return to the south, where the MPLA were advancing, and the track to the east was impossibly hard for little Alicia and Raymundo. He had taken a gamble on finding places on a boat across the Congo into Zaire, or a ship that was passing en route to some far away destination. So far, his gamble had been unsuccessful.

At six o' clock in the morning he walked into town to Port M'Pinda, as he had done every day. At the sight before him he started to run towards the dock. A small steamer was moored alongside, smoke coming from her funnels. She had obviously just arrived. A couple of men were carrying stores down the gangway. They were delivering foodstuffs to the town. A burly, scruffy-looking half-cast wearing a sweat-stained blue shirt and a captain's hat was yelling instructions to the crew. There were already more than a hundred refugees clamouring around the gangway, trying to buy or beg a passage in the vessel.

Sergio managed to push himself through the crowd until he was close enough to the captain. "Where you heading?" He shouted to the man.

"Brazil, Rio," he replied, not taking his eyes off the workers.

"When you casting off?"

He looked at his watch. "Soon as we finish unloading this lot and loading some other stuff. About seven."

"How much for a passage?"

"I've got ten already, there's no room for any more."

"I said, how much?"

This time the captain looked at him. The young man looked serious, and desperate.

"How many are you?"

"Just my wife, two small children and me. How much?"

The captain thought of a number, doubled it, then added some more. He quoted an outrageous price.

Sergio calculated quickly. He would still have about fifteen hundred dollars, plus the diamonds. There might not be another chance to get away.

"Can we have a cabin and food?"

Now the captain was taking him seriously. He could make some good money out of this idiot. "For five hundred dollars more, you can have my cabin. It's big enough for you and your family at a squeeze. In any case, it's all I've got to offer."

Sergio hesitated. That left him just over a thousand dollars, plus forty or fifty thousand in diamonds. They could get started in Rio in good shape. Elvira couldn't stay on that beach, sleeping in the back of the cramped truck with the children. She needed a proper bed and so did the kids. He took his decision.

"Here's half now. I'll be back in thirty minutes and pay you the rest."

Forty minutes later, Sergio and his family were piling the few clothes and possessions thay had fetched with them into the captain's small, smelly cabin. The man obviously smoked a pipe, since the walls were brown and everything stunk of nicotine. But they had a porthole to let in fresh air for Elvira and they had a bunk bed, which was more than the other poor passengers who were spread out on the deck, trying to create a little comfort for their long sea trip.

At seven fifteen, the five crew members cast off from the jetty and the ship headed out across the Atlantic towards Recife, over five thousand kilometres away, its first stop on the way to Rio de Janeiro.

FORTY-ONE

Tuesday, August 5th,1975
Geneva, Switzerland; Tangiers, Morocco

Angela was late. It was Tuesday and she should have arrived in Geneva on Monday. They were moving the diamonds from Malaga in batches. Laurent knew the risks, and had decided that it was better to lose one batch than to jeopardise everything if it went wrong. This was the seventh of ten trips. Angela had successfully made three and Lorenzo, her boy-friend, had made the others, also without any problems.

"Where was she going?" Charlie was trying to think logically, to make a plan.

"Morocco. She has three routes, all by ferry. Barcelona to Tangiers, Algeciras to Ceuta, and Almeria to Nador." Laurent had a small map from a ferry company. He showed the other two men the routes she might have taken. "It depends on the day of the week. She mixes it up, sometimes she travels the same route twice in a row, other times... Well, you get the point."

"So we don't actually know, specifically?"

"We don't. I doubt that she went via Barcelona, because she was up that way a couple of weeks ago. Ceuta has its problems because it's still part of Spain, but she knows one of the Customs guys there. Almeria is possible, but hell, I simply have no idea." The Frenchman looked worried. He had only three people who worked with him regularly and they were like family. In Angela's case, she *was* family, his favorite niece, the daughter of his wife's sister.

Laurent and his Spanish wife, Elena, had been married only two years and had no children. There were no close relatives on his side of the marriage, the French side, but in her family there was no shortage of young people to spoil. Angela was an example, she was the eldest child of one of Elena's sisters and they both loved her like a daughter. Although she looked several years younger, she was actually twenty-five and had been working for him for seven years, since the IOS days. She and Lorenzo made a great team, occasionally working together as a couple when it was more suitable to the job in hand. She lived with her parents in Antiquerra, up the road from Malaga. They knew about Angela's work and didn't disapprove. They could all do with the generous commissions that Laurent paid and there had never been a problem, until now.

"Where does she go from Morocco?"

"Either from Tangiers to Genoa by ferry, the Italian border is fairly soft. Or back over to Gibraltar. That's still UK, so she can fly to London and then back to Geneva. It sounds complicated, but it's actually a great route."

The men talked the matter over for a long while, but there was absolutely nothing they could do. They had no idea where the young woman was. They could only pray that she was safe and would turn up tomorrow, alive and unharmed.

Tangiers, Morocco

The only item in the abandoned house was a filthy rug, the one Angela was kneeling on. The house was falling to pieces in a slum area on the outskirts of Tangiers. The man who had kidnapped her was a *Pied-Noir,* a half cast, French and North African, wearing a faded tee shirt and jeans. Lank hair hanging over his neck, nicoteen stained teeth and a foul breath. *Probably Algerian,* she thought. He had brought her here in a beat-up old Citroen *deux chevaux*, on the back seat, wrapped in the rug.

She was furious with herself. On the ferry from Barcelona she thought she recognised him from her trip a couple of weeks before. He came up to her, asking if she wanted a lift when they arrived in Tangiers. She told him that she was meeting her boy-friend at the port but she knew he wasn't fooled by this. He had her figured for a *courrier*, carrying something out of Spain to some more hospitable place. The question was, what?

She didn't want to give him a chance to get close enough to find out. Getting off the boat she attempted to shake him off but he was smarter than she expected and came around the port building from the other side. She walked right into him. He had a pistol, so she didn't resist. Behind a wall in the car park he tied her hands, rolled her into the smelly rug then threw her onto the car seat and drove out to the house.

Now he was pulling her rucksack to pieces. *Probably looking for drugs*. People who took the ferries regularly, especially young people, were usually running drugs. The customs agents were often involved. It was a business, just like any other. He threw her papers and the few items of clothing aside. Then he pulled out the pouch and emptied the rough diamonds onto the floor.

"*Qu'est-ce que c'est cette merde*? What's this shit?" He didn't know what they were. "Is that all you're carrying?" He demanded in French.

The pouch contained only about twenty stones. The rest were packed with vaseline into the hollow, metal frame of the rucksack. Fortunately he hadn't figured that out.

"They're my beads from Africa. I'm going to make them into a necklace to sell. What did you expect? I'm just a student, I don't know what you want of me. Just let me go, I won't tell anyone." Her French wasn't perfect, but good enough.

"When I've finished with you, you won't be able to tell anyone anything, so shut your stupid mouth. What else do you have? Where's your money?"

"I've got no money. I'm broke."

He slapped her across the cheek so hard that she fell sideways onto the rug. "Everyone has money you lying bitch. Where is it?"

"It's here. In my jeans, on the belt."

The man unbuttoned her jeans and pulled down the zip. She had a belt on underneath with a small flat purse on it. He undid the belt and ripped it off her, counted the bills in the wallet. "Two hundred dollars! Where does a kid like you get that kind of money?" He slapped her across the face again.

"OK, don't hit me again, I'll tell you. I go with men. They pay me, I'm very good."

He looked at her lying on the rug and licked his lips. "*Putain!* Slut! Sit up!"

"I can't, you can see I can't. My hands are tied."

He grabbed her, manhandling her back to a kneeling position, and ripped off her blouse to reveal her small breasts, covered by a black bra. He kneeled beside her and pulled the bra off, stroking her breasts with his calloused fingers then pressed his mouth against hers. She almost fainted from the stench of his breath.

"Undo my hands. I can do things for you. You won't be sorry."

He sat back on his knees and thought for a moment. She couldn't lie on her back with her hands tied behind her. And she was no threat, she hardly weighed fifty kilos. In any case he was going to kill her soon. *One fuck and bang.* "OK. But no tricks or I'll break your neck." He undid her hands.

She rubbed her wrists. They were sore from the rope. "I'll let my hair down, it's too hot like this." Angela's long hair was done in a bun, fastened up with hair clips. She reached up and undid the clips. When she brought her hands down, she was pointing a small gun at him.

He looked at the gun. It was tiny. He laughed out loud, showing his yellow teeth. He reached out to grab it. "Stupid bitch."

It was an American Derringer Colt, just twelve centimetres long. It only fired two bullets. One was enough. She pulled the trigger. The man was staring at the gun, he couldn't believe his eyes. Suddenly a third eye appeared in the centre of his forehead. He fell onto the rug, dead.

Angela caught the ferry to Gibraltar, then flew to Geneva via Heathrow. She was two days late. On her remaining trips she was on time.

FORTY-TWO

Friday, August 15th, 1975
Geneva, Switzerland

Alberto arrived at Klein, Fellay's offices at 10:00 am and was shown into Miriam's conference room, where the others were waiting. After a friendly reunion, the four new partners held their first annual meeting of the Angolan Clan. Charlie chaired the proceedings, explaining their thinking on the long term, softly, softly approach to the business. Everyone agreed with the proposal. They were content to look forward to a continuing revenue stream from the diamonds for as long as it lasted.

The Englishman's partnership concept was equally cautious. "We don't want a regular company, with share certificates and all that corporate stuff. The problem there is that someone might be tempted, or forced, to sell his shares. Then we could find ourselves in bed with a partner whom we can't get along with and it could endanger the partnership.

"So I propose that we form an offshore company with registered shares and we restrict the transfer of shares. Just like an old-fashioned partnership agreement. That means that we can only sell our share back into the company, or pass it onto our nearest of kin or their spouses or descendents when we snuff it. It's also essential to keep quiet about the business. Nick is convinced that we'll be in big trouble if word gets around that we've got this massive stock of Angolan diamonds. I recommend that you don't even tell your nearest and dearest. I certainly don't intend to. We're entering into a long term partnership, so let's try to avoid any pain or risk down the road. If you all agree, then we just need to decide on the share split. OK?"

The other partners took heed of his advice and unanimously agreed to his proposals. No one wanted to endanger this opportunity. They then opened up the discussion on the partnership shares.

Laurent had readily accepted to work with them, to develop the market, using his financial contacts and building a distribution network. Alberto couldn't commit himself to any involvement but was modest in his attitude towards his share. It was finally settled at thirty percent each for Charlie and Nick, twenty-five for Laurent, and fifteen for Alberto.

The problem that took the most time to resolve, was the name to be given to the partnership. It was Nick who found the solution. He wrote down, Charlie, Laurent, Alberto and Nick. The initials spelled ***CLAN***. In deference to Henriques and Manuela, the partnership was to be called the ***ANGOLAN CLAN***.

Miriam opened the accounts for them with Klein, Fellay. One in the name of the partnership, operated by any two signatures, and one for each partner. They made the initial distribution transfers to each account, leaving Nick's hundred thousand dollars in the Angolan Clan account for operational requirements.

After the meeting, the four partners said goodbye and went their separate ways, for the time being. They had made a long term committment and they knew they would be seeing each other often in the future.

Alberto went back to Lisbon, but it was clear that he didn't intend to stay there much longer. The deaths of Olivier and the others had had a profound effect on him, and events in Angola had caused him to question his own convictions. In November he would finally be able to celebrate the independence of his country after five hundred years of occupation. Only to see thousands of

Cuban soldiers march in to replace the Portuguese. Was that a good solution? He knew it was not.

Nick decided that Switzerland was as good a base as any. He obtained a temporary residence permit and rented an apartment overlooking the *Jet d'Eau* in Geneva. He joined the Geneva Golf Club in Cologny, although he didn't get the chance to play as often as he would like. He took Miriam Constance out for dinner and they started going out together when he wasn't travelling about, managing the processing of the diamonds. He found out that Swiss woman were no different from South African or Australian women.

Laurent returned home to Monaco. To Elena and their friends at the Monte-Carlo Country Club. He had always found the golf course to be a great place to do business. He used his network of financial and banking contacts to move stones and funds around and start creating market opportunities.

Charlie stayed in Geneva for a few more days. It was a perfect place to set up the company and commercial structure. Ellen and Ronnie joined him at the Majestic when he returned the following weekend and he transferred funds from his account at Klein, Fellay to the Banco de Malaga. Within a month they had found a lovely old hacienda in Mijas village. They moved in in October 1975, just in time for her birthday.

FORTY-THREE

Friday, August 15th, 1975
Rio de Janeiro, Brazil

The rent on the one bedroomed flat in Rio de Janeiro was one hundred dollars a month plus another hundred deposit. The ship had been met by traders and conmen of all description, trying to squeeze some money out of the ragged band of refugees who came down the gangway. One of them had a small apartment for rent on Rue Nascimento, behind the Copocabana beach, and Sergio quickly snapped it up. After stocking up on provisions and household requirements for the family he had almost eight hundred dollars left. He also had the diamonds. The pouch had remained hidden and intact during their whole trip, carefully folded each day into Raymundo's nappy.

The voyage across the Atlantic had been relatively uneventful. The captain turned out to be a man of his word and left the family in his cabin in peace. Sergio realised that he'd paid through the nose when he heard how much the other passengers had been charged. But he reasoned that it was worth the money for his family to be safe and fairly comfortable in the cabin. There had been many arguments and fights amongst the refugees on deck and one man had been lost overboard in the night. Only the captain's quick and decisive action had prevented things from descending into all out war.

Although he had enough cash left for two or three months, Sergio needed to sell one of the diamonds. Elvira's condition hadn't improved. She was constantly wheezing and the effort of gasping a little air into her lungs was taking all her energy. Pale and skinny, she had no appetite and not enough strength to look after the children. He had to look after his whole family so he couldn't even go out to try to find work. He had called a local doctor, at a cost of ten dollars, who gave Elvira a quick examination and told her that she should go into hospital for proper rest and treatment. But they had no insurance, and hospitals cost money. He needed to get some cash for their comfort and security and for the hospital. It couldn't wait.

He walked along Calle Almanteja, a street where there were several gem dealers, until he came to a store with a name that he thought looked Portuguese. He knew nothing about Brazilians and he didn't trust what he didn't know. The store owner was Sr. Ferreiro, a short fat man with a bald head, about fifty, who smoked cigarillos and confirmed that he was from Coimbra. He and his wife had emigrated from Portugal fifteen years before and he had been in business for five years, buying and selling diamonds and other gems.

Sergio had taken one diamond, which he showed to the man after he'd talked with him for ten minutes and felt that he was an honest dealer.

Ferreiro whistled through his teeth when he looked at the one carat stone through his lens. "Angolan, eh. Have you got more of these?" He asked.

"Depends. How much is it worth?" Sergio countered.

"I could go to three thousand dollars."

"I could go to some other dealer."

"OK. Three thousand three hundred a carat. I have to make a living too. What'd you say?"

Sergio knew that Ferreiro was right. His brother, Henriques, had quoted four or five thousand, but that was a top price in a quality market, not a shitty little corner of Rio. Also, he was used to selling rough diamonds at four hundred dollars. This was almost ten times that price, he wouldn't get more. He agreed.

"I don't have that much cash here," the dealer said. I'll have to go to the bank this afternoon. Keep the stone and I'll come by your place tonight and we'll do the swap then. OK?"

Sergio was relieved. He could pay for Elvira's hospital treatment and look after his family for a year with that much money. Ten years of security from all ten stones, enough to set up a business and make a living in this new country. He blessed his brother's foresight in leaving him the diamonds. He gave Ferreiro the address and went home to share the good news with his wife.

The doorbell rang at seven thirty. Alicia and Raymundo were already in bed and Elvira was sitting with them. Sergio didn't want her disturbed by the transaction. The single diamond was in his pocket, the others hidden in a trunk in a closet in the bedroom.

He opened the door and was surprised not to see Ferreiro. The man who stood there was huge, almost two metres tall. A massive body topped by a surprisingly small head, covered with long, lank, blonde hair.

"Sr. d'Almeida?" he asked. His voice was high, almost a falsetto, totally out of character with his physique. His Portuguese was guttural and accented.

Sergio felt uneasy. He didn't like the look of this man. "What is it?"

"You have some merchandise for a friend of mine."

"You mean Sr, Ferreiro?"

"That's right. I'm his collection agent."

"Do you have the money?"

"Where's the stones?"

When he heard, *stones,* plural, Sergio's eyes flickered towards the bedroom where the diamonds were hidden. That was enough for the stranger. He pushed Sergio aside and opened the bedroom door. Elvira was sitting by the bed. The two children were fast asleep. She swung around, alarmed at the intrusion.

"Get out of my wife's bedroom, she's not well and you're frightening her. Where's the cash?"

He tried to pull the man away. The blonde giant turned and hit him across the face with an enormous backhand and he fell to the floor, his nose broken, blood running down his chin. He scrabbled around trying to find his spectacles. Elvira screamed and ran to help him. The children awoke and started crying, alarmed by the noise.

"There'll be no cash. Just give me the diamonds and I'll leave you alive. Otherwise it could turn out very nasty. For you and your family" The stranger pulled out a folding knife from his belt. He slowly opened it up. It had a long, thin stiletto blade.

Fifteen minutes later the blonde man left the apartment, all ten diamonds in his possession. Sergio was lying on the floor of the living room, three ribs cracked and his nose and two fingers broken. Even when the man had kicked her husband in the side and stamped on his fingers for the third time, Elvira had managed to stay quiet about the diamonds, for the sake of her children's future. But when he took Sergio's hand, raised the knife and threatened to cut off his fingers one by one, she hadn't been able to stand any more. She begged him to stop and brought out the diamonds, even finding the last one in Sergio's pocket. Their fortune was lost. It was the price she had to pay to save her husband's life.

Sergio scrabbled around on the floor and found his spectacles. He straightened out the plastic frame. Only one of the lenses was cracked. Ignoring the pain that racked his body, he helped Elvira up to lay alongside his frightened children on the bed. She was wheezing badly from a panic attack.

He sat on the side of the bed, dabbing the blood from his face. The diamonds were gone, he was hurt, Elvira was sick and he had less than eight hundred dollars to support his family. His head drooped as he reflected on his predicament. *Where the hell is Henriques? What would he do now?* He asked himself.

FORTY-FOUR

November - December 1975
Luanda, Angola; Lisbon, Portugal

After Mozambique's independence in June, the Marxist-led *FRELIMO* took over the government, plunging the country into seventeen years of civil war. Immediately after the declaration a bloody government clampdown left thousands of Portuguese and Mozambique civilians dead in the streets of Lourenco Marques. The first action of Samora Machel, the new President, was to execute all five of his political opponents, including Joana Simeão. During the civil war, over a million Mozambicans perished and almost two million left their country, never to return. Carlos Souza Machado was not the only loyal citizen to be fooled by the Marxists, nor to sacrifice his life for his country.

On November 11th Angola gained its independence. Over half a million Portuguese and Angolan citizens had aready fled from the civil war that was engulfing the country. Thousands of Cubans were shipped in during the week before independence and many Soviet officers arrived on November 12th. Luanda, Malanje and Cabinda were swiftly taken by the *MPLA* and in January, 1976, backed by Cuban forces, they defeated the *FNLA* and captured Ambrizete, extending their control from Luanda to the north west border with Zaîre. As foretold by Henriques, the rebels grabbed control of all mining operations in the country to finance their armies. Angolan diamond production ceased overnight.

South Africa and the other western nations withdrew their troops within a year and the *FNLA* crumbled, leaving only the *MPLA* and *UNITA*, the remaining moderate rebel movement, to fight each other and continue the destruction of the country. The twenty-seven year civil war became the longest, bloodiest war in recent African history and one of the great Cold War conflicts, a bloody reminder of the political divide between Russia and the USA.

In December, a moderate government under Colonel António dos Santos Ramalho Eanes took back control of Portugal. A state of emergency was declared, *COPCON* was disbanded and two hundred extreme left-wing military were arrested. Major Otelo Saraiva de Carvalho, the hero of the Portuguese Revolution, was stripped of his position and a new Democratic Voting System was inaugurated. The communists were ousted from power.

What had been foreseen by Charlie and his friends many months before finally became clear for the rest of the world to see. Why Álvaro Cunhal had been rescued after eleven years in a Portuguse prison and taken to Russia. Why he was so valuable to the Marxist regime that they had looked after him for another fourteen years in Moscow and Prague before bringing him back again to his homeland.

Cunhal had succeeded in doing what no one had done in recent history. What the power and might of the Russian State had tried and failed to do for so many years. He had, almost single handed, converted a right-wing, capitalist controlled European country into a Marxist state. In less than a year, he had subverted the military leaders into appointing a communist government whose first actions were to destroy the capitalist system in Portugal. And although this situation lasted for only a year, it was a long enough time to achieve the objective.

And that objective, the strategy behind this apparently senseless and short term change of power now became apparent. A strategy born of many years of planning and preparation between Cunhal and his masters in Russia, from his escape in 1960, until his return in 1974. The Russians knew that even if they lost control of Portugal, there was a bigger prize to be won. Africa! They had fomented dissatisfaction in the army by financing increased guerilla activity in the colonies long before the death of Salazar in 1968, in the hopes of instigating a sea change. Then, when the change came, they hijacked the Revolution of the Carnations as a means of destabilising and radicalising the country and pushing it towards Marxism. This rape of Portugal had been executed to win a fabulous prize. To take possession of Angola and Mozambique.

This was the strategy that Cunhal and the Russians had planned for so long. This was why they had financed the murder of thousands of innocent young soldiers in Africa. Why they had nurtured the revolution in the minds of the many unhappy elements in the army. This was what Cunhal had somehow managed to orchestrate over the long, almost thirty year period, while he was in prison in Portugal and then exiled from the country. Álvaro Cunhal was not just a Portuguese communist. He *was* Portuguese Communism.

At New Year, Nick came down to Mijas and they made a toast, both to the past and their old, lost friends, and to the future and their newly found friends. 1976 was the beginning of a new life. For those of them who had survived 1975.

FORTY-FIVE

April 25th, 1976
Geneva, Switzerland

Before the four partners returned home, they had agreed to hold a meeting of the Angolan Clan each year. Somewhat nostalgically, they chose to meet on the anniversary of the Revolution of the Carnations, the 25th of April, at ten in the morning in Geneva.

Their first meeting was in Miriam's conference room at Klein, Fellay. Charlie hadn't released any financial information, so there was an air of expectation in the room.

The Englishman, looking fit, tanned and relaxed, opened up the proceedings.

"Welcome to the first annual meeting of the Angolan Clan. It's great to see everyone here. First of all, Nick will give us a report on the diamond production."

"I'll keep this short and it's not a monologue, so if you have any questions, just fire away." The South African took up a hard-backed ledger and consulted the pages as he spoke. "The exact count of rough diamonds that we started with was seven thousand one hundred and ten stones, with a total weight of just over twenty-two thousand carats. So we actually had more than the number of stones and weight that we expected.

"Since last November we have gone through a baptism of fire. I won't bore you with the many problems and disappointments along the way. But thanks to Laurent and Charlie and a lot of lateral thinking, we have created a viable business model. We've moved our rough diamonds up the food chain, by processing them and marketing them successfully. We've actually proved that we can do what we set out to do.

"The first good news is that by going slowly and low profile we've cut and polished exactly one hundred and twenty stones, with a rough weight of three hundred and seventy carats. We processed them in New York and Montreal and we've forged a great relationship with the companies involved. So we have the cutting and polishing operations sorted.

"The next good surprise is that the average loss on converting the rough stones to finished gems is less than we expected, at slightly below fifty percent. Henriques chose well shaped stones which are easier to work with than I had feared. These African diamonds are very hard, so you can get some surprises, but so far our net weight is more than half of the rough weight.

"We split these hundred and twenty stones into one hundred and sixty-five finished gems, with a net weight of one hundred and ninety carats. The stones are in a good commercial range of sizes for pricing; half a carat to two carats, average weight just over one carat. Not small enough to be rubbish and not large enough to raise any eyebrows.

"Let's have a look at what we're talking about here." Nick pulled out a small pouch from his case, it was actually one of Henriques's original pouches. He tipped the contents onto the table. Five magnificent diamonds spilled out, sparkling in the light from the overhead lamps. Each stone was about two carats in size. He moved them with his fingertips and they shimmered and reflected the light, like clear drops of spring water. The stones were brilliant cut, the multiple facets catching and reflecting the light from every angle.

He handed the stones to Alberto. "These are the pick of the crop. I would qualify the clarity as pure. If you look at them through the lens, you'll see no inclusions - that's imperfections. In these stones there aren't any. The colour is finest white, the best there is. The cut is also ideal. The rough stones were of just the right shape to obtain perfect proportions in the finished article. From the first hundred rough stones we produced fifteen of this size and quality. Laurent sold ten of them and I kept the remaining five back to show you. The other hundred and fifty stones are excellent gems, but of slightly lesser quality, in colour and cut."

He took another pouch out of his case and sprinkled a number of smaller stones onto the table. "These are some of the gems of lesser purity, but you need a lens to see that. They're beautiful stones for high quality jewellery."

Alberto passed the large diamonds to Laurent who sprinkled them from hand to hand, like a miniature waterfall. Alberto did the same with the smaller stones. "They all look the same to me, absolutely perfect."

Nick nodded in agreement. "That's right. All our diamonds are highly saleable. Some at excellent prices and the rest at reasonable prices. I can't promise that they'll all be the same but I'd be surprised if they're not."

He turned to Charlie. "Your turn to knock them out."

Charlie got up, notebook in hand. "While I've sat around doing nothing and Nick's been producing these fabulous stones, Laurent's been travelling the world and spreading the gospel, to great effect. First, he placed a few stones into Sotheby's and Christies' sales in London, Geneva and New York. We got decent prices, with no disruption in the market and with no publicity. Now he's got several private dealers taking stones as well. So far, we've sold one hundred and forty gems with a total weight of one hundred fifty carats.

"We set up a Geneva trading company to do this business. To run the paperwork, buy in the diamonds and sell them legitimately to the ultimate customers. It's called *International Diamond Dealers SA. - IDD.* A bit corny, but at least it's clear what we do. We have a small office just around the corner, near the railway station, with a secretary and an accountant. He's a French Swiss, called Rolf Besson. A clever, hard-working man and also very discreet.

"The diamonds are brought into view by *Angolan Clan Ltd,* an offshore outfit we registered in the British Virgin Islands. When we bring stones from the vault to process and market, we sell them from the BVI company to IDD. Then they become documented and legitimate. The accounting requirements in the BVI are fairly non-existent, so there isn't any scrutiny on where the diamonds came from, where they're going, or what pricing policy we implement. We opened an account for IDD with the Banque de Commerce, near the office, and we simply use the Angolan Clan account here at Klein, Fellay, for the BVI company.

"We can't provide any certification of the origin of the gems and we don't want any visibility, so we're selling at a big discount to the market. On the other hand, our tax liability is minimal, because between BVI and Switzerland we match the pricing with only a nominal profit for IDD. This keeps us in good shape with the Swiss, because we cover our costs and make a small profit and the BVI doesn't care what we do. Unless something changes to convince us otherwise, we'll continue with this formula. It works so we won't fix it.

"What we've managed to do is to bring the stones from nowhere, through the BVI company and into the Swiss company, so that we can process, present and commercialise them internationally, with the proper paperwork and a very low tax exposure. It's about as efficient as you can get without trying to be too clever."

He looked at his notebook again. "The current top market price is around five thousand dollars per carat for this quality. Our average sales price was about sixty-five per cent of this marker, at three thousand two hundred dollars per carat. So the hundred and fifty carats sold by Laurent produced a total revenue of four hundred and eighty thousand dollars in six months.

"Our processing costs, office and operating expenses and sales commissions were about a hundred and sixty grand. So in cash terms we have an actual operating profit today of three hundred and twenty thousand dollars. Then there's the value of the finished stock, less the selling costs, which is about a hundred grand, net. That makes a profit to date of over four hundred and twenty thousand dollars, from just one hundred and twenty rough stones. And we still have about seven thousand of them in the vault.

"I won't bullshit you about the future, but this means that we are way ahead of the rough diamond prices that Henriques used to get. If we can keep this up, selling two to three hundred stones a year at these prices, we can make a lot of money over the next few years."

Nobody spoke for several moments, then Alberto started to clap his hands and continued until the others had joined in.

"That's enough guys. This is a three man team," Charlie responded.

"What are the chances of a fall in prices?" Alberto asked.

"I suppose it's possible, but it seems highly unlikely for a few reasons. First, prices are actually as low as they've ever been in recent years. Most analysts consider that an increase in value is more likely than a fall. The market has already started to move slightly up during the last couple of months.

"Second, the war has virtually stopped the output from Angola. Henriques, God rest his soul, was right. The mines have been taken over by the rebels and official production has halted. They'll mine and sell what they can to finance their war, but there is no more official Angolan diamond production. This probably explains the upward movement that is occurring.

"Third, our stones are the best African diamonds now available. As long as we don't screw it up we could actually benefit from this situation."

The mood in the conference room was ebullient. After the horrors of Portugal and Angola, they couldn't believe their good fortune.

Charlie continued. "You'll remember that we left a hundred thousand dollars in the Angolan Clan account. Well, I've made a few transactions with companies that I know well, and we've managed to make a profit of thirty thousand dollars. So, after Nick's net revenues, plus these profits, plus the original float of a hundred thousand grand, we're sitting with about four hundred and fifty thousand dollars in the account. The Angolan Clan is in good shape.

"Now," he finished, "we haven't talked about dividend distributions, so why don't we agree on that, then go to the Hotel des Bergues for lunch?"

They agreed on an annual distribution of eighty percent of the cash profits from the diamond operations and investments and twenty percent retained in the partnership account for operations, emergencies and investment. The four partners would share a first dividend of over a quarter of a million dollars. As long as no one wanted to buy a yacht, they'd get by.

They had an excellent lunch. Laurent ordered a Chateau Cheval Blanc from St. Emilion and they raised their glasses to the success of the Angolan Clan. The Bordeaux wine was delicious, full bodied and fruity.

FORTY-SIX

April 25th, 2007
Geneva, Switzerland

The Angolan Clan had been in business now for over thirty years and was still going strong. The partners were once again seated around a conference table in Klein, Fellay's offices, which had moved about ten years before to the area of Plainpalais, on the other side of the lake, where several banks had built new headquarters. Miriam Constance was no longer there. After years of waiting vainly for Nick to make a commitment, she had married an Italian client and moved to Lake Como.

Although it was still a private investment bank, Klein, Fellay had now been taken over by a multinational clearing bank which operated in most countries of the world. International business could be transacted on a twenty-four hour basis, virtually seven days a week. Charlie found this useful in his investment dealings. He had set up an Internet banking system with the bank. It was highly secure and extremely functional.

Laurent had lost his wife the previous year and they had never had children, but he kept himself busy and in good shape, either on the ski slopes or the tennis courts of the Monte-Carlo Country Club. He continued to manage the sales activities for the partnership and maintained contact with Nick and Charlie via his indispensable BlackBerry.

With his first dividend in 1976, Alberto had bought a house in Chelsea. After the Communist Party was defeated in the democratic national elections his job in Portugal was over. Cunhal no longer needed a bodyguard. He had confided to Charlie that he was totally disillusioned with the way the Soviets were raping the ex-Portuguese African colonies. He was an idealist, a believer in and a fighter for improvement. After seeing so many years of bloodshed he couldn't stomach it any longer.

He told him, "The only difference from before is that the people getting killed are no longer Portuguese soldiers, they're Angolan and Mozambique civilians. We haven't fixed anything, we've made it worse. I wish Olivier was still alive, so I could tell him he was right all the time. I'm fifty-six now, and thanks to you, Inês and I can afford to spend our remaining years in a place of our choice and we've chosen London. Come and visit us when you can."

With the passage of the years, his health deteriorated and his leg gave him more and more trouble. He was obliged to walk with a stick, which he hated. He predeceased his wife by just a few months in the millennium year, 2000. He was eighty years old.

His son, Raffael, had replaced him in the partnership in accordance with their agreement. He had left London after the death of his parents and now lived in the US. Unlike his father, whose contribution had been vital to the existence of the Angolan Clan, he didn't actually do anything and never contacted the others. He just arrived at the annual meetings and happily accepted his dividends. The other partners didn't know much about Raffael. He had secrets that he didn't disclose to them and although they found his manners rather unsavoury, they never forgot the debt they owed to Alberto, the reward for which had been agreed many years before.

Nick now lived in South Beach, Miami, with the latest of several attractive, younger women. But even after all this time he'd never been able to get Rachel out of his mind. A few years before, he had enlisted the help of a private detective to find out what had happened to her. He needed to know how she was, where she was, what she was doing, who she was with.

When he examined and analysed the information he got back, he came to a breathtaking conclusion. He didn't know how to cope with this revelation, but as a first step he asked Laurent to open up business with a promising young gem and bullion specialist who traded out of Durban, South Africa.

Charlie was fit and well. Despite losing Ellen in dreadful circumstances several years before, he was still living in their home in Marbella. He had been comforted in his loss by Leticia, a lovely Angolan-Portuguese girl who had started working for them as a housekeeper. They had a one year old son called Emilio Salvador but only Leticia's parents and Charlie's lawyer knew of this fact. He was not one to bare his soul to the world at his time of life.

Not even his son, Ron, knew about his half-brother and Charlie was biding his time for the right moment to disclose it to them both. The same thing went for the Angolan Clan. Ron had never been able to understand the secrecy that he maintained around the source of his wealth. As a result, their relationship had broken down many years ago. He had gone to live in England and each year Charlie found it more difficult to pull down the barriers that he had erected to protect his family and friends but which had only served to alienate them over time.

Nick got up to make his diamond report. He kept it very short. "Our policy has always been to only process the number of stones we planned to sell in each year. On average we have produced three hundred finished stones with a weight of just over three hundred carats. We've always sold them at good prices, with no fuss or visibility – a very profitable, low profile business. Our annual revenues have risen to four million dollars, with average profits over seventy percent, so we've had a good run for our money.

"This year," he continued, "we have decided to process all the remaining stones. The first lot is already with the processing company in Brazil that we've been working with for the last few years. I expect to get all of them finished within six months. Charlie will explain the reasons for our change of thinking to you now." He sat down again, looking a little weary.

Charlie thanked Nick and Laurent for their contribution to the many years of success. The diamond market had been good to them. Nick's *"Oh my God. I have to have that"* approach had been more successful than they could have foreseen.

He distributed a set of accounts and outlined the results from sales and from his management of the partnership funds for 2006. The balance on the Angolan Clan account had increased with every passing year. They were all very wealthy men.

"Now I have a couple of important points," he continued. "The first is that Rolf Besson, our accountant, is retiring after thirty-two years. He's sixty-nine. Even older than me! I suggest we give him a handsome farewell bonus for his retirement. We've hired a replacement on a consulting agreement, name of Kurt Vogel. He's a Swiss German. Not much personality but lots of experience. He's already started part time, to take over from Rolf next month. And Gloria Smouha, our secretary, is still with us after almost twenty years, so we're in good shape.

"Now I'll explain why we're processing our remaining stock of rough diamonds." Charlie paused, weighing his words. "First, it's my belief that we are heading towards the end of another economic cycle. I think the next year is going to show up some serious defects in the financial markets. The world has been living on a credit binge for the last decade and it's going to go bust sooner or later. Probably sooner, in my opinion.

"We have lived through previous recessions and we got out in good shape because we were well diversified, as we are at the moment. However, this time, everything is pointing to a general fall in values. In the markets, in property and in commodity prices. I've therefore asked Nick to finish our diamond processing so that we'll have a stock of completely finished diamonds, ready to market, by the end of the year.

"Then we either continue with our distribution channels over the next few years until we liquidate our stock, or we find a buyer for the whole stock. Personally, I favour the latter, for several reasons.

"The first reason is simple economics. If we go into a recession and the shit really hits the fan it will affect our pricing. Diamond prices have increased by about four hundred per cent since the Angolan Clan was formed, so our decision to sell little and slowly has been vindicated. But I think it's time to change that policy to avoid being caught in a falling market.

"The second reason isn't commercial, it has to do with world opinion. We're very fortunate that IDD has never been accused of selling conflict diamonds and become tabloid fodder. The world press has been red-hot on this since the atrocities in Sierra Leone, Liberia and Congo. We've remained under the radar because we operate through BVI and Switzerland and we don't make a noise in the market. Thanks to Nick and Laurent, our processing, sales and distribution are out of the limelight.

"But now that the Kimberley Process has been globally accepted, it's becoming more difficult to sell uncertified diamonds. Our stones are not conflict, or blood diamonds, but we can't prove it and we don't want to be accused of it. It's too risky to continue like this for much longer. It's time to get out of the business while we still have a good reputation.

"Laurent and I have talked about this and he feels that we can find a buyer for the remaining stones in a single lot. It should be about a thousand stones and Nick expects to have them ready by the end of the year." He looked at Nick, who nodded his confirmation. "This will be one last confidential transaction, low profile, as always and we'll be out of the game. So, I propose that we pursue that course. We'll still sell our usual number of stones to our regular customers, but if we can sell the balance of the stones by the end of this year then we think we'll still hit top market prices and we'll be safe from any future controversy. If we wait, we take a substantial downside risk."

"The last reason is a very personal one." Charlie looked around the table at his partners, old and new. "The Angolan Clan has existed for thirty years and I think that we all agree that it has been successful beyond our wildest dreams. However, we are not getting any younger. In fact some of us are getting really old." He paused for the inevitable laughter. "Some of you don't have direct descendents to pass your share on to and it would be unfair if anything happened to you and you lost that share.

"For all these reasons, I propose that we should cash in all of our assets and have a last meeting next April to transfer all funds to the partners and close down the Angolan Clan. We can then go off to our retirement projects with a chunk of cash to survive on.

"Of course," he added, "nothing prevents us from meeting every year just to enjoy a good lunch together."

As usual, Charlie's logical thinking and foresight convinced his partners to follow his advice. The four men agreed to close down the Angolan Clan in April 2008.

BOOK TWO

PART THREE: 2008

FORTY-SEVEN

Thursday, April 17th, 2008
Marbella, Spain

It was after eleven in the morning when Jenny and Leticia finished reading Charlie's narrative. He had written in a diary style. Dates, people, places and a short summary of the events. But despite the factual and understated manner in which his text was written and presented, they were mentally and emotionally drained by the mass of information that he had revealed. Reading between the lines, they had lived with him through the dramatic and complicated history of the Portuguse revolution, the harrowing consequences of the relinquishing of its African colonies and his life over the last thirty-two years.

At the end of the text, Charlie had added another teaser. It was dated February 27th, 2008.

> *"Jenny, Leticia,*
> *You have got this far. Well done.*
> *Leticia has a key in her possession. It is for safety deposit box no. 328 at the Banco de Iberia in Marbella. Just follow the trail and take care.*

Good luck and love to you both.
Charlie."

They sat quietly for a moment, trying to assimilate his life story and the events he had experienced. Jenny couldn't believe that Ron's father, a wealthy, apparently unadventurous man who didn't seem to care much about anyone, had lived through such chaos and mayhem and been close to so many people in Portugal and Africa. And he had managed to get out. Not just alive, but having amassed a substantial fortune in the process. For himself and for the friends who had emerged unscathed with him.

She tried vainly not to be influenced by her memories of her own father and after a while, she said, "So Charlie's fortune was built on death and diamonds. Maybe that's why Ron moved away from home. He must have found out and he didn't like it. I think I'm beginning to see what happened and I would probably have agreed with him. "

Leticia shook her head, "No, I don't think it was like that. I'm sure if my parents had a chance to leave Angola with money they would take it. You don't know what it was like to escape with nothing and have to start again. Charlie and his friends were not responsible for those deaths. Not for the revolution, not for the wars. They had a good business and it was taken from them, like everybody in Portugal and Africa. What happened was crazy politics, communism and wars and they weren't responsible. They were victims like my family, but they were clever enough to get out with the diamonds and then to make a marvellous success."

She took Jenny's hand. "Ellen was right. It would be stupid to leave that fortune to be stolen by somebody. Henriques gave it to them and they were supposed to make the business together. I think Charlie was right to set up the Angolan Clan. The others would have done the same but maybe not so well. We have to think of the good things that Charlie did. Trying to save his friends and family and looking after Nick and Alberto. He was the only one who could get it done and he did it. I think Ron would understand if he read the story. His father was a good man, an honest man. Not a thief or a murderer. We should be proud of him."

"Hmm. Perhaps." Jenny wasn't convinced. She didn't trust anything to do with large amounts of money. But she didn't want to shake Leticia's faith in Charlie. He had been her lover and was Emilio's father, so she had to tread carefully. "Maybe Ron didn't understand because he didn't know the full story. He must have been ashamed of his father and now it's too late to explain it to him. Perhaps I was being naïve and Charlie and his friends were heroes, not villains. Anyway, I hope Emilio is proud of him when he learns this history."

Whatever the truth behind his fortune, Jenny began to understand why Charlie had become so unsociable. *He probably wasn't always like that,* she thought. He'd lost so many of his friends, then his family. He was getting old and lonely. *Thank God he met Leticia,* she concluded. *She and Emilio were probably the only reasons he still had to enjoy life.*

She was also shocked again that she had known so little of the history of Portugal's brief, but bloody flirtation with communism. Even Leticia, who knew a little of the history, was amazed. She explained parts of the story to her mother, who responded in voluble Portuguese.

Leticia translated for her. "My mother says this part of Portugal history is full of shame. Nobody wants to remember. She says the Portuguese government made a.. What is *decreto*?"

"Decree?"

"Yes, they made a decree to say this period was not legal. Afterwards they gave back all businesses and properties to the owners. But all fortunes were lost, all companies were bankrupt. It's a very bad history for Portugal. Not so bad as Angola, but very bad."

"And Charlie was part of that history. Ellen too. But she never mentioned a word of any of it when we were together."

"And he never told me any of it either. In five years he never said anything to me about Portugal. I'll keep the story for Emilio to read when he grows up and learns English."

Leticia took up the last page of the history and re-read the note from Charlie. "I think Charlie wants us to finish his work," she said. "What do you think we should do now?"

Jenny wasn't happy about this turn of events. Clearly, Charlie expected them to finish what he had started but again it meant more complications in her life that she didn't need or want. More unknown things to fear. Vague worries about motives for Ron's and Charlie's accidents were tugging at her subconscious, but she pushed them away.

"Don't you think we should just let sleeping dogs lie?" she replied.

"Charlie gave me that key to keep for a reason, Jenny. We can't just ignore his wishes, can we?"

Reluctantly, Jenny replied, "I suppose you're right. We'll have to go to the Banco de Iberia in Marbella to see what's in box number 328."

Leticia checked her watch. "We could go now. The banks are open until half past two."

"Very well. In any case, we'll have to meet the person who looks after our account. I'll ask José Luis to arrange a meeting for us."

The older lawyer was busy, but Francisco answered. "I'll give Patrice a call now, he's a good friend of mine. I'm sure he'll receive you. I'll call you right back."

Encarni was back at the house with Emilio. He was playing in the pool. The police had removed their plastic tape that morning, leaving Juan to spend two happy hours pushing around the vacuum cleaner and checking the water purity. It was as pristine as ever.

By the time they were ready to go, Francisco called back. "Patrice can meet you right away. Ask for Patrice de Moncrieff, he's a client manager for Andalucia. He's actually French but he's been down here in Marbella for the last year. Patrice is a great guy, you'll like him.

"By the way," he continued, "I spoke to the Chief Inspector and we can hold the funeral on Monday morning. The church secretary proposed eleven thirty, if that's alright with you?"

Jenny agreed and thanked him. She was happy to let the lawyers take care of the arrangements. She was still thinking about Charlie's note. What was in that safety deposit box? There was something else she didn't know and she didn't like not knowing.

On the way to the bank they stopped off at Leticia's parents' home. The fifth floor apartment was surprisingly large. Soft light flooded into the living room from the south facing windows which looked out towards Marbella harbour. Emilio's bedroom was furnished with colourfully painted furniture and a crotcheted quilt covered the bed. Family photographs and a few childish drawings stood on a dresser. Some of his clothes lay on the bedspread, tiny sizes. Looking at them, Jenny felt a momentary pang of sadness.

Standing on a chair, Leticia reached up to retrieve the key from the top hem of the curtain where she had hidden it several months before. "Here it is. Time to go and look in that box."

They drove down to the car park behind the *Parque de Alameda* and walked along to the bank. By now it was almost two, and shops and offices were starting to close, the streets busy with people going off to enjoy their lunch and their afternoon siesta.

Patrice de Moncrieff strode across the banking hall to introduce himself. After greeting Jenny, he shook hands with Leticia and said, "You probably don't remember, but we've met before. At Mr. Bishop's house last year. You were kind enough to look after us when we were sitting talking on the terrace."

"*Si Si. Seguro.* It was after Charlie was sick. How are you, Patrice?"

"I'm fine and it's a pleasure to see you again, although I'm very sorry about the dreadful circumstances" The man gave her a sympathetic smile. She appreciated this small sign of friendliness, nervous in her new role as an important client of the bank. Jenny watched her reaction with interest.

"My office is up on the first floor. We can use the stairs, no need to take the elevator." His English was perfect, but with a noticeable French accent. Jenny suspected that he put it on a little. *He speaks English a bit too well to need that accent.*

Once installed in the large corner room, Jenny appraised the man sitting opposite them. Patrice was dressed in a dapper, light-blue suit made of a linen material, slightly creased. A darker blue handkerchief poked out of the breast pocket. His blue striped shirt also had a slightly wrinkled look. A button-down collar and a wide, light blue tie finished off the sartorial display. His dark hair was swept back with gel, leaving a wave falling down over his brow. *It must have cost him a lot of money to look sloppy. French couture, in Marbella,* she thought. *Spanish bankers must be well paid.*

Patrice said, "I must tell you how much I liked and admired your father-in-law, Jenny. We had a good rapport. He was a clever man. A very good nose for business and investing."

Neither of the women wanted to dwell on Charlie's demise, so Leticia asked, "Francisco told us that you only came here a year ago. Did you come from France?"

"Not at all. I was originally hired by the BIP in South America, in Sãu Paulo, actually. Then they transferred me to Geneva and because of my Spanish I was transferred again to Madrid when they bought the Banco de Iberia a few years ago."

"The BIP? Is that a very big bank?" Jenny had never heard of them.

"The *Banque International de Paris.* It's one of the biggest international banks. We have branches all over the world."

"And they sent you from Madrid to Marbella! You must miss the life in the capital."

"On the contrary! I asked to be transferred down to Andalucia. I don't like big cities. I love the outdoor life in Southern Spain. It suits me perfectly. And I have clients in other countries, especially in South America, so I spend quite a lot of time travelling."

The lawyers had obviously advised him of the terms of the will, since he discussed Charlie's accounts and produced various documents for their signature. Title could only be transferred when the estate was settled but he confirmed everything José Luis had told them.

When Jenny saw him glance at his wrist watch, she asked about the safety deposit box.

"If you have the key, you can open it now," he replied. "We don't need any documentation for that."

Leticia showed it to him. "It's box number 328."

"Fine. Let me call Señora Lopez, she's in charge of the safety deposit vault. We close at two thirty, so I'll just make sure she stays." He spoke quickly in Spanish then put the phone down. "She'll meet us down at the vaults on the lower ground floor. Follow me."

At the door to the vaults he introduced them to a young woman, shook hands with them both and gave Leticia his card, assuring them that he was at their disposition whenever needed.

As he turned to go, he added, "Would you mind if I came to

the funeral to pay my respects?"

At their acceptance, he thanked them and loped athletically back up the stairs.

Sra. Lopez was a tall, willowy blonde. She was dressed like a would-be model and glanced admiringly at Leticia's classic features and careless grace as she signed the visitor's register. She opened up the massive door that led the way into the vault. It was decorated with a mural of soft Andalucian landscapes painted in muted tones, which ran around the walls above the banks of safety deposit boxes. In the centre of the marble floor was a multi-coloured motif in polished tile, with a long, old fashioned table standing over it and eight leather-backed armchairs around.

Their box was in the corner of the room, a small-sized door in the middle row of boxes. Sra. Lopez inserted the bank's key and Leticia did the same with hers. The lock release clicked and the door opened, revealing the metal box.

"Do you know the procedure?"

Leticia nodded, "*Si. Gracias, Señora.*"

The woman left them and Leticia placed the box on the table. She opened the lid.

Jenny breathed a sigh of relief. There was nothing inside but a brown A4 envelope containing a single sheet of paper. She held it up so that they could read it together. It was written in Charlie's hand and dated February 20th, 2008.

> *Dear Jenny, Leticia.*
> *Your next stop is Klein Fellay SA, Geneva. Safety Deposit Box 36.*
> *Good luck and much love,*
> *Charlie.*

"That's the bank the Angolan Clan used, Charlie as well. That must be what José Luis meant, *bank accounts in Geneva.*" Jenny shook the envelope upside down. A single key fell out. It was a silver-coloured, double-sided key with no indications on it at all. She put the note and the key back into the envelope. It was too large for her handbag, so she tucked it under her arm. She double checked that the box was empty and replaced it. "I think we're done here. Let's get Señora Lopez to lock up and she can go for lunch."

In his office, Patrice had switched his computer system onto the CCTV network. He found the channel for the camera at the entrance to the vault just in time for the large flat screen to show the three women going in and then Señora Lopez coming out. He kept an eye on the screen while he worked. After a few minutes, the Spanish employee went back into the vault then they all came out together and walked up the stairs towards the exit. Jenny was carrying a large brown envelope.

He rewound the recording until he had a a clear shot of the women, then froze the frame and printed it out. *Hm. Two very beautiful women,* he reflected, looking at the image. Picking up the telephone, he speed-dialed a number and talked for a few moments. Then he locked his office and left the bank, the printed photo in his pocket.

On the way back to the car park, Jenny thought about this last message. "Did Charlie ever mention the bank or his business in Geneva?" She asked. "Anything you can remember?"

"He never talked about those things." Leticia racked her memory. "But there was something. I went into his office, it was a few weeks ago. He was on the phone. He said something like, *Don't worry about it. If you find anything, call me back, or I'll see you in Geneva.* He told me that it wasn't important but he had to go to the bank in Geneva at the end of the month. He went every April. For the Angolan Clan meeting, I suppose."

"Maybe he's left instructions for us in this safety deposit box and we're supposed to go and sort it out." Jenny's tried to control her apprehension. *More unknown events to discover.*

Leticia nodded absently, thoughts of Charlie flooding once more through her mind. She concentrated on driving them back to York House.

Jenny was now thinking about the funeral on Monday. She snapped her fingers. "You know what? We should let Charlie's partners know about his accident. I'm sure they'll want to come to the funeral. Then we can meet them and find out what's going on."

"But how? Did you find some phone numbers in the computer?"

"No, but I think I know how to contact them."

At the house, Jenny opened up Charlie's email files in Outlook. She found unfiled messages from Laurent and Nick, from the days before his accident, confirming that they would be in Geneva for the Angolan Clan meeting on April 25th. Nick's message was sent from Miami. Laurent's was from his BlackBerry. He was still in Verbier, skiing. He was going home, then to Paris and then to Geneva for the meeting. She found Raffael's email address in the address book.

"Right, I've got them all. Shall we send an email to invite them to come and meet us and pay their respects?"

"I think you should send it alone. It's better to not make it too complicated, telling them about me and Emilio."

She wrote a message advising them that, sadly, Charlie had died in an accident and his funeral service would be held in the church at San Pedro de Alcantara, near Marbella, next Monday. If they could attend, she would be pleased to meet them. She signed it, *Jenny, Charlie's daughter-in-law.*

Encarni grilled some fresh sea bass on the barbecue and they had an al fresco lunch on the terrace. Leticia opened a bottle of rosé, cold and fruity, trying to cast off her gloomy mood. Jenny thought that she could get used to this kind of life, although she missed Cooper.

Fuente wandered over at the end of their meal before they cleared away. He went straight to Jenny, rubbing himself against her legs, his jet black coat glistening in the sunlight.

"He must have smelled the barbecue. Clever cat, aren't you Fuente?" She gave him some fish pieces. The cat ate his snack then padded off again.

Later that evening, after Leticia and her family had gone and the house was quiet, Jenny sat in the kitchen, going over the day's happenings and jotting down items in her notebook. She re-read her notes, then looked at the calendar on the wall. Today was Thursday, April 17th and the Angolan Clan were due to have their annual meeting next Friday, the 25th.

Now, just one week before what might be their last reunion they had been informed of Charlie's death, by his daughter-in-law. How would they react to it? They might not even have known who she was. Even if they did, they may have been informed about

Ron, but they probably wouldn't know that she was the next in line to become a partner. *And they almost certainly don't know about Leticia and Emilio.*

Her head started to ache with all of the possible permutations in this confusing situation. Then she wrote down *Geneva* and underlined it twice. She got undressed for bed, determined, supressing her inner fears. Whatever was waiting for them, she couldn't put it off for ever. Her mind was made up. She was ready for the next move.

It was eight days until the meeting of the Angolan Clan.

FORTY-EIGHT

Thursday, April 17th, 2008
Divonne, French-Swiss Border

It was ten o'clock when Gloria got back to her flat. Her mother had finally fallen asleep and she'd sneaked quietly out, exhausted from the strain of trying to hold a one-sided conversation for hours on end. She went to the nursing home each evening when she was working, taking something especially tasty for their supper together. It had been two years since the effects of the stroke meant that she had no longer been able to look after her at home. Gloria was a small woman and she didn't have the strength to help her now that she couldn't walk at all. Tonight her mother had been much worse, hardly recognising her and becoming confused and upset at the visit. It broke Gloria's heart to see the deterioration in her.

When she wasn't working, visiting the home or taking her mother out, she spent most of her time shopping, or in the kitchen preparing meals for her. The freezer was full of meals for two, waiting to be defrosted and cooked. Her mother's favourites. She had bought a specially equipped van so that on her days off, if the weather was fine, she could take her for a drive along the lake or up into the mountains, just to get her away from the home. She would push the wheelchair down the ramp and they could picnic and chat by the lake or in one of the many rest areas by the autoroute, surrounded by trees and greenery. Just like the garden they'd had many years ago. It was true that her mother couldn't really have a conversation any more but Gloria was sure that she heard and understood everything she said.

Gloria had no children, no husband, her mother was all she had. But it hadn't always been like that. She'd been married at the age of twenty-two, when she lived in Paris. Her husband was the concierge at the Villa Patrick, a small hotel on the left bank. Their life together had been punctuated by violence. When Grégoire wasn't working nights at the hotel, he was getting drunk and beating her up in their two-roomed apartment in the cinquième Arrondissement. She was so desperate to please him that she put up with it for four years, until she discovered that most of his night shifts were spent, not at the concierge's desk but in the bedrooms of a succession of women whom he apparently didn't need to hit.

On the night she found out from one of the maids at the hotel, he screamed at her, "If you didn't look like a bloody horse and didn't screw like an old maid, I wouldn't need to play around. You deserve everything you get." He hit her once more, bursting her lip, before packing his bag and leaving the apartment for good.

Gloria couldn't get over those last remarks. She had always been ashamed of her looks and her body and Grégoire had never made her feel pretty or sexy, or anything but a prostitute and a punch bag. Retreating into her shell, she went to live with her mother in Divonne, across the French border from Geneva. She applied for a Swiss work permit, in her maiden name of Smouha, and got a job with IDD, a diamond trading company in Geneva. She was near her mother, her job was interesting and her hours were flexible. She was happy. She didn't need a husband, or any man in her life.

Once or twice she was invited out by men, but she was terrified of showing her body, or disappointing them in bed, so it never lasted long. Then, eighteen months ago, in November of 2006, a miracle happened. She met a man and fell in love, really in love, and was wonderfully happy for six whole months. Gloria discovered, for the first time in her life, what sex was all about.

It was a Friday morning and she was shopping in Geneva for a birthday gift for her mother. The stroke had happened just two months previously and the seventy-eight year old was left crippled and almost without speech. Gloria was devoting herself to getting her mother well again but so far there was little progress. She took her bags into a café on the Place de la Fusterie and sat at the bar with a cup of coffee and a croissant. A man of about thirty stumbled over her bags and some items fell out onto the floor. Stooping down to retrieve them, their heads bumped together. Instead of being embarrassed he laughed uproariously, until she had to join in. He ordered a coffee and sat on the stool next to her and they talked.

Gino was a good looking man. About thirty, with dark brown hair and brown eyes. Just looking into them made her feel weak at the knees. And he looked at her and talked with her in his charmingly accented French in a way that no man had ever done. As if he found her attractive and interesting and someone special. Not a punch bag who looked like a horse. She was smitten.

He told her he was from Genoa, but based in Lugano, selling computers in northern Italy and the Italian part of Switzerland. He was visiting Geneva for the weekend. Gino asked her out for dinner that night and she hesitated, thinking of her mother, then quickly made up her mind. Her mother wouldn't know if she'd missed a night's visit, or even a week's, for that matter. She would visit her early, before dinner. She accepted and her romance began with dinner at the Café de Paris, near Cornavin station.

Later, in Gino's hotel room, Gloria had the most unforgettable night of her life. She discovered that sex was exciting, satisfying and fun and she loved every minute of it. With his help and encouragement, she threw aside her inhibitions and used her body as if it had been made only for that purpose.

They were both replete with passion when she fell asleep in his arms at two in the morning but she woke up at six and quickly aroused him again. They spent the weekend together at her apartment and she felt guilty at visiting her mother so little, but not so guilty that she could deny her newly discovered passion. Gino had to leave for Milan on Sunday evening but he promised to call her on his return the following Friday. She passed the week in a dizzy haze, waiting impatiently for his call and running up to meet him at the train station at Cornavin like a lovesick teenager.

For six months he managed to get most weekends off and they spent them at her apartment. She now had someone else to cook for besides her mother. She spent every evening of the week visiting her so that she wouldn't have a guilty conscience when she hardly visited her on the weekend. Even when she was with her mother she was counting the hours to Friday evening, when he would get off the Milan train in the station and take her in his arms.

Gino was everything that Grégoire wasn't. He was funny, loving, tender and apparently madly in love with her, despite her looks. He was interested in her mother's condition, although he never visited her, it would have confused her too much. He asked her about her job, about IDD and the diamond business. She was proud to be able to show off her knowledge and he admired her for holding down a high profile job on a part-time basis.

Then in April, 2007, he told her he'd been transferred back to Genoa and would no longer be able to travel to Geneva at weekends. She was heart-broken, but suspected he was returning to a wife and family in Italy. In any case, she could do nothing, her idyll was over. It had been the happiest and most fulfilling period of her life, but her mother needed her more and more, so perhaps it was just as well. She wept all day when he left, then cooked supper to take to the nursing home.

A few months ago, Gloria had begun to suspect that something was wrong at IDD. She couldn't put her finger on it, but after a while she called Charlie Bishop, her boss, who lived in Marbella. The poor man had suffered a heart attack last August and she hadn't seen him since October, but she felt obliged to advise him of her misgivings. It was her duty.

At his request she had looked more deeply into the matter and her suspicions increased. There *was* something wrong and she knew how to confirm it. She would be alone in the office on Tuesday and could access the bank statements she needed to be sure. If she found what she expected, she determined to call Charlie and warn him before he arrived for the annual meeting the following Friday.

FORTY-NINE

Friday, April 18th, 2008
Marbella, Spain

Jenny was up at seven and immediately checked the laptop for emails, but there was nothing. She walked around the garden and up the staircase to the lake, past the little ponds and waterfalls so painstakingly tended by Juan. The sun warmed her skin. Ipswich seemed to be a million miles away. A dark, dank place in winter, where she had spent such a miserable time over the last four months. She felt a change in her physical and mental state, a kind of metamorphose. The Spanish climate and relaxed way of life had brought a feeling of wellbeing to her body. And just getting a sound, natural night's sleep was invigorating. She was starting to feel good about herself again.

Leticia arrived with Emilio at eight and saw the breakfast already prepared. When she protested, Jenny simply replied, "We're both co-owners of the house now and today it's my turn to do the household chores." It was going to take some time before the younger woman came to terms with her new status in life.

They drove to the beach and Jenny watched her trying to teach her son to swim. The sea wasn't yet warm, but Emilio splashed about without caring until his mother was as thoroughly soaked as him. Then they walked along the beach for a drink at one of the *Chiringuitos.*

Leticia seemed to be shaking off her depressed mood, and listening to her chatter away in her fast improving English, Jenny began to bless her good fortune. After the trauma of losing both her husband and father-in-law, she had inherited what were effectively a sister and a nephew and she found that she had never felt so happy and comfortable with the people around her.

As they sat with their coffee, she explained to Leticia her thinking of the previous evening. Charlie had told them not to waste any time and that the next stop was in Switzerland. Despite her apprehension, she knew that Leticia was right. They had to follow his instructions. His story had to be finished.

She took out her pocket diary and went through the dates with Leticia. "The funeral is on Monday and the Angolan Clan meeting will be held on Friday. Why don't we try to get a flight to Geneva next Wednesday, the 23rd? That should give us time to organise ourselves. I imagine we'll just need a document from José Luis to prove that we are Charlie's surviving relatives. Then we could visit the bank on Thursday and attend the meeting on Friday."

"And we'll meet Charlie's three partners." Leticia thought for a moment. "It's going to be strange, isn't it? We have read all about them, but we don't know them at all. And for sure they won't be expecting to meet us."

"Right, that's settled." Jenny jumped up, the school teacher in her taking over. Let's get back to the house and start making arrangements."

Jenny looked through the various files in the office, but she could find nothing to do with Klein, Fellay, or the Angolan Clan business in Geneva. "I'm not surprised," she said to Leticia. "After what José Luis told us, I didn't think he would have kept anything here in Spain. Everything must be in Geneva. I suppose we'll find out when we get to the bank."

She got the number from international enquiries and called right away, asking for the person who dealt with Mr. Bishop's account, since Charlie had not specified any name. *Charlie makes things very difficult,* she thought to herself. *There must be a reason.* She didn't realise that the reason was not to make it complicated for her, but impossible for anyone else.

After speaking with two people whose jobs were clearly to provide a security blanket around their customers, she was put through to a Mademoiselle Rousseau. Jenny explained the situation to her and after a few moments, she was transferred to Monsieur Eric Schneider. Although he wouldn't admit that he'd ever heard the name Bishop before, Schneider, a pompous sounding man, told Jenny that if she represented a client who was now deceased, she needed to provide documentation to prove she was the new beneficiary. He specified the items needed and Jenny noted them down.

She was about to call the lawyers when Francisco rang to confirm the funeral arrangements for Monday. After noting the details and the name of the English-speaking priest he had asked to hold the service, she told him she needed to speak to them about another matter. A moment later José Luis also came on the line.

Jenny was circumspect in her explanation. "It seems there may be an account with a bank in Geneva and we intend to go up there on Wednesday. We won't put you in a difficult position, José Luis, but we need some documents signed by you as executor of Charlie's estate."

She read from her notepad the documents which M. Schneider required:

A copy of Charlie's death certificate.

An affidavit that José Luis was the executor, signed by a Spanish Notary.

An affidavit from José Luis, naming Jenny and Leticia as beneficiaries.

These papers, plus their passports, should get them past the Swiss Guard at Klein, Fellay. Leticia held a Portuguese passport, since her parents had become naturalised citizens in Cascais. An Angolan passport might have been more problematical at the Swiss immigration.

José Luis confirmed that everything could be prepared and notarised by Wednesday morning. Jenny was again impressed at how things seemed to get settled so easily in Spain.

"If you'd like," Francisco added, "I could accompany you to Geneva. It's a lovely city and I know it quite well. I could perhaps be useful and even show you around a little."

"Yes," José Luis agreed. "If Francisco was to go with you, it could be helpful and not improper. He is not an executor and is not required to make tax declarations, etc."

Jenny was amused at the way that José Luis could separate what was acceptable or not. The two lawyers were only five metres apart in their offices. *Chinese walls, or Spanish walls, perhaps,* she thought. *What a sensible system.*

She rang off and explained to Leticia. "We'll have to think about Francisco coming to Geneva. I'm not sure it's a great idea. But right now we'd better get our trip organised."

"I'll call my friend, Louisa," said Leticia. "She has a travel bureau in Marbella. Shall we go in business class?"

"I'm used to easyJet," Jenny answered. "Do you think we can afford it?"

Louisa advised her that Iberia operated daily flights to Geneva, via Madrid. If they left Malaga in the early afternoon, they would be in Geneva by six in the evening. *Perfect timing.*

"Let me see if there's a special excursion ticket I can get you. It's an expensive flight."

"We'll be travelling in business class," Leticia said, to her friend's surprise.

Louisa was still keen to save her money. "I know a small family hotel near the lake, only ten minutes out of town. It's charming and not too costly, not like the big fancy places. Shall I book two rooms for you?"

Leticia happily agreed and the agent gave her the details of the Hotel de La Grange. "It's just by the Parc La Grange, with views over the lake and the mountains. You'll love it."

In order to help her put aside her forebodings about what awaited them in Geneva, Jenny had started to compile a *To do* list in her note pad. She took it out and ticked off several items. Travel plans and lawyer's documents organised, the women could forget their Geneva trip for now and prepare themselves for the funeral on Monday.

At Klein, Fellay, Mr. Schneider dictated a note about his conversation with Jenny to his assistant, Mlle. Rousseau. When she got back to her office she made a call on her mobile phone. "*Bonjour chéri*. I have some news for you."

It was now seven days until the meeting of the Angolan Clan.

FIFTY

Friday, April 18th, 2008
Washington DC, USA

Project Fairy Tale was proving to be a gold mine of precious information and Sonia Nicolaides was digging away at it, carefully and expertly. She was now in the process of preparing a chart, showing the interconnecting structure of those members of the ring she'd identified. This, in turn, would permit her to compile a hierarchy of these members. To establish their position in the process of creating and distributing the material and running the sickening international trade in innocent children. So that she could work out who were the top dogs, the people they should manage and cultivate in order to tie up the whole network. By setting a trap all the way from the top to the bottom of the stinking pile.

One of the reasons it was so time consuming was that all of them used pen names. Da Silva was a good example. He had three pseudonyms, of which "*silver.rod*" was the most revolting. Many of them also used fake email addresses from a remote Internet Provider, often several in a row, to hide their origin. It was often impossible to know where they were physically located. Some names corresponded with the members of rings in her other dossiers. This didn't surprise her, dealers and users of such filth were bound by a common sickness and it was contagious between groups. It could help the investigative work to find out who and where these people really were, a combined effort between many different sections of the department, behind the scenes and on the ground. And enormous international cooperation between the agencies and police forces of just about every western nation.

She opened up da Silva's computer and downloaded the messages for his four accounts. There were five messages in the dirty addresses. One of them asked why he hadn't joined the weekly "chat-room" the previous Wednesday. The 'I am travelling' message had been sent, but she dreaded to think how she would cope with this problem when she went live. Another was a reminder that his subscription to the '*Top Shelf Video Club*' was due. She didn't want to imagine what further horrors might be in store, but she knew that she was going to have to cope with them. Casting these thoughts aside, she dragged the messages into the corresponding files for further examination over the weekend. It was time to start playing the game. She would ask her Case Director permission to open up communications the following week. She'd also have to ask for a credit card number to renew the subscription. They seemed to have an unlimited supply of anonymous credit card numbers in the financial department.

There remained one new message, the first she had received on the clean *r.da.silva* address. She read it a couple of times then looked up the names of the sender and the recipients in all the address books. The names and addresses appeared nowhere in the computer. She realised that da Silva had been cleverer than they had imagined. He must have systematically erased all messages of any importance on the *r.da.silva* address, together with the names and addresses of the senders and recipients. She didn't know why they had been erased, but assumed it was to avoid any possible contamination with the other, dirty addresses. As far as she could see, the message was innocuous and had nothing to do with her investigation, but she couldn't leave it to chance that it might be a thread that would lead somewhere.

After thinking for a while, Sonia called an ex-colleague at the NYPD and asked him to do her a favour. He was just about to leave on a weekend trip, so he promised to look into it on the following Monday. It would take him a day or two to get the information, but he was pleased to be able to help. He had never plucked up the courage to invite her out when she worked alongside him, and had been gutted when she had left New York. Maybe this was his lucky day.

FIFTY-ONE

Saturday - Sunday, April 19th - 20th, 2008
Marbella, Spain

On Saturday, Jenny accompanied the da Costas to the market and then to the beach. Surrounded by her family, Leticia was in a more cheerful mood, which infected Jenny in the same way. They passed a pleasant, relaxing morning, putting the mixed emotions of the last week behind them for a while.

Lunch was a happy, family affair. Delicious, freshly grilled fish at a chiringuito on the beach, near the Hotel El Fuerte. Leticia explained their travel plans to her parents and they willingly agreed to look after her son while the women were away for three days. They dropped off Emilio and his grandparents at their apartment and went off to the fashion shops at Puerto Banus to spend a little of their inheritance on some warm clothes for the trip to Geneva.

On the way back to York House, Leticia took a detour through the area surrounding the Las Manzanás urbanisation. She told Jenny that there were four golf clubs within a radius of ten kilometres, and several more a little further away.

"They call this area "Golf Valley" because there are so many *campos de golf.* Many rich foreigners are living in the big villas around here." Leticia was pointing out some enormous properties, most of them with huge walls to keep out prying eyes. Only the roofs could be seen from the road.

They look more like mansions than villas, thought Jenny, *but not many of them compare with Charlie's property.*

There was a huge amount of construction going on, even in this exclusive and expensive neighbourhood. Driving around the perimeter of the Las Manzanás urbanisation, above York House, the paved road ended and they came upon a narrower lane, just a dirt track covered in gravel. The track turned and ran for a couple of kilometres until it came past a large forested area then alongside a wide, rolling valley, populated by small groups of olive trees and flowering bushes, with a small river running through it. It seemed that the land around the river was being shaped into a golf course by massive earthmoving machines. Hills were being flattened and new hills recreated to replace them. But there was no one working on the site, the machines were standing idle and the whole area was deserted. There was no activity at all.

Further along, at the side of the track there was an enormous, crater-like excavation for an apartment development. A large, painted sales sign was erected in front of the huge hole, which had a wooden barrier around it. The sign announced a magnificent new golf course and country club on the site. It had an artist's impressions of the course, with the apartment building and swimming pool in front. The development was called ***AVENIDA PARC***, but the empty shell of the building standing there looked derelict and abandoned. The biggest crane Jenny had ever seen towered over them, reaching up out of the depths of the excavation. There was enough construction equipment in and around the hole to build a city. Judging from what was going on everywhere else on the coast she had no doubt that was the intention.

Fortunately, it was on the other side of the forested land from Charlie's property and far away enough not to affect their tranquillity, if it was ever completed. *I suppose it's always been like this,* she thought to herself. *Just as you think the area is finished and settled, they start all over again. Except this time it looks as if they've run out of money, or clients, or both.*

They continued on the track for another kilometer, emerging higher up the main road to Coin, which brought them back down again to the entrance of the urbanisation. Preoccupied with their sight seeing, the women didn't notice the small black car that had been following them all afternoon.

"I don't understand," Jenny said, as they arrived at the house. "How are they going to take all the traffic on the roads and provide the water and infrastructure needed for such an influx of newcomers? And where are they going to find all those wealthy foreigners to buy apartments and houses and shares in more and more new golf and country clubs? It looks like they're already too many of them under construction."

Leticia shrugged, "Spanish promoters are not worrying at all for such matters. They sell everything from the plans before it's built and they take the money for the next project. Nobody cares for finishing anything."

"I've heard that saying before. Spain will be a lovely place when it's finished!"

"If it gets finished," added Leticia.

Jenny checked again that evening for emails. There were still no replies. *Strange,* she thought, *you'd think his friends would be in touch as soon as they heard of his accident.* She went to bed early and fell immediately into a deep sleep.

It was nine thirty and José Luis was already sittting at the table with a glass of *Fino* sherry when Espinoza arrived. They had arranged to meet for dinner at the Posada de Antonio. The restaurant, owned by Antonio Banderas, the actor, was not usually within Espinoza's budget, but his invitation was an official one and he could enjoy a good dinner on his expense account.

He had known the lawyer for twenty years and they had been good friends for the last twelve, when he had been promoted to Inspector in the Homicide squad and was immediately thrust into a murder case in nearby Estepona. It had taken him only three weeks to solve the crime, using old fashioned detective work, with an unorthodox, politically incorrect approach.

The victim was a real estate promoter whose brutally beaten

body had been found in the cellar of a half-finished apartment complex on the marina. When Espinoza examined the contracts and accounts of the development, he began to conceive a solution which presented both a motive and a most unlikely suspect. But in order to follow the trail back to the suspect he had to find a way of infiltrating the network of Spanish notaries and lawyers, all the way from Malaga to Madrid.

With unofficial help from José Luis, he had managed to bluff his way to the truth and set a trap for the murderer, who had covered his tracks with clinical and callous professionalism. It was only Espinoza's refusal to follow the rules and cut through the red tape obstacles so cleverly erected by the culprit that permitted him to find the motive and reveal the truth.

The man, who was now serving a thirty year sentence in a maximum security prison near Cordoba, was a highly respected Madrid lawyer with an international reputation, a brilliant mind. Not all of the villains of the world were IQ-challenged thugs, as Espinoza well knew.

Not all policeman are IQ-challenged either, he had decided, after the verdict.

José Luis and he had been firm friends ever since and had collaborated on a couple of other investigations. Tonight, he had invited him for dinner to pick his brain, but also from friendship, knowing that they would otherwise both be alone, since the lawyer was a widower and he and Soledad were in a state of limbo.

"*Holá. Que tal, José Luis?*" He sat at the table and ordered a beer. His expense allowance would stretch to one decent bottle of wine, but little more. Best to save it for dinner. He enjoyed few good meals since his separation and the consequent strain on his resources. The two men chatted for a while before ordering their meal then Espinoza started his word game.

"So. I suppose the two women were surprised at the terms of Sr. Bishop's will?" He asked ingenuously.

The lawyer was taken aback at the question. He had surmised that the policeman wanted to talk about his separation from Soledad, since it was he who had advised a trial separation to avoid the distress and ruinous cost of divorce proceedings. He thought back to the end of his meeting with the women. "Jenny was definitely astonished at the news about Emilio," he chuckled, "but the will itself was not really surprising."

"And what are Sra. Bishop's plans now? Will she be staying here at her new house? Just in case I need to contact her," he added, looking earnestly at the lawyer.

At his age, José Luis found it difficult to control his garrulous manner. "Actually, Pedro," he sipped the last of his *fino*, "the two of them are off to Geneva next week to visit a bank."

"Geneva?" Espinoza's brain started whirling. *Find a motive for the crime,* he thought to himself. *A Swiss bank sounds to me like a possible motive.* He threw out a few more subtle questions but saw from the lawyer's answers that he didn't have anything further to disclose. He let the subject drop and perused the wine list for a bottle in his price range. Their meals arrived and the evening passed pleasantly, with no further discussion of the Bishop affair.

As he walked home, Espinoza's mind was still revolving around the lawyer's slip-up in mentioning the Geneva bank. He knew exactly who to call. Inspector Andréas Blaser, one of his Swiss opposite numbers in Interpol. They had been on a conference together in Berlin and had got along well. Blaser lived in Carouge, a suburb of Geneva. He would know how to find the women when they arrived and how to watch what they did while in Switzerland. He would call him first thing next week.

On Sunday morning Jenny went down to the gym in the basement. It was equipped with more expensive and complicated machines than her fitness club in Ipswich. She spent thirty minutes running, lifting and stretching until she was in a fine sweat and feeling fit again.

Later, she drove the Mini to the lovely old church in San Pedro, to attend morning mass and meet the Reverend Macintosh, a small chubby man, who emanated an aura of calm and peacefulness around him. They chatted for a while after the service and Jenny told him as much about her father-in-law's life and family as she was able, without revealing any secrets.

She passed the rest of the day quietly. Reading, pottering in the garden, feeding the fish and watching the golfers hit their balls into the lake. It was a bit like being at home in the UK, but bathed in warm sunshine. She opened up Outlook again to check for any messages. There was still nothing. It seemed the other partners were either too busy, or simply hadn't switched on their email over the weekend. She would check again in the morning.

Fuente came along as she was making herself a snack in the evening. His timing was perfect, as usual. He wandered away after his meal and Jenny wondered if he went off to visit someone else, or if he was a permanent resident at York House. The property was certainly big enough for him to get lost in without any difficulty.

She lay in bed that night, mentally ticking off the items in her notebook. Things seemed to be falling into place. *Apart from contacting the other Angolan Clan partners,* she thought. She lay awake for a while, wondering what that meant, then she fell into a sound sleep.

It was now five days until the meeting of the Angolan Clan.

FIFTY-TWO

Monday, April 21st, 2008
San Pedro de Alcantara, Spain

At eleven o'clock exactly, the funeral car left York House to follow the hearse towards the San Pedro cemetery, about seven kilometres west of Marbella. Francisco had arranged for the body to be brought up to the house earlier that morning so that the two women could say their last goodbyes.

Charlie looked so well that they half expected him to sit up and climb out of the coffin; a tribute to the cosmetic skills of the undertaker's staff. Tears poured down Leticia's face as she took her last look at the man she had loved, the father of her son. She gave him a farewell kiss on the forehead. His skin was cold and slightly clammy. She shivered at the sensation.

They sat with Emilio in the back of the car as it wended its way slowly along the coast road in the warm sunshine. José, Encarni and Juan were in their car behind and there were another eight cars following them. Friends who had come along to pay their respects and share this last journey together with them and Charlie.

Reverend Mackintosh welcomed them and ushered the family

into the front pew of the small church. Some people were already there, probably friends from areas around Marbella. The coffin was surrounded by wreaths and floral arrangements. The church looked beautiful.

The service was brief and the vicar succeeded in making it both friendly and respectful. His short conversation with Jenny had enabled him to get an insight into a man he had never met. His address was delivered in a soft Scottish accent and he managed to raise a few tears and smiles without appearing too light-hearted. *You'd think he'd known him personally,* mused Jenny. *What a good choice. Well done, Francisco.*

She gave a short address, reminiscing about pleasant memories. Speaking fondly of Ellen and Ron, Charlie's late wife and son. Hinting that there was more to him than might appear and regretting his disappearance but giving away no details about his extraordinary past.

Leticia was in tears for most of the service, sobbing gently and leaning into her mother's shoulder. Jenny had asked her to say a few words but fortunately she had refused. She saw that the young woman would have been incapable of speaking, she was too distressed.

The vicar continued with the service. "We'll now listen to Charlie's favourite piece of music, a very interesting choice. The words are on page three of the Order of Service. If you'd like to sing along I'm sure he would be delighted." From the loudspeakers placed in the corners of the Church there came the rhythmic sound of *Waterloo.* By the end of the first chorus the whole of the congregation was singing away heartily.

At the end of the service they left Emilio in the churchyard with his grandmother and walked across to the immaculate cemetery where the few mourners were assembled by the grave to witness the burial.

Jenny said, "I'm sure that Ellen and Charlie will rest better here under the Spanish sunshine than in the cold, wet earth of the UK."

Leticia nodded. "It's not difficult to choose. Spain has problems like every place, but everything seems easier when the sun is shining. Now they are together again, in the sunshine." She blew her nose violently and Jenny put her arm around her shoulder as they stepped away from the grave.

Back in the churchyard, they stood beside the vicar, shaking hands with the visitors as they left. "Thank you for coming. Charlie would be happy that you came. God bless you."

The last to leave were José Luis and Francisco. The two women thanked the young lawyer for having arranged everything. On this occasion he was not wearing jeans, but had on a navy-blue suit and a black tie. Jenny noticed that his steel-rimmed spectacles were tinted for sun protection. Again she was uncomfortable to register his good looks.

Just then Patrice walked up to them, wearing a smartly cut, double-breasted black suit. "Sorry I'm late, but I was tied up in a meeting." He took their hands and kissed each of them on both cheeks. Jenny noticed that he held Leticia's hands longer than was strictly necessary.

He greeted José Luis politely and Francisco grabbed his hand. "*Come ésta, amigo?*

He explained to the women, "Patrice and I are skiing and climbing partners. We go up to the Sierra Nevada whenever we get the chance."

"Did you go this weekend?" Leticia tried to shake off her gloom and enter the conversation. She had never been to the mountains. Maybe she should take Emilio up there some time. It was time to start doing things with him again, Charlie would want that.

"I'm afraid not, we were both travelling. With our travel and work schedules we maybe get up there once a month if we're lucky." The Frenchman looked disappointed, he clearly treasured his climbing trips.

"Why do you travel on weekends?" Jenny asked Francisco. "That doesn't seem fair."

"Tell that to our clients, Jenny. I go when and where they ask me. That's what José Luis hired me for." He looked at the old lawyer for confirmation.

"I'm exhausted just thinking about your schedule, Francisco. Better you than me. Although I agree with Jenny, travelling on weekends doesn't really seem fair."

While they were speaking, Jenny noticed a young man, alone,

apparently waiting to pay his respects. She didn't know him and Leticia showed no signs of recognition.

José Luis turned to them. "Well, I think it's time to leave you two young women with your family. I hope you have a quiet and restful evening. Francisco and I will see you tomorrow morning. The first batch of documents is ready for your signatures and the others you can collect on Wednesday. In the meantime, don't hesitate to call if you need anything at all." The women shook hands with the three men and they walked off towards the car park. The vicar went back into the church, leaving them alone with the last visitor.

They turned to greet the stranger. He was a pleasant looking man, medium height, with light brown hair, brown eyes and a slightly tanned face. Jenny noticed that his nose was a little crooked, as if it had once been broken and then fixed.

He shook their hands. "Please forgive my intrusion. I'm sorry to introduce myself on such a sad day. My name is Adam Peterson."

He spoke with a slight but noticeable accent. *Australian,* wondered Jenny?

She and Leticia introduced themselves. *He's not one of Charlie's partners,* Jenny thought. "Were you a friend of my father-in-law?"

"I've only met him once on a business matter, so I never knew him on a personal level. But," he added quickly, "it was some time ago. I found him to be a very clever and agreeable person."

Before she could find out anything more, he said to Leticia. "Is that your little boy over there? I heard him speaking Spanish in the church."

She brought Emilio over to shyly say, "Hello" and the man tried unsuccessfully to have a conversation in English with him.

Jenny tried another tack. "Are you staying down here in Marbella?" She wondered how he could have known about Charlie's death and the funeral.

"I just arrived yesterday and I'm leaving again this afternoon, but I wanted to pay my respects." His glance encompassed both women. "You have my deepest sympathy."

They talked inconsequentially for a few minutes before the stranger looked at his watch. "I'm sorry, but I must get on my way to the airport or I'm going to miss my flight."

"Do you need a taxi?"

He shook his head. "That's kind but I have a rental car." He shook hands with them both, tousled Emilio's hair and strode off out of the churchyard without looking back.

Leticia looked quizzically at Jenny. "You know who was that?"

"I've no idea. I wonder how he knows who we are and about Charlie's death and the funeral. I can't imagine how he could have found out. It was only settled on Thursday."

"So someone we don't even know has arrived, but none of Charlie's partners. Why do you think no one from the Angolan Clan has come?" Leticia furrowed her brow. "Of course they had not got much time to make arrangements."

"I wouldn't expect Nick or Raffael to make it here from the States but you'd think that Laurent would have been able to come from Monaco. It's not all that far away."

"Did you look to see if we had an email from anyone?"

"I looked yesterday but there was nothing. We'll check when we get home, maybe there's something today."

"It seems there are still many puzzles to solve. And who is this man, Adam Peterson?"

"I don't know, maybe time will tell. Let's get your parents and go home for lunch."

Leticia returned alone to the graveside to say her last farewell and Jenny went to join the family. She noticed a slight fragrance in the air. Not the churchyard flowers, something artificial, like a woman's perfume. She put her hand to her nose and smelled a faint scent on her palm. *Hmm, someone's wearing a nice after shave. Could be Hugo Boss?* It had been one of Ron's few extravagances, she remembered sadly.

On the drive back to Marbella Leticia was in a quiet, pensive mood. Now that Charlie had gone she realised that her life had changed and would continue to change in many ways.

Memories of the events of the past few years tumbled through her mind. Ellen's death in Yalta had been the tragic catalyst for Charlie's growing reliance on her. Not just as a housekeeper, but as a friend, a companion, a confidante and then almost by accident, a lover.

It had started after his first attempt to socialise again, by arranging, with her help, a dinner party for some friends. She had come from the kitchen to say goodnight to Charlie but couldn't find him. He was sitting on the wall of the terrace, sobbing quietly, his shoulders heaving with the emotion. He didn't hear her come up behind him.

"Shhh, Charlie, it's alright." She put her hand on his shoulder, squeezing it, as if to inject some of her positivity and vibrancy into the older man.

"No it's not, Leticia. It's bloody terrible." Charlie didn't turn around. He lifted his head, looking out over the pool into the night. "I can't even remember a word that was said at the table this evening. It was a nightmare. Just sitting, trying to smile and make conversation when you've already forgotten what was said. Everywhere I looked I saw images of Ellen, nothing else, nobody else, just her beautiful face. We built this house together but it's stamped everywhere with her personality. Since she's been gone it's like I'm just a lodger living in her home and I don't really belong here without her.

"It's as if my life has just come to a standstill. I don't know why I bother getting up in the morning. Without Ellen, the day holds absolutely nothing. Just one day after another with no point to them at all. I should have died instead of her. She was much better than me at coping with life, she coped for both of us."

Leticia wanted to comfort him but she knew her English wasn't good enough. She just said, "You need a good night of sleep, Charlie. Tomorrow will be better."

Over the next few months they slowly grew closer. Charlie was quite different to Spanish men, whom she thought either immature and frivolous or suffering from a male macho complex. He was considerate, funny and interesting and with her help he began to shake off the mood of depression he'd suffered after Ellen's death. He took up golf again and started socialising. She felt that she'd helped him to regain his equilibrium. In addition to this, her English had improved dramatically so she could enjoy a proper conversation with him.

One day in September, she was about to leave after her morning's work. Charlie was relaxing by the pool. It was a very hot day and he persuaded her to stay for a swim. Afterwards, lying in the sun together, it seemed the most natural thing in the world for them to make love. Charlie was self deprecating. "It's been a long time, Leticia. I hope you won't be disappointed. And don't look too closely at my physique, it's not what it was."

Leticia had started to pick up his very English sense of humour. "If you are fit to play golf then I think we can manage."

He was sensitive and considerate. Taking his time, ensuring that he gave her as much pleasure as he was able. It was one of the most tender and pleasurable experiences of her life. With his hands and lips, Charlie paid tribute, slowly and tenderly, to every part of her lovely body. She had never achieved an orgasm in such an unfrenzied, gentle and relaxed fashion before. The sensation resonated deeply throughout her body. Lying on the lawn by the pool, in his arms, under the warm Spanish sunshine, she felt totally fulfilled and happy.

Afterwards, Charlie gazed at her exquisite, perfect body, and marvelled at his good fortune. "My God, Leticia. You're so young and beautiful and I'm so old and decrepit. Do you realise that I'm old enough to be your father?"

She kissed him gently. "I already have a father, Charlie. I think it's better if you just be my lover."

And that was what happened. Over the next months and years they fell deeper and deeper in love. It was not a passionate love, it was a mature and appreciative love. Although the physical side of it was a joy to both of them. "I think you're getting more fit all the time, Charlie. Is your golf getting better also?"

Having given up on boyfriends, it had been a long while since Leticia had taken any kind of protection. When she fell pregnant, Charlie immediately suggested that they get married.

She refused. "I don't want your friends at the club to think you take advantage of your employees. I think it's better to not change anything."

Initially her parents were worried and sceptical of the outcome. But when they saw how happy and fulfilled their daughter had become they came to terms with the situation. Then at the birth of their first grandson they were ecstatically happy. The christening was a private ceremony. Just the small family together, at the Iglesia Cristo church in Coín.

Shortly after Emilio's birth, Charlie told her, "We're going to have to face up to telling Ron about Emilio one day. They have to meet each other. It's not going to be easy, Ron's going to wonder what the hell I've been up to. If I've lost it in my dotage. But it's not fair for neither of them to know they have a brother."

"I think it's better to wait a few years until Emilio is old enough to understand," she replied. "Nothing is going to change, only that it is probably easier to explain later on."

The next month he returned from Malaga to tell her that he had looked after them both in his will. "I'm getting too old to take chances. Now José Luis has all the details in his hands, so you and Emilio won't have any problems when I go. He won't say anything."

Although she scoffed the idea she realised he was right. And when he suffered his heart attack she was sure she would lose him. She stayed with him night and day, caring for him, instilling him with her youth and energy, willing him to get better. And he did. After two months he was like a new man, fit, happy and living life to the full again.

But just weeks later, tragedy struck again. Charlie lost his only son. Their Christmas was overshadowed by the shock and grief that Ron's death brought and it took all of her love and understanding to help him out of the depths of his despair. He lost interest in his business, going just once more to Geneva on a February morning and returning that same evening.

Then, after his accident, their happiness had ended. She had Emilio, their beautiful son, but she had lost Charlie, her friend and lover. And Ron had disappeared before he had met Emilio. Without discovering that he had a brother. *Who could have known?*

Now she was facing another new phase in her life. No longer a housekeeper, no longer an unmarried lover. A young, wealthy woman with the world at her feet, a whole new life ahead, for her and for Emilio. She would have to get used to mixing with people who had always been outside of her social circle. She frowned at the thought.

One thing at a time, she told herself.

Back at York House, Jenny opened up Outlook again. There were two emails. The first, a very brief message from Laurent, sent from his BlackBerry, conveyed his sadness at the news but apologised that it was impossible for him to attend the funeral. He was travelling and would be in contact again in a few days. The second was from Nick and though it contained a warm message, reflecting his feelings of shock and loss, the answer was the same. Neither man could be present and they would be back in touch soon. There was no message from Raffael, but the women were not surprised at this. Charlie had said he was less involved than the other partners.

That night, Jenny fell into a deep sleep, as if she had taken a sedative. She woke at five in the morning, still tired after a series of disturbing dreams, and went down to make a cup of tea. As she sat on the terrace in the pre-dawn darkness, the last dream sequence came back to her.

It was a pitch black night and she was walking alone through a darkened graveyard when a figure appeared before her. It was a man, but she couldn't make out his face. Surprised and frightened, she ran back through the darkness, tripping over gravestones and undergrowth, bruising and cutting her hands and knees. Each time she got to her feet she could hear the soft footsteps of the man behind her, getting ever closer.

She took shelter in the entrance of an old ruin at the edge of the churchyard, holding her breath, standing motionless against the moss covered wall. She waited a couple of minutes, her heart thumping so hard she thought it would give her away. There was no sound. He had gone.

Emerging from the entrance, she walked towards the path to leave the place. The man appeared on the paving directly in front of her. He stepped quickly up to her, took her in his arms and kissed her passionately, moving his hands about her body. At first Jenny didn't resist him, but responded to his touch. Forgotten feelings awakened again after the last few lonely, miserable months on her own.

Then a shaft of moonlight illuminated them for a moment and she saw his face. "I know you," she cried out, pushing him away from her. "But who are you?"

"What's wrong, Jenny?" He stared at her. "It's me, Adam Peterson."

Jenny shivered. Both from the recollection of her dream and

from the cool morning air. She went down the stairs to the pool. The surface of the water was still and shining with the reflection of the moon. She looked down at the water, seeing her own face looking up at her. A slight breath of wind ruffled the surface and it seemed for a moment that the reflection changed into the face of the young man at the funeral. She felt a sense of dread, then went back into the house to get ready for the day. *Who is Adam Peterson,* she asked herself?

It was now four days until the meeting of the Angolan Clan.

BOOK ONE

PART FOUR: 1979 - 1998

FIFTY-THREE

September, 1979
Durban, South Africa

When Adam was four he was enrolled at Glenwood Preparatory School, not far from their home and near Durban University. He started in the September term, just after his fifth birthday and was the youngest boy in his class. Two weeks after the start of school he was brought home by the headmistress, Mrs. Connolly, who had been Rachel's primary school teacher many years previously. Adam was crying and Rachel saw that he had a large bruise on his forehead and there was blood on his lip and on his school blazer.

"Have you had an accident, sweetheart?" She picked the little boy up and held him to her. At this, his crying increased in intensity and became hysterical sobbing. Adam could put on a good show, even at that tender age.

"I'm sorry, Rachel," the school teacher said, "We've had a bit of a battle in the playground. But Adam's fine. Unlike little Lawrence Callim, poor child."

"He called me a bastard!" Adam turned and glowered at the woman.

Rachel suddenly felt sick. She had been dreading this day and had hoped it would never arrive, but now it had. "Do you know what it means, Adam?"

"No, but all the other kids were laughing, so it must be something nasty."

"So what did you do?"

"I fought him. And I won," he added proudly, putting aside his tears.

"But he's almost two years older than you and much bigger. How on earth could you win a fight against him?"

"I'm afraid it wasn't exactly like that." Mrs. Connolly intervened. "Lawrence is in the hospital. He was hit with a rock. He's got a lump on his head the size of a football. I'm surprised he wasn't killed."

"He had me on the ground. I had to bash him with something, he was hurting me. He's a rotten bully."

It took Rachel a half hour and two cups of coffee to convince the headmistress that her son wasn't a danger to the community. Then they went to speak to Lawrence's mother, to ensure that the matter would end there.

Rachel now had to explain to the children the discrepancy between their parent's wedding anniversary and Adam's birthday. Sitting with them on the garden terrace she explained that after the death of Mammy Matja their father had been lonely. They had fallen in love and decided to get married and bring another child into the family. They wanted the four children to be as close together as possible, so they made sure that the new baby came very quickly. Soon after the wedding they became a family of six, wasn't this wonderful?

"Then Adam isn't really our brother is he, Mammy?" At seven years old, Greg could already understand the implication.

"Greg, do you think of me as your mother?"

"You know I do, but.."

Catrine immediately jumped into the conversation. "Of course you are our mother. I'm sorry, but I can't remember Mammy Matja any more, I've forgotten her face." She burst into tears. Her younger sister immediately joined her in crying and Rachel held the two girls to her.

"It's the same for me. Mammy Matja is gone and you are the only mother I want," Greg cried. "But Adam is only our half brother. Arthur Lumley told me in school."

"That's not true!" Adam said to his elder brother with a scowl. "Your mammy and daddy are the same as mine." He broke into tears again.

"The most important thing is that daddy and I love you all just the same. Greg, you and Catrine have been lucky enough to have had two mothers. But all of you have the same father and for all these years you have had the same mother. So it means that now we are just a nice ordinary family of six. No differences any more."

The children seemed mollified by this explanation and Rachel hoped that it would put the matter to rest. In any event, it was never brought up again by them. And there were no further incidents at school since none of the other children wanted to end up in hospital. However, Adam began to get the feeling that Greg looked down upon him as a lesser member of the family. There was no reason behind this, but he began to suffer from a feeling of inferiority with regard to his step-brother.

FIFTY-FOUR

September, 1979
Favela Morro do Cantagalo, Rio de Janeiro, Brazil

Sergio d'Almeida was counting his money. He had seven dollars to his name. Enough to buy supper tonight. Knowing how much Alicia and little Ray could eat between them and how much would be left for him, he bought nine sardines from the fish seller in the next alley then a small loaf of bread and an apple from the stall on the corner. He had only four dollars left, but he had a broken fridge to repair and a lighting system to set up in someone's garden. That would bring in fifteen dollars, so he could finish the week in credit.

After recovering from the injuries inflicted on him by the blonde giant, Sergio had tried every way he could think of to find Ferreiro and recover something from the catastrophe. But the gem dealer was no longer there. His store was closed and shuttered and obviously had been for several weeks. Neither he nor his attacker was to be found, although he wasn't keen on coming across that man again. He knew that with fifty thousand dollars worth of diamonds Ferreiro could pack up and start again anywhere, just as he had dreamed of doing.

Elvira was no better and he couldn't afford a doctor, even less a hospital. After paying two months rent during his recuperation, he now had only five hundred dollars left in the world. He couldn't afford to pay rent either, so he wandered through the nearby shanty town, the *Favela Morro do Cantagalo*, next to the park and behind the beach. The third time he strolled through the mean, filthy lanes, he saw a man taking a couple of battered old chairs from a shack and carrying them across the street into another, slightly larger, smarter place.

Intrigued, he asked what was going on. The man's uncle had just died and he was improving his own shack with anything of use. Like Sergio, Eladio was an Angolan refugee but his family had arrived the previous year, in time to buy a couple of huts before the massive influx of refugees made it impossible to find any kind of a dwelling, no matter how decrepit.

"What are you going to do with your uncle's shack?" Sergio asked.

"I'll sell it for whatever I can get. I can't use it to enlarge our place, it's on the other side of the lane, so I'll try to get a few bucks for it."

Sergio bought the 'dwelling' for fifty dollars and made a good friend into the bargain. Eladio and Tanya had two children a little older than Alicia and Ray, and after moving in, the two men saw each other often, usually just sitting in the filthy lane with a beer, talking about the old days. He found a bed and a few more pieces of furniture and made a ramshackle sofa in the corner of the shack where Elvira could rest. Her health wasn't improving.

The rainy season started in December and the lanes in the favela became streams. The foul air was even more hot and humid. It was like breathing in steam. Elvira's asthma was even worse. She couldn't get any fresh air into her lungs. There wasn't any. Their daughter, Alicia, started to suffer from the same problem. Sergio had three hundred dollars left. He couldn't leave his wife and children to go out and find work and if he didn't do so they would run out of money in a few months. Every night, he lay in the bed that they shared, listening to their laboured breathing, trying to think of some kind of a plan, a solution, some way to improve their lives. But he couldn't. They were trapped in the favela and they would die there. There was no way out.

In February, Elvira had a terrible attack. She wheezed and gasped until her face turned blue. She was suffocating for lack of air. Sergio couldn't stand seeing her like that. She was dying in front of him. He asked Tanya to look after his family for a few minutes and ran along to the doctor's surgery. He gave the quack ten dollars and they ran back together with medication to help Elvira's breathing, even temporarily, to alleviate her suffering.

Tanya was at the door with the children. She was crying, they all were. "It's too late," she said. She took Ray and Alicia across to her place and left Sergio alone with the doctor.

Sergio went into the shack and saw his wife lying on the bed. She looked better. For the first time in months she wasn't red or blue in the face. She wasn't gasping or wheezing. She was finally beyond suffering and pain. She was at peace.

"No! No! No!" Sergio screamed out in the tiny, shabby room that had become their home. The doctor gave him back the ten dollars and left him alone with his wife.

Since then, Sergio had managed to find a way to look after the children and do a little work. Either taking in machines for repair, or helping with electrical installations in nearby, wealthier neighbourhoods. He was a good engineer and electrician and had some regular customers. Eladio and Tanya helped out sometimes, looking after the children when he was out working. Somehow they survived.

He fried the sardines in some oil and carefully divided them up. Two and a half each for Alicia and Ray and four for him. With a couple of slices of bread and a piece of apple, it was enough for supper. Better than some days, worse than others. After putting the children to bed, he sat in the lane with Eladio and drank a beer, his one luxury, and they talked about the old times. The good times, in Angola.

FIFTY-FIVE

1984 - 1994
Hampshire, England

Hanny had insisted that Adam should go to boarding school in England when he was ten years old. Greg was already at St. Jerome's, in Hampshire, and they would be company for each other. Their two daughters were ensconced in the local school system in Durban. Catrine was preparing for her GCEs as well as coaching her younger sister.

Although she wanted to keep her daughters at home, Rachel was happy for the boys to go to the UK. The school system was suffering from the active opposition to the curriculum by the growing anti-apartheid movement. They had successfully organised boycotts of the coloured and Indian elections for the Tricameral Parliament. Under Prime Minister PW Botha, South Africa was sliding towards complete anarchy. International opposition to the Botha regime was decimating the economy, as US and European companies pulled out of the country.

Rachel applied to the Irish Embassy in Johannesburg and obtained a passport for her son. It would make travel much easier in

Europe. She and Hanny shed a tear when Adam waved them goodbye at the departure gate at Durban International Airport. He would be met by the Housemaster when he arrived in London, like many other boys at the start of the school year.

Greg was three years ahead of him at school and Adam enviously watched him progress through his last years, winning just about every trophy, both academic and sportive. It had been difficult for the younger boy, always being the runner up in the family. Greg was only three when his brother was born and he was determined not to be upstaged by the new baby. As a result, Adam would often throw histrionic tantrums to gain his parent's attention. He was endowed with a true Irish temper, and he used it to great effect.

The previous year, Adam had noticed the time difference between his parents wedding anniversary and his own birthdate. He realised that he been conceived out of wedlock and although he said nothing, it increased his sense of inferiority towards his step-brother. What exacerbated the feeling was that Greg was smarter and more gifted than him and he started to show this in spades. He finished his last year as school captain and obtained eight GCE "O" Levels and four "A"s. The school rugby team won the county championships under his captainship and he was voted Student of the Year.

Adam, on the other hand, was a very average student and didn't fit well into the sports curriculum. He was too much of a loner, failing to mix with the other boys and lacking a team mentality. The school sports master had given up on him competing for anything until they went for the Junior School's first year's skiing trip to Chamonix. Adam turned out to be a natural skier. By the end of the week he had moved to intermediate level and he won the final race of the programme, competing against much older boys.

He continued to improve every year and each summer when he went home, he would open up his case and take out his ski trophies, proudly showing them to his parents. "See what I've won this year." He'd line them up in the study alongside the few others he'd won, next to the impressive, expanding collection amassed by his brother. In addition, during his visits to Chamonix, he showed an aptitude for the French language. After a few years, he was able to communicate well enough to show off to the other boys in his class.

In 1992, Adam left St. Jerome's after scraping an admission to Trelawney College. Greg was already there, in his penultimate year. He was Captain of Chapman House, captain of the rugby and cricket teams and had been singles tennis champion two years running. Six months before he left the college, in January, 1993, he was summoned by his Housemaster, Professor Bellamy. The housemaster of Adam's house was also there and there was a policeman present.

"This is Sergeant Jeffries from the local constabulary. We'd like to ask for your help with a matter that has arisen." The Professor was wearing his customary red and blue striped bow tie, a matching handkerchief tucked into his breast pocket. He looked like an antiques dealer.

Greg was mystified by the request. "Ask away, Professor. I'll be happy to help if I can."

"There's been a bit of a problem in Smithfield House."

Greg stiffened, that was Adam's house."What kind of a problem?"

"Nigel Stanford was attacked outside the school last night. He was on his way back from the Grey Horse." The pub was the most popular venue in town for the undergraduates.

"Attacked? That sounds serious. Was it a robbery?" To Greg's knowledge there had never been a robbery involving boys from Trelawney.

"Yes, it seems Stanford was wearing a diamond ring and it was stolen from him."

"Do you know who's responsible?"

"Unfortunately not, that's the problem. Stanford was alone because his friends were still in the pub. The assailant came from behind so he couldn't definitely identify him or her. He was hit on the head, but when he fell he apparently bashed his head again on the pavement and was rendered unconscious for a few minutes. He's still in the infirmary."

"Poor kid." He turned to the policeman. "Do you have any information about the crime?"

"Sergeant Jeffries is here at our request, Greg. It's rather a delicate situation. We need to ask for your assistance."

"I'm confused, Professor. Why is it delicate and what assistance can I possibly give?"

"It seems that your brother was fascinated by the diamond ring. Apparently he had offered to buy it several times, the last time being yesterday. Stanford inherited the ring from his grandfather so he isn't interested in selling it and he says he told Adam, in no uncertain terms, to drop the subject."

"You're not suggesting that Adam…?"

"I'm not suggesting anything. But Stanford says he is convinced that Adam knocked him down and took his ring. As I say, there were no witnesses and the police have been unable to find any evidence at all."

The police officer coughed apologetically. "It was freezing rain last night, Greg, so the pavements have been washed clean. That is, if ever there was anything there in the first place."

"How do you mean, *if there was anything there*? You think that Stanford's lying?"

"Well," interjected Dr. Clarence, Adam's housemaster, "there seems to be a bit of bad blood between the two boys and since we don't actually know what happened, it's put everyone into a very difficult and embarrassing position."

Greg looked at the three men, feeling perplexed and worried. "So, Stanford could actually have slipped and fallen and banged his head and there was nobody there at all?"

"Well, it is odd that Stanford didn't make this accusation until Dr. Clarence visited him in the infirmary late last night. It might be that he was a bit concussed." Sergeant Jeffries coughed again. "However, if the ring has been stolen then we have a different situation."

"What does the ring look like?"

"I've seen it several times," answered Dr. Clarence. "It's a gold ring with a yellow stone embedded in it. I know nothing about jewellery, but it is obviously quite old and Stanford says the stone is a yellow diamond."

Greg knew if it was a yellow, or fancy yellow diamond, as they were known, it would be quite valuable. "So have you interviewed my brother? What does he have to say about it?"

"I have talked to Adam, but he says that he was studying in his dorm until the other boys who share with him came back from the pub. They found Stanford and helped him back to the college infirmary. That was the first he heard about the matter, according to him."

"Was Stanford unconscious when they found him?"

"Apparently not. He was standing, rather shaken, with a nasty cut on the back of his head where he'd fallen."

"Had he had much to drink?"

"Two pints of beer, I understand. Not enough to make him fall over in the street."

"Has Stanford actually pressed charges, Sergeant?"

"He has not. He said he wanted to find the ring. If Adam had it, he would press charges."

"So, Stanford has no proof that my brother attacked him or stole his ring, but based on his accusation that Adam did it, we're faced with a scandal which could be totally unfounded."

"I entirely agree, Greg. We all want to avoid a scandal if possible, but I have to try to do my job." The policeman was also not at ease.

"So what happens now?"

Professor Bellamy replied. "Sergeant Jeffries has a proposal to make."

"What is it, Sergeant?"

"It occurs to me that this could just be a bit of fooling around between two young men. Stanford maybe just had a fall in the street. It was quite slippery last night in the freezing rain. He doesn't seem to be too fond of your brother and he was put out that he kept going on at him to buy the ring. So he invents this story that Adam took it, to make him sweat a bit. Stanford hasn't pressed charges, so Adam isn't yet involved in a police matter. I suggest that you have a word with him. Ask him if he knows anything about this. Was it a bit of tomfoolery? Does he have the ring in his possession? "

Greg was mortified. He had to ask his younger brother if he'd attacked and robbed a school friend. *My God! What a mess.* "Very well, I'll go and see him right now. But I'm sure he'll deny any knowledge of the affair, so what happens then?"

"In that case," replied Professor Bellamy, "we must search his dorm and all his personal effects. If we find nothing, then we will have to recommend to Stanford to drop his accusation, since it will only be his word against Adam's. If he agrees, then Sergeant Jeffries will continue his investigation for an unknown assailant and that will be the end of it."

Adam was mad with rage when his brother recounted the discussion to him. "That lying bastard, Stanford! I never tried to buy his ring, it's a piece of cheap crap. It's a battered old ring, made of dull gold with a tourmaline in it. It's not even worth pinching. And to suggest I might go around bashing people on the head in the street! I didn't budge from my dorm last night, everybody knows I'm cramming for the exams. I was studying when the other boys went to the pub and I was still at it when they got back. We're not all geniuses you know, Greg, some of us have to study to get a pass."

Greg ignored this jibe at his academic ability. "The thing is, Adam, he's accusing you of assault and theft. It's not a trivial matter."

"Well, let him go and accuse some other poor sod, 'cos it wasn't me. Now I really do feel like bashing his head in. Serve him right, the vindictive little prick."

"But why would he invent such a story? Is there something you're not telling me?"

"It's just a clique thing, that's all. They're all conspiring against me, Stanford's cronies. Little rich boy, buying his friends with his grandad's money. Bunch of bloody lying sods."

Greg was amazed to hear this abusive talk from his brother, though this was not the first time he had seen Adam become semi-hysterical when things didn't go his way. He sounded as if he was suffering from a victimisation complex.

"Adam, there's only one way to settle this. We have to make a search of your dorm and all your stuff. We'll prove that you don't have the ring then it won't matter what Stanford says. No one saw anything, so he'll have to retract his story and the business will be over."

At this, Adam went into paroxysms of rage and it was only after a very stern lecture from his elder brother that he agreed to this solution.

They searched the dormitory and Adam's personal effects with great care, but found nothing. When they explained the situation to Stanford he agreed not to press charges, so Sergeant Jeffries left them, to make other lines of enquiry. The housemasters reported the outcome to the principal and it was agreed to drop the matter. Greg was relieved at the result, but felt a nagging doubt at his brother's extreme reaction to their discussion.

Things settled down at Trelawney, and the strange business of the vicious attack and theft of the diamond ring was relegated to a historical anecdote. The ring was never found and the police failed to find or even identify the attacker. Stanford left the college that year and went up to King's. Greg and Adam never mentioned the matter again, but Greg didn't forget it.

Greg gained a first in economics and won the tennis singles championship again. The Trelawney cricket team carried the Southern College's Tournament and the rugby fifteen won the Inter-College Trophy. He went back home to Durban in a blaze of glory.

FIFTY-SIX

January, 1991
Rio de Janeiro, Brazil

There was no reply when Ray d'Almeida knocked at the door of the house on Centennial Drive, so he he tried the door handle. The dwelling was a small bungalow in Leblon, a pleasant, but not expensive area of Rio. The door opened and he called into the hall, "Hello Sra. Lindosa, it's Ray. I've got your groceries."

Ray was sixteen years old and working at three jobs. First thing in the morning he sold newspapers on the street corner. He made grocery deliveries in the afternoon and in the evening he was a waiter in a small café near the beach. No salary, tips only.

Times were tough and Ray's father, Sergio, had little work and even less money. His sister Alicia suffered from the same asthmatic condition that had killed their mother fifteen years ago and could just about look after their shack in the favela and cook what little food they could afford.

It was thanks to his father that Ray was still on the straight and narrow. Like all the kids around, he had been approached many times to get involved in the thriving drug business. After the third time it happened, when Ray was ten years old, Sergio took him to a shack at the poorest end of the track, where the Caldeira family lived. The place was in darkness. Not even a candle lit up the shed, which reeked of stale food, dirty bodies, animal detritus and worse.

"Bento!" Sergio called twice into the darkness. He struck a match and lit a taper which shone into the doorway. Ray stood nervously at his side, not knowing what to expect.

"*Sim*?" The voice that answered was weak and hoarse, accompanied by a wracking cough and a hacking sound.

"Can I come in?" Sergio didn't wait, but pushed his son ahead of him into the room.

In the flickering light from the taper Ray saw a scene more frightening than any of the nightmares that had plagued him since his mother's death.

Lying on a filthy, stained couch at the end of the room was a naked man. Long, matted hair and a mangy, unkempt beard. Vivid bruises and weeping sores covered his stick-thin arms and legs so that the skin looked like a grotesque graffiti design.

His eyes were puffed up and almost closed and he peered blindly through the gloom to see who was disturbing him. Even from several feet away, they could smell the feral stench of his breath as he gasped at the effort of trying to sit up on the couch. After a moment, he fell back again and lay motionless.

Sergio took his son to the bedside. Discarded hypodermic needles, teaspoons, match ends and candle stubs lay on the floor around the bed and on a table nearby. The man still didn't move. It was as if he was in a coma. Sergio said, "He'll be dead by the end of the week. That's what drugs do. If you want to be like that, you're on your own."

Bento died on the Friday. Ray had worked at three jobs ever since.

There was still no sound in the Lindosa's house so Ray walked along to the kitchen and dumped the paper bag on the table, checked the bill and laid it beside the groceries. Turning to leave, he saw a handbag lying on a chair at the table. He went into the living room and back into the hall, looking around and listening carefully. There was no one in the house.

The purse inside the bag contained thirty dollars. He removed a five and two dollar bills, slipped them into his back pocket, replaced the purse and bag and went back to the hall.

"Hello, Ray. What are you doing here?" A woman in a gardening smock was coming in through the door. She had been working in the garden and hadn't heard him.

Confused, he replied. "*Bom dia, Senhora Lindosa.* I was just delivering your groceries. I put them in the kitchen."

"Oh, thanks. Come back in, I'll get something for you."

Anxious now, he said, "Don't bother. I'll be back next week."

"It's no bother. Come into the kitchen."

Ray followed her back in and she picked up her bag and took out the purse. "That's strange. I could swear I had five dollar bills in here." She looked up at d'Almeida and saw from his flushed face what had happened.

"I'm sorry, Senhora. Here's the money." He pulled the notes from his pocket and placed them on the table. "Please don't say anything. I'll lose my job and be nicked. My father's broke and my sister's sick. My family needs me to work. Please don't report it. I'll do anything."

The woman appraised Ray as if he was a potential purchase in a boutique. He was taller than her husband and better looking, with a muscular build, a light olive skin and dark, curly hair. In fact, she registered, Ray was a good looking young man.

"I think we can work this out," she said, and took him by the hand towards the staircase.

An hour later, Ray rode off from the house on his bicycle to make his last deliveries. He'd avoided being fired and probably going to jail, but he wasn't too happy about the weekly duties expected of him by Sra. Lindosa.

FIFTY-SEVEN

1996 - 1998
Durban, South Africa

After finishing at Trelawney, where he gained a pass in modern languages, Adam returned to Durban in 1996, two years after Mandela's swearing in. Apart from holidays, he hadn't lived with his family for twelve years. He had missed living through the most tumultuous times in recent South African history. When he left, his homeland was divided by race and mutual hatred. It seemed that the country would be torn apart by a storm of violence and go the way of so many other African nations, towards civil war. The nation had to endure another ten years of trauma before Mandela's African National Congress won the first non-racial democratic election and he was sworn in as President of the country. Adam came home to a democratically governed republic. The storm had abated.

His sisters, Catrine and Birgitta, were now married, with a little boy and two girls respectively. Their husbands both worked in Hanny's business as store managers. And Greg, who had returned three years previously, was engaged to be married and also working with his father, preparing to take over the business.

Hanny, who was now fifty-six, was working less and playing a lot of golf. He'd encouraged Rachel to take it up and she was a natural golfer, winning many competitions, to the envy of the other ladies at the Chukka Country Club.

"You should see her, Adam. Your mother's got the most natural swing I've ever seen. She hits the ball further than me and straighter, too." Hanny still thought that his wife, at fifty- one, was the cleverest and loveliest woman he'd ever known. They were perfectly happy together.

Rachel had taken up her cancer research work again after Adam's birth. With some help from her father and Hanny and a modest financial contribution, she had convinced the Royal Albert Hospital to introduce a cancer research programme. Twenty-two years later she was still involved as a regular consultant, having an unusually deep knowledge of the disease.

Two years before, she had conceived the idea of opening a hospice. She set up a registered charity to finance the project and with the help of all the family, she organised dances, dinners, sports days and every possible kind of event where she could raise money, either through contributions, or lotteries, or sponsorships. Within a year she had raised enough to convert an old warehouse that Hanny still owned from his grandfather's days into a comfortable, well-equipped rest home for terminal cancer patients.

At all of the functions she addressed the audience, exhorting her friends and the other attendees to give generously. "We owe it to our community to provide a place where terminally ill patients can be cared for during their last days. Where they can end their lives in comfort and with dignity, surrounded by family who care about them."

Rachel would use her personal experience as an example. "My own father has just died after a long fight with cancer. He was one of the fortunate few whose family could look after him, even though my mother had already passed away. But he was in a lucky minority. There are thousands more sufferers who have nowhere to go to and we must do something about it."

Research was all very well, but Rachel wanted to become personally involved. To invest her knowledge in a more direct, more caring way. She was so happy when the first 'guests' came to stay in the newly appointed accommodation. She spent more time than she should at the hospice. But when Hanny saw how much satisfaction it afforded her, he didn't mind.

And when her family asked her how she had the energy to start the project and see it through at her age despite all of the obstacles in her path, she replied to them as she had done many times before, simply reflecting her basic philosophy of life, "If you decide that something needs to be done, you can't put it off for ever. Now's the best time. It always is."

Back at home, Adam once more felt the pressure of competing with his brother. His parents had never deliberately favoured their eldest son but he envied Greg his place as top dog and still felt that he looked down on him. He wanted to succeed on his own and show everyone what he was capable of, to prove himself to his parents as a winner, not a second best.

He rented an apartment and a nearby office in downtown Durban and working with some funding and advice from his father he set up a trading company specialising in gemstones, gold bullion and other precious metals. His reputation as a smart businessman quickly spread in a highly competitive and ruthless industry. He showed that he could be as competitive and ruthless as the best of them. His success was admired by his family and friends but he constantly sought for more. He was a very ambitious man.

"Old Willy Martin called me. He's closing up, he's tired. He must be eighty years old if he's a day. He's offered me some nice stuff, very good prices."

It was March, 1998. Hanny had arranged to buy a selection of jewellery from a Joburg dealer who was retiring. He had been dealing with the man for many years, so he was buying the merchandise sight unseen. He prevailed upon Greg to drive up there to pick up the goods.

"This leg's bothering me a bit. It's that bloody thrombosis that I had last year. I'm just going to sit in the garden this weekend. Your mother will play golf then we'll have supper on the terrace. A perfect weekend. You don't mind, son, do you?"

Adam had a customer there whom he could visit so he and Greg agreed to go up together. It was Friday afternoon when they set off, aiming to spend the night in Joburg, do their business on the Saturday and return on the Sunday.

"Right, Adam. Two shifts, three hours each and we'll be more or less there." The two men climbed into Greg's battered Range Rover and drove off, en route for Joburg.

Adam was taking the first shift. He was wearing the driving gloves which were one of his affectations. He had several little foibles like that. He needed to appear different from the crowd and got upset when anyone questioned his habits. He had gone out with a lovely girl called Judith for several months the previous year but she had dropped him for that very reason. She said that he wanted to appear eccentric but he ended up looking peculiar. Adam had gone bananas and screamed at her to apologise. She left him instead. He was glad to see the back of her. *What did she know?* It was strange that all of his short relationships with women had ended the same way. *Stupid bitches,* he always thought to himself.

They arrived in Joburg late that evening and spent the night in a hotel near the dealer's store. On the Saturday, after depositing the three boxes of valuables in the hotel safe, they went for supper to the Long Bar, a popular establishment near their hotel. At the table, Greg noticed that his brother was sporting a gold ring on his right hand that he'd never seen before. This wasn't surprising, since they didn't spend much time together. Greg preferred to pass his leisure time with Alison, his fiancée.

"That's a nice ring you're wearing. Where did you pick it up?" He reached over to turn his brother's hand around for a closer look.

Adam pulled his hand away quickly. "Just a bauble I picked up in London on a business trip. I've got several of them. Little artisan in the city. Makes nice stuff, very wearable and not expensive." He jumped up. "Must visit the gents. Back in a sec." He went down the stairs to the toilets. When he returned, Greg noticed that he had removed the ring. He decided not to mention it again for the moment, it might spoil the weekend.

Driving back to Durban, with the merchandise safely stowed in the back of the Range Rover, they found themselves in the middle of a torrential rainstorm. Greg slowed down to the pace of the other cars. The vehicles were bunched into small groups at intervals along the road, the cars in each little convoy going nose to tail in the difficult driving conditions. Dirty water was being thrown up from the slick, muddy surface by the vehicles in front. With this and the driving rain, the windscreen wipers could hardly keep up.

The incident with the ring and his brother's erratic behaviour had jogged Greg's memory as he lay in bed last night. He remembered clearly the business with young Stanford, five years previously at Trelawney. From the brief glimpse he'd gotten last night, the ring that Adam had taken considerable trouble to conceal looked like a gold ring with an embedded yellow diamond. Greg was a very upfront man. He didn't like subterfuge of any kind, especially where he had been personally involved.

"So, Adam, that ring last night. You got it from a jewellery designer in London?"

"Oh, that ring. Yes, a little artisan down in the east end of town, near Hatton Garden."

"Do you have it handy? I liked the look of it. It would probably sell well in our shops."

"It's in the case with my stuff. Remind me when we get home." Adam switched the radio on. "Let's see if we can listen to something other than the windscreen wipers."

Greg was not to be put off. "How much does he sell them for?"

"The rings you mean? About four or five hundred quid, depends on the stone, of course."

"Is that in bulk, or just a one off?"

"I've only bought the one, so I don't know for sure. But I suppose you could do a deal."

"Really? I thought you said last night that you'd bought several of them."

"You must have misunderstood me. That's the only one I've bought." Adam shuffled uneasily in the passenger seat.

"Well, I don't usually forget what someone has told me within twelve hours of hearing it. And now that you mention a misunderstanding, it seemed to me that your ring looked very much like the one that was stolen from Stanford at Trelawney five years ago."

"What in hell's name are you talking about? You never even saw Stanford's ring, it was nothing like the one I was wearing. What are you trying to insinuate?"

"Dr. Clarence described the ring to me and it was similar to your ring. And you told me that it was yellow gold with a tourmaline in it. That's like a yellow diamond. Isn't that right?"

At this, Adam almost jumped out of the car. He turned to his brother with a furious expression. "Listen you suspicious, sanctimonious bastard, I've just told you that the two rings were nothing alike. If you don't believe me you can go and screw yourself."

Greg forced himself to remain calm and concentrate on the treacherous road. *Maybe I picked the wrong time for this discussion,* he thought. "Alright, keep your shirt on. I'm just interested in buying some of those rings for the business. What's the name of the jeweller in Hatton Garden?"

Suddenly, Adam lashed out at Greg's head. "You lying prick, you've always had it in for me. You've hated me ever since the day I was born. You think I'm inferior to you. I've known it for years. Now you're trying to implicate me in something that happened five years ago, just so you can add another trophy to the Greg Peterson collection. You're a bloody retail jeweller, not Sherlock fucking Holmes. Leave me the fuck alone." He took another swipe at his brother.

"Jesus Christ, Adam. What in hell do you think you're doing? Are you insane?" Greg took his left hand off the wheel to defend himself from the blows. Adam grabbed his hand, twisting it as if to break it. Greg pulled violently away and fell sideways against the driver's door, his foot pressing down on the accelerator. They had just come over a rise and were now headed downhill. The heavy vehicle speeded up, starting to sway on the road, closing up on a white truck ahead of them. Greg pulled himself back up and grabbed the wheel again. They were about to ram into the truck. He braked and pulled the wheel to the left.

"Shit!" Adam saw the smash coming up and grabbed the armrests to hold himself steady.

With a screech, the Range Rover spun around on the slick asphalt and its back end smashed into the truck. The vehicle rebounded and Greg almost managed to bring the wheels back in line on the road. He glanced in the rear view mirror and saw there was a black Jaguar behind him. The driver had also stepped on the brake and it was sliding towards them on the slippery surface. It struck them on the rear left-wing, thrusting the car towards the ditch at the side of the road. The front near wheel dropped into the ditch and the Range Rover turned over sideways, tumbling through the bushes lining the road. Rolling over again they smashed into a tree stump and came to rest on all four wheels in a muddy banana plantation.

Both brothers were wearing safety belts, but the car was an old model and there were no airbags. Because Greg had been gripping the wheel so tightly he had been able to hold himself in position in his seat. Apart from bruising in his shoulders and legs where he had been thrown about by the rolling vehicle, he was unhurt. He unfastened his seat belt and turned to his brother. Adam was bleeding from the forehead and the nose. He had been smashed against the doorframe when the car had rolled over. The passenger door had been pushed in onto him and his legs were twisted under the folded metal of the door. He was unconscious.

Greg reached over and felt his pulse. It was beating regularly. He made no attempt to try to move his brother, but left him as he was. He grabbed the carphone and it fell to pieces in his hand. He didn't have a mobile phone but he knew Adam did. He looked desperately around for Adam's mobile. It was nowhere to be seen in the jumbled interior of the vehicle. *It must be in his pocket,* he told himself, but he didn't want to disturb his brother. Greg knew that some other driver would have one. He jumped out of the vehicle into the pouring rain and clambered up the muddy bank to seek help.

The scene was chaotic. There were cars all over the place, on both sides of the road. It seemed that one of the cars behind them had slid right across the tarmac and collided with the oncoming traffic. He could still hear the noise of other cars coming from both directions, as they screeched to a halt, trying to avoid the multiple collision.

Greg ran to the Jaguar. It was damaged in front where it had hit his Range Rover and there was another vehicle rammed into its rear.

The driver was still sitting at the wheel, rubbing his neck as if he'd suffered a whiplash. Then Greg saw him pull out a mobile phone. He ran around the front of the car to speak to him.

Julius Oösterhoozen was beat. He'd been up for 24 hours straight, driving his semi-remorque up to Joburg from Cape Town to pick up a container that had to be in Durban by Monday morning. His lorry was in front of a group of eight cars making up the convoy some distance behind Greg and Adam. They were travelling at only seventy kilometres an hour, approaching the top of a long straight rise, with no other vehicles on the road. Conditions were so bad on the slippy road that the cars behind hadn't dared to overtake the long vehicle. He rubbed his eyes and reached down to get his thermos, still half-full of sweet, strong coffee.

As he came over the rise, starting on the descent, he saw the jumble of cars in front of him, emergency lights flashing. He slammed his foot on the brake, struggling to hold the massive vehicle in line. The trailer jack-knifed behind the cab, sliding sideways and pushing him across into the path of the oncoming traffic which now appeared, coming up the slope. He hauled the wheel over and the trailer reversed direction, turning him around backwards, then the twenty foot container slammed into the first of the cars in front of him. The cars were pushed forward in series by the impact, like dominoes. The black Jaguar was the third car in the line.

As he passed in front of the Jaguar, Greg heard a bang and the car suddenly shot towards him. His immediate reaction was to turn to try to push it away. The car fender hit him in the knees, breaking the kneecaps and femurs in both legs. Although the car was moving at less than twenty kilometres an hour, the counter-reaction of his upper body to the impact against his legs caused his hips to dislocate as he fell violently forward onto the bonnet of the car. Three of his ribs were broken and his head smashed down onto the metal surface, breaking his jaw and nose and cracking his skull, just above the right brow. The top of the grill pushed into his stomach, almost tearing the kidney from the renal artery and severing the pancreas from the small intestine. He bounced off the bonnet onto the ground and the car wheel crushed his shoulder and broke his right humerus as it rolled over him. He lay still, half under the Jaguar, sprawled in the mud in the beating rain.

One of the doctors from the Emergencies Admissions Dept. came into the waiting room where Hanny, Rachel and the whole family had been sitting for almost two hours since receiving the telephone call from the police. They all jumped up apprehensively.

The two brothers had been rushed down to the General Hospital in Durban and had gone straight into surgery. Eighteen cars on both sides of the road were involved in the multiple collision due to the appalling visibility and treacherous conditions. The first police had arrived on motor cycles within a couple of minutes of receiving the call from the Jaguar driver and immediately ordered up a helicopter from the accident rescue service. The jumble of vehicles on the road prevented the ambulances from arriving for over an hour.

Greg had been taken to hospital in the helicopter, while the remaining rescue team was forced to wait until the fire brigade could get through to cut the door off the Range Rover, to extricate Adam from the wreck and transport him by ambulance. The road was closed for three hours, but because the traffic had been moving fairly slowly there were no other serious injuries, apart from one or two cases of whiplash and some minor cuts and bruises.

The family had not been given details of the condition of the injured brothers. The police had simply described the circumstances of the accident. It was ironic that Greg had emerged unscathed from the crash in which Adam had been injured, only to be knocked down by a car that was hardly moving.

The doctors had been working on both men in separate operating theatres since they were brought in. The doctor who came in now had been operating on Adam.

He smiled at them. "Adam's a very lucky man, considering the circumstances. He has a slight concussion which should be gone by tomorrow morning. He also had a broken nose which I've fixed better than the original. I'm afraid that he has multiple fractures to his legs, but they are not complex. The door panel simply impacted the shins and caused several clean breaks in both legs. I expect a full recovery in not more than three months. He's in plaster casts and he's sedated, so you won't be able to see him until the morning. It's better to let him sleep it off for now."

The family gave him their heartfelt thanks then asked about Greg. He had no knowledge of Greg's condition, he was still undergoing surgery. They resigned themselves to wait for further news.

It seemed a lifetime before the second surgeon came through to meet them. His face was grey from fatigue and he was not smiling. Hanny took Rachel's hand and they braced themselves for his words. She was trembling with fear and worry over the fate of their eldest son, Hanny's son. The doctor asked them to sit down again and he sat alongside them.

"I'm desperately sorry," he started.

Rachel and the other women hardly heard the rest of what he said. Those three words confirmed their worst fears. They held each other and sobbed helplessly at the death of their son, brother and fiancé. Hanny tried desperately to concentrate on the doctor's voice, as if it might somehow explain to him why his son's life had been so swiftly and mercilessly taken from him.

The surgeon stoically continued with his explanation. "Even though the vehicle that hit Greg was moving quite slowly, he sustained a number of severe injuries from the impact. It's not uncommon to suffer more damage from a slow collision than from a fast one. We see this a lot in sports accidents. In a fast collision, or a high speed fall, the body is often thrown away from the impact zone, suffering bruises, contusions and broken bones, but nothing worse. No complicated breaks or damage to internal organs." He took off his spectacles, wiping them absent mindedly with the hem of his white gown as if he was giving a lecture to a group of students.

"When the collision is slower, but with great impetus, the damage can be much worse. The body is put under enormous pressure and cannot escape, causing undue stress on the skeleton, the muscles, the joints, the organs, etc. Unfortunately, this is what happened in Greg's case. The momentum of the car was too great for his body to resist, and he couldn't get away from it. It literally pushed him to the limit, and the damage he suffered was very difficult to repair. I have seldom seen such terrible injuries and I hate to say it, but," here he looked at Rachel and Hanny, "your son is better off not surviving than living with the physical disabilities that would have devastated the quality of life in his remaining years.

"Strangely enough," he went on, "we were able to repair most of the life-threatening injuries to his internal organs. In reality, Greg died because the blow to his head caused pressure on his brain and we had to try to relieve it before it caused permanent damage. But because we had to cope with that at the same time that we were working on those vital organs to avoid a complete failure of the system, it was more than his body could withstand. Although he was a very fit and strong man, I'm afraid that it was just too great a shock for his heart, and combined with the loss of so much blood from all the haemorrhaging in his body, his system couldn't cope with all of these stresses. In other words, I'm afraid that there was simply too much damage for us to repair before he succumbed to his injuries."

Adam never told his parents about the ring, or the fight in the Range Rover. He convinced himself that to lose one son was as much as they could bear. If he told them the truth, they would feel that they had lost both sons and that would be truly unbearable for them. He spent the rest of his life trying to convince himself that he was not responsible for his brother's death.

FIFTY-EIGHT

March, 1998
Favela Morro do Cantagalo, Rio de Janeiro, Brazil

Ray d'Almeida walked wearily home to the shack in the favela. It was after midnight and he'd just finished his shift as a waiter at the Hotel Dominico. He currently had four jobs. At six in the morning he started his day gutting fish at the open market in the harbour then at nine thirty he drove a delivery truck, swapping empty gas cylinders for full ones at shacks and trailers around the beach area. This was his best paid job, made possible by the few dollars he'd saved the previous year to get a driver's license, after learning in a beat up old Dodge truck belonging to one of his few friends who could afford to run a car. Between four and seven he washed cars in a garage near the favela, before starting at the hotel.

Alicia still suffered from the same asthmatic condition and couldn't hold down a job. His father was still working as an odd job man, fixing TVs and washing machines for those families who could afford such luxuries. Between the two of them they just about scraped up enough to eat three times a day and buy a change of clothing once in a while.

Ray was still wearing the waiter's outfit supplied by the hotel, a white shirt and black waistcoat and trousers. His head down, he trudged along, entering the first crowded lane of the favela, the noisome smell already permeating the air. A few shanty dwellers were sitting on their stoops and a man's body was lying drunk, drugged or dead at the side of the lane.

He turned a sharp corner to start climbing the path towards his home on the high side of the shanty town. There were fewer people around. He could hear music and shouts and screams from further down the hill. It sounded like a party was in progress. Then his sharp hearing caught a shuffling sound and murmuring voices from behind him. He looked around and saw a couple of figures slip into the shadows of the tumbledown constructions. His waiter's outfit had made him a target before, he might have a pocketful of tips. *Some chance,* he thought. He had less than four dollars in his pocket.

Tensing himself, he continued walking and groped for the only weapon he had available. It was a folding penknife, with a corkscrew bottle opener that he used in the restaurant on the rare occasions that a customer ordered wine. He took the knife from the pocket of his waistcoat and opened the corkscrew, gripping it tightly in his fist with the screw protruding between his first and second knuckles. A moment later he heard the footsteps right behind him and swung round to confront two muscular black men in T-shirts and jeans, hefting short sticks in their hands.

The first of them ran at him, smashing the cudgel towards his head. Ray sidestepped and as the mugger plunged past him he lashed out at the man's face, the corkscrew slicing through his cheek like a melon.

He yelped with pain. "Fucking dago. I'll kill you for that."

The second man was on him immediately, swinging his stick into Ray's kidneys. He staggered and the first man turned and kicked him in the shoulder, knocking him to his knees.

The man aimed his foot again at Ray's face and he dodged the kick, grabbed his leg and savagely twisted it around. There was a crack and the man cried out and fell backwards on the ground, holding his broken knee. The second assailant caught Ray around the neck and headbutted him in the face. He felt his nose break and tears sprang to his eyes. The man positioned himself to hit him again with his head, his drug tainted breath panting into Ray's face. He blinked away the tears, and desperately focusing on the face in front of him, he positioned the corkscrew on his fist and punched straight into the man's eye. The mugger screamed as the metal screw penetrated his eye, going straight through into the socket, blood and mucous from the wound mingling with the blood from Ray's nose, dripping onto his waistcoat.

"Now I'm really pissed off," he shouted. "You've ruined my fucking outfit, you bastards. You're gonna pay for that!"

Ray limped slowly away from the two dead or unconscious bodies in the lane, he didn't know which and he didn't care. He was holding his side where the stabbing pain from the kidney blow was hurting him. He was richer by three dollars, which was all the two men had on them, but it would cost him a dollar to have his waistcoat cleaned. He took it off and rolled it up so that the bloodstains couldn't be seen, washed the blood off his face in the outside sink and tried painfully to push his nose back into place. He didn't want his father and sister to notice anything that might worry them. They already had enough on their minds.

BOOK TWO

PART FOUR: 2008

FIFTY-NINE

Tuesday, April 21st, 2008
Malaga, Spain

Leticia came to the house early to discuss matters before they drove together to the lawyers' office. First, Jenny called back Monsieur Schneider at Klein, Fellay. She confirmed that they would come to see him on Thursday morning at eleven with the documents he had requested. He seemed surprised to hear back from her so quickly, complementing her in a patronising fashion, and said he looked forward to seeing them.

"I think it's quite normal. M. Schneider must be German Swiss, very efficient." Leticia grimaced at the prospect of dealing with the Swiss banking system. "Why didn't Charlie put his money in Marbella? Everything is more easy in Spain, no?"

Jenny laughed. "Not if you want it still to be there after thirty years."

"Good point, the Swiss Guard is protecting our money. *Merci beaucoup*."

"Anyway, we don't know what there is at that bank, if there's anything at all. Let's wait and see," Jenny said cautiously. "Although

I suppose there must be something to do with the Angolan Clan." Jenny was thinking about Francisco's offer to come to Geneva. "You realise we can't let José Luis and Francisco learn about the Angolan Clan? Charlie kept it a secret for thirty years and he must have had good reason to do so. In any case, the partnership should be terminated this year so we should just let it fade away without any publicity."

Leticia nodded. "We'll have to tell Francisco that we don't need him."

"Right, that's settled. Time to go to see José Luis."

At Klein, Fellay, Mlle Rousseau made a call on her mobile phone. She just said, "*Bonjour mon amour.* They're coming here on Thursday morning."

José Luis was tied up and Francisco ushered the women into the conference room. He assured them that everything was in order. They signed several documents concerning the estate, then Jenny said diplomatically, "We hope you don't mind, but Leticia and I think it's better for us to go to Geneva alone. We need to start sorting our new lives out without a chaperone. If we have any problems we'll call you but we don't anticipate any difficulties that we can't cope with."

The lawyer seemed disappointed, but said he understood, then added, "The documents for Geneva will be notarised in the morning, so I can bring them to the house if it would help."

"There's no need to bother. We can collect them on our way to the airport." Jenny didn't want them to be stuck with visitors while they were preparing for their departure.

They drove into Marbella and picked up their air tickets from Louisa, then walked along to the Banco de Iberia. Jenny had persuaded Leticia to call Patrice to arrange to change some money into Swiss Francs for them. "We're sure to get a better rate than anywhere else," she reasoned.

The Frenchman came down as soon as they arrived at the bank and they went to the currency desk to purchase a couple of thousand Swiss Francs. Jenny had brought sufficient money with her in Sterling and the rate against the Swiss currency was quite good. It cost her less than a thousand pounds. With that amount and their credit cards they expected to be solvent for three days, even if Geneva was as expensive as Louisa had warned.

While they waited for the currency to arrive, Leticia said, "We've never been to Geneva before. What's it like?"

"Well, it's nothing like living in Marbella," Patrice replied. "Quite the reverse in fact. A lot of work and not very much fun. But it's a great city to visit. You'll like it. You should try to go up to the mountains, it's really spectacular. Francisco and I were skiing there earlier this year and it was marvellous."

Jenny forestalled the conversation, "That's a nice idea, but we won't have time this trip. Maybe next time." She was careful to reveal nothing to the banker. The less said the better.

Patrice nodded. "Well, I know a lot of people in Geneva, so if there's anything I can do please just ask. What about your hotel? You need to watch out, they can be very costly."

Leticia was determined to take credit for her arrangements. "I booked us into La Grange Hotel. I've heard it's very comfortable and not expensive."

"I know it well. It's a good choice, I'm sure you'll be well looked after."

Jenny left them talking and went to a screen showing the latest Swiss franc exchange rates against the Euro and the US Dollar, scribbling them in her notebook, just in case.

Turning to go back to the counter, she collided with a man standing behind her. Unshaven and wearing a scruffy anorak and jeans, he looked out of place in the crowded banking hall. He gave her a blank stare when she apologised then walked over to the exit, looked back at her and went out into the street.

Jenny put the Swiss Francs carefully into her purse, separate from the Sterling and Euros. The purse went into her bag, which she held by the strap, over her shoulder. Patrice escorted them out, wishing them *au revoir* and an enjoyable trip to Switzerland.

He watched them until they were out of sight then pulled out his mobile phone and set off in the opposite direction, speaking quickly in Spanish as he strode away from the bank.

The women walked back through the Alameda gardens to the underground car park. As they turned to go down the staircase, Jenny felt her bag being torn from her shoulder. She held onto the strap and was swung around to come face to face with the scruffy man from the bank.

"*Déme el bolso o tu es la carne muerta!* Give me the bag or you're dead meat!" He held a vicious looking knife in his hand. It was twenty centimetres long, with a wide, serrated blade. Looking at Leticia, he said, "Yours as well. Hand it over or your friend is history."

Leticia gasped and stepped away. "Give him the bag, Jenny. Don't argue, he'll kill you!" She held out her own bag for the man to take.

Jenny took her bag from her shoulder, gripping the strap in her left hand. "*Muy bien,*" she said, offering it to the thief and showing her other hand, palm upwards, in surrender.

"*Ciuidado,hembra*! Careful, bitch!" Brandishing the knife in one hand, he took hold of the bag with the other. Jenny grabbed the hand and crouched on the ground, pulling him forward in an improvised judo throw. Astonished, he fell straight over her, still clutching the bag. He slashed out wildly with the knife and the blade cut across her arm.

The mugger fell heavily to the ground and the knife spun out of his grasp. He scrambled to retrieve the weapon. Quick as a flash, Jenny jumped to her feet and kicked him in the face. She was wearing leather walking shoes, and the toe caught the man on the temple. He fell back and dropped the bag, holding his hand to a gash on his forehead, blood running down his face.

She picked up her bag. "Get the knife, Leticia!"

Leticia was looking on in a daze, sure that her friend would be stabbed to death. She kicked the knife away from the man's reach then grabbed it and handed it to her.

Blood was running down Jenny's arm and dripping from her hand. "You tried to kill me, you son of a bitch. I'll slit your filthy throat." She raised the knife over the cowering, would-be mugger, ready to slash him.

Leticia grabbed her arm and screamed, "Stop it, Jenny. You'll do something crazy."

She took a deep breath and shook her head. "Right! Tell him I won't hurt him if he goes away now. Tell him, Leticia!" Jenny stood over the terrified man, pointing the knife at his face.

The man had understood her. "OK," he said. "Let me up and I'll go. Don't hurt me."

She stepped back and the man jumped to his feet and sprinted away across the park.

The women watched him run from their sight then Jenny walked across to a bench on the edge of the park and sat down. The knife was still in her hand. She looked around. Nobody had witnessed the scene. It was lunch time and some couples were sitting eating sandwiches near the fountain, but they were on the other side of the trees, out of hearing range.

"Are you all right, Jenny?"

The English woman's heart was pounding. She breathed deeply to calm her nerves. "It's a long time since I had to do that. More than ten years. Last time it was a thirteen year old emotionally disturbed kid, not a fully grown mugger. Thank God for the judo lessons."

"You might have been killed. *Dios mío,* I was so frightened for you."

"Don't be silly, Leticia. The papers and money and keys are in our bags and we're going to Geneva tomorrow. I couldn't let a dirty Spanish thief steal them, could I?"

"Let me see your arm." Leticia rolled up her sleeve. The wound was no more than a long scratch. It had almost stopped bleeding and wouldn't need stitching. "Here." She tore up a handkerchief and tended the wound then tied a piece of the cotton around the arm.

Jenny got up and went over to a rubbish bin to throw the knife away then had second thoughts. "I'd better keep it. If somebody else finds it they might get similar ideas."

They sat quietly in the park for a few more minutes then went to recuperate the car.

In the underground car park, the man standing behind the concrete pillar watched the women walk from the ticket machine towards the Mercedes. He saw that they were still carrying their bags and Jenny held what looked like a long knife in her hand.

"Shit!" He knew now that the mugger would not be coming to collect his fee, because he had somehow failed to steal the bags. He tried to imagine what had gone wrong. It was such an easy job. A professional thief with a vicious knife against two defenceless women was a piece of cake. He should have the bags and their contents in his hands, but he didn't. Someone must have intervened. Some bloody interfering passer-by must have gone to help them. There was no other explanation. He hadn't witnessed the fight or he would have reassessed his opinion of the two 'defenceless' women. It was a mistake he would live to regret.

As he watched the Mercedes drive slowly through the barrier he banged the pillar with his fist in frustration. Now he needed a new plan and time was running out.

Leticia drove without speaking, waiting until Jenny had recovered from the incident. She couldn't believe that this slightly-built ex-school teacher had bested a vicious mugger armed with a murderous weapon. The knife was lying on the floor by Jenny's feet. Leticia shuddered at the sight of its wide, serrated cutting edge. *Crazy woman,* she thought. *Brave but crazy*. Reaction set in and Jenny slept all the way back to Marbella.

In the house, she disinfected and bandaged the cut then went to put the knife in a kitchen drawer. She changed her mind and hid it where no one would come across it by accident.

In Charlie's office she checked his email again but there was nothing new. As she switched off the machine, the phone rang. She picked it up. "Hello, Jenny speaking."

A woman's voice with a strong French accent said, "Good afternoon. This is Gloria, from the Geneva office. Can I speak to Mr. Bishop please?

Jenny remembered that the IDD secretary was called Gloria. She said, "I'm afraid that Mr. Bishop's not here. This is Jenny Bishop, his daughter-in law, can I help you?"

"How do you do, Jenny, my name is Gloria Smouha. "I need to speak to Mr. Bishop. When will he be back, please?"

Jenny realised that she couldn't continue in this vein, so she steeled herself. "The fact is, Gloria, that Mr. Bishop had an accident in his pool. He fell and hit his head and was drowned. It was just a few days ago. That's why I'm here, for the funeral and everything."

She heard a sharp intake of breath. "So, he's dead? Charlie's dead?"

"I'm afraid so. I'm sorry to have to tell you like this. Is it something I can help with?"

There was a pause then Gloria replied, "There's some information he asked me to confirm and I wanted to explain it to him, but... Well, it's difficult to tell you on the phone, because you don't know me or the business or anything."

Jenny thought for a moment. "Listen, Gloria. I'm coming to Geneva on Wednesday evening. I can come and see you on Thursday and you can tell me about it when we meet."

The other woman was relieved. She explained to Jenny how to get to the IDD office and gave her the telephone number. She only worked three days a week but she would be there all day on Thursday. Jenny agreed to meet her there in the afternoon.

"It must have been her on the phone with Charlie!" Leticia exclaimed when she told her.

"That's what I thought."

"Did she say what was the problem?"

"She didn't want to tell me on the phone, but I suppose we'll find out on Thursday."

I wonder what the call was about? Jenny thought. Gloria had sounded rather concerned. Once again there were things that she didn't know. Her sense of foreboding returned, but she said nothing more to Leticia. Time enough to worry when they got to Geneva.

It was Tuesday afternoon before Chief Inspector Espinoza found the time to call Inspector Blaser in Geneva. The Swiss policeman immediately agreed to his request to 'take care' of the two women when they arrived in Switzerland. It seemed that things were very quiet in Geneva and the surveillance would keep a junior agent busy for a few days.

During an earlier call with José Luis, Espinoza had managed to glean the name of their hotel from him. The women had left the address with Francisco in case of any emergency. He was probably unaware that he'd mentioned it, so subtle was the questioning. It made Blaser's task easier, knowing where they would start and finish each day. He promised Espinoza a detailed report first thing on the following Monday morning. The Spanish officer hoped that it would throw up something, something he could get his teeth into. He was still convinced there was a motive and a crime. Time would tell.

To prepare for their Geneva meeting, the women went back through Charlie's narrative and Jenny read out the key points in the history of the Angolan Clan. Revisiting the people and events in Portugal, Angola and Geneva that had been thrust into their lives by Charlie's story.

"You know, Leticia," she said. "This isn't going to be any easier for the other partners than it is for us. Instead of their friend and genius business partner, Charlie Bishop, they're going to meet two women with no business experience at all. It's going to be a big shock for them and we don't know how they'll react. We have to be careful."

"If they were people that Charlie trusted then I think we have to trust them also. Everyone is in a new, different position. It's not only you and me." Leticia was right, things had changed for everyone.

But how do we prepare ourselves to meet three men whom we don't even know, but who are now our business partners? Jenny asked herself. There was enough background on Laurent and Nick for them to form an impression, but Raffael remained an enigma. She couldn't get her head around it all, so she put it aside until later.

Over the last few days, Jenny had become more and more impressed with Leticia. She was clever, quick on the uptake and had a wonderful sense of humour. Endowed with a genuinely affectionate nature, she had a positive vitality which fairly radiated from her and made everyone around her feel good. Despite her initial forebodings, it was impossible for Jenny not to become fond of her, like the younger sister she had never had.

As she had become closer to Jenny, Leticia had also revealed to her the gradual transformation of her relationship with Charlie. There was no doubt it was a true love story, despite the disparity in their ages. It was sad, Jenny thought, that Charlie had been able to enjoy her youthful company and love and the growing up of his son for such a short time. *Still,* she mused, *short, but so very sweet. Lucky Charlie.*

Leticia went back to her apartment to pack and spend the evening with her family. Her parents were delighted to have Emilio staying with them for several days and José had asked for a couple of days off work so he wouldn't miss sharing this break with his grandson.

It was now three days until the meeting of the Angolan Clan.

SIXTY

Wednesday 23rd April 2008
Geneva, Switzerland

A young, dark haired concierge welcomed them as their taxi pulled up in front of the Hotel de La Grange. He spoke French with a strong accent. "Portuguese," Leticia whispered to Jenny.

The hotel was situated on the left bank of *Lac Leman,* the Lake of Geneva. It was after eight o' clock and too dark to see the lake directly in front of them. A line of faint lights could just be discerned, shimmering on the far side of the water, which was not very wide at that point.

It was a very chilly evening and a soft rain was falling. They pulled their new, warm coats around themselves and hurried into the hotel. It was charmingly old-fashioned, clean and comfortable. Their rooms on the third floor faced the lake and promised to offer vistas in the morning, over the water to the Jura Mountains beyond.

They unpacked and freshened up and after Leticia had called her mother to check on Emilio they went downstairs to the bar where she ordered two glasses of white wine, in French.

Jenny laughed. "You're determined to make me feel inferior in languages, aren't you? Though I don't know if ordering white wine qualifies as speaking French!"

"Just wait a moment. I have to ask for my supper next!"

On the way to the airport, they had picked up the documents and a scribbled note of apology from José Luis's secretary. He was busy with a client and Francisco was on his way to London. *He certainly gets around,* thought Jenny. *Good job we didn't want him to come to Geneva.*

Their business class seats on the Iberia flights were comfortable and although the change-over in Madrid was delayed, they managed to sleep for a while on the Geneva section. They had waited to have dinner in their hotel. Nine o'clock wasn't late by Spanish standards. Jenny wasn't convinced that it was worth paying all that money for business class. She thought of herself as an easyJet kind of traveller and told Leticia this. The younger woman disagreed.

Now, sitting in Le Parc restaurant in the hotel, listening to her order her dinner in French from the Maître d'Hotel, Jenny wondered if all their preparations would be enough. Despite what Leticia had said about trust, they were entering a world of men and a world of money. Large amounts of money. How would they handle themselves? In Jenny's experience, large amounts of money seldom brought happiness and often brought problems. She put aside her trepidation and they had an enjoyable dinner together. Tomorrow would arrive soon enough.

It was now two days until the meeting of the Angolan Clan.

The man in the brasserie watched the women go up to their rooms. He got up and stretched himself. He was stiff and tired after sitting there for the last three hours. Going out into the street to find his car he pulled out his mobile phone and spoke for a few minutes. It took him only fifteen minutes to drive to his apartment and he was in bed by eleven. He would need to be up at six to get back to the hotel, but he was a good sleeper.

As usual, Gloria had been to visit her mother at the nursing home. It was after ten o'clock and she was about to get ready for bed when the doorbell rang. Surprised, she went into the tiny hall and asked who was there. When there was no reply she cautiously unlatched the door onto the landing.

"What on earth are you doing here at this hour?" She exclaimed, before the visitor pushed her aside and stepped into the apartment.

Gloria's body was found the next morning, Thursday, at 6:30 am, when the first early morning riser went to get her cycle to ride to the bakery for fresh croissants. She was lying on the flagstones that surrounded the building, directly under the little balcony of her fourth floor apartment. On the other side from the entrance, where the rubbish containers and cycles were kept. That was why the body hadn't been noticed the previous night.

The gendarmes found bloody marks on the lid of one of the containers which matched bruises and contusions on her shoulder and head. Neither they, nor the doctor who arrived shortly after, could find any marks on the body which were not consistent with a fall or a jump from the balcony. They deduced that the actual cause of death was a broken neck sustained when she had landed on the corner of the container lid.

The ambulance took the body to the morgue and the pathologist confirmed the cause of death, and that Gloria's injuries were consistent with a fall from the fourth floor balcony. She examined her hands for evidence of a struggle. There was none, but she noticed a bruise on the upper arm and some chafing to the lips. This could indicate that Gloria had been held from behind with a hand over her mouth, in such a position that she couldn't defend herself. She was a small woman, and could easily have been overcome in such a way, but there were no other indications of foul play.

The pathologist also observed a very faint, perfumed odour. Lifting the right hand to her nostril she tried to identify the scent. She thought that she could also discern the perfumed smell on Gloria's neck or head. Could it be a man's cologne or after shave, or a woman's scent? She added this to her report, but there was not enough evidence to arrive at a definite conclusion as to the reasons behind the death. It was a frustrating question of, did she fall, or was she pushed?

After finding documents in the apartment concerning Gloria's mother, the Gendarmes arrived at the nursing home to interview her on Thursday afternoon, unaware of the severity of her condition. She couldn't remember who Gloria was and became distressed, believing that they had come to arrest her and take her away from the home. She was so disturbed that the doctor was called to sedate her. When the nurse told them that Gloria had become more and more upset at her mother's condition, a theory of suicide began to emerge.

A request to interview her fellow workers at IDD, her employer in Geneva, was transmitted to the Geneva authorities and on Friday morning an officer from the Sûreté went to the IDD offices, but they were locked and empty. The police found the address of M. Kurt Vogel, the local director, from the Registre de Commerce, but there was no one at his apartment. Since the next day was Saturday, they contacted the Divonne authorities to inform them that they would follow up the visit to the office on the following Monday. They made another trip to Vogel's flat on the Saturday, but there was still no one at home.

The only other two directors of the company lived in Marbella and Miami and the head of the Swiss investigative team determined to contact the local police there on Monday if there were no further developments in Divonne.

Over the weekend, more gendarmes and a Sûreté officer came from Gex to question the neighbours at Gloria's apartment building. No one had seen anything or anyone. Some of them had never ever seen Gloria. There were no clues in the apartment, no clues at all. The French authorities could only wait until Monday to find out if Kurt Vogel turned up. If not, they would put out an Interpol alert for him. He was the only line of enquiry they had, but he was missing.

Like most cross-frontier investigations, communications were not perfect and progress could be slow. Gloria's death might remain a mystery for a very long time.

SIXTY-ONE

Thursday 24th April 2008
Geneva, Switzerland

Jenny and Leticia arrived at the bank at 10:30 am. They paid off the taxi driver and looked up at the impressive building, six floors of glass, metal and stone, taking up the whole street corner. An ornate double main door decorated with wrought iron was flanked by two squarely carved stone pillars. On the right hand pillar a discreet brass plate read:

Klein, Fellay SA.
Membre du Groupe BIP.

"Look! It's the same group that bought Banco de Iberia. See, BIP, *Banque Internationale de Paris.*"

"Of course! That's why Charlie changed banks in Spain, because it was easier to deal with BIP, both in Geneva and in Marbella." Things were falling into place in Jenny's head.

"But this must be where Patrice worked in Geneva, so why did he never mention it?"

"Maybe he didn't know Charlie was a client. I'm sure he wanted to keep things separate. I'd be very surprised if he even transferred money between the two."

"He probably wouldn't make a mistake like that. But it's a peculiar coincidence."

Another coincidence, Jenny registered uncomfortably, but she said nothing more.

Leticia pushed the automatic doors open and they walked across the magnificent lobby to the reception desk. They asked to access their safety deposit box before meeting M. Schneider and after a few moments a young man came and escorted them downstairs to a large, high ceilinged vault. It was very modern, with an enormous glass topped table and high-backed chairs in the middle of the room. Several abstract paintings hung on the stuccoed walls. Not as impressive as the vault in the Banco de Iberia. *But probably more efficient,* thought Jenny.

After going through the register signing and dual key opening ceremony, the bank officer rolled out a leather mat onto the table top and politely left them. The box that Jenny removed was larger than the one in Marbella. About the same width and length, but deeper. She couldn't become accustomed to owning these safety deposit boxes in banks all over the place. She didn't know what was in them and it made her nervous. She breathed deeply and slowly opened the box.

Although the box was larger, the contents were very similar. This time there were three A4 sized envelopes inside. She opened the first envelope and removed two printed documents, both with the name of Klein, Fellay embossed in blue on the top. They were printed in French, German and English.

The first document was a single sheet, headed:

**PROCURATION – VOLLMACHT -
POWER OF ATTORNEY**

It concerned a numbered account 421-75 at Klein, Fellay, with the rubrique '*Triumph TR4*'. The beneficiary of the account was not shown. It was in favour of Jennifer Margaret Bishop and

Leticia Lurdes da Costa as joint signatories. There were places for the two women and a witness to sign the form. It already carried Charlie's signature and the rubrique 'Triumph TR4 421-75', in Charlie's hand. Someone called Emilie Thonney had witnessed his signature, adding *assistante administrative* as her occupation. It was dated February 23rd 2008. Jenny felt a moment of panic when she saw alongside her name; 'Civil Status: Widow'. A thought flashed through her mind, *Written by a dead man for the widow of his dead son. Everything happens for a purpose.*

She pulled herself together and said, "So it seems there is an account here. And so much for our preparations, Charlie is always one step ahead of us."

"February 23rd. That must have been the last time he came to Geneva, when he flew here in the morning and came home in the evening. He must have come just to make these arrangements." Leticia shook her head, pushing away the memories. "Well, I think it makes it more easy for us. No need for all the papers from José Luis."

"I'm quite sure that the mysterious M. Schneider will agree with you."

"He will consider that we are very efficient, like him. Very German Swiss, no?"

"I certainly hope so. Although I don't understand the bit about the car and I have no idea how we're supposed to sign the form."

The second document was also a power of attorney. This time for a numbered account 427-75 at Klein, Fellay, with the rubrique '*Angolan Clan'*. It was also in favour of Jenny and Leticia. Once again, no beneficiaries were shown. The document was already signed by Charlie, and witnessed and dated like the other. It specified that either of the two women could sign with any of the other signatories on the account.

"So, one of us has to sign together with Laurent, Nick or Raffael." Jenny had tried to memorise Charlie's story in detail, but she knew they needed to be sure of themselves when dealing with the Swiss bank. "We'd better not sign anything until we see Mr. Schneider. We don't want to mess it up when Charlie has gone to so much trouble."

She replaced the documents in the same envelope, then

opened the second one. It contained a single sheet of paper, in Charlie's writing.

> *Well done again, my dears. So far, so good.*
> *Next stop: Safety Deposit Box 72, Ramseyer, Haldemann & Company, Geneva.*
> *Think of Ellen.*
> *Much Love, Charlie.*

She shook the envelope onto the table and two keys fell out. One was a small, hollow barreled key, well worn and obviously very old. The other was flat and larger and had a yellow elastic band through the hole in the end. *More safety deposit boxes, more unknowns,* she thought unhappily.

She shook the third envelope upside down. Another key, for a Yale automatic door lock, fell onto the table. The envelope also contained another single sheet of paper, written once again in Charlie's hand.

> *Hello again.*
> *This key is for the IDD office at 362, Rue de la Gare, just opposite the Cornavin Hotel, at the train station. I don't know whether you'll need it or not. The accountant is there on weekdays, his name is Kurt Vogel. The secretary is part time, her name is Gloria Smouha.*
> *Love, Charlie*

"Gloria should be waiting for us there this afternoon, so we won't need the key," Leticia observed. "But better to be safe than sorry. Thank you, Charlie"

The women split the keys between them, Leticia guarding the two safety deposit box keys, and Jenny placing the other two in the zipped part of her own purse. She put all the papers and notes into one envelope and called back the bank employee. Then they went out to the reception and waited nervously for Mr. Eric Schneider.

SIXTY-TWO

Thursday 24th April 2008
Geneva, Switzerland

Eric Schneider was only in his early forties but he had already lost most of his hair. What was left was combed across from a parting on the left, so that it covered his head with a sparse layer, like wisps of brown thread. He was tall and thin and rather pompous and constantly blew his nose into a white handkerchief, quite vigorously and loudly. The handkerchief must have been doused with some kind of cologne. Each time he pulled it out there was a slight whiff of a pleasant fragrance.

They were in a comfortably furnished meeting room on the sixth floor of the bank. On the wall behind the banker's desk was a large poster of Zermatt. A skier dressed in plus fours stood in front of an old lodge with a steam train behind him. He was holding an ancient pair of very long, wooden skis and poles. The poster said "*Willkommen in Zermatt. Die Schweizerische Spitzenskistation.* Welcome to Zermatt. The Top Swiss Ski Station"

The two women sat in armchairs across the desk from Schneider and he served them with coffee and water from a small side table.

"Welcome to Genève, Mesdames," his English was perfect, but with a slight Germanic lilt. He had a haughty way of addressing his clients. "Is this your first visit?"

After a few moments of smalltalk, the banker addressed the matter in hand. "Do you have the documents we discussed on the telephone, Mme. Bishop?"

"Well, we have better than that. It seems my father-in-law did the work for us ahead of time." She laid Charlie's documents and the Spanish affidavits in front of him.

He examined the papers and opened up a dossier on the otherwise empty desk. He compared Charlie's signature on the forms with another sheet from the file, then, at his request, the women both handed over their passports.

"This is excellent. With these documents I don't need any further confirmation of your beneficial ownership. We just need to witness your own signatures on the forms and we can make the necessary changes in our records immediately.

"Please sign first with your proper signature and underneath it the numbered account signature, the way that Mr. Bishop has done it. In future you must only sign with the special signature to operate the account. We have a sophisticated scanning system here to authenticate the signatures, so it is highly secure. You should never sign with your own name."

Schneider called in his assistant, Mademoiselle Rousseau, an attractive, shapely woman of about thirty, wearing a tight blue sweater. She witnessed their signatures and added her occupation and the date.

"*Merci, Mlle. Rousseau.* Would you please make copies of these documents?"

She exited the office with the forms and the banker blew his nose enthusiastically, folded his handkerchief back into his pocket and said, "Please accept my condolences for the death of Mr. Bishop. He was a very pleasant and clever gentleman who had more financial expertise than most of the people in this bank. But please don't repeat that to anyone."

Addressing Jenny, he went on, "It's a pleasure to meet you, Mme. Bishop, and to welcome you as a new client of Klein, Fellay. I hope that you will stay with us for many years."

Jenny noted that he hadn't mentioned Ron, although he had seen from the form that she was a widow. She nodded and said nothing. She didn't have the nerve to ask him to call her by her first name. It might not be appropriate in Swiss banking circles.

"And I'm delighted to meet you too, Mme. da Costa. May I ask what your relationship with Mr. Bishop was? It's only for our files, we have certain reporting requirements."

For the first time, Jenny saw Leticia blush. The slight colouring of her cheeks made her look even more lovely. Knowing that her English tended to let her down when she was flustered, Jenny waited to see how she would handle the question.

"Yes, Mr. Schneider. You see my English is not like Jenny's, but I will tell you." She paused, then blurted out, "Charlie and me, we had a baby two years ago. A baby son, Emilio!"

The women sat quietly, waiting for the banker's reaction. He said nothing for a moment then he pulled out his handkerchief and blew his nose again and they smelled the slight aroma of cologne. Replacing the handkerchief in his pocket, he stood up and reached across the desk to shake Leticia's hand. "Many congratulations Mme. da Costa. I am very happy for you."

Nonplussed, the two women looked at each other. *Should we blow our noses now?* thought Jenny. *Perhaps it's an old Swiss banking custom.*

"Now, ladies," Schneider continued. "I understand the circumstances behind your visit. What exactly can I do for you this morning?" He looked at his watch, then back up at them in an impatient way, as if his time was really too valuable for this meeting.

Jenny indicated the file on the desk. "We'd like to talk to you about these two accounts, we actually know nothing about them. Can you bring us up to date please?"

"Of course. I have here the latest statement for Mr. Bishop's account. You and Mme. da Costa have the right to all available information, copies of documents, statements, anything that you need for this account, for the last five years. That is the mandatory preservation period for the bank documents, but I doubt that we will need to consult anything from so long ago."

He opened the file and removed two sheets. "For your information I am a Senior Vice President of the bank and was personally responsible for Mr. Bishop's affairs. Because it is a numbered account, in the interests of security and confidentiality, only you and I and the Board have access to the full details. My assistants and some senior staff know certain signatory details and they may see transactions as they are processed. But they can never access the financial status of the account. This is for your own protection, and that of the bank."

He handed the sheets to Jenny. "Here is the latest statement. You will note that it carries only the rubrique "*Triumph TR4*" and the account number." He gave a wry smile. "I have no idea why Mr. Bishop chose that name, but I am sure there is an interesting story there. The statement runs from October 1st up to 31st March of this year. Mr. Bishop had already received the statements up to September last year. The balances are now entirely in cash deposits, in accordance with his instructions. The various currencies are shown, with the corresponding balances in Swiss Francs."

"Very efficient, Mr. Schneider, thank you." Jenny and Leticia scanned the sheets together. On the first page was a list of transactions executed over the last six months and on the next page several balances were listed, in Euros, US Dollars, Pounds Sterling and Swiss Francs. The amounts were converted into Swiss Francs in the right hand column. The total on the bottom of the statement was fifteen million two hundred and twelve thousand Swiss Francs.

The two women looked at each other in disbelief. From the exchange rates that they had seen in Marbella, the balance was equal to slightly less than ten million Euros.

Just then, his assistant came back into the room with the copies she had made.

"*Merci Mlle. Rousseau.* That will be all for now." She placed the documents next to the statement on the desk.

The door closed behind her and the banker said. "I see that you are a little overcome by the news, ladies. May I first congratulate you, and repeat that Mr. Bishop was an unusually competent investor. I have no knowledge of his other affairs, but in the case of his accounts with Klein, Fellay, he has left you with an impressive legacy."

"Perhaps we need another coffee, Mr. Schneider." Leticia took Jenny's hand and squeezed it, as if to wake them both from a dream.

After Mlle Rousseau brought fresh coffee and water they discussed the account with the banker for another few minutes. He considered that the cash deposit position was prudent, the world might be facing a difficult period. His advice was to do nothing until they had had time to review their new situation then he would then be delighted to help them. He also mentioned that they had a highly secure system of Internet banking which Charlie had used. They might consider implementing that when they had time to think about it.

Leticia changed the subject. "We noticed that your bank is part of BIP, we understand it's a very large bank." She didn't mention Patrice. If Charlie hadn't done so, it was best ignored.

"That's quite right, in fact one of the largest in the world. When Mr. Bishop first came here back in the seventies, we were a small private bank, with branches in Geneva, Zurich and London. That was before my time, of course. But I was already here when we were acquired by BIP, about fifteen years ago. Now we operate in just about every country in the world, all the way from Alaska to New Zealand. This is most useful to our international clients of course."

They were suitably impressed with this news. "Thank you very much for all of this information and help, Mr. Schneider. It will take Leticia and I a little time to come to terms with all of this. There have already been a lot of surprises that we are still digesting."

The banker nodded and said nothing. Jenny continued, "Now, would you kindly help us to understand the other account, for the Angolan Clan?"

The two women waited while Schneider went through his nose blowing routine once more. He put away his handkerchief and said in his pompous tone, "I cannot deny that there is such an account open with us, since you now have signatory powers on it. However, without the agreement of another signatory I am unable to disclose any further information. You will understand that the same rules apply to everyone for reasons of security and confidentiality."

"Of course," Leticia interjected., "Jenny and me did not understand exactly the signature part. So, the best is for us to come tomorrow for the annual meeting. That will be alright?"

"I was about to suggest the same thing. When your three partners are present you will be able to access everything you wish. If you come to the bank tomorrow morning at ten, I will be pleased to introduce you to them. After all, I have known them now for fifteen years.

"Now, Mesdames," he said importantly, "I'm afraid I have to prepare for another client." He called in his secretary to clean the things away, and helped the women into their coats. "Are you comfortably installed in Geneva?"

"Yes, we're in a small hotel next to the Parc La Grange. It's très cosy. I booked it myself." Leticia gave Jenny a haughty look. Even the banker smiled at her pantomime.

As Mr. Schneider escorted them out of the meeting room towards the elevator, Mademoiselle Rousseau went back into her next door office and made a call on her mobile phone. When the number answered, she said, "*Bonjour, chéri.* I have some more news for you."

SIXTY-THREE

Thursday 24th April 2008
Geneva, Switzerland

"Ten million Euros. ***Diez millóns*****! I never knew there was so** much money in the world!" Leticia took a large sip of her mineral water and looked at Jenny in amazement.

After leaving Klein, Fellay they had walked across the Plaine de Plainpalais. The weather was cool, a slight breeze blowing, but it was a fair and refreshing day. Even though they were near to the lake, the air smelled clean and dry, unlike the humidity of Marbella. There were several cafés in the area and they chose one to go in for lunch.

Jenny didn't reply. All this money was starting to make her uneasy. She remembered Espinoza's questions about a motive for the deaths. *Ten million Euros is a fairly big motive.* She put the thought behind her, she didn't want to consider it.

While the waiter brought them their *Plat du Jour*, they looked up Ramseyer, Haldemann & Company's address in the phone book. Then they located the street on the city map the concierge had given them. The office was on the other side of the lake in an area called Pâquis. It was not far from the station and therefore near to the

IDD office. They decided that they had time to go there on their way to visit Gloria.

After coffee they asked the waiter to call a taxi to take them to Pâquis. He gave them a strange look then went to make the phone call. The cab driver asked them to repeat the address then he shrugged and set off. Going over the Pont du Mont Blanc, the main bridge that links the two parts of the city, they had a fine view of the famous Jet d'Eau, the one hundred and forty metre high fountain which stands at the edge of the lake. The water tumbled down from its great height like a waterfall over a cliff, and splashed into the lake below.

There were ferry boats moored at the shore and a couple of passenger boats were crossing under the bridge. Further away on the water they could see the brightly colored spinnakers of yachts making their way across the still surface towards Lausanne. Large flocks of swans and ducks crowded the jetty area, where some bird lovers were throwing bread for them. In the distance they could see the outline of mountains, virtually all around the city.

Only a couple of blocks from this beautiful area, the taxi deposited them in an unprepossessing part of town. They were surrounded by run down bars, amusement arcades and night clubs with lurid posters and photographs in the windows and at the door. There were a few seedy looking hotel entrances and many restaurants and cafés specialising in cuisine from all over the world, multi-lingual menus in their windows. Despite the time of day, several premises had neon lights on, spelling out *Sex Shop,* and a few young women in unseasonably flimsy attire were standing smoking on the street corners. Groups of men of all nationalities and colours stood in side streets, glancing around furtively as they talked.

Jenny looked around. "We'd better get inside before they think we work here."

Leticia just giggled. Her good humour was returning and she was fazed by very little, as the English woman had discovered.

No. 475, Rue de Mauvergny was a solid six story edifice faced with white stone. There was a metal plate on the double doors to the building, announcing:

Ramseyer, Haldemann & Company.
Sécurité Privée et Commerciale.

They rang the bell and then replied to a male voice that came over the intercom. A moment later one of the doors swung back and a young man in a smart grey suit appeared.

"*Bonjour Mesdames. Soyez les bienvenues. Veuillez me suivre s'il-vous-plaît?* Welcome, ladies. Please follow me."

As they followed him to the reception desk, Jenny said, "Can we speak English, please?"

Not surprisingly, he replied with an impeccable accent, "With pleasure, ladies."

The young man, Gilles Simenon, was in charge of the safety deposit boxes. He asked them to sign a register, then escorted them to an elevator which he opened with a code punched into a key pad. He inserted a key card into the panel and pressed a button. They descended two floors and emerged in an anteroom with a steel grid which he opened with the key card. In front of them were massive steel double doors. Gilles entered another code on the keypad and the doors swung back. They entered an enormous, almost completely empty room.

The young man stood to attention, as if he was in the Swiss army. "Mme. Bishop, Mme. da Costa, welcome to one of our safety deposit vaults.

"This building is exclusively for the safety deposit vaults and related activities. It's one of our main businesses," he explained. "There are five levels of vaults below and above us. It was specially built when the company moved its headquarters here from Berne almost forty years ago. The walls are constructed from triple layers of reinforced concrete. It's still the most secure design in Switzerland." He pressed a button and the doors slammed shut behind them.

The room was built in a circle, with no windows or doors apart from the one they had entered through. The wall was constituted by a continuous series of metal boxes surrounding them. Some of the boxes were from ceiling to floor and others of every height in between. There must have been thousands of them built into the circular wall. A long polished steel table with a wooden top stood across the centre of the room, with six chairs around it.

"We have installations in Zurich, Berne, Basel and other cities in Europe, and an even bigger vault on the outskirts of Geneva," he added proudly. "I'll get the key for your box."

He inserted the key card into the lock of a full length door adjacent to the entrance, then entered a code on a keypad and opened the door. The cupboard, as it was revealed, held rows of keys on a rotating cylinder, covering it from top to bottom. He turned the cylinder, removed a key and took them across to box no. 72. It was a quarter size door on the bottom row.

"Please enter your keys, *Mesdames*." He indicated two keyholes, midway down and near the bottom of the door. There was also a keypad on the door.

"Is there not one key from you and another from us, Mr. Gilles?" Leticia had in her hand the larger key from the Klein, Fellay safety deposit box, the one with the yellow elastic band. Neither woman understood his instruction.

"My key goes into the top lock, Madame, this one here." He indicated a third lock at the top of the door. "Your two keys go in these locks underneath."

The women looked at each other anxiously. *Why had Charlie left them only one key?*

Jenny explained, "Actually, Mr. Simenon, we only received this key this morning, it was left to us by someone who passed away. We didn't know we would need another key. Is there some way we can obtain a duplicate?"

"That's impossible I'm afraid. The third key looks the same but it is quite different from the others, there are no two keys the same. The access code completes our security measures – three levels of protection. Some companies are more sophisticated, or technological, but no one else provides three security barriers. That is one of the reasons for our success. "*Security is our Watchword*"." He coughed, looking slightly embarrassed. "That's our company motto, you'll see it on our brochure. Well, it seems that we have a problem here. If you'll just wait a moment, I'll bring our directeur, Mr. Jolidon, I'm sure that he can assist you."

The man who approached them must have been about forty, but trying to look thirty, with brown hair almost down to his shoulders. Clad in a tight blue suit, he walked with a mincing step. He wore a pleasant aftershave, but which didn't disguise his sour breath. After listening to Jenny's explanation, he replied, "I'm awfully sorry, Madame Bishop, I've only been in this job for six months and I didn't know your father-in-law. I sympathise with your problem but I'm afraid there's nothing I can do. We need three keys to open the box and between us we have only two and each key is unique, as is, of course, the access code." He pushed his long hair back in place, revealing a silver ring in his ear. "I hope it's nothing too valuable?" he said to Leticia ingenuously.

"It might be very valuable." She immediately regretted her answer, and the warning look that Jenny gave her. "But we don't really know," she added, rather lamely.

"Then I hope you can find the other key and return when you've done so."

Jolidon escorted them back through the security lift and up to reception. "I assume you're staying in town, so you can easily come back when you've resolved the problem?"

"We're staying on the other side of the lake, at the Hotel de La Grange, only ten minutes by taxi." This time it was Jenny who replied.

"Oh yes, I know it well. A lovely, quiet hotel. It's in the park right next door to the Restaurant des Eaux-Vives. You really should try to dine there if you have the chance. Elegant, historic building, wonderful views over the lake and the food is divine. I highly recommend it, but you'll need to book. It's awfully popular with the Geneva set."

The women thanked him and exited the building.

The directeur stood watching them until they walked out of sight. Going inside, he read the women's names from the register, then went into his office, picked up his notebook, then went down into the circular room and walked over to box number 72. He remembered the look that Jenny had given the other woman. After making a couple more notes, he came back upstairs and pulled out his mobile phone. "It's Claude calling. There's something I think we should talk about. I'll come over about eight tonight."

"Well, that was very disappointing," Jenny said. She avoided mentioning Leticia's error.

"I know. Charlie is making this difficult for us. We have to think like him, very clever."

"Well, I suppose there can only be one explanation."

"Yes, one of the other partners has the third key. It has to have two people."

"Exactly! Charlie didn't use the safety deposit at Klein Fellay and he arranged this box with double keys so that no one could open it alone. He was smart and he was suspicious."

"But why didn't he say this in his story? There are lots of things we don't understand. We don't even know what's in that box."

"I know." Jenny shook her head. "But in each note he has told us enough to work out the next step. Like the safety deposit boxes. The first key came from you, the second from Banco de Iberia, the third from Klein Fellay. Now, where will the next one come from?"

"Like you said, he was smart. So, tomorrow we'll find out who has the next key, right?"

"Right. My bet is that each partner has a key, but Charlie's is the master key and the others are all the same."

"And what about this access number we need? Where do we find that?"

"I think I know the answer. We'll see, tomorrow."

They were very near to the IDD office on the Rue de la Gare and decided to walk over to the office to meet Gloria. The appearance of the area improved as they made their way up to the Rue de Lausanne and walked towards Cornavin Station. No. 362 was half way along the Rue de la Gare and they saw from the post boxes that the IDD office was on the third floor. When they rang the bell, a square-built, burly man with a small moustache came to the door.

"Good afternoon. Mr. Vogel?"

The man didn't smile. He said, in English, "What can I do for you?" He had a thin reedy voice, not at all in keeping with his appearance, and a hard, Swiss-German accent.

"My name is Jenny Bishop, Charlie Bishop's daughter-in-law and this is Leticia da Costa, Charlie's companion." Leticia blushed at this description of herself, but said nothing.

Vogel hesitated, looking uncomfortable. "Oh, I see. Well, er, come in, ladies." He stepped aside and ushered them into a small reception area-cum office

This was apparently the secretary's domain, but there was no one there. A smart looking wooden desk was situated opposite the entrance door, with a PC placed under it on the floor and a keyboard and screen on the working surface. Apart from the equipment and a filing tray and telephone, the desk was bare. Gloria was obviously a very tidy person. On the wall above her desk was a map of Africa and a large photograph of polished diamonds, spilling onto a silver tray. A cabinet with a printer-photocopier and a fax machine on it stood next to a water machine murmuring in the corner. Another wall housed open shelving units full of box files of several different colours. The files were labelled in neat handwriting.

Vogel led them into another, larger room. It was very untidy and smelled of cigarette smoke. A navy blue raincoat and felt hat hung on a coat stand in the corner of the room. Books and papers covered every available surface. A battered partners' desk had a pile of open dossiers on it. A briefcase lay open on a table by the desk, it was full of papers and files. On a sideboard against the wall was a pile of travel books and in the corner stood a metal filing cabinet with two of the drawers open, more files lying on the floor below.

"Please sit down." The accountant gestured to two office chairs ranged in front of his desk. He removed a number of ski magazines which were strewn over the chair seats.

He sat in a leather armchair on the other side of the desk. On the wall behind him hung a certificate with Vogel's name on it, *Diplôme d'Expert Comptable,* Qualified Accountant. There were also several diplomas from a ski academy. He looked at the women, saying nothing.

"You may be unaware that Mr. Bishop passed away a short while ago. That's why we're here in Geneva." Jenny decided to avoid any small talk, this man didn't seem the type.

"I was advised of this by Mr. Schneider, at Klein, Fellay, just yesterday. I'm sorry."

"Yes, well the thing is that we have now become part owners of IDD. We wanted to meet you and Gloria, but it seems that she isn't here today?" Jenny didn't mention their appointment with Gloria. She might get her into trouble.

"No, she's not. She should be in on a Thursday and she never said anything about it yesterday. She usually takes the Friday and Monday off. She only works three days per week."

"Is she married?"

"I don't think so, but Gloria doesn't talk much about her private life. She is very busy with her work, only coming in for three days."

"How long have you worked for IDD, Mr. Vogel?"

"I started part time last April, and took over last June. So it's a bit less than a year."

"Did you know my father-in-law well?"

"Not very well. He interviewed me before I started, but I've only seen him twice since then, in July and then in October after his heart attack. Our business was mostly done by email, telephone and fax. He came in December, but I was off skiing and he hasn't been back since."

Jenny thought back. *Charlie came here in February, but not to the office. Why?*

Leticia interjected. "Probably you know Nick Martinez and Laurent Bonneville as well."

"I've met them a couple of times."

Jenny said, "Can you provide us with a copy of the accounts and bank statements, Mr. Vogel? We are coming to the meeting tomorrow and we'd like to be up to date."

Vogel's eyes were darting about. He waved his hand around the messy room. "Well, I'm busy getting the accounts ready for tomorrow. I expect Mr. Bonneville or Mr. Martinez to come by in the morning, prior to the meeting and collect everything. I believe that's what has been done in the past."

"So, you can't let us have them today?"

"I'm afraid not. I'll be working quite late this evening to get them ready, I'm sorry."

"Very well, Mr. Vogel. We look forward to seeing everything at the meeting tomorrow."

They got up and Jenny asked, "You don't happen to know where Gloria lives, do you?"

"She lives in Divonne, just over the French border. She's not resident in Switzerland, she's got special papers as a French frontalier worker."

"Do you have a phone number for her?"

Vogel pulled out a phone book from his desk drawer and jotted a number on a slip of paper. "You have to dial 0033, then 450 for the frontalier zone," he informed them.

They left him surrounded by his paperwork and walked down the Rue du Mont-Blanc.

"That's the third disappointment today. We're not making much progress, are we?"

Leticia was looking thoughtful. "Jenny, what is your impression of Mr. Vogel?"

"He certainly seemed very nervous and I can't think why. He's got to prepare a set of accounts. How difficult can it be?"

"No, not that. I mean a different thing."

"I'm not sure I understand?"

"I think he looks like a man who is clearing up. He has his briefcase, lots of files and papers and I think he was sorting them out. Also, he has piles of travel and ski books, like when you go away for holidays."

"I don't know, Leticia. The problem is that we don't have any idea about him or the business and he doesn't know us, so it's difficult for us to insist. I'm sure everything will be ready for the meeting in the morning. But I wonder why Gloria wasn't there." She pulled out her mobile phone. "I'll try her number, see if we can meet her."

When there was no reply, Jenny said, "She must be out. Perhaps she's got a problem and hasn't gone to the office. But you'd think she'd call and leave a message. Especially when we had an appointment." Trying to sound unconcerned, she put away her phone and said nothing more.

It was four-fifteen in the afternoon. The breeze had dropped and it felt warmer. Since they could not achieve anything further, the women decided to look around the town. They strolled back across the bridge, enjoying the vistas to the East, over the lake to the mountains ranged along the horizon, snow visible on the peaks.

The Jet d'Eau was still propelling its waterspout skyward and planes passed high above their heads, coming and going from Cointrin airport.

In the Place du Molard, stalls were selling freshly cut flowers. A rich combination of aromas permeated the square. The smell of coffee from the cafés mingled with the the scent from the flowers and the perfumes of the shoppers. Everything was clean and smart, the people, the cars, the streets and sidewalks and the blue and white trams and orange buses which ran constantly in every direction. It was as if everything had been through a giant washing machine and put back all cleaned and polished, to brighten up the city.

They wandered through the narrow streets of the Old Town, full of antique shops, bars and restaurants, admiring the Cathédral de St. Pierre and the Confédération Centre, then walked past the elegant shops on the Rue du Marché on their way back to the hotel.

"If we have time, we should come here tomorrow for some shopping. We need to check out the prices. It's right, Jenny?"

"Perfectly right. Let's check them out."

Back at the hotel they sat talking in the lounge for a while, until Leticia announced, "I have to go and do two things now. I need to call Emilio and I need a hot bath."

"Bonsoir Monsieur Jolidan." The well built man standing in the hall of the Casino de Divonne was an expert in both martial arts and physiognomy. He never forgot a face.

"Bonsoir Mathieu." Jolidan greeted him then walked through the magnificently decorated gambling hall. There were few players at the tables, but he knew that some would be dining in the hotel and more would arrive much later in the evening. He entered a small office at the back where two large men were waiting for him. They were dressed in over-tight tuxedos, which made them look like badly creased penguins.

The directeur sat opposite the men. "I think I may have found the answer to our problem," he announced.

"It's not *our* problem, Claude. It's yours. A fifty thousand Euro problem, to be precise." The man took out a pack of cigarettes and offered one to his colleague. They both lit up, looking keenly at Jolidon.

He waved the smoke away and coughed nervously. "Well, I think there's a chance of making a lot more than that. Let me tell you what happened today."

At dinner in Le Parc restaurant, the women discussed the day's events and didn't notice a man in the brasserie reading *Le Temps*. But he watched them, as he had done all day.

It was now one day until the meeting of the Angolan Clan.

SIXTY-FOUR

Friday 25th April 2008
Geneva, Switzerland

It was one minute past ten on Friday, 25th April, 2008, the thirty-fourth anniversary of the Revolution of the Carnations. Thirty-four years since the lives of everyone in Portugal and in their African colonies had been changed for ever. Now Jenny and Leticia were waiting to meet Charlie's partners, men who had confronted dangerous and life-changing experiences with him and had emerged safe and wealthy. Unlike so many others who had not.

They were back on the sixth floor of the bank, sitting in a large conference room around a fine Louis XVI table with a delicately worked marquetry inlay. A series of hunting prints lined the walls, which were clad in a patterned fabric. It all looked very chic. From the ten available chairs they chose the two at the end of the table, furthest away from the door and nearest the double French windows. There was a small balcony outside, but it was a chilly morning so the windows were closed. Mademoiselle Rousseau brought them fresh coffee then left them alone and Leticia poured out two cups.

Jenny sipped her coffee thoughtfully. *Why did Olivier, Carlos, Manuela and Henriques have to die, when Charlie and the others survived? What extraordinary turn of fate decreed the destiny of so many people whose lives had become inextricably intertwined? Deciding who lived and who did not.* She shivered, remembering the deaths in Charlie's narrative. Little by little she was changing her views on her father-in-law and the origins of his wealth. *Maybe there are fortunes without crimes,* she wondered. *And maybe Charlie was the exception.*

She was still lost in thought when Leticia said, "It's ten twenty now and nobody is here."

"I don't understand why not. They've had this meeting every year for thirty-odd years. What's so different this year?"

"This is the last year, so it can be different I suppose. We are different partners from last year, but they don't even know about us. Anyway, we are ready for the meeting, aren't we?"

"Not quite," replied Jenny. "That man Vogel isn't here either, with the accounts." She took out her mobile phone to call the accountant.

Just then the door opened and Mr. Schneider entered, looking more pompous than usual. "I have some news for you, Ladies. let me introduce Mr. Adam Peterson. A new partner!"

Adam walked slowly into the room, looking slightly sheepish. Immediately behind him entered Mademoiselle Rousseau, bringing them more fresh coffee. Jenny put away her mobile and looked at Leticia in astonishment.

The Swiss banker introduced them rather formally. "Madame da Costa, Madame Bishop, Mr. Peterson." They shook hands with Adam for the third time in almost as few days, utterly confused. "Mr. Peterson has produced the necessary documents and signed our internal *formulaires,* so I can confirm that he is a new partner of the Angolan Clan. I'll leave you to conduct your meeting. Please call me if you need anything."

The banker left the room, closing the door behind him and they heard the sound of a nose being blown violently.

Adam sat opposite them at the other end of the table. He kept as much space between them as he could. The women looked at each other. Things were not proceeding at all to plan. What was going on? Once again they were faced with more surprises, more unexpected events.

Jenny sat in silence, her mind feverishly trying to fit this latest piece into the jigsaw puzzle that had become their lives over the last few days.

Leticia broke the ice. "I think we need many explanations, Adam. Jenny and I are very confused."

"Can I get myself a coffee? I'm a bit out of sorts today myself, actually." He poured himself a cup. Absently, Jenny noticed that he took three spoons of sugar.

Marshalling her thoughts again, she said, "Adam. Is that your name, Adam Peterson? It's true that Leticia and I only became new partners yesterday, because of Charlie's death. However, we do understand the rules of the Angolan Clan. We don't want to be rude or offensive, but we don't understand how you can become a partner, because the others, Nick, Laurent and Raffael, have no children. And they certainly don't have any children called Adam Peterson."

"It's exactly the problem, Adam. And also, where are the other three partners? They should be here. Now it is half past ten and nobody has come. They sent a message to Charlie to say they are coming and they are not here, but you are here. Something is not right."

Adam sipped his coffee and settled in his chair with his hands crossed on the table top. "It's quite complicated, but I'll try to explain." He looked at the ceiling for a moment and then back at the women.

"First of all, I have never met Raffael and I don't know where he is. But Laurent, Nick, Charlie and I have done a lot of business together. Like you, I was expecting to meet some of them at this meeting and I was looking forward to it."

"But how did you meet Charlie? And now you say that you also know Laurent and Nick. How do you know about the Angolan Clan? How did you know about Charlie's funeral? I mean, just tell us. Who the hell is Adam Peterson?" Jenny didn't swear much unless she was in a rage and it had usually been restricted to Ron. She blushed with embarrassment but sat still, like Leticia, waiting for his answer.

He sighed, shifting uncomfortably on his seat. "This is going to be very difficult for you to believe. I'm Nick Martinez's son."

Leticia jumped out of her chair. "But Charlie never said to us anything about this. We never knew that Nick Martinez has a son."

He took another sip of his coffee. "Neither did he. And strangely enough, neither did I."

BOOK ONE

PART FIVE: 2002 - 2008

SIXTY-FIVE

July, 2002
Geneva, Switzerland

In July 2002, Nick Martinez suggested to Laurent Bonneville that he might want to contact Adam Peterson, a young diamond dealer from Durban. He'd heard a lot of good reports about him and thought he could be a suitable channel for a steady flow of business. He was reputed to be honest, clever and discreet. This latter quality was of prime importance to the Angolan Clan.

Laurent met him in Geneva and Adam was immediately intrigued by his presentation of IDD. They had a selection of fabulous Angolan diamonds of the highest quality, in purity, colour and cut. Apparently they were not interested in marketing through the mainstream channels and extracting top rates. At the prices they offered, there was a substantial margin for him, so he was very keen to develop the business with them.

However, because of the global condemnation of the exploitation of the blacks in the diamond mining industry and the financing of bloody conflicts in African countries, there was a lot of international concern about African gems. Adam knew that he could ruin his reputation if he made a mistake over such a sensitive matter. He wanted to satisfy himself on that point.

"Tell me truthfully, are these conflict diamonds, blood diamonds? Have they been mined over the dead bodies of the black workers?"

Laurent turned his still piercing blue eyes on him. "We would never stoop to do such business. These diamonds come from a source we have had for more than twenty-five years. They came exclusively from Angola and they have not been mined during the wars."

Adam was intrigued by the Frenchman's reply. The sample stones shown to him by Laurent were by far the best he'd ever seen. He questioned him to find out more and racked his brains to try to work out how IDD came to have such a store of fine Angolan diamonds, but in vain. He put the question away for later and the two men shook hands on the deal.

Over the next few years he was a consistent and reliable source of business and eventually became their largest customer. This access to fine diamonds brought him even more renown in his specialised field and it also brought him very substantial profits. He bought as many stones as he could get from them, only twenty or thirty per year in the beginning, then about one hundred for the last couple of years. He was clever in his marketing of the gems, causing no ripples in the market place, which suited IDD perfectly.

Laurent began to rely on him for a guaranteed thirty or forty per cent of his annual sales, and the two men enjoyed a trusting relationship. He never gave Adam any further information about the stones, nor the names or even the existence of his partners, Nick and Charlie. From time to time Adam wondered about IDD and reflected on Bonneville's explanation of the source of this apparently endless supply of Angolan diamonds, but he never renewed the discussion. He just took as many stones as they offered, paid his bills on time and continued to wonder where the diamonds came from.

SIXTY-SIX

November, 2004
Las Vegas, Nevada, USA

It was three-thirty in the morning when Ray d'Almeida carefully opened the door of suite 1627 at the Golden Nugget Hotel in Las Vegas and looked out into the corridor. There was no one in sight, so he closed the door behind him and strolled along to the bank of elevators. Paco was waiting in the lobby and they walked out of the hotel together.

"How much?" asked Paco.

"Hundred bucks. You?"

"Seventy-five."

"I keep telling you that size does matter." Ray laughed. "When it comes to screwing that is," he added.

He had been picked up at the bar by a fifty-three year old woman from Palm Springs, whose husband was enjoying a winning streak on the blackjack table. After a couple of drinks, she took him up to her room. She was very demanding and he had to work hard for his money.

Paco's 'date' was a late fifties, bottle-blonde divorcee, who thought she looked like Marilyn. His job was easier, since she was completely plastered by the time they went upstairs and he had to wake her up to collect his pay.

The two men had met up several months previously in Arizona, climbing in the Mohawk mountains near Yuma. Paco was from Zaratoga, in central Spain, and had been drifting around the US for over two years. He was the same age as Ray and they decided to team up, both enjoying hiking and climbing in the deserted, mountainous expanses of the southernmost states.

Ray and his family had left the favela eighteen months before, when his father was finally offered a job in Rio. It was ironic, almost comical. After starving in Brazil for over twenty years, just when his father was almost too old to work he was suddenly in demand. He had got a job with a company that was set up to process rough diamonds. Sergio was an expert diamond cutter, having been trained in Luanda when he was young. He had also found a place for Ray in the company, where he learned to keep the books. They could afford to move to a small apartment in the same area. Close enough to go back to the favela if they had to.

After making a little money and seeing his father finally earning enough to look after his sister, Alicia, Ray had decided to go walkabout. Fortunately and surprisingly, he had never been in prison and was able to obtain a Brazilian passport and get out of the country.

He travelled around the coast by sea from Brazil, working his way on a freighter to Venezuela, then on various vessels up through central America, until he reached Mexico. He drifted from Mexico through California, Arizona and Nevada, working at just about every job under the sun. Waiter, gardener, delivery man, even a bank clerk for a couple of months, until he found his true forte as a gigolo.

This latter was the best paid job he'd found, and he and Paco made a great team, working in tandem. The Spaniard was the same age and height as Ray and with their similar build and Mediterranean looks they were usually taken for brothers. The older women in the bars and casinos couldn't resist them. Paco wore spectacles and had a rather shy demeanour, whereas Ray was loud and flamboyant, projecting a raunchy image.

A couple of months before, they had pooled their savings and acquired a beat-up old mobile home, in which they lived and drove from town to town to ply their wares. They had made good money in Vegas this last week. The women were falling over them, but Ray was tired of the scene.

"How much you got in your pocket?"

"Eight hundred bucks, give or take."

"That means we've got amost two thousand between us. How about we take off for the mountains again. I've had it with boozing and screwing old ladies."

They climbed into the Jayco camper van and headed off into the desert, towards Arizona. At nightfall, they camped out on the slopes of the Black mountains and heated up some supper on a petrol stove, then climbed into their sleeping bags and spent the warm night under the clear, star filled sky. They were back in paradise.

The next morning they set off at first light, walking and climbing further into the mountain chain, ropes and equipment in their backpacks, along with a few provisions. They stopped for a bite on a high sloping rock face, crisscrossed with narrow crevices. Paco was fascinated by the depth of the fissure that ran alongside them. It seemed to descend forever, but he could see what seemed to be the glint of water at the bottom.

"I'm going down to see if there's an underground lake down there."

He hammered a metal peg into the rock face and they snagged his rope around it and around a rocky outcrop, to take more strain.

"Look after my stuff for me. I'll be right back."

He took off his spectacles and handed them to Ray for safekeeping, then climbed down into the fissure and disappeared from view, the rope tightening as he used it to slow his descent, performing a kind of abseil, finding what purchase he could on either wall of the crevice with each foot.

Ray picked up the Spaniard's backpack and looked through the few items inside. Surprisingly, his passport, driver's license and wallet were wrapped in a cloth at the bottom of the bag. There were eight hundred and twenty dollars in the wallet.

He looked at the passport. It had been renewed in Los Angeles and was valid until 2012. He put on the spectacles and roughed up his hair like Paco's. When he peered at his reflection in the blade of his pocket knife it was like looking at the passport photo. The driving license was the same, it was valid and the photo looked like him.

Ray sat and thought to himself, *A valid Spanish passport and driver's license, with a photograph that looks like me. That's worth a lot of money, much better than Brazilian ones. And two thousand dollars is twice as good as twelve hundred. Same thing with the Jayco. Why have half when you can have the whole thing?*

A dreamy look came into his eyes. Almost absent mindedly he started to saw away at the taut rope with the pocket knife. The fibres split apart, until, with a snap, the rope was pulled down over the edge of the fissure. A second later he heard a shout from Paco. He looked down into the crevice and saw the Spaniard straddling the fissure, a foothold on either side holding his weight.

"What the fuck are you doing?"

"Just saying goodbye," he answered. "It's been great. See you around."

Paco looked down at the drop below him then back up to Ray. The movement caused him to lose his footing on the steep walls of the crevice. With a scream, he fell straight down like a rock. He had disappeared completely from view before Ray heard the splash of water from the bottom.

He was right, he thought to himself. *Probably an underground lake.*

The following month, Ray drove back into Las Vegas and went to a discount call shop to phone his sister and father, to wish them a happy Christmas.

"Hi, Alicia. How's things?"

"Ray. Thank God you've called. Dad's sick. He's lost his job. You've got to come home. Right away!"

SIXTY-SEVEN

November, 2006
Rio de Janeiro, Brazil; Haute Nendaz, Swiss Alps

"Take care, Alicia. I'll call you a couple times a month. Don't fret and make yourself sick, you've got enough money to get by and I'll soon send more."

Ray d'Almeida climbed into his friend, Lorenzo's cab, waved to his sister through the back window and settled down for the thirty minute drive to the Antonio Carlos Jobim airport. His Varig flight to London left at seven that evening and his easyJet connection to Geneva was at ten o'clock the following morning. He'd booked the flights separately, using his Brazilian passport for the Transatlantic flight and Paco's Spanish one for Geneva. Once through UK immigration, he would go back through check-in and fly to Switzerland as a good, honest citizen of the European Community, not a suspicious immigrant from South America.

There was a good train service from Geneva to Sion and a postal bus to Haute Nendaz, so he would be up there by late afternoon, in time to claim his room. Despite early snow, the resorts were still quiet and there was plenty of available accommodation.

His job interview wasn't until the next afternoon, so he had time to get himself sorted out.

He had fifteen hundred dollars and some Swiss Francs in his wallet, enough to get him by until he started earning a salary, and he'd left Alicia with five hundred dollars, which would see her through for quite a while. She was used to living on very little. Since Ray had returned from the US, almost two years ago, he'd made more money than ever before but he'd had to save as much of it as he could for this trip, so they had continued living in their normal, frugal way.

Until their father, Sergio, died of a second heart attack the previous year, the medical bills that they had to face, although not enormous, consumed most of Ray's income and some of his savings. It was only by a lucky chance that he had been able to land a job with enough pay and tips to manage. With the experience of the Las Vegas hotel and casino scene that he'd acquired during his time there, he had talked the manager of the Gold Coast Casino, on the Copocabana beach, into giving him a try out as a croupier. His good looks, easy charm and skill in languages and numbers soon confirmed him as the new 'king' of the roulette table and he finally started earning a decent income. The money also enabled him to buy the books that he needed, to learn some new skills. Skills that would be necessary for his project.

He had devised and started his project shortly after he returned and was looking after his father, whose first heart attack and deteriorating eyesight had caused him to lose his job at the diamond processing plant. Sergio had described to Ray, batches of diamonds that they were receiving for cutting and polishing from a Geneva company called IDD, International Diamond Dealers. He was sure those diamonds were Angolan alluvial diamonds. And he was almost certain that they came from pre-war Angola, and probably from his own mine.

Ray and Alicia had been too young to understand the catastrophic events which had condemned them to live in the favela for most of their lives, and Sergio had never found the courage to divulge the story to them, but now he needed to unburden himself to his son. In his declining state, it took him a lot of time and much gentle probing from Ray to bring back to mind the details of their flight from the d'Almeida's mine in Angola over thirty years ago and the subsequent theft of their only source of money.

As he learned the history of his family's lost fortune, Ray became overcome by a great sense of injustice, which gradually transformed itself into a burning rage. His rage began to consume him and his mind turned to restitution, and to vengeance. He vowed to find the family's lost fortune and to reclaim it, whatever the cost. But he knew that it would take every skill he possessed, and some new ones he would have to acquire. He made a list of the things he needed to learn, and started to conceive a project to right the wrongs suffered by his family. It became an obsession that filled his every waking minute from that moment on.

With his first pay cheque from the casino, Ray bought himself a monthly user card at a local Internet café. He had never owned a computer, so he got friendly with the owner, who taught him the basics. Ray quickly became an expert on Google and his research was extremely rewarding. Between Googling and dredging into his father's failing memory, he began to improve his knowledge base and to plan his project.

He said nothing to Sergio about his plan. He didn't want to distress him any further during what was evident were his dying days. His father had become so weak that he spent most of the day on the same bed that they had owned in the favela. He now ate very little, even by comparison with the minimum food supply that they had been used to all their lives and he was as skinny as a rake. In June, at the age of sixty-two, he suffered a second heart attack and this time he didn't recover.

Alicia and Ray were heart-broken. Sergio was the only family they had really ever known. He had somehow managed to look after them all their lives. Despite having to flee from his homeland and being robbed of the small fortune that he'd smuggled out, and suffering the loss of Elvira and the foul conditions they'd experienced in the favela, he had survived. And he had ensured that his children survived. Sergio had been a fine and loving husband and father to his wife and his children and now he was gone.

The cost of a headstone was out of their reach, and his grave, next to Elvira's in the public cemetery, was marked only by a wooden stake carved with their names and dates of birth and death. After the local priest had said a few words, Ray knelt at the side of the grave and prayed as he never done before. He prayed for his father's and mother's souls and he vowed to bring justice to avenge his family's lost birthright. His furious rage was now transformed into an inexorable determination. He would perfect and execute his project, and God help anything or anyone that got in the way.

Over the next year he spent all of his spare time working on the computer at the Internet café and studying in the apartment or at the library, preparing himself for the greatest test of his life. In addition to Google, he mastered Word, Excel and PowerPoint. He also became an expert in other new and useful subjects. His project slowly took shape.

The afternoon after his arrival in Haute Nendaz, Ray went to the *SoftSnow Ski Shop,* and thanks to his proficiency in languages and confident manner and looks, he was taken on immediately with responsibility for renting skis, boots and snowboards. He would start training the next week, both in the shop and on the piste, and go onto a salary from December 1st. The pay was sufficient for him to send a small amount to Alicia each month. Phase one of his project was in place.

The following week, he got a lift into Geneva with Jean-Pierre, another ski-bum who had an old van. It was time to initiate phase two. A more delicate task, but one he was well equipped to perform.

SIXTY-EIGHT

December, 2007
Geneva, Switzerland

Adam had driven over to his parents' house on his way to the airport. Rachel came out to the driveway with him and he kissed her on the forehead then climbed back into his Land Cruiser. "I'll be back at the end of the week. Don't worry about me and don't work too hard at the hospice. Look after dad and make sure he takes his pills."

His flight to Geneva at eight that morning was complicated and tiring, requiring stops in Johannesburg and Zurich. The appointment at the Crowne Plaza Hotel was fixed for tomorrow morning at ten thirty, so he would get some sleep there tonight if his flights were on time. He would be back home in five days, hopefully having concluded the largest deal of his life.

Adam had now been working with IDD for over five years, making good money from the small number of stones they would supply, but always wanting more. Then, a couple of weeks ago, he had received a call from Laurent.

"You've been bugging me for a larger supply of stones."

"I'll take as many as you can deliver."

"Even if it's as many as a thousand, possibly more?"

Adam was nonplussed. For five years he'd been trying to squeeze more stones out of IDD. He'd already had his year's supply of one hundred stones and now they wanted to flood the market. *Where the hell do these diamonds come from?*

"It's possible, but I'll have to check with my channels. How many carats?"

"About a thousand. Between half a carat and two carats per stone as usual. Same purity, colour and cut."

"What price are we talking?"

"We're prepared to sell to you at a flat rate. The whole shipment at the same price, irrespective of stone size. This is actually a hell of a deal for whoever comes up with the cash." Bonneville quoted a price, putting on a bad impression of a Jewish accent. *To you, my boy.*

Adam did the maths. This could be the deal of a lifetime. "That might work," he said. "Are they on the market?"

"Not yet, you've got first shot. You've been a solid partner for quite a few years. We've done good business together."

"When you say "done" does that mean this is the end?"

"Look, Adam, IDD has been in this business for over thirty years. Don't quote me, but we're looking to close it down."

"Right, I understand. So, I'd better take this stock 'cos I won't get any more. Correct?"

"That's about the size of it."

"How long do I have to respond?"

"Call me by the end of the month with a yes, no, or maybe and we'll try to work it out. I want to have this tied up by January, latest."

"Trust me, I'll come back with a yes."

Adam spent the next month working the telephones. He knew that to suddenly push out a thousand top quality Angolan stones into the market place would cause a few ripples and IDD had always wanted to avoid that, so he had to find a more subtle solution. In addition, he knew that the price was very keen. He could make a margin of twenty percent and probably more, but it would require finessing. And of course, he wondered why IDD suddenly wanted to cash in all their remaining merchandise. *And how come they still have a thousand stones in stock after thirty years?* If he knew the answer to that, maybe there was an even better deal to be done. Whatever the answer, he wanted to get control of those gems.

He called Bonneville back at the end of November. "I think there's a deal to be done. Can we meet in Geneva?" They fixed an appointment at the Crowne Plaza Hotel, next to the airport, on December 10th.

Laurent called Nick, in Florida. "You were right about Adam Peterson, he's very interested and he's just the profile we need. Good volume of business, doesn't attract attention and pays on the nose. I'm going to see him in Geneva next week."

Nick breathed a sigh of relief. "That's perfect. I'm expecting the last batch of stones back from the Brazilian processing outfit at about the same time. Everything should be in the safety deposit in Geneva by the time you get there. I'm pissed that we're running a bit late, but last week I was down in Rio again, for the fourth time this year. We've had a lot of problems since they lost their chief cutter."

"Don't stress over it Nick, it's not your fault, you're travelling too much as it is. We've shipped all my sales for the year now, just got to collect from the usual late payers, and there's a hundred stones left in the vault. So, if you're right, we should still be able to close everything out by the April deadline. Do you have a final count yet?"

"The last batch will be a thousand stones, so, with what's left in Geneva it's going to be just about what we expected, eleven hundred stones, twelve hundred carats."

"Anything I can do to help?"

"I've arranged with Charlie to fly up and get things sorted. He was going anyway to see the banks, because he hasn't been since October. He's just waiting for the word. If Peterson's for real, we should be able to do a deal by the end of the year."

Nick prayed silently that Adam would turn out to be for real.

"If Charlie's coming up then I'll help him to sort out the new batch and the stones in the safety deposit and he can help me in the meeting with Adam. Two heads are better than one."

"Perfect. Team work, I like it. I'll ask Charlie to get there at the same time as you and Adam, and I'll make sure that the stones are there for you. I'll be at home all through the holidays, so call me when you have something definite. Just one thing. Don't tell Adam anything he doesn't need to know. We need to get this done quickly, but confidentially. It's the biggest deal we've ever done or likely to do, so let's play it close to the chest."

"Understood. And if you need me, I'll be in Monaco until New Year, then I'm going skiing."

"Sounds cold."

"How are things in Miami?"

"Hot."

"The weather or the girls?"

"Both."

Nick sounded tired and coughed a lot during the conversation. *Running about getting the diamonds finished,* Laurent assumed. *He can take a holiday soon. We all can, when we finish.*

The courtesy coach dropped Adam off at the hotel at one thirty am. He managed a few hours sleep before going down to meet Laurent at ten thirty.

"So, how was the flight? Or I should say the flights."

"They don't get any shorter, that's for sure."

"Too many people flying. All the security, the waiting in line. It's no fun any longer."

The two men sat in a small conference room on the first floor of the hotel. After the usual small talk, Laurent produced, as usual, several stones of different weights.

"A random sample, from half a carat to just over two, as good as always. The final count is twelve hundred carats. Our word is our bond. What about you, Adam?"

The South African admired the Angolan diamonds. They were magnificent. He knew that he had to have the whole allotment, but there was just one problem. He had to play on Laurent's strongest characteristic, his trust.

"I have a proposal to make and it relies upon trust from both sides. I've flown up here to demonstrate my total commitment, but I need your help."

Laurent, sanguine as ever, said only, "Go on."

"I've placed the diamonds with four buyers, guaranteed,

but.." He pulled a notebook from his pocket. "Today is December 10th, it's Christmas in two weeks, so we've missed the end of year buying season."

The Frenchman saw the logic in this argument, but he said nothing.

"My buyers are finished business for this year. There's no cash around for the minute."

"So why fly all the way up here if that's the case?"

"Listen, Laurent, everyone except the big boys is going to tell you the same thing and I understand that you don't want to deal with them. Right?"

"Right."

"Remember, I said I've got four guaranteed buyers. That's what I want to work out with you, guarantees. So that you know you've sold the stones and you'll get paid. And I know that I'll get the stones when I pay."

"So what are the guarantees?"

Adam counted on his fingers. "Number one, I'll pay you a million dollars to seal the deal.

"Number two, you place the cash in escrow with your bank and it's forfeited if I don't complete.

"Number three, I take down all the stones by latest 30th April, either in batches, or all in one lot. I pay cash each time and you keep the escrow money until I've taken all the stones and paid for them. Then you release it.

"Number four, I'll show you copies of my commitments from my customers. You know the companies anyway. The conditions are basically the same, but I've blanked out the prices."

The Frenchman smiled at this. He didn't expect Adam to be doing this for charity. He knew that there was a nice margin to be made, but he didn't mind and neither did his partners. That was why they'd been successful for so many years. No need to change it now.

The South African had one condition to add to his list. "Number five. I have sight of the diamonds, but they stay with you until I complete. And I get twenty stones of my choice to present to my customers as soon as we sign the contract and I transfer the million dollars."

Laurent asked him for a few more details. He had no need to take notes, he had the memory of an elephant.

"So, what do you say, Laurent? Can we do a deal?"

"I can't decide alone. It's a decent offer, but I need my partners to agree."

While Adam took an afternoon nap, Laurent went up to Charlie's room. They called Nick on the speakerphone and Laurent summarised Adam's offer. After discussing it for a while, they decided to let Charlie hammer out a secure deal. Surprisingly, Nick insisted that he wanted to meet the buyer and sign the final contract. The other two agreed, this was his baby and so far he hadn't dropped it. They would have to explain this to Adam. That was their decision.

Nick changed the subject, "Is everything OK at the banks, Charlie?"

"I presume so. But I came up to see Schneider and Brigitte Aeschiman about the accounts, and there's nobody here." Aeschiman was the manager of IDD's bank in Geneva. "She's still on maternity leave. Now they've had an early snowfall and everybody else's gone skiing, Kurt Vogel's gone off as well. It's incredible! In England, if you have any snow they close the country. The problem is that I have to go back tomorrow after the diamond delivery, for, er, a birthday." He bit his tongue. He'd almost said, *for Leticia's birthday*.

"I'll have to get back here again before the annual meeting to check on everything and get ready for the distributions. I called Kurt on his mobile and everything seems to be under control. I got the whole situation up to date when I came here in October, so it's no big deal to check the transactions since then. We'll be in good shape for the next meeting. Especially if this deal with Peterson is for real"

Before ringing off, Charlie asked, "Are you feeling OK, Nick?"

"I'm fine. Why?"

"You sound terrible, really tired. You sure you're fine?"

"Charlie, I'm in great shape. Too much travelling down to bloody Brazil and feeling the stress of getting this deal done is all. Just send Adam over here and we can all relax."

"What do you think?" Charlie asked Laurent after they closed the call.

"He sounds tired. But after thirty years at this game, it's to be expected."

The two men met Adam in the hotel bar before dinner. They sat in a quiet corner to talk.

"This is my partner, Charlie Bishop, the cleverest man I know. He wants to haggle. OK?"

"Ready, willing and able." Adam eyed the Englishman up. About five eleven, a large imposing man, full of quiet confidence, a certain aura. Charlie looked in charge. Adam wished he could appear so in control of things.

"It's a pleasure to meet you, Adam. You've been a good customer for some years, so my job here isn't to screw up the deal, it's to try to make it safer for everyone concerned. OK?"

"Go right ahead, Charlie. I'm sure you've got a lot more experience than me in this field, so I'm all ears."

"Right. Basically, we've decided to close up IDD. We've been running it for thirty years and we're getting tired. We still have a stock of diamonds that Laurent has described to you, and our deadline to sell them was December 31st, but we've missed that, so our new date is 31st March. For reasons of our own, we want the cash in the bank by April 1st. OK?"

Adam nodded his understanding and said nothing, he saw that Charlie was a man who built a platform of logic, so it was best to let him get on with it. *In any case,* he thought to himself, *it still gives me three clear months to execute. That should be no problem.*

"Under your offer we may have to wait three months to know if we have sold either a part, or all of the stones. But they are ready for delivery now. You want us to take a risk on timing and completion. Why would we take that risk?"

Again Adam waited for him to answer his rhetorical question.

"First, because we have commitments from your clients.

"Second, because we have fixed a firm price today, irrespective of what might happen during the next three months.

"And third, you are offering us an insurance policy of a million dollars."

Adam murmured his agreement with Charlie's summing up.

"I want to agree one more condition and I think we can move forward."

"Alright, I'm listening. What is it?"

"If you don't succeed in completing by 31st March, it will probably be because of a falling market. Your margin might screw the deal."

Adam moved uneasily on his seat. He didn't care for the direction this discussion was taking. "Go on."

"We need clearance to approach your customers directly if you don't complete by that date. Our price will still be competitive, because we have your margin to play with. If we can sell directly to your customers we can probably still do the deal we want, at the price we want."

"But what happens to me in that case? All the work I've put in. I can't be held accountable for a falling market." Adam was panicked by the proposal.

"But that's what would happen anyway under your proposal. If the market tanks then you either drop your price or you lose a million dollars. We still have our diamonds."

Adam looked at Laurent, who had said nothing. "This is too hard, guys. I can't turn my customers over to you and get nothing in return."

Now Charlie had him exactly where he wanted him. "OK, I agree. If that happens and we sell directly to your customers, you get a commission of five per cent on the total proceeds."

"And I get my million back?"

"Fine, we're not looking to steal your money."

"How about ten per cent? Nobody makes five per cent in the jewellery business."

The three men finally agreed to this formula, but Adam was shaken. Charlie had manipulated him like an amateur.

Laurent spoke for the first time. "There's one more thing we'd like you to do. Our third partner is the guy who has created these stones and these are his last, so we'd like you to go and meet him. You take the contract and sign it with him. It's just a formality, but it's our way of showing our respect for his work in the partnership over all these years."

"Florida!" Adam had never heard of any of the other IDD partners. Now, he learned that they lived in Marbella, Monaco and Miami. "I've never been there. I'll probably have to fly through London, but I need to check it out. Tell me when I have to go and who I have to meet."

"You're going to meet Nick Martinez, a gem expert and mining engineer. We've been working together for over thirty years. You'll like him, he's a great guy."

"Is he flexible, I mean for the date when I go over?"

"Well, Christmas is just around the corner, so it's got to be just after New Year. We need to make time to get this deal signed with you, or go to one of our other customers."

"You won't need to do that, I promise. Let me get home and arrange the travel and I'll call you immediately. Let's fix provisionally for the second week of January."

Over dinner, Adam asked a lot of questions about the partnership, but the others revealed virtually nothing. He was also very interested in Laurent's life in Monaco and his skiing seasons in Verbier. He'd love to go sometime. Like Bonneville, he was a keen skier.

He talked about his family and his schooling and college in the UK and Charlie mentioned that his son Ron, lived with his wife, Jenny, in Ipswich.

"I love England," Adam said, "Great memories, despite the crap weather. Actually, I'll be in London for a few days on my way home." He sipped his wine. "Is Ipswich near London? If you give me Ron's address, I could try to pop round and say hello. I'd like to meet him."

The men finished their wine and retired early, they had an important deal to complete.

The next morning Laurent and Charlie met the Securitas van at the IDD office. Kurt Vogel was on a week's skiing holiday, and it was Gloria's day off, so they had the place to themselves.

"It's typical." Charlie was irritated. Everybody's gone skiing. What a bloody shambles!"

Laurent signed for the parcel from Rio and they took it inside.

They took out the eight pouches and sprinkled the contents onto a leather mat on Gloria's desk. There were no surprises. Eight piles of exquisite diamonds, sparkling and shimmering in the overhead light. They replaced everything in Charlie's old briefcase then took a cab to Klein, Fellay. In the safety deposit vault they opened the box and took out a key. They closed it again and left with the diamonds still in the briefcase. They took a bus to the Place du Molard then a taxi to Ramseyer, Haldemann & Company's offices, as they had done for the past thirty-odd years.

Gilles didn't appear and Monsieur Jolidon introduced himself to them as the new Directeur. He accompanied them to the circular room, where they put their two keys into the locks of box no. 72. He opened the third lock, then left them. They removed the two pouches of diamonds and pooled them with the new delivery, leaving five bags and taking the other five with them in the briefcase.

After escorting them out of the building, the directeur went back down to the vault. He had a small pad with him and wrote down the number of the box, together with a few notes, underlining the word *briefcase* a couple of times.

In the cab, Charlie explained, "Either Adam will complete or he'll have to drop his price if the market turns. In any event, we're covered with the escrow money. I've already drafted the contract, but we'll wait and send it by email. Mustn't appear too keen to deal."

Laurent sent a message from his BlackBerry to Nick, in Miami, to confirm the successful delivery of the stones from Brazil and their agreement on the contract.

At Ramseyer, Haldemann, the man who had been following them all morning introduced himself to Monsieur Jolidon as a potential client. The directeur showed him their pamphlet with the photographs of the safety doors and the circular room and extolled the virtues of the double key and access code security. The visitor was duly impressed and promised to return to initiate a relationship. He caught a taxi at the corner and was driven to Cointrin airport.

Back at the hotel, Charlie and Laurent met with Adam again in the conference facility. "You wanted sight of the diamonds. We've brought about half of them, the rest are just as good." Laurent opened the case and removed the five pouches and the leather mat.

He carefully poured the diamonds into five separate groups on the mat. "Take a look."

Adam was entranced by the sight. He had never seen such a quantity of unique, perfect diamonds in his life. The reflected light from them hurt his eyes. They measured between two carats and a half carat. He breathed deeply and fingered the stones, cascading them from hand to hand to see them glitter and sparkle. He took out his jewellers lens and examined the larger stones. They were perfect, he had to have them.

He said, "Put them away before I hit you over the head and steal them." He was almost tempted to try it.

Laurent laughed. "No chance. I'm a black belt in martial arts. I'd break your neck."

Adam suspected that he might be telling the truth, so he didn't reply.

He went to his room and fetched a tan leather presentation case, like an ultra slim briefcase. He chose twenty stones of various sizes, which he placed lovingly in the case. He left the case in Laurent's care until the contract was signed and the escrow funds transferred.

That afternoon, Adam left for London, and the two partners took a bus to the Place du Molard, then a taxi to Ramseyer, Haldemann & Company's offices. The directeur took them downstairs again, where they replaced the briefcase in box no. 72. Once again he jotted down some notes on his pad after they had left the building. They took a cab back to Klein, Fellay, replaced the key in the vault, then went to Cointrin airport to catch their flights to Malaga and Monaco. It was now up to Adam Peterson to fulfil his promise.

SIXTY-NINE

December, 2007
Durban, South Africa

It was less than two weeks to Christmas and Adam had invited his parents out for dinner. They went to a Japanese restaurant near the harbour. They were all fond of sushi, although Rachel believed it could be harmful if eaten to excess. She was still slim and hyperactive and tended to dictate her own dietary preferences to the rest of her family. They pretty much ignored her, but she continued to do it anyway.

Hanny was in a fine mood. He was with his adorable wife and his only son, who had an important transaction in hand. He was waiting to hear all about it tonight. He also suspected that he might be asked to lend a hand, since it sounded like a very substantial deal.

Once they'd ordered and the Japanese waitress had poured the wine, Hanny raised his glass. "To my favourite wife and my favourite youngest son."

"To you and mom," Adam responded. Despite Greg's death, as usual, his father had said "youngest son," not just "son." *I'm going to make him so proud of me,* he thought.

"So, how was your trip to Europe, successful?"

"It was terrific. Geneva was good for business. Then I spent a few days in the UK. It was just like being back in school or college. Rubbish weather, but good pubs and restaurants. England still rocks. It's a fun place, especially London."

Rachel was impatient to hear his news. "Your father says that you're on the verge of an important business deal. Do you want to tell us about it?"

Adam went through his relationship with IDD and explained the main details of the transaction. He showed them his calculation of his expected profit, it was very substantial.

"How can anyone have a thousand fabulous Angolan diamonds? Rachel responded. The Angolans have hardly recovered from their civil war and the rebels have had control of the mines for over twenty-five years." The Angolan war was still a very recent memory to South Africans.

"Mom, I asked Laurent Bonneville, he's the guy I'm dealing with, about the diamonds before I started doing any business. He swore to me that they are not blood diamonds. He told me that they came from a source that IDD has had for twenty-five years. That was in 2002, so if it's true, that source is now over thirty years old. I've sold hundreds of them over the past few years and they're always the same, magnificent."

"I've seen them, Rachel, and I don't believe they're blood diamonds. They're too perfect. I'm sure these diamonds were mined and processed by a professional mining company."

"That's right, dad. They showed me another five hundred in Geneva. I took them in my hand, looked at them through my lens. They're superb, the best I've seen in any market. If the world doesn't end next week, I'll finish this deal in a couple of months and make a fortune."

"I suppose it's the million dollars in escrow that you want to talk to us about, son."

"That's it, mom. I can put together a half a million and I could easily raise the other half from outside sources but I wouldn't do it without talking to you first." Adam was gilding the lilly. Borrowing half a million dollars these days wasn't exactly a walk in the park.

"Listen, Adam, it seems to me that the only real danger here is that you fail to complete the deal and IDD decides not to sell, or they sell to someone who isn't your customer. Then you forfeit the million dollars. That's the real risk." Hanny had done a lot of deals in his life.

In his desire to obtain the diamonds at any cost, Adam had overlooked this possibility He blamed it on Charlie' negotiating ability. "I'm sure I can solve that," he said, "But first, take a look at these copies of the commitment letters from my buyers. What do you think?"

Hanny knew all four of the companies concerned, two in the UK and two in the US. They were all solid businesses and he would bet on them completing. He showed them to Rachel, "These customers are as good as they come. We've worked with two of them ourselves."

His wife glanced at the letters. "They're certainly very reassuring."

Adam knew this to be true. They were much more concrete and reassuring than the fairly vague originals that he'd used to fake up these copies. *Well, fake up is a big word. Improve, let's say.* If they fooled his father then they should certainly fool the IDD partners.

Rachel said, "We need to be sure the million dollars is safe. It's an awful lot of money for the family."

"What if I can make the million refundable if they decide not to sell to my customers?"

"Then," his father looked at Rachel, who nodded her assent, "I think we can help you."

Adam begged his parents not to tell the family about this transaction. He wanted to show what he was capable of, landing a big fish and getting a trophy for it. In reality he was terrified that someone, maybe one of his brothers-in-law, who might know the buyers, would check out the commitment letters and find out that they were forgeries. He knew his father wouldn't think of doing this, but he didn't want to risk anything at this stage.

Hanny and Rachel agreed. "This is not money from the business, it's from our savings. If anything goes wrong, we don't want the family to feel that we were foolhardy. Let's keep it to ourselves until you complete everything and we can share the news. Then we'll open a bottle of Krugers with them all. They'll be happy for you. We all will."

They raised their glasses again. "To Adam, and his Angolan diamond business. Success."

Adam received Charlie's draft contract by email the next day. His message said he would step out of the transaction as soon as the terms were agreed. Laurent and Nick would close this out.

He printed out the contract and showed it to his parents. "This is from Charlie Bishop, one of Laurent's partners I met in Geneva. He's an Englishman, very smart and very straight. That's who we have to convince to change the conditions for the escrow money."

He and Hanny drafted a new clause, specifying that IDD would reimburse the escrow money if they refused to sell to him or his customers at his contract price or better. He returned it to Charlie, confirming that he had the million dollars ready to deposit. The next day he received a new draft, including the proposed change. Charlie had also sent a copy to Laurent and Nick, handing the deal over to them, for execution.

"The final contract's back already!" He printed out and checked the whole document once more. It was exactly as he had corrected it.

"These guys are the most honest businessmen I've ever met, dad."

"Either that, or they've thought of a way around this clause that we haven't. Anyway, son, your mother and I are backing you, not them. Just get out and do the deal."

Adam didn't tell his parents that he had to pass another hurdle before he was home and dry. The meeting with Nick Martinez, in Florida. They might have second thoughts about the half million dollars. He decided not to mention his Miami trip at all, only that he would meet IDD and get the contract signed in the US while he was visiting his two American customers. He checked the flights and arranged to meet his buyers on Tuesday, January 8th, in New York.

"That gives me three months to complete by March 31st. That's more than enough time." Then he emailed Laurent that he could get to Miami to meet Nick on Wednesday the 9th.

Hanny and Rachel urged him to get firm delivery commitments from his buyers. They were as excited as he was at the prospect of doing this deal.

SEVENTY

January, 2008
South Beach, Miami, Florida

An attractive blonde woman in a pink sweater and shorts opened the door to Nick Martinez's penthouse apartment on Ocean Drive. It was half past four on the afternoon of Wednesday, January 9th. "Hi," she said, "you must be Adam. Come in. Welcome. I'm Suzie."

He left his travel bag in the hall and followed her into an enormous living room with full length windows looking straight out over the sea. She was wearing a delicate perfume. He tried to identify it, but couldn't.

A tall, tanned man with a Latin look got up from the couch. He appeared to be in his mid-sixties. He put out his hand. "Nick Martinez. Nice to meet you, Adam. How was the trip?"

Nick tried to appear calm and aloof, but inside he was shaking with emotion. He wanted to take Adam in his arms and hug him, tell him everything. *I'm your father, you're my son. Our son, mine and Rachel's.* He tried to formulate the words. *But where do I start? What do I say without screwing it up and scaring him off?* He remained silent and appraised the younger man with a long stare, taking him in from head to toe. *He's a good looking kid. Got Rachel's colouring and looks. I'll have to wait for a while. Time to get to know each other. No hurry.*

Adam was saying, "I decided to blow the budget and fly first class, so the trip was fine. And the limo you sent to pick me up, that was a nice touch. Thanks for inviting me to stay with you, instead of a hotel." Nick nodded and said nothing. "Anyway, I'm happy to meet you too." He looked around. "Marvellous place you've got here."

The warm sunlight was streaming into the living room. It was furnished with comfortable chairs and sofas and tasteful pieces of antique furniture. The floor was littered with oriental rugs and there were several very abstract, modern paintings on the eggshell painted walls. *Interesting, probably expensive, but not my style,* thought Adam. Through an archway he could see a dining room, then another arch led into a kitchen, spotless white, with a huge island in the centre. The apartment must have been about thirty metres long.

The overall ambiance was relaxing; pastel shades and lots of flowers. *Woman's touch,* he decided. A circular staircase went from the hall to the floor below. He supposed there were bedrooms on that floor. A couple of doors led off from the other side of the entrance hall.

"What can I get you, Adam? Coffee, martini, soft drink?" Suzie went over to a fully equipped bar built against the wall.

"To tell you the truth, I'd kill for a cup of tea," he replied.

"Fortnum and Mason's English Breakfast? Digestive biscuit?" He smiled his thanks, it seemed that Suzie was prepared for anything. She went through the dining room to the kitchen.

"It's too cool to sit outside, but come see the view." Martinez slid open a pair of French windows and they stepped out onto a wide wrap-around terrace, full of recliners, sunbeds and teak furniture, with flower boxes running along the front and sides. Beyond the display of flowers and plants, the ocean shimmered in a slight haze. Speedboats and yachts moved across the flat surface of the water. Dog walkers were trekking across the beach and some folk were skating up the sidewalks and the road on roller blades. Adam could see why Nick had decided to live there.

"Absolutely breathtaking! How long have you been here?"

"In Florida, over twenty years now, but only twelve years here. I used to rent a house near Doral golf club, but it was too complicated, having a house just for me, so I bought this place off plan during the construction. Previously, I lived in Geneva for a long while."

Adam could detect a slight accent in his speech. It could have been American, but it was so faint that he couldn't place it. He put it aside. "Quite a change. Geneva, where everything closes at nine at night, then Miami, that's when places start to open up."

Nick laughed. "Geneva is quiet, but it's very civilised. Everything works, so if you have a good reason to be there, it's a great place to live. Especially if you can afford to travel and get away from time to time. How about you? Have you always been in Durban?"

"Apart from school and college in the UK, yes. But I travel a lot, so I can't complain."

"I don't suppose you can spot my accent?" Nick asked nonchalantly.

"I was wondering about that. It's so faint it sounds like several accents all mixed together and cancelling each other out."

"That's pretty much what happened. I've lived here and there, but originally I'm from your neck of the woods."

"You're not South African?"

"Joburg, no less. I'm a Wits scholar, mining engineering. I even worked for those bastards at Imperial Diamond for a few years." He waited to see if this news would provoke a reaction, find out if Rachel had spoken about him.

Adam replied, "My God, I would never have guessed. I would have said US West Coast, very faint. You must have left quite young."

"It's so long ago I can't even remember."

"And you've never been back?"

"Never. I guess it didn't figure in my itinerary."

"Do you have any family over there?"

"Not any more. My mom went to the UK twenty years ago, but she passed away soon after. Nobody else around, I'm afraid."

The two men chatted as they watched the activity on the beach and the sea. Martinez had divulged all he wanted, or dared to, and despite Adam's prodding he didn't talk any more about his past, nor did he mention the diamonds. After a while standing on the terrace, he shivered. "Getting chilly, let's get inside."

Suzie had placed a pot of tea and a plate of biscuits on a low table in front of a deep sofa. Adam put three spoons of sugar in the cup, "Thanks, just what I need."

Nick declined her offer. "Adam and I have a couple of things to discuss, Suzie. Have you got something to do?"

"I'll find something, darling, don't worry." She kissed him on the forehead, left the men and went through a door at the far end of the hall.

"Lovely girl." Adam sipped his tea. It was hot, sweet and refreshing after his long trip.

"We've been together ten years, that's pretty good for me. I'm not great at relationships."

"I know what you mean. Women are still outside my comprehension zone. I guess I'm not old enough to figure them out yet."

"The sad thing is when you get to my age and you still can't figure them out."

Adam studied the man opposite. His hair must once have been black. It remained thick, but it was predominently grey. And his complexion wasn't as dark as it had first appeared, under the tan, he looked a little pasty and he had dark shadows under his eyes. He was also slimmer than at first glance. Although heavy-boned, he must have lost some weight recently, his long sleeved shirt was quite loose around the collar.

"Laurent tells me that you've been a good customer of IDD for several years," Martinez said, trying to move onto safer ground.

"Not as good as I'd have liked. He only let me have about a hundred stones per year. Can't make a fortune with those quantities."

"So that's why you want to buy the rest, to make a fortune?"

"Right! I'm not in business for altruistic reasons. I've already sold them."

"That's good news. This is strictly an end game for me and my partners, Charlie says cash is king and that's good enough for us. So, where's the cash?"

Adam extracted the revised contract from his briefcase. "I suppose you've seen this?"

Nick took it from him. "I have, but I don't understand why you want three months to pay. We've never had that problem before."

"You've never sold a thousand stones before, it's a whole different ball game. That's what I explained to Charlie and Laurent. And at this time of year it's difficult to get people to make a move. They're still wrapping up last year's business and are not ready for this year's."

"Laurent says that you've got firm commitments though?"

Adam took out the letters. *Now or never.* "Take a look at these."

"Are you sure you want me to see your customers' names before we sign the contract?"

"Nick, the contract is signed, I shook hands on it in Geneva and that's good enough for me. And I met two of my buyers in New York on the way here and it's a done deal."

Martinez leaned forward to take the papers. He winced and sat back on the settee again.

"Are you OK, Nick?"

"Just a bit of a stomach ache. It's been nagging me for a week or two, must be Suzie's cooking. Better take some Alka Selzter." He laughed, took the letters from Adam and read them carefully through. Adam waited, apprehensively. *Have I screwed something up?*

"Very reassuring." Unknowingly, Nick repeated exactly what Rachel had said. He looked at the contract again. "OK, you've had sight of the diamonds. Can I have sight of the funds?"

Hanny had already deposited the half million dollars into Adam's business account. He handed Nick an affidavit from his bank confirming instructions to transfer the sum of one million dollars to IDD, upon receiving details of the escrow account from Mr. Peterson.

"I'm impressed. You've thought of everything."

"Thanks. I don't have your experience, but I have a reputation for being a serious businessman. I won't let you down."

"Did Laurent or Charlie tell you why we want to close this deal by the end of March?"

"Only that you've been in the business now for over thirty years and you want to retire."

"It's more complicated than that, but basically, you're right. It's time to close it down."

"So what's the story behind these diamonds, Nick? Thirty years is a long time to run a business without supplies."

"Maybe I'll tell you one day, but right now I think we should have a drink with Suzie. Tomorrow, if I'm up to it, we'll sign the contract and make the the escrow money transfer."

"Why wouldn't you be up to it?"

"Oh, I'm just a bit under the weather these days. Bit tired, not quite up to scratch. I'm sure it's nothing. Let's rescue Suzie from her room, she hates being separated from me."

"And vice versa, right?"

"That's right, Adam."

Supper was a pleasant, quiet affair. Nick opened a fine bottle of Cabernet Sauvignon from Napa Valley, delicious with the tuna steaks that Suzie had grilled. Adam noticed that he ate very little and drank half a glass of wine.

At nine thirty, Nick said, "You must be dead after your flights. Why don't we have an early night and a sharp start in the morning?"

Adam was lodged in one of the guest rooms on the floor below. When Suzie came to ensure that he had everything he needed, he said. "I hope I'm not intruding on you and Nick. I could have easily stayed in a hotel, there's one right next door."

"Don't be silly, you're very welcome. We're pleased that you're staying with us, we've got so much space it's nice to see it used once in a while."

"Well, I really appreciate it. By the way, I hope you don't mind me mentioning it, but Nick seems a bit off form. Is he OK?"

"Well, he's been feeling tired and listless for a while now, got no appetite. But he won't talk about it and refuses to go see the doctor. Nick's not the best communicator in the world. 'Grin and bear it', that's his motto."

"You'll have to talk him into getting a check-up. I hear he's been running around a lot. He needs to take more care."

"Don't worry, I'll do better than that. Just as soon as you've gone I promise to drive him to the doctor myself. Good enough? Anyway, time for shut eye now. We'll see you bright and early in the morning. Good night, Adam." She gave him a peck on the cheek.

He was again aware of the subtle aroma of perfume. "Sleep well, Suzie."

She smiled and closed the door behind her. Adam slept like a baby.

SEVENTY-ONE

January, 2008
South Beach, Miami, Florida

The following day, Nick didn't emerge from his bedroom until midday. Adam was up with the larks, and met Consuela, a round Cuban lady, who was bustling about the apartment, vacuuming up invisible dust and polishing the immaculate furniture.

While he drank his first coffee of the day, Suzie fixed some eggs and bacon and they ate together. She gave no explanation for Nick's absence, except to say he was having a lie-in, but she had instructions to take Adam for a drive around South Miami.

After breakfast they took the elevator down into the car park under the building and she opened up a double-door garage. There were three impressive machines inside. A blue Jaguar 4.2 litre XL open-top sports car stood alongside a bright red, 1968 Cadillac de Ville convertible. By the wall at the side was a 1975 Harley-Davidson XL-1000, in the original, shiny, light brown factory paint. All the vehicles were in show-room condition.

"You choose." Suzie gave him an infectious grin.

"It has to be the Cadillac. I've never even seen one before, never mind ridden in one."

She handed him the keys, "The gear shift is on the column. Apart from that it's easy. Long, but easy." She seemed unaware of the double entendre.

Adam negotiated the enormous car out of the garage and onto Ocean Drive. It was a fine, warm day, and they drove with the top down, Suzie wearing a blue baseball cap to protect her long blonde hair from blowing about in the rush of fresh, bracing sea air. She looked beautiful, sitting alongside him on the wide bench seat.

They turned up onto Collins Avenue then drove through the historic art deco area and across to Biscayne Bay as she pointed out the sights.

"Miami seems a fun place. Something like Cape Town," he told her.

They drove over Biscayne Bay on the MacArthur Causeway and stopped for coffee in the Palm Island Park. Adam soon realised that Suzie was a surprising woman. Intelligent and well informed, she was far from being the dizzy blonde he had expected. She seemed totally unaware of her feminine attraction, laughing and talking animatedly, apparently with no sexual agenda. Adam was captivated by her natural beauty and poise. When she laughed out loud, opening her eyes wide and showing her perfect white teeth, he was smitten.

She was fascinated by Rachel's work in cancer care. "They're starting to build hospices over here too. There are lots of charitable foundations raising money. Our welfare programme isn't great and so many people can't afford to die with dignity. It's awful"

She told him her parents were living in Orlando. "They're golf fanatics. Everyone seems to start playing golf when they can't play tennis any more. It's a great retirement project. *Tour the world's best golf courses. Travel and sport.* I'll be into that when my time comes."

Adam laughed at the idea of this lovely young woman planning her retirement. "Do you and Nick play?"

"I've tried a few times, but it's so infuriatingly difficult. Nick plays well, although it's been a while since he's had a game, what with travelling and being under the weather and all."

Adam didn't pursue the matter, he expected that Nick would tell him if he wanted to.

They drove the giant car back to the garage and went upstairs. Standing close to Suzie in the elevator he was once more aware of her perfume. "What's that lovely scent?"

"It's Clinique. Elixir Aromatique. Like it?" She put her hand to his nose.

He breathed in the lovely fragrance. "Delicious." He didn't know if it was the perfume or her skin. *I could fall in love with this woman,* he thought to himself. *Dangerous business.*

Back in the apartment, she said, "That was nice. How about a drink before lunch?"

She made a couple of martinis and they sat out on the terrace watching the animation below. It was midday and the sun was warm and relaxing. Nick came out wearing a bathrobe, towelling his hair dry. "Sorry to be such a drag. I seem to need a lot of sleep these days. Probably been doing too much running around."

"Hello, darling. Adam and I went out in the Cadillac. He wants to make you an offer."

Nick gave her a kiss and sat on the arm of the terrace chair. "You can't afford it, Adam, nobody can afford to buy that car. I bought it when I made my first million, I'll never sell it."

"Just as well, it's a bit large for Durban. I'll take the Jag instead."

Over lunch, Suzie mentioned to Nick that Adam's mother, Rachel, was running a cancer hospice that she'd set up in Durban.

"Rachel? Is that your mother's name?" Nick asked, ingenuously.

"That's right. She's a wonderful woman. You'd absolutely love her, everybody does. Especially Hanny, my dad, he adores her, and she likewise."

Nick winced at these words, but simply asked. "And she works with cancer patients?"

"She has done for years. She started the hospice that she runs, raised the funding, got it built, got the staff and the volunteers. She's really incredible."

Nick didn't want to say anything more in Suzie's presence, so he put it off again. *How many times can I postpone this conversation,* he asked himself.

Adam rightly got the impression that he was preoccupied with other thoughts and changed the subject. Once again Nick ate hardly anything and when Suzie took away his still-full plate, she joked, "Shall I put this in a doggy bag for you?"

That afternoon, the two men discussed the final details of the transaction. Adam took out the contract again and put it on the coffee table.

Martinez looked at it and asked, "What time is your flight tomorrow?"

"I'm taking the five o'clock flight to London."

"That means you have to leave here at latest two thirty. Fine. I have to make a call to Laurent and Charlie in the morning, so let's sign the contract before you leave. OK with you?"

"Not a problem, we'll sign it tomorrow." The two men shook hands. Nick's hand was cold and clammy and he looked pale.

"Are you feeling all right, Nick?"

"I think I'm coming down with something. I'll go visit the quack tomorrow after you've gone home, see what pills are in vogue these days."

Adam's room on the floor below was spacious, with a large bathroom and wide, full length windows and a terrace running along the front. It was after eleven o'clock. Once again they'd had an early, light dinner and gone to bed by ten thirty. He was lying awake, wondering why Nick hadn't signed the contract. *Why is he calling his partners tomorrow, is there something I've missed? Maybe the commitment letters, something wrong with them?*

He heard the door open. "Adam, you awake?"

"Suzie?"

The bedcovers rustled and he felt her slide in beside him. She cuddled up against his body and turned his face toward hers. "Hi, Adam." Her breath was sweet and warm. She touched his lips with her fingers, then taking his face in her hands she kissed his forehead, his cheek, his nose, then his mouth. He responded to her kiss. She kissed him more deeply, her lips opening against his and he felt her tongue slide against his teeth. He opened his mouth a little and her tongue pushed right inside, a warm, sinuous feeling as she curled her tongue around his. It was wet and sweet, like a slice of fresh peach.

He returned her kiss furiously, pushing his tongue into her mouth in turn. He was only wearing shorts and he could feel her naked body press against him. She took his hand and placed it on her breast, the nipple was hard and erect. He stroked the soft, smooth flesh of her breasts, rubbed his fingers over the nipples, which became more aroused.

She pushed her hips against his body and moved her hands over his bare chest. "I want you Adam. Please make love to me."

Adam couldn't believe this was happening. He'd never before been seduced by a woman. His penis thickened, growing with every thrust of her tongue and movement of her hands on his body. Suzie pushed the sheets back and kissed his chest, his nipples, nuzzling them like a baby. She stroked his stomach, moving her hand down his body to his shorts, then caressed his penis beneath the material. Her hand sneaked inside them and moved slowly down to the now fully erect organ. She wrapped her fingers around it. His head spun with emotion.

Suddenly he panicked. *There's something wrong here. Why would Suzie bother with me?* His voice thick with passion, he asked, "Where's Nick?"

She smoothed her fingers over the tip of his penis, then took him completely in her hand, gently squeezing and lifted her leg across him. He smelled her odour, the scent of her arousal. "Nick's asleep, he took a pill. He needs a good night's rest, he's been sleeping badly for a while now. Just relax, he won't disturb us."

"Suzie, I can't. I'm sorry, but I can't do this, I'm really sorry." He pulled her hand from his shorts and moved away from her.

"Don't worry, Adam, Nick won't mind. In any case he won't know, but even if he did, he wouldn't mind, I promise." She moved back against him, embracing him and kissing his neck. "I want you so much."

He felt her soft breasts against his back and her hands started to stroke his stomach again. He was giddy with desire for her but he struggled to master his emotions. Somehow he managed to extricate himself from her arms and sat up on the bed. He switched on the light. "Suzie, you have to go. We can't do this and I can't resist you any more. Please go. Please."

Suzie lay still for a moment, her face pushed into the pillow.

Then she gave a deep sigh, turned over and sat up beside him. "OK, Adam. If that's what you want, I'll go."

"God knows it's not what I want, but you have to go. This is all wrong."

She got down from the bed and faced him, naked and exquisite. *Jesus, she's the most beautiful girl I've ever seen.* He felt awful. "I'm so sorry, I don't know what to say."

"No need to say anything, Adam, just one of those things, ships that pass in the night and all that. I'll see you in the morning. Good night and sleep well." She kissed him softly on the mouth and walked to the door.

"Good night, Suzie. Please try to forgive me."

She smiled at him then turned and left the room, closing the door quietly behind her.

The next morning it was nine o'clock when Adam finished dressing. He went up to the kitchen, Suzie wasn't to be seen and Nick was talking on the phone. He went out on the kitchen terrace to let him finish his call. It was already busy outside. People were rushing about doing all kinds of recreational activities. Someone was water skiing behind a blue and yellow speed boat and a couple of large yachts were cruising by.

Suzie came through the kitchen and joined him on the terrace. Her hair was still damp from the shower. She looked amazing. "Good morning." She gave him a kiss on the cheek. "I hope you slept well."

"Not great, I'm afraid." He tried to cover his embarrassment. "You look as if you did, more lovely than ever. How do you do it?"

"Clean living and a clear conscience." She laughed at his discomfort. "Just joking. Come in and I'll fix some eggs."

Nick had finished his call. The two men sat over mugs of coffee while Suzie prepared breakfast. "Charlie and Laurent are happy with the deal, so we'll sign the contract after breakfast. How about we have a very light meal then Suzie and I will take you along for lunch to the Hard Rock Café on Biscayne Boulevard on the way to the airport. You have to experience some real American culture before you go."

Adam hid his elation. The contract would at last be signed, his letters had passed muster. "I've never been in a Hard Rock, we don't have them in South Africa. That'll be a real treat, a genuine American burger."

Suzie prepared scrambled eggs on a toasted English muffin, light and tasty.

Nick ate hardly anything. "Bit of a tummy ache this morning. I'll leave room for the burger," he said. Adam wasn't convinced.

While she cleared away, the two men went to sit on the living room couches. Adam pulled out two copies of the contract, signed them opposite his name and passed them to Nick, who signed for IDD. They shook hands, Adam felt relieved, he'd passed every test.

Nick handed him a sheet of note paper. "Here are the details of the IDD escrow account. You can send the fax to your bank from the machine here in my office. Laurent is in Geneva, so I've asked him to fly to London with your presentation case and all the documentation and you can meet up in Heathrow. I'd like to tie up everything today to make the deadline, so we need to get moving right away."

They spent the next hour in Nick's office, sending the required messages and calling Laurent to arrange the meeting. Then the two men went back to sit in the living room. Suzie could be heard still fussing about in the kitchen.

Nick braced himself to turn the conversation to their relationship. *It's time to break it to him. I can't let him go home without knowing who I am.* Aloud, he said, "Adam, there's something I have to tell you."

Adam smiled at him in a conspiratorial manner. "You mean the Suzie test, right? Well, I guess I passed it."

Nick was completely thrown. "The Suzie test?" He glanced towards the kitchen then back at Adam. "Oh, I see." He paused. "You must think we're pretty cynical folks."

Adam realised he'd made a big mistake. "I'm sorry, Nick, I jumped to a stupid conclusion. I couldn't believe that Suzie would fancy a guy like me, I still can't believe it. My mistake! I apologise, I didn't mean to offend you, nor her."

"Let me tell you something." Adam winced at Nick's stare. "Suzie and I have been together for ten years and we have a very liberal relationship. I don't ask her what she does when she's not with me and she doesn't ask me. Even so, I know that she has rarely, if ever, done anything that would upset me. The thing is though, she's thirty years younger than me. She has her needs and I can't always fulfil them. Like at the moment, I haven't been a hundred percent right for a while and she misses, well, the physical side of our relationship."

"I understand! I totally misread the situation. I can't apologise enough."

"You don't need to apologise to me, it really doesn't bother me, but I'll tell you one thing. If Suzie has a thing for you, you are a bloody lucky man, a rare breed. She's an exceptionally picky woman and you should count your lucky stars. If you feel the need to apologise, then apologise to her, not to me."

Adam felt like a complete idiot. *I don't think I can apologise again, I said enough last night.* He really couldn't figure women. *Stupid bitches,* he had always said. *But this time it's me who's a stupid prick.*

Nick got up and went into the kitchen. He felt sick to the stomach. The moment was gone and there wouldn't be another opportunity. *I can't try again. I just don't have the courage.*

Suzie pulled the Cadillac up in front of an admiring crowd at the BA terminal. They'd managed to get through lunch at the Hard Rock without any further discomfort, mainly thanks to her light hearted banter. She was a clever woman. *What an asshole you are,* Adam thought to himself again. Well, he had the contract, the million dollars and he'd soon have the diamonds. No time for regrets. He picked up his cases and turned to say goodbye to Suzie.

"Have a good trip, Adam, and come and see us again. Nick and I would both like that." She hugged him warmly and kissed him softly on the mouth.

He whispered in her ear, "I'm really sorry. Sorry for everything."

She gave him an affectionate smile. "Rain check, OK?" She went back to sit at the wheel of the enormous car in case it was towed away.

The two men walked to the entrance of the terminal. Adam had noticed that Nick had seldom spoken and eaten hardly anything at lunch, his burger was virtually untouched when the waiter cleared away the dishes. He seemed to be preoccupied with something. *It's probably my fault, that stupid remark about Suzie.* He turned to apologise again.

Before he could say anything, Nick grabbed his hand and shook it warmly. "Travel safely and I'll see you either in Geneva or here, when we've completed the transaction."

"Nick, it's been a real pleasure, I hope I didn't bugger it up too badly."

"Don't worry, I've forgotten it already. By the way, this little health thing, it's nothing serious. You don't need to mention it to my partners, they worry about me enough already."

"I won't say a word, but please go to the doctor tomorrow. Better to be..."

"I know, safe than sorry. I promise to go tomorrow. See you soon, God speed."

As Adam walked towards the check-in counters, Nick took from his wallet a well-thumbed, creased photograph, the colours faded with age. It showed a young woman in a blue halter top and shorts, standing in the shallow surf on Clifton Beach, her lovely blue eyes smiling at the camera, and at him.

Sitting in his first class seat with a glass of champagne, Adam read and re-read the contract. Even though he knew it by heart, he had trouble registering the words. He couldn't get Suzie out of his mind. *I still don't get it,* he thought. *What does she want with me?*

SEVENTY-TWO

January, 2008
Durban, South Africa

The whole family was in the garden of Hanny and Rachel's house. It was Saturday, the day after Adam's return and he'd slept for twelve hours. He'd come straight from the airport to his parents' house to spend the weekend with them. He came out to a blazing hot day and a blazing hot barbecue. The kids were playing in the pool and the adults were sipping fruit punch on the terrace. Adam greeted everyone in a relaxed fashion. He felt comfortable, he'd gotten his deal under control. His parents would be proud of him.

He sat on the terrace with the others and his sister, Catrine, brought him a glass of punch. "Thanks, Catty, just what I need. Cheers everyone." He sipped the delicious, cool mixture.

Rachel came to sit beside him. "Welcome home, dear. How did it go in the States?"

He kissed her on the cheek. "Couldn't have been better, mom. Whilst I was there I met another IDD partner and we agreed on the last details and signed the final contract. I've already transferred the escrow money, so we're in business."

"That's wonderful, Adam. Your father will be proud of you. We'll talk about it when the family's gone."

The afternoon was an enjoyable break for Adam after the stressful visit with Nick and Suzie. His aunt Josie was there with her brood. She was a lot of fun. They played with the kids in the pool and Tom, Birgitta's husband, organised a game of cricket on the lawn. The South Africans were crazy about cricket, the children even more so.

"Goodbye folks, see you soon." Josie drove her family off at last, waving back at the house.

Rachel walked back up the driveway with Adam. "Let's go sit with your father and you can tell us about your trip."

Hanny was sitting on the terrace, smoking a cheroot. His leg was bothering him and he no longer joined in the games with the children. "How's my boy, everything in good shape?"

"Hang on, dad, I'll just get something to show you." Adam went up to his room and brought the signed contract, the documents given to him by Laurent, and his presentation case.

He opened up the case, revealing the twenty diamonds he'd selected the previous month.

"Just look at these, mom. I know you're still madly in love with dad, but you'll be crazy about these fabulous gems as well, I guarantee it.

"Oh, my!" Rachel had seen many impressive diamonds in her life, but nothing like this brilliant display. "Now I see what you've been talking about. They're absolutely stunning."

He handed over his magnifying lens and his father looked closely at several of the stones. "Incredible!" He shook his head. "I've never seen such perfect clarity and colour in my whole life. You could easily increase your price, nobody has stones like these."

"Too late, dad, my customers are already biting at the bit. And I don't want to get the reputation of being a price hitcher." Despite his reply, Adam was mentally kicking himself for not going for better prices. Hanny was right, he'd never seen better stones in his life.

He produced the documents he'd received from Laurent. A certificate of ownership from IDD, an authorisation to carry the diamonds on their behalf and the VAT and other documents for the customs post at the airports, en route to visit his customers in the US and UK.

"Everything seems absolutely professional, son. That's usually a very good sign."

"And here's the final contract. Your idea about the funds was brilliant. I transferred the escrow money by fax from Florida. Everything went as smooth as clockwork. It's a done deal." He handed the contract to his father.

"Whose is the signature for IDD? I can't read it." He gave the contract back to Adam.

"It's another partner I met in Florida. I think there are four of them altogether. I met Laurent and Charlie in Geneva, and in Miami I met the guy who signed the contract, Nick Martinez. He's the diamond expert who's been processing their stones for the last thirty years. He's a really nice guy, lives in Florida. But you won't believe it, he's originally from Joburg."

Adam was looking at the contract in his hand, intent on getting his story right. He failed to notice his mother's shocked expression at the mention of Nick's name. His father remained impassive, somehow controlling his astonishment at hearing this name from the distant past.

Rachel gave a gasp and Hanny took her hand. "Are you all right dear?" To Adam, he said, "Your mother's been a bit off colour this week, son. I'll just take her in for a lie-down. I'll be back in a moment and we can continue."

"Are you sure you're all right, mom?" Adam was concerned, his mother was never sick.

"I've probably been overdoing it at the hospice. Don't worry, I'm fine." She pulled herself up and went inside with Hanny. Adam realised that his parents were getting on in life.

His father came back a little while later. "Right, let's have all the gory details."

Rachel begged off supper that evening and stayed in her room. The two men opened a bottle of Merlot and sat outside, nibbling at some of the leftovers from the barbecue. They talked a lot about

Adam's business. Hanny was very interested in the IDD partners, especially Nick Martinez. Adam gave him an abbreviated version of his trip to Miami, saying that he'd had a call to invite him down when he was in New York. He mentioned that Nick spoke with a soft accent. "I would never have guessed he was from Joburg, his accent's got lost in his travels, that's for sure." He told his father what he knew about the man, which wasn't much, but it was enough for Hanny.

It was after ten when Adam said goodnight and went upstairs to his room. Hanny went into his office. After a short while, he emerged and went to their bedroom. It was in darkness. Rachel was in her armchair by the window, looking out at the harbour lights.

"How are you feeling, my love?" He saw that she had been crying. She looked worn out.

"Darling, I suppose it's not possible that this is an incredible coincidence? That there's another Nick Martinez in the world, a different man altogether, not the man that I knew?"

"Well, if you answer me two questions, we'll know for sure."

"What questions?"

"First, did he attend Witwatersrand and obtain a BSc in mining engineering?"

She didn't reply, just nodded.

"And was he Director of Diamond Mining Operations at the Imperial Diamond Exploration Company, in Joburg?"

She took his hands and looked him in the eyes. "It's him, it's the same Nick. Where did you find all this out?"

"I cheated. I looked up IDD on Google and found the directors. Charlie Bishop, FCA, BSc, and Nick Martinez GIA, BSc, from UK and Joburg respectively. Added to what Adam told us, there's no doubt it's the same man. The problem is, what do we do about it now?"

"Oh, Hanny, this is all my fault. I should have known that it would come out somehow. Now everyone will find out about my sordid past, the unmarried mother, saved by a Prince Charming. Adam is thirty-three and he has to learn that the father he has always known isn't really his father. I'm so terribly sorry." She burst into tears, shaking her head from side to side.

"After Greg's death, I thought we'd, you'd suffered as much as any parent could cope with. Now, because of my stupidity, Adam and the whole family are going to have to go through another awful trauma. And a man I loved and thought I'd forgotten has suddenly reappeared in our lives. I just don't know what to do, what to say, to try to put things right."

Hanny put his arm around her shoulders. He kissed her wet face and stroked her hair back in place. "Now then, Rachel, please stop crying. We have to talk sensibly about this and it's not going to be easy if you're blowing your nose every two minutes."

When the tears had stopped flowing the two of them sat side by side, holding hands like young lovers. They talked the matter through backwards and forwards. Hanny confirmed that Nick had left Joburg and had never been back. He'd lived in Geneva and Florida and elsewhere. It seemed that he had done very well for himself over all these years. He was one of the owners of the fabulous Angolan diamonds and Adam was doing business with him.

He had to be told. Somehow they would have to explain it to him and to the family as well. Hanny insisted that they would understand, even sympathise with Rachel's unfortunate situation, it had happened over thirty years ago. It didn't change anything today, the family wouldn't fall apart because of this. But that wasn't the problem, the problem was Adam.

After an hour's talking, Rachel made her decision. "I have to tell him myself, it's the only way. He's my son and Nick is his real father. You've always been the best father he could have wished for, but I have to tell him about Nick. He's met him, he's doing business with him and he doesn't know who he is. I've got to face up to it, there's no other way."

They held each other in bed as they had done for the last thirty-three years. Now that Rachel had taken her decision she felt relieved. She had a good night's sleep, but Hanny didn't sleep so well. He lay awake, thinking about his own son, Greg, taken from him at the age of twenty-six, in a tragic, senseless accident. Now, his adopted son, whom he loved as his own, was about to find out that he wasn't his real father. That he'd been lied to for all these years. Was he now going to lose his only remaining son? Then there was Nick. He knew that Rachel had never really forgotten about him. His whole family life was under threat and there was nothing he could do about it. He dreaded finding out what tomorrow would bring.

When Rachel came down the next morning, Adam was already having breakfast. He had vowed to lose the couple of pounds he'd gained travelling, so he was eating fruit and yoghourt. She declined anything to eat and poured herself a mug of coffee.

"I hope you're feeling better, mom?" He was concerned that his mother had missed supper and gone to bed early. He couldn't remember her ever doing that.

"I'm perfectly fine, don't worry. I was a bit tired last night, having all the family over for the day. I think I'll take a few days off from the hospice. But don't worry, I'm really fine."

They sat talking quietly over their coffee and Rachel summoned up all her courage. She said, under her breath, *I can't put it off for ever. Now's the best time, it always is.*

"Come and walk a little in the garden with me. There's something I need to tell you."

He looked worriedly at her, but said nothing, took her by the hand and helped her up. They walked across the lawn together, arm in arm.

"It's about something that happened a long time ago, Adam, before you were born."

SEVENTY-THREE

January, 2008
Cape Town, South Africa

Adam was sitting at a café on the Waterfront in Cape Town. He had a double whisky in front of him. It was six o' clock in the evening of Monday, 21st January, a very hot day. He had flown down the previous night and checked in to the Raleigh Hotel, right on the harbour, but he hadn't slept a wink that night.

After the conversation with his mother, he had walked from the house to Durban harbour, about two kilometres. He had no idea where he was going, his head was spinning and he felt sick and frightened. He walked along the waterside for what seemed like hours, trying to make sense of the story she had recounted. It had hit him like a bombshell. Hanny wasn't his father. For thirty-three years he'd been another man's son. His real father had left his pregnant fiancée and had never been seen again, until, by some Machiavellian stroke of fate, his son had gone to visit him in Miami. *My real father. I'm doing a multi-million dollar deal with my own father.*

I'm really just a bastard, he told himself. *If Hanny hadn't taken pity on mother, I wouldn't have a father.*

Rachel had told him that she and Nick had been very much in love. They were together for a year and were to be married, but they had a falling out. It was to do with apartheid. *Maybe,* he thought. *Or maybe he just didn't want to have a kid. Maybe he knew Rachel was pregnant. Maybe he'd walked out on both of them.*

The other thing was that Catrine and Birgitta were not his sisters and Greg had not even been his half-brother. He recalled the time they had talked about it when he was a child. Greg had said that he wasn't really their brother. *He must have known. Maybe everyone knows. Maybe I'm the only person who didn't know.* That's why he'd always felt inferior to his brother, because he was. Greg had made him feel it too, and now that he was no longer there, he would never be able to ask him, to find out if that was the reason for their incompatibility.

Adam felt like throwing himself into the harbour. He was in a state of despair. He didn't realise it but tears were rolling down his cheeks. If anyone had seen him they would have taken him for a crazy person. He was talking to himself and crying. He *was* a crazy person.

After trying to walk away the nightmare, he had gone back to the house and booked a flight that evening to Cape Town. He came out to the terrace where his parents were sitting. "I need to get away for a few days. This is just like a bad dream, I need time to sort it out."

Hanny tried desperately to comfort him. "Adam, whatever happened, whatever you think, you are my son. I married your mother because I loved her and I still do. And I love you in the same way. You are my son, not somebody else's, mine. I was lucky enough to have two sons but now I still have one, and that's you, Adam. And I'm proud of you and I always will be. I can't change what has happened but I love you and I always have, always will."

"So why did nobody tell me then, dad? Why was I left to find out like this? To go to Miami and do a deal with a sixty-five year old guy who turns out to be my own father. You couldn't write this script if you tried. It's just too bloody ridiculous."

Rachel's heart was breaking. She didn't know what to do or say. *First Nick, now Adam,* she thought. *I've estranged them both. Oh my God.*

Hanny tried again. "We didn't tell anyone, Adam. Neither your brother nor your sisters knew. Auntie Jodie was the only person in the world who knew about your mother's pregnancy. We never imagined in our wildest dreams that this would come out, even less that you would meet Nick. We made a mistake and we're deeply sorry for it. But we tried to do the best for you. If anyone else had known, your life might have been a misery, you would have felt...I don't know how you would have felt, but we didn't want to take that risk. I wanted to be your father, it wasn't forced on me and I'm happy that I took the decision to marry your mother. Not through pity, but for love, love for her, and for her unborn child."

Adam realised that further talk was futile. He said, "I've booked on a flight to Cape Town. I'm leaving in a few hours, I don't know how long for. I'll send you a text message when I find a hotel, I need to get away and straighten out my head."

He had walked into the Raleigh Hotel at eight o' clock and was lucky enough to find a single room, moderately priced. It was high season, so Cape Town was frenetic. The hotels and restaurants were overflowing with tourists from every part of the world. He tried to lose himself in the crowds, dined alone in the hotel, had a drink and went to bed. He didn't sleep.

That morning he'd wandered about, looking at the boats and window shopping along the shops and boutiques on the Waterside. He bought an ice cream, it was cool and refreshing in the heat. He didn't think too much about his quandary, his father, mother and Nick, or whatever they should all be called. Somehow the day passed.

Now, he was sitting by the harbour, sipping a whisky. A young busker with dreadlocks was strumming a guitar and singing "Blowin' in the Wind." He was quite good, making pleasant background music, not noisy. Adam absently walked over and dropped a twenty rand note into the singer's hat. He nodded his thanks and started on "Tambourine Man." *Must know I'm a Dylan fan,* Adam speculated.

A young woman came and sat at a table right next to him and he heard her order a Campari and soda. *English,* he registered, *London accent.*

The waiter poured the drink and managed to spill the soda. It splashed down onto the woman's dress. It looked like a new holiday outfit. She jumped aside and her purse fell onto the ground, spilling money and credit cards. Adam got up to help her gather everything back again. "I'm sorry," she said. "That's very kind, thank you."

Adam replied, "No reason to be sorry, it wasn't your fault." He'd never understood why English people always apologised for everything. He supposed that if she got run over by a car, she'd spend her dying breath apologising for being so clumsy.

It turned out that she was on a ten day holiday with a girlfriend. They came from Surrey, where she was a nurse at the local hospital, in the cancer ward. She was easy to talk to and he needed that. Some semblance of normality from an unknown third party. He told her his mother was a cancer specialist and had been for over thirty years. When he mentioned the hospice she was duly impressed and said all the right things. Before he knew it, he'd invited her for dinner at his hotel. The restaurant was quite good, he'd eaten there the previous evening. Old fashioned and comfy, not sparse and modern.

They had another drink then walked along to the hotel. The Waterfront was bustling with visitors coming down for the evening, to have dinner and enjoy the ambiance. Music blared out from the many restaurants which had live entertainment. Buskers and local bands were playing against each other so you couldn't make out any tune at all. The head waiter found them a table by the window, where they could see the activity outside.

"Where's your friend tonight, Lucy?"

"My friend? Oh, you mean Pam. She found a chap the first night we arrived and I've hardly seen her since. I suppose she's out with him for dinner or whatever."

Lucy was quite pretty in an English way, light brown hair, brown eyes in a round face with a snub nose. She gabbled away, talking so much that he could hardly get a word in. They had two bottles of wine with their dinner and afterwards they went up to his room.

As soon as they got through the door, she threw her arms around him, kissing him fiercely, trying to thrust her tongue down his throat. She pulled his sport shirt open so the buttons burst and pushed him onto the bed, unzipping his flies. She was like a wild animal, not concerned about his satisfaction or needs, only intent on satisfying her own sexual desire. There was no passion, no tenderness, only lust. He felt cheap, almost as he imagined a prostitute might feel. He decided to act like her. They didn't make love, they had sex three times, in all sorts of positions, until he was completely exhausted. She was insatiable. In the end she was still sitting on top of him trying to climax one more time when his penis was shrunken and sore. He felt sickened, dirty and for some reason, guilty.

So that's a one night stand. It could have been anybody who came along, he realised. *She and Pam came here with only one thing in mind, sex. Or, maybe two things, booze and sex.*

They fell asleep. The two bottles of wine finally kicked in. She woke him with her snoring at five o'clock in the morning and he went to shower himself clean and brush his teeth.

Adam sat on the balcony of his room, looking at the harbour in the pre-dawn gloom, thinking about things. *Was Rachel's affair with Nick like that? Like a one night stand? Just about sex, nothing else? No!* He knew it wasn't possible, his mother was loving, tender, considerate and affectionate, all the things that Lucy wasn't. Nick must have been the same. *It couldn't have worked otherwise. Not to be together for a year, to live together and plan to marry. It had to be love.* He had to be the product of love, the alternative didn't bear thinking about.

And Hanny, there wasn't a day went by when he didn't show his love for his family. He wasn't to blame for Adam's predicament, neither was his mother, nor was Nick. He hadn't even known about his son, he still didn't know. Adam realised that he couldn't blame anyone, it was one of those things and he had to get over it. Time would heal the wounds. It always did.

He thought about his feelings for Suzie. His passion had almost forced him to make love to her, *love, not lust.* He knew she was a special person, maybe she really did have feelings for him. Nick seemed to think so. *It's funny. I've got Nick's blessing to woo his girlfriend. From father to son,* he thought. But he knew it wasn't like that. Nick wanted Suzie to be happy, he'd succeeded in that for ten years and now he realised that it was coming to an end. He had to go back over there soon to see her. To find out if it was something more than just a momentary need for physical contact. *And I have to go over to introduce myself to my father,* he realised.

Just before six in the morning, the golden orb of the sun climbed up over the horizon, flooding its precious light across the sky from the east, colouring the few scattered clouds with a crimson sheen and casting a brilliant reflection onto the calm waters of the harbour below. In the distance, a lonely fishing boat was making its way across the shining surface of the ocean, leaving a shallow, white-topped wake behind it. The seabirds' chorus heralded the birth of a glorious new day. A new day for South Africa, and a new day for Adam Peterson.

Nothing really changes, he thought to himself. *The important things stay the same. You just have to recognise them.* Adam felt a sense of peace. He was starting to see clear, he was ready to go home. He went inside to wake Lucy up and get rid of her.

SEVENTY-FOUR

February, 2008
South Beach, Miami, Florida

Suzie opened the door for Adam and Rachel. "Adam, how great to see you." She looked wonderful.

His heart flipped. *She's still the most beautiful woman I've ever seen.* She gave him a hug and a kiss, saw some lines of stress in his face and squeezed his hand.

"Suzie, you look marvellous. This is my mother, Rachel."

"I'm so pleased to meet you. Adam told me a lot about you." She hugged her too.

Adam was relieved at the reception. When his mother had told him that she had to come to see Nick with him, he'd panicked. *What's Nick going to think? We're supposed to be doing a huge deal and suddenly my mother wants to meet him.* Then he realised it had to be done, it was a kind of catharsis for everyone concerned. But how could he explain it on the telephone?

Hanny gave him an idea. "Tell Nick that your parents have put up part of the million dollars escrow money and I'd like to come over and meet the people we're dealing with."

"But..." Adam didn't follow.

"Wait, son. Just before we're due to go, tell him I'm not feeling up to it, but your mother would like to come in my stead. She has never been to Miami, so she'd love to use the ticket and come over and meet him. He can't refuse a perfectly normal request like that."

Nick was rather subdued on the phone. Adam told him he was coming over to close the two US customers and he'd like to come down to see him. He gave Hanny's version of the story and Nick said he would be pleased to meet Adam's father.

Two weeks before the trip, Adam called back and announced that his father wasn't well, but his mother, Rachel, would love to visit Miami and meet Nick. Did he mind if she came in his place? "It'll be good for her to get away from the cancer hospice, she works far too much."

At the thought of seeing Rachel again after all these years, Nick's mind went into a nervous spin. Falteringly, he said, "I would love to meet her, but are you sure that she really wants to come all the way over here? It's a very tiring journey."

When Adam insisted that his mother was looking forward to the trip, Nick said, "Well, in that case, you have to come and stay here again. Suzie would be upset if you went to a hotel."

Adam could hear him coughing at the other end of the line. "Are you all right, Nick? Mom and I don't want to invade your home if you're not up to it."

"Don't worry about me, I'm fine. I'll see you and Rachel next Thursday. Have a good trip. Suzie will make sure you're comfortable when you get here."

They had come via London again and Rachel didn't approve of first class, so they were feeling a little jet-lagged. It took them over an hour to get through immigration and Nick hadn't sent a limo this time, so they'd taken a taxi for the short run to South Beach. The Vietnamese driver dropped their luggage on the pavement. "Too hot to take them up."

Adam paid him off with a very small tip and took their bags up in the elevator.

Suzie picked up his briefcase at the door. "Let me show you straight to your rooms and you can dump your stuff and clean up."

Adam noticed that the door to the living room was closed. He supposed that Nick was busy with something. He carried the other bags downstairs. The two women were chattering away already, Rachel trying to hide her nervousness. She told Suzie she loved the beach that they'd seen from the taxi, white sand, turquoise sea. It was beautiful, just like Durban.

"Wait 'til you see the view from the terrace, mother, it's magnificent."

Adam had the same room as previously. Suzie took Rachel to another guest room along the hall. Like Adam's, the room looked across the beach to the sea, it seemed that every room in the apartment did. He waited while Suzie showed Rachel around.

Rachel's mind was seething with emotions. She was about to meet the father of her son. The man she hadn't seen for more than thirty years but had never managed to get out of her mind and her heart. She fussed nervously with her bags for a few moments then said, "I think we should see Nick now. We'll clean up later. It's not polite to keep people waiting."

"Sure, let's go up. He was sleeping before, so let's be quiet."

Rachel gave Adam an anxious look. He shrugged, as if to say, *I don't know.*

Suzie led them back up the stairs and opened the door to the living room. Unlike Adam's last visit, the blinds were half closed and the room was in semi-darkness. Nick was lying back on a settee, his feet up on an upholstered stool. He seemed to be dozing. The room was stiflingly warm, but he was wearing a flannel dressing gown and had a blanket across his legs. Several cushions had been piled up so that he could lie back against them.

Adam couldn't hide his shock. Nick looked to have lost ten kilos or more since last month. His face, in the poor light, was haggard, deep shadows under his eyes, and the skin had a yellow sheen, as if he had jaundice. His thick hair was now almost completely white and had been cut quite short. He seemed smaller, wrapped up in the blankets, as if he'd shrunken since Adam had last seen him. He turned to look at his mother.

Rachel gasped, it was the last thing she could have imagined. For fifteen years she had cared for hundreds of terminal cancer patients with only a few months to live. Now, she was looking at the father of her son, the man she had never stopped loving, and she knew that he was one of those statistics. Nick was dying, and he didn't have long.

She steeled herself and stepped forward into the pool of dim light. "Hello, Nick."

Nick's eyes opened. He peered into the semi gloom, tried to sit up and leaned up on his elbow. Standing in front of him he saw a lovely, twenty seven year old woman, shining auburn hair and a fair Irish complexion. She was wearing a blue halter top and shorts. "Hello, Rachel," he said. "I'm sorry for being such an asshole. I love you so much."

"Don't be an idiot, Nick. I love you too, always have done." She went forward and sat by him on the settee. She put her arms around him and kissed his head, his face, his lips, gently and lovingly, like a mother.

Adam stepped forward. "Hello, Nick."

Before he could continue, his mother took his hand. "Adam's our son, Nick. Your son."

"I know, Rachel. I've known it for a while, there were lots of clues. He looks just like you. He's great, a wonderful son. Come here, Adam." He took his son's hand as he sat on his other side. Despite the warmth of the room, Nick's hands were freezing cold.

Suzie stood in amazement, tears flooding to her eyes. She had known nothing of this. She tried to cope with the revelation that Adam was Nick's son, and yet, just a month ago, they had never, ever met. But it seemed that Nick had somehow known of his son's existence. That's why she'd been drawn to Adam, he was his father's son. And Nick and Rachel were still in love, after all this time, more than thirty years. And they'd all found each other, just... *Just in time, I suppose. Don't fool yourself Suzie, Nick doesn't have long, and Rachel knows it.*

"I've got a lot to tell you both. Thirty-four years worth, to be exact."

"And we've got a long story for you too, Nick."

"Well we'd better get started, because I may not have that long. How about some tea, Suzie my darling?"

"English breakfast? Digestive biscuits?" Suzie went out with a cheeky grin on her face.

Adam watched her go, *God she's so beautiful.*

Rachel and Nick watched Adam, then looked at each other. *Life goes on.*

"Promise me you'll never leave me, Rachel."

"I'll never leave you Nick, that is if you don't leave me again." But Rachel knew he was going to leave her again in a short while, and this time for ever. She had to make the most of this, Hanny would understand. Her life had gone full circle. It was time to close out the circle.

"Let me tell you about Hanny, and Catrine, Greg and Birgitta. And Adam." she said.

PART FIVE : 2008

SEVENTY-FIVE

Friday 25th April, 2008
Geneva, Switzerland

Adam stepped out of the conference room and called Mademoiselle Rousseau. "Could we have some fresh coffee please?

It had taken him an hour to relate an expurgated version of his story. It was now eleven-thirty and he looked beat. Reliving all the emotion of his and his parent's lives, especially the last few months, had clearly taken a lot out of him.

The two women were in a state of shock. Jenny was thinking, *This is just like an Agatha Christie novel. Nothing is as it seems.* She had made several pages of notes in her jotting pad, but Adam's story was much too long and complicated to record properly.

She said to Leticia. "Did you understand everything? What do you think of it all?"

"I think I understand everything he has told us. But I suppose we must wait for the rest of the story. This Angolan Clan is like Spain, nothing is ever finished.

Adam sat back down opposite them and the secretary brought more coffee. He poured himself a cup, with three sugars. The women refused, they were coffee'd out.

"Adam, we're dreadfully sorry about Nick, you have all our sympathy. It seems that we've all lost close ones lately. When did you leave? How were things?" Jenny was trying to fit these events into the time frame of the last week.

"Nick, my dad that is, died two days ago. I just got back in time from Charlie's funeral to be with him at the end. He didn't want any treatment, no surgery, no chemo, just the morphine for the pain. I think finding Rachel again after all those years was all the medicine he wanted. The problem was that by the time he was diagnosed it was too late. He'd ignored it for too long and he knew it. It's a bloody vicious disease, pancreatic cancer. Takes no prisoners.

"Apart from a week in March when she went home to see the family, my mom was with him for two months. They were so much in love. If it's possible for anyone to die happy, then I suppose he did. It was wonderful to see them talking, catching up on two whole lifetimes apart. We both spoke to Hanny each week and he was so understanding about it. He insisted that Rachel should stay as long as she needed, for everybody's sake. Then he came over to Miami at the beginning of April to be with them both. He's a wonderful man. I guess I've been the luckiest guy in the world, I've had two super fathers. Don't know what I did to deserve them. "

He stopped, took out a handkerchief, blew his nose and took a deep breath. "They're both still there with Suzie. They get on just great together. I flew to London last night and on to Geneva early this morning."

"I'm so sorry, I can't imagine how painful it was for all of you."

Leticia added her condolences. Then she paused. "But why did you come to Geneva when your father is just passed away?"

"Because he asked me to come. He told us all about his work in Portugal with Charlie and Olivier and about the Revolution of the Carnations. Everything about Angola, Henriques, the guerrilla wars, about Cunhal and his bodyguard, Alberto. I've never heard such a story in my entire life. It was like reading a book on African colonial history. Then he told us about the Angolan Clan and their thirty years of incredible business. And of course, he wanted me to take over from him, so I came straight here for the meeting."

"Except it seems that there is no meeting. What's happened to Laurent and Raffael?"

"I haven't got a clue. I don't know how to get in touch with Raffael, but I emailed Laurent to arrange for the completion and I got a reply saying he wanted to do it in Geneva this week and he'd confirm the details later. I naturally assumed that he'd be here for the meeting."

"That reminds me," Jenny said. "I sent emails to each partner about Charlie's funeral and I got a reply from Nick and Laurent, so who answered my mail to Nick?"

"My mother did. My father asked her to and I agreed. He had already sent a message to Charlie and Laurent about the completion of our deal and about the annual meeting just as if everything was normal. He didn't want anyone to know how sick he was. Then when my mom and I came over to see him, it started to get very complicated. And when we got your message about Charlie's accident, things went from bad to worse. He felt he couldn't tell you about his illness or about me when Charlie had just died.

"He was sick and he was emotional and he didn't know what to do for the best. He was upset over everything. He didn't know how to handle it, so we decided that it was best for me to come and explain everything to you myself."

"But you couldn't have come from Florida to Charlie's funeral in such a short time, it's not possible." Jenny's forebodings were returning. Some things didn't seem to add up.

"I wasn't in Florida then. I left at the end of February to go to New York and London because I had contracts to finalise to sell a thousand diamonds by the end of March. I was flying backwards and forwards for the whole month. And when I called my mother that day from London and she told me that they'd received your email, I couldn't believe it. I couldn't believe that Charlie was dead and Nick was dying. That's the two main partners gone! She told me my father's opinion and we both agreed it was the best solution. So I took the flight that night from London to Malaga for the funeral the next morning and went back to London that afternoon and on to Florida to see my parents again."

"But why didn't you tell us all this at the funeral? You didn't even mention Nick, or Laurent, or the Angolan Clan. We had no idea who you were until you told us your story today."

"Jenny, when I got to Marbella, I honestly didn't have the nerve to tell you. It was your father-in-law's funeral and you and Leticia were very upset. I just didn't think the funeral was the right time to tell you all this. And what do you want me to say? *Sorry Charlie's dead. By the way, Nick will be too in a few days. And how do you do, I'm the son he never had.*"

"So you haven't told Laurent, either?"

"Just the same. My father didn't want any of his friends to know that he was dying, nor that the man they'd been dealing with was his own son. And after he heard about Charlie, there was no way he was going to upset them any further. Soon enough to tell Laurent about Nick and myself when I arrived for this meeting. It's very difficult to do these things from a distance, he couldn't face it and neither could I."

"I understand very well, Adam, we have the same trouble to tell everyone who we are," Leticia said sympathetically.

"Well, now that Mr. Schneider has vouched for me, you know it's all true. I'm sorry for the subterfuge, but it hasn't been a very easy time for me."

"Nor for us either."

"I'm sorry. I meant for all of us, for everybody. My mom, Nick, Hanny, Charlie, and of course, you two as well. I know that, I'm really very sorry."

Adam asked cautiously about Leticia's involvement. Without blushing this time, she proudly told him that Emilio was Charlie's offspring. Adam was delighted at the news. "So the Angolan Clan has you two as partners and there's a new life to celebrate. It's about time."

Just then, there was a knock on the door and Mr. Schneider came in.

"I'm sorry to disturb you, but the bank closes between 12:15 and 14:00. If you haven't finished your meeting I can reserve the room for you again later."

Jenny said, "There's a very good café around the corner. Why don't we go there for some lunch and continue at two o' clock?"

"I'll call home first. Just to see if everything is fine, I'm sure Emilio is missing me." Leticia took her mobile phone from her handbag.

Adam excused himself, he'd wait for them at the door. He too pulled out his mobile phone and walked to the elevator.

Remembering the absence of the accountant, Jenny made a call to the IDD office, but the phone rang out unanswered. She tried Gloria's number with the same result, then folded up her mobile, a thoughtful expression on her face.

After her five minute call, Leticia said, "I think we have to go home tomorrow. My mother says Emilio is upset with me to leave him so long."

"That's fine. I think we're both ready to go home. We'll stick to the flights we've booked for tomorrow and you'll be in time to put Emilio to bed."

"We'll have to wait 'til next trip for the shops in Rue du Marché. What a shame."

As they walked across the lobby a smartly dressed man emerged from one of the elevators. He handed in an identity badge at the reception desk, then went to the main doors.

"I don't believe it. It's Patrice!" Leticia grabbed Jenny's arm and they walked towards him.

At the sound of her voice the man turned towards them. It was the French banker. His face registered confusion, his eyes darting left and right. Then regaining his composure he came towards them with a broad smile. "Good heavens. What are you two doing here?" He embraced both women. "I didn't know you were coming to our bank."

Jenny's mind was working overtime. *Another coincidence? Maybe!* She squeezed Leticia's hand to warn her. "Hello, Patrice. We had no idea it was your bank. We've finished our business and we're checking out some banks in Geneva, just in case we need one."

"There's one on every corner. Just like bodegas in Spain!" Leticia had caught on.

Adam came back into the lobby, pushing his phone into his pocket. "There's a taxi outside for a Mr. Moncrieff."

"Thanks, it's for me. I'm just off to the airport," Patrice answered. Jenny breathed a sigh of relief. *No more explanations necessary*. She introduced Adam as a family friend as they walked out to the street.

Patrice embraced the women again. "I'm sorry I have to rush off. I look forward to seeing you back in Marbella. Let's have lunch together next week." He climbed into the taxi and they watched it drive off.

"Small world, isn't it?" Adam said. The women exchanged glances and didn't reply. Leticia was beginning to share Jenny's mistrust of too many coincidences.

During lunch, they managed to clarify the rest of Adam's story. He told them that Nick had called his lawyer over and had made a will. He left a substantial legacy to Suzie and the balance of his estate, including the apartment, to his son. Perversely, he also left the Cadillac to him, and the Jaguar to Suzie. His lawyer contacted Mr. Schneider at Klein, Fellay and completed the paperwork requested by the banker and Nick signed it. He gave Adam a key, with details of his safety deposit boxes in Miami and Geneva. It seemed he had adopted the same stratagem as Charlie to cover up the trail.

Adam visited the Florida bank and found the second key for Klein, Fellay. He had now been down to the vault and had the third key for the box at Ramseyer, Haldemann & Company.

"It's just like our puzzle, but we didn't have such good explanations from Charlie."

"He set this system up cleverly. You need two signatures for the Angolan Clan account at Klein, Fellay and two keys for the safety deposit box at Ramseyer, Haldemann. Nobody can access the box alone. This is Nick's master key and you must have Charlie's." He pulled out a leather pouch from a buttoned, inside pocket of his jacket and removed a large flat key, identical to the one Leticia had in her handbag but with a green rubber band instead of yellow. "Laurent and Raffael each had a secondary key, so you needed the two masters, or one master and one other. Nick and Charlie would lend each other their key when necessary."

"That's what we worked out, four keys, but only two types." Jenny frowned, "But I still don't understand. What's in that box?"

"That's where the diamonds are. Klein, Fellay is just a dupe, the bank account is there, but not the diamonds. Now we can access that box too."

"I'm getting confused. So you haven't already sold the diamonds? But you put up that guarantee and agreed to sell them by the end of March."

"Jenny, I have sold them. I finalised my contracts when I was in Europe and the US in March. But everything got delayed because of Nick's condition, so I missed the date by a few days. Then when I emailed Laurent to arrange delivery, he replied that he would do it with me in Geneva this week. I've got the buyers calling me every day and I can't deliver. I don't know what's going on."

"And Laurent isn't here. In fact, only we are here and we are the new partners." Leticia sighed with frustration. "Where are Laurent and Raffael?"

"And Vogel. Where is he?" Jenny said. *Where was the accountant, where was Gloria, where were the other partners? What was Patrice doing there?*

There were too many coincidences and too many unanswered questions for Jenny. She didn't like not knowing things and it was worrying her.

SEVENTY-SIX

Friday 25th April, 2008
Malaga, Spain

Chief Inspector Pedro Espinoza drank the rest of his café solo and said to the young woman standing next to him. "Look, Laura. Wouldn't it be easier if your mother came to see me herself? I know she doesn't want to meet me in the house or her flat, but we could see each other somewhere else. This is not a bad place to meet." He waved his hand around the tiny bodega in central Malaga. They had just had a lunch of tapas, with a glass of Ribuero del Duero, spoiled only by the tongue-lashing he'd received from his daughter, while she told him why her mother wouldn't talk to him.

"Dad, you're not listening to me and that's why Mamá won't talk to you. Because you don't listen to her, either. You're so bloody tied up in your murders and robberies that you don't have the time or the patience to listen to anyone except your pals in the force."

Espinoza winced at the severity of his daughter's scolding. The worst part of it was that she was right. Since he had been promoted to Chief Inspector his job had taken over his life. He had fallen out of love with his wife and fallen in love with catching villains. Soledad had left him six months ago after he had worked four straight days on a murder case and never bothered to come home. Sleeping in the office was not conducive to a happy marriage.

"It's a very simple problem. The allowance you're paying Mamá isn't enough. It hardly covers her rent on the flat and she's got no money to enjoy her life at all. She doesn't say much to me but I know she's broke and she can't go looking for work at her age. It's not fair and I feel really sorry for her. I even give her a few euros from my salary and I can't afford to continue doing that. You have to sit together and work out a new deal, or she'll have to go to the court and that'll cause you all kinds of problems that neither of you need."

His arrangement with his estranged wife had been made amicably, shortly after she moved in with their daughter. Neither of them wanted, or could afford a divorce, for the moment. With the help of José Luis, they had agreed to a cooling off period, a trial separation. They had agreed on a percentage of his salary, enough for her to find a flat to rent and live on her own for a while, until they decided if they had any kind of a future together.

In practise it hadn't worked out like that. He had agreed to pay the mortgage on the house until they could sell it. But the property market was so lousy that he hadn't had a single offer, except for one joker who'd offered ten percent less than the balance of the debt. The monthly payments to the bank and to Soledad were crippling him and he couldn't see a way out.

It's insane, he thought to himself. *We used to live comfortably together in a beautiful house and now we live seperately in a house and a flat and we can't even get the formula right. She's paying too much and I'm not earning enough.*

"Right," he said. "I have to go to a conference in Holland this evening and I'll be back on Sunday night. Can you ask your mother if she'll please have lunch with me on Monday? I'm sure we can work things out over a glass of wine. I promise to be patient and listen and do whatever's necessary. I don't want her to have financial difficulties on my account."

He knew that the best way to help both Soledad and himself to avoid difficulties was for them to get back together again. Two people together could live more comfortably on one salary than two people apart. But it wasn't the right time to suggest that. It wasn't the right time to suggest anything. Laura was right, the time was right for only one thing. Just to listen.

He kissed his daughter and they parted. He was returning to the house to pack a bag for his trip, she was going to the real estate broker's office where she worked on a small salary and large commissions, which were becoming scarcer and scarcer as the economy faltered. It seemed that everyone was going to have to adjust to new economic conditions, including him.

SEVENTY-SEVEN

Friday, 25th April, 2008
Geneva, Switzerland

After blowing his nose in a triumphant manner, Mr. Schneider produced a large file with the name, *ANGOLAN CLAN,* printed on the front. His three clients waited expectantly for his revelations. The other partners had still not arrived.

He removed some sheets, closed it and pushed it aside. "I have here the latest statement of the account. In accordance with Mr. Bishop's instructions, countersigned by Mr. Martinez," here he looked apologetically at Adam, "we have liquidated all investments and the entire balance has been transferred to the current account, in US Dollars. It seems there was to be a general distribution this year, and Mr. Bishop wanted it to be as simple as possible."

"That's right, Mr. Schneider. In fact, the partnership is to be dissolved this month." Jenny paused. "The only problem is that we are missing two partners."

"I appreciate your dilemma. I'm disappointed not to see M. Bonneville and Sr. Pires da Silva. I was also expecting Herr Vogel to pass by. He collected a copy of all the statements to prepare the accounts for the meeting."

Jenny wondered again where Vogel was, with his up to date accounts. This was not looking good. *Leticia could be right,* she thought.

Schneider continued, "All I can do is to provide you with the relevant information and since you can operate the account by your two signatures, I must accept whatever instructions you give me." He pushed the statements towards them. "Here you have the current status of the account. Once again, it carries only the rubrique "*Angolan Clan*" and the account number. Another interesting story, I'm sure.

"The statements show the last liquidations, running from January 1st to 31st March. The final balance, in dollars, is at the bottom of the third page."

Jenny said. "Adam, come and sit over here, we'll discover this together."

The first two pages listed the transactions executed since January and there were several more on the third page. The names of many well known companies appeared. The sales proceeds were recorded in various currencies then converted into dollars and interest had been added at 31st March. The balance printed on the bottom of the third page was twelve million three hundred and forty thousand dollars.

Leticia and Jenny said nothing, just looked at the statements, then at each other.

"Twelve million dollars! My God." Adam's share of this money, together with his inheritance of the five million dollars Mr. Schneider had shown him in Nick's account that morning, meant he had become richer by about nine million dollars in the space of four hours. His head spun with the news, he was a very, very rich man. *And this is without the proceeds of the last diamond sale,* he thought to himself.

Jenny was doing similar sums. Thirty per cent of that amount was over two million Euros. Their cash legacy from Charlie was now twenty million Euros. Her share was ten million; over eight million pounds. She'd learned the hard way that too little money was a bad thing, but too much was even worse. *It can't be right to come into such a fortune without earning it,* she thought. *Something is sure to go wrong. There's just too much money involved.* Once again she remembered Espinoza's question. The motive was getting stronger.

Leticia smiled contentedly. This meant that she and Emilio could travel in business class for the rest of their lives.

Jenny tried to think pragmatically. There were still two partners missing. "I think," she said, "that we need to discuss things together again in private."

"Of course. I'll be in my office when you need me. Is there anything you would like?"

"A cup of tea would be just the thing please." Adam suddenly thought of Suzie. The tea wouldn't taste the same without her making it for him.

Schneider left them and within a couple of minutes his assistant arrived with the tea. She fumbled the teapot and spilt some on the table. Wiping it down with a Kleenex, she moved the statements away from the damp patch. She exited the office and Jenny poured tea for everyone.

"What should we do now?" Leticia's head was aching from all of the English conversation she'd faced that day.

"Well, this meeting was supposed to be to liquidate the Angolan Clan, but we can't really do anything until we get hold of Laurent and Raffael. And Vogel, the IDD accountant, hasn't come, so where are the accounts? I've called the office and he's not there."

She pulled out her mobile phone again. "Leticia was already suspicious of him yesterday. I'll see if he's come back." The office number rang out without answer. She tried Gloria's home number once more, but she didn't reply. "That's not a good sign. Gloria's still not there, Vogel's not there and there's nobody here. I don't like this at all. There's fortunes of money being thrown at us from every direction and lots of peculiar things happening that we don't understand." She racked her brains. "The problem is, I don't know what we can do now."

"I don't think there's anything we can do." Adam put three spoons of sugar in his tea. "We need Laurent to complete my diamond sales. Then when we get the funds in, we liquidate everything. We need everyone together to do that."

Jenny thought of something else. "I'm sorry to mention this, but when is Nick's funeral? We have to go back to Marbella tomorrow and I suppose you have to get back to Florida. I'm wondering how we're going to get everything sorted out before we leave."

"It's on Tuesday morning. I have to be in Miami by Monday latest, to help with the final details. I can't miss my father's funeral at any cost."

Leticia sighed, "But how can we try to make some progress before we all leave?"

Jenny had worked out the only option. "We're going back to Ramseyer, Haldemann's. Now we've got both keys we'll see what's really in that box. There may be some explanation there from Charlie." She picked up the folder with the statements. "Let's go."

Schneider came from his office and Jenny explained the situation to him. They would contact him when things were clear. Since they had to leave the next day, he may have to act upon instructions from Spain or some other place.

"Then you can use our Global Internet Banking system," he announced importantly. Mr. Bishop and Mr. Martinez used it all the time. It's absolutely secure and you can access it from anywhere at all. I'll explain to you how to operate it, it will take just a few minutes."

In his office, Schneider went through the procedure with them. He explained the Internet indemnity documents and other bank precautions. They signed the authorisation documnts then used the keyboard on his desk to introduce their new PIN numbers into the system.

"I'll get the new parameters set up this afternoon and courrier the countersigned documents and everything else over to you at the hotel before you leave. Now, is there anything more I can do for you?"

At this, Jenny had another thought. "Could you let me have a copy of the Angolan Clan bank statements for last year?"

The banker returned with the statements in a plastic folder and Jenny placed the others with them.

He accompanied them to the main doors. "I'm sorry that you've had such a fruitless visit, on top of the bad time you've been through. I look forward to hearing from you when you have located your other partners. I'm sure there is a perfectly simple explanation for their absence."

After shaking hands and thanking him, they went out to find a cab to take them to *Pâquis*. The sound of a loudly blown nose drifted through the closing door behind them.

In her office on the sixth floor, Mademoiselle Rousseau took out her mobile phone. "*Bonjour, mon amour.* I have lots of news for you."

SEVENTY-EIGHT

Friday, 25th April, 2008
Geneva, Switzerland

When they got out of the taxi, Adam took in the surrounding red light area with surprise. "I guess Charlie must have had a good reason for choosing this place, I just hope it wasn't what it looks like."

Leticia punched him on the arm. "Don't be disgusting. Charlie didn't do things like that. He didn't need to."

Gilles Simenon welcomed them at the door of Ramseyer, Haldemann and Company. "Mr. Jolidon asked me to advise him when you returned, I'll just call him."

The directeur minced over to them and shook hands. "Good afternoon, ladies, I assume that you have found your missing key, since you are back again." He looked Adam up and down, as if expecting an introduction. The South African said nothing.

Jenny was cautious. "We are ready to open the safety deposit now, Mr. Jolidon."

"There is just one formality before that, if you don't mind. We must try to maintain our register of safety box owners up to date. It's difficult, because keys get handed down without our knowledge. Since there have been some changes in your case, I have the forms here."

"We thought there is no need to record our names. Isn't this an anonymous safety box?"

"It is anonymous to everyone except our company, Mme. da Costa. But we need to advise the banking authorities that we have been diligent in our customer management. There are lots of regulations now. It's awfully tedious." He placed the forms on the reception desk and handed Leticia a pen. Each of them filled out their name and address and signed the forms.

Jolidon said, "Mr. Peterson, is it? I'm pleased to make your acquaintance." He gave Adam an approving smile. "Now if you'll just sign the register, we'll go down to the vault."

They all signed as requested then went through the security lift and steel doors into the enormous circular room. Adam looked around, impressed with the security in the building.

"If you'll kindly produce your keys, we'll open up box no. 72."

Jolidon inserted the key that Gilles handed him from the cupboard, and Leticia and Adam entered theirs in the other two locks. They turned the three keys.

"Now Mr. Simenon and I will turn away while you enter the access number. I just want to ensure that you have no further difficulties."

Jenny wasn't keen on doing this while Jolidon was in the room, but positioning herself between Leticia and the two men, she entered into the keypad on the door, one, five, eleven, four five. Ellen had been a Scorpio, born on the fifteenth of November. Leticia looked at her with relief. *Another clever clue from Charlie.*

"*Et voila!*" Jolidon turned and gestured like a magician as the door released. He made no attempt to leave.

Jenny said, "Thank you, Gentlemen, we'd like to be alone now." The directeur looked rather put out, then he took Gilles by the arm and they exited the room.

When he got back to his office, Jolidon made a call on his mobile phone. All he said was, "The women are back. They've found the other key."

"I don't know what that was all about. We've never had to give any information to the banks where we have our other safety deposits." Jenny was becoming suspicious about the directeur. She reflected that she was becoming suspicious of almost everyone she met recently.

Adam peered around the massive vault at ceiling level. The circular band of safe doors seemed to be unbroken and there was nothing on the ceiling except spot lights arranged in a pattern, spelling out R. H. C.

"What are you looking for?"

"CCTV cameras, I wouldn't like to think that anyone else is privy to our business."

Leticia looked around. "I can't see anything. In any case, I think it's not possible to have such cameras in a private vault."

"When we ship the diamonds to my customers we won't need this place any more, so we'll just let it go. Speaking of diamonds, shall we open the box?" Adam extracted the box from the safe and placed it on the table. It was larger than the previous boxes, and heavier. "After you." He invited Leticia to open it.

"Even if I know what's inside, I'm still very nervous." She opened the lid.

Inside the box there was a battered old leather briefcase, like a lawyer's document case.

"Charlie's case!" Jenny's eyes pricked with tears. "Thirty years, and still going strong."

She put the briefcase to one side. Underneath it in the box there were six cardboard files, labelled with dates from the past. The first file was labelled *Angolan Clan Account. 1975-1980.* It was full of financial documents from the earliest days of the partnership. In the front were fastened the bank statements and transaction slips. Behind them were typewritten listings of the transactions, each entry carefully ticked off with a red pencil, closed off on the twenty-fifth of April 1980. The statements changed appearance over the years and the listings changed to Excel print-outs in the nineties. The last statement in the file was dated 30th September, 2007. *Charlie must have put it in when he came in last October*, she realised.

Putting down the last file, Jenny picked up the briefcase, undid the strap fastenings and unlocked the clasps with the small key from the safety deposit box at Klein, Fellay. When she pressed the lock, it opened. "Amazing," she said to the others, "Charlie didn't lock it with the code. Good thing, since I don't know it." For once he'd made things simple for them.

She took out the contents of the case and placed them on the table. There were ten chamois leather pouches, each tied with a string like an old fashioned lady's purse. They were the original pouches that Henriques had filled with the rough stones.

Adam unfastened them and emptied the contents into ten piles on the leather surface. The two women gasped at the lustrous brilliance before them. One pile was comprised of stones of about two carats, large and brilliant cut, the facets showing the reflection of every available ray of light. The other piles were of smaller stones, but just as radiant. It was as if a bright fire had suddenly been lit on the table.

Jenny took some of the diamonds and poured them from hand to hand, just as Laurent had done, three decades before. The gems flooded with light, like a stream of brilliantly lit clear water trickling through her hands. *So this is what Olivier, Manuela and Henriques died for. Beautiful, but deadly. Is anything worth that sacrifice?*

"*Dios mío. Qué magnífico*! My God. How magnificent!" Leticia couldn't believe her eyes, she had never before seen anything so exquisite. She took one of the large stones and held it on her finger, like a ring. "Maybe Adam will let us have one each, as a reminder of the Angolan Clan." She smiled mischievously at the South African.

Adam said nothing. He was looking at the piles of stones with a trance-like expression.

There was still something in the briefcase, a soft felt bag. Jenny carefully removed it and took from it the last three items.

The first was a small silver frame. Inside the frame was a one thousand dollar note. It was obviously extremely old, with a picture of a moustached man from the forties, wearing a wing collar. *One of Henriques's notes, part of the half million dollars,* she realised.

"Look at this." She showed it to the others. "I wonder how much it's worth today."

"Probably as much as the original half million," Adam said seriously.

There was another frame, a simple wooden one, containing a faded article cut from a newspaper, with a photograph. In the centre of the photograph was a very young-looking Charlie Bishop, long sideburns and moustache, shaking hands with a tall, stern-faced, prematurely balding man wearing an army uniform. Dozens of medals adorned his chest. On the other side of the officer was a smartly dressed, dark-haired, latin-looking fellow. He was laughing at the camera as if he'd just heard a good joke. At the other side of Charlie, three more army officers stood, their smiles not quite hiding the smug expression on their faces.

The caption underneath the photo read:

Primeiro-Ministro Gonçalves visita APA.
Outra história de sucesso de Governo.

Someone had written the date of the article in the corner of the paper, *27th May, 1975.* "What does it say, Leticia?" Jenny handed her the frame.

Leticia looked at the article. Tears came to her eyes at the sight of the handsome young Englishman in the photo. *Oh, Charlie, why did you have to leave me?*

She pulled herself together. "It says, 'Prime Minister Goncalves visits APA. Another Government success story.' I remember this from Charlie's history, it's the Nationalisation Committee, on the TV."

"I don't think Nick told me about that. I'll ask you for the full story when we've got more time." Adam looked at the article and handed the frame back to Jenny

"So that's Olivier." She looked thoughtfully at the photo. "What a nice-looking man." Memories of the dreadful end to the Angolan adventure flooded into her mind.

"Finally we can see what one of Charlie's partners looks like. It's funny, the only one we have seen and he died thirty years ago, but we haven't seen any who are still alive." Leticia shivered at the thought.

She picked up the last item from the briefcase. It was a small ring box. She undid the old fashioned clasp and opened it. The solitaire diamond in the ring glistened in the light from the ceiling spots. As she showed it to the others, it seemed to wink at them.

"It must be Ellen's ring, the one that Nick gave her." *I wonder what became of Maggie Attwell, and her son, Alan,* Jenny mused.

"I think you should have this, Leticia, from my father. It'll be thirty-five years old soon, same as you. Happy birthday." Adam slipped it onto her engagement finger.

"That's the wrong hand. Men, honestly!" Jenny transferred it to the other hand.

"It's beautiful. Are you sure? It was from Charlie, don't you want to wear it, Jenny?"

"It fits your finger perfectly. Too perfectly to change." Jenny held up Leticia's hand, admiring the lovely diamond. "Charlie would want you to have it and so do I."

They turned back to the safety deposit box. Lying at the bottom was the last item, another brown envelope, A4 size. Leticia picked it up and, from experience, she shook it upside down and three sheets of paper fell out.

The first sheet was a signature form from Banque de Commerce de Genève. It referred to an account in the name of *International Diamond Dealers SA.* The names of Jenny and Leticia appeared with an empty signature box against each. It was undated and the sheet was signed by Charlie, as a director of the company.

The second sheet was a Resolution from a meeting of the Board of IDD, appointing Jenny and Leticia as directors of the company. It was also undated and signed by Charlie, as chairman.

The third sheet was in Charlie's handwriting, dated February 23rd , 2008. Jenny read it out loud.

> *Dearest Leticia and Jenny,*
> *You've reached the end of the trail. Congratulations.*
> *I'm sad to say this is my last message. The bank is just 100 metres along from the IDD office, on the corner of the Rue du Mont Blanc. The manager's name is Brigitte Aeschiman. I hope that everything has worked out as planned. I love you both and wish you and Emilio much happiness.*
> *Love from Charlie.*

"That's the bank I sent the million dollars to." Adam stopped speaking and looked at the two women. They were both silently rereading the note, tears running down their cheeks.

"What is it?" he asked.

"It's Charlie's last message," Leticia said sadly. "He's been leading us from place to place, as if he was still there. But now it's over. He's not there any more." She put her arm around Jenny's shoulder and they looked at the small pile of items on the table.

"Goodbye, Charlie. Thanks for everything." Jenny had finally come to terms with his story and the truth behind his fortune. Leticia had been right. Charlie was a hero, not a villain. She picked up the photograph and banknote and placed them in the felt bag. They both felt as if an invisible guiding cord had snapped and now they had to find their own way forward.

Adam tried to lighten the atmosphere. "I'll have to be extra nice to you in future. You're in control of my money now."

Jenny looked at her watch, it was three forty-five. "You're right, Adam. Put the diamonds back and let's go straight to the bank, they should still be open. We need to get our signatures recorded before we leave tomorrow. Now that Charlie and Nick are gone there is nobody who can sign for IDD. We've got to be ready to deliver the diamonds and operate the bank account. If we don't do it now, it might mess up your transactions."

He carefully poured the stones back into the pouches and replaced them in the briefcase, put everything in the box and closed the safe door. Leticia pressed the bell to call for Gilles.

Mr. Jolidon came back in. "Gilles has gone out for a while, can I help you?" He seemed rather uneasy, pushing his hair back several times.

Jenny was succinct. "We'd like to lock up now, we've finished our business, thank you." Adam turned his key in the lock, Leticia did the same.

"Oh. You're leaving already?" Jolidon looked flustered. He turned his key in the lock and replaced it in the cupboard. He followed them through the steel doors and they got into the lift. As they walked towards the outside doors, he said, "If I may make a suggestion."

They turned, not wishing to waste any further time. "Yes?"

"I was thinking. To avoid having any future difficulties in accessing the vault, perhaps I could have a copy of one or both of the keys made for you. It could be done quite quickly."

Jenny replied. "I don't think that's a very good idea. As you told us yourself, each key is unique and I think it's better to keep it that way, don't you, Monsieur? Now we're in rather a hurry, so anything further can wait until we return."

At this, he opened the main doors for them. They walked out and crossed the street towards the Rue du Mont Blanc, heading for the bank.

"I don't trust that man," said Jenny. "How can he imagine that we'd let him copy our keys? The sooner we move everything from there, the better."

"I absolutely agree," said Adam. "Shifty-looking bloke with a bad breath. I wouldn't trust him an inch."

As they turned the corner, a black BMW drew up in front of the Ramseyer, Haldemann building. Two men jumped out and ran to the door, which was being held open by Jolidon.

"You've just missed them," he said petulantly, flicking a hand in their direction.

"*Merde*. Fucking traffic!" The two men turned and ran to the corner just in time to see them walking away. They stopped, came back and went inside with the directeur.

Adam had turned to look behind him as they turned the corner. He saw the two men run towards them then stop when they walked onto the main street. He said nothing to the women.

Brigitte Aeschiman was a striking-looking brunette in her early forties, with a full figure, still carrying a little extra weight after the birth of her first child. Like almost everyone they had met in Geneva, she spoke perfect English, this time with a charming French accent, almost like a lisp. She showed them a photograph of her new daughter, Camille. She had only been back at the bank for a month, after five months of maternity leave. It had been a difficult pregnancy.

She was devastated to learn of Charlie's accident and Nick's demise. They had apparently had a client-banker relationship for over ten years, although she told them that since Charlie's heart attack he had seldom been to Geneva.

The women handed over the documents signed by Charlie, together with their passports, and their signatures were recorded so that they could now operate the accounts. They then authorised Adam to be added as a signatory, to replace Nick.

Jenny asked about the other signatory powers on the accounts. They learned that Mr. Vogel could sign for any amount up to fifty thousand Swiss Francs, enough to cover normal monthly expenses, salaries, etc. Any larger amount had to be countersigned by Charlie or Nick. They, mainly Charlie, had done this by fax, from their homes.

Mme. Aeschiman printed out a statement of the transactions for the last year for them. There were two accounts. The balance on the first, the operating account, was a little over two hundred thousand dollars, Nick and Laurent's operating cash. There were a number of entries on the account. Sales receipts, payments for salaries and expenses, and transfers to the Angolan Clan account. In a separate, *IDD Escrow Account,* there was only one entry, Adam's million dollars. It had accrued some interest over the last few months. Jenny placed the statements into Schneider's folder.

She explained to Mme. Aeschiman that there would be some substantial transactions with Adam's customers within the next couple of weeks. Funds would arrive and transfers would be required. The banker confirmed that they could send their instructions by fax, to execute these transactions without coming to Geneva.

Mme. Aeschiman escorted them to the exit. "I'll send confirmation of any receipts by email and wait for your instructions. I hope everything goes well for you in the future." They shook hands and left her. Their business had taken less than an hour.

"You realise that you might have to come back with me to ship the diamonds?" Adam said, worriedly. "That's if we can't find the other partners, I mean."

"We'll deal with that in due course, Adam. For now I just wanted to make sure that we can operate the accounts so you can execute your transactions. Now you can relax and go back for Nick's funeral without worrying." Pragmatic as always, Jenny continued,

"We just have time to take you to the IDD office before it gets too dark. It's almost right next door."

They entered no. 362 Rue de la Gare and went up to the third floor. The door to the IDD offices was locked and no one answered when they knocked. Jenny took out the Yale key, opened the door and found the light switch. Gloria's office looked exactly the same, vacant and tidy, but Vogel's office looked different, it had been tidied, virtually emptied. The piles of travel books and ski magazines were gone, the filing cabinet was closed. The accounting certificate and ski diplomas were missing, the wall still showing the light patches where they had hung. The desk was bare and there was not a document or a file to be seen.

""Curiouser and curiouser," said Alice."

"Sorry, Jenny. What did you say?"

"Oh, I was just being an English Literature teacher for a moment. It's a line from Alice in Wonderland. What I mean is, *what's going on?*"

"I think it's what I said. It looks like Herr Vogel has gone for a long holiday."

They looked through the files in the cabinet. There were corporate and other documents concerning the British Virgin Islands, and tax and administrative papers for Switzerland, as well as accounts and financial reports for the company. The last was for 25th April, 2007. There were no accounts for 2008.

They went back into Gloria's office and took down several files from the shelves. They were all two pronged dossiers in hard covers, with the documents fastened over the prongs and clipped down. Leticia opened up the first of them. It was labelled *IDD Diamond Transactions Account. October, 1975 – April, 1976.* Inside were all of the transaction documents for that period concerning the sale of diamonds, the costs of shipping, insurance, cutting, polishing, commissions, travel and other expenses. All the transactions were listed on typed sheets with details of each item and the account balance. The statements for the IDD account at the Banque de Commerce de Genève were at the front, showing all receipts and expenses and the regular transfers into the Angolan Clan account at Klein, Fellay. Like the statements at Ramseyer, Haldemann, the entries were ticked carefully off with coloured pencils. The other files were for May to April for each succeeding year. There were thirty-one of them in all.

Jenny took up the last one, *May, 2007* –, it was quite thin. Gloria hadn't closed this one off and it was unlikely to go beyond 2008. She opened it up and looked at the last quarterly bank statement from the Banque de Commerce de Genève, it was dated 31st March, 2008. She compared it with the Excel listing in the file, it showed the same balance. She pulled out the statement given to her by Mme. Aeschiman and compared the balance at the same date, it was identical. *If something is going on, I can't spot it for the moment.* She put the file into the large plastic folder with the bank statements.

On a lower shelf, there were ten old fashioned ledgers. They were divided into sections for the same periods as the files. They contained very complete entries, in Nick's handwriting, concerning the numbers of rough stones, the finished gems, weights before and after cutting, losses in processing and a variety of other details. In a separate section, they found records of the various processing companies and customers that IDD had worked with over the past thirty-odd years. Adam looked through the pages and found his name on the list.

Nick had also added information on price fluctuations and market trends, year by year, illustrated by carefully drawn graphs. Charlie's prognosis concerning the price of diamonds had been well founded. The market continued to be strong and values increased almost every year up to 2000, when highest quality finished stones gradually settled down to between fifteen and twenty thousand dollars per carat - four times their 1975 value.

Looking over this data, carefully compiled by his father over the last three decades, Adam was lost in admiration for him. Together with Charlie, he had worked out a way to avoid the big corporations and create a hugely profitable business, a business that had produced millions of dollars for its partners. Charlie Bishop was certainly a very clever man but Adam realised that Nick Martinez had been equally clever in his own way.

Jenny said, "This is very impressive work. Your father was a true professional. I'm sorry that we won't ever meet him." Adam looked gratefully at her, struggling with his emotions.

Leticia looked up from the ledger in her hand. "This makes me think of something. We have to do this last transaction with you, but we don't know any details yet."

"Nick and I executed a contract in January. I have to complete the purchase of the remaining diamonds at a price of exactly ten million dollars, that's twelve hundred carats at eight thousand three hundred and thirty three dollars a carat. They're very precise guys."

Once again, the amount involved made the women's heads swim. That was about seven million Euros, on top of all the money they'd already discovered. *This is just like winning a lottery jackpot,* thought Jenny. *And we know how they often turn out.*

"I have four buyers who are ready to complete. All we have to do is to prepare the diamonds into four batches, I know what the customers want, so I can do that. Then we deliver them to Securitas, in Geneva. They confirm that they have the merchandise, the customers transfer the funds to my bank and I transfer the ten million to the Banque de Commerce."

"Then we pay you back the million dollars?"

"Right, then we transfer everything from the IDD account to the Angolan Clan account and make the final distribution of all the Angolan Clan funds to the partners. It's really quite simple, except for a couple of things."

"We don't know where are Laurent and Raffael."

"Number one, right."

"And someone has to be with you to get the diamonds from the vault and deliver them to Securitas."

"Right again, number two."

Jenny had a sudden thought. "I wonder." She picked up the phone on Gloria's desk, pressed the menu button and then the phone's internal directory, looking under G, for Gloria, then S, for Smouha. There was what looked like a mobile number for Smouha, G. She dialled it, but the phone was switched off. She redialled the secretary's home number from her own mobile, but once again it rang out without a reply.

"Still no sign of Gloria. She and Vogel have disappeared off the face of the earth. I simply don't understand it. And it's Saturday tomorrow, and we have to leave anyway, so we can't get anything done before next week. It looks like you're going to have to come back after the funeral, Adam. Unless we can get hold of Laurent and handle the dispatch of the diamonds with him."

It seemed to Jenny that things were getting seriously out of control. She didn't like the feeling at all. She looked at her watch and gave a frustrated sigh. "It's five thirty and Leticia and I need to make some telephone calls and I would like a hot bath. We'd better get back to the hotel. Where are you staying?"

"I haven't actually got a reservation. What with all the rushing about I guess I just didn't get round to it."

"I'll make a call." Leticia pulled out her mobile and dialled a number. After a short conversation in Portuguese, she said, "*Isso está perfeito. Muita obrigada Senhora.* That's perfect, thank you. " She winked at Adam. "Right, you are staying with us, lucky you!"

Jenny could hardly contain herself. "What's wrong with the French?"

"*Dios.* I don't believe this city, half the staff in the banks and hotels is Portuguese. It's easier to talk English or Portuguese than French. I think I'll give up learning the language."

Adam laughed. "Wherever the hotel is, let's get a cab at the station, I'm too weary to walk anywhere."

At Klein, Fellay, Mademoiselle Rousseau brought the material for the Global Internet Banking system into Eric Schneider's office. He examined and countersigned the new signatory forms and indemnity documents and she went out to photocopy them. While she was absent, he checked the three small electronic security number generators against the account number and put them in three envelopes addressed to Adam, Jenny and Leticia. Mlle. Rousseau brought back the documents, carefully folded them and placed them in the envelopes and sealed them.

"Call the courier service and get them delivered to the Hotel de la Grange this evening, Mademoiselle. And then you can leave for the weekend, thank you."

His assistant looked at her watch. "It's almost six o'clock, Mr. Schneider. I'm not sure that we can get a delivery in time. But I'm going into Eaux-Vives this evening. I can drop them off if you like. That way we're sure that they'll get them before they leave."

Schneider was relieved. His new clients would see that the bank's service was second to none. He blew his nose enthusiastically and consigned the envelopes to Mlle. Rousseau.

SEVENTY-NINE

Friday, 25th April, 2008
Geneva, Switzerland

Leticia claimed their keys from the hotel receptionist. Their rooms had old fashioned locks, not the modern swipe card locks that are common in the big hotels. They went upstairs to make their calls and left Adam to sign in. It seemed that he had been lucky to get the last room. It was on the second floor, below their accommodation.

They didn't notice the man sitting in reception with his back to them, reading the Tribune de Genève. But once again he noticed them and he heard everything.

Emilio was excited to hear that his mother would be home the next evening. Encarni told her that they were already planning the weekend, the weather was fine and there were lots of beach activities involved. Leticia then called Juan to ask him to pick them up at Malaga airport. Juan didn't ask a single question, he was a very quiet man.

Jenny called Linda, at the kennels. She told her that Cooper was eating well, he was in great spirits and he wasn't pining for Jenny. This news quite upset her.

When Adam got to his room he called his mother. Rachel was relieved to hear from him. She was fine, Hanny was fine, the family was fine and Suzie was wonderful. Despite her own feelings after losing Nick, she had been a great comfort to them. The funeral arrangements were all settled and he had to be home by Monday evening. He then called his customers and arranged to see them on his way back to Florida.

Jenny called Leticia's room. "Why don't we take Adam out for dinner? It's our last night in Geneva. That *Eaux-Vives* place sounds good. Shall we splash out with some of our newly acquired wealth?"

"Let me book, Jenny. I am the only one who speaks Portuguese!"

Esther Rousseau left Klein, Felly, with the three envelopes in her handbag and caught the number one bus from Plainpalais to Place des Eaux-Vives. She walked along to the Hotel Mercury, went straight up to the third floor and knocked at the door of room 310. "*Chéri!*"she cried, as a man opened the door and took her in his arms.

It was eight o' clock when the two women knocked on Adam's door on their way downstairs.

"I'll be down in five minutes," he called.

As they were waiting in the lobby, Leticia's phone rang. It was a Spanish mobile number which she didn't recognise. She pressed the green button. "*Si, diga me.*"

It was a very bad line, but above the crackling she managed to make out a man's voice speaking in Spanish, "Hello, Leticia, this is Francisco calling. How are you?"

Hiding her surprise, she answered. "Francisco, I'm fine. How are you? Where are you?" When Jenny heard this, she raised her finger to her lips. *Don't say too much.*

"I'm in London. Sorry I didn't see you, but I had an urgent call from a client. I just wanted to be sure that everything is OK with you and Jenny. Are you in Geneva?"

"Yes we are and everything is going fine, thanks. We've managed to get our business done." Leticia took Jenny's cue.

"I'm glad to hear it. When will you be coming back to Marbella?"

"We'll be home tomorrow evening. We're just going out for dinner at a posh restaurant in the park next door, you probably know it. Eaux-Vives, it's called."

After a few more words she thanked the lawyer and rang off. "That was thoughtful of him. He says the restaurant is very good and he sends you his fond regards. Lucky you."

Jenny flushed. *That's not so funny,* she thought. Aloud, she said, "Where's Adam?"

She went to the courtesy phone on the reception desk and rang his room. There was no answer. She was just about to go back up again when he came running down the stairs.

"Sorry. Had to make one more phone call. Right, let's go. On the town with two gorgeous women, the champagne's on me."

They walked out of the hotel past a man in a raincoat standing in the shadows, smoking a cigarette. It was too dark to make out his features under the brim of his hat. After they went by, he threw his cigarette down, spoke on a mobile phone then walked up the stairs into the hotel, passing another man who was coming out behind the others. He waited a few minutes in the reception area and was then joined by Esther Rousseau. Together, they walked up the stairs to the third floor of the hotel.

The restaurant building was magnificent, a cross between a chateau and a chalet in the middle of a delightful park. The *Maître d'Hotel,* slim and erect in his morning coat and patent leather shoes, reminded Jenny of Fred Astaire. He whisked them across the room to a table looking right over the lake. They had a memorable evening.

The man sitting in the bar kept his eye on them while he wrote up his notes for the day's activity. He listed every place they had been and the name of the man who had joined them, which he'd overheard in the hotel reception. His boss would be pleased with his diligence.

"Goodnight, ladies, see you early for breakfast. Moving day tomorrow." The women left Adam at his bedroom door and walked up to the next floor. They kissed good night and Jenny went along to her room. It was ten thirty and she was beat. *What a day! I'll be glad to get home.*

As she entered her room, Jenny noticed a slight aroma. It could have been a man's after shave but it was too faint to identify. She threw her handbag on the bed, undressed and went to the bathroom to clean her teeth. There was no safe in the room, but the top drawer of the chest of drawers had a lock. She took the key from under the lamp on her bedside cabinet where she'd hidden it and opened the drawer to put back the watch and rings she was wearing.

Jenny was a very, almost obsessively tidy person. Every shoe in her wardrobe had its own place. Her sweaters were ranged by colour, as were her blouses, her dresses, even her underwear. The few items of jewellery that she had with her were no exception. The Ebel steel and gold watch that Ron had bought for her went on the left of her wedding and engagement rings and Ellen's eternity ring. They were on the left of her mother's pearl necklace, which was on the left of her opal earrings and pendant. At the right side was her bead necklace from Tunisia and the small leather box that was full of odds and ends. Ron's cufflinks and wedding band, the locket with his photo in it. Old items that were never used but that she kept close.

The leather box was placed with the front stud facing her and the hinge behind. *That's not right!* It was facing the wrong way. At one glance, she knew that someone had opened the drawer and moved her precious belongings. Everything had been replaced in the right position, but slightly out of line. She spilled out the contents of the leather box, there was nothing missing. She looked through the other drawers and the wardrobe, nothing seemed disturbed.

She picked up her handbag from the bed where she'd thrown it and took out her purse. The keys she was guarding were in the zipped part of the purse where she'd placed them. Putting on a dressing gown from the bathroom, she walked along to Leticia's room.

Leticia saw from her face that something was wrong. "What is it? What's happened?"

"Where do you keep the safety deposit keys?"

"In my purse, inside my handbag."

"The one you had with you tonight?"

"Of course! I don't leave them somewhere else, it's too risky." She went to get her purse. "Here." There were two keys inside, the Klein, Fellay key and the Ramseyer, Haldemann key.

Jenny explained what she'd discovered. "Have you noticed anything odd in here?"

Leticia opened the locked drawer, examined the few items, shook her head and closed it again. She looked around the room, then went to the wardrobe and took out a second handbag, a spare. "Look, the inside pocket is open. I always button it, it's *defectuoso*. You know?"

"Faulty, you mean. Doesn't close properly?"

"The bag keeps falling open. You have to button the pocket. It needs tiny fingers to button it up, like mine. Things fall out if you don't do it. I always close it carefully."

"Someone is after the keys, it's the only explanation. They know we're in this hotel and somehow they've managed to get into our rooms. We'll have to tell Adam."

As they walked down the stairs to his room, Jenny's mind was whirling. It seemed that everyone was after their money or the diamonds. Who could they really trust? *There must be something we can do to protect ourselves,* she thought. *But what?*

Adam was in his pyjamas and had thrown a dressing gown on. "What on earth is the matter?" He stifled a yawn.

The women went inside and explained what they feared. "I doubt that anyone could get in here. It's one of those card swipe locks." He was obviously very tired or a little drunk.

"Let's check the secret place." He took his jacket from the wardrobe and unbuttoned the small inside pocket. "This is for any loose diamonds I might be carrying. Safe as houses." He searched vainly inside the pocket then looked around, shaking his head, trying to concentrate.

"False alarm," he said. I changed my jacket to go out for dinner and steamed it over the bath. I must have forgotten to switch the key over."

Jenny was standing by the bathroom door. "I'll get it while you look around the room."

Leticia checked his jacket again while he looked vaguely in the wardrobe and opened a couple of drawers. He saw nothing amiss, he was not as neat and tidy as the women.

Jenny emerged from the bathroom with the other jacket and Adam searched in the same inside pocket. His face blanched. He rifled through the other pockets, finally throwing the coat on the bed. Picking up the first jacket, he searched it again without success. "Jesus Christ, I don't believe it. It's gone. The key's gone!"

"Let me have a look." Jenny picked up the jackets and searched them carefully, feeling through the material in case it had slipped inside the lining. There was no key there. "Are you sure you didn't put it somewhere else? We've had a pretty tiring day."

When he shook his head, Leticia asked, "Who did we tell about the hotel?"

"We told Schneider and we told Jolidon, no one else."

"I bet it's that bloody Jolidon. None of us trusted him and for good reason. I didn't tell you at the time, but there were a couple of villainous looking blokes chased after us when we left his office. I didn't want to worry you, but in my book, the guy's definitely not straight."

"So, you think he's broken in here and stolen the key?" Leticia began to feel very uneasy. *Thieves in their bedrooms in a Geneva hotel?* She shivered at the thought.

"I've got no idea, but the bloody key's gone and now we can't access the vault. What an imbecile I am, I should never have left it in that jacket."

Jenny was thinking hard. "Jolidon would certainly be the obvious candidate. He must know there's something valuable in that box. Thank heavens he doesn't know exactly what. At least I hope to God he doesn't. On the other hand," she added, "Maybe you've simply lost it. We've really no proof that anyone's broken in."

"I don't know whether it's been lost or stolen. I'm so sorry. How could I be so bloody stupid?" Adam sat down in the bedside chair. He was trembling with reaction. "I thought you couldn't get past those card swipe locks," he said, looking over at the door.

"I suppose there's always a way to break in somewhere if you're a professional," Jenny observed. "We'll have to call the manager. Probably the police as well, I suppose." She picked up the phone and called reception.

The manager, Mr. Leboeuf, was about sixty years old and apparently lived in the hotel, since he arrived five minutes later. He was dumbfounded at Jenny's report. "Mme. Bishop, I can assure you that in the twenty two years that I have been running this hotel, we have never, ever, had the slightest problem."

He insisted on coming to check the door locks and look at the drawers and wardrobes, listening carefully to their explanations.

"We're in the process of changing all the locks to swipe card technology," he explained. "The second floor is finished and the third floor will be done next week. That's why you ladies have keys and Mr. Peterson here has a card.

Before Jenny could interject, he added, "However, it really makes no difference. We're not changing for security reasons, it's a matter of efficiency. All the good hotels are doing it."

His protestations and alternative hypothesises almost convinced them that they had imagined everything. Finally he agreed to call the police, but not until the next morning. "If the key was stolen then nothing we do tonight will change anything. We'll call in the morning and you can make an official complaint, although frankly I think that nothing will come of it."

After he left them Jenny said to the others. "We have to be very discreet about this. We can't tell the police that we've lost a key worth millions of dollars. They'll start all kinds of enquiries, mostly into us. Think we're an international drug syndicate or something. So I doubt very much that there's any chance of them finding out who broke in."

She thought for a moment. "But don't forget that both Laurent and Raffael have the second key. I'm not saying that this isn't serious, because someone definitely broke in and it was most likely to steal the keys. But at least it means that we can sort things out when one of them turns up. So it's not a complete catastrophe."

"But Jenny," Leticia interrupted. "If someone came and stole that key, it must mean we're in danger. They'll come after the other one, and I've got it!"

EIGHTY

Friday, 25th April 2008
Washington DC, USA

Sonia Nicolaides was fed up and tired. It had been a long week, the latest of many long weeks. She was supposed to be working shorter hours for the last three months but the days always turned out to be longer than before. Now it was Friday evening and she was still trying to catch up with paperwork to close out the week. *How come I'm the only one in after six on a Friday?* She asked herself. *I must be a slow worker. Either that, or I've got too many cases.*

She had known when she was requested to move from the NYPD to work for the Justice Department in Washington that this might happen. But after two years with the Child Exploitation and Obscenity section, the work seemed to be multiplying exponentially. For the zillionth time since she had started, she thought to herself, *what a sick and depraved world we live in.* She went to get herself another coffee and came back to her computer terminal, took out her written notes and documents for *Project Fairy Tale.*

She took a swig of coffee and waited for her computer files to update themselves. *Underpaid and overworked,* she said to herself, pushing her hands up over her head and stretching her arms and neck. But Sonia's main motivation in her work was not a salary, however good it might be. It was a very primitive emotion - revenge. And she knew that if she could help just one child to avoid the fear, horror and pain that she had endured for more than six years then she could keep on going.

Sonia had suffered abuse from the age of six until twelve, at the hands of her step-father and her uncle, her mother's brother. Like most victims of abuse, she had been threatened with terrible reprisals if she reported it. So it had gone on for night after dreadful night, year after horrible year, until her step-father had overdosed in the lavatory of a strip joint in Queens.

The next night, her mother had left her alone as usual, to go and get drunk out of her mind in some sleazy bar. "Your uncle Kevin will probably come round to sit with you. Don't worry, I won't be late."

Sonia had lain in her bed, the covers pulled over her head, terrified that her uncle would come back. But he never did, she never ever saw him again. Still, for years she lay waiting, dreading his return. The waiting was sometimes worse than the abuse. And even now, after all these years, somewhere inside her she was still waiting.

And so she never told anyone, until she got her first job at sixteen and could just about afford to pay a therapist's fees. It had taken her three years of therapy to partially get to grips with the physical and emotional scars she'd suffered. Even after ten years with the NYPD, as a policewoman and then detective and now two years working with CAPP, she couldn't sleep without taking tranquilisers. And she couldn't bear to let a man touch her.

She had already written up her notes and prepared the monitoring and fishing proposals for the following week for five of her cases. *One more to go.* She would discuss them all with her Case Director on Monday morning.

In *Project Fairy Tale,* she was now playing the game and communicating with the other members of da Silva's ring. She had even participated in the sickening "chat-room" exchanges of real and imagined experiences of two dozen vicious, depraved perverts. The mental images created by those sixty loathsome minutes had kept her awake all night, even after taking a tranquiliser. The filth she had to read and reply to, composed as if it came from a corrupt, perverted mind, often made her physically sick, but she persevered in the knowledge that she was doing something to make a difference. Something that could save one child, or maybe many children from harm.

She opened up the *r.da.silva* account but there were no new emails, none since the message she had received the previous Friday. There was also no news from the NYPD and she made a note to call when she finished for the day. She had just opened up the first of the dirty accounts when her phone rang. It was Jack Pearson, her ex-colleague in New York.

"Sorry to take so long to get back to you, Sonia, but it's absolute hell here right now, you're well out of it. We're in the middle of a management review and a crime wave at the same time. So the bosses are doing exactly what they do best, preventing us from getting any real work done. Anyway, here's what I've been able to find out."

After recounting the results of his enquiries, Jack summoned up the courage to tell her that he'd be in Washington the following month and would like to catch up with her. She thanked him and promised to call back when she'd checked her diary. He put down the phone with a feeling that she never would call back.

Sonia digested the information he'd given her. It was clearly not relevant to her investigation of the CAPP project and normally she would have simply filed it away in case anything subsequently materialised to bring it back under scrutiny. In this case however, the instincts born of her years of detective work with the NYPD took over.

She looked up the European data base and found the name and contact numbers of the person she thought would be interested. Then she composed a fax, revised it and re-read it again. *That should do it.* She printed it out and took it down to the coms room to be transmitted. It would have been quicker to send an email, but she knew that a fax was much more secure. After two years in CAPP she didn't trust emails, even encrypted. She passed it through the machine and received a confirmation that it had been transmitted at six forty-five, Friday evening, local time, and twelve forty-five, Saturday morning, Central European time. She filed the fax and turned back to *Project Fairy Tale.*

Three more hours and I can go home for the weekend. Big deal.

EIGHTY-ONE

Saturday, 26th, Sunday, 27th April, 2008
Marbella, Spain

The Iberia flight to Malaga, via Madrid, took off on time at midday on Saturday, 26th April. Adam had left for London just an hour before. He had managed to arrange meetings with his two UK customers on the Sunday morning to organise the completions for the week after Nick's funeral. The US customers were easier to meet. He would stop off in New York on his way back to Miami to set up the arrangements with them. Of course, everything was dependent on finding Laurent or Raffael.

The interview with the Geneva Gendarmes that morning was a complete farce. They clearly agreed with the hotel manager. People didn't break into hotel rooms in Geneva and the supposed victims could produce no proof to contradict that rule. When Adam admitted that he could have simply lost it, the police lost interest and the meeting was closed. A report would be filed on an unconfirmed crime, possibly committed by a person or persons unknown. Jenny had enough experience of such reports to know that they seldom led anywhere.

The manager saw them off in a taxi to the airport. He was apologetic, but obviously happy to have deflected any scandal away from his hotel.

"He must have thought we want a reduction in the price." Leticia was shocked at the bill. "It's outrageous," she said, impressing Jenny with yet another display of English vocabulary.

"Well, we didn't get one, all we got was a complete whitewash. I don't think the Swiss like to be criticised much. It's against their efficiency rules."

They had discussed the mystery of the two missing partners again, without any conclusion. They didn't know how to contact Raffael and when Adam tried calling Laurent's mobile number the message said it was switched off or out of coverage.

"We've got to find one of those guys or I can't execute my transactions. This is an insane situation." Adam was still agonising over the missing key. "I'm so sorry," he kept repeating, shaking his head in frustration.

Before he left, Jenny announced that if they didn't hear anything by Monday, she would call Chief Inspector Espinoza. *How difficult can it be to find two grown men,* she reasoned?

Adam left for his flight, still apologising, and they agreed to coordinate their actions after Nick's funeral, hopefully after having made contact with at least one of the missing partners.

Jenny made another effort to contact Gloria. She got a "not available" message from her mobile number again and there was still no reply from her home. *I hope she's OK. I wonder what it was she wanted to tell us.* She decided not to say anything to Leticia. She was already very uneasy. The women went to catch their plane to Madrid. At seven forty-five they were met at Malaga airport by Juan, who said as little as usual, and fifteen minutes later they were on their way back to Marbella, after the most momentous week of their lives.

Jenny didn't want to spoil his mother's homecoming for Emilio, so they dropped Leticia off at her parent's apartment and went on to York House. Juan left her at the door with a shy, "*Buenas noches, Jenny.*"

It was a warm evening so she sat on the terrace with a glass of wine, the air sweet from the white Dame de Noche flowers planted along the wall. It was warmer than Geneva, and certainly much warmer than Ipswich. She would have to get her head around things tomorrow, but tonight she needed a good sleep. She went up to bed and fell asleep immediately.

In Geneva, the man who had followed them for the last three days finished his report and emailed it to his boss. His assignment was satisfactorily terminated. He called his girl friend and arranged to take her out for lunch the next day. He was feeling very pleased with himself.

On Sunday morning Jenny woke to a constant drumming noise. She struggled to identify the sound. It was rain. Torrential rain that had started in the night and hadn't let up. The terrace at York House was like a pond, water pouring down the rain spouts to the swimming pool level. *What a difference a day makes,* she thought. The house felt cool, the rain had pushed the temperature down by several degrees. Rather than try to adjust the heating system, she put on a pair of cotton trousers and a blouse, with a long sleeved cardigan on top.

In the kitchen, she switched on the coffee machine and took out a couple of slices of brown bread from the freezer to make toast. There were a couple of remote control devices lying near the flat TV screen on the wall above the counter. One was marked with a ***sky*** button. After fiddling with them for a few moments, she managed to find the UK news channel, where the weather lady was describing a huge low pressure area, extending across most of Europe, and forecasting with it the usual accompanying stormy, rainy, cold conditions. It seemed that Marbella wasn't the only place that was suffering from this awful weather.

Jenny switched the depressing programme off and sat in the kitchen with her coffee and toast, looking thoughtfully out the window at the downpour. The rain was so heavy that she couldn't see across the garden to the golf course. Memories of their momentous trip to Geneva ran through her mind, especially the things that had gone wrong, or hadn't occurred as planned. The non-appearance of Laurent and Raffael and the appearance of Adam. Meeting Patrice in the bank. The disappearance of Gloria and Vogel. The break-in at the hotel. *Lots of coincidences?* She took her dishes over to the sink and noticed that the message light on the telephone was blinking.

She pressed the button on the machine and a mechanical-sounding woman's voice told her, in Spanish, that there were four new messages. The first two were from golf partners on holiday from the UK, who were unaware of Charlie's accident. The third was from José Luis, asking her to call him when she returned. It wasn't urgent. The fourth message had been left on the previous Thursday, at nine o'clock in the evening.

It was a man's voice, deep, with a soft French accent. "*Hello. This is Laurent Bonneville, with a message for Jenny. I was very sorry to get your email about Charlie, it's a terrible tragedy, shocking. But I wonder if you will be going to Geneva for the annual meeting of the Angolan Clan? If you are, I'm sorry, but I have been detained here in Paris and I won't be able to meet you. I don't have a mobile number for you, so I'll try to call the bank tomorrow to see if you're there, but I'm under time pressure. If I can manage it I'll put a call through to Nick as well. If I can't get hold of you before, I'll call back at the weekend, or you can call me on my mobile.*" He gave a number starting with 00377. "*I look forward to speaking to you.*"

The message was so unexpected that she didn't listen to the number properly the first time. She played it again and wrote it down. When she dialled it, the screen on the handset came up with *Laurent Bonneville.* It hadn't occurred to her to check the phone for his number. The line rang a few times then the same voice replied.

"*Oui, allo. Ici Laurent.*"

"Laurent, this is Jenny Bishop, how do you do?"

"Jenny! I'm so glad to finally get hold of you. I'm sorry, but I had a terrible day on Friday, and I had no time to call the bank and I didn't know where you'd be yesterday. Did you go to Geneva for the annual meeting? Where are you now? Oh, I'm sorry, I forgot to say how sad I am about Charlie. He was a marvellous man, please accept all my condolences."

"Thank you, Laurent. I'm in Marbella, we got back from Geneva last night. We were worried when we didn't hear from you and I just remembered to check the messages. Are you still in Paris?"

"I'm in Paris, but I'll be leaving this evening for Monaco, after I finish my business here. Were the others there, Raffael and Nick? Did you have a good meeting?"

"There was nobody there but Adam, Leticia and I. We weren't able to do anything."

There was a pause at the other end of the line. "I'm getting really confused, Jenny. I suppose Adam was there to complete the diamond sale, but you say that you couldn't get anything done? Why weren't the others there? And why was Leticia there, I don't understand?"

Jenny realised that the Frenchman had no idea what she was talking about. This was going to be very difficult on the telephone. "Listen, Laurent, there have been a lot of developments. I'm not sure that I can explain it very well on the phone, it's a long and complicated story."

There was another pause, then he said, "Jenny, I'll call you back. I'm going to check the flights and see if I can come down there before returning home. It sounds as if we need to meet, and the sooner the better. I'll call you within the hour."

"I'll be here. It's pouring with rain, so I don't expect I'll be going anywhere."

"OK. *A tout de suite, Jenny. Au revoir.*"

Jenny immediately called Leticia. "Finally, it looks as if we'll get some answers."

"I think Laurent will need a lot of answers also. It's hard to know where to start."

"I'll start by calling Adam, he'll be relieved to hear the news. I'll call you when I've heard back from Laurent. Is everything fine at home?"

"Apart from the weather. Emilio is very upset with the rain, he thinks it's me who brought it from Geneva."

Jenny called Adam's mobile. He told her he was in Oxford in a rented car on his way to see a customer. She explained the situation to him.

"That's great news. I've just got these two visits to make, then I'm heading back to Heathrow. Call me as soon as you know something, I'll answer even if I'm driving."

"Take care on the roads, if the weather is like it is here, you'd better drive carefully." She put the receiver down and went to make another cup of coffee.

Laurent called back less than an hour later. "I can get a flight down to Malaga at six thirty, getting in at eight forty-five. I only have carry-on baggage, so I could get to Marbella by nine thirty or so. Would that be acceptable?"

"That'll be fine, you can stay here at York House tonight. Juan can pick you up."

"It'll be simpler and faster if I just get a cab at the airport. Don't worry, I know the way."

"That's great. I look forward to meeting you at last."

"And me you, Jenny. Will Adam and Leticia be there? It sounds as if there's a lot to explain, and Adam and I need to settle the delivery and payment of the diamonds."

"I hope that they can manage to come. I'll get onto it now, to make sure." Jenny said nothing about Nick. It was better to explain things face to face, not on the telephone.

"Good, I hope I'll see you all tonight. *A ce soir,* Jenny."

"See you later, Laurent, have a good flight."

She rang Adam first, and brought him up to date. "What do you think?"

"I already called the airline. I could get down to Malaga by eight thirty."

"That means you'd be at the house by about nine fifteen. That's just before Laurent."

"The problem is that I'd have to leave at five in the morning to get connections back to Miami by Monday evening. Your opinion?"

"Well, I don't want you to get stressed out before your father's funeral, but you'll probably be happier if you can get back to Miami having met with Laurent. At least you'll know you can get your transactions completed."

"Fair enough. You're right, as usual. I'll get the flights organised and see you later."

Jenny repeated her offer of Juan's services, but he told her not to bother. He'd take a taxi.

"See you this evening then. We can't go on meeting like this, you know. People will talk," she joked.

"A girl in every port, that's me. See you tonight."

Leticia was reassured by the developments. "Can I bring Emilio over and stay the night? He won't be happy if I leave him alone again so soon."

"Come over sooner, early evening. Bring some cartoon DVDs with you and we'll have some fun, despite the rain. I'm sure he'll love it."

Jenny spent the rest of the morning tidying the house, sorting out her travel bag and other mundane chores. She realised that if she decided to stay in the house they'd have to get another housekeeper. Leticia was now co-owner of the property and too hooked on shopping.

Braving the teeming rain, she took an umbrella and went down to the gate to open the mail box. It was cold outside. The rain was heavier and the storm clouds that filled the sky made the day dark and depressing, a total contrast with the days before her trip to Geneva. She ran back to the house with the few items of mail, glad to be out of the cold and wet.

In the kitchen, she put some cat food into a deep dish so that it wouldn't get blown away and placed it outside in the most protected corner of the terrace. Fuente would be disappointed if he arrived in the rain and had to go hungry.

She heated up some chicken soup and drank a dishful of it, putting on the light so she could read the few pieces of mail. There was nothing of importance except for a bank statement from the Banco de Iberia and some utilities bills. A large envelope contained a cruise brochure from a company called *Silver Sailings. Maybe I should try that sometime,* she thought, remembering how much her parents-in-law had enjoyed their cruises. Then the events of the last week finally caught up with her and her eyes started to close. She lay down on one of the couches in the living room and fell fast asleep.

Jenny woke with a start. She'd had a vivid, frightening dream that was still clear in her mind.

She was playing tennis inside a huge circular room. Her opponent was a masked man wearing a blue raincoat, with a dark blue handkerchief poking out of the breast pocket, and old fashioned, plus four style, skiing trousers. They were both holding racquets made from hard-backed green ledgers, with long silver keys as handles. The net was made from plastic file covers, alternate squares of red and green, so that it looked like a patchwork quilt.

It was a sweltering day and even though they were inside, the sun was beating down unmercifully. There was a crowd of spectators, holding umbrellas to ward off the hot sun.

The man was about to serve. He threw up a wad of thousand dollar bills and smashed his racquet into them. The notes disintegrated and confetti flew though the air, covering the court and the players. A vicar, sitting in the umpire's chair, called "Game, set and match."

A woman wearing a veil and wedding dress ran out onto the court and threw diamonds to the crowd, who caught them in their upturned umbrellas. The man in the raincoat removed his mask and kissed the woman. He turned to bow to Jenny. It was Kurt Vogel!

Jenny went to get the bank statements given to her by Eric Schneider for the Angolan Clan account and the statements she'd received from Mme. Aeschiman for the IDD accounts and the file she'd taken from the office. She sat down at the kitchen table with a pencil and started ticking the items off. After fifteen minutes she found what she was looking for.

From September 30th, the last day that Charlie had checked the books, up to 15th March, there were seven receipts in the IDD account. These were no doubt from Laurent's last diamond sales. The total amount was nine hundred and seventy thousand dollars.

There were corresponding entries on the Excel sheets showing transfers of the same seven amounts, minus the IDD profit, to the Angolan Clan account.

There were seven corresponding debit entries on the IDD bank statements.

But there were no corresponding entries for funds received on the bank statements for the Angolan Clan account. The money had never arrived there, it had disappeared.

Almost a million dollars had gone. And so had Kurt Vogel!

Jenny thought about Vogel and Gloria, about Jolidon and the diamonds, about Patrice and the BIP, the break-in at the hotel, about the missing partners and about Ron and Charlie and the money. She remembered what Chief Inspector Espinoza had said and she began to feel very frightened.

EIGHTY-TWO

Sunday, 27th April, 2008
Marbella, Spain

At five fifteen, Jenny heard the sound of a car horn. Through the pouring rain she could see Leticia's Vitara outside the gates. She pointed the remote control towards the gate. Nothing happened. She went to the security camera control unit in the hall but the screen was blank and when she pressed the release button the gates remained stubbornly closed. Finally, she grabbed her umbrella and ran down to the gateside to turn the emergency switch and the gates rolled back. When the car was through she turned the switch to close them again. Then, thinking of Adam and Laurent, she opened the small gate and left it ajar. Leticia parked as close to the house as possible and they ran up the stairs with Emilio.

The main door was at the side of the house, facing the waterfall and a large pond, full of water-plants and surrounded by flower beds and shrubs lovingly planted and tended by Juan. The waterfall was now rushing down so strongly it was threatening to cause the pond to overflow and flood the entrance area and the staircase but there was nothing they could do about it, except to hope that the rain would ease.

"What's wrong with the gates? My control wouldn't work at all."

"It must be the storm. The system seems to be bust. Never mind, come in from the rain."

Leticia left their raincoats and overnight bag in the hall. She and her son were both warmly dressed in trousers and woollen jumpers against the cool temperature.

"What is it, Jenny, has something happened?" Despite the other woman's calm demeanour, Leticia sensed that something was wrong.

"It's nothing to worry about, I'll tell you later. Let's have some fun with Emilio now." Jenny picked the little boy up and he kissed her fondly. *"Holá, Jenny."*

"Holá, Emilio, qué tal?" She almost wished he was her own child. *Anyway, he's my nephew, or something like that.*

They went downstairs to the games room where there was a large television screen, and watched cartoons for an hour or so. Then the three of them tried to play *Chopsticks,* all together on the piano. This was funnier than the cartoons.

Afterwards they sat in the kitchen and Leticia made tea. She heated up the remains of Jenny's soup for her son's supper, with a glass of fruit juice and a couple of slices of nutty bread that she'd brought with her. She wanted him to be in bed early this evening, the excitement of being reunited with her had exhausted him.

Jenny was reflecting that the house was much too large to be comfortable. Since she had arrived they had spent most of their time in the kitchen. They were all happiest there and the other rooms seemed to be such a long way away. For a moment she was nostalgic for her semi-detached in Ipswich, where she could light an open fire and sit right in front of it, warm and cosy in the small living room. She would watch TV, with a snack on a tray on her knee, then go straight up the stairs to bed. No wasted space, just enough to be comfortable.

Leticia interrupted her reverie. "I must go for some shopping. There is almost nothing left in the fridge." She laughed. "We must be very poor."

"We can't shop on a Sunday, so that's for tomorrow. Now come over here for a moment, I've got something to show you." Jenny spread out the papers on the kitchen table. They sat on the bench seat with Emilio and she pointed out the fraudulent entries.

The younger woman was startled. She had never had money before and had little knowledge of fraud or criminality.

She sat back on the bench seat, her hands to her face. "So, now we see why he was packing up. He can pay for a very long holiday with all that money."

"It's not so funny, Leticia. Remember, this is our money now and that's a lot to lose to a crooked Swiss accountant."

"You're right. And Charlie didn't find it out, because of his heart attack. And Vogel wasn't skiing, he was hiding from them. Then Charlie never went back to the office after Ron… Anyway, he didn't like the cold weather, he liked more to play golf in Spain." She shivered. "I wonder where he is now, Vogel. We should get Chief Inspector Espinoza to go after him."

"You remember that Mme. Aeschiman was having a baby at the time? I bet she would have seen this swindle if she'd still been at the bank."

Leticia said, "Jenny, never mind the police thinks nobody broke into our rooms, I'm sure it's true. I don't believe Adam just lost the key. Somebody stole it and they must be looking for the other one, and now there's a crook in IDD. I'm beginning to be afraid now, we have to do something. But what?"

"You're right. We should call Chief Inspector Espinoza and we should do it now. I thought of it yesterday and then forgot about it. Where's his card?"

Leticia found the card amongst the photographs in her purse. She picked up the kitchen phone and listened for the dial tone. "It's not working." She replaced it on the stand, picked it up and tried again, shaking it. "The phone's not working, the dial tone isn't there."

Jenny tried. It was dead. "It's the weather. I bet there's a telegraph pole down somewhere. Or maybe it's the electric circuit in the garden. That's probably what's wrong with the gate system," She got her mobile. "What's the number?"

"I'll use mine, it's a Spanish one. No need to make international dialling, and it's easier for me in Spanish." Leticia rang the policeman's office number. A recorded voice advised her that Espinoza was away on police business until Monday. She left a message asking him to call her or Jenny back as soon as possible.

"I'll try his mobile number." This time it told her that the phone was either off or out of coverage. She left the same message.

Leticia thought for a moment. "I don't know if Francisco's back from London, but we could call José Luis. What do you think?"

"He's seventy years old and it's a Sunday night. It wouldn't be fair to call him. Anyway, what could he do? We have to wait for Espinoza, he can do something."

"And we can't expect Juan to come out to check the phone and electricity in this awful weather. We'll have to wait for the morning," Leticia added.

Jenny said nothing, just nodded her head. *More coincidences,* she thought. First the camera and the gate didn't work and now the phone. *Everything happens for a purpose.* But she didn't know what purpose, and Jenny didn't like not knowing things.

"I think Emilio should sleep now, it's almost eight thirty." Leticia said, stroking her son's face. The little boy was yawning, his eyes were getting drowsy. "I'll put him in the spare bedroom along the corridor. No need to put him upstairs until we go up. I won't bathe him tonight, he's too tired after all the excitement and the games." She took her child along to the visitor's bedroom, washed him and cleaned his teeth in the adjoining bathroom.

Jenny watched her as she prepared her son for bed, folding up the little items of clothing and laying them on the bedside chair. She dressed him in the blue pyjamas that she had brought with her, then turned back the crisp white sheets and dimmed the light. The little boy climbed up onto the bed and lay on his back, smiling up at his mother. Leticia looked at Jenny and saw the longing in the other woman's expression, the unsatisfied need to share her love and affection. "I forgot his teddy bear," she said. "Why don't you tuck Emilio in, while I go quickly to get it from my bag?"

Jenny bent down, gently arranged the sheets around the child, then sat on the side of the bed. He reached up and pulled her face down, so that he could give her a goodnight kiss. "*Buenas noches, Jenny.*" His breath was pure and clean, his skin smelled of lavender soap.

"Good night Emilio. Sweet dreams." He smiled, not understanding, but happy to be there with her. Leticia came back into the room and put her arm around Jenny's waist, sitting with her on the side of the bed. Emilio immediately fell into a deep sleep. They sat watching him, the sound of his soft, regular breathing hardly distinguishable against the steady drumming sound of the rain outside.

Looking at his innocent little face, Jenny wondered how the night was going to end. Was he safe? Were any of them safe? She had never been surrounded by so many unknowns. She took Leticia's hand and they went back into the kitchen. *Maybe we've bitten off more than we can chew. Where's Chief Inspector Espinoza? Why didn't I call him sooner?*

EIGHTY-THREE

Sunday, 27th April, 2008
Schiphol Airport, Amsterdam, Holland

"Good evening again, ladies and gentlemen, Captain Haan speaking. I'm pleased to inform you that I've just received a confirmed departure slot from the control tower for twenty minutes to seven. This means that I'll be starting the engines and pulling back in just ten minutes time. I apologise once more for the delay, but as I explained, the awful weather all over Europe has caused chaos, so we're not the only flight to be held up. I estimate that we'll be about one hour late, which would make our arrival time in Malaga at twenty-one fifty-five. That's five minutes to ten. But you can be sure that Mikael and I will do everything possible to catch up on that. I invite you now to relax, watch our safety demonstration carefully then enjoy our in flight service."

Chief Inspector Pedro Espinoza roused himself and checked his watch. He had been dozing in the plane for forty minutes, while they waited to start the engines. The captain had got them on board so that they would be ready to depart as soon as a slot came up. Now it had, evidently. He removed the marker from page two hundred and eight of his latest tome, *Living in the Criminal Mind.*

He took another sip of water and started reading. *Fascinating stuff!*

The policeman had been on a conference with his Interpol colleagues at the Amsterdam Sheraton. It was near the airport and they had assembled there on Friday evening, attended a conference all day on Saturday and Sunday morning, and closed the meeting down that afternoon. *Most interesting,* was the general consensus. *Very boring,* had been his own assessment. Modern technology made international policing a lot easier but as Espinoza kept reminding everyone, nothing replaced good old fashioned detective work. Toil, imagination, patience and psychology. That was the secret to solving crimes and nailing criminals. Get into their mind, work out their motivation and modus operandus, then ask yourself, *What would I do next? Y vamos!*

Espinoza had worked through his fair share of crimes in Malaga. The successful investigation of the Madrid lawyer, with José Luis's assistance, had kick-started his career as a Detective Inspector and he had never looked back. A few years after his initial success his rank had risen to *Inspector Jefe,* Chief Inspector. Since then he had been allocated more than his quota of violent crimes, usually involving the most common motives for villainy of any kind all over the world since time immemorial; sex, power, fear, revenge and money.

He was appalled to witness the recent huge and rapid increase in criminal activity in southern Spain. The most telling example was that recently, the UK police had instituted a large scale effort to locate and apprehend the twenty top criminals on their most wanted list. Espinoza was proud, but equally ashamed, that five of them had already been caught on the Costa del Sol. It seemed incredible to him that his territory attracted such a huge number of miscreants, including some of the big-time villains of the moment. He had been asked to talk on this subject at the conference and had heard, not for the first time, the phrase, *Sunny place for shady people.*

Now, as the plane taxied to take off, he put aside his book, leaned back in his seat and closed his eyes again. He planned to wake up in time for the inflight meal, he was starving.

Jenny looked out the kitchen window, then at her watch. The time was just after nine. "That's strange," she said thoughtfully.

"What's wrong?" Leticia looked up at Jenny's tone.

"The garden lights aren't on. They usually come on at eight-thirty and they haven't." After failing to pierce the heavy rainclouds all day long, the sun had finally given up and slid below the horizon and it was completely dark outside. The pouring rain could be seen against the glimmer of the street lights beyond the wall at the bottom of the drive. But the gardens, the driveway and the gates were cloaked in darkness. The property was so large and surrounded by so many trees that the house seemed to be lost in the middle of a forest, far from civilisation.

"Do you know where the outside switches are?" Jenny knew the outside lights had to be on a different circuit. "The circuit breaker must have gone and blown all the outside connections. That's why nothing's working."

She followed Leticia downstairs and through the labrynth of corridors in the basement that led to the games room, the wine cellar, the gym, the massage and steam room and several storage areas, then through the garages to the machine room. It looked like a NASA missile-launch control room. Cables, pipes, valves, stopcocks and switches were connected to pumps and machines of all types and sizes. Computer screens showed the temperature, pressure and humidity of the various areas of the house, the pool, even the wine cellar. There were two tall electrical cabinets, each containing dozens of switches, buttons and dials, all labelled in Spanish, in Juan's erratic script.

The women scanned down the list of labels. "We're never going to find what's wrong like this, we don't know what to look for. In any case I think it must be something in the garden that's gone wrong in this lousy weather. We'll have to wait for Juan to check it tomorrow, like you said. If he can't fix it, we'll call the phone and electricity companies. At least the house is alright." Jenny dusted her hands off and started back towards the door to the garages.

Leticia shivered and looked around the room. "It's freezing down here. It's always hot, not cold." She went over to the outside door, the one that led to the driveway. She pushed against the large security handle. "Look. The door's not locked. Juan always locks it. And there's water on the floor. It must have come in from outside."

"Strange," said Jenny, walking back to her, "the key's here."

A rusted steel key was hanging on a hook at the side of the door. She pushed the heavy door open. A blast of cold air rushed in. The women peered outside. The light from the room illuminated the pitch black night and they could see the rain pouring down. It seemed to be getting stronger. Spray from the raindrops splashed into the room onto the tiled floor.

"He must have forgotten to do it when he went home on Friday." Leticia shivered again and went to pull the door shut. "What was that?" She turned quickly and grabbed Jenny's arm. "Over there!" she said, pointing at the shadows behind the machines in the corner of the room.

Jenny had heard the noise too. A sound like a child whimpering. "Who's there? Come out of there, now!" She grabbed the key from its hook and hurled it into the corner.

There was a loud squeal and Fuente came racing between the machines and shot out of the door and down the driveway. The women almost collapsed with relief. "My God. He almost gave me a heart attack." Jenny put her arms around Leticia, she was trembling like a leaf. "How on earth did he get trapped down here? He can't have been here since Friday, can he?"

"I don't know and I don't care. That cat scared me almost to death." Leticia closed the door and pushed the handle into the locking position then went across the room to retrieve the key. "There." She turned the key and hung it back on its hook. "Fuente can stay out tonight."

The women went back upstairs to the kitchen. Jenny's mind was whirling again. *How could the cat get down here? The doors were all closed. And why was the outside door unlocked? Another coincidence? There are too many of them by half. It's time we did something.* She picked up her mobile from the counter. "I'm going to try Espinoza again."

The phone started ringing in her hand. It was Adam, he had found a taxi and was leaving the airport. "I was lucky, only a half hour's delay. The flights are in chaos with this rotten weather. I tried the house phone but it was off. Is everything OK?" He sounded a little worried.

Jenny forced herself to remain calm. "Everything's fine, don't worry. It must be this storm. I think the outside electricity circuit must have blown. It should take you about forty-five minutes to get here in this storm. Leticia and Emilio are here too. We'll sort something out for supper, I bet you're starving, and Laurent's sure to be, too." She gave him instructions for the taxi driver to get to the house and told him about the open gate.

Leticia went along to check on Emilio. He was in a sound sleep, his arms stretched out above his head. She kissed him on the brow and closed the door. The bedroom was along the corridor at the other end of the house from the kitchen, so he shouldn't be disturbed.

She came back to the kitchen. "I'll see what we have to eat. You're right, Adam and Laurent will be hungry and we need to have something too." She started rummaging through the fridge and the pantry for anything still fresh after their absence.

To take her mind off her mounting misgivings, Jenny picked up her notebook and started skipping through it, thinking about the last week's events.

"Another problem solved." Leticia showed her what she'd found in the fridge and the pantry. They could manage a cold snack, at least. "I'll get a bottle of wine. I think we need a drink." She ran down the stairs to the cellar, where she had a choice of thousands of bottles of fine Spanish wines, and brought up a 1994 *Tondonia Gran Reserva.*

She opened the bottle, tasted the wine and poured two glasses. "Have a glass, Jenny. We have to cheer up, we are starting to worry too much."

Jenny still had her nose in her notepad. "Not now, thanks." She looked up at Leticia, her brow furrowed. "I was thinking about the diamond contract that Adam signed with Nick. We haven't seen the contract. For such a lot of money we really should, it's only common sense."

"So you don't trust Adam? You mean he might cheat us like Vogel did?"

"Leticia, apart from you, I don't know who to trust. I'm just trying to be careful and not make a stupid mistake that could hurt us. We're amateurs, with no business experience. We've just been robbed of hundreds of thousands of dollars. We need to check everything to be sure."

Leticia said, "I remembered one thing on Friday night. When we went to the restaurant in the park, he kept us waiting fifteen minutes, then when we came back again, the rooms were searched. It might be just a coincidence, but we need to check. But how?"

Then Jenny had a brainwave. "Come along to the study, I think I know how to do this."

In Charlie's office, she started up his laptop again. Under *Documents and Settings*, she found *A C Business*. She looked down the list of files and found a folder labelled *IDD*. She opened it up and saw that the sub-files were labelled by year, all the way back to 1992.

Scrolling down the list of the 2007 sub files, she got to December, 2007. There was only one Word file listed, labelled *A. Peterson & Co. Final Dec. 07*. She opened it up, it was the final contract sent by Charlie to Adam to take to Florida, to be signed by him and Nick.

Jenny read through the text on the screen. The conditions were spelled out clearly in Charlie's methodical way and they corresponded with what Adam had told them. She came to the price clause, gasped and sat back from the machine, looking as if she'd seen a ghost.

Leticia looked over her shoulder at the computer screen. "What is it?"

"The price that Adam told us was ten million dollars exactly, right?"

"That's right. He said it was eight thousand three hundred and something dollars per carat, I remember perfectly, it was such a lot of money. So what does it mean?"

"Look at this!" She put the cursor over the price clause and ran it along the text. "It means that Adam is trying to steal two million dollars from the Angolan Clan, two million dollars, from us, and from his other partners!"

The price quoted in the contract was shown as:

> *Take down price, partial or total:*
> *1,200 Carats @ $US 10,000- per Carat.*
> *Total Net Price payable on completion:* *$US 12,000,000-*

Jenny stared disbelievingly at the screen. She couldn't believe that Adam could attempt this. He might have fooled her and Leticia, and maybe Raffael, but Laurent would spot it immediately. *He must have some kind of a death wish,* she thought. *Nobody could be so stupid, or dishonest, to try to carry off such a brazen deception.* She thought again about the break-in. Someone was definitely after the diamonds. But who? And where were they?

She had another thought. "Maybe the contract was changed again and Charlie didn't keep a separate copy. He just made the changes in this one and then forgot to save it as the final one." Knowing Charlie's obsession for doing everything correctly, Jenny didn't think this likely, but she was trying desperately to find a way of absolving Adam. After their recent disappointments, she wanted, needed to believe in him.

"But how can we tell without seeing Adam's contract? What a mess, everybody wants to steal, even when they have got plenty of money. It's crazy." Leticia ran her hands nervously through her hair.

"There's one way to try to find out, look." Jenny went to *File,* up in the top left hand corner of the screen. Scrolling down, she opened up *Properties,* then *Statistics,* displaying a list of all of the data concerning the document, when it was created, modified, printed, etc. "You see, the file was created on December 10th, but it's probably been modified several times since then. It says here that the last modification was on Dec. 15th 2007." She stopped. *Two days before Ron's death. My God!* Her eyes misted over. She pushed the thought away and read the data labels, wiping her eyes dry. It was impossible to know if the correct version had been saved or not. "No good. I can't tell whether or not there was a different final version."

"Wait." Leticia pointed at the screen. "Look what it says under *Printed.*"

"It was printed out on April thirteenth, 2008, at seven twenty-two in the morning. That was the morning that Charlie died, he must have been working before he went in for his swim."

"Jenny, it's not possible. I was with Charlie the night before. He told me he was getting up for his swim at seven and playing golf at eight-thirty, like always. Just think. It takes him fifteen minutes to swim, then he has to shower and get ready for golf, go for coffee at the club. And he likes to practise before he plays." Leticia was adding up the minutes on her fingers. "He didn't have time to work before his swim. Besides, Charlie never worked on a Sunday. I always came to see him after his golf and in three years he was never working on a Sunday."

The only explanation was obvious and terrifying. Someone had been in the house immediately after Charlie's death. Someone who knew the computer passwords. The women looked at each other in dread. *Vogel, Gloria, Jolidon, the break-in at the hotel, the difference in the contract, the telephone and electricity cuts, Fuente trapped in the basement.* Now they were alone in the house, waiting for two men to arrive, men that they didn't know at all. Could they trust them?

They walked back along to the kitchen. "I'm going to call Espinoza again. This could be evidence concerning Charlie's death. We've got to let him know right away." Jenny couldn't find the card with Espinoza's number, so she took Leticia's mobile and pressed the call button again. The officer's phone was still switched off and she left another message, telling him that they might have found important evidence.

As she switched off, they heard the front doorbell ring. Jenny looked at her watch, it was nine forty-five. "It's too early for Adam, it can only be Laurent, his flight must have been on time. He's probably left the taxi outside and walked up the drive, he'll be soaked in this downpour."

They walked along the corridor from the office. Jenny tried to suppress her forebodings and calm the other woman. "Don't say anything about this. We're probably imagining things. It's this awful weather and the things going wrong in the house. It's making us paranoid. There must be some simple explanation. Let's wait and see what happens. At last we might get some answers, instead of just questions." She went into the hall and unlocked the door.

"Hello, Laurent. Welcome to sunny Marbella."

He was standing in the porch with his back to the door, shaking the water off his raincoat. The porch light wasn't on, but in the light from the hall she saw that the shoulders of his jacket were damp and his shoes and trouser cuffs were soaking. The thunderstorm seemed to have moved away but the rain was still hammering down remorcelessly. The rainwater was rushing down the staircase alongside the waterfall, causing the pond to flood the flower beds and plants around the entrance porch.

"You must be wet through and freezing. Come in."

He removed his hat and turned around to face her. "Hello, Jenny. How are you?"

BOOK TWO

PART SIX: 2008

EIGHTY-FOUR

Sunday, 27th April, 2008
Malaga, Spain

Along with just about every other person on the flight, Chief Inspector Espinoza switched his mobile phone on as he was standing in the aisle with his carry-on bag, waiting to get off the plane. The flight had made up some of the original delay so by the time they taxied across and arrived at their stand it was ten minutes to ten. He saw that his battery was getting low, but the beeping noise told him he had messages. He dialled his answering service. There were five calls to listen to and a text message. *On a bloody Sunday evening,* he thought to himself. *Is there no one who can do anything without calling me?*

There were two messages from his daughter. She wanted to speak to him again about her mother's allowance. She'd spoken to Soledad and wanted to tell him what had transpired. *It'll have to wait until tomorrow,* he decided, *it's too late for a fight tonight.*

His secretary had sprained her ankle. She would be out for a week. *Marvellous!*

The fourth message was from Leticia da Costa. Could he call back as soon as possible.

The fifth was from the same number, but it was Jenny Bishop, who repeated the request. This time, she said that they might have some evidence about Mr. Bishop's death. His pulse quickened and he ran through the teeming rain to his privileged parking place next to the arrivals hall. As he drove to the airport exit he returned the call to Leticia's number, but her phone was off. He didn't know where she was and he had neither her nor Jenny's home number with him, so he'd try again from the landline when he got to the Comisaria.

Even though it was Sunday night, Espinoza didn't have anything to go home for. Since the 'trial separation', he lived in an empty house that he couldn't afford and wasn't worth the money he'd paid for it. He would pop into his office to check his desk and emails and then go for a beer at the tapas bar next door then back to the house to sleep. *What a life I've created for myself. Fifty-two years old and nobody waiting for me at home.*

Despite the weather, the traffic was light on Sunday night and he was at the station in just twenty minutes. The duty officer was half asleep at her desk.

In answer to his question, she replied, "Nothing special, *Inspector Jefe*, it's been a quiet night. How was your trip?"

He went up to his office and saw his phone was blinking. *More messages.* There were only two, his secretary again and Leticia da Costa. Reaching for his phone book to look up her house number, he saw there was a fax on his private machine. He tore it off while he rang Leticia's number. It was headed, "*US Department of Justice*", sent by a Special Agent in Washington, Sonia Nicolaides. *Must be Greek origins,* he thought.

A woman answered the phone. "*Si. Diga me.*"

He asked for Leticia. The woman told him she was her mother. Her daughter was at Sr. Bishop's house with Jenny.

"Do you have the number handy?" She gave it to him.

"*Gracias, Sra.* Oh, is her little boy with her?"

"*Por supuesto, Sr.* Of course."

"*Gracias Sra, y buenas noches.*"

He dialled the number and started reading the fax.

Chief Inspector Espinoza.

In the course of investigating another matter, I have come across some information which may be useful to you. On April 17th, an email, signed, "Jenny, Charlie's daughter-in-law", was sent from a Spanish email address, to three men. It informed the addressees that Charlie had died in an accident. I have traced the email address used by Jenny, to Marbella, which I understand is in your jurisdiction.

You should be informed that one of the three men, Laurent Bonneville, died in suspicious circumstances in Verbier, Switzerland, on April 2nd. The second man, Raffael Rodrigo Pires da Silva, known as 'Roddy', also died in suspicious circumstances in New York, on April 11th. He is involved in my present investigation. I have no information concerning the third man, Nick Martinez, who lives in Miami.

The email address that Jenny transmitted from, and the other two recipient's addresses seem to be clean. As far as I can ascertain, none of the persons concerned, except for da Silva, is implicated in, or connected with my investigation. I hope that this information is of value and I am at your disposition for any other clarifications you may need.

Sonia Nicolaides, Senior Case Manager, CAPP.

The Bishop's phone gave a disconnected signal. Espinoza raced out of his office and into the waiting elevator. On the way to his parking place he called his subordinates at the Policía Nacional in Marbella. He jumped into his car, switched on the siren and emergency beacons and accelerated up the rainy street to the Autopista. The clock on the dashboard read ten twenty-three.

EIGHTY-FIVE

Sunday, 27th April, 2008
Marbella, Spain

Jenny stepped back in surprise, her hand to her mouth. "Francisco? What on earth are you doing here? It's almost ten o'clock on a Sunday night."

"I'm sorry, Jenny. I know it's not convenient, but I must talk to you. I have important information and you need to know it right away. May I come in?"

Jenny's heart started pounding. What was happening now? She said, "Well, of course you may. But Leticia's here and what can be so important that it can't wait until tomorrow?"

"Leticia's here too? Good, that will save time, my news concerns her as well. You have to listen to what I have to say. It could be vitally important."

She stepped aside to let the lawyer into the hall and closed the door behind him. He hung his raincoat and hat on the hall stand. They walked into the kitchen and Leticia turned in surprise, repeating Jenny's question. "*Qué haces aquí, Francisco?*"

"*Buenas noches,* Leticia. I'm afraid I have some worrying

information."

Jenny tried to manage the situation. "Sit down, Francisco, you look soaked and cold. Have a glass of wine to warm you up and you can tell us why this is so urgent."

He sat at the table and took off his spectacles, wiped them with his handkerchief, then took a healthy swig of the Rioja. "That's delicious. *Salud*."

Jenny sat on the bench seat next to Leticia. "So, what's this about, Francisco?"

"Well, as you know, I was in London and I just got back an hour ago. I was there to meet one of my clients, Raffael da Silva."

"Raffael? That's one of Charlie's partners." Leticia gave Jenny a worried look. *How did Francisco know him?*

"That's right. It's the most incredible coincidence. I only discovered it yesterday, after making enquiries with my US counterpart."

"What enquiries, I don't understand?"

"Last night I discovered that Raffael died two weeks ago, in New York."

A cold chill ran down Jenny's spine. *Charlie was dead, Ron was dead and now Raffael too.* She didn't want to think about the implications.

"But how was he your client? He was in New York, not Malaga. I don't understand."

"He's been my client since I worked in New York for TMTP, sorry, Thompson, Mather, Trelawney & Prescott. He didn't turn up for our meeting in London, so I asked them to investigate. They called me last night and told me that he'd died."

"And they'd discovered that he was Charlie's partner?"

"Yes. The Angolan Clan, but I suppose you know all about that, don't you?"

Now, Jenny was totally confused. From previously knowing nothing about their business in Geneva, it seemed that Francisco was suddenly aware of everything. He'd mentioned the Angolan Clan, but was that something that da Silva's lawyers would know about? Did he know about the diamonds, the bank account, Adam's transaction? What exactly did he know?

She tried to find out indirectly. "How did Raffael die? He was quite young, wasn't he?"

"It was a drug overdose, but the police aren't sure if it was accidental or deliberate."

"My God. You mean it could have been a murder?"

"I'm sorry, I didn't come here to frighten you, but it seems that's the case."

Jenny sat back in alarm, trying to digest what she had just heard. Raffael, one of the missing partners was dead, possibly murdered and Francisco had come to tell them about it at almost ten o'clock on a Sunday night. *There's something he's not saying here,* she thought.

"Why exactly have you come here, Francisco? You could have called us, or waited until tomorrow. What's so urgent that you have to come here on a Sunday night?"

The lawyer paused, looking apologetic, even distressed at what he was about to say. "Jenny, TMTP informed me that the police believe that the deaths of Raffael and..." He looked even more uncomfortable, before continuing, "your father-in-law could be connected."

Leticia was listening anxiously to the conversation, also adding up the ominous list of accidents. She said to Jenny, "You remember the Chief Inspector asked if someone might have a reason. But he was talking about Charlie and Ron. And now there's Raffael."

"Don't be so silly, it's just a coincidence." She glared at the younger woman. *Don't say any more! Where is Adam? Where is Laurent? Where is Espinoza? Far too many coincidences.* Her mind was seething with terrifying possibilities but she was unable to confront them.

She thrust those thoughts aside and considered what the lawyer had said. "So, on what are they basing that theory?"

"They think there could be a conspiracy. That there are other partners involved. Apparently there's a lot of money at stake and they're trying to grab it for themselves."

"Other partners?"

"A South African and a Frenchman. The police say that one or both of them may be imposters. Dangerous criminals, pretending to be partners of the Angolan Clan."

Adam and Laurent! Leticia's blood ran cold. They were awaiting the visit of two possible murderers.

Jenny's mind raced, remembering the clues that she'd chosen to ignore. *Adam's five year relationship with Laurent and IDD, the trips to Geneva, London, New York and Florida. The mysterious appearance at the funeral, Laurent not turning up in Geneva, the break-in at the hotel,the two million dollars difference in the contract.*

She cleared her mind again, still puzzled by the lawyer's nocturnal visit. "How did you get all this information on a Sunday night? Does José Luis know anything about this? Have you informed Chief inspector Espinoza?" She sat nearer to Leticia, taking her hand in her own. The young woman was staring at Francisco, her eyes wide with fright.

"The New York police contacted TMTP, they're gathering information. I got the call when I landed and drove straight here from the airport. I haven't called anyone else yet, I wanted to explain it all to you first." He took a gulp of wine and poured himself another glass.

Jenny's mind was off on another track. *Where does Nick fit into this? Was Adam's story invented? If Nick is dead, how did he really die?* She shook her head. It wasn't possible. She recognised genuine bereavement when she saw it. And Laurent had been Charlie's partner and friend for thirty years. There must be a mistake, some simple explanation. Francisco had got hold of the wrong end of the stick.

He reached for the telephone. "But you're quite right. I'll call Espinoza and José Luis now, if you think it's best."

Leticia said, "That phone doesn't work." She handed the lawyer her mobile. "Use mine, the numbers are in it."

Before he could make the call, the doorbell rang again. It was just before ten. Jenny turned to go to the hall. "It's either Adam or Laurent. They were due to get here about now. They must have walked up the drive as well."

The lawyer jumped up in alarm. "They could be the men I've been warned about. Why are they here? Do you know how dangerous this could be? We have to be extremely careful."

"They're coming because we asked them to come. It's too long to explain now, but I can't believe that they're implicated in any murderous conspiracy. Just act naturally and don't say anything about Raffael. Let's try to find out what's really going on."

When the other two nodded their understanding, she opened the door. The rain had increased in intensity, it was beating down like stair rods, and there were impressive flashes of lightning across the sky, followed by the noise of thunder rolling around the hills on the other side of the golf course.

EIGHTY-SIX

Sunday, 27th April, 2008
Lyon, France; Marbella, Spain

Just before ten o'clock, Esther Rousseau walked towards the immigration desk at the Aéroport St Exupery in Lyon, her ID card in her hand. She had taken the train from Geneva at six thirty and her Air France flight to Heathrow left at ten thirty, so her timing was perfect. She was using the French ID card in her maiden name of Esther Bonnard, which was still valid, since it was issued only six months before her marriage to her Swiss husband, which had lasted less than a year. Up to the day she met Ray d'Almeida.

Her suitcase was already checked in. It contained clothes for both of them. Mainly beachwear. Ray had told her that Panama was a very hot place. Hotter than the South of France, which she had often visited before she moved from Toulouse to Geneva after marrying Gaston. Esther was happy to leave Switzerland. It held too many bad memories, mainly because of Gaston, who turned out to like men more than women. And that sexually-frustrated, nose-blowing, arrogant bastard, Eric Schneider, who spent more time in his office looking at her tits than dictating letters. Ray had come along just at the right time. For them both.

Only another five hours and they would be together again, this time for good. Then off to a safe, sunny place, with a fortune in the bank. She tried to keep the smile off her face as she handed her ID card to the immigration officer. People don't smile at immigration officials.

Chief Inspector Pedro Espinoza was driving his SEAT Léon through the pouring rain at a hundred and fifty kilometres an hour on the autopista near Cabopino. It was as fast as he could risk with the bad visibility and rain-soaked road surface. He'd plugged his mobile into the car battery-charger, but it was the radio-telephone that now started squawking. It was Martín, one of the Policía Nacional officers from Marbella that he'd sent to York House.

"What's going on?" Espinoza asked.

The distorted reply came back, "We've just arrived at the security post. The others aren't here yet. The guard says he's seen no unusual activity on the CCTV."

Espinoza hesitated, weighing up the options. The problem was that he didn't have any real information apart from a fax from a woman agent in the US. "OK. Wait for the others and for me. I'll be there in ten minutes. I want to see for myself before we take any action."

Just as he finished speaking he saw the glare of the braking and emergency lights of the cars ahead slowing down and he jammed his foot on the brake. A moment later he passed a Municipal Police car parked on the hard shoulder. Two policemen, wearing fluorescent yellow rain jackets, were placing accident signs on both sides of the road.

"What's happening?" he called to the nearest officer.

"Good evening, *Inspector Jefe.* There's been a crash further along the road, between the Marbella Golf course and the hospital. With this shitty weather we're slowing the traffic all the way back here so it doesn't get any worse."

Espinoza thought for a moment. "Call your colleagues and make sure the hard shoulder is free all the way past the accident spot. I'm on an emergency and I need to get through."

The officer saluted and pulled out his walkie talkie. Espinoza put his foot down and drove onto the hard shoulder. The dashboard clock read ten forty-four.

"Here we are again. I was supposed to be on my way to Miami by now. Sod's law." Adam dropped his bags on the hall floor and hung his raincoat in the hall.

"I hope you agree it was the best thing to do." Despite the contract and what Francisco had just told them, Jenny wanted to hear Adam's side of the story. She also believed he was worrying about his father's funeral. She knew how stressful funerals could be.

"On one condition. Make me a pot of tea and all is forgiven. I'm absolutely freezing. It's like a bloody swimming pool out there. This is not what I expected in the Costa del Sol." He went into the kitchen and Leticia came to greet him, then turned to introduce him to the lawyer.

"We haven't met, although I saw you at the funeral. I'm Francisco García Luna, how do you do?" The two men shook hands.

"Francisco's one of our lawyers, Adam," Jenny said.

"Nice to meet you. I'm Adam Peterson." He looked worryingly at Jenny and Leticia. What was this lawyer doing here on a Sunday night? He thought about the contract. *They've seen the difference in price. Shit!*

Francisco removed his steel rimmed spectacles and pushed them into his lapel pocket. Without them, Jenny saw that his eyes looked different, no longer soft and kindly, but somehow arrogant, even cruel.

"So you're Adam, Martinez's bastard. You useless piece of shit. You stupid, incompetent prick! You're the asshole who's cost me twelve million dollars." He smacked Adam across the face so hard that he fell to the floor.

Jenny and Leticia screamed "What are you doing Francisco, are you crazy? Leave him alone, we don't know that he's done anything wrong."

Blood poured from Adam's nose. His head swam and he saw stars. He suddenly thought of Stanford all those years ago in college, when he'd knocked him down in the street. He'd been terrified that he'd killed him, but he'd been lucky. He sat up, holding his nose. "What in God's name is going on here? Who the hell do you think you are?"

"Who am I? I'm just the poor schmuck who's been screwed out of a fortune, that's all!"

Jenny couldn't fathom the lawyer's words and actions over the last twenty minutes. He was behaving like a drunk. She said, "Have you been drinking, Francisco? You're not making any sense. You'd better leave now before you make things even worse for yourself."

Adam staggered to his feet and sat in one of the kitchen chairs and she went to the sink to wet a towel with cold water. He took it and tried to staunch the flow of blood from his nose.

"I am making perfect sense, my dear Mme. Bishop. You're just being a bit slow to catch on." Francisco took another swig of the wine.

Like a flash of lightning, the truth finally burst into Jenny's head. Everything the lawyer had told them was a lie. It was he who was planning to steal the Angolan Clan fortune. He was a crooked lawyer, a thief, just like Vogel. He was probably in league with Raffael and had lied about his death. He had told them the story to get inside the house. To attempt to steal the money and the diamonds. She suddenly felt better, finally knowing what was happening. This was something she could cope with. His tactics were to frighten them. Well, two could play at that game.

"I've had enough of this, Francisco. You can't come barging into our house and behave like this. You're deranged, or drunk or something. If you don't get out, I'm calling Chief Inspector Espinoza."

She picked up her mobile and looked for the policeman's card. Francisco punched his fist down onto her hand, smashing the phone onto the floor. Shattering it into fragments.

Jenny looked at the remains of the mobile phone then at the lawyer's smug expression. *SMACK!* She slapped him across the face with all the strength she had. "Don't you dare behave like a vicious gangster in front of me and my friends. Now get out before we call the police."

Francisco fell back against the table. He raised his hand as if to return the blow, then touched his fingers gently to the scarlet weal on his face. "Aren't you a tough cookie, Jenny? Well, well, who'd have guessed?" He gave a grim smile. "I was trying to be nice to you, don't you know how much I like you? Well, it's too late for that now, it's time to get serious."

He reached into his jacket pocket and took out a gun. A pistol with a plastic grip and frame and a metal barrel. "If anyone gives me trouble, I'll shoot them. It's really very simple, you misbehave, you get shot."

"Stop acting like a bloody idiot, Francisco. This is not some kind of a children's game. Put that stupid gun away before you hurt someone, and get out of here." Jenny went to grab the weapon from his hand.

The lawyer held her away with one hand and pointed the gun at one of the wall cabinets. A loud blast rang out, followed by the sound of smashing china, and a round hole appeared in the wood. Jenny screamed and turned away from the pistol. An acrid smell filled the room.

"This is not a stupid gun, Jenny. It's called a Sig Sauer P226 DAK, it cost me three hundred Euros and it kills people. Now get back, all of you and give me some space. He poked the gun into Jenny's shoulder, then flashed it around the room, pointing it at each of the others in turn.

Jenny backed away from him, away from the weapon, and went to stand beside Leticia. She was rooted to the spot, trembling with shock and fear. Jenny put her arm around her shoulder to instill some calm into her. Neither of them had ever seen a handgun before, except on TV and in the movies, even less been threatened by one.

She wiped a hand across her brow, the hand she'd slapped the lawyer with, and noticed a faint perfumed aroma. Putting her fingers to her nose, a memory flashed through her mind. *The hotel bedroom in Geneva. After the break-in, the smell of perfume. It was Hugo Boss aftershave, the same as at Charlie's funeral. Could he have followed us to Geneva? What on earth's going on here?* She pulled Leticia closer, trying to convey a sense of composure.

Francisco picked up the house phone from the kitchen counter and listened for a moment. "Good." He gestured at Adam. "Switch your mobile off and put it here." He took Leticia's mobile from his own pocket and laid it down on the table. He had already switched it off.

Adam didn't move. He couldn't believe this Spanish lawyer was in the house, waving a loaded pistol about. The only gun he had ever seen close up was a big, old service pistol in Hanny's office drawer. He had come across it when he was a kid, looking for change to buy candy. This maniac was holding one that seemed a lot more dangerous. An ugly, square shape, like a weapon in an American gangster movie. It looked deadly. He was paralysed with fear.

Leticia tried to overcome her terror. She spoke in Spanish, desperately attempting to get through to the man. "Why are you doing this? We're friends, there's no need to threaten us. We've done nothing to hurt you. Put the gun away and tell us what this is about."

"*Feche sua boca, cadela!* Shut your mouth, bitch!" He shouted in Portuguese. "I said mobile off, Peterson, now!" He raised the pistol and pointed it at his head.

Leticia gasped with shock at this obscene outburst in her native tongue. She fell back against the counter, her hand to her mouth, her eyes wide with shock and fear. Adam pulled out his mobile phone, his trembling hands fumbling to switch it off, then placed it on the table.

"That's better!" He took another swallow of the wine.

Now, Jenny realised that it was the lawyer who had interfered with the house phone and probably the outside electricity. *He must have been in the house, downstairs in the machine room. He must have a key!* Despite her rising panic, she tried to talk to him quietly and calmly to find out what was going on. "Francisco, you're a lawyer, you haven't been trained to hurt people but to help them. We've done nothing to harm you, why are you threatening us?" *Be sensible, reasonable.* She was shutting her mind to the dreadful thoughts that were closing in on her. She didn't want to let them in.

"You're partly right, Jenny. You and Leticia haven't harmed me, unlike your father-in-law and his cronies. As a matter of fact, I have nothing against you, but because of this useless prick, my 'reward' for three years work will be half of what it should be."

"He's talking about the delay in the sale of the remaining diamonds. He's after the money, it's quite clear." Adam had come to the same conclusion as Jenny. Despite his fear, he looked disgustedly at the lawyer. "Just an amateur bloody crook, trying to steal our money."

Francisco smashed his pistol across Adam's face, knocking him off the chair onto the floor again. The women screamed and went to help him, but were pushed back by the lawyer.

Adam sat up and shook his head, his hands to his face. Blood was running from a cut on his forehead and a red gash on his cheek.

His left eye was starting to close up and his cheekbone felt as if it was broken. He tried to push aside the pain and fear and adopt a tone of bravado. "Is that the best you can do? Women and children are your usual victims, I suppose." He staggered back to his feet and leaned against the counter.

Francisco lifted the weapon again then thought better of it and pushed him onto the bench seat. Leticia sat down next to him, dabbing the blood from his face with the wet towel.

"You stupid Irish bastard, I'm not stealing from anybody, I'm reclaiming what's mine. It's you lot who are the thieves. It's not your money in the first place, it's money that was stolen. You think people died making that money so that you could steal it? Think again!" He poured himself another glass of wine and sat at the table, waiting for his words to sink in.

Jenny tried to analyse his words. *He knows about Charlie and Nick, and that Adam was born Irish. He knows about the money, the people who died, the sale of the remaining diamonds. But how?* She looked blankly at the other two.

She tried a new tack. "You're wasting your time trying to steal from us. There's nothing here in the house to steal. Just leave now and we'll forget the whole thing."

"Thanks for the advice, but no thanks. I'm not some dumb-ass Spanish lawyer. I know exactly where the money is and how to get it and you're going to help me."

"You're saying that you're not who you pretend to be, is that it?"

"Well the first thing you can do is stop calling me Francisco. It's been over a year now and I'm pissed off with it."

"So, what's your real name?"

The lawyer swigged his wine again. "I was baptised Raymundo Jesus Melo d'Almeida, after my father's brother, Henriques. Does that ring a bell?"

Oh my God! Henriques was the owner of the mine in Angola, the one who had a brother. He's Sergio's son! Jenny sat down beside the other two, racking her brains to try to understand this new twist. Adam looked at her vacantly, he couldn't remember who Henriques was, but Leticia was staring at the man in amazement. The truth was dawning on her too.

He said to her, in Portuguese. "*Entende agora?* You understand now?"

"So you're Angolan, like me?" Leticia replied in Portuguese. She had finally found some kind of link that might help them deal with this monster.

"*Não sejas tão estúpido, cadela!* Don't be a stupid bitch!" He switched back to English. "Neither of us is Angolan. We were both lucky enough to get out of that hell-hole thirty years ago. Except your family got to Portugal and found work and we ended up starving in Brazil. Big difference! So now you're a first-class Portuguese and I'm a second-class Brazilian"

She tried to remain calm. "But now you can change that. If you want a share of money from the diamonds, why don't we just talk and arrange things? There's no need to hurt us."

"I think you're missing the point." Adam sat up straight, his mind clear. "He doesn't want a share, he wants it all. Right, Raymundo?"

"It's Ray, actually, and yes that's right, it's only fair. Those diamonds were mined by my father and we got nothing and you've got everything. If it wasn't for him, you'd be scavenging to survive like we were for thirty years in Rio."

"So how did you end up in Brazil?" Jenny tried to get him to continue talking. *Let him tell his story. Play for time.*

"You couldn't imagine in your worst nightmare, Jenny. We had to flee from Angola after Henriques was killed. The soldiers came, the rebels came, Cunhal's people came. My parents had to run for their lives, with two kids. I was just a year old and my sister was three.

"It took us weeks of running and hiding before we found a boat for Rio, and my mom got so sick she never recovered. She died before I was two. We starved for thirty years. My father couldn't work and we had nothing. When I was eighteen I had four jobs and we were still starving." He took another drink. "You people have no fucking idea of the real world."

Jenny was cursing her lack of attention, there had been so many clues she had missed. *I've got to keep him talking. Let him get it all off his chest. Finish his story.* She said, "So, how did you become a lawyer? Come to Spain and work for José Luis?"

"You must be joking! Me, a lawyer?" He laughed cynically. "Just because that senile idiot José Luis was fooled by my diplomas, it doesn't make me a lawyer. The man's a moron, he doesn't even know how to check a CV."

"You mean all that business about Berkeley and Washington and New York?"

"You shouldn't believe everything you hear. I've never even been to school. I read a few books about international law and taxes, it's not complicated. The rest of my story was total rubbish. I arrived in Malaga a year ago and José Luis was stupid enough to hire me. Then I was able to get into Charlie's house last year when he was sick. Pretty clever, eh?"

"So you found out everything about the diamond business?"

"You mean the Angolan Clan? Of course. I read it on his computer at the house. It's actually an interesting story, but just a high class robbery in the end. And the office files told me all about the bastard he had with his housekeeper. Disgusting old pervert."

Leticia gasped and took Jenny's hand, looking at her helplessly. *Where did this creature come from? How do we get away from him?*

Jenny squeezed her hand. The man was a monster, but if all he wanted was money they must be able to work it out. She kept on trying to make him talk, to placate him. "So what happened in Brazil? Why did you come here to Spain?"

"When my dad was almost sixty, he got a job with a company that was set up to process rough diamonds. He got me a place in the company, helping out. "After I'd made a little money I went off to the States. Just drifting around. That's where I got the Spanish passport. Friend of mine called Francisco, everybody called him Paco. Fell down a crevice, poor sod.

"Then I called home and my sister told me my dad had had a heart attack, so I went back. They'd fired him from his job. He told me they'd been getting rough diamonds from a company called International Diamond Dealers, IDD. He was convinced they were pre-war Angolan diamonds, like the ones he'd mined."

"But why didn't he say something to his company, or to IDD?"

"And get fired from the only job he'd had for thirty years? Don't be so bloody naïve. Anyway, I found it out myself. I looked IDD up on Google. Do you know Google? It's amazing. I found the IDD directors, Charlie Bishop and Nick Martinez. Bingo!"

"How did you know the names?"

"I didn't. But my dad remembered Henriques telling him about three guys who were going to save their bacon, Olivier, Charlie and Nick. Too big a coincidence to be wrong."

"So you came to claim your family's inheritance." Against her better judgment, Jenny found herself starting to sympathise with the Angolan.

"First I had to read a few books and save up some money. I got a job in a casino and looked after my sister and my dad. He took a long time to die. He weighed nothing at the end. I couldn't even afford a headstone for him. Do you have any idea what I'm talking about? Shit!"

He swigged from his glass. "Two years ago, I was ready. I worked the winter season in Haute Nendaz, near Geneva, then came down to Malaga. Just in time, almost too late."

"But how did you know José Luis was Charlie's lawyer?"

He laughed out loud at this question. "Stupid woman. I just told you, you understand nothing about the real world. Have you ever heard of Gloria Smouha?"

Her hand went to her mouth. She looked at the others. *What had happened to Gloria?*

D'Almeida saw the name register. "Have you ever seen her?"

He was teasing her, playing some kind of a game. She shook her head.

"She's forty-something, looks like a horse, but she's a hell of a screw, never had it for bloody years. She fell madly in love with me. They mostly do."

He'd said he'd stayed near Geneva. He knew where the IDD office was and he must have known about the keys. It was him who broke into our rooms. Everything suddenly fell into place. Gloria had betrayed them, for sex. Ray was an extremely clever man, a corrupt, brutal monster, but very clever. She had to find a way to play him along. *But how?*

She glanced at the stainless steel clock on the wall. It was twenty past ten. Her brain was calculating times, people. Laurent should be there by now. *All he wants is the money.* She tried to win some time. "Leticia's right. I'm sure we could arrange some kind of a fair share. We can talk it through with the other partners. One of them's coming here any minute."

"Oh yes. Your friend Monsieur Bonneville is expected, *n'est-ce-pas*? Well, I'm sorry to inform you that he has been delayed, permanently delayed!"

The other three looked at each other blankly then back at d'Almeida. *How did he know about Laurent coming down?*

Jenny resisted the temptation to ask him anything more. "Stop trying to scare us, Ray, it won't work. I just spoke to him a little while ago and he'll be here any minute. Right, Leticia?"

"For sure he's coming. He called us twice." A spark of hope kindled in her mind, she'd almost forgotten that Laurent was on his way.

The Angolan reached into his jacket pocket and took out a BlackBerry phone. He put it to his mouth, speaking into it with a convincing French accent. "Oui, allo. Ici Laurent." He looked at Jenny, grinning like a naughty schoolboy. "Sorry, Mme. Bishop, Laurent had a nasty accident, there's a lot of it about. He definitely won't be coming, ever."

"What do mean, an accident, you mean he's dead? You murdered my friend, a sixty year old man? You cowardly piece of shit." Adam jumped up and tried to grab the gun. D'Almeida held him off and kicked him in the groin. He fell to the floor again, doubled up, pain shooting through his body.

"I told you, he had an accident. Dangerous business, skiing in Verbier when there's nobody around. For amateurs that is, not for professionals. The point is, I thought you had sold the diamonds like you were supposed to and the money was in the account. Bonneville was no longer necessary, just another complication. I don't like complications." He gave Adam a malicious stare. "And I don't like people who don't do what they promise."

The women listened to this exchange in silent fear. The man that Jenny had talked to and invited to their house was not Laurent Bonneville, Charlie's partner. It was the man who had killed him. This Angolan self-confessed murderer. Suddenly their lives had been invaded by robbery, brutality and now murder, and the murderer was standing in front of them, boasting of his crime.

He'd set a trap for them and they had walked right into it, like lambs to the slaughter.

Jenny thought about what he'd just said. "*Just removing a complication.*" *Who's going to be next*? She asked herself. *What does he really want?*

Adam had managed to pull himself up to the counter again. "OK, so you're not just an amateur burglar, you're also a bloody amateur murderer, you disgusting piece of African filth."

D'Almeida grabbed him by the throat, the gun against his head. He stared into his eyes, looked around at the two women, then back to Adam. "Nobody who kills four men without getting caught could be considered an amateur. I'm a professional, and if you don't shut your fucking mouth, I'll make it five, happily."

EIGHTY-SEVEN

Sunday, 27th April, 2008
Marbella, Spain

Espinoza was driving on the hard shoulder of the *autopista* past the Marbella Golf Club at over a hundred kilometres an hour. He could see the blinking, yellow lights of the emergency vehicles as he slowed down at the scene of the accident. There were cars all over the road and he'd heard on his radio that there were casualties. The rain was pouring so hard that visibility was almost zero. He assumed that was the cause of the crash. In any case traffic accidents weren't in his jurisdiction and he couldn't stop.

A yellow-jacketed police officer waved him on and he saw two Municipal Police cars and an ambulance as he went past, so the response seemed to be well organised. He drove back onto the autopista. He was almost at Marbella, his lights flashing and siren blaring. But he'd lost a lot of precious time. The dashboard clock said ten fifty.

My God! He's either a pathological killer or completely insane. But where's Laurent? Is he really dead? Jenny's mind was spinning. Trying to digest all of these frightening revelations and somehow devise a plan of action.

D'Almeida checked his watch. "We're wasting precious time with all this chat. Jenny, there's a roll of tape in my raincoat pocket. Go and get it. Any stupid moves and someone gets shot."

Jenny said nothing and went out to the hall. She seemed to be in a frightened daze. A moment later she came back into the room with a roll of duct tape and put it on the table. She had taken off her cardigan and placed it on the end of the bench seat.

D'Almeida poured the last of the Rioja, took another gulp and put the empty bottle back on the counter. He pointed the gun at Adam, "Turn around, asshole, hands behind you. OK, Jenny, wrap the tape around his wrists, tight. Don't play games, fasten his wrists together."

Jenny looked despairingly at Adam. He put his hands behind him and gestured to her to do as he said. She wrapped the tape around his wrists, bit it with her teeth and snapped it off.

"Sit down on the floor." Adam did as he was told. "Now tie the tape around his ankles."

D'Almeida made her fasten up Leticia in the same way. When she and Adam were on the floor, he got Jenny to help him to sit them up against the cabinets, under the window.

"Right, your turn now." He put the pistol on the table and stepped across to her. "Give me the tape and turn around."

She handed it over to him. As he reached out to take the roll, it fell from her hand and rolled across the marble tiles.

"Clumsy bitch!" He stooped to get the tape.

Jenny grabbed the empty wine bottle from the counter and smashed it down at his head. Sensing the movement, d'Almeida looked up and raised his right arm to fend off the blow. The bottle struck him on the right shoulder and bounced out of her hand. It shattered on the tiles, fragments flying through the air. He fell to the floor with a cry, holding his injured shoulder.

Leticia and Adam watched in disbelief as she quickly retrieved the serrated knife from under her cardigan on the bench seat. The knife that she had taken from the mugger in the park and placed out of reach of unwary hands. On the shelf above the coat rack in the hall.

"Lie still, or I'll stick this in you!" She waved the knife in his face.

"You fucking piece of work! You've broken my shoulder!" He reached up with his left hand to hold the edge of the counter and pull himself to his feet.

"I told you not to move!" She smashed the knife down onto his fingers. He pulled his hand away and the blade slid across his knuckles. He fell to the floor again, blood welling from a gash on the back of his hand. The knife rebounded off the granite surface of the counter, jumped from her grasp onto the marble tiles and skidded across to the other side of the kitchen.

She turned, grabbed the pistol from the table and trained it on him, holding the weapon with two hands, arms outstretched. "Don't move or I'll pull the trigger. I don't care if I kill you, it's what you deserve."

The Angolan gazed implacably into her eyes. He pressed the back of his left hand to his mouth, staunching the flow of blood from the incision then wrapped a handkerchief from his pocket around the wound. "Good try, Jenny, I'm very impressed." He pulled himself to his feet. "Only problem is, you forgot to release the safety catch, stupid woman!"

Jenny knew nothing about guns. She looked at the pistol, trying to work out what to do. D'Almeida stepped towards her, his hand out to take the weapon. She pointed the gun at his head and pulled the trigger. A loud crack rang out. The recoil from the gun pushed her backwards and pulled her hands up so that it was pointing over his head. A small hole appeared in the middle of one of the copper bottomed pans hanging over the ceramic hob and they heard the smack of the bullet penetrating the plaster.

She jumped back and dropped the gun onto the floor in fright. D'Almeida stooped down and snatched it up.

"Christ Almighty. I don't believe it!" He turned the gun on her. "You're a quick learner, Jenny. Firearms lesson number one, aim at the chest and pull the trigger. This gun doesn't have a safety catch, but it does have quite a kick. If I didn't need you to perform for me later on, I would show you how it's really done."

He transferred the gun to his injured hand and gave Jenny a

mighty smack across the face with the other. "Now, behave yourself. I'm starting to get really annoyed with you."

She fell against the table, holding on tight to it to stop from falling down. Her knees felt weak and her face and head were pounding.

"Leave her alone, you cowardly bastard! Was that your speciality when you were a gigolo, beating up women?" Adam was trying desperately to sound brave, but inside he was shaking with fear. He knew the man intended to kill them. It was just a matter of time.

D'Almeida ignored him and went back to stand by the counter, covering them with the handgun. He rubbed his shoulder with his left hand, wincing with the pain, blood from the wounded hand leaving a stain on his jacket. "Normal service is resumed. Come here, Jenny."

She came slowly back to the counter, breathing deeply. Trying to calm herself down after the rush of adrenalin that had spurred her on through the fight. A feeling of overwhelming tiredness swept over her and her cheek was burning where he had hit her. Suddenly, she felt like a little girl, frightened and lost amongst a group of crazy adults. She tried to push the fear and pain away. Tried to think and plan. She'd seen him wince when he rubbed the damaged shoulder. *It must be badly bruised, or maybe even broken. How can I take advantage of that?*

"Now, turn around and put your hands behind you." Holding the gun against her back with his injured hand, he clumsily wrapped the tape around her wrists. He pushed her down to sit with the other two then did the same to her ankles.

Adam tried to encourage her with a smile, despite his fear. He'd been mesmerised by her attack on the Angolan. He hadn't seen her in action before. He couldn't credit his eyes when she smashed the Angolan's shoulder with the bottle. And to have smuggled in that murderous looking knife. She'd almost cut his hand off. *My God! She's twice the man I am. I'm sitting here, incapable of doing anything, while she's trying to save us all. And she almost succeeded!*

Leticia had her eyes tightly closed. She pretended it was just a dream, a bad dream. If she didn't look at him, maybe he would go away and leave them without harming her little boy.

"Very good. Now we can get on with our business." D'almeida

picked up the wet towel, rinsed it in the sink, and wrapped it around his hand. The bleeding had lessened but it was stinging and his fingers were cramping up. He sat in one of the kitchen chairs in front of the hostages and swigged back the last of the wine. After the initial shock of the blow, his shoulder was starting to throb with pain. A deep, nagging ache that ran through his shoulder and up into his neck. His head was pounding and he felt nauseous. He shrugged off the pain and looked at Jenny, a cynical smile on his face. *You'll pay for that, later,* he seemed to be thinking.

He studied his watch then pulled out a pack of cigarettes from his inside pocket and lit one up. The cigarette smouldered a lot, it looked wet. He inhaled the smoke deeply.

Adam's head and cheekbone were throbbing. He could hardly see from his left eye, the wound on his cheek was stinging and his face was covered with dried blood. He realised, like Jenny, that their only hope was to attempt to win time. To give them a chance to find a way out, or be rescued. *But by whom? On a Sunday night in Marbella in the torrential rain. Who's going to come to our rescue? This maniac will kill us and the gardener will find our bodies tomorrow morning.* His blood ran cold at the thought.

Desperately trying to pull himself together, he looked straight at the Angolan, taunting him to get him to continue talking. "So, it's the *Raymundo Melo d'Almeida, the Homicidal Maniac Show,* is it? How come you're bragging about four murders? Taking your sick dreams for reality? Is that how you jerk off every night before you go to sleep?"

D'Almeida ignored the jibe. "If you make the calculation, it isn't very profitable work. Two years of hard graft, busting my balls to learn how to pass for a lawyer. Raising enough money to come and get back my family's fortune and then working for that idiot José Luis. And what's my reward in the end? Twelve million dollars for four bodies. That's only three million a head. If you'd made the last transaction it would be six million a head. That's twenty- four million dollars. Now that's worth killing for. I felt like killing you when I found out you missed your deadline. But I waited. No need to rush, we've got time."

He came over to Adam and kicked him in the hip, almost absent mindedly. "You just can't get good help these days."

Adam winced, but asked him again,"What are you talking about, four bodies?"

"Well, as I said, there's been a lot of accidents about." He took a drag on the cigarette. "I mean, take Charlie, for example. That was most unfortunate, he seemed like a nice guy. But he'd had a long and happy life, and it was virtually painless. Anyway, I don't approve of screwing your employees when you're nearly seventy years old."

"It was you who printed out the contract from Charlie's machine, after you drowned him in the pool." Jenny's heart was beating as if it would burst. She felt sick, light-headed, as if she would faint. Over the last week, Charlie had become a kind of a hero figure to her, he had achieved so many amazing things and never even spoken of them. Now she realised that his life had been snuffed out by this crazy, monstrous creature.

Leticia burst into tears at this cold blooded confession. She had loved Charlie and he had loved her. Their child would grow up without a father because of this man's murderous greed and hatred. She was incapable of speaking, terrified by the ranting, evil creature who had suddenly burst into their lives. Frightened of saying something that might put them into even more danger. Not just the three of them, but also her son, asleep just twenty-five metres away. She closed her eyes and tried to shut the scene out of her mind, but there was more to come.

"I already had the contract from Bonneville's BlackBerry," the Angolan continued, "I was just confirming the date, to be sure the money would be there." He looked balefully again at Adam, took a drag on the cigarette and went on, "Anyway, don't get so upset about Charlie. Just think of that shit, Raffael, or Roddy, as he called himself in the bars and on the Internet. That bastard didn't deserve to live. The guy was a paedophile, a bottom feeder. A sick, disgusting animal, who preyed on kids and vulnerable women. He never did anything worthwhile in his whole existence. He got his money from his old man and he pissed it down the toilet all over the world. Wherever he could buy the crap he fed on.

"Huge, fancy apartment on Central Park, full of the most sickening filth I've ever seen. You couldn't imagine it in your worst nightmares. Do you know his Internet name was "*Silver Rod*"? Fucking arrogant pervert, he was a disgrace to mankind. Made me ashamed to be born in Angola. That was a service to humanity getting rid of him. I hope he burns in hell!"

He didn't mention Cindy, the prostitute. *Shame about her,* he thought. *Nice tits.*

"You crazy, pathological, inhuman piece of garbage. How can you sit there and tell us that you've served humanity by murdering four people. Tell us that they were accidents, that they deserved it, trying to justify your insanity to us. You're never going to get away with this. You think that the police won't come looking for you in every corner of the world when they find this out?" Adam struggled to get out of the bindings. His wrists were red raw with the twisting, but the tape wouldn't give.

"Ok, you don't believe me? Here's a genuine accident, the fourth one. Actually, it was the first one, but it makes no difference."

"NO!" Jenny gave a strangled scream. She felt a red mist come down over her eyes. She knew what was coming next. She had known for a long time but she didn't want to hear it, she didn't want to know for sure.

He ignored her and pulled on the cigarette again, it was almost burned down to the end. "I don't know how you can live in that wet and miserable place, Ipswich, Jenny. It was freezing rain when I was there. I rented a car, just to have a look around. I was kind of reconnoitring, you know? I found the garage and by an amazing stroke of luck, while I was sitting there Ron came out. I could see him under the street light. I'd seen him when he came to stay at Charlie's house when he was sick. He was with some young chick. He walked her across the road to her car, gave her a big kiss and she drove off.

"He stood looking after her for a while, stupid prick. It was dark and wet and when he stepped onto the road to go back in, my car just kind of jumped forward and knocked him over. I honestly didn't mean it. It was just an accident. I was really lucky there was no damage to the car. Just a couple of tiny scratches on the wing. I went through the car wash twice and gave it in at the airport. They didn't see a thing, didn't charge me.

"I was surprised when I got back and José Luis told me he was dead. That's when I realised that accidents can be very unpredictable.

So I became a bit of a specialist. I got rid of all the complications like that, and now here we are, just the four of us together. Clever me."

"You murdered my husband. You knocked him over and left him to die in the rain, in the dark, on the road, like an animal. YOU SADISTIC, FUCKING, MURDERING MANIAC!" Jenny couldn't go on. She couldn't find any more words. She just wanted to crawl away into a corner and sit and cry. To grieve for Ron at last, knowing who was responsible for his death, why he had died. For no good reason at all, just for money.

"But Jenny, he was having an affair, he was screwing his secretary or whoever. I was doing you a service, people shouldn't treat marriage so lightly. You're a lovely woman, he should have respected you."

"YOU HAD NO RIGHT! You had no right," she sobbed. "He was my husband. For better or for worse he was my husband and I loved him. We had a life. I had a life. You took away my life and left me with nothing.

"So Ron wasn't perfect. Are you? Am I? Is anybody perfect? NO! In your deranged mind you've decided that all of these people are better off dead and you're some kind of avenging angel, cleaning the world up. WELL, YOU'RE NOT. You're a sick, twisted, calculating, cold-blooded murderer. That's all, nothing more, nothing less."

She sat forward, staring the man down, trying to force her words through, into his mind. "Maybe you had a miserable childhood. Yes, you lost your mother and you lost your father. Is that our fault? We've lost our families too. We didn't start the war in Angola. We didn't make you work at four jobs to feed your family. We were unaware of your existence. It's not our fault, how could we possibly know? What could we have done? What could Charlie and his friends have done? Nothing, nothing at all! Because in the middle of a war-zone nobody knew anything about your father or his family. You've just told us they were running and hiding, so how could anyone know?

"You think you've all been cheated? Maybe that's true, but it doesn't give you the right to go around murdering innocent people. Did it ever occur to your sick mind to contact us and tell us this story before starting on your murder spree? Before kidnapping us and tying us up in our own home?

"And in the end, why are you doing it? For justice? To avenge your family's honour? To put the world to rights, as written in the bible according to St. Raymundo?" She laughed contemptuously. "No, you're not doing it for any of these reasons. You're doing it for only one reason. Just for the money. All the money! And that's why you're threatening to kill us too, just so that you get everything. Not a share. Not what your father, or Henriques would probably have asked for and we would certainly have given, willingly and we still would. But it's not enough is it Ray? It's got to be all or nothing. But in the end, that's what you're going to get, nothing, because that's what you deserve. You're going to get what you deserve and it won't be a bucketful of money."

Jenny was now past tears, she was as mad as hell. She sat back against the wall and turned to Adam and Leticia. "Don't let this crazy, sadistic pervert get to you. We'll make it through this, I know we will."

Adam looked at her in consternation. He hadn't known the details of Ron's death. This murdering bastard had just admitted that he'd killed her husband and he'd been more concerned about scratching the car than about the man's life. And Jenny had given back as good as she'd got. She'd refused to be browbeaten by his insane ravings and pathetic excuses. She was incredibly brave. Braver than him. He was scared to death. The man was a maniac, a pathological maniac. There was no way they would get out alive.

Leticia sat immobile. White faced, still saying nothing. She was terrified that d'Almeida would discover that Emilio was asleep just along the corridor. She was praying silently under her breath. Praying that if she died, her son would survive.

"Well, Jenny, that's all very well, I have my point of view and you have yours. I do love a good argument, but time is short and we have business to attend to." The Angolan stubbed out his cigarette in the sink and looked at his watch. "Almost eleven, time to send some messages, with your help."

Wincing again at the movement, he took out Laurent's BlackBerry and a sheet of paper from his inside pocket and placed three small electronic keys on the table. Thanks to Esther Rousseau, they were labelled 'J', 'L' and 'A'. "Let me see." Holding the BlackBerry clumsily in his left hand he typed a few phrases and numbers from the paper onto the keyboard. "Twelve million dollars exactly. Sounds good, doesn't it? Right, Jenny or Leticia, tell me your PIN number."

"Don't do it! He's going to transfer the money by the Internet. He'll never be able to do it if you don't give him the number. He's murdered four people and he probably killed the real Francisco too. Let him rot in hell." Adam was still struggling to get free.

Leticia opened her eyes and looked at Jenny. Neither of them spoke. D'Almeida picked up the pistol and went over to Adam. He pressed the muzzle against his forehead. "You have exactly five seconds. Then whatever brains this idiot has got are splattered all over the floor."

Adam's face blanched, but he said again. "Don't do it, he's bluffing."

The murderer's finger tightened on the trigger. They heard the first click of the double action firing mechanism. Adam closed his eyes, waiting for the shot. His mind spun away, thinking of all the things he wouldn't be able to fix. He'd attacked and robbed Stanford. He'd lied to his brother and provoked the car crash that had killed him. He'd faked letters and showed them to his parents and to Nick and the others. And after all that, he'd tried to steal from these two women. He'd tried to steal from his new partners. He felt nothing but contempt for himself. *Payback time,* he thought.

"Thirteen, ten, sixty-nine." It was Ron's birth date. He had been a Libra, true to his sign.

"Thank you, Jenny." D'almeida put down the gun on the table and entered the PIN number in the BlackBerry. He looked at his watch, it was ten fifty-five. He entered the security number from the electronic key marked 'J' and pressed *Send.*

"Well, that wasn't too bad was it?"

Adam was sweating. He'd been prepared to take the bullet, but he knew it was stupid. Sometimes he was stupid. *Why die for a few million dollars when I've just inherited a fortune.* He thanked God that Jenny had intervened. He looked at her sitting next to him. Chin up, her cheek bruised, but a determined look in her eyes. *I'll make it up to you, I'll make it up to everyone,* he thought.

She smiled, saying, *Don't worry,* silently with her lips.

"Did Schneider tell you that they have banks all over the world?" d'Almeida said smugly, bragging his inside knowledge. "It's really convenient on a Sunday night when you've got an important transfer to make. Well, maybe not for you, but definitely for me."

The sound of La Marseillaise blasted out. It was the BlackBerry. He read the message. "Please enter second PIN. *Muito bem. Merci, Esther,*" he said.

He walked over to Leticia, BlackBerry in one hand, gun in the other and said to Adam, "So now you know why you're still alive, even though you don't deserve it. What's the second PIN number? And don't let's go through that same charade again, because this time it's Leticia who'll die. Then there's only you and Jenny left. And if I don't get the money, then I really have no reason to leave anyone alive." He stood over the young woman and held the revolver against her head. Leticia had her eyes shut tight again, praying silently.

"Well, Adam?"

"You complete and utter shit, Fifteen, zero three, ninety-eight." It was the date of his brother Greg's death.

The Angolan entered the number and the updated security number from the third electronic key. He pressed *Send* again and sat back down. A fraction of a second later, twelve million dollars started out on a six-stage route from Geneva to the Marshall Islands, Goa and three other insignificant tax havens, before arriving in a numbered account at the Union Bank of Panama, awaiting d'Almeida's visit.

"That was a clever system that Charlie devised," he said. "It just made it complicated to get the three of you here together. But as you've seen, I'm pretty good at sorting out complications."

The hostages didn't respond to this show of arrogant self-congratulation. They sat in silence, now clearly seeing the trap that d'Almeida had set for them. And wondering just how it would end.

And he got me to do the job for him. The spider and the flies. Not for the first time, Jenny recognised the twisted brilliance of the murderer.

A few moments later the phone rang once more. He looked at the message. "Well, it seems that I'm twelve million dollars richer than I was this afternoon. It's not as good as twenty-four, but it'll have to do. Lucky me!"

Adam cursed Schneider's name. *That stupid, hyper-efficient Swiss banker.* His Internet banking, high security system had just cost them all the money in the Angolan Clan account. A chunk of data, containing twelve million dollars, had left Klein, Fellay and was speeding through the ether on its way to God knew where. The money was gone. *Who the hell is Esther, anyway,* he wondered?

D'Almeida typed in another short message on the BlackBerry, then pressed *Send* again. He turned his attention back to the three hostages. "Now, what shall we do next?" He said with a broad smile on his face.

EIGHTY-EIGHT

Sunday, 27th April, 2008
Lyon, France: Marbella, Spain

Esther Rousseau installed herself in the middle seat of row 23 on the left side of the plane. She had gambled on the flight not being busy and maybe getting three seats to herself. Unfortunately the window seat contained a very large and sweaty Frenchman, who looked at her in the same way that Schneider had. Just below the neck. She put a wrap around her shoulders and when all the passengers were aboard she moved into the aisle seat.

The flight had been delayed for half an hour because of the storms across Europe, but she hoped that she'd still be in time to meet Ray's plane. She kept her mobile phone on, in her hand, until they were ready to taxi away. Just as the announcement came to switch off phones, a short text message arrived. It said simply, *"12 million. XXX."* Esther laughed out loud and settled back in her seat.

Espinoza had just turned off the autopista at La Cañada and was racing up the Coin Road towards Las Manzanás urbanisation when the radio-telephone squawked again.

"What is it?" He shouted.

Martín's voice screeched out. "Where are you? We've all been here for ten minutes."

"There's a crash on the highway. I'm less than five minutes away. What's happening?"

"Still the same. No activity in the neighbourhood. I'm not surprised, in this pissing rain."

"Hang on. I'm almost there." He pushed his foot flat on the floor and acelerated up the deserted road. The dashboard clock said ten fifty-eight.

D'Almeida winced again as he put the BlackBerry back into his inside pocket. "Now, last item on the agenda. The keys to the safety deposit. Since I can't have the money from them, thanks to this Irish imbecile, I'll take the diamonds, they're no good to you lot. When things settle down, I'll sneak back to Geneva and get them out of the vault. Nobody else will know about them once you three are gone. That's the balance of my reward, another twelve million, poetic justice. So, I know there are two keys, where are they?"

Jenny's brain started racing again. *Leticia's not up to this. She'll crack and give him the key to save Emilio. But there could be a chance here.* She looked across at Adam, trying to work out a plan of action.

The other two had only really registered the words, *once you three are gone*. It was a sentence of death. They would not leave the house alive!

"You first, ladies. Where's your key? Leticia, have you got it?" He held the pistol against Jenny's head. "Speak up, I haven't got time to waste."

Leticia sat immobile, paralysed. Unable to move a muscle or to make a sound.

"I asked you a question, Leticia, where's the key? I'll count to three, then Mme. Bishop will be reunited with her husband. And it will be your fault."

"She hasn't got it. I took control of it when we left Geneva." Jenny was totally convincing. D'Almeida looked at her. Knew she wasn't lying.

"So you've got one and Adam's got the other. Clever of me

finding out about the double key security, wasn't it?" He laughed, delighted to brag about his inside knowledge again. "So, where is it, Jenny."

"It's in a safe place in my bedroom. The first one at the top of the stairs."

Adam and Leticia looked blankly at her. What did she mean? She didn't have a key.

Before d'Almeida could notice their air of surprise, she went on, "In the third drawer of the bedside cabinet, there's a key inside a decorative box. Not the porcelain one, the other one. The key opens up the mirror above the dresser and there's a safe behind. The combination is..."

"Jenny, shut your mouth. It's so bloody complicated, you're going to show me. My head is pounding like a drum and I haven't got all night." He looked at his watch again. "I've got a date, a very important date. You're coming with me to get the key, and no tricks this time."

He turned to Adam, "And where's your key? You must have it with you and it better be easy to find. I'm in a hurry."

Adam played along with Jenny's game, whatever it was. He said. "When you get Jenny's, I'll tell you where mine is. Provided you release us and let us go. That's the deal."

D'almeida laughed. "Fine with me, Irish asshole. You give me the key and the access code and I leave you in peace." They knew this promise was worthless, but it might win them a few precious minutes.

Clumsily, protecting his injured shoulder, D'Almeida pulled Jenny to her feet to lead her to the hall. She fell to the floor. "I can't get upstairs with this tape on, I can't even walk."

"Useless bloody woman!" He took out a pocket knife and cut the tape around her ankles. She struggled to stand and he pushed her to the staircase in the hall and up the stairs. The pistol was pressing against her back. Jenny's mind was whirling again and she was hyperventilating. *There must be a way to turn the tables here.* It was the last opportunity she'd get before he realised she was lying about the key. But what could she do with her hands tied behind her?

He switched on the bedroom lights. "Right. Where's the bloody key?" He pushed her inside.

The lamps illuminated the spacious room and the double bed in front of them. Lying on the bed was Fuente, looking as if he'd just fallen into the fountain again. His long, thick hair was soaked through. A large damp patch surrounded him on the counterpane. He looked up at the intruders, his big green eyes blinking in the lamplight.

"Fuente, you poor thing, you're absolutely drenched through. Did we frighten you from the cellar. I'm sorry, we didn't know it was you. Did you have to climb on the roof to get back in?" At the sound of Jenny's voice, the cat lay on its back, purring. Inviting her to stroke it.

"What the hell are you worrying about a stupid cat for? Get that filthy animal out of here." Realising that Jenny could do nothing with her hands tied, he pushed past her and bent down to grab the cat. It jumped up and lashed out at him, raking its claws across his cheek. D'almeida put his hands to his face and staggered back towards the door.

Jenny ran straight at him, smashing solidly into his damaged shoulder with her own shoulder, pushing him backwards from the doorway onto the landing. Before he could recover, she hit him again, knocking him over the top stair. D'Almeida lost his balance and with a cry, plunged down the staircase, his head smashing onto the hall floor below with a sickening thud.

Racing down the stairs after him, she checked his body. He was unconscious and blood was trickling from his face and head onto the marble tiles. She looked around for the gun. It wasn't in sight. *He must be lying on it.* She tried desperately to turn his body over, but with her hands tied behind her, it was impossible.

She left his motionless body and ran into the kitchen. Before the amazed stares of the others, she sat down on the floor to pick up the serrated knife, her hands behind her back. Turning the blade inwards, she sawed through the tape around her wrists. She dropped it twice when she caught her flesh with the blade. Free now, she went over and released Adam and Leticia from their bindings.

"What happened, what did you do?" Adam rubbed his wrists, sore from the tight binding.

"I'll tell you later, there's no time now. Quick, Leticia," she instructed, "Get Emilio, we'll take the Vitara and get out of here."

Leticia ran along the corridor to the bedroom and came back into the kitchen with her son in her arms. He was still asleep.

"Where are the car keys?" Jenny was searching the table and the counter.

"In my bag in the hall." Leticia turned to lead them out of the kitchen.

"You fucking cow! You almost killed me." D'Almeida was standing in the doorway, holding onto the frame. He was shaking his head and swaying slightly on his feet, but pointing the pistol firmly in their direction. The scratch across his cheek looked like parallel ski tracks running down to his chin. The blood dripped onto his shirt collar and the lapel of his jacket.

The three hostages stared at him in dismay. They had been within seconds of escaping, but time had run out for them now.

He looked at his watch again. "Thanks to you, you interfering bitch, I'll have to come back for the keys. But now I know you haven't got one and you've turned out to be a big complication. I dislike complications. Goodbye, Jenny." He turned the pistol on her and squeezed the trigger.

EIGHTY-NINE

Sunday, 27th April, 2008
Marbella, Spain

Espinoza's car screeched to a halt in front of the security post at the entrance to the urbanisation. Two blue and white Policía Nacional cars and a Municipal Police car stood waiting, engines running. The security guard sat in his cabin looking at the CCTV screens. Six police officers crowded in the doorway, trying to shelter from the rain.

"Well?" Espinoza went to look over the man's shoulder at the screens.

"Still nothing. Some guy arrived in a taxi about an hour ago and went in through the gate. He had bags with him, like he was going to stay. Since then I've seen no movement at all."

"Why aren't the garden lights on? You can hardly see anything."

"I don't know. They didn't come on tonight but I figured it was this shitty weather had knocked them out."

Espinoza's mind went into overdrive. "What about the inside lights?"

"I can just see the reflection of some lights. The downstairs ones have been on all night and the upstairs just lit up. But we're not allowed to see in the house."

"What's going on Pedro?" Martín, the Policía Nacional officer, lit a cigarette, blowing the smoke out the door.

"We've got a possible hostage situation up at Charlie Bishop's house." The Chief Inspector gave them a rapid summary of the evening's happenings. "The child is there too. I don't know what's going on but my nose tells me it's not looking good. And I don't like this problem with the outside lights."

"So what's the plan?"

"We go up to the house by both streets, from the west and from the east. I want the lights, the sirens, the works, to try to scare the hostage taker. At the house we block both sides of the entrance. If the gate's locked we go over the wall and get inside the house, firearms cocked and ready. I think this guy, if he's there, is a multi killer, so take no chances. If he blinks, hit him. If we're wrong and there's nobody, no harm done. But I'm not taking bets on it."

"*Inspector Jefe*." One of the local policemen spoke up. "There's another road, well, more of a dirt track, going up around the urbanisation, at the back of the Bishop's house. It goes by the new *Avenida Parc* development. Why don't me and Felipe go up the Coin road and drive in from the other end? Then we've got all the exits covered in case he gets out the back." Espinoza gave his agreement and they screeched away from the urbanisation. Back towards the main road, to come in from the opposite direction.

"Take this." The Chief Inspector handed the security guard a walkie talkie unit. "If you hear or see anything, press this button and shout for help."

The remaining three cars set off towards York House. Martín on the east side of the golf course and Espinoza and the third car on the west side. The storm had returned and occasional flashes of lightning were reflected on the surface of the lakes between the fairways. The police cars sped up the deserted access roads, sirens blaring, emergency lights flashing. Competing with the streaks of lightning and rolls of thunder.

The property looked dark and menacing. Light was escaping from a few rooms on the ground floor and one upstairs room.

Espinoza parked on the grass verge, almost touching the wall. The accompanying car straddled the width of the road, blocking any passage. The main gates and the small gate were closed. He waited until the third car drew in against the other side of the gate. Everyone drew their pistols and waited for a few seconds. No one appeared in the driveway. They couldn't see the main door, situated at the side of the house facing the waterfall.

He called down to the guard at the entrance to the urbanisation, "Anything?"

"Nothing at this end," came the distorted reply.

"Right." The Chief Inspector got out of the car into the downpour and shouted to his men above the noise of the rain, "On the roofs, over the wall." The six policemen climbed onto the car roofs and prepared to scale the three metre wall.

NINETY

Sunday, 27th April, 2008
Marbella, Spain

As d'Almeida squeezed the pistol trigger, Adam jumped forward, making a grab for the gun. There was a loud report and he fell back against the wall, a burning sensation in his hand. The bullet had pased between his fingers and thumb as he yanked the gun muzzle aside, but he had hardly even felt it. Now the powder burns were starting to sting.

"You stupid shit! I'm going to shoot you first for that, you Irish bastard." He trained the pistol on Adam's chest. His head and shoulder were throbbing so badly he couldn't think straight.

Adam braced himself. He had known that there wasn't much chance of surviving, but at least he'd tried to save Jenny. He'd tried his best, although it wasn't much good.

D'Almeida hesitated, trying to concentrate, thinking about the diamonds. *I can't shoot him, he must have one of the keys.* Then his confused mind realised that he didn't know who had any of the keys. It could still be Jenny, even after her play acting. And he still needed to obtain the access code.

Leticia had her arms tightly around Emilio, putting her body between the gunmen and her son. The sound of the shot had woken him and he looked around sleepily and started crying, confused at the unfamiliar surroundings.

The Angolan shook his head and turned the gun away from Adam, pointing it at Leticia. "Shut that bastard up or I'll shoot both of you. My head's ringing like it's got a bell in it."

Jenny saw the approaching lights through the window. "It's a siren, a police car. It must be Espinoza." The noise accentuated until it was a constant blare, coming towards the gates.

The Angolan ran to the window and saw the cars pulling up at the gates. "I don't fucking believe it!" He turned to face them, waving the pistol. "Who called the police? How did you call the police?"

He studied his watch again. "Shit!" He looked desperately around the kitchen, thinking furiously. Everything had been going so well and now it had suddenly gone terribly wrong. He was out of time. If he shot them all he would never get the keys and the diamonds. He'd have to wait and try again, but he needed a bargaining chip, some kind of leverage. He herded the others at gunpoint to the back of the room and pushed them into the pantry. Shoving Leticia back against the wall, he grabbed Emilio from her arms. "*Diga adios a seu pequeno canalho.* Say goodbye to your little bastard, Leticia."

"No!" She screamed and tried to wrest the little boy from his hold, but he pushed her back again so that she fell on the floor. She pulled herself to her feet, trying to get hold of her son. The Angolan pointed the gun at Emilio's head and stepped back to the door. Adam pulled her back, holding her away from the murderer. She tried desperately to wrestle free from him, shouting and struggling in her frenzy.

D'Almeida held the screaming child against his legs, still aiming the gun at him, and stepped out of the room. "This is not over. I'm coming back and if you want this kid to stay alive, you'd better get me those keys." He slammed the door shut and they heard the key turn.

"Emilio!" Leticia screamed and pummelled at the closed door. Then she collapsed to the floor, curled up in a ball, huge sobs racking her body.

The Angolan went to the front door, took his navy blue raincoat, wrapped it around the struggling child and fastened it with the belt. He switched off the hall light and opened the door. It was pitch black and freezing cold. The rain was bouncing up off the ground and water was cascading over the flower beds and down towards the driveway. He looked towards the entrance gate and saw the lights from the police cars. Taking hold of the raincoat belt with his good hand, he hoisted Emilio up like a parcel. He threw the key to the pantry door into the garden, put on his fedora, slammed the door and ran towards the flooded staircase.

Esther refused the inflight meal. She hardly ever ate meat and all they had on offer was a ham and cheese sandwich. She lay back in her seat, trying to block out the noise of her neighbour chewing with his mouth open and slurping his beer. She was calculating whether she'd be in time to meet Ray's flight. It would take her over two hours to collect her bag and get to Luton on the shuttle bus from Heathrow. Her plane was scheduled to arrive at eleven thirty, UK time, and his flight was due in at two in the morning. He would soon be boarding in Malaga, on his way to meet her. Twelve million dollars richer, thanks to her clever inside work at the bank.

She fell into a doze as the aircraft cruised through the stormy skies across France towards the English Channel. She dreamed of running up to kiss him in Luton airport. Then hiding out for a few days in a small hotel room somewhere. Making love all day and night while they waited to swap the cold climate of the UK for the sun-soaked beaches of Panama.

D'Almeida pounded up the staircase at the side of the stream. The stairs were awash with water, splashing up and soaking his shoes and trousers as he ran. The stream was now a river, rushing down alongside him in a torrent, boosted by the torrential rain. His head, face and shoulder were killing him. But his thighs, muscled by climbing and skiing over the last few years, pushed him rapidly up towards the perimeter wall. Under his arm he was carrying Emilio, wrapped in the blue raincoat. The little boy was crying and screaming, but his voice was virtually unheard against the sound of the rain and running water.

The tree branch was wet and slippery and he almost dropped Emilio. He scrambled over the wall and staggered across the forested area, climbed into his car and dumped the screaming child on the back seat. The car screeched away on the dirt track towards the Coin road. The pain from his shoulder was intensifying, it felt as if hot needles were being pushed up into his neck. The bleeding from his hand and face had stopped, but his hand was stiffening up. The cut was severe. His head felt as if it had been hit with a steam hammer and Emilio's crying wasn't helping, but his mind was calculating madly, trying to find a solution to this new situation.

He looked at the clock on the dashboard, it was eleven fifteen. He had a seat on the Luton flight, leaving at half past midnight from Malaga. There was also an ID card in his pocket in the name of Jean-Pierre Bastien and the photograph wasn't very good. He could easily have got through immigration. He wondered fleetingly if the guy's body had ever been found in Haute Nendaz when the snows melted. *Stupid French asshole, trying to steal from me. Who tries to steal from a ski bum? He knew I had nothing to steal.*

His plan had been perfect. *I would have been in the UK with Esther by two in the morning. Lost amongst the millions of illegal immigrants before breakfast time. Before the gardener came and found the bodies in York House, before the alarm went off in Spain. Easy to get out by boat to Ireland, then on to Panama when things quietened down. Easy to sneak back for the diamonds when the time was right.*

Thanks to that bitch, Jenny Bishop, it was no longer a perfect plan. He was hurt. He was covered in blood. He didn't have the safety deposit keys and he had the police on his tail.

Shit. Those interfering fucking police! Where the hell did they come from? He knew he couldn't make it to the airport now, the police were too close. But he had the child. If he could get onto the highway he might stand a chance. They wouldn't take any risks with Leticia's little boy. *Twelve million dollars. The hard part's done, stay calm and you can make it.*

Emilio was still screaming for his mother, the noise intensifying the pain in his pounding head. "Shut your mouth, you little bastard!" He drove as fast as he was able.

NINETY-ONE

**Sunday, 27th April, 2008
Marbella, Spain**

Espinoza jumped down from the wall, stumbling and almost falling into the rush of water that was pouring down through the gate. The others followed on his heels up the driveway, running through the deluge, holding their guns ready as they ran. The stairway from the drive was flooded and they splashed up to the entrance porch. The front door was locked but through a side window they could see lights in the kitchen and living rooms. They hammered on the door but no one came.

Espinoza shot the lock away and they ran inside. He was terrified at what they might discover. They raced through the hall into the kitchen. It was deserted, the floor littered with broken glass and pieces of duct tape. They heard the sound of banging and shouting from the pantry door at the back of the room. There was no key in the lock.

"Who's in there?" Espinoza shouted.

"It's Jenny. There's three of us here. We're alright but we can't get out."

"What's been going on?" Espinoza motioned one of the policemen forward. He brought out a vicious looking knife, like a jemmy with a sharp blade, and tried to force the door open at the lock.

"It's Francisco, he's a murderer, he's got Emilio. We're all right, but he's taken the boy with him." Jenny shouted the words out over the noise of the jemmying. There was a crack as the blade snapped off clean in the policeman's hand.

"Francisco? You mean the lawyer?"

"He's not a lawyer, he's a fake and a killer!"

"Jesus Christ!" Espinoza took out his pistol. "Can you stand to the other side of the door from the lock? I'm going to shoot it out."

There was a loud gunshot. The door swung open and the three hostages emerged.

Adam blurted out, "He's got Emilio and he's got a gun."

The policeman looked at Adam's bloody, battered face. "Who are you?"

"He's Adam Peterson, a friend from South Africa. He saved our lives." Jenny looked around desperately. "Francisco's just escaped. He's carrying Emilio. He can't have got far."

Espinoza looked around, "Well, he hasn't come out the driveway and he hasn't passed the guard at the entrance."

Leticia cried out in Spanish. "He must have gone up the garden to the top wall. He's going round to the Coin road. You've got to find him, he'll get away with Emilio." She ran to the door and down the staircase, forgetting that she couldn't follow them alone.

Espinoza spoke on his walkie-talkie. "Felipe, he's a villain and he's coming your way. He's armed and he's got the kid. Stop him but no shooting!" The policemen ran to the door. "*Vamos.* Miguel, we'll follow him up the back. Martín, you go around behind Felipe and block the road." He turned to Adam, "I'm calling an ambulance for you."

Adam had wrapped a handkerchief around his burned fingers. "I'm fine. I don't need an ambulance. I'm coming with you to nail that bastard."

The policeman decided not to waste time arguing. "What about you?" he asked Jenny. She nodded and they followed the officers out of the kitchen, running after Leticia, down the drive and out the small gate. The two women climbed into the back of Espinoza's vehicle and Adam went with Martín, the Policia Nacional officer. They sped down to the main entrance and separated. Two cars swung around to the right to drive up the side of the urbanisation and follow the direction of Ray's car and the other made for the Coin road.

D'Almeida had the sidelights on, but not the headlights, the police didn't need any help. There were no street lights and it was so dark that only the occasional flashes of lightning helped him to see the road. When he reached the forested area there was no light at all. He took the corner too fast and had to press hard on the brake. The car skidded on the slick, muddy track. *Shit!* It slid towards the trees. He swung the steering round again and felt a stab of pain from his injured shoulder, winced, and tugged the wheel too far over. The back end of the car spun round and hit a rocky outcrop. He pulled the wheel round the other way, crashed the front wing into a tree on the verge and there was the sound of smashing glass.

The car wouldn't pull back in reverse. It was a front wheel drive and the wheels were spinning in the mud. *Lousy piece of crap!* He got out and pushed the front end out of the mud, his shoulder screaming with the effort. It was a small car, not very heavy. It slid over the slick surface and he got it onto the track again. He climbed back in, soaked and hatless, his trousers covered in mud and blood on his face and jacket. His shoulder and hand were throbbing with pain and his head was pounding. Emilio was screaming even louder than before on the back seat. In Spanish, he shouted, "Keep your mouth shut, you little shit. You're my ticket out of here."

He pulled away and switched on the headlights this time. One was dead, the other pointed away at an angle, but he could see the road. The noise of sirens was approaching from behind as he accelerated along past the forest and looked in his mirror. The sky was lit by the flashing lights of the police car. They were maybe a kilometre behind. He drove through the curve before the *Avenida Parc* project, still accelerating.

"There he is!" Coming from the opposite direction, Felipe Montero jammed on his brakes and swung the wheels across the track in front of the construction site. The two officers jumped out of the car, guns in hand.

The Angolan pulled the steering violently to the left and stamped on the brake, desperately trying to avoid the police vehicle. His car mounted the verge and smashed into an upright supporting the huge sales sign. The support was pushed over backwards and the sign detached itself with a loud crack. It fell sideways, held only by the one remaining post. The back end of the car hit the barrier, pushing it over so that the stanchions were pulled almost out of the sodden earth. The car was stuck against the barrier.

"Come here you little prick." D'Almeida grabbed Emilio from the back seat with his injured hand and climbed out into the rain, his gun in his right hand.

"Police! Stop there! Drop your weapon and put down the child." As Felipe stepped forward into the light from his car's headlights, d'Almeida raised the pistol and shot at him. The policeman clutched his chest and dropped to the ground. The Angolan turned round as Espinoza's car pulled up behind him.

As they raced along, Jenny breathlessly told Espinoza about d'Almeida. How he'd killed at least four people and he'd just stolen a fortune from them by Internet. She omitted the part about the Angolan Clan and the remaining diamonds. It was too complicated.

"You were right, Chief Inspector, I'm sorry, but you were right. There was a motive, there was money in Switzerland. He's the killer. He killed my husband and my father-in-law and two other friends, in New York and in Switzerland. He's not Spanish, nor American. He's from Angola and Brazil, a pathological murderer. I can't believe you got here in time, he was just about to shoot us because he's got the money now. We should all be dead. I can't believe it."

Leticia said nothing. Her mind was hardly functioning. She kept repeating to herself, in Portuguese, *Please God, save Emilio. Please God.*

At the dirt road Espinoza had to slow a little, it was pitch black. The siren was still blaring and the emergency lights were flashing red. As they drove through the edge of the forest the branches above their heads glowed scarlet. The rain fell through the glow like a blood-coloured waterfall. It was like driving through hell.

Jenny said, "But I don't understand what made you come over here so quickly? Our messages weren't very urgent. When we phoned we didn't know that Francisco was really someone else. We just saw something in the computer that put the wind up us. "

"You can thank your email to Pires da Silva for that. A young woman in Washington put two and two together and faxed me. Then you said you might have some evidence and your phone was off. So I feared for the worst. It's just instinctive." He rubbed the mist from the inside of the windscreen. "Look, you can see his tail lights, we've got him. Just in time"

Leticia roused herself. "Señor Espinoza, we are only in time if we save Emilio. We must stop that monster. Please promise me that you'll save my son."

"We've got him now, Leticia, he can't get out, he's in a box and we're about to close the lid. He won't do anything to Emilio. It won't help him and we'll have him completely covered." Espinoza sounded more confident than he felt. Crazy people with guns did crazy things. "Please try to stay calm and leave it to us. This is our job."

More lights appeared ahead. They were at the *Avenida Parc* development. Espinoza slowed again as they approached, then stopped, the other car pulling up alongside them. They climbed out into the torrential downpour, to be confronted by a nightmare scenario.

NINETY-TWO

Sunday, 27th April 2008
Marbella, Spain

A small black car was jammed against the barrier around the excavation. Two wheels were on the grass verge and the driver's door was open. One headlight was on, shining into the void, the other was dead. Broken glass littered the verge and there were skid marks on the track. The *AVENIDA PARC* sales sign was hanging from a single upright at a crazy angle above the car and one of the fence support posts was lying back, just holding in the ground, almost detached from the barrier. On the other side of the road, the local police car was parked diagonally across the track, its headlights illuminating the scene. Felipe, the local policeman, was lying on the ground on his back under the pounding rain. He was bleeding from the chest, the blood forming a dark pool on the dirt road. The other policeman was sheltering behind the open door of the car, holding a pistol in his hand.

D'Almeida was standing at the side of the black car. He had no raincoat or hat on. His face and clothes were covered in mud and blood and the rain was pouring down over him, soaking his jacket and trousers. He was holding Emilio in front of him.

The little boy was still wrapped in the blue raincoat, standing immobile. Too frightened to make a move. The Angolan was pointing his gun at the child's head.

"Emilio! Emilio! *Oh, Dios mío.*"

The boy looked around at the sound of Leticia's voice, squinting through the rain in the half-light. "*Mamá, Mamá.*"

Leticia tried to run towards her son. "*Vengo, Emilio.* I'm coming."

The Chief Inspector stopped her. "Don't move. You'll endanger your child. Wait, we'll get him." He barked out an order to the remaining policeman.

Just then, the other blue and white police car pulled up behind Felipe's vehicle. Adam got out with the two officers. He stared in disbelief at the scene, then looked across at Leticia and Jenny.

He shouted to the Angolan. "What do you want, Ray, if that's really your name? What do you want the boy for? Are you a paedophile like da Silva was?"

"Keep your fucking nose out of this, you interfering bastard. Shut your filthy mouth up. I've shot one asshole already. How'd you like to be the next?" D'Almeida tightened his hold on Emilio, pressing the gun against the terrified child's neck.

"Why don't we make a swap, you take me and let Emilio go? What do you think, you cowardly Angolan pervert? Let the kid go and take your chances on a grown up." Adam stepped away from the police car. The officer tried to grab him but he avoided his grasp. He walked towards the murderer. His hand and head were throbbing with pain and he could hardly see straight. The whole side of his face around his eye and cheek had turned black and blue. It hurt him even to speak, but he went on. This bastard was going to kill that innocent little boy. *Better he kills me,* he thought. *I've managed to screw things up really well. Time to do something decent for a change.*

"Leave this to us, Señor, this is a police matter," Espinoza shouted. "Step back please and don't interfere, he might harm the child." He pulled the women back behind his car. He didn't like the way things were shaping up. Taking out his gun, he disabled the safety catch. Shouted to his officers to do the same.

"Everybody get back or the kid's a goner. Walk away and leave the police car. I'm cold and wet here. It's time for me to leave for warmer climes." D'almeida lifted Emilio up in his arms and pressed the gun against his head. The little boy started screaming again, fighting to get free and looking around in the darkness for his mother. "You've got ten seconds to get away from the car. If not. Bang! It won't be my fault, it's up to you to decide."

Adam continued to walk slowly towards him. "What do you say, Ray? Leave the kid and take me. You can't kill everybody. I've.."

"I warned you, Irish bastard!" The murderer shifted his aim with the pistol and fired it at Adam. There was a flash from the barrel and the shot rang out loudly above the sound of the storm. The bullet caught him in the left side of the chest and spun him round. A second shot came and he fell to the ground on his stomach, blood starting to soak through the back of his coat from the exit wound.

Leticia screamed Emilio's name and tried to run towards him. Jenny put her arms around her and held her back behind the police car.

As the gun recoiled, d'Almeida felt another deep spasm of pain from his shoulder. The fingers of his left hand were cramping and his hold on Emilio slackened. The little boy squirmed out of the raincoat onto the ground and crawled away from his grasp then scrambled up and ran towards his mother. "*Mamá, Mamá.*"

The Angolan pulled up the gun again, pointing it at the running child. Espinoza aimed his pistol with both hands and fired two shots into the middle of the murderer's chest. Leticia ran to scoop up her son, and brought him back behind the police car, holding him to her, out of harm's way.

The gun blasts slammed d'Almeida back against the barrier. The weakened stanchion lifted from the sodden earth and the fence fell to the ground. With a cry, he fell backwards towards the edge of the crater. As his head went back, he saw the *AVENIDA PARC* sign hanging right above him. He reached up to grab the frame around the edge of the huge billboard with his left hand. The cramped fingers throbbed with the effort, but he managed to hang on and stay on his feet. He lifted the gun to return Espinoza's fire.

His weight caused the remaining upright to lean towards him and the sign slipped further down, forcing him backwards over the crater. He realised that he couldn't hang on with his left hand alone because of the pain in his fingers. Desperately trying to avoid falling into the void, he dropped the pistol. He took hold of the sign with his other hand, ignoring the stabbing ache in his shoulder and attempting to pull himself back onto his feet. The upright leaned further over and creaked, almost painfully, as it tried to withstand the uneven contest. The billboard fell slowly down towards the excavation. His hands gripped tighter until his knuckles whitened as he tried to prevent the massive board from collapsing behind him and taking him with it. The effort forced the veins on his neck to stand out like cords.

The group stood stock-still as they watched the scene, unable to move, mesmerised by the final dramatic act of the night's events. Leticia held her son in her arms, and turned his head away from the awful sight. D'Almeida, blood soaking through his shirt from the pistol wounds, was desperately clinging onto the sign and slowly slipping backwards towards the deep pit behind.

With a sharp crack, like another gunshot, the remaining upright snapped half way up and the sign fell away towards the crater, dragging the murderer back off his feet. Still hanging on to the billboard, he was projected back over the edge of the excavation, flying headfirst and backwards into the void. He passed through the glare from the car headlight and with a final cry, disappeared into the darkness. Into the depths of *Avenida Parc.*

Jenny ran over to Adam. He was lying on his stomach, still breathing, still conscious. She knelt beside his head, whispering into his ear. "Adam. Thank God you're alive. It's all over. D'almeida's gone. Hang on for the ambulance. Just hang on and you'll be alright."

Leticia carried her son over towards them. She leaned down to speak to him. "Thank you Adam. For Emilio's sake. Thank you."

He opened his eyes and looked at her, struggling to speak. There was blood around his mouth. "It wasn't just for Emilio. It was for him and Greg."

The Policía Nacional officer motioned them away. He placed a cushion from his car under Adam's head, a rug over his body. Leticia took hold of Jenny's hand and they walked back to Espinoza's car.

Martín, the other officer, was kneeling beside Felipe. His body was sprawled out in the road, motionless. He checked the pulse at the wrist and at the neck, then looked across at Espinoza and shook his head. The Chief Inspector was standing at the edge of the crater, looking down into the void and shouting into his mobile phone. Organising an ambulance and other back up support. He saw the sign from Martin and shaking his head, he spat down into the darkness. Then he looked over at the two women. He nodded at Jenny, *Gracias, Sra. Bishop.*

Martín drove the women and the little boy back to the house. The other Policía Nacional officer took notes as they gave him the details of Adam's family name, his parents, his Durban address, that his mother was in Florida for his father's funeral and they should call her there, and other responses to his questions. It all seemed so complicated to Jenny when they had to explain it like that.

When they arrived at York House the rain had slackened off, but water was still flooding down to the street from the staircase. The small gate was still ajar. Jenny turned the emergency switch again to open up the big sliding gates and Martín drove up the driveway. He insisted on searching the property from top to bottom then saluted and went to sit in his car. Espinoza had ordered a twenty-four hour guard in case the murderer had any accomplices. Martín waited for the first patrol to arrive before leaving.

Emilio was fast asleep again, his fingers gripping his mother's hand. He was dirty and scratched, so Leticia gently woke him and they tended his wounds and bathed him. She put him back to bed in the small bedroom, tucked him in and they kissed him goodnight again. He fell asleep immediately. She left the door open so they could hear him should he awaken. They hoped that he would soon forget the trauma of the last hour. Or, if he didn't, that he might recall it only as a bad dream.

The women cleared up the debris in the kitchen and mopped up the traces of blood in the hall. They talked quietly about the dreadful scenes of violence they had just witnessed and wept at the deaths of d'Almeida's victims, some known, some unknown. They thanked God for their own and Emilio's safe delivery and prayed that Adam would also survive the murderer's savage attack without permanent harm. They talked for a long while, trying to put the night into some kind of perspective so that they could accept it and understand it for what it was. The work of a madman. A brilliant, pathological madman.

Finally, Jenny said, "It's strange, but this story didn't just start tonight, or last week, or even with Ron's or Charlie's death. It's been going on for a long time, for over thirty years. The day Charlie and his friends brought those diamonds from Angola they started a chain of events that kept going, like a train or a juggernaut. Nothing could stop it and tonight it finally caught up with us.

"And Adam and Ray were caught up in that momentum. They were both after the diamonds, but for different reasons, and tonight their paths crossed. The momentum finally caught up with them and we happened to be in the way." She shivered, remembering the awful events of the night.

"But it's over now, Jenny, isn't it?"

"I don't know. I hope so, but I honestly don't know," she replied. "There are millions of dollars of diamonds sitting in a vault in Geneva and you have only one key. I'm sure that Ray didn't have one, or he wouldn't have been so obsessed with getting them both. So maybe it wasn't him who broke into our rooms. Was Adam's stolen or did he lose it, or is there another explanation?"

"You mean that someone else stole it and is still out there, waiting to try to get the second key, the one I've got?"

"I can't tell you. But we may be the only surviving members of the Angolan Clan and we can't get those diamonds with one key and we probably can't recuperate the stolen money. It's probably a very good thing. The diamonds and that money were never ours. They belonged to many people, most of whom have disappeared. Maybe we should just leave them and their fortune in peace. We don't need it and we don't deserve it."

When they had talked themselves out, Leticia carried Emilio upstairs and laid him in the double bed in Jenny's bedroom. The counterpane had dried out. There was a slight stain to be seen, but there was no sign of Fuente. She slept in the bed next to her son and

Jenny slept in the bedroom next door. It was four in the morning before sleep came, but it was a dreamless sleep.

Esther Rousseau waited in the arrivals hall at Luton airport until the very last passenger from the very last flight had left. Ray hadn't turned up. She had called his BlackBerry at least a dozen times, but it was switched off or out of range, she didn't know which. She didn't leave a message. Ray had told her never to do that, something about it being traced.

She looked up when she heard the ground staff attendant's question. "I'm fine thanks," she replied, then got up and walked out of the building, pulling her suitcase behind her. She had five hundred pounds in her purse and a case full of beach clothing. It was freezing outside.

NINETY-THREE

Monday, 28th April 2008
Miami, Florida

Chief Inspector Espinoza called the Miami Police Dept. on Monday at six o'clock in the morning, Florida time. He had worked through the night after returning to Malaga and had received the report from the hospital at five thirty am in Spain. He decided to grab a few hours sleep in the office before making the call, he didn't want to give the family such news in the middle of the night. He recounted to Detective Sergeant Giannada a complete history of the night's events, to complete the three page report that he'd faxed through earlier. Then he gave him Nick's address on Ocean Boulevard.

Giannada and his partner, Detective Debora Allen, rang at the intercom in the lobby at seven-thirty. Rachel and Hanny hadn't come up from their bedroom yet and Suzie was preparing breakfast when she answered. It took her a few moments to understand the policeman. On hearing that they needed to speak to Mr. or Mrs. Peterson, she knew there was something wrong. She opened the door as the two officers emerged from the elevator. "It's Adam isn't it?

What's happened to him?"

When they advised her that they could only explain to Adam's parents, she hurried downstairs to wake them, her mind filled with dread. Hanny and Rachel were still in their dressing gowns. They came into the living room in a daze, not understanding why the police officers were there. Rachel repeated Suzie's question, "What's happened to Adam?" Giannada asked them to sit while he made his report.

Detective Allen sat with Suzie on one of the couches. She took her hands in hers. Hanny sat with Rachel opposite Giannada, holding her hand. They all waited in fearful silence for the policeman to speak. He didn't mess around, he kept the story brief and to the point. He'd been contacted by a Chief Inspector Espinoza, of Malaga, in Southern Spain. A serial murderer had tried to kill Adam, Jenny and Leticia, while robbing them in their house in Marbella. He had been caught and killed. But Adam had been shot twice, trying to save Emilio, Leticia's son. The women and little boy were unharmed. Adam had been taken to the hospital and had been in surgery for three hours.

Hanny's face blanched and he took Rachel's other hand, squeezing until it hurt. They were too shocked to speak. Rachel's mind went back to the waiting room of the hospital in Durban, ten years ago. Then they had lost their first son. Surely it couldn't be possible that they had now lost their second. *Adam has to come back for Nick's funeral tomorrow*, she thought to herself. *He has to come home*. She held her breath, praying that the news would be different this time.

The sergeant paused and took a deep breath before continuing. "I'm very sorry to be the bearer of such terrible news, but your son, Adam, died at five am this morning, Central European Time, in the intensive care unit at the Marbella General Hospital, in Spain. The cause of death was breathing failure subsequent to lung damage sustained from a bullet wound."

"No! It can't be true. Adam's coming back today for his father's funeral. It's not possible." Rachel turned to Hanny. "Tell them. Tell them he's coming back. It's a mistake. Tell them, Hanny."

Hanny couldn't speak. Tears ran down his face as he held Rachel tightly in his arms, stroking her face and head, her wracking sobs piercing him like sharp arrows. Detective Allen put her arm around Suzie's shaking shoulders.

Giannada waited respectfully before continuing his report. "It seems that the first bullet was lodged dangerously close to Adam's heart and his right lung was torn by the second bullet. The left lung was working overtime and threatened to push the lodged bullet into the heart. They tried to patch up the torn lung again and again, so his breathing would be stabilised and they could get out the bullet before it moved. But the damage was too severe. It just kept tearing and the lung wouldn't reflate."

"And so he suffocated to death. Oh, my God. Adam." Rachel collapsed back into Hanny's arms.

Giannada said nothing more, leaving them to cope with the shock and distress.

After a few minutes, Rachel's weeping subsided and Hanny said, "What can you tell us about this killer? This man who killed our son and his friends. What kind of a monster was he?"

Giannada told them what Espinoza had told him of d'Almeida's history and his aborted plan. "Espinoza lost one of his men, a local policeman," he added. "The Angolan just shot him out of hand, just another murder. God knows how many people he's killed all together. He told me he'd never witnessed anything like it."

He continued, "I'm afraid there's another thing. They were too late to prevent him from transferring a large amount of money from Adam's account, over the Internet. I doubt it can be traced. Usually these crooks transfer the money several times over, until you can't find or retrieve it."

The others knew, even if the policeman didn't, that the reason for this attack was the Angolan Clan. *Those cursed diamonds from more than thirty years ago.* Fleetingly, Hanny hoped that there would be no consequences for them or the women as a result of the police enquiries. All of them had already suffered enough.

When the two officers were satisfied that they could do nothing more, they gave Hanny the contact details for Espinoza and the hospital. Arrangements had to be made for Adam's body to be returned home to Durban.

Hanny thanked the officers and escorted them out. Rachel and

Suzie were holding each other tearfully on the couch. He closed the door behind them and stood in the hall, alone, tears running from his eyes as he tried to come to terms with the loss of his remaining son. His adopted son. Rachel and Nick's son. In just a few days Rachel had lost her lover and her son. He knew that the next few months would be much more difficult for his wife than for him. He went into the kitchen to make tea and brought it in and poured it for the women.

Rachel sipped her tea distractedly, her mind wandering everywhere. Memories came flooding back, some happy, some sad. Apart from her father, whose life had ended at the age of seventy-six, she had lost three men that she loved dearly, taken from her before their time. Her lover, Nick, lost to her for many years, then taken by a vicious cancer. Her stepson, Greg, victim of a tragic accident. And now Adam, her true son, murdered by a madman, for money.

She looked over at Hanny. He was speaking quietly to Suzie, comforting her in her loss. Just as he had comforted Rachel every day of their life together, for the last thirty-four years. Even during the last days of Nick's illness, Hanny had never begrudged her the long hours she spent tending to his needs. He knew that she had never stopped loving Nick. It was something that he was prepared to accept because he loved her so much himself. Now, Nick was gone, Greg was gone and Adam was gone, but Hanny was still there. As he had always been. At her side.

At that moment, Rachel took an important decision. *When I get home, I am going to hand over the management of the hospice and give up my consulting work at the hospital. From now on I'm going to share every minute of my life with Hanny, for as long as we have together.*

She went over and gave Hanny a loving kiss on the lips. Then they sat together and talked with Suzie.

NINETY-FOUR

Monday, 28th April 2008
Marbella, Spain

"Please come in Chief Inspector Espinoza. José Luis, how are you?"

Before calling Giannada, Espinoza had phoned José Luis. He gave the lawyer a similarly succinct account of the night's happenings and the tragic news that he'd just learned. The death of Adam Peterson. For once, the old man was speechless.

"Can you come over to York House with me? We need to close this off with the two ladies. I think it'll be better if you're there."

He called Jenny and sadly informed her of Adam's death. Although the women were half expecting the news, it was a terrible blow. Yet another death caused by d'Almeida in his murderous quest to steal their fortune. As she had foretold, he had ended up with nothing, but he had left them with a dreadful legacy. She thought about Adam's parents, attending Nick's funeral whilst preparing for their remaining son's. It was too much for anyone to bear.

Espinoza agreed that he and José Luis would come over at one in the afternoon. Jenny wanted to have time to talk to Leticia and agree on what they needed to tell the policeman. As José Luis kept saying, *sometimes it's better not to know everything.*

For the first time since she'd come down to York House, Jenny led the way into the sitting room. The marble floor was covered with silk rugs from Iran, in soft pastel colours, and there were several fine pieces of antique furniture, as well as the comfortable couches and armchairs. A lovely old grandfather clock stood against one wall and many paintings, a mixture of classical and modern, adorned the walls. Ellen's magnificent Steinway grand stood towards the back of the room. Jenny hadn't had the time or the nerve to try it yet. She made a mental note to try to do so before leaving.

The two men sat facing the French windows looking over the swimming pool across to the golf course. It was completely flooded. The weather had settled again and the reflection of the sun was sparkling on the natural lakes created on the fairways by the flood water. It looked as if there wouldn't be any golf for a while. Dozens of striped whoopee birds could be seen, pecking away at the soft, wet turf, in search of insects and grubs for their lunch.

Juan was still mopping down the terraces and pool area. He'd had to catch several fish which had overflowed from the lake and ended up in the swimming pool. Apart from that, the property looked beautifully clean after the rain. No dust, no dirt. It reminded Jenny of Geneva. As if everything had been taken away, spring cleaned and put back in place again.

Leticia came in looking forlorn, having left her mother up at the lake with Emilio. He had taken a liking to feeding the fish. They had not told Leticia's parents the full story of last night's events. It was over, and the less said about it the better. Emilio seemed to have put it out of his memory. He hadn't mentioned it yet and she prayed that he never would. She shook hands with Espinoza and kissed José Luis on both cheeks.

The lawyer looked weary. "Leticia, Jenny, what can I say? I'm so terribly sorry that you've been put in harms way through my stupidity. I blame myself completely. It's an awful situation, and it's all my fault, I had no idea, no idea at all."

"Well, let's try to make sense of this business. This murderer seems to have devised a very complicated plot, but I'm not sure what the real reason for it was. Why don't we start at the beginning? Jenny, can you enlighten us?" The policeman switched on a small recording device and settled back into the depths of the armchair. Jenny reflected that it was the first time she'd ever seen him look comfortable.

"This is for you, Chief Inspector." She handed Espinoza a printout of the Angolan Clan narrative, explaining where it came from and what it described. Then she and Leticia recounted their journey through Charlie's maze of clues. They left nothing out. The story poured out of them, a kind of catharsis needed to regain their peace of mind. After the many tragedies that had occurred, first in Angola, then over the last few months, culminating in their terrifying ordeal with d'Almeida, they wanted nothing more than to regain that peace of mind.

After almost an hour, the two women ended their story with the transfer of the funds from the Angolan Clan account and their near death experience before the policemen's arrival.

"So that's why he needed to get you together with Adam. To get both PINs. Of course! Now I see the reasoning behind the whole plan. He got rid of Raffael and Laurent and then Charlie. Ron was already.. I'm sorry, Jenny, gone, so he needed you two and Nick, either in Geneva or in Marbella. Then either of you could authorise the transaction, together with Nick. It must have been quite a shock when he learned that the one person he'd left alive was now dead. He must have had an accomplice at the Swiss bank. That's how he got the account details and the security devices. Brilliant!" He looked extremely satisfied with the plan, as if he'd devised it himself.

"Esther!" Leticia remembered what the Angolan had said, "*Merci, Esther.*" "You're right, it must be someone in the bank. She was helping him, like Gloria."

"Right, I'll get the Geneva police to check on the bank employees. And who's Gloria?"

When they explained, Espinoza made a quick note, then continued, "He'd made a big mistake, killing Bonneville before he knew that the deal was done. Now he knew he couldn't lay his hands on the whole amount. His only chance would be to somehow get the two keys from Nick and from you in Geneva and steal the diamonds from the vault."

The women looked nervously at each other. They didn't know what the policeman's attitude would be to the matter of the lost or stolen key.

Espinoza seemed not to notice their discomfort, and went on, "And when he found out about Nick and Adam it was too late. You'd been and gone from the safety deposit and he didn't have the keys. Somehow, he knew the system at Ramseyer, Haldemann, that two keys were needed, so he was desperate to get them from you. He must have searched your rooms but he'd know it was unlikely that you'd have left the keys behind unattended and it was much too risky to try to attack you in Geneva.

"Now he had to concentrate on getting the money. He had already left a message on your phone. He planned to trap you and get you to transfer the funds when you were back in the house in Marbella. That would also be his opportunity to get both the keys."

"I suppose that if I hadn't phoned him back he would have called again," said Jenny, reflectively. "Whatever happened he was a good enough psychologist to know that we would walk into his trap."

The police officer breathed a deep sigh. "It's an amazing story, and that's not the end of it. The only reason that I came racing along to the house was because of da Silva, the paedophile. It was another big mistake for d'Almeida to kill him.

"Your email about Sr. Bishop's funeral set off alarm bells at the Child Abuse Prevention Programme in Washington. Several suspicious deaths, including this paedophile, and I was convinced you were in danger. I had no idea how much danger." He stopped, thinking how lucky they had been. *A difference of a minute or two. Not more.*

"What about Vogel, Chief Inspector. Do you think he'll ever get caught?"

"There's an Interpol arrest warrant out for him, Leticia. But I'd be surprised. There are lots of those crooks running around the world. It's very difficult to catch them, unless they make a mistake. We'll see. Anyway, he's no threat to you, so don't worry."

Espinoza switched off the recorder and the women went to fetch coffee.

As they came back into the sitting room Fuente came padding in with them. He jumped up on the couch beside the lawyer, who stroked his head.

"José Luis, you must have a very strong feminine side. Fuente doesn't generally like men, you're very privileged."

The old lawyer smiled and continued to spoil the cat. Fuente purred contentedly.

Chief Inspector Espinoza put three spoons of sugar into his coffee. "Ladies," he said. "I have a confession to make. Last night I downloaded the data and the calls from the BlackBerry. We found it undamaged in the murderer's pocket."

"Laurent's BlackBerry!" Jenny took Leticia's hand. She had suddenly become uneasy.

"Yes, M. Bonneville's device. A lot of what you have told me I already pieced together from the data - the Angolan Clan. I got a good idea of why d'Almeida was killing people off. Each one was disguised as an accident so they wouldn't be connected until it was too late. What I didn't know was why he left Nick and then Adam alive, but now I understand. He expected to have all three of you at his mercy in Marbella, with the two PIN numbers and the keys between you.

"You have been open and honest with me and I greatly appreciate it. José Luis here has heard everything and I'm sure that he is as impressed as I am with the way you have handled yourselves. In my opinion, it would have been impossible for you to save Adam. It almost seems to me that he wanted to commit suicide, but your actions saved the two of you and his sacrifice saved Emilio. You are both brave and resourceful women."

"It was Jenny, Sr. Espinoza. She's the brave one, not me." Leticia said. "I was terrified and I think Adam was as well. Jenny saved us both, but then Adam .. Well, I don't understand why Adam did that, but he saved my son and I will never forget it."

"Then we have Jenny and the Chief Inspector to thank for preventing even more deaths."

"You forgot Fuente, José Luis. He helped to delay d'Almeida just long enough for the Chief Inspector to get here."

"Then he deserves a double portion of supper."

The cat jumped down and strolled into the kitchen, as if he'd heard all he wanted to hear.

The lawyer watched him go out. "What a beautiful creature. God makes all kinds. It's hard to understand."

Jenny said. "We have a favour to ask of you. Can you trace Ray's sister, the one in Rio?"

"Why do you want to do that?"

"Because she is an innocent victim in this terrible business and we want her to enjoy some benefit from the Angolan Clan. All we know is her family name, Melo d'Almeida."

"But I know exactly where she is. Her name is Alicia Beatriz Melo d'Almeida and apparently she lives in a poor suburb of Rio."

"But, how..?"

"Because, every month since Francisco came to work for me he has transferred ten per cent of his salary to her. I have sent it for a year now to a Western Union office in Rio. He told me it was a distant cousin. Obviously because the name would have given him away."

This time it was Espinoza's turn to say, "*Incredible*. As you said, José Luis, it's hard to understand. How can such a cold blooded, ruthless killer be so thoughtful with his family?" He shook his head. "I suppose it's a kind of schizophrenia."

He glanced at his watch. He was going to be late for tapas with Soledad if he didn't leave right way. She'd agreed to meet him at the bar in Malaga at three and he couldn't be late this time. Getting up from the sofa, he said, "It's time for us to leave you in peace and to forget this business. Come on, José Luis, I'll drive you back."

At the door, Espinoza turned and said, "I don't work for the tax department, nor for the financial fraud office. As far as I can ascertain, this man committed these murders and came to your house with only one thing in mind. To steal the legacy left to you and Adam Peterson."

Jenny and Leticia waited apprehensively as he continued.

"I have no reason to believe that any of you were involved in any kind of improper financial dealings, since all of this is a legacy issue. I assume that you will be addressing the matter of the robbery with the bank in Switzerland, and since the culprit is dead, it is no longer a police affair here in Spain.

"The same goes for the possible attempt to steal the keys and the diamonds. According to the copy of the Geneva police report which I have already seen, there is no proof of any robbery. There were no keys on d'Almeida, nor on Adam, and from what you say, it's quite possible that he just lost his key. So unless you make a formal complaint that something has been stolen, there is no reason for the police to intervene." He didn't disclose the existence of the surveillance report he had received from Inspector Blaser. It had thrown up nothing of importance and might only serve to alienate them.

The women looked at each other in relief. They hadn't imagined that Espinoza would check for a police report in Geneva. But apparently he had, and it was inconclusive.

"I'll make further enquiries into the two women, Esther and Gloria. But unless those enquiries produce anything material, I will be closing my dossier on this unfortunate business after I read the manuscript you have given me. It sounds to me as if it's a story worth reading. Then this recording," he showed them the little cassette from the machine, "and the manuscript, will go into the archives and I doubt that either of you will be bothered any further." He smiled for the first time since they had met him.

"*Gracias, Chief Inspector. Gracias José Luis.*" Leticia kissed both men on the cheeks and said goodbye. Jenny did the same. The two men walked down the driveway to their car.

The women went into the garden to find Encarni and Emilio. It was time for a late lunch.

NINETY-FIVE

Thursday, 1st May, 2008
Cointrin Airport, Geneva

Jenny retrieved her hand luggage from the conveyor belt at the security installation and put her shoes and coat back on. Leticia was already set to go. They went to the nearest departure area, which was not in use and sat on the hard metal seats, talking quietly.

Jenny was still coming to terms with the tragic consequences of Charlie's legacy. *So many people lost because of those diamonds. It should have been called the Angolan Curse, not Clan.* Chief Inspector Espinoza had called her in the afternoon after their meeting to inform her that he had heard from the police in Geneva. His Interpol colleague had advised him there was an alert out for Kurt Vogel in connection with the death of Gloria Smouha. Inevitably, it seemed that Gloria was probably another of d'Almeida's victims.

It was the last straw. The reality of what they had experienced suddenly overwhelmed them and she and Leticia spent the rest of the day crying and consoling each other until they couldn't grieve any more.

Now it was time to go back to Ipswich. She'd looked at the

weather forecast, it was quite warm and dry at home. *Home, where's home? It's not Marbella, not yet. Maybe some time, but I need to get back to normality for a while. Back to making Cooper's supper and walking him in the park. I need to talk to Cyril about the garage. Get some exercise at the tennis club with Audrey. Go to the gym and the hairdresser. Lots of things to do.* Aloud, she simply said, "I can't wait to see Cooper again and take him for a walk. He must have missed me."

"Maybe I should get a dog for Emilio." Leticia said thoughtfully. "I think it's very good for children. In the house we have plenty space for a dog, it's better than the apartment."

"Be careful that Fuente doesn't get jealous. He's a mean cat when he gets upset."

Leticia gave her little giggle. "I need a dog with a strong feminine side, like José Luis but tough, like you. I'll get a lady dog and call her Jenny."

They had returned to Geneva the previous day and sat with M. Schneider in his conference room. He had obviously spent a long time with the bank's lawyers since their last visit. He sounded as if he was reading from a script.

"I set the Internet system up with Mr. Bishop, almost ten years ago," he told them. "I never imagined it would be abused like this. Of course, I couldn't have foreseen that the perpetrator would murder several people in order to access your funds." He looked incredulous. "Nor that he would try to murder all three of you, and kill poor Mr. Peterson in the process. It really defies the imagination."

The women said nothing and Schneider moved uneasily in his chair. "Our lawyers have examined the matter and I'm afraid that the news is rather bad. Internet banking is a fairly new innovation and there is always some risk attached. The terms and conditions of our Internet Banking Agreement are very specific. Because the two correct PIN codes and security numbers were entered, despite the very dreadful circumstances, our bank cannot accept any liability. We have endeavoured to trace the funds, but without success. The money is irretrievably lost. I am deeply sorry for this, but I'm afraid there is absolutely nothing we can do."

Jenny replied, "We have already discussed the whole matter with our own lawyer, Mr. Schneider, and we have an entirely different point of view. We're not going to accept your position, since there are a lot of extenuating circumstances. Not the least of them is that your own assistant, Esther Rousseau, was obviously involved in these crimes."

"Well, Madame Bishop, in that respect, our lawyers considered position is that there is actually no evidence that Mademoiselle Rousseau was connected in any way with the murderer. She is presently missing and until she is found, this is all circumstantial. Even then, the legal situation is not at all clear, so I'm afraid that the bank cannot accept any responsibility." The banker took out his handkerchief and blew his nose with evident relief. He had delivered the message that his masters had trained him for.

Jenny laughed scornfully. "Mr. Schneider, in view of your attitude, there is no point in continuing this meeting. We will appoint a Geneva lawyer to represent us and we'll let the lawyers fight it out. We don't particularly want to get into a law suit with a Swiss bank, but we also don't want to be treated like idiots. One day the matter will be settled and the insurance company will, no doubt, pay the bill."

For once, Schneider looked embarrassed and dropped his pompous tone. "I understand, Madame Bishop. It's most unfortunate, but it's out of my hands. The truth is, I'm sorry to say, that in today's world we can all find ourselves victims of crime, in one way or another. Modern technology certainly has its place, but perhaps not in anonymous transfers of millions of dollars."

The women said nothing further. They had made their attempt and it had failed, for the moment. Jenny was profoundly depressed at the result. She felt cheated, not just for herself, but for everyone concerned. She and Leticia had lost, Ray had lost. Most likely Esther had lost. Adam, Gloria and everyone involved with the Angolan Clan who had disappeared, had lost, not just money, but their lives. The only participant in this dreadful adventure that had not lost was the Swiss banking system.

Jenny had already decided that she didn't like the way that Klein, Fellay ran its business. If she had known what was going through the banker's mind she would have liked it even less.

Schneider didn't mention the substantial funds in the accounts still held in the names of Laurent Benoît de Bonneville, Raffael Rodrigo Pires da Silva and Adam Henrik Peterson. Unless he was advised that any of them had bequeathed the funds to anyone, they would remain at the bank along with thousands of other unclaimed balances until the powers-that-be decided to release them for some purpose. It was not part of his duties to bring attention to such matters. It was not in his script.

He accompanied them down to the reception to call a taxi, then left them, the familiar sound of his nose being blown drifting back along the corridor.

Their meeting with Mme. Aeschiman, at the Banque de Commerce, was quite different. She was aghast at the story. "I'm so sorry for Mr. Bishop and for you, of course. It's a tragedy. Such a clever, nice man, and his partners too, and now Mr. Peterson. I can't believe it."

When they told her about Kurt Vogel, she was sympathetic. "I'm going to make a complete investigation of these transfers. If this is an embezzlement, I'll pass it on to our fraud department. Our lawyers will decide what can be done, if anything. I believe that if a signature was forged then our insurance is engaged. I certainly hope so. I'll contact you as soon as I have any news."

Hanny had called Jenny on the Monday, after the detectives' visit, to sympathise with her and Leticia for their ordeal. Leticia spoke to him, describing how Adam's bravery had saved her son. She would never forget it.

Jenny had asked him for the details of his bank account. They could now draw a line under this last aborted transaction of the Angolan Clan. They transferred the million dollars back to him and closed down the IDD account.

When they left, Mme. Aeschiman was sorry to see them go. It was the end of a long relationship. *Although,* thought Jenny, *I think I'd rather prolong that relationship, if possible, than continue to deal with M. Schneider. We'll see what happens.*

Now, in Cointrin as they sat talking, Leticia took out the key to the Ramseyer, Haldemann safety deposit. Charlie's key, the one with the yellow elastic band. "What should we do about this? And what should we do about the diamonds?"

"Tell me, Leticia. If you could go and get those diamonds, would you do it? Do you really want all that money?"

"Anyone would want that much money, Jenny. But I think it's very dangerous. We don't know who has the other key, but they know who has this one. And I'm sure they will want to get it."

"So there's nothing we can do. Twelve million dollars of diamonds locked away in the red light district in Geneva and you only have one key. We can't exactly run a small ad in the newspaper. We'll just have to wait and see what happens, if anything happens."

"I don't want to keep the key, Jenny. I don't want to keep it in the house. I'm frightened for Emilio that something bad will happen."

Jenny took the key from her hand. "Then I'll keep it. You can forget it ever existed. I promise nothing bad will happen to you, nor to Emilio."

They walked towards the gate for Madrid. The flight was boarding. Leticia put her arms around her. "Take care, Jenny dear. Please come and see us in your house soon. Emilio and I will miss you." She wiped the tears from her eyes.

"No crying, Leticia, I always want to think of you laughing. In any case I'll be over often, just wait and see."

"Jenny." She paused nervously. "I have something to tell you."

"I hope it's something nice?"

"I think so. Patrice called me. He is very sorry about Ray and everything. He sent his best wishes to you and… he invited me to have dinner with him when I get home."

"And did you accept?"

Leticia looked at her in surprise. "Of course I did, why should I not? I still miss Charlie so much, but I think he would want me to get on with my life. He would have understood."

Jenny could have bitten her tongue off. Her question reflected the pang of envy that had momentarily stabbed her. This young woman had delightful parents and an adorable little son. Now it seemed, a good looking young banker was setting his cap at her. *What have I got? A semi-detached in Ipswich and a West Highland Terrier called Cooper.*

She pulled herself together. *It's the start of a new life for both of us. She's just sprinted ahead a little, that's all.*

Leticia was watching her apprehensively, looking for Jenny's approbation, just as she had always looked for Charlie's, still unsure of herself in this new episode in her life.

"I think that's absolutely wonderful. Just make sure that his intentions are honourable, and try to get him to dress down a little. He looks a bit too French, in my opinion."

Leticia relaxed again and giggled. "I think it's better than being too Swiss."

"That's more like it. We've got you laughing again. Goodbye, Leticia, have a safe flight. Give Emilio a big kiss from his Aunt Jenny."

"You too. Say hello to Cooper for me." The two women embraced and parted, for the time being.

Leticia waved as she went through the gate to claim her business seat on the Iberia flight to Madrid.

Jenny walked slowly towards her departure gate. She took her purse from her bag and opened the zipped part. She placed Charlie's key with the yellow elastic band next to Nick's key with the green band. The key she'd taken from Adam's jacket in his bathroom at the hotel. Now they were side by side, together, as they should be.

She wasn't in a hurry, she had plenty of time. She'd paid a speedy boarding supplement on the easyJet flight to Stansted. It had cost her ten pounds extra. *Time to change my spending habits,* she thought, *I can afford it.*

THE END

CHRISTOPHER LOWERY is a 'Geordie', born in the northeast of England, who graduated in finance and economics after reluctantly giving up career choices in professional golf and rock & roll. He is a real estate and telecoms entrepreneur and has created several successful companies around the world. Chris wrote the Angolan Clan after the Revolution of the Carnations forced him to flee Portugal in 1975. He also writes patents and children's books and composes music. He and his wife Marjorie live between Geneva and Marbella. They have one daughter, a writer/photographer who is resident in Geneva.

LOOK OUT FOR CHRISTOPHER LOWERY'S
NEXT THRILLER:

The Rwandan Hostage

the sequel to
The Angolan Clan
and the second in the *African Diamonds* series.

ALSO BY CHRISTOPHER LOWERY:

The House that Jack Built:
A modern fairy tale
(Illustrated)

The second and third books in this
series coming soon:

Captain Jack and Jack and the ET Folk

Visit www.unclechrisproductions.com
for news, humour and stories.

URBANE